CRITICAL ACCLAIM FOR BARBARA ERSKINE AND HER EXTRAORDINARY FIRST NOVEL

LADY OF HAY

"ALMOST IMPOSSIBLE TO PUT DOWN! . . . has everything that readers of racy fiction could ask for: beautiful characters, exotic settings, and passion. It also has something such readers rarely find in their favorite stories—situations and characters that are so completely convincing that they come to life."

—*The Philadelphia Inquirer*

"FASCINATING . . . a unique journey into another place and time . . . rich with historical detail."

—*Book Alert*

"A BONA FIDE PAGE-TURNER . . . Erskine writes richly and well about reincarnation . . . she keeps your interest, draws you relentlessly back for more, makes you care about her characters . . . and what more can a reader ask?"

—*The Times* (London)

"SUPERB! . . . A BLOCKBUSTER! . . . WILL HOLD YOU EN-THRALLED."

—*Boston Post-Gazette*

Also by Barbara Erskine

LADY OF HAY

KINGDOM OF SHADOWS

Barbara Erskine

A DELL TRADE PAPERBACK

A DELL TRADE PAPERBACK

Published by Dell Publishing
a division of
Bantam Doubleday Dell Publishing Group, Inc.
666 Fifth Avenue
New York, New York 10103

MICHAEL JOSEPH LTD

Published by the Penguin Group
27 Wrights Lane, London W8 5TZ, England
Viking Penguin Inc., 40 West 23rd Street, New York, New York
10010, USA
Penguin Books Australia Ltd, Ringwood, Victoria, Australia
Penguin Books Canada Ltd, 2801 John Street, Markham, Ontario,
Canada
L3R 1B4
Penguin Books (NZ) Ltd, 182–190 Wairau Road, Auckland 10,
New Zealand

Penguin Books Ltd, Registered Offices: Harmondsworth,
Middlesex, England

First published in Great Britain 1988

For information address:
Michael Joseph Ltd, London, England.

The trademark Dell ® is registered in the
U.S. Patent and Trademark Office.

ISBN: 0-440-50200-4
Reprinted by arrangement with Michael Joseph Ltd.

Printed in the United States of America
November 1989

10 9 8 7 6 5 4 3 2 1

MV

For
ADRIAN JAMES EARL
and
JONATHAN ERSKINE ALEXANDER
also descendants of The Bruce

Acknowledgments

I should like to extend my thanks to all those who have helped me with information for this book and who have so patiently answered my questions on so many diverse subjects.

Among them I must mention especially the Rev. Edgar Pearson, the Rev. Brian Toll and the Rev. Peter Disney for their advice on the subject of possession and exorcism; Janet Hanlon for her expertise on childbirth; Ann and Michael Grieve; Richard Smith-Carington; Michael Unsworth for all his help on the subject of the oil industry. Also my husband Michael for his information on the City and the way it works, and for his tolerance in putting up with a diet of spaghetti for two years while I wrote the book.

I am very grateful to the Sheldon Press for allowing me to use the extracts from the prayers of exorcism from *Healing and the Family Tree* by Dr. Kenneth McAll.

Thank you too, to the people of Buchan, especially David Rennie at Dundarg, who welcomed us into their homes and showed us the ancient castles which form the frame for this story.

Duncairn does not exist. Had it done so, it would have been very near to Old Slains, and looked not unlike Dunottar!

Barbara Erskine
Great Tey 1988

Tain

Dundarg

Old Deer

BUCHAN   Duncairn

Ellon   Slains

MAR

Kildrummy

Aberdeen

Dunkeld

Coupar
Angus

Methven
Perth   Scone

Dail Righ
Glen Dochart

Stirling

Bannockburn

Edinburgh

Berwick

Rathlin

KINGDOM OF SHADOWS

The Dream

It came again that night with the silent menace of a cloud sliding across the moon. In her sleep her hands, slippery with sweat, began to clench and unclench. Her breathing became short and irregular, her heartbeat increased, and she threw herself from side to side, moaning with fear. Then she ceased to move. Beneath her eyelids her eyes began to flick rapidly from side to side.

Panic-stricken, she fought to escape, her hands groping in the darkness while something held her back, trapping her, holding her immovable. There were bars above her head, behind her back, on every side of her, and beyond the bars, eyes. Faces, staring, mouths moving, teeth glittering with spittle, like the fangs of animals. Only they weren't animals. They were people, and only the bars could save her from them. She cowered back now, on her knees, her arms about her head.

When she looked up, they had gone. All was empty again.

Slowly she stood up. Now in her dream she was a bird. Her wings were stiff with disuse, the feathers dusty and brittle. To spread them hurt the muscles in her breast and shoulders. She tried to beat them. Faster and faster, willing them to carry her outward and upward toward the sky. But the bars held and the feathers beat against them—beating, beating until her wings were broken and bloody and she was exhausted. Hope died; she knew again she was a woman.

The dream began to lift and with it the immobility that comes with the deepest sleep. Tears filled her eyes and slipped from beneath her closed lids. She moved her head restlessly again, her hands groping in an echo of the dream, seeking the bars, afraid they would still be there when she awoke. She was fighting the dream now yet still ensnared.

1

One hand, flailing in the darkness, caught something and held it until her knuckles whitened. It was the chained door of the cage.

As her eyes flew wide she opened her mouth and began to scream.

❦ Prologue ❦
1970

Margaret Gordon looked down at the two children at her feet and smiled. James, his cheeks pink and shining, his hair neatly brushed, the checked shirt and jeans clean for once, was sitting fidgeting on the footstool, near her chair. At eight, he was already a tall, athletic boy, showing promise of being as handsome as his father. She shook her head sadly, then she turned her attention to Clare. Four years older than her brother, she was a dark-haired, slim child, with the grace and elfin beauty of a fawn. Her short, wavy hair framed a delicate face, dominated by the huge gray eyes.

And the eyes, as always, were fixed unwaveringly on her great-aunt's face.

"Go on, Aunt Margaret, let's hear the bit about the spider." James leaned forward, elbows on knees. "And how the king escaped from Scotland."

Margaret smiled indulgently. "Again? You ask for that story every time you come to see me.

"And Clare?" She turned and smiled at her great-niece. "Which story would you like?"

As soon as the words had left her mouth she regretted them, knowing what the answer would be. She felt her stomach muscles tighten warningly as she met Clare's steady gaze.

"I'd like to hear about the Countess Isobel who crowned him king," the girl whispered. "And how they put her in a cage. . . ."

Margaret swallowed. "That's not very cheerful, my dear. I think perhaps we should stick to the spider today, as it's nearly teatime." She hesitated, uncomfortable beneath those

3

huge, expressive eyes. "Besides, your mother and Archie will be back from their walk soon."

"Go on then, Aunt Margaret," James said. "It happened on Rathlin Island . . ."

Margaret looked down at her hands. The slim, aristocratic fingers were thickened and knotted with arthritis now, so she could no longer wear rings or push a bangle over her swollen knuckles. How silly at her age to care for such vain, inconsequential things. Surreptitiously she glanced at Clare again. When the child was a little older she would give her the jewelry. For the rest Clare would have to wait until she was dead.

She gripped one of the walking sticks tightly and rested it upright against her knees so that she could lean on it, perched on the edge of the high seat to ease the pain in her back. The child's mother said she often had nightmares. Had she already had the dream? There were dark shadows under her eyes that should not have been there in a girl her age. Margaret felt a warning shiver of apprehension. Abruptly she brought her mind back to the story. "On Rathlin Island there was a cave, and there the king and his followers hid the whole of that long, vicious winter. . . ."

If only Isobel had gone with him. If only he had allowed her to stay at his side as he longed. If only he had not sent her away.

The long silence stretched out as her thoughts went back over the story, the story that had obsessed her as long as she could remember, the story she had told these two children again and again.

But how had she heard it herself? She couldn't remember who had told her first. The story had always been with her, part of her bones, part of her soul! The joy, the pain, the love, and, at the last, the fear and despair. And with it the recurring nightmare.

"Aunt Margaret?" James gave a tentative cough. "The king . . . on Rathlin . . . ?"

With a start she dragged her thoughts back to the present. She forced herself to smile.

"I'm sorry, James. I think I must be a little tired." She

glanced at Clare, almost afraid the girl had read her thoughts, but Clare was no longer looking at her. Her eyes were fixed on the window, staring up at the thick mat of gray cloud that hung over Airdlie House. Her eyes were full of pain.

"Clare!"

Only the astonishment in James's face made Margaret realize how panicky her cry had sounded.

The girl jumped up. "Yes, Aunt Margaret?" She came to stand at the old woman's side, her face full of anxiety. "What is it?"

"Nothing, my dear, nothing." Margaret raised herself up to her feet. Her imagination was running away with her again. It was crazy to think one could unwittingly pass on an obsession. Another fear to lay at the door of her overfertile brain. The child was growing up, that was all. On the threshold of womanhood. Soon she wouldn't want to listen to an old woman's ramblings anymore. She would be far more interested in boys and pop music and clothes. There would be no time then for a story so many generations old. No time at all. She would forget.

Margaret took a stick in each hand and gripped them firmly, placing the two black rubber tips squarely on the polished boards on either side of her swollen feet. "Let's go and start making tea, shall we?" she said. "The Bruce and his spider can come later."

Chapter One
THE PRESENT DAY

"You know, you are being bloody unfair to Paul!"

Gillian Royland reached for the tumbler and sipped lazily at the fruit drink. She pushed her sunglasses up into her hair and peered at her sister-in-law myopically from beneath her shady hat. "Don't you want children, for God's sake?"

"You know I do." Clare eyed the other woman's hugely pregnant bulk beneath the expensively cut sundress, then she lay back on the towel and closed her eyes, one hand dangling in the pool feeling the silkiness of the water against her fingertips.

"Then why won't you have some proper tests to find out what's wrong?"

Clare sighed. "Paul and I have both been to Dr. Stanford."

"Oh, yes, a chat with your GP." Gillian heaved herself up higher on the cushioned chair. "What does he know about it? I told you, you must go and see my gynecologist in Harley Street."

"There is nothing wrong with me, Gill." Clare clenched her fist in the water, unwilling to talk about the questions, the tests, the humiliations she and Paul had already faced. "John Stanford said I should learn to relax a bit more, that's all."

"And you respond by going to this crazy guru!"

"He's not a guru!" Clare sat up impatiently, shaking her wet hair back from her face. "He teaches yoga. Millions of people study yoga. There is nothing wrong about it. You should try it. Yes, even in your condition!"

"Hey, keep calm." Gillian hastily dropped the glasses on her nose, retreating at once from the threat of an argument. She eyed her tempestuous sister-in-law wryly. "You certainly need to learn how to relax." When Clare didn't respond, she went on tentatively, feeling more secure behind the glasses. "Everything is all right between you and Paul?"

The question hung for a moment between them. Clare clasped her arms around her knees, her shoulders hunched as a breath of cold touched them. "Why shouldn't it be?" she said at last.

Gillian watched her covertly. "No reason at all. You are both coming to our party on Saturday, aren't you?" She changed the subject so abruptly that Clare stiffened.

"If Paul can get away from London this weekend." Clare stood up suddenly with effortless grace and stood poised by the side of the pool, conscious for a moment of her sister-in-law's critical stare. Then she dived into the water. The cold was biting, invigorating, touched already by that frisson of autumn in the air. It was the first day of October.

By the time she pulled herself up the ladder at the far end of the pool, she was shivering violently.

"He's still furious about your great-aunt's will, isn't he?" Gillian's cool voice brought Clare up short as she stooped for her towel.

"He told you that?" Clare swung to face her.

"He told David about it, in the end. But we'd guessed something was wrong. Everyone thought she would leave you and James half of her money each."

"It was hardly everyone's business!" Clare retorted.

"Oh, come on, we are family." Gillian began to lever herself to her feet. "Paul isn't worried about money, is he, Clare?"

"Paul?" Clare stared at her, visibly shocked by the question. "What on earth makes you ask that?"

The two women eyed each other for a moment, Clare's steady gray eyes meeting Gillian's pale watery ones. "Nothing. Nothing at all. He just seemed so upset about the money, that's all."

"He was upset for me." Clare rubbed her hair energetically. "He thought I minded."

"And don't you?"

Clare shook her head. "I wanted Duncairn, that was all."

* * *

She stood for a long time after Gillian had gone, gazing down at the pool as another shower of golden leaves pattered onto the water. She had minded about the money, of course. She had minded dreadfully. It would have given her her freedom.

She dried herself lazily and dropped the towel as the breeze died away again and the sun reappeared, warming her chilled skin. As she ran her hands slowly down her own slim, tanned body she scowled, thinking of her sister-in-law's swelling, fertile figure. Then she noticed that behind her a woman had appeared at the gateway in the high hedge that enclosed the pool area. She waved. "Come on, Sarah, and have a swim while the sun is out," she called.

Sarah Collins frowned. Tall, smartly dressed, in her early fifties, she wore an apron over her skirt. In her hand was a pile of letters.

"The mail came just as Lady Royland was leaving," she called back. "I thought I'd bring yours over. I can't swim now. I've an enormous amount to do this morning."

Had she imagined the slight emphasis on that last pronoun? Clare wondered. The unspoken implication that Clare of course had nothing to do at all?

Clare smiled at her determinedly. "I'm sure things in the house can wait, Sarah. I doubt if we'll have many more beautiful days like this, this year."

She knew the woman wouldn't swim. She never did. For all Clare's determined efforts to make a friend of her, Sarah Collins seemed equally determined to keep her distance, to draw demarcation lines. Mistress and servant. Lady of the house and housekeeper. Confidante—that was a traditional part of the role—but giving nothing in exchange, so not a real friend. Ever.

Clare shrugged. She picked up the towel again and, after drying her hands, she took the letters. She glanced at them without interest then threw them down on the white-painted wrought-iron table.

Already Sarah was walking back to the house. The gate clicked behind her and Clare was alone again. Sighing, she poured herself some juice from the jug on the table, but she didn't drink it. Instead she walked over to the mat on the pool's edge. She would do twenty minutes of yoga practice now, while her body was clean and invigorated and relaxed from the swim.

She slipped out of the wet bikini and tossed it to one side, sitting, gracefully naked, on the mat. Taking a deep, slow breath, she closed her eyes and began deliberately to relax, muscle by muscle, limb by limb, letting her mind float blankly as, slowly, she drew her legs up into the first asana.

"Yoga, meditation, relaxation. First class, my dear. They're all first class." She could still hear John Stanford's slightly patronizing tones. "Anything to help you unwind and remove the stress. Now don't worry about it at all. The tests are going to prove there is nothing wrong. You'll see. When nature thinks you're good and ready you'll conceive and not a moment before. We can't hurry these things, you know."

"But don't I have to go into a hospital or anything?" She had expected worse than those tests—a hospital appointment, talk of a D and C—*something*. Not a pat on the back for going to yoga classes.

He had shaken his head. "You've been on the pill for five years, Clare. It can take a while for your fertility to return. I'm sure in my own mind that's all it is. Is Paul putting the pressure on you, my dear? Wanting a son and heir and all that? I'll have a word with him about it. Leave it to me."

And that had been that. And meanwhile Paul's family surrounded her reproachfully with their children. Gillian with three and another on the way. Chloe, her other sister-in-law, with two, and even Em, her best friend, Paul's baby sister, had Julia.

She opened the first of her letters as she walked back toward the house, once more clad in the bikini for the sake of Sarah's susceptibilities. She was reading it as she reached the soft mossy grass of the back lawn.

We understand that you are the owner of the hotel, castle . . . and policies of the area known as Duncairn . . . Scotland. Our client has indicated that he would be interested in pur-

chasing the above-mentioned property in its entirety . . .
negotiation of a price to be undertaken . . .

Clare stared down at the letter in disbelief. A wave of
anger swept over her. Did they seriously imagine she would
sell Duncairn? Sell her birthright, sell seven hundred years of
history, her inheritance from Aunt Margaret, sell all that
beauty and wildness and memory? The letter had a demanding tone that implied knowledge of the place and of the
extent of her ownership. Suddenly she was filled with panic.

The letters clutched in her hand, she began to run toward
the house, her bare feet silent on the old polished boards as
she pushed open the French door. The drawing room was
cool, shaded from the sun by half-drawn curtains, and Jo-
casta, her long-haired golden retriever, was lying there in the
cool, asleep.

Not even pausing to read the letter again, Clare sat down
at her desk, pulled a piece of letterhead from one of the
cubbyholes in front of her, and grabbed her pen.

Nothing, nothing would ever induce her to sell! No amount
of money would be sufficient incentive. Her pen raced over
the paper. The property was not and never would be for sale.
How dare Messrs. Mitchison and Archer even ask? She
scratched her signature and folded the paper into an envelope. It was then she realized her hands were shaking with
fury.

With a loud sigh and a smacking of her lips the dog lay flat
again and closed her eyes. Clare stared at Casta for a moment, then slowly tore the envelope in two. She took a deep
breath. Body awareness, Zak called it. Be aware of your body;
notice when it's under stress. Be conscious of your pulse. Your
heartbeat. Feel the heat in your face. Notice how you are
breathing. Give yourself more oxygen. Nothing is worth that
much hassle. . . . His cool voice came back to her. Time.
Take time. She hadn't realized she was trembling; reacting to
the threat as if this man, this unknown lawyer with his impor-
tunate letter was in the room with her.

Slowly she stood up. There was no hurry. The letter could
be mailed anytime. He could do nothing. The land was not

for sale. Whatever his client wanted it for, they could find somewhere else. Nothing and no one could force her to sell. . . .

She thought suddenly of Paul, and she found herself swallowing nervously. What would Paul say when he heard about the offer? And with the same thought she knew with calm certainty she would never tell him.

Upstairs she showered, then, wrapping herself in a bathrobe, went into her bedroom. It was a pretty room, full of sunlight, the dust-pink curtains and frills making it warm and friendly while the silver-gray carpet gave an impression of cool self-possession. She could smell the roses from the silver-and-glass bowl on the table by the window. Meditate. That was Zak's remedy for situations she couldn't handle. Meditate, relax, take time. Then face the problem and do something about it. Then forget it.

She opened the closet in the corner of the room and brought out a candle in a squat cut-glass holder and some matches. After lighting it and placing it carefully on the carpet, she drew the curtains, then she sat down cross-legged before it, eyes closed, wrists hanging loosely on her knees.

She set her mind on the first visualization exercise Zak had taught her. "Close your eyes and think of your favorite place. The place you feel happiest and most relaxed. Picture the scene. Make it so real you can smell it, feel it, hear it, feel the sun on your skin, hear the birdsong, smell the grass, make a mental ashram there." She always chose Duncairn.

It was in June she had been there last, on Midsummer's Day, just after she and Paul had had their first quarrel.

The will had been quite explicit. To Clare came the ruined castle, a thousand or so acres of moorland around it, the old-fashioned, sleepy hotel, and some rents from the fishing village that nestled at the foot of the cliffs. As she had a rich husband to support her, she had no need of money, so the three farms and the money, all of it, went to James, who was so like his dead father, as did Airdlie, the Perthshire house and estates, although their mother and her second husband, Archie, had life tenancy there.

"Did you know what the old bat planned to do?" Paul turned on her the moment they were alone in their hotel room after the reading of the will.

"No, I didn't know." Her voice was bleak. "She always said she would leave everything to us both. I was to get Duncairn —I've always known I'd get Duncairn—but I thought she'd leave me some money too."

"Some money!" Paul lowered his voice. "Margaret Gordon was worth over one and a half million, Clare, in securities alone. With the farms another three at least." His handsome face looked drawn and pale as he caught her arm and swung her to face him. "And she left it all to James! You will have to contest it."

"No!"

"No?" He stared at her.

"No, Paul. I won't contest it. She's right. You're a wealthy man. My brother had nothing, nothing at all. He never even had a father. Daddy died before he was born!"

"He had Archie—"

"Archie hates us. He has always resented us for being there; he thinks of us as coming between him and Mummy, you know that as well as I do." Clare's eyes were blazing. "No, that money is James's by right. I have everything I want." Abruptly her anger subsided. She put her hands on Paul's shoulders. "Come on, darling. We don't need any more money."

Paul caught her wrists and pushed them away. "Everyone needs more money, Clare. Duncairn's worth *nothing.*" His voice was harsh.

For a moment she stared at him, shocked, then she turned away and walked over to the window, staring down over the rooftops at the back of the hotel toward the distant Firth of Forth. "Well, it's worth everything to me," she whispered. "Everything. Don't you understand?" She spun around. "It's been in our family for seven hundred years!"

"Then perhaps James ought to have it as well. He is, after

all, the heir to whatever pretensions your family has to gentility, not you." Paul's voice was deliberately cruel.

She gasped. "Paul!"

"Well, it's true. Or are you claiming some feminist right of inheritance because you are the eldest? Perhaps it is *I* who should have taken *your* surname when we married!" His voice was heavy with sarcasm.

"Well, at least it's a name to be proud of!" she flashed back at him, suddenly not caring what she said. "After all, what are you? The third son of a family who can't trace their ancestors back more than one generation! I never could understand why you were so anxious for an heir. He'll have nothing to inherit from you!"

"Apart from the wealth that everyone keeps talking about, you mean," said Paul. His voice was ice-cold.

Clare stared at him, furious to find herself near tears. To conceal them, she turned back to her scrutiny of the rooftops, watching with anguished intensity a gull wheeling around the distant chimney pots. She hunched her shoulders.

"Apart from your wealth," she echoed.

"So. At least I now know what you think of me," he went on quietly. "May I inquire why you lowered yourself so far as to marry me?"

"You know why I married you!" She didn't turn around. "I loved you."

"*Loved,* I notice. Not love."

"Love, then! Paul, what's the matter? What's wrong with you? Why are you like this?" She pushed herself away from the windowsill and came to stand in front of him.

He stared at her. The frail beauty of her pale face with the expressive gray eyes and the dark frame of her hair never failed to make him catch his breath. The frailness, of course, was misleading. Clare was as tough as old boots, even if she was a bit highly strung. He noted the tears on her cheeks now and felt a sudden twinge of contrition. He hadn't meant to hurt her.

It was just that the disappointment and the anxiety had been so intense. Dear God! how he had relied on that money. It was to have been his lifeline, his only way out of the hell he had found himself in. He could feel the sweat starting out on the palms of his hands just at the thought of what had happened. Abruptly he began to peel off his jacket. "If we're to meet the others in the bar before lunch we'd better get ready," he said abruptly, throwing the jacket down on the bed. "No doubt your brother will want to buy a bottle or two of Bolly to celebrate his little windfall."

"Paul—"

"No, Clare. Don't say another word. Not another word. I think you've said enough." He pulled off his tie and shirt and threw them down too before disappearing into the bathroom and slamming the door.

Clare stared after him in silence. She was overwhelmed by a sense of utter loneliness, as if she had found herself suddenly in the room with a stranger. A stranger of whom she had been for a moment almost afraid.

Her gaze fell on the dressing table where earlier he had thrown his car keys. Less than a minute later she grabbed them and, with a glance at the closed bathroom door, let herself out of the room, and began to make her way quickly down the hallway.

Dazzled by the blaze of the hot afternoon sun, Clare had stared around at the castle ruins. Behind her the cooling engine of the British racing green XJS ticked quietly, pulled up on the grass at the side of the track. The cool wind carried the scent of the sea, sweetened by the dog roses that climbed the crumbling gray walls. Slowly she walked out along the promontory toward the cliff and cautiously peered over. Perhaps a hundred years ago railings had been put up across the massive breach in the walls where the seaward stones had begun to fall down the cliffs, but now they sagged drunkenly over the gap. She peered down toward the water, gray-blue, opaque, cold even beneath the blazing June sky, and watched the gulls circling in the air currents. All around her the sound of birds was deafening: kittiwakes on the cliffs, their cries echoing off the granite shell of the tower, the yelp of a jackdaw hidden somewhere in the crumbling walls, a blackbird high in the rowan that grew in the space between the walls where once the chapel had stood.

The castle was deserted. Well off the tourist trail and unsignposted, only the visitors to the hotel ever came here, and there were few enough of them. She glanced over her shoulder toward the gray stone walls of the Duncairn Hotel, nestling behind the deep windbreak of birch and fir. It was losing money, that she knew, but it would be hard, very hard, to bring herself to change things. She loved Duncairn for its solitude. Behind it the distant low silhouette of the hills could be glimpsed. A successful hotel would end that solitude overnight.

Slowly she strolled over the grass. In the center of the walls someone had mown roughly, just enough to make for easy walking among the ruins—Jack Grant at the hotel, she supposed. She would stay the night there before driving back to Edinburgh. It would give both her and Paul time to cool off. And she couldn't face going back to Airdlie. Not now that it belonged to James.

She was no longer shaking. She had expended her fury and her pain by hurtling up the throughway at over a hundred miles an hour, not looking or caring if the police were patrolling, and then on the long narrow road north. But she was still tense, still depressed after the ordeal of the formal reading of the will, knowing that she had been the only person in the room who truly and desperately mourned Margaret Gordon.

She jumped as a shadow fell across the grass near her and looked wildly around, but it was nothing. Just the wind flexing and tossing the graceful branches of a birch. Slowly she began to walk around, every now and then reaching out to touch the warm, gray-pink stones of the castle walls as if greeting them ritually, taking possession of her inheritance. After picking her way through the thistles and rank grass and wildflowers toward the stone steps, she climbed precariously up to what remained of the second floor of the old keep. The floor had half collapsed and two of the walls had gone, but one high, rounded window on the seaward side remained intact and she made her way carefully to it. She stood in the embrasure, her hands on the sun-warmed sill, looking out to sea. There was a bank of mist out over the water now, pearly in the diffused sunlight.

A man was standing watching her from about twenty feet away, leaning against the crumbled remains of the eastern tower. Instinctively she drew back into the shadow of the window arch. He must be a guest at the hotel, she supposed. She studied him covertly, noting the patched khaki sweater, the threadbare cords, and the more than serviceable binoculars slung around his neck. He was a tall man, in his mid-thirties perhaps, good-looking in the rugged Scots fashion, very fair. And he was an intrusion. She felt a wave of resentment at his presence. She needed to be alone. Angrily she turned back and descended the steps once more, conscious that she was in full view of him. She wondered suddenly what he must make of her, still dressed for the Edinburgh solicitor, in a dark-blue silk dress and high-heeled shoes, scrambling over the ruins. Only her hair was fitting now, torn from its neat style by the wind and whipped into wild tangled curls.

She expected him to retreat as she walked near him, but he didn't move. Folding his arms, he leaned comfortably against the wall, and she thought she saw a flash of grim humor in his eyes as she walked past him, her heels catching in the grass and stones, before he turned away.

It was as she was making her way slowly back across the high bank of turf that covered one of the collapsed walls that she felt it. Suddenly, from nowhere, a wave of grief and despair swept over her, so tangible that it stopped her in her tracks. It was as if the mood came from outside herself, an atmosphere borne in on the cold wind. Behind her, the banks of haze had drawn closer; a sea mist was beginning to drift soundlessly up the huge granite cliffs, lapping among the fissures in the stone. Even the birds had fallen silent.

She glanced up at the sun, which moments before had been shining hotly down out of a blue sky. Now it was a cold white disc, shrugging into the mist banks and out of sight.

For no reason she was suddenly afraid.

In spite of herself she glanced back over her shoulder toward the stranger, seeking the comfort of another human presence. He was standing now beneath the rowan tree, staring up at the broken arch of the high window that had once dominated the chapel. And without even seeing his face, she knew that he too had felt something of the cold shadow that had crossed the castle.

Lost in her meditation, Clare frowned, guiding her mind back into the sunlight as she had been taught, driving away the North Sea mist that had cast its cold fingers over Duncairn, driving away the despair and fear that had persisted until she retraced her steps to the car and drove on to the hotel. She had not seen the stranger again.

Sarah Collins was in the kitchen polishing the silver when the phone rang. She waited meticulously for four rings, to see if Clare was going to answer it upstairs, then she picked up the receiver.

"Hello, Mrs. C. It's Emma Cassidy. Is Clare around?"

Sarah frowned. She resented deeply being addressed by anything other than her proper name. "I believe she's upstairs, Mrs. Cassidy. If you wish, I'll call her." She didn't wait for a reply. After dropping the receiver on the worktop with a rattle designed to illustrate her irritation, she began to walk slowly toward the stairs.

The door of the master bedroom was shut. Sarah listened for a moment, her ear almost against the wood paneling, then, very gently, she knocked.

There was no reply. She pursed her lips slightly and was about to turn away when, on impulse, she gripped the handle and twisted it quietly until with a *click* the latch slid back and the door opened. Clare was still seated on the floor, her legs crossed, her hands resting loosely on her knees. Her eyes were shut. Sarah watched in horrified fascination, noting the candle, the wax dripping slightly on the side away from the gently blowing curtains, the pale ice-green bathrobe slipping so that it revealed one long tanned thigh and most of Clare's left breast. Her breathing was deep and completely regular, her body relaxed, her face a picture of calm serenity. Sarah shivered. It might be an Indian summer in the garden, but in this shaded bedroom, it was suddenly very, very cold.

Turning, Sarah almost ran from the room. She pulled the door closed silently behind her, then hurried back down to the kitchen. Her hands were shaking as she grabbed the phone. "I'm sorry, Mrs. Cassidy, but I can't find her. She must be outside somewhere. Shall I get her to call you back later?"

She did not wait for Emma to ring off. She slammed down the receiver, took a deep breath, then picked the phone up again and began to dial.

She was put straight through to Paul's office. Gripping the receiver tightly in her left hand, she glanced nervously toward the kitchen door. "She's doing it again," she whispered into the mouthpiece. "Now, this minute. The candle and everything."

"It's good of you to call, Mrs. Collins." At his desk in the dark, oak-paneled room, Paul stood up slowly. "But I don't think there is any cause for alarm. I gather contemplation of a lighted candle is a well-known meditation technique."

Sarah took another deep breath, clearly audible down the phone. "I think it is more than meditation," she said darkly. "I've seen meditation on TV and when that dreadful man Zachary came over here to give her those lessons. What he showed her was quite different. What Mrs. Royland is doing is wrong. It's very, very wrong."

Paul leaned against his desk wearily. "In what way wrong, Mrs. Collins?"

She bit her lip, rubbing her fingers distractedly through the iron set of her hair. "It's just *wrong,*" she repeated stubbornly. "You must stop her doing it, Mr. Royland."

"I doubt if I could do that." She heard with surprise the bitterness in his wry laugh. "I doubt if I could stop Clare doing anything she really wanted to."

He hung up and stood looking down at the telephone for several minutes without seeing it. Then he threw himself down once more into the deeply buttoned leather desk chair, gnawing his thumb. His office was large, with paneled walls hung with oils of former directors of the bank. When, as now, the sun was not shining directly into the window, it was a dark, depressing room.

When the sound of the phone interrupted the silence once more, he turned back to it, irritated.

"Paul, I would like you to look in, if you would, when you come back this weekend." It was the Roylands' doctor, John Stanford.

Paul frowned, automatically reaching for his appointment book. Then he pushed it aside without opening it. "What is this all about, John? Do I gather it is not a social call?"

"I've had the results of the tests we ran on you and Clare. I'd like to discuss them with you before I talk to you both together."

Paul closed his eyes. Slowly he sat back in the chair.

"Which is as good as saying that we have a problem. And as you want to see me, do I gather it's in my department?" He took a deep breath. "Come on, John. Don't pussyfoot with me. I don't need anyone to hold my hand and look into my eyes while they talk to me. You can tell me over the phone."

"Very well." There was a pause as if John Stanford, far away in his Suffolk surgery, were choosing the right words. "It is the sperm count, Paul. It is low. Very low. We could repeat the tests, but the results are consistent. I'm afraid that it is very unlikely that you would ever be able to father a child. Under the circumstances, I think we can rule out the need for any further tests on Clare." There was a long silence. Then: "Paul? Are you there? Listen, we should discuss the situation. Will you look in anyway when you get back? There are avenues you should consider pursuing at this stage."

"You mean it's curable?" Paul was twisting a pencil between his fingers.

"No, Paul. I'm sorry. But there are other ways. Adoption, artificial—"

"NO!" Paul slammed his fist down on the desk. "If it is irreversible, then there is nothing to discuss, John. Nothing. Forget it. Do you understand? And John, I forbid you to tell Clare or to discuss this with her at all. Is that completely clear? I absolutely forbid it. I will tell her myself when the right moment comes."

He put the phone down and stood up. The bottle of Scotch

in the drinks cupboard in the corner of the office was still unopened. Paul broke the seal as he unscrewed it, then poured himself half a tumbler and sipped it slowly, his mind mercifully blank as he walked over to the window and stared down into Coleman Street. The traffic was at a standstill, the pavements crowded.

He had been watching for several minutes when slowly his attention focused on the far side of the road. A woman was standing there waiting to cross. She was holding a small boy by the hand. As they waited, the child began to jump up and down with excitement, looking up at her, and he saw the woman's face as she smiled down at him. It held an expression of such tenderness that for a moment he found himself biting his lip.

With a groan he turned from the window and hurled the whisky glass across the room.

Chapter Two

Emma Cassidy was in the bath when her brother called. Wrapped in a dark-green bath sheet, she sat down on the edge of her bed.

"Hi, Paul. How are things in the City?"

"Much as usual." He sounded depressed. "Em, I want to talk to you about Clare."

"Oh?" Emma was suspicious.

"You know she's got very involved with this yoga stuff. She's taking it very seriously."

"That's a good thing, surely." Emma threw herself back on the heaped pillows. Downstairs, her daughter Julia was sitting watching children's TV. For five minutes the house was peaceful. "I've done some yoga myself. It did wonders for my figure."

"No doubt. But she is doing it because she is obsessed with this idea of having a baby." Paul's voice was hard. "It's crazy. She must stop thinking about it. I am sure now in my own mind that children would not be a good thing. Not for us. We manage fine without that encumbrance in our lives, and we've got to find a way to put an end to this obsession of hers."

There was a short silence, then Emma laughed uncertainly. "My God, Paul. I thought it was you who kept on about having a son all the time. It was you who was making poor Clare feel so bad about it."

"In which case I must disabuse her of the idea." Paul was abrupt. "I've changed my mind."

Emma sat up straight. She frowned. "Has something happened, Paul? What is it?"

"I'm thinking of Clare. She's been under a lot of strain." He sounded severe. "And she is taking this yoga too far. I don't like the sound of this man who has been teaching her, or the thought of him wandering around my house. He's beginning to get her involved in some weird practices."

"Really?" Emma gave a breathless laugh. "You know, I think I like the sound of that. I wonder if they'd let me join in!"

"I'm being serious, Emma. Something has to be done, before it gets out of hand. I want you to try to talk her out of this whole stupid business."

"Why me, Paul? Why can't you do it?" Emma was serious again.

"Because she won't listen to me. You know what she's like. She can be so damn stubborn."

Emma frowned. "I always thought you two could talk, Paul. Have you been quarreling again?"

"We have not." He was growing exasperated. "Just help me in this, Emma! You have always got on well with her. She'll listen to you. I have to nip this thing in the bud. When did you last speak to her?"

"I tried to call her at Bucksters today, but your terrifying Mrs. C. said she was out. I'll try again when she comes up to town tomorrow. We'd vaguely arranged to meet on Friday anyway. But, Paul, surely yoga isn't bad? I don't understand why you're so worried about it."

"It's not the yoga as such, it's what goes with it—it's the meditation this man is teaching her—the mind bending—the attempts to conjure a child out of the air—"

"Is that what she is doing?" Emma was horrified. "Oh, Paul, that's terrible. Tragic."

"Exactly. So will you help me?"

"You know I will. Oh, poor Clare, that's ghastly."

She looked up at Julia who, bored with television, had wandered into the room, chewing on an apple, and suddenly her eyes filled with tears.

Rex Cummin was standing on the balcony of his penthouse apartment in Eaton Square. It was eight in the morning and the air was still cold as he absently studied the trees while waiting for his car to arrive outside the front door four floors below.

"Here's the mail, honey." His wife stepped out next to him with a handful of letters. They were a good-looking couple in their mid-fifties, both immaculately and formally dressed for the day. "Do you want me to get you some breakfast before the car gets here? Louise is late again, I'm afraid."

He looked up from thumbing through the pile of envelopes. "Don't be too hard on that kid, Mary. She's efficient enough, and she has a long way to come on the bus. Toch!" He gave an exclamation of disgust and handed the mail back to her. "Still nothing from that Scottish solicitor! Damn it, Mary, when is that woman going to answer him?"

"You only instructed him to make an offer for the estate last week, honey." She did not have to be told what he was talking about. "It could take months for them to get around to discussing it."

She noticed with a worried frown that he had clenched his fists and that the vein in his temple was beginning to throb again.

"Months is no good!" he shouted. "Sigma has got to have that land all signed and sealed before any breath of suspicion about the secret seismological surveys leaks out. Hell, Mary, what we've been doing is strictly against the law in this country. You can't go around doing surveys on other people's property without permission. We've got to cover ourselves. That's why this place is so perfect. We make Mrs. Royland a good offer for that hotel—which must be losing her thousands a year. Okay, so everyone realizes why we did it later, but by then it will be too late. My God, even Bob Vogel in Houston isn't onto the implications of those surveys yet." He slapped his fist into his palm. "And we have to wait for some goddamn British solicitor to ass about—" He winced suddenly, his hand going to his diaphragm.

His wife's practiced eyes missed nothing. "I'll get you some Maalox, honey. It'll line your stomach." She turned back toward the windows, then she hesitated. "Did you make offers on any of the other properties in that area?" It was a seemingly innocent question.

He shook his head. "There are going to be problems with the rest. Most of it is owned by the National Trust for Scotland and people like that. We'll put in bids later if the British government gives us exploration licenses. Besides, those test bores may not strike so lucky." He paused thoughtfully. "No, Duncairn is perfect. The test results; it's privately owned; and there's the hotel—the perfect excuse for the offer. My God, Mary, do you know there's even a ruined castle!"

"I know, Rex. You already told me." Did he really think she could have forgotten? The letters from the Scottish-American societies, the passionate delving into his ancestry, the genealogists in London and Edinburgh, the excitement when he found he might be descended from an ancient Scots family—a family who had once owned, among many other things, a castle on the wild northeastern seaboard of Scotland, a castle that now was possibly sitting on seven million or so barrels of oil. She smiled indulgently. "Now, you promise me you'll eat something on the plane."

"Sure, honey." He was impatient. "And you call me, at once—*at once*, if that letter comes."

"Of course." She walked ahead of him back into the large drawing room with its modern tubular steel-and-glass furniture.

Something crossed her mind suddenly. "Why did you ask him to send his letter here, Rex? Why not straight to the office?"

He scowled, running his fingers through his hair. "Not a word of this must get out, Mary. Not one word. I sometimes think not everyone in that office is entirely loyal. No!" He raised his hand as she was about to protest. "No, I can tell. Ever since I was ill they've been watching, waiting to see if I'm still on top of things. Nothing is said. To my face they're all great guys, but I can sense it. And I'm not going to lose this opportunity to prove old Rex Cummin is still one step ahead. And I am not going to lose that castle! That is why I'm going to Houston in person."

Mary sighed. "What if Mrs. Royland turns down your offer?" she couldn't resist asking.

"I'll make a bigger one." He flipped open his black leather

attaché case, deftly checking that passport and documents were in place. "The lady is a Scot. I'm sure she appreciates the value of money." He smiled wryly.

"Even if she doesn't you can make sure you get in the best tender later," she said quietly.

He snapped his case shut and stared at her for a moment out of very blue eyes. "I don't just want the license, Mary. I want to own that land. I want Duncairn."

Paul Royland had agreed to join one of his junior partners for lunch in the City Club. Both tall, impeccably clad in the City uniform of dark suits, striped shirts, and sober ties, Paul dark, Henry very fair, they made a striking pair as they threaded their way toward their table. Henry Firbank was on edge. Several times as they ate their hors d'oeuvres he glanced across at Paul as if trying to pluck up the courage to say something. Finally he managed it. "Old Beattie asked me in for a chat yesterday. He—" He paused, chewing on a mouthful of melon. "He mentioned you several times."

"Oh?" Paul looked up, his fork halfway to his mouth.

"He was a bit concerned about some of the deals you've been involved in over the last few months. I can't think why. I told him everything was going fine. I told him you've always had an idiosyncratic way of handling things, that's all." Henry gave an embarrassed smile, his florid face even more pink than usual. "But he did seem a bit worried. I thought you'd better know."

Paul gave a grim smile. "Beattie should worry about getting himself measured up for a wheelchair. The bank's getting beyond him."

"Right." Henry grinned amiably, obviously relieved to have gotten his remarks off his chest.

"I must get Penny to check that my filing is up to date, I can see that," Paul went on sarcastically. "I had no idea I was being investigated."

"Oh, it's nothing like that, I'm sure. There has been some muddle over old Mrs. Barlow's investments, I gather, and—" He broke off. "What is it, old boy? Is something wrong?"

"Nothing." Paul closed his eyes and took a deep breath. He

put his fork down and pushed aside his plate. He had hardly touched his food. "I'd better have a word with Beattie about this. You forget it, Henry. I know what's happened. There's been a foul up between the old girl and her broker. She's reluctant to change over to BCWP." He took a long drink from his glass of wine and changed the subject. "You're coming to this reception at the Guildhall tonight, I hear. Clare is driving up from Bucksters for it. I'm sure she'll be pleased to see you there."

"How is Clare?" Henry looked up, his face alight. "It's ages since I saw her."

Paul, beckoning the waiter to take away their plates, gave Henry a hard look. "She's well. Radiant as always."

"Radiant?" Henry echoed. "She's not—that is, you're not— I mean, I know she hoped . . ." He floundered to a standstill, embarrassed.

Paul frowned. He closed his eyes for a moment as a wave of anger and despair swept over him. "If the word you're looking for is pregnant, the answer is no. She's not."

Clare had arrived in London late that morning. She drove straight to their house on Campden Hill. It was a pretty, white-painted Regency cottage, hung with clematis. In front of it there was a small paved area, starkly bare save for an Italian stone urn that contained an ornamental bay tree and two large terra-cotta pots overflowing with geraniums and lobelia. After letting herself into the hall, she paused and listened. She had left Casta at Bucksters with Sarah Collins; otherwise the small elegant rooms would have been filled immediately with bouncing, grinning retriever. The house felt very quiet and empty.

She was exhausted by the long drive, and there were dark rings under her eyes. She had had the nightmare again last night, waking at three in the morning to the sound of her own screams. It was the third time in as many weeks. Again and again the dream had come back since she had gone to Duncairn in June, as if somehow that lonely ruin had stirred some sleeping demon in her brain. If only Aunt Margaret were there. She had understood. Once, when Clare was a child, they had talked about the dream. Clare, tearful and shaking after it had come again, had run not to her mother's bed—Archie had long ago forbidden that—but to Margaret Gordon's, snuggling into her great-aunt's arms in the four-poster in her room in the cold north wing at Airdlie. "One day I'll explain, Clare," Margaret had whispered. "Dear God, the nightmare is mine, not yours! You shouldn't have to suffer it as well. Be brave, my child. Remember, morning always comes, the sun returns, and it will stop. I promise, one day it will stop."

And for several years it had not returned; not until that midsummer night at the Duncairn Hotel. Since then she had had it four times, and then again last night. As she sat up in bed trembling Clare had heard the creak of floorboards on the landing. She held her breath, desperately trying to calm herself, praying it wasn't Sarah coming down from her top-floor apartment, but the urgent scratching at the door followed by a pleading little yelp reassured her.

She shot out of bed and ran to let Casta in, flinging her arms around the dog's neck as she wept into the thick golden fur. She had spent the rest of the night with the light on, the dog lying next to her on the bed.

Paul called her at the house in Campden Hill just after lunch. "I thought I'd see if you'd arrived safely," he said. His voice was strained. "What sort of journey did you have?"

"Tiring." She was sitting at the Queen Anne bureau in the front room. "I left later than I meant to, so the traffic was bad. Where shall we meet this evening?"

They talked almost as strangers these days. Polite—there had been no more quarrels—but slightly distant, as if those unpremeditated words, hurled at each other in the bedroom of the Edinburgh hotel, had unlocked some secret hostility that neither had recognized before, and that they were both terrified they might loose again. Even the intimacy of the visits to the doctor and the terrible embarrassing tests and all that went with them had been conducted on a strangely impersonal level.

"Why don't you come to the bank at about six, and we'll go

on from here. I'll take you out to dinner afterward, if you like." Suddenly Paul was sounding more relaxed.

Clare brightened. "I would like that, darling."

"Good. By the way, John Stanford called yesterday with the results of our tests. They all proved normal. And I agree with him now that we should leave things there. Give it a rest. Leave it up to chance. Stop worrying. Forget about doctors. Forget about having a baby. Let the whole thing go, now. Get on with our lives."

"But, Paul—"

"No, I mean it, Clare. This has all been too much strain on you. I don't want you cracking up. I don't even want to discuss it anymore, do you understand? We have both been in danger of becoming obsessed by the subject, so let's drop it for good. No babies. No children. I've come to think we'd be happier without them in the long run anyway." His voice tightened. "Right? Now, I'll see you later, and we'll have a pleasant evening without that subject hanging over us. Agreed?"

It was only after she had hung up that it dawned on her to wonder if he had sounded slightly drunk.

Carefully she unpacked the candle and set it on the floor of the bedroom. A bath, then half an hour's meditation would restore her energy before she changed for the reception. She walked into the bathroom and threw open the window. It looked out onto the tiny garden with its trellised roses and mossy paving stones. One or two rather dog-eared blooms still clung to the wall below the windowsill.

After turning on the bath water and tipping in some bath oil, she stepped in, lay back, and, closing her eyes, thought about Paul.

He very seldom drank. Unlike his two brothers, who indulged their appetites if not to excess, then at least without too much soul-searching, Paul had an almost ascetic approach to food and drink. In spite of this, however, he was a large man—all three Royland brothers were tall and broad-shouldered. But unlike the other two his late thirties had not produced a paunch or a thickening of the flesh. She couldn't believe he had been drinking. Perhaps it was euphoria because the tests had proved normal, after all their worries. If so, she desperately hoped it would last.

Drying herself slowly, Clare wandered back into the bedroom. She dropped the towel now and stood in front of the long mirror scrutinizing her figure critically. At twenty-eight, ten years younger than her husband, she was as slim and taut as she had been when she was eighteen.

She lighted the candle solemnly and raised her arms as Zak had told her, to signal the start of her meditation. Then slowly she sank down into the half-lotus position.

She had written back to the solicitor the afternoon before, a considered, firm letter in the end, politely informing him that Duncairn was not, and never would be, for sale, and she had driven into Dedham with it and caught the evening mail. As far as she was concerned the matter was closed. Duncairn was safe. Her haven, her refuge. As Zak had promised, the problem, once faced, had gone away.

For a moment, on the brink of closing her eyes, she hesitated. Her last visualization of Duncairn hadn't been as she intended. It had brought back unbidden memories of Midsummer's Day. She shivered. That experience she did not want to relive. This time she would be more careful. She would picture the moors beyond the castle, and perhaps, if she concentrated, she could summon Isobel back, the Isobel of Aunt Margaret's stories. . . . The Isobel who had been the heroine of all her daydreams as a child, her imaginary playmate in her loneliness. Carefully she began to construct a picture in her mind of the moor near the castle as she had seen it so often when she was a child. She saw the blaze of heather beneath the torrid sky and the hills, misty in the distance. Overhead, slowly rising on the invisible spirals of the wind, a buzzard was mewing, the lonely call echoing across the moorland. She could feel the sun on her back, smell the soft honey of the wild thyme and moss, even hear the gentle ripple of the brown water in the burn at her feet. Now, with the scene set, perhaps the story could start again. . . .

* * *

Shaking her long hair back from her face, the child threw herself down full-length on the grass and began to scoop the cool water into her mouth. The young man standing behind her eyed her bare legs and naked brown feet doubtfully. "You'll be in trouble when your nurse finds out where you are," he said, his face unwillingly relaxing into a smile.

"Nurse!" She sat up. Some of her hair had slipped into the water and it dripped onto the shoulders of her thin woolen gown. "I don't have a nurse. I'm a grown woman, Robert of Carrick, and don't you forget it."

"You are?" The young man laughed out loud. "I beg your pardon, my lady Isobel. But all the ladies I know have bevies of maids and attendants following them everywhere, and men-at-arms to watch over them when they stir from their castles!"

"I do too." She clasped her knees with a shiver. "I ran away from them when I knew you were riding up here. I wanted to come too. I get so bored doing what Lady Buchan tells me all day long, Robert."

"Nevertheless, you should obey her." Robert looked troubled. "If you are to marry the earl it is important that his mother teaches you all she knows. Lord Buchan is a great and powerful man, Isobel. He will expect much from his wife."

"Pooh." Isobel flung herself backward on the grass, shading her eyes to stare up at the sky. "He'll never marry me! He barely knows I exist. Do you know, when he comes to Duncairn or Slains to see his mother he sometimes takes me on his knee and tells me stories. He gives me presents and sweetmeats, just like the children of his brothers. I'm sure he thinks I must be one of them."

"I doubt it." Robert stood looking down at her. "You and he have been betrothed since you were a small child. He's only been waiting for you to grow up. That is why your mother gave you to Lady Buchan to bring up, when your brother was sent to England after your father died."

There was a long silence as his words sank in. She sat up again, pushing the hair back off her face. It was a small oval face with huge gray eyes, set below straight dark determined eyebrows, a face that promised great beauty. Defensively she hugged her arms around herself, unconsciously hiding the budding breasts that barely showed yet beneath the loose folds of the dusty gown. "Then perhaps I'm not grown up," she said at last in a whisper. "Perhaps I never will."

The betrothal had taken place before her brother was born. She remembered vividly the day at Falkland Castle when her father had told his wife what he had arranged. Neither the earl nor the beautiful Joanna de Clare had realized that their small daughter was listening and taking in every word of their conversation. It had been after Duncan of Fife, young and inexperienced as he was, had been chosen as one of the two earls on the small council appointed to rule Scotland after the death of King Alexander. He had received the news of his appointment confidently, attributing it to his own undoubted qualities, becoming since that day more conceited than ever, flaunting his position, using it everywhere to his own advantage. Later Isobel had learned the truth— that the earldom of Fife had to be represented because of its preeminence among the seven ancient earldoms of Scotland. Before she had believed it was because her father was a great and good man.

The earl had glanced down at his daughter as she played near him. "I have been speaking to my lord of Buchan. He is willing to agree to her betrothal to his heir." Duncan had preened himself, waiting for his wife's reaction. Isobel too had waited. And she had seen the horror and disbelief on Joanna's face.

"You wish to betroth that child to Lord Buchan's son?" Her eyes had grown enormous. "But, my lord, she is only a baby, and John Comyn is a grown man. He would never want a child for a wife!"

"He will wait." Duncan had given a snort of laughter, throwing back his head so that Isobel could see even from where she sat on the ground the gaping hole in his teeth where the surgeon had pulled a great aching molar. "By the saints, he's waited long enough to take a wife as it is!" He had grown serious suddenly, sitting forward on the edge of the

wooden bench, resting his chin on his hand so he could gaze
into his wife's face. "Don't you see what a marvelous union
this will be? The Comyns are the richest and most powerful
family in the land. The old earl is, with me, one of the six
guardians, but when he dies, which must be soon, Joanna, it
would be expedient if our two families were linked by more
than just friendship. Our lands in the north march together—
what could be better than to bring them closer? After all," he
had added bitterly, "it looks as if that puny girl will be my
only heir." He had paused, and Isobel, hugging herself with
sudden devastating misery, saw the sparkle of tears in her
mother's eyes as he rushed on in a bluff attempt to cover his
cruel remark. "Think, think of the power this will bring us. If
it hadn't been for this little queen of ours far away across the
water, it might well have been a Comyn chosen as king.
Think of that."

And now that little queen had died without ever coming to
Scotland, and as Duncan had predicted, a member of the
huge Comyn family had been chosen as king—John Balliol,
Lord Buchan's cousin.

Only six weeks after that terrifying news of her impending
betrothal had come tidings of the death of the old Earl of
Buchan. Joanna had been afraid that now he was free of his
father's influence John Comyn would repudiate the agreement. She had heard, and so had Isobel, all eyes and ears as
usual, near her, how he had sworn and flown into a rage
when told that his father's choice for his bride was only four
years old, but then he too had seen the strength that would
lie in such an alliance. Only two weeks after his father's death
he had come to Fife for the betrothal ceremony and Isobel
had seen him for the first time. He had brought a fine filigree
brooch of silver for Isobel's mother Joanna and a heavy ring,
engraved with the Buchan seal, for Isobel; her small finger
had not even the strength to hold it. Once the ceremony was
over he had galloped out of the castle courtyard, followed by
his retinue. Two days after that a messenger had arrived
from him bearing a doll. The riders had, it seemed, passed a
traveling packman, and the earl had found a gift more suited

for his little bride. They had heard nothing of him after that until Isobel's father died.

Robert rode ahead of her to within sight of the castle, then he drew rein. "You go on, back to your attendants," he said. "I think it better we're not seen together. I'll ride on south to Mar, as I intended in the first place." His smile softened the rebuke.

"If you see my great-grandmother at Kildrummy will you give her a kiss from me?" Isobel smiled suddenly. Malcolm, Earl of Fife, had died some twenty years before, long before Isobel was born, and his widow Eleyne had remarried the powerful Earl of Mar, but she had kept her interest in her Fife family, particularly Isobel, in whom she recognized much of herself when she was young. Isobel, in a world devoid now of close family, loved her dearly.

"Why don't you get into trouble if you ride without attendants?" Isobel asked Robert suddenly. "It's just as dangerous for you to ride the hills alone."

"My attendants are waiting for me, as you well know." He slapped the neck of his horse affectionately. "Besides, I am a man." He frowned. "Will you get into bad trouble when you go back?"

"I'm bound to." She looked up at him unrepentantly. "But Mairi, who has charge over me, never does very much, even though she says she will. She says I'm uncontrollable."

"I can believe it!" He laughed. "I'm glad I'm not to have the marrying of you, cousin. I doubt if I could cope."

She giggled. "No, you couldn't. I shall be a shrew and a scold and no man will want anything to do with me! I shall ride the hills dressed in men's clothes and be my own mistress. Then my lord Buchan will wash his hands of me and marry an old docile lady who can give him ten fat babies!"

This time they whipped her. They took her into the great hall at Duncairn where Elizabeth, Dowager Countess of Buchan, was sitting on the low dais.

Isobel stood before her defiantly, her fists clenched in the folds of her skirt, as Lady Buchan distastefully looked her up and down, taking in the ragged gown hitched up in her girdle and revealing her muddy, scratched legs and feet.

"So, where did you find her this time?" she asked. "In the byre with the animals?"

Mairi, a stout woman of indeterminate years and unswerving loyalty to her young charge, shook her head miserably. "She went out riding alone, my lady. She told her escort to go back without her."

"And they obeyed her?" Lady Buchan's eyebrows shot upward toward her fashionably plaited and netted coils of hair.

"Oh yes, my lady. The men always do as Lady Isobel says." Mairi bit her lip. "She's awful determined, for a lass."

"Is she indeed." Lady Buchan's face was growing more and more grim. "And did you set off to ride looking like that, my lady?"

Isobel colored a little at the sarcastic tone. "I took my kirtle and my stockings and shoes off and bundled them up in the heather so they'd not be spoiled," she said defiantly.

"I see. And what were you intending to do, that they might get spoiled?" The older woman rose to her feet suddenly. Her face had sharpened with suspicion. "Was there someone with you out there?"

"No, my lady," Isobel blurted, suddenly guilty. "There wasn't anyone there."

"Are you sure?" Taking a step toward her, Lady Buchan seized her by the wrist. "No young man? No love to amuse you? Where is my son?" She turned abruptly to the attendants who encircled them.

"He's just returned to the castle, my lady," a voice replied. "He said he'd be in to greet you directly."

John, Earl of Buchan, was as good as his word, striding into the castle hall only a few minutes later, his spurs ringing on the stone flags.

"So, what is this? A trial with so small a prisoner?" He dropped a kiss in the air some inches above his mother's head and then straightened to look at Isobel, standing before Elizabeth, her arm still firmly clasped by the wrist.

He was a tall, hirsute man in his late thirties, good-looking, with hard brown eyes. Isobel took a step back as his gaze fell on her.

"This child has been roaming again. She behaves like a strumpet." Although near sixty, Lady Buchan was still a slim, graceful woman, without a streak of gray in her dark, lustrous hair. She was almost as tall as her son as they stood facing each other across Isobel's head.

"A strumpet, is it?" John looked down at Isobel with sudden interest, his eyes traveling down her slight form.

"Aye, a strumpet. And her maidenhood will be long gone before you get around to making her your wife!" Elizabeth of Buchan tightened her lips primly. "She is uncontrollable."

"Surely not." John stepped forward and, taking Isobel's arm, pulled her away from his mother. "How old are you, sweetheart? I thought you were still a child, but I gather you are not content with a child's games any longer."

Too proud to shrink away from him, Isobel straightened her shoulders and stuck out her chin. "I am fourteen, my lord."

"So you are indeed. Old enough to be bedded it seems, so old enough to be wedded. Who did she lie with?" He shot the question over her head at the unfortunate Mairi. "Whoever it was, he'll pay for it with his life."

"There was no one, my lord." It was Isobel who answered, her eyes blazing. "Your lady mother seems to think I would lie with stableboys and serfs. I, the daughter of the Earl of Fife, a descendant of the ancient House of Duff!"

"Hoity-toity!" The dowager countess gave a humorless laugh. "If you behave like a strumpet, madam of Duff, you may expect to be treated as one. She has disobeyed me too often, John. She should be whipped."

Isobel bit her lip. She stood her ground, though, her wrist still firmly held in John's rough fingers.

He seemed to be considering, and for a moment she dared hope he would reprieve her, but it was no good. He released her wrist.

"Very good, Mother. Perhaps a lesson in obedience now will make her a gentle wife later. But don't hurt her too much. I'd hate to see such a pretty child marked."

Almost blind with rage and humiliation, Isobel barely noticed as she was led, stumbling, to the chamber she shared
with Mairi and two of Countess Elizabeth's grandchildren,
and there made to take off her gown. Standing shivering in
her shift, she watched dumbly as one of the countess's ladies
appeared, carrying a hazel switch.

She was too proud to cry. When it was over she pulled her
gown back on with Mairi's help and then walked in silence to
the deep window embrasure. Only there, behind the heavy
curtain, did she allow herself to waver for a moment, kneeling on the cushioned window seat, staring out across the
glittering sea.

The telephone made Clare jump nearly out of her skin. It
was several moments before she could gather her wits
enough to stagger to her feet to answer it.

It was Emma.

"I thought I'd missed you again. Are we still going out
tomorrow evening?" Emma's voice was down-to-earth,
cheerful.

"Tomorrow?" Clare was dazed.

"You remember. We agreed we'd have a meal together—
just us, without husbands—to try that new place we were
talking about. Are you all right, Clare?"

"I'm sorry." Clare pushed her hair back from her face
distractedly. "I must have been asleep. What time is it?"

"Just after five—"

"Five?" Clare's eyes opened wide. "My God, I'm due at the
bank in less than an hour. I'll talk to you tomorrow, Em,
okay?"

She sat still for a minute after she put down the phone,
trying to gather her wits. The meditation, if that is what it
had been, had been a terrifying reality. It was as if, in sitting
down and opening the secret, closed recesses of her consciousness to the past, she had allowed someone else's memories to come flooding back. It was as if she were Isobel and
Isobel were she; as if she had entered completely into the
mind of this child who had, according to Aunt Margaret,
been her ancestor, and as if Isobel had entered into hers.

Shaken, she stood up and gazed into the mirror, trying to catch a glimpse of those other eyes that had, in the silence of her meditation, looked out through her own. But it was no use. They had gone. All she saw were the eyes of Clare Royland, a twentieth-century woman who was late for an evening with her husband.

Shrugging off her mood as best she could, she began at last to get ready. She slipped into the green silk dress with its swirling calf-length skirt and reached for Aunt Margaret's gold pendant to clasp around her neck, staring at herself in the mirror for a moment one last time before reaching slowly for her hairbrush. Already it was nearly half past five.

The taxi dropped her opposite the broad flight of steps that led up to the door of the Merchant Bankers, Beattie, Cameron, at six-fifteen exactly. Slowly, trying to compose herself into the role of partner's wife, she walked up the steps and smiled at the doorman who unlocked the door for her.

"Good evening, Mr. Baines. Is Mr. Royland in his office?"

"Good evening, Mrs. Royland. It's a treat to see you again, if I may say so. I'll just check at the desk." He led the way to the reception desk and picked up the internal phone.

Clare glanced around at the huge entrance hall. This was still the old building, for all its modern plate-glass doors. The broad flight of stairs and the oak paneling betrayed the office's solid Victorian origins. Above the grotesque marble fireplace at one end of the hall was a large portrait of James Cameron, co-founder of the bank, and opposite him, hanging over another equally imposing fireplace, Donald Beattie, grandfather of the present senior partner. Paul's office was at the top of the first flight of stairs.

As Baines hung up she turned toward the stairs with a smile. "All right to go up?"

"He's not in his office, Mrs. Royland." Baines came out from behind the desk. "He's in the new building. If you'd like to follow me, I'll show you where to go."

He opened a door in the far wall beyond the stairs and ushered her through. There, a glass walkway lined with exotic plants led directly into the new tower building where the bank and the stockbrokers Westlake Pierce, where her brother worked, now formed the nucleus of a new and powerful financial services group.

Clare followed him into the fluorescent-lit building until he stopped outside a row of elevator doors. "This one will take you straight to him, Mrs. Royland. The penthouse conference room. Nonstop. You get a breathtaking view from up there. You haven't been in the new building before, have you?"

He paused, his finger on the button as the elevator door slid back. "Mrs. Royland? Are you all right?"

Clare had closed her eyes. Her fists clenched tightly as she felt her stomach turn over in panic. The elevator—a steel box with deep-gray carpeting on floor and walls—was waiting for her, the door open, the little red eye above the call button alight and watching.

She swallowed desperately. "Are there any stairs?"

"Stairs?" He looked shocked. "There are thirty-two stories, Mrs. Royland! Don't you like elevators? I don't like them much myself, truth to tell, but they're fast, these ones. You'll be all right." He gave her a reassuring smile.

She bit her lip. "Would you come up with me?"

"I can't." He shook his head. "I'm not supposed to leave the desk. By rights, I shouldn't even have come through here. . . ."

There was no alternative. Giving him a shaky smile, Clare stepped into the elevator, clutching her leather purse tightly to her, and watched as the door slid shut.

How could Paul have forgotten her claustrophobia, her terror of elevators? Why couldn't he have waited downstairs and come up with her, rather than making her travel up alone? Breathe deeply. Relax. Use what you've been taught. And count. Slowly count.

The elevator was slowing. She braced herself for the slight jolt as it stopped. Relieved, she waited for the door to open. There was total silence around her. Nothing happened. Even the slight hum of the mechanism had stopped. Then the lights went out.

"Oh, God!" Clare dropped her purse in the darkness, the

adrenaline of panic knifing through her stomach. Desperately she reached out in front of her until her hands encountered the heavy steel doors, groping frantically for the crack between them. She could hear her breathing, hear her own sobbing as she clawed desperately around her. It was like the nightmare all over again—the nightmare of the cage, but this cage was real and solid, and it wasn't a dream. Was there an escape hatch? A telephone? She couldn't remember. Frantically she tried to keep a hold on the threads of reason as she hammered on the heavy, carpet-deadened walls. But there was nothing. Just a square, empty box.

"Oh, Christ! Oh, God, please don't let this be happening! Please!" Already it was growing hot and airless. The darkness was absolute, tangible, like black oil swirling around her.

Falling to her knees, she put her hands over her face, trying to cut out the darkness, rocking backward and forward on the soft executive carpet, and at last, uncontrollably, she began to scream.

Chapter Three

"Clare? Clare darling, you're all right. It's all over. You're safe."

Paul was squatting beside her in the elevator, his arms tightly around her. Behind him, the broad penthouse reception area was bright with light. "Come on, Clare. Can you stand up? Nothing happened. There was some sort of power failure. It was only a few seconds, darling."

Shaking like a leaf, with her husband's arm around her, Clare managed to rise to her feet and Paul helped her out of the elevator. "Come on, darling. There are chairs in the conference room. Penny, could you get some brandy. Quickly." Paul's secretary had been hovering white-faced in the doorway.

Clinging to him, Clare followed Paul into the huge conference room with its floor-to-ceiling windows. Some were screened with blinds, but no blinds were drawn on the western side, and the whole side of the room was a blaze of fiery red from the setting sun. After helping Clare to a chair, Paul took the proffered glass from his secretary and held it to his wife's lips. "Drink this. My God, woman, you frightened me. Why on earth did you scream like that?"

"I'm sorry, Paul, but I couldn't help it—"

"Of course you couldn't." Penny put a comforting hand on her shoulder. She was a plump, pretty woman of about thirty, smartly dressed in a dark suit with a frilly jabot at the collar of her blouse. Next to the green swirl of silk under Clare's mink coat it looked odd, even indecently sober. "I hate that elevator myself. I'm always terrified it might get stuck."

"It didn't get stuck." Paul sounded irritated. "It stopped for a couple of seconds when the electricity went off. That's all."

"It was several minutes, and it probably seemed like several hours to poor Mrs. Royland," Penny retorted stoutly, glaring at her employer.

Shakily Clare took another sip of brandy. "I'm all right now, really." She managed a smile.

Behind Paul the sunset was fading fast. Grayness was settling over the city. No one had switched on any lights in the conference room itself, and it began to seem very dark.

Paul was watching his wife closely, as if undecided what to do. The wave of tenderness that had swept over him as he helped her from the elevator had passed, leaving him strangely detached once more. When at last he spoke, his eyes were cold. Whatever regret and sadness still touched him when he thought of their longing to have a child had been firmly suppressed. He had far more immediate worries on his mind.

"You look very pale, Clare. I don't think you should come to the reception after all."

"Nonsense, Paul. I'm fine."

"I don't think so." Paul was firm. "Penny, would you go back with Clare? Get a taxi and see her to the house. I have to go on to this wretched do, but I'll come on home straightaway afterward. You should go to bed, darling. You look completely overwrought."

"I'm not, Paul." Clare was suddenly angry. "I'm perfectly all right. If you'd been waiting in your office none of this would have happened."

"I thought you'd like to see the view."

"But you know how much I hate elevators. Couldn't you at least have waited downstairs and come up with me?" She knew she sounded petulant, and the realization made her even more angry.

He was looking at her thoughtfully. "I suppose I should have. I'm sorry."

"Oh, Paul." She bit her lip suddenly, desperately wanting him to put his arms around her, but it was Penny who kept ineffectually patting her shoulder.

Paul had reached into his pocket for his wallet. He extricated a ten-pound note. "Here, Penny. Would you take her home now please, then go on yourself. I'll see you in the morning."

Clare swallowed her anger and disappointment with difficulty. Paul was treating her like a spoiled child who needed punishing. She wanted to shout at him, to defy him, to go to the party in spite of him, but then again, for his sake, she did not want to argue in front of the other woman, and she had to admit her legs did still feel shaky. She glanced up at him, suppressing with difficulty the new wave of fear that swept over her at the thought of getting into the elevator again. "But what about you? Why can't you come down with us?"

"I'll follow in five minutes or so. I have a few papers to sort out." He glanced at the long conference table. At the far end his briefcase lay open, a neat pile of documents beside it on the polished surface. His gold fountain pen lay meticulously aligned on top of the papers. "You will be all right, Clare. Penny will look after you."

Unceremoniously he ushered them both to the door. He didn't wait to see them call the elevator.

Penny pressed the button, her arm firmly linked through Clare's. As the doors slid open she glanced up at the small glass-fronted cabinet in the wall high up near the elevator buttons. Inside it were all the emergency power switches for the top floor. She had gotten up to close the door to the landing after Paul went out to the cloakroom. She was sure she had seen him standing there near the switches. Then all the lights had gone out and, dazzled by the sunlight behind her, she could see nothing on the dark landing at all.

"The club is almost empty this evening." Paul's brother-in-law Peter Cassidy greeted James Gordon in the changing room at Cannon's as the latter, having fitted his card into the electronic door, came in carrying his sports bag. "We needn't have bothered to book a court." He stooped to retie the lace on one white tennis shoe. "How is your sister, James? Em seems to think she's going through a rough patch."

"Is she?" After putting his card back in his wallet, James ripped off his tie and pulled the Turnbull & Asser shirt up over his head without undoing more than two buttons. "I haven't talked to Clare for ages. I think she was a bit miffed about me inheriting Aunt Margaret's money. I mean, the old girl had a very good reason for doing it, but Paul and Clare didn't see it that way. Paul wanted to contest the will and have her declared senile."

"Which she wasn't, I gather." Peter sat down on the bench in the middle of the room to wait for him.

"No way. She was right on the ball up to the last five minutes, Ma said. Clare knew that, of course. I don't think she cares, actually. It's Paul. You'd think with all his money he'd leave it alone, wouldn't you? But perhaps it's a habit with him." He paused reflectively. On the whole he was a great admirer of Paul's. "Anyway, I thought Clare might be too embarrassed by the whole stupid thing to want to talk to me for a bit." He grinned, flicking his dark hair back from his face. "Besides, she hasn't been much fun lately. She leads such a boring life, stuck in that house in the middle of no-where." He stepped out of his trousers and reached for his shorts.

"It doesn't sound boring from what I've been hearing." Peter laughed. "She's having private lessons in body-building from a continental Lothario."

James had been rummaging in his sports bag for a shirt. Abruptly he straightened. "Oh, come on. That's one of Emma's stories!"

"No, you ask Clare."

"I will." James laughed. "Good old sis. Perhaps she's finally kicked over the traces. I always knew she would in the end. I wonder what Paul thinks?"

"He's horrified. He was the one who called Em. He wants her to talk Clare out of it all. Apparently he thinks it's all some sort of compensation for not getting pregnant."

"What a load of crap." James had finished putting on the white socks and shoes. After stowing the last of his things in his locker, he picked up his squash racquet. "It's Paul who is neurotic about having a son. I don't think Clare gives a screw. Come on. I'm going to thrash you tonight, then last man to finish twelve lengths of the pool pays for dinner."

* * *

James looked distastefully around at the disordered living room of his apartment in the Barbican when he got home that evening and sighed. The cleaning woman had failed to come for the second time running, and it was thick with dust. Dirty plates and glasses littered every free surface, and there were clothes scattered on the floor. The air smelled stale. After throwing open the windows, he went into the kitchen and opened the refrigerator. It was empty of food. Tonics, cans of beer, two bottles of Bollinger, that was all. It didn't matter. He wasn't hungry. Peter had gone home to Emma for supper in the end. James had been invited, but he hadn't wanted to go. There was always tension in the Cassidy house. He helped himself to a can of beer and, going back into the living room, threw himself down on an easy chair, picked up the phone, and, after extending the antenna, began to punch out a number.

It was some moments before she replied, and when she did she sounded depressed.

"Hi, Clare, how are you?"

"James?" From the slight sniff he wondered suddenly if she had been crying and he frowned. Deep down, beneath all the aggression, he was very fond of his sister.

Once home, Clare had gone straight upstairs to lie down, not even bothering to remove her dress. Still indignant at Paul for sending her home like a child who has been forbidden a party because she has misbehaved, she was even more cross with herself for allowing him to do it. She had been lying gazing up at the ceiling, still feeling very shaky, when the phone rang. It was James.

"It's a long time since you bothered to call. What do you want?" she asked, forcing herself to sound cheerful.

"I don't want anything. I can afford my own now, remember?" he said maliciously. "No, seriously, Sis. I've been hearing weird stories about you and your body-building. What gives?"

There was a puzzled silence, then Clare laughed. "Body-building? Who told you that?"

"A reliable source. Actually it was Peter Cassidy. Emma told him. Tell me about it."

"It, James, is yoga, that's all."

"What, no dumbbells? No rippling muscles and black satin G-strings?"

"No." It was her old infectious laugh.

"And no continental Lothario?"

There was a pause. "No, Californian actually."

James whistled. "What does Paul say?"

"He's not interested, and if he was I wouldn't care." She sounded rebellious. She didn't want to think about Paul, so she changed the subject abruptly. "James, you haven't had any letters about selling any of the estate, have you?"

"No. Why?"

She hesitated. "I had a letter from a solicitor in Edinburgh —Mitchison and Archer—saying they had a client who wanted to buy Duncairn."

James gave a soundless whistle. "I wonder why. Did they name a price?"

"No. They said it would be negotiable."

"Are you going to sell?"

"Of course not. That's my inheritance. All there is of it," she couldn't resist adding.

James ignored that. "I can't think why anyone would want Duncairn," he went on relentlessly, "unless—" He stopped suddenly. "You know, there were some rumors in the City last month about the oil companies sniffing around the northeast coast again. Maybe they're looking for somewhere to put a new terminal." He was intrigued. "That would be a wonder, Clare, if old Duncairn turned out to be worth a fortune. Whatever they want it for, if it is an oil company, they would offer good money."

"Even if they do, I'm not selling." Clare was appalled at the thought. "Listen, James. Don't mention this to anyone. I haven't told Paul about the letter and I don't intend to. There's no point."

"There would be if they offered you enough money, Sis. I'll ask around and see what I can find out for you."

Clare walked across to the window after James had hung

up and drew back the curtains. The night was cold now, after the hot day. She could smell smoke; someone had been burning dead leaves in one of the squares and the scent flavored the night with autumn.

With a sigh she closed the window and walked slowly downstairs, still wearing her green dress. The skirt dragged on the steep uncarpeted staircase behind her with an exotic rustle. She went down the second flight to the basement kitchen, wondering if she should find herself something to eat—she hadn't eaten properly since breakfast that morning —but she wasn't really hungry.

Damn James. She hadn't wanted to think about that letter anymore. And damn Paul. She had been looking forward to the reception. And damn the elevator! She shivered. Baines had been amazed when Penny asked him about the power cut. None of the building seemed to have been affected except the top floor. Of course none of the other elevators had been in use at the time, but he would call the engineers at once and have them checked. He had been indignant, asking why they hadn't called him on the internal phone, and scolded them for using the elevator again. Clare had clenched her fists tightly as they waited for the taxi, her eyes firmly on the locked glass doors. Only when she was out on the pavement once more did she begin to relax at last.

She went back upstairs into the living room. The original two rooms had been knocked through into one, so there were windows at both ends. She walked across and drew the front curtains briskly, then went to stand looking out into the darkness of the back garden beyond her own reflection. It was probably damp and misty in the country by now, but here the night was clear and luminous even where it lay beyond the reach of the light from the window. She could see the pale, blighted rosebuds clearly, clinging to the trellis behind the oak garden seat.

She brought the candle downstairs and set it in the middle of the Persian rug in the front half of the room and lighted it. Then, kicking off her shoes, she turned off all the lights. She unplugged the phone, then, quietly shutting the door into the hall, she turned back to the candle and, closing her eyes, raised her arms above her head.

Isobel was wearing a beautiful deep-red full-skirted gown with a long train. It was held in place with a plaited girdle and she wore a gilded chaplet over her hair, which hung loose over her shoulders. She was a little older now.

She was standing in the shadows at the back of the great hall, watching eagerly as the page made his way to the Earl of Carrick's side as he sat talking with a group of men. She saw the boy sidle up to him and whisper in his ear, and she saw Robert look up, his eye quickly scanning the great hall. He couldn't see her, hidden as she was in the shadow of one of the pillars that soared up into the darkness to support the massive roof timbers. Outside, night was falling.

The moment she saw Robert stand up, she turned and slipped out of the hall, picking up her skirts to run, threading her way swiftly through the crowded passages of the castle towards the chapel.

The door was heavy. Grasping the iron handle she turned it with an effort and slipped inside. The chapel was almost dark, but a candle burned before the statue of the Virgin in a niche beside the altar, another on a ledge beside the door. The air was sweet with incense. There was no one there. Breathing a quick prayer of gratitude that the place was empty she curtseyed before the statue and crossed herself, then she waited, her eyes fixed on the huge arched window above the altar. With darkness outside she could see none of the colors in the patterned glass, only the fluted stone tracing that held it in place.

When the door opened again with a slight creak she gave a little gasp, but it was he.

"Robert!" She flew to him. "I had to see you. Why have you come back to Duncairn? Where is Lord Buchan?"

Robert caught her as she threw herself at him, holding her at arm's length. "I came here to meet with him, Isobel, but he and I could not agree." He tightened his lips. "I leave now and I do not intend to return to this castle or any other held by Lord Buchan."

"But, Robert—" She looked up at him pleadingly.

"No, little cousin. He has seen how worthless the Balliol is as king, yet still he supports his claim to the crown against that of my father because the Comyns and the Balliols are kin. He even arranged that John St. John should place the crown of Scotland on John Balliol's head in the name of your young brother." He smiled wryly. "Your House of Duff has power indeed, my Isobel. The hereditary right to crown a king! It was that crowning which gave weight of custom to Edward of England's choice for Scotland's king." He paused. "Perhaps when the people of Scotland come to their senses, we can bring your brother back from his place at the King of England's side, and then, one day, he can crown me! But until the Bruce claim is recognized and Balliol dispossessed, your betrothed and I cannot agree. Now"—he smiled at her in the darkness—"what is so urgent you have to see me alone?"

"They have fixed our wedding day." Her whisper was anguished. "If the king gives his permission, we are to be married at Martinmas. Oh, Robert, I can't bear it. It mustn't happen. You have got to help me."

For a moment he looked down at her, his face sorrowful, then, almost reluctantly he drew back. Briefly he touched her cheek with his hand. "Poor Isobel. There is nothing I can do, you know that."

"But there is. There must be." Her voice rose in panic. "That is why I wanted us to meet here. It is the only place in the castle we can be alone. Please, Robert, you have to think of something. You have to get me away."

She took a few paces from him toward the altar, then turned back, her red skirts sweeping the stone flags impatiently. Behind her the candles flickered and smoked. "Please, Robert. Any moment Father Matthew may come back. You've got to think of something."

He studied her gravely—the beautiful, anxious face beneath the long, curling black hair, the huge gray eyes, the slight but undeniably feminine figure beneath the figure-hugging red cloth. She was close to him now, and he could smell the sweet musk of her skin and the slight scent of lavender from her gown. Unexpectedly he felt a wave of intense desire sweep over him, and, surprised and embarrassed, he took a step back.

"Isobel, nothing can be done. You have been betrothed to Lord Buchan since you were a child. A betrothal is binding, you know that."

"But it can be broken. Somehow it must be broken. If you are going to be king, you can do anything! You must marry me instead, Robert. Please. You like me, don't you?" She took a step toward him, putting her hands on the front of his surcote, her eyes pleading.

"You know I like you," he whispered, his hands gently covering hers. "Isobel, this is foolish. It cannot be."

"Why?" Instinctively she knew what to do. Gently, standing on tiptoe, her hands still pressing against his breast, imprisoned in his own, she kissed him on the mouth. It was the first time she had kissed a man.

He groaned and pushed her away violently. "Isobel, don't you understand? It can never be. Never. I too am betrothed, remember? And I too have fixed my marriage date. It was one of the reasons I went to Kildrummy. Isabella of Mar and I will marry at Christmas."

Stunned, Isobel stared at him. "Isabella of Mar," she echoed dully. "You prefer that milksop to me?"

"Aye, I do." He looked at her coldly. "I'm sorry, but that's the truth."

He tried not to see the hurt and rejection in her eyes, hardening his heart against the pain he knew he had caused her. He had in fact only spoken half the truth. He loved his betrothed; she filled him with tender protectiveness, making him feel strong and chivalrous, her knightly protector, a role that appealed to him greatly, but, he had to admit, he felt very strongly attracted to Isobel of Fife too, although in quite a different way. He closed his eyes. He was a man, not a boy. He knew the difference between courtly love and lust. What he felt for his gentle, beautiful betrothed was the former. Isobel of Fife, on the other hand, stirred him to passionate longing. She was exciting, a temptress, though she scarcely knew it yet herself, and undoubtedly she was trouble. The feelings she aroused in him shocked him. One should not feel desire such as that for any lady of high birth, never mind one so young and destined to become another man's wife.

With an exclamation of anger he turned from her, staring hard instead at the serene painted wooden face of Our Lady in the niche.

"You are making yourself unhappy," he said curtly. "There is no point, can't you see that? There can be nothing between us, ever. And there can be no escape from your betrothal."

He saw that his blunt words had stung her. She straightened her slim shoulders. "Oh, but there can, Robert," she retorted, her eyes flashing rebelliously.

He wasn't sure to which of his two statements she was referring. Perhaps both, he thought, and in spite of himself he felt a little shiver of excitement. But his voice remained firm. "You can't escape, Isobel. Make up your mind to accept it."

She shook her head. "I don't accept things," she retorted. "Even if you do. I'm a fighter, and I'll fight this. If you won't help me, then I'll manage alone. Now you'd better go, or your men will miss you in the hall."

He hesitated. "Don't do anything foolish."

She tossed her head. "I don't intend to."

"You won't try to ride anywhere alone?" Almost unwillingly he had stepped closer to her again. His hand strayed to her shoulder, touching her hair.

"It's none of your business where I go or what I do," she replied softly. "Not now." Her mouth was close to his. He saw the tip of her tongue for a moment between her lips, unconsciously teasing.

Unable to stop himself, he held out his arms and drew her to him, his mouth urgently seeking hers, crushing her breasts against his chest, imprisoning her arms against her sides.

"Oh, God forgive me, but I do love you," he breathed.

"Then help me." Somehow she freed her arms, winding them around his neck. "Please, Robert."

"And make you my little queen, love? I can't. Don't you see, I can't." Anguished, he kissed her again, stifling her words.

Isobel stiffened, then with a sob she tore herself free of his arms. "Then go!" she cried. "Go now. I never want to see you again! You shouldn't have come here! To kiss a woman in here before Our Lady is wicked—it's sacrilege!"

"Then it is a sacrilege I gladly commit." Gravely Robert took a few steps toward the door. "May Our Lady protect you always, Isobel, my love. I wish I could," he said. Then he was gone.

The ground-floor office in the sixteenth-century building on the north side of the Grassmarket in Edinburgh was untidy, piled high with books and pamphlets. Files overflowed from shelves and chairs onto the floor, and posters covered more posters on the walls. Sitting at the desk in the center of the room, Neil Forbes paused in his writing and, dropping his pen, stretched his arms above his head with a sigh. He glanced at his wristwatch. It was after 9 P.M. Behind the blind, the Grassmarket was deserted, the dark street wet in the windswept rain.

He gave an exclamation of irritation as the phone rang.

"Neil? I'm so glad you're still there. I didn't have any other number—"

He frowned momentarily, not recognizing the voice.

"It's Sandra Mackay. You remember. I came to the Earthwatch meeting when you were talking about pollution. We had a drink afterward . . . I'm a friend of Kathleen's . . ." Her voice trailed away uncertainly.

"Of course I remember." He squinted up at the ceiling, noting a new place where the wallpaper was beginning to peel away. "What can I do for you, Sandra?" He had a pleasant voice, deep and musical with a slight Scots inflection.

She gave a strange half sigh. "It's difficult. I know I shouldn't tell anyone this—it's breaking the rules of the office. I'm supposed to keep everything I see and hear confidential. I always have, but . . ." He could hear the indecision in her voice.

"Sandra, if it is something that worries you, and you think Earthwatch should know about it, then you have done the right thing in calling me. Personal loyalty is a wonderful thing, but not at the expense of the environment or the safety of the people as a whole. These days we must all learn to accept that." It was what he always said. Trite but true, and something he passionately believed. "Now, can you tell me over the phone, or would you like to meet me somewhere?"

"No, no." She sounded terrified. "Listen, I've only five minutes to talk before my mum gets back." She paused for a moment, then began in a rush.

"I typed out a letter last week to a Mrs. Royland in England. We were transmitting a client's offer to buy her estates. She owns about one thousand acres up on the coast at Duncairn, including the village and the old castle. Today she wrote back refusing to negotiate. She said the estates were not for sale and never would be. Well, Mr. Archer called me in to dictate a reply without even consulting the client again. They are offering more money than you can imagine!" She paused. "When I'd taken down the letter he told me his client was prepared to go much higher if necessary to get it."

Neil had risen to his feet. Still holding the telephone, he walked across to the map of Scotland pinned on one wall of the office. The phone in one hand, the receiver in the other, he peered at the map, even though there was no need. He knew only too well where Duncairn was.

"Mr. Archer said there were rare birds and plants on the cliffs there and he thought they had some sort of development in mind, and he said he didn't like the sound of the offer at all," she went on.

Neil scowled. "Neither do I," he said grimly. "And I would guess they are offering well over the normal market price. Do you happen to know the name of the prospective buyer?"

"I shouldn't tell you."

"You have already told me most of it, Sandra." He was at his most reassuring. "And no one will ever know how we found out any of this, I promise."

"Well." She sounded only half reassured. "It was a man called Cummin. He works for something called Sigma Exploration."

Neil stood staring at the map for several minutes after she had hung up, then slowly he returned to his desk. He took a file out of one of the drawers and opened it. So it was true, the rumor that someone had been carrying out surreptitious geological survey along that stretch of coastline. And it looked as if the worst had happened. The surveys had been encouraging.

"Gossip has it that it is onshore oil, Neil," Campbell had said in his note. "I can't believe that, unless the geological structure of Scotland has changed recently, but for what it's worth someone has been surveying pretty thoroughly up and down the coast over an area of several miles. And doing it far from openly. It is an area that contains several Sites of Special Scientific Interest and some of it is owned by the National Trust for Scotland and is Heritage coastline . . ."

"And some of it is owned by Mrs. Clare Royland," Neil murmured to himself. He threw down the file and, standing up again, began pacing the short space of empty floor between his desk and the window. He was remembering the visit he had paid to Duncairn in June shortly after Jim had sent in his report.

It was a place he knew well, a place he had visited on several occasions as a student, a beautiful place, ruinous—including the hotel, he thought wryly—wild, unspoiled, peaceful, with several miles of rocky, dramatic coastline, which had to be preserved at any cost. He had wandered around all morning, going to the hotel for a pint of Export and some sandwiches for lunch. Then, drawn back almost against his will, he had walked back to the sprawling ruins of the castle for one more look before driving back to Edinburgh.

It was then he had seen her. He was certain it had been Clare Royland. Who else could it have been? She had arrived in a flashy green Jag, dressed for a London garden party, even to the high-heeled shoes. Young, beautiful, oh, yes, undeniably beautiful; rich, aristocratic—looking at him as if he had no right to be there, which, strictly speaking, he hadn't, and then, later, looking through him as if he weren't there at all. He remembered how the whole place changed after she arrived. The joy had gone out of his visit. It was as if her arrival had released strange, unhappy memories in those ancient stones. He shivered at the thought. The mist had come in off the sea, drifting up the cliffs, cutting off the sunlight, and he had left her to it.

She looked the type who would sell, damn it. She might protest her love of the place, but in the end she would sell. After all, she was married to Paul Royland. And he had good reason to remember Paul Royland of old.

Henry Firbank paid off the cab at the bottom of Campden Hill and began to walk slowly up the road. When he had met Paul at the Guildhall, Paul was deep in conversation with Diane Warboys, one of the new brokers at Westlake Pierce, but he had paused long enough to explain that Clare had had a fainting fit at the office and decided to go home rather than come to the reception.

Later, when Paul had offered to take Diane out to dinner, Henry had made up his mind. He wasn't being disloyal to Paul. It was merely natural concern for how Clare was. He would knock, perhaps not even go in, just see she was all right. . . . It never crossed his mind to telephone instead.

He could see a faint light showing at the crack in the heavy pale-aquamarine silk curtains. Straightening his tie, he lifted the knocker and let it drop, wishing he had thought to stop off and buy some flowers somewhere on the way. He waited, then he knocked again, louder this time. Perhaps she had fallen asleep in front of the television.

He wasn't sure, afterward, what made him do it, but when she failed to answer his third knock he found himself slinging one long leg over the low railings at the side of the steps and stepping into the paved front garden so that he could peer through the crack in the curtains.

Clare was seated cross-legged on the floor in front of a guttering candle. She was facing the window and he could see her clearly. Her face was serene, blank, her eyes closed, her whole attitude completely relaxed as the flickering candlelight played over her, illuminating her features, turning them to alabaster, picking out the glint of gold at her throat and wrists and on her fingers, sending darting shadows into the deep folds of green silk piled so carelessly around her on the floor.

Henry caught his breath. He watched her, fascinated, unable to tear his eyes away, as the candle slowly died, leaving her sitting in darkness alleviated only by the thread of light thrown across the floor by the streetlamp behind him. It was only the sound of footsteps walking down the road in the distance that made him straighten suddenly, realizing how he must look to a passerby, doubled up with his eye to a crack in the curtain.

After vaulting back over the railing, he stood uncertainly on the step, wondering what to do. Tentatively he knocked again, then, bolder, he rang the doorbell. It pealed through the house, making him jump. He waited breathlessly. Moments later a light came on in the hall and the door opened.

"Henry?" Clare stared at him, dazed.

"Clare." He bent forward and kissed her cheek. "I'm sorry to call so late. If you'd rather, I'll go away at once. Only Paul asked me to look in on my way home and see you were all right. He has met up with a client, I gather, and he'll be a bit late back—you know how it is." Paul hadn't asked him to do anything of the sort.

Clare bit her lip. She looked tired and strained in the harsh light of the hall.

"That was good of you, Henry. You'd better come in." She backed away from the door.

He followed her into the living room and he found himself looking at the rug where she had been sitting. There was no sign now of the remains of the candle, but he thought he could smell it, mixed with her subtle perfume in the air.

"You're sure you're not too tired, Clare? Paul told me you weren't feeling very well."

"No, I'm fine. Come on down and talk to me while I make us both some coffee. The elevator at Coleman Street got stuck with me in it and I made a bit of a fool of myself, that's all. I'm afraid it will be all around the bank tomorrow." She smiled wanly.

"Oh, Clare, how terrible." He followed her down the steep flight of steps.

"I've been claustrophobic since I was a child. So silly, really." She busied herself filling the kettle and plugging it in while he sat down on a stool watching her, his long legs folded under the breakfast bar.

"Clare. I couldn't help seeing, through the curtains, upstairs. What were you doing with that candle?" He hadn't meant to ask, hadn't meant to admit to spying on her.

She glanced up at him sharply, but she smiled.

"Meditating."

"You mean like praying?" He looked embarrassed.

"Perhaps, a little. Although, not the way I do it." She was playing with her sapphire engagement ring, twisting it around her finger so the facets caught the light. "It's very strange, Henry. Something I started doing to help me unwind a bit." Suddenly she found she had to tell someone about it. Strangely, she knew Henry would understand. "When I was a child I had a sort of imaginary playmate—I think a lot of children do. She was called Isobel." She paused for such a long time he wondered if she had forgotten he was there.

"Go on," he said at last.

"My brother was four years younger than I, and we never got on, really. We still don't." She smiled wistfully. "So I was a lonely child." Isobel's brother was four years younger and a posthumous child, like James. She paused, recognizing the strangeness of the coincidence for the first time. "I suppose that's how children always react to loneliness: an imaginary friend."

Henry said nothing, afraid to interrupt her train of thought.

"She was a real person," she went on at last. "An ancestor of ours. My great-aunt used to tell us stories about her. Long, involved, exciting stories. I don't know where they came from or if they were true but they caught my imagination.

"I hadn't thought about her for years—not until I went to Duncairn again in June. Now she has come back. Not to play with." She laughed, embarrassed. "Not like when I was a child, but when I meditate. It is as if I am opening a door, and she is there waiting. . . . She is much more real than before. No longer my creation. It is as if she has a life of her own."

Henry could feel the skin prickling slightly on the back of his neck. He cleared his throat. "I expect the meditation technique allows your imagination a free hand," he said slowly. "But if it upsets you, you should stop."

"Oh, it doesn't upset me. I enjoy it. It's so much more exciting than—" She stopped abruptly. "I was going to say than real life, but that sounds so awful."

Henry grinned. "It's not awful at all. It's quite understandable. Real life is—well—real. Your Isobel presumably has more fun in her life."

Clare smiled. She was thinking of Robert's kiss. "Indeed she does. Do you think I'm quite mad?"

"Only marginally." He was relieved to see the strain leaving her face.

"Please don't tell Paul. I don't think he'd understand. Paul thinks I should be happy pottering about like Gillian and Chloe or your partners' wives, doing good works and going shopping, but I'm not like that. I need something more, something different from them. The trouble is, whenever I try to explain to him that I would like to get a job, or do some really serious studying, we get back to babies." Her jaw tightened.

"Babies?" Unobtrusively Henry leaned forward for the jar of instant coffee and drew the empty mugs toward him.

"Paul wants me to have babies."

"And you don't?"

"Oh, I'd love to have one; I sometimes think I can't live without one. But then I get depressed about it and want to forget about babies altogether." She paused for a moment, thinking again of Paul's phone call earlier that day. The tests were okay and yet suddenly he'd changed his mind. Now he too wanted to forget about babies. She bit her lip. Somehow it didn't ring true, but that was something she could worry about later. "I wish Paul really could forget about babies for a bit. In fact, I wish the whole Royland family weren't so obsessed with procreation."

Henry laughed. "Tough. Tell him you're on the pill, taking a degree in Oriental studies and about to rebuild your fairy-tale castle with your own hands once you've finished your bricklaying apprenticeship, and there will be no babies until you're forty at least. I gather motherhood late in life is all the rage these days. That should fix him."

She giggled delightedly. "Oh, Henry, I'm so glad you came over. You put everything in perspective. Bless you."

Henry picked up the kettle. Suddenly he felt ridiculously happy.

James was surprised Paul agreed to meet him so quickly.

"So." Paul looked at the younger man with some curiosity as they made their way briskly along Coleman Street. "What is all this about?" James was very like Clare to look at. Roughly the same height, which was fairly short for a man, slim, dark-haired, the same large gray eyes, but curiously, on him, the features made him look rugged and handsome. Handsome enough to pull women in droves, according to his sister, even before he had inherited his fortune.

"I wanted to know how Clare is." James looked him straight in the eye.

"She's fine. That was a stupid incident last night. She has to learn to be less neurotic, that's all."

"Last night?" James raised an eyebrow. "What happened last night?"

"She was trapped in an elevator for a minute or two and it shook her up. Isn't that what you meant?" Paul asked mildly.

"No." For a moment James looked uncomfortable, then with a slight shrug, he went on. "No, I was talking about this man teaching her to cope with mental stress or whatever it is. Why is she so stressed?"

Paul gave a deep sigh. "I wish I knew. But, as to her handsome yoga teacher"—he gave a half smile—"I think you can take it he will shortly be getting his marching orders. Clare's neuroses, such as they are, are better served by rest and quiet than by some quasi-spiritual mumbo jumbo. I'm sending her

on a holiday next month. That will help her more than anything else."

"Lucky Clare," James said dryly. "Does she know yet?"

Paul caught the note of sarcasm and looked up. Unexpectedly he smiled. "No," he said. "She doesn't know yet."

It was not until they were sitting at their table downstairs
at Gows and their food had arrived that James dropped his
bombshell.

"What do you think about the offer for Duncairn?" he
asked innocently as he picked up his fork.

"The what?" Paul stared at him.

"Clare received an offer for Duncairn. Didn't she tell you?
She turned it down, of course. I gather they didn't mention a
figure—"

"Who? Who wants to buy it?"

"Ah well, that's the interesting point. Clare didn't know—
the offer came through a third party, but I've done some
nosing around among my pals." James stopped and put a fork
full of fish into his mouth, chewing slowly, well aware that
Paul was waiting.

"And?"

"And I gather there is some speculation about surveys
they've been doing up that coastline. Word is, one of the oil
companies might have put in a preemptive bid just in case
they decide to test drill. The bet is that the offer is from one of
the big consortia or, just possibly, from an outfit called Sigma
Exploration, a U.S.-based company that is trying to get a
larger foothold overseas. There's been a lot of talk about
them in the City lately. You must have heard of them.
They're trying to raise some big bucks."

"And you think some of it is to buy Duncairn?" Paul's eyes
narrowed. "For God's sake, Clare never mentioned it!"

"She doesn't know," James put in hastily. "Not about
Sigma." He hesitated, suddenly half regretting that he had
betrayed Clare's confidence. "She'll put up a hell of a fight for
Duncairn, Paul—"

He stopped, astonished, as Paul laid down his knife and
fork, his food untouched, and pushed back his chair. His face
was white. "Fight," he said slowly. "She doesn't even know

the meaning of the word. If someone is offering big money for that heap of stones, and she opposes the sale, I'll make her sorry she was born!"

Turning on his heel, he headed for the staircase.

Chapter Four

Clare was out in the tiny sun trap of a garden at the back of the London house when Paul arrived. An open book had been discarded on the paving stones beside her chair as she lay, dressed in a low-necked cotton blouse and shorts, soaking up the afternoon sun.

"I've just had lunch with your brother."

"Oh?" Clare felt her stomach tighten. She resisted the urge to scramble to her feet. She stared hard at the litter of crisp dead leaves nestling in the moss against the bricked border of the flower bed and waited.

"He tells me someone has offered to buy Duncairn." His voice was even.

"That's right." Clare tried to sound casual. "Crazy, isn't it? I expect they wanted to develop the hotel." She carefully avoided looking at him.

"No doubt. May I ask how much they offered you?"

"They didn't mention a figure. They said if I was interested we could discuss a price, but as I have no intention of selling, there is nothing to discuss."

"And you weren't even interested enough to find out how much they were considering offering you?" His tone had a mocking, dangerous ring.

"No." She stood up abruptly, her shoulders hunched, and took a few steps away from him, studying a bruised rosebud with exaggerated care.

"What if I told you that it was worth a fortune to the right person?" he said quietly.

"It wouldn't make any difference." She turned to face him. "I suppose James told you he thinks they want it for an oil terminal or something. Well, even if they do, I don't care. I'm not selling."

"Not a terminal, Clare. They think there is oil there."

She stared at him. "I don't believe you!"

"It's true. Whether you believe it or not, and whether there is really oil there or not, is immaterial. The fact is, one of the oil companies believes there may be, and they want to acquire the land. Now, under different circumstances, I might have agreed with you and said keep the land, although rents and revenues are unlikely to be worth much, but we need the capital, and with the oil industry in such turmoil, the sensible thing is to go for money in the hand. Now. If this company wants to invest in a speculative deal, then you should take their offer. It will be a big one." He was watching her intently, his voice still carefully even. "They might change their minds later."

"No. I don't want to sell. Aunt Margaret left Duncairn to me. She meant me to have it forever." She was trying to breathe calmly.

"And pass it on to your children?" Paul's voice was acid.

Clare froze. "Mine or James's," she whispered at last.

Paul sat down on the wooden bench near her. Behind him the mellow redbricks of the wall radiated a gentle heat from the sun. He took a deep breath, determined to seem calm. "Clare," he said with exaggerated patience, "I do appreciate your feelings, darling, but they are totally irrational. When the price is right one must always sell."

"And everything has a price, of course." She sounded very bitter. "So, tell me, Paul. What is the price for Duncairn? Were you thinking of driving them up? Holding an auction perhaps in a marquee on the castle grounds? What is it to me, after all? Just some scrubby moorland, some inaccessible cliffs, the rents from a fishing village, a ruin, and a hotel that makes no money! You're right. I should sell it at once! I can't think why I should have delayed." She turned toward the door. Then she stopped and faced him again. "Money! That's all you think about! For God's sake, why do we need any more capital? Haven't we got enough?"

"No, we haven't got enough. As I told you before, Clare, one cannot have enough money," he replied coldly. "And as your aunt failed to leave you any at all to administer the estate, and as you seem convinced she had your welfare at heart, I can only assume that she had some idea of its worth. It may be that she did, after all, leave her property divided equally between you and James. And if that was the case, she expected you to sell."

"She did not." Clare stared down at him. "You know perfectly well she did no such thing. I don't understand you anymore, Paul. If we needed the money, this would make sense, perhaps. But we don't." She pushed her hair back from her face. "Do we?"

For a moment he hesitated, then he shook his head. "I need all the money I can get, Clare. For investment." He gave a hard, humorless smile. "And I intend to get it. And I am not going to let you stand in my way."

There was a moment's stunned silence as Clare stared at him. "What do you mean?" she managed to ask at last.

"I mean I intend to see to it that you accept that offer. You'll have no children, Clare, to pass on some stupid old woman's sentimental vision of a family seat to. The Gordon connection with that land would die with you anyway, because I'm damned if you're leaving it to your brother. He's got enough as it is."

"I could still have children, Paul." In her confusion at his sudden rage Clare seized on her one bit of hope. "You said there is nothing wrong with me—"

"No! Accept the fact. You will never have children. John Stanford told me so, Clare. We didn't want to hurt you, we didn't want you to blame yourself, so we agreed to say nothing to you. But it's you—*you* who can never have a baby!" He stood up, his face taut, his bitterness, anger, and impotence focusing at last on her, battering her, determined to hurt her as he had been hurt. "Inheritance means nothing when the line is barren, you might as well face it. Do you think if you did decide to leave Duncairn to James that he would keep it for one single minute? Of course he wouldn't. He would sell."

"Paul—"

"No, Clare. No more crazy excuses. I want you to give me that letter. I'll contact the solicitor—"

"I burned it." Quite suddenly she was completely calm.

She looked at him coldly. "I have no intention of selling, Paul, or of letting you do it for me. The land is mine. And it will remain so."

Their eyes locked. For a moment she thought he was going to hit her. Then, abruptly, he pushed past her and went into the house. A few minutes later she heard the front door bang.

For a long time she sat quite still on the bench, her mind a blank. The October sun had slipped behind the rustling, paper-dry leaves of the plane tree in the garden behind theirs, throwing cold, flecked shadows over the paving. She shivered violently.

Barren. The most desolate word in the English language. No pregnancy, no baby; no sons, no daughters. Just a useless empty woman, hated by her husband. The look in his eyes had been more eloquent than any of the words he had thrown at her. He disliked her and he despised her. The change in him, which had started the day Aunt Margaret's will was read, was now complete. The Paul she knew, the Paul she had married had disappeared. His charm, his sense of humor, his carefree extravagance, all had gone. Had he never loved her then, at all? Was the acquisition of money going to take the place of the family they would never have? She stood up and blindly turned and ran into the house. After picking up the phone with a shaking hand, she began to dial. Dr. Stanford was not in.

For a long time she sat staring into space, then at last she stood up. She walked slowly upstairs and went into her bedroom and drew the curtains.

Her legs crossed, her hands resting loosely on her knees, she tried to force herself to breathe steadily. She could hear her heart pounding in her chest, feel the throbbing of her nerves, like electric shocks in her stomach. Calm. She must be completely calm before she lighted the candle.

But it was no good. Slowly she pushed her body into a series of yoga movements—the cobra, the swan, the shoulder stand, the stork. But her mind was still racing, her muscles contorted. She could find none of the usual comfort in the asanas. Lying down flat on the floor, she tried to relax, bit by bit, starting with her feet as she had been taught, but that was no use either. Exasperated, she gave up. What was the point of trying relaxation methods now? She never would conceive. There would be no baby. She was barren.

Then she reached for the phone again and dialed the Cambridge number.

"Zak, it's Clare. I'm sorry to call you, but you did say—"

She told him everything. His calm voice reassured her, stilled the urgent jangling of her nerves, and he had promised to come the next day. Meanwhile, she would try to meditate again, as he suggested, and if it didn't work at once, she would go on trying. There was no hurry. She had all evening. But somehow she had to find a way of getting back into Isobel's world. There she could forget her own.

She lighted the candle and stood looking down at it for a while, breathing slowly and rhythmically, then slowly she raised her arms. She closed her eyes and sank down to the floor. "Be there," she murmured out loud as she began to build again her laborious picture of the empty moors. "Please, be there for me. . . ."

Isobel was on horseback, a bundle of clothes tied behind her on the wooden saddle, a cloak around her shoulders. A heavy fur-lined hood bounced behind her on her back and her hair was loose, streaming in the wind as she bumped up and down to her horse's trot. She was alone.

She glanced behind her apprehensively, but the castle, silhouetted blackly against the blaze of the sunrise, was quiet. She had not been missed yet. Her heart gave a little lurch of excitement as she kicked the animal into a canter.

It was a year since Robert had left Duncairn, and still she was unmarried. Martinmas had come and gone and Lord Buchan was too busy to arrange his marriage. He was constantly absent from the castle. As one of the most influential men in the land, he was helping to direct the nation's affairs, helping to balance the delicate political maneuvers needed to keep Scotland an independent nation, free from English domination.

Having been asked to choose Scotland's king from among

the several claimants to the throne after the direct royal line had failed with the death of Scotland's little queen Margaret, far away in Norway, seven years before, Edward of England was not inclined to retire now from Scottish politics. His aim was to be overlord of Scotland, if not king himself. The nation was in deadly danger. In March Berwick was captured and sacked, and then the Scots had been defeated at Dunbar. Lord Buchan had not returned to his northern lands. Isobel, with everyone in the Countess of Buchan's household, heard the news from the south and waited anxiously to see what would happen next, but her anxiety had a very personal twist to it. She did not want the Earl of Buchan to come back at all, unless perhaps he had had second thoughts and still thought his betrothed too young for marriage.

Nothing was said and Isobel prayed the marriage was forgotten. Then to her horror she found that it had merely been postponed while lawyers wrangled. Once again, she now knew, the date for the wedding had been set. So now she was having to carry out her plan.

Robert's departure the year before had left Isobel very thoughtful. If he would not help her, would anyone? She was alone. Alone in every sense but the true one, for not for a moment was she allowed out of sight of one of Lady Buchan's attendants; on every side there were eyes watching her.

They could watch, but they couldn't read her thoughts. Her vague, childish optimism that the earl would forget about her was gone, so every waking second of her day was filled with plans of escape. She was cautious now, and outwardly docile, but inwardly she was defiant. She would not marry the Earl of Buchan.

She still hugged the thought of Robert to her secretly. His words had shaken her but, unknowingly, he had offered her a challenge. It was one she could not resist, and the reward for success was freedom. He was married now to another and he could never marry her, but he loved her. He had kissed her, and that kiss, she knew instinctively, had sealed a bond between them that had to be redeemed.

And to redeem it she had to leave Duncairn.

She did not doubt she would succeed; there was no possibility of failure. Carefully she laid her plans. Calmly practical, she had rejected the romantic notion of climbing the castle walls. She had to go out through the gates, but invisibly, covering her tracks, so no one would see her go and no one would miss her. And that meant going at night.

The horse had been easy. She bribed Hugh, the handsome son of the farrier, to take one of Lady Buchan's palfreys from the stables under the west wall and leave it overnight in the stall next to the forge. Reluctantly she decided against her own showy, spirited gray pony and selected instead a sturdy bay, a horse that would excite no attention on the road. Hugh knew what he had to do.

The bundle of clothes was easy too. She gathered them together over two days, stuffing each garment down behind a coffer in a corner of the dark sleeping chamber. It was the actual leaving of the curtained bed she shared with Mairi and Alice, one of Lady Buchan's granddaughters, that would be very hard.

She tried getting up before dawn to see what would happen. Grumpily Mairi turned her head on the pillows. "Where are you going, my lady?" The woman's eyes were still puffy with sleep.

"Where do you think!" Isobel slid out of the high bed.

In the privy she waited, counting slowly to see if Mairi would get up to see where she was or go back to sleep.

Mairi got up.

The second idea was more daring. She announced she had decided to go to keep a dawn vigil in the chapel to pray for the soul of her dead father. Grumbling furiously, Mairi accompanied her there too, and Isobel was forced to kneel on the cold stone for an hour, her eyes fixed on the statue of the Virgin, before she would admit she could stand it no longer and creep back to the warmth of the bed.

In the end the solution had presented itself. Mairi was so tired after her disturbed nights that she nodded off once or twice in the course of the day. Isobel noticed, and waited, and managed to whisper to Hugh.

That night she was deliberately restless, kicking her companions, tossing and turning, determined to keep them

awake as long as possible so their exhaustion would make
them sleep through her exit from the bed, though she had to
acknowledge she could not have kept still if she had tried.
Keyed up beyond endurance as she was with the thought
that Hugh would be waiting at dawn, she was terrified that
she would fall asleep herself and miss their assignation.

As the first lark soared upward into the black sky, Isobel lay
completely still at last and held her breath. Beside her Mairi
groaned and, punching the soft pillows, turned on her side.
Within a few minutes her breathing had steadied and she was
deeply asleep.

On the other side of her Alice muttered incoherently and
let out a gentle snore. Isobel breathed a little prayer, wriggled toward the foot of the bed, and pushed her way out
between the heavy curtains.

The spiral stair outside the door was pitch-dark, the light in
the sconce long since burned out. Holding her breath she
listened, then she pulled her kirtle on over her head and
wrapped herself up in her cloak. She began to feel her way
down the steep stairs barefoot, her hand pressed against the
cold, curving wall. In the silence of the predawn she could
hear everywhere the sigh and shift of the sea below the castle
walls. It was almost high tide.

The great hall was full of sleeping figures, men lying on the
rushes, wrapped in cloaks or plaids. The air was fetid. Wrin-
kling her nose, she crept along the wall toward the door. She
used every ounce of strength to lift the latch and pull it open,
then slipped through. Beside it the door ward, an empty ale
tankard beside him on the floor, sprawled against the wall.
He never heard the latch lift or saw the slim dark figure slip
out of sight among the shadows.

The cold morning air was sweet and intoxicating. After
waiting only to pull on her shoes and take a firmer grip on her
bundle, Isobel ran down into the outer bailey, praying Hugh
had remembered.

He was waiting at the postern with the horse, the keys in
his hand. When she had gone he would relock it, slip the keys
back into the gatehouse, and crawl back to his pallet at his
father's side.

* * *

Isobel was exultant. She had not dreamed it would be so easy. Staring up into the brilliant blue of the sky, she felt her heart soar up with the lark. She would show Lady Buchan and her son! And Robert! Other women might meekly marry and submit to their fate, but not she! She felt the wind lift her hair and, dropping the reins, she flung out her arms toward the sky. She was free!

She rode all day without seeing anyone, carefully avoiding the wider tracks, keeping to the deer paths through the heather, always alert for the movement of horses or the alarm calls of the buzzards, which would tell her she was not alone. Two days' ride, she had heard, that was all, two days with her back to the rising sun and her nose to the land where it sets, then she would reach the territory of the Gordons, the sworn enemies of Lord Buchan.

As night came near she grew less certain. She was desperately hungry, and she was cold. A heavy dew was falling as she stopped at last in a small glen with a creek running through it. It seemed a safe enough place, with shelter and grazing, but as the shadows lengthened and the soft darkness deepened around her, she felt for the first time a shiver of fear. After tethering the horse, she lifted down the heavy saddle with difficulty, and, wrapping herself in her cloak, she settled herself to sleep.

It was impossible. Her mind was racing in circles; pictures of her life in the Buchan castles, at Duncairn and Slains, Kinedar, Ellon and Rattray, and the others flashing before her eyes, and with them visions of the countess, the earl, their household—and Robert. Again and again the face of the handsome young earl appeared before her. She scowled, shifting her weight as she leaned against the saddle, feeling the damp from the ground working its way into her clothes. Somewhere nearby an owl hooted and she shivered at the sound.

If only Mairi could have come with her. She prayed silently that Mairi wouldn't get into trouble for letting her escape. She loved Mairi, who had looked after her since she was a baby, going with her when, at the age of four after her father was brutally murdered, the Countess of Fife had sent her to the Buchans. Joanna de Clare, distraught and preoccupied after the death of her husband and the traumatic early birth of her son, had not had the strength to stand up against the earl's demands that Isobel be brought up by his mother. The owl hooted again and seconds later Isobel heard the agonized scream of a small animal dying in the heather.

She was frozen and aching in every limb by dawn. Sleep had come in the end, but only in short fits and starts, interrupted by every night sound. She had been reassured by the steady, single-minded grazing of the horse and its relaxed dozing—it sensed nothing to fear—but her senses were overstretched and exhaustion had made her too tired to sleep deeply. By dawn she was again in the saddle, her back resolutely to the crimson blaze of the sunrise in the sky behind her.

Lady Gordon was completely confused by the arrival of her young visitor. The disheveled clothes, the dusty, exhausted horse, the absence of escort or anything to prove her identity beyond the haughty demeanor and Isobel's insistence that she be received at once by the lady herself were all most perplexing.

"But who are you?" Lady Gordon stared at her visitor in astonishment.

"I am Isobel of Fife; the earl is my brother." Isobel smiled demurely, only half aware that she looked more like a peasant than a lady, with her peat-stained face and hands. "I have been held prisoner at Duncairn castle. Lord Buchan wants to force me into marriage. I knew you would help me."

She was thoroughly enjoying herself now, her hunger and exhaustion temporarily forgotten, as she became conscious of the circle of men and women behind her, listening open-mouthed to her dramatic appeal.

She held her breath, her eyes pleading, as Lady Gordon stood up. The reference to the Earl of Buchan had evidently struck a chord with her. Her pale cheeks had colored violently. "Nothing would surprise me about that man! You poor child. What a terrible thing! Of course we will help you!"

Isobel sighed with relief. She was safe.

Within an hour she had been fed and wrapped in warm blankets and put into a bed. Only minutes later, hugging herself with excitement, she was fast asleep.

It was two days before she discovered her mistake.

Isobel paused outside the door to the solar where she was to join her hostess who was spinning in the room's comparative comfort as soft rain fell outside. A male voice full of excitement sounded from within. Almost without realizing it, she stopped to listen.

"My God, Mother! Do you realize what a strong hand it gives us? That child was no prisoner! She is Buchan's betrothed. She has been lined up to be his bride practically since she was born. And we have her! It gives us the key, don't you see? If we hold her he'll have to agree to our demands over our boundaries and give us back our lands. All we have to do is say he must agree or he won't see her again! She'll have an accident of some sort, and disappear!"

On the landing, Isobel closed her eyes.

In the solar, Lady Gordon stood up, agitated. "How could you be so stupid, my son! He would never allow himself to be blackmailed! He'll come and take her by force, killing every man, woman, and child here and burning our roof over our heads while he's at it." Isobel could hear the sound of her skirts catching on the dusty heather strewn on the floor as she paced back and forth. "Dear God, I wish Patrick were here. He would know what to do! We cannot defy Lord Buchan, we cannot!"

"You were prepared to hide the girl."

"That was because I believed her. I thought she was being held against her will."

There was a laugh. "She probably was. She probably has a lad somewhere she would rather marry. She'll learn." He sounded cynical. "When she's a countess."

Isobel waited to hear no more. Cold with horror, she turned and fled down the long staircase.

The servants had been given no orders about her, and the surly groom was leading out her palfrey in response to her imperious demands when from the gatehouse they heard the sound of the watchman's horn. She froze as the heavy gate opened, staring at the white mist of rain beyond it, her mouth dry with fear. Hope died as she saw the band of horses milling around the gate. More than half of them wore the livery of the Earl of Buchan.

Sir Patrick Gordon looked her up and down as he dismounted from his horse. "So, the rumor is true." He turned to the grim-faced man who waited, still mounted, at his side. It was Sir Donald Comyn, steward to the household of the Countess of Buchan. "It appears, sir, that the lady Isobel is indeed our guest, but not, I think, an unwilling one." He glanced at the doorway behind her where his son had appeared. "We have resolved our differences with Lord Buchan," he said curtly. "The matter has been settled. And now I am glad to see that we can give his lordship earnest of our good intentions by returning to him his lady. There was a rumor at Scone that she had been kidnapped. I knew that could not be the case. I am glad to see that she found a friendly roof to shelter her until Lord Buchan's men could come for her."

Behind her in the doorway Isobel heard the sharp hiss of breath as the younger Gordon turned toward his father.

The young man glanced at her, and for a moment Isobel was terrified he was going to tell them her story. He looked at her thoughtfully, and she saw his eyes soften. Whatever he had been prepared to do to her to get his own way, he was not going to betray her now.

"I understand Lady Isobel was lost on the moors while flying her hawk," he said slowly. "It was lucky she found her way here. Because of the mist we had not yet managed to dispatch a message to Duncairn to say that she was safe."

Isobel saw the naked relief in Sir Patrick's eyes. Turning to his son, she gave him a grateful smile, then slowly she began to descend the stairs toward the horsemen.

"I have summoned my son from the south." Lady Buchan was standing by the table sorting through a pile of bright silks as Sir Donald ushered Isobel into the solar. "He shall know of your escapade in person."

Isobel raised her chin a fraction. "I got lost on the moors. The Gordons were most hospitable and kind." She turned to Sir Donald in mute appeal.

He nodded. "I gather the little lady was out with her bird," he said. "She became confused in the mist. She was lucky to have found shelter."

"Rubbish." Lady Buchan swept the silks together into an untidy heap and turned her back on them. "You do not have to leave the castle alone at dawn in order to go hawking. Were you running away, my lady? Trying once more to avoid marriage with my son? He does not meet your requirements, I gather." There was no humor in the cold eyes.

Isobel clenched her fists. She held Lady Buchan's gaze as firmly as she could. There would be another beating, but the pain would soon be over and then there would be another chance to escape. "I do not wish to marry anyone, my lady," she said.

Lady Buchan gave a harsh laugh. She glanced at her steward then back at Isobel. "Indeed. So you intend to enter a convent?"

"No! Yes. . . ." For a moment Isobel looked away from her, confused.

"There is no other use for a woman. Either she belongs to God or she belongs to a man." Lady Buchan walked thoughtfully toward her accustomed seat and sat stiffly down. "If I thought God had called you to his service, Isobel, neither I nor my son would dispute the right of the church to take you. But you have no such calling. You are destined for a man. Your father and he settled it many years ago, and the king has agreed." She gave Isobel a cold smile. "You belong to my son."

"I shall belong to your son at Michaelmas, my lady. Until then I belong to no one but myself." To Isobel's surprise her voice sounded determined, even defiant.

Lady Buchan smiled. "A Michaelmas wedding would have been very pleasant," she said quietly. "As it is, I think a summer wedding would be even better."

Isobel's eyes widened. "What do you mean?"

"Why do you think my son is returning? To reprimand you

again? To punish you? I can do that without his presence. He is returning so that the marriage can be brought forward. There is no need for delay, and once you are his wife you will have no further opportunity for these rash sorties into the hills." She smiled coldly. "I understand that the bishop of St. Andrews will be accompanying him to perform the ceremony."

"No!" Isobel stared at her, terrified. "No, he can't do it so soon, he can't!"

"He can and he will." There was no pity in Elizabeth's eyes as she looked at her future daughter-in-law's face.

There was a guard on her door. For three days they had kept her a prisoner at the top of the keep, alone but for one of Lady Buchan's waiting women, who sniffed and moaned and sat huddled and unmoving over the empty hearth. Even her friend, Alice, had been forbidden to come near her.

Isobel was standing at the eastern window. It was unshuttered, looking directly out to sea, and the cold wind was funneling through the deep embrasure into her face, making her eyes run, but she did not move. It seemed terribly important to watch the shifting gray slopes of the water as the night fell, with the white specks that were the gulls, wings folded, seemingly asleep on the heaving, ever-changing mass. The room was full of the sound of the waves. She pulled her cloak more tightly around her and shivered.

The door opened, and she turned, her face setting automatically into an expression of stubborn wariness.

The Countess of Buchan stood in the doorway for a moment, fighting for breath after the long climb, one hand braced on the door post, the other still gathering up the folds of her heavy dark-red skirt.

"My son and the bishop have arrived," she announced as soon as she could speak. "The chapel is being made ready for the nuptial mass. My ladies will dress you now." Behind her three figures had appeared carrying armfuls of clothing.

For one wild moment Isobel thought of escape as the women laid the heap of bright fabrics on the bed, but there was nowhere she could go; nothing she could do, save submit with every ounce of dignity she possessed as they gathered around her, chattering happily among themselves, to pull off her everyday woolen gown and replace it with shift and gown and kirtle of silk and velvet in crimson and azure and gold while Elizabeth watched, her face curiously abstracted.

The chapel was lighted by a hundred candles, and crowded. Isobel gasped. She stopped in her tracks, conscious of the three women closing around her, realizing she could not breathe, again feeling the tight panic closing over her as Elizabeth took her arm. "My son is waiting for you," the countess whispered.

Isobel could feel her heart beating unsteadily beneath her ribs; her mouth had gone dry and she felt very sick.

"No," she whispered desperately. "Please, no."

The fingers on her elbow tightened. "He is waiting," Elizabeth repeated.

The Earl of Buchan, his constable, Sir Donald, the chamberlain, and the bishop of St. Andrews, followed closely by the castle chaplain, were standing near the door to the chapel.

John stepped forward and took her hand. "The time has come sooner than expected, it seems, for us to exchange our vows, my lady." He looked at her impatiently.

She felt the bishop's eyes on her, and she looked up at him, half hoping he would see the monstrousness of the act he was about to perform and refuse, but the stern, unsmiling gaze swept over her almost without interest and lighted on the countess at her side. The bishop gave a slight bow, then he turned back to the earl.

Isobel gritted her teeth, her hand cold in that of her betrothed. She was determined he would not feel her tremble.

The vows took only a few minutes to exchange. She thought of remaining stubbornly silent, refusing to say a word, but she knew it was no use. They would find a way of making her swear or they would ignore her altogether. She was there at the earl's side before the bishop. That was enough.

Together she and Lord Buchan made the short walk to the altar to hear the hasty mass. Then it was done. When she rose

from the faldstool it was as the new Countess of Buchan.
Elizabeth, standing so tight-lipped behind them, was rele-
gated finally to the position of dowager.

There had been no bridal attendants, no flowers for her
hair, no lucky charms to bless her with, and now there was to
be no celebration banquet. John took her straight to the
bedchamber in the high keep and dragged the door closed
behind them.

"So, to bed with my new wife." Up until now he had not
even looked at her. Now he turned and glanced at her face. It
had lost its customary defiance. The expression he saw there
was full of fear.

He frowned. "Shall we call the bishop to bless the bed with
holy water? It might be fitting to double bless this union,
unwilling as it seems to be." Slowly he lifted his heavy mantle
from his shoulders and threw it down on a stool. Beneath it
he wore a long tunic, fastened by an ornate girdle.

"Our union will never be blessed, my lord." Isobel stepped
back from him, feeling the solid oak of the door behind her.
"You have married me under duress. You know I have no
wish to be your wife."

"I think few women go happily to their husbands, if the
truth were known," John said slowly. "But in the end they
get on well enough. It is not so bad to be Countess of Buchan,
is it?"

He made no attempt to touch her. Turning away, he
walked to a side table and poured himself some wine. Her
face had shaken him. He had always thought her a child,
playing with his niece to whom she was so close in age, so
alive, so vibrant, so happy. Beneath her silken veil her
pinched, unhappy face was transparent with emotion. He
could see the fear and doubt and defiance chasing each other
through her eyes. She was like a little trapped bird, pressed
there against the door of his room. He gave a deep sigh. She
looked very young and vulnerable. Too young. His tastes
were for more mature women. Yet he had to bed her, and at
once, then he could get back to more important matters, like
the war with England in the south.

He downed the wine and set the goblet with a bang on the

carved wood of the side table, then he turned to face her. "You look cold, my dear. Why don't you take off that gown and climb into bed. Let me bring you some wine."

"No." Her voice was tight with fear.

John sighed again. "Isobel. You know what must be done. Come." He held out his hand.

Stubbornly she shook her head.

He caught her arm, exasperated. "I shan't be a cruel husband, Isobel. If you obey me, we shall be content together. Come." As he pulled her toward him his hand strayed to her face. "You aren't a child any longer, sweetheart. There is strength here, and beauty. I'm a lucky man." He leaned down toward her and kissed her on the forehead.

Isobel stiffened and, with a little cry, stepped back, but he tightened his grip on her. "You mustn't be shy with me. Come, show me a proper kiss. I am assured you know how." He was beginning to grow impatient. His moment of concern had passed. He was remembering his mother's warnings, her insistence that Isobel had a lover somewhere out in the hills, her reiteration that the girl had bad blood and that she was a devil's tease, sent to tempt men from their wives. Her skin was soft and yielding beneath his fingers. At last he was beginning to desire her.

He released her abruptly and turned back to the goblet, which he refilled with wine. "Drink." He handed her the goblet. "Now. Every drop." He put his hands on her shoulders as she raised the goblet to her mouth. The rough Gascony wine was warm against the cold metal beneath her lips. She sipped it, then obediently sipped again, feeling the warmth traveling through her veins. "And again." He fetched the jug and filled her goblet anew, watching as she drank it. She felt a wave of nausea and protested, but he pushed it to her lips again. Her head was beginning to swim, and the room spun around her, but still he forced the wine down her. Then he took the cup from her fingers.

She felt him lift her off her feet and lay her on the bed, and she thought she raised her hands to defend herself. But nothing seemed to happen. The room was growing dark.

The branch of candles on the table was dripping wax onto

the embroidered cloth in the cool breeze that was blowing in from the sea. Outside, the long summer evening was drawing to a close as bats flitted past the high, narrow windows. In the room there was a deep silence, broken only by the sound of the earl's heavy breathing as he held his young wife down and began to remove her clothes.

Chapter Five

Clare sat completely still. She was numb from head to foot. Disoriented, she glanced around her, then she heard it again. Someone was ringing the doorbell.

Beyond the curtains it was dark now. In the shadowy bedroom the only light came from the flickering candle. She was shivering violently.

Emma was standing on the doorstep. "I was just going," she said as Clare opened the door. "I thought you must have forgotten and gone out." She was a tall, striking young woman with glossy chestnut hair and the dark Royland eyes. Beneath her coat she wore a pale-blue silk shirt and skirt. "Are you all right?" She peered at Clare suddenly. "You look frightful. Is anything wrong?"

Clare laughed uncomfortably. "I'm sorry, Emma. I forgot you were coming this evening." She stepped back to allow her visitor inside. "What time is it?"

"After seven. What have you been up to? You weren't asleep?"

Clare hesitated, then impulsively she clutched at Emma's arm. "I've got to tell you. I've got to tell someone. It was so awful, so . . . so real." Suddenly she buried her face in her hands.

"Clare?" Emma stared at her in dismay. "Come on, what's the matter? Is it Paul? What has that bloody brother of mine been doing now?"

Wordlessly Clare shook her head.

"Then what?" Emma's voice was gentle. "Come on, Clare. You must tell me. Is it—is it about those tests you and Paul went for?"

Slowly Clare raised her face from her hands. She sat down

83

limply in the Victorian chair near the fireplace. "Oh, that!" Could she really have forgotten that? "The results have come back; I can't have children."

"Oh, Clare." Helplessly Emma stared at her. "I'm so sorry." She didn't know what else to say.

"I was so sure there was nothing wrong." Clare stared straight ahead of her at the pattern on the rug near her feet. "It's strange, but I thought I would know if it were me, know in some subconscious part of myself. But I didn't. I can't come to terms with it yet."

"Are you going to think about adoption?" Emma asked cautiously.

Clare shrugged. "I don't know what we're going to do. Paul was foul about it."

"The bastard!" Emma threw herself down on the sofa opposite her. "He has got to be the most insensitive, unfeeling, boorish man I've ever met!"

In spite of herself Clare smiled. "So much for sisterly love."

"You know there's not much of that lost between Paul and me. We've always hated each other." Emma grinned. "I never could see what you saw in him. But you know that."

Clare smiled. "Oh, he has his moments." She hesitated, then she frowned. "But he has changed lately. He seems to have a lot on his mind, and it's not just the baby business. At least, I don't think so. He seems to have got some sort of an obsession about money at the moment, almost as if he's worried—" She stopped abruptly, shaking her head. "Maybe there are problems of some sort at the bank. He never talks about what goes on there." She sighed, leaning back in the chair. "I've been trying to think of ways of taking my mind off everything. And I think I've found one. It's not a permanent solution, but it's a sort of temporary counterirritant. Inflicting one kind of pain to distract oneself from another worse one. That is what I was doing when you rang the doorbell."

Emma frowned. "I take it that this is something to do with the yoga I've been hearing about."

"Who on earth told you about that?" Clare stood up restlessly. "But, yes, it's to do with that. Meditation. It's the most

incredible experience, Em. It's exciting, frightening sometimes—mind bending. One empties one's mind and concen-
trates, in my case on Duncairn, and after a bit all these images start to appear—people, places from long ago. It is an
amazing way of escaping reality!" She grinned suddenly. "It's
as if I were conjuring up the spirits of the dead!"

Emma stared at her, her eyes wide. "You're not serious!
What happens?"

"First I do some yoga to put me in the right frame of mind,
then I have a little ritual with a lighted candle that I learned
from Zak—that's the man who taught me the technique. It is
a way of opening the doors to some sort of altered state of
consciousness. I'm going to buy some incense while I'm here
in London—that helps too, apparently. Then I begin to meditate, and it all starts to happen—scenes from the past, with
real people who talk and move and seem as solid as you or I,
and it's so vivid I feel as if I were there. It is as if, if you had
been here, you would have seen them too—seen everything
that happened."

"It sounds incredible! You're loopy, Clare! You do know
that?" Emma grinned fondly.

Clare smiled. "I know, it's frightfully shocking, isn't it? I
dread to think what Paul would say if he knew."

Emma raised an eyebrow. "What makes you think he
doesn't?" She grimaced.

"There's no way he could. I've never told him. Oh, he
knows about the yoga, but lots of people do that."

"What you're doing frightens you, though, doesn't it?"
Emma was not to be distracted. "You were in quite a state
when you opened the door."

"Was I?" Clare looked surprised. "The doorbell startled
me, that's all. Although—" She hesitated. "It was rather horrible."

"What was?"

"Nothing." Clare shook her head. Her face sobered as she
remembered the dark, echoing chamber high in the keep at
Duncairn, full of the sound of the sea.

She pushed the picture away firmly. The only merit in the
scene she had been witnessing was that Paul had not been

able to follow her there too. "Come on. Give me ten minutes to change and we'll go out. I have a feeling Paul has gone back to Bucksters without me—he doesn't want to miss the party tomorrow." She stopped suddenly. "Are you and Peter going?"

"To David and Gillian's?" Emma shook her head. "No fear. We're going to the theater. Clare, seriously—"

"No, Em. I don't want to talk about it anymore. Let's go out. Please. You won't say anything about any of this to Paul, will you?"

"Of course not. What do you take me for?"

Clare smiled. "A friend. Otherwise I wouldn't have told you anything."

The Reverend Geoffrey Royland sat back comfortably at the breakfast table and opened his copy of *The Times*. At the table with him, his wife Chloe and their two teenage children were immersed in the mail. The large untidy kitchen, the only modernized room in the sprawling Edwardian rectory, smelled comfortably of coffee. Emma had just arrived.

"What brings you out so early?" Geoffrey asked.

"Coffee, Emma?" Chloe slid an extra cup off the sideboard with a surreptitious glance at her sister-in-law. Emma looked tired, and there were dark rings under her eyes. Her normally cheerful face was very sober.

"Please."

"Is something wrong, Emma?" Chloe put the cup down in front of her.

"I don't know. I wanted to talk to you, Geoff, about Pete and me. It's nothing very dramatic; I just feel I want someone to talk to." She smiled apologetically at Chloe.

Geoffrey interrupted her with a gesture of his hand. "Why don't you bring that coffee into my study. We'll talk there." Then, turning to Chloe, he said, "Excuse us, Chloe, will you?"

Geoffrey led the way out of the kitchen. His study was a ground-floor room, overlooking a quiet, tree-lined street. Outside he could see Emma's car parked beyond the gate.

Gesturing her toward what his family referred to as the interrogation chair, a deep-buttoned shabby leather armchair opposite his desk, he lowered himself into his own place. "You and Peter have been having problems for a while, haven't you?" He glanced at her, concerned.

"Is it that obvious?"

"Perhaps only to people who love you. Has something happened?"

She shrugged. "Nothing special, I suppose." She sat back in her chair and sighed. "It's just, well, he's never there. I went out last night with Clare because I was all on my own again. Then when I got home the house was so—so empty!"

Geoffrey sighed. "Poor Em. But from what I hear he won't change his job. Wheeling and dealing in the Far East is his whole life. Can't you and Julia go with him sometimes?"

She raised her hands helplessly. "If I give up working in the gallery I can."

"Ah." Geoffrey looked at her thoughtfully. "And you don't want to do that."

"No, I bloody well don't! It's not even as though Pete is away at the moment. He came back later from his beastly meeting and of course we had a row! The trouble is we never go out, Geoff! Even when he is home. It's all work, work, work!" She smiled ruefully. "I'm sorry. I don't know why I came to dump all this in your lap. I suppose it was talking to Clare last night. It made me realize how important it is to have something else if your marriage falls apart."

Geoffrey raised his eyebrows. "Oh, dear. Don't tell me that is what is happening to Clare and Paul too?"

"They've found out it is she who can't have a baby."

"Poor Clare. I know how heartbroken she must be, but surely that is not going to destroy their marriage?"

"It's helping. She's discovering fast just how rotten Paul can be." Emma shook her head sadly. "She has got nothing now. No job. No children. And probably no husband. Poor Clare. All she is left with are her daydreams and her visiting spirits!"

"Her what?" Geoffrey looked startled.

"Oh, Lord! I'm not supposed to tell anyone." Emma put her hand to her mouth. "Well, not Paul, anyway. She's doing some kind of weird meditation and conjuring up the spirits of the dead." She paused, then, seeing her brother's face, she was unable to resist dramatizing her statement. "With candles and incantations and incense and spells!"

Geoffrey was looking at her closely, unable for a moment to decide whether or not she was joking. It took only a moment to convince him that, in spite of the dramatic whisper, she was not.

Uneasily he rubbed his hands together. "I think you'd better tell me all about it," he said after a moment. "How did she start all this?"

"She met someone who taught her yoga. She met him at a party. He comes from California."

"It follows," Geoffrey said dryly.

"And he's gay, so he's not after her body, only her mind." She laughed.

"Or her soul."

"Geoff, you mustn't tell Paul about this."

"Emma, this could be serious. If you are correct, then Clare could be playing with fire. So many people get involved with these things without realizing how dangerous they are." Geoffrey stood up and walked across the room. Absentmindedly he picked up his pipe from an ashtray and tapped it against the white plaster molding of the mantelpiece. "I really ought to talk to her," he went on after a long pause.

Emma watched him uneasily. "Geoffrey, I promised I wouldn't mention it to anyone."

"I'm glad you did, though."

He paused. "Are you sure it wasn't this you came to tell me about, Emma? You're worried about her, aren't you?"

"I'm worried about myself, Geoff. That is why I came."

"Of course." He smiled. "And we must talk again. Don't do anything too precipitous, Emma. Peter is a good man. I think you'll work it out. I think you both still love each other. And as for Clare—" He hesitated, frowning. "I really do feel I must do something for her. Unfortunately I have to go away next week, but in any case I must think about this very carefully, and . . ." He hesitated with a quick glance at his sister, "I must pray."

Emma snorted. "What else?" she said, then grinned. "Will you pray for me as well? I need it." Then her face sobered. "Don't say anything to her, Geoff, please. Whatever it is she's doing, it matters to her. It is all she's got at the moment."

Geoffrey frowned. "That is the danger," he said. "That is exactly the danger. Poor Clare! I feel guilty that I haven't noticed that she was so unhappy. But we don't see her and Paul that often, and when we do she always seems so self-contained. Chloe is very fond of her."

"So am I. And I don't want to see her hurt. Leave it alone, Geoff, please."

"I can't do that, Em. Not until I've found out what she really is doing. I have to, don't you see? And something else. I think I should talk to Paul."

"No!" Emma jumped to her feet. "No, you mustn't. Look, maybe it's not as bad as I've made it sound." She stopped as she caught sight of the expression on Geoffrey's face. "Blast you, Geoff! Leave Paul out of it!" She put her hands on the edge of the desk. "Don't mention it to Paul. Don't you know yet what a bastard our brother can be?"

Paul had taken Casta for a walk across the fields. The grass was white with dew and a thick mist still clung among the trees; it was cold. Hands in pockets, he strode down the lane and up the edge of a field, watching with only half an eye as the dog ran back and forth, plumed tail wagging, flushing rabbits and partridge out of the hedgerow. He was still seething with anger. The drive back to Bucksters, always agonizingly slow on a Friday evening, the realization that he should have brought Clare back for the party—David and Gillian would raise their eyebrows when he turned up without her—and the continuing nagging worry about the money, all had contributed toward a sleepless night and a king-size headache. He was well aware that he was being unfair to Clare, but he could no longer think about things rationally. He kicked at a stone that lay in his path. Across the fields a tractor was slowly pulling a plow parallel with the hedge away from him, a cloud of gulls following it, hovering excit-

edly as the dull dead stubble turned methodically into huge
scoops of shining clay.

She had to be persuaded to sell; it was imperative that she
be made to see the sense of whatever offer was being made.

He drew off his boots in the back porch and walked into the
kitchen. Sarah Collins was rolling out some pastry at the
table, her hands covered in flour. She glanced up as he
walked in.

"The mail and papers have come, Mr. Royland. They're
there, on the side."

One of the envelopes was addressed to Clare—typed, with
an Edinburgh postmark. Thoughtfully he turned it over,
then with sudden attention he ripped it open. He read the
contents twice, carefully, standing with his back to the fire in
the drawing room. Then, after throwing the letter down on
the low coffee table in front of the sofa, he went to the French
doors to stare across the garden. At last the mist was lifting
and the sun was coming out. Slowly Paul smiled.

"I managed to do it again after I spoke to you, but I don't
think I'm doing it right. Suddenly there is no peace in the
scenes I see."

Zak came as he had promised. He listened to Clare intently
as she told him what had happened in her meditations and he
frowned.

"Why don't we meditate together? I can see how you do
it."

Reluctantly she agreed. When they were both sitting quietly she closed her eyes. As she did so, Zak opened his own
surreptitiously.

Elizabeth de Quincy, dowager Countess of Buchan, had
ordered the lighting of a hundred candles. The hearth was
empty. In the doorway the King of England stopped and
looked around him. His followers crowded around him staring at the two women at the far end of the hall. Around the
walls of the castle the household and the servants stood peering over each other's shoulders in awe. Edward's reputation
was that of a formidable and a vengeful man.

Elizabeth, who had not yet departed for her dower lands, stood on the dais in the great hall, with her new daughter-in-law at her side as King Edward entered. It was a violently hot day. Outside the sea murmured against the cliffs; the birds were silent, roosting in the shade or rocking gently on the sleeping waves. Behind Edward his followers filed into the courtyard and spilled out across the bridge to the meadow beyond the castle.

He was tall, a good-looking man still, in his late fifties, his dark hair graying at the temples beneath the gold coronet he had elected to wear on his triumphant journey. Beneath the cream woolen mantle he was wearing a full suit of mail. He alone among his sweating followers looked as cool as an ice floe in the winter hills.

By that midsummer of 1296 the Scottish armies were scattered and in defeat. King Edward was triumphant.

Lord Buchan had come back briefly to Duncairn with Scotland's elected king, John Balliol, his cousin and the Lord of Badenoch, and sat up all night grimly discussing policy with his cousins. He left with scarcely a word for Isobel. They had decided to beg for terms. The only policy possible at the moment was to be received into Edward's peace.

The King of England's terms were harsh. At Brechin, King John of Scotland and his followers were told their fate. The kingdom of Scotland was forfeit and its most sacred treasures, including the Stone of Scone and the Black Rood of St. Margaret, were removed to London. King John and his Comyn friends and relatives were to be sent south into England, the Earl of Buchan with them. Lord Buchan was luckier than his kingly cousin. He was not destined for the Tower. Instead he was merely required to remain south of the River Trent, beyond the sphere of Scottish politics.

His new wife was not required to go with him. She had her own appointment with Edward of England.

At Duncairn the news of John Balliol's humiliation was greeted with horror by the dowager. At Montrose his abdication of the kingdom had been followed by the ritual tearing off of the royal arms from his surcoat—an action that was to gain him the nickname of Toom Tabard throughout the land.

He was then sent south, the prisoner of Thomas of Lancaster, while King Edward turned his attention north. Slowly and inexorably the royal train began touring the defeated land, stopping at every town and castle of note on the way to demand the abject homage of every important person left behind after his prisoners had been sent south. On July 22 he had at last arrived at Duncairn.

"So." He did not appear to raise his voice, but it carried with ease across the hall to the dais. "This is one of the strongholds of Lord Buchan, who is at present our guest in England. I shall require the keys of this castle and homage from its keeper." His eyes strayed from Elizabeth to Isobel. He gave a slight, humorless smile. "Lady Buchan? The keys, if you please."

The keys lay on the table, beside Elizabeth. Automatically she reached for the heavy ring. Then she drew back. "You are the countess now, child," she whispered hoarsely.

Isobel froze. Her mouth had gone dry. To pay homage to the King of England for a single stone of Scotland was heaping insult on their already pitiful humiliation, but she dared not refuse. Slowly she picked up the keys. She stepped off the dais and began the slow walk down the hall, aware that every eye was on her. She held her head high, walking with slow dignity, her eyes fixed on the face of the king.

After reaching him, she dropped a deep curtsey and handed him the keys. He tossed them to the knight standing at his side. "So, you are Lord Buchan's bride. My congratulations, madam. I am sorry to have had to deprive you of your husband so soon." His face was cold. "Our cousin, your mother, sends you greetings; and your brother who is in the household of our son."

"Thank you, sire." She curtseyed again. She had seen her mother so seldom in the last few years she could barely remember what she looked like; her brother she had never seen, save as a baby.

"And your uncle, Macduff, who appealed to us at Westminster last year, if I remember right, against your late lamented King John's decision to imprison him." Again the humorless smile. "It was astute of him to recognize us even then as overlord of Scotland."

Isobel could feel her cheeks coloring in indignation. "My uncle, sire, was bitter at the injustice done him by our elected king." She emphasized the penultimate word. "Had Scotland's true king been chosen to rule, my uncle would not have needed an arbitrator."

She heard the gasp of horror from the onlookers at her temerity, and she felt a little clutch of fear but she kept her head held high.

"The true king?" Edward inquired with deceptive mildness.

"Robert Bruce, the lord of Annandale, sire."

"Ah." He nodded. "The man who thinks I have nothing better to do than win a kingdom for him. His claim was dismissed as invalid at my court, Lady Buchan, with those of the other rabble of claimants to the throne of Scotland. And now John Balliol has proved himself traitor to his overlord, Scotland can do without a king at all. I shall rule this country myself from now on. I require your homage, madam."

She swallowed. "You have my homage and my loyalty, sire, for our lands in England."

"And now you will kneel before me for your lands in Scotland."

There was a slight movement around them, whispering among the Buchan household as they watched the young woman standing before the king. Elizabeth de Quincy raised her hand to her mouth to hide a smile. Her own mortification at their defeat was lessened by the sight of Isobel's dilemma, and not for the first time she felt a secret grudging admiration for her rebellious daughter-in-law.

Isobel had clenched her fists. "I will give my allegiance only to the King of Scotland, sire," she whispered. Her courage was fast oozing away.

"There is no King of Scotland." Edward was peremptory. "You will do homage to me as overlord of Scotland, madam, or you will be sent a prisoner to England after your husband. Choose."

She gave in. Kneeling in the dried heather at the king's

feet, she put her hands in his and repeated the oath in a voice so quiet he had to bend to hear her.

Twenty minutes later the king rode out of the castle, leaving a token garrison behind to hold it in his name.

It was a year before she saw her husband again.

The following summer King Edward granted Lord Buchan a safe conduct to travel north for two months only, to visit his lands in Scotland and to see his wife.

Isobel was pacing up and down the deserted tower room, kicking at the hem of her skirts with every step, her arms folded, her face set with fury. She was alone. The servants had fled downstairs. Lord Buchan had still not come to greet her.

For months she had remained alone at Duncairn. The morning after the King of England's departure, Elizabeth had removed most of the household to Slains Castle, a few miles along the coast. Isobel was left behind. It had been her husband's orders before he left under escort for England. She was to remain at Duncairn with the garrison and a handful of women and learn the duties of a wife.

Frustrated, bored, and angry, she had begged and railed and sworn at her husband's steward, demanding to be allowed to ride out of the castle, but he was adamant. The earl's orders were to be obeyed. She was a prisoner.

And now Lord Buchan had returned. The night before she had heard the horses and men ride into the castle and she had waited in her room, trembling, for him to come, but he had not appeared. Now her fear had passed and the anger had returned. How dare he ignore her! She was the countess —that much she had learned in her solitude in the castle, and she deserved his attention.

With a whirl of scarlet skirts she stormed back to the window and stood in the embrasure looking down at the sea, drumming her fingers on the stone. The tide was high and the waves were crashing onto the base of the rocks, casting clouds of spray into the air. The sun was shining directly into the window—a brilliant September sun, highlighting the granite cliffs and turning the dry soft grasses to gold. When the door opened behind her and slammed back against the wall, she did not turn.

"So, this is where you hide yourself. Can you not even come down to the great hall to greet your husband?" Lord Buchan's voice was acid as he banged the door shut behind him.

She swung around. "I am not a groom to attend at your stirrup, my lord."

"Indeed not. You are the lady of this castle, the hostess I expect to find in the hall greeting my guests."

"I was unaware you had guests"—Isobel stepped down from the embrasure—"as no one had the courtesy to tell me!" She had a sneaking feeling she was in the wrong, but nothing would make her admit it, even though the sight of her husband's tall, muscular figure beneath the dark-green mantle had brought back her fear of him with a sickening jolt.

He sighed. "Isobel, I do not want us to be enemies," he said slowly. "Nothing will be served by your temper. Come." He held out his hand. "Let us go down now."

For a moment she hesitated, then, reluctantly, she put her hand in his. If the only way to get out of the castle and ride free was to appease him, then appease him she would.

The truce lasted until dusk. At the high table in the great hall she was seated between her husband and his guest, his cousin John Comyn. As a succession of courses came and went before them, their talk was all of politics.

"You agree King Edward of England is making more and more impossible demands of the Scots people. We have to find a way of being free of his ambition." Lord Buchan leaned forward, his elbows on the table.

Comyn nodded gloomily. "Our cousin, King John"—his voice was full of irony—"does not dare cross him now. He is useless. We have to throw the weight of tradition and the wishes of the community of the realm into the scale. All the lords of Scotland are with us."

Buchan frowned. "Nearly all. There are some who put their arrogance and personal ambition before Scotland's good."

Comyn nodded. "The Bruces, you mean. They are still with us at heart, even if they appear to support Edward. Young Carrick is a fine fighter." He sighed. "They find it hard to acknowledge their claim to the throne was overturned and John Balliol made king. They will come around slowly if we can find a way to make them turn their allegiance back to Scotland without rubbing their noses in the act."

Isobel looked from one man to the other. The mention of Robert's name had set her heart beating very fast. "Robert will never swear allegiance to Balliol," she said firmly. "The Bruce claim was far the stronger!"

Both men looked at her in astonishment. "So, you are an expert on the law, little cousin!" John Comyn smiled at her patronizingly.

Isobel could feel herself growing red. "I know who was the rightful heir to King Alexander's throne," she said tartly.

"But it was a representative of your own brother who crowned Balliol king, surely." Comyn was enjoying himself. "The seal of approval from the Earl of Fife himself—who else could have put the crown on King John's head?"

"My brother is in England, sir, and a mere child," she retorted. "He knew nothing about it. He would never have set the crown on Balliol's head of his own choice."

Buchan's face darkened. "That is enough! John Balliol is our king for better or worse, and we must abide by the court's decision. Now the important thing is to see that Scotland regains her independence and rights as a kingdom."

"To do that, she must have a strong king!" Isobel put in.

"And you think old Robert Bruce of Annandale is the man to fill the position?" Comyn asked, still amused. "A man whose wife, if the story is true, threw him across her saddle when she took a fancy to him and carried him off to force him into marriage! A strong man indeed!" He leaned back with a roar of laughter and raised a goblet of wine in mock salute.

"I think it is the younger Robert Bruce she means," Buchan put in coldly. "Am I not right, my dear? It is his son, Lord Carrick, we are talking about, are we not? The one who paid you so much attention when he was here last."

Too late, Isobel saw how she had betrayed herself. Desperately she put her hands to her flaming cheeks, conscious that the eyes of both men were upon her. "I haven't spoken to Lord Carrick for more than a year!"

"But when you did?" Buchan was watching her face thoughtfully. "You spoke to him alone, did you not? It was reported that you were both seen leaving the chapel."

"Perhaps. I don't remember." She raised her chin defiantly. "What does it matter now?"

"It matters not at all. Now," he said quietly.

Alone in their chamber later, he turned on her. "You will not see Lord Carrick again alone, do you understand?"

Isobel, wrapped in the pale-green bed gown Mairi had given her after helping her undress, shivered. The room was dark now and full of shadows as the candles streamed in the draft from the window.

"I doubt whether the occasion will arise, since you are enemies," she said sadly. "And he has no interest in me anyway. He is married." Her eyes betrayed her pain for a moment.

Lord Buchan saw it. "So. That is it. You would have preferred a young, handsome husband, a man whose father claims a kingdom. That appeals to you, does it?" His face was hard with anger. "Not the stableboy my mother thought you were involved with, but an earl! So much more fitting for the great Lady of Duff. Far more to her tastes, although not perhaps to Carrick's, as you came to me a virgin! Or was he still so recently knighted that he was mindful of his vows! Well, you are married now, madam, and to an earl of ancient lineage. To me! And you will play the part of my wife in every particular until the day you die, do you understand me?" He caught her shoulders. "Your first duty being to provide me with an heir!"

He took no pleasure in her body. Her slim, almost boyish figure, her pale skin and delicate bones excited him hardly at all as he pulled open her gown and pushed her down onto the bed. Only her rebellion raised him to passion, and then it was anger, not desire, that inflamed him.

He stayed at Duncairn for three weeks as he discussed with the Scottish lords their plans for rebellion and made the decision at last to defy King Edward openly by breaking his parole and joining them. By the time he left the castle with them, Isobel knew that she hated him as she had hated no one in her life before; and she also knew that she was pregnant.

As he rode away down the track at the head of his men, she called Mairi to her.

"A bath," she commanded. "Have them bring a bath up here and fill it for me!"

"My lady?" Mairi stared at her. "Up here? Now?"

"Now." Isobel was imperious. For once she did not care how much work it made for the servants, or how hard it was to carry water up the high, winding stairs. She waited in the chamber she had shared with the earl for the men to drag the heavy wooden tub up the stairs and fill it with bucket after bucket of rapidly cooling water, then, alone save for Mairi, she began to remove her clothes.

She heard the woman's quickly smothered gasp of horror as she saw the bruises on Isobel's arms and shoulders, and the lacerations where her husband's brooch and buckles had caught at her bare skin as he took her again and again over the weeks, not even bothering to undress himself, but she ignored the woman's unspoken sympathy. She gritted her teeth. If she wavered even for an instant in her resolve she would begin to cry, and that she would never do.

As she helped Isobel climb into the high-sided tub, Mairi was blinking back her tears, but Isobel was uncowed. "Fetch me that box, standing on the coffer," she commanded as she lowered her aching body into the water.

Mairi did as she was bidden, wiping her eyes surreptitiously on her sleeve as she picked up the small carved box.

Isobel held out her hand. "Now leave me alone," she commanded.

"My lady—"

"Leave me! I'll call you when I'm ready." Her voice wavered for the first time.

She waited for the door to close, then, carefully holding the box clear of the water, she opened it.

The powders were ready: crushed herbs and tree bark, the

ash of a burned piece of parchment on which a spell had been written, and the charcoal remains of a poor burned frog. With a shudder she tipped the mixture into the water. Then, throwing the box to the ground, she gently stirred it in around her. She had already swallowed some of the powder, dissolved in wine; this ritual cleansing would complete the spell that Mairi had herself told her, long ago, and would rid her of Lord Buchan's child.

When the water was quite cold and she was shivering violently, she called Mairi back.

"Quick, give me a towel." She climbed awkwardly from the bath and ran, swathed in the towel, to stand by the fire. Her teeth were chattering audibly. "Throw on more peats, Mairi, I'm so cold." Outside the wind was rising; the polished horn shutters in the windows rattled and the dried heather on the floor stirred uneasily in the draft.

"I won't bear his child, Mairi!" Isobel cried as Mairi approached with a neatly folded clean shift from one of the coffers. "I won't. I'd die rather!"

Mairi shook her head sadly. "It will be as God wills, my lady."

"No! It will be as I will!" Isobel shook out her hair. She snatched off the towel and stood for a moment, naked in the firelight, looking down in distaste at the roughly woven unbleached cloth covered in little bits of the herbs and bark that had been clinging to her damp skin.

Mairi shrank back. Such blatant nakedness was shocking. The child she had bathed a thousand times before had become a stranger.

As she watched, Isobel held the towel high and flung it on the fire. It smoked and blackened on the smoldering peats, then it burst into a brilliant flame that leapt crackling up the chimney. Both women stared at it for a moment, then, shaking with fear, Mairi hurried forward and wrapped Isobel's chilled body in the shift. When she turned away the little hairs on the back of her neck were standing on end. Glancing over her shoulder at her mistress, Mairi crossed herself secretly.

"You're not afraid of me, Mairi?" Isobel asked suddenly.

"Of course not, my lady." Still unnerved, Mairi didn't look at her. She stooped to pick up the box near the bath and, after closing it, reverently she put it down on the table.

"I meant it, Mairi. I will not carry that man's baby." Isobel spoke with a new authority, no longer a child.

"I believe you, my lady." Mairi shivered again.

"And now it is over." Isobel was staring into the fire. "Soon the blood will come, and I shall be free of it!"

Chapter Six

It was with some curiosity that James obeyed Paul's summons to his office. As he sat down opposite his brother-in-law, he frowned at Paul's opening words.

"I want this conversation to be completely confidential. As you predicted," he went on, "Clare is adamant in her refusal to contemplate the sale of Duncairn. Irrationally so." He paused again, allowing the words to hang for a moment in the air. "It is, of course, a very difficult time for her. The discovery that she can never have children has upset her enormously. It is perfectly understandable that her entire outlook on life is a little disturbed at the moment. The problem is that she is allowing her emotional distress to interfere with her business acumen."

"I never thought my sister had any business acumen at the best of times," James said.

Paul looked at him sharply. "Indeed?" he said. "Well, I assure you she has. Which is why she would be the first to be furious if she found that she had missed out on a massively profitable deal while the balance of her mind was disturbed."

James let out a soundless whistle. "That's a bit strong, surely."

Paul stood up restlessly. He walked across to the window and stood looking down into Coleman Street for a moment in silence. When he spoke it was with extreme care. "I understand that there have been times, even from her earliest childhood, when Clare has had periods of, shall we say, strangeness?" He put his hands in his pockets, leaning forward slightly, as if studying something below on the pavement.

"Hardly strangeness." James was staring at Paul's back.

"She's always been highly strung, I suppose. And Aunt Margaret used to call her fey. But I don't think that means what one thinks it does, does it?" He gave a forced laugh.

"It means doomed to die young." Paul turned sharply, leaning against the windowsill.

James licked his lips. They had gone rather dry. "I'm sure Aunt Margaret did not mean that."

"What then?"

James hadn't realized before what hard eyes Paul had. Brown, like nuts; expressionless in the handsome face.

"I think she meant slightly spooky; seeing ghosts, that sort of thing. Like those nightmares she used to get all the time."

"She still has them."

"Does she?" James glanced up at him.

"And she is still suffering from claustrophobia. That has something to do with the nightmares, I think."

James hesitated uncomfortably. "I don't know that it does, actually," he said at last. "I think that may be my fault." He stood up and slowly paced up and down the carpet. Paul was watching him, a frown on his face. "It was when we were children," James went on after a second or two. "A game that got out of hand." He glanced up at Paul with an apologetic smile. "Aunt Margaret used to tell us stories about Robert the Bruce: Scottish history—battles and stuff." He paused again. "One of the stories was about a woman who was put in a cage and left there to die." He shuddered. "It was pretty horrible, really. Clare was obsessed by it and Aunt Margaret would go on about it; it never seemed to dawn on her that Clare was really upset by the whole thing. Anyway, we used to play Robert the Bruce games—the Battle of Bannockburn, that sort of thing. And once we played the woman in the cage." There was a long silence. "Kids can be pretty cruel, can't they, and there were times that I thought I hated Clare. She was older than me, and I always thought she was mother's favorite, so I didn't have too much conscience about what I did." He stopped pacing the floor. Looking down, he kicked viciously at the carpet.

"And what did you do?" Paul prompted softly.

"I locked her in a cage at Airdlie." James resumed pacing

the floor. "There was a cage at the back of the stables—a small run really, where grandfather kept his dogs. I found an old padlock and pushed her in and left her there. It was quite late at night. Completely dark. There was no one around."

"How long was she there?" Paul's eyes were fixed on his face.

"All night. We started playing after we were supposed to be in bed. The grown-ups were having a dinner party. No one noticed she was missing. No one heard her call."

"What happened?"

"In the morning I went to let her out. I thought it was a great lark, but she was unconscious. I can still remember how frightened I was. I thought she was dead. I didn't know what to do. The woman who looked after Aunt Margaret came and I helped her carry Clare to bed. She was terrified because she was supposed to have been looking after us. She put hot-water bottles at her feet and smacked her hands and face and in the end Clare woke up."

"And?"

"That's the strange part. She didn't seem to remember anything about it. And no one ever said anything. You're the first person I've ever told." James gave an embarrassed laugh. "It was shortly after that that she started getting attacks of claustrophobia—quite serious ones."

James continued, "Aunt Margaret blamed herself. I think she suspected that it was to do with the woman in the cage, but she didn't know what I had done. She never told us that particular story again." He paused again. "The woman in the cage—I think she died at Duncairn."

"I see." Paul turned away, walking back to the window thoughtfully. There was a long silence, then at last he spoke. "It is my opinion, and that of our doctor, that Clare is heading for a nervous breakdown. To avoid such a thing happening, I am going to take as much as possible off her shoulders: take over the management of her affairs; send her away for a long rest so that she can get things back into perspective."

"And sell Duncairn while she isn't looking," James said almost under his breath.

Paul swung around. "I can see no merit in keeping the

property. That hotel will be nothing but a drain on our resources. However, if there is really some family attachment
to the place, I am prepared to offer it to you first."

"At the same price Sigma is offering?" James raised an
eyebrow.

Paul inclined his head slightly. "The property has become
valuable and I am a businessman."

"How do you propose to get Clare's agreement to all this?"

"I will see to it that I get power of attorney."

"You mean you're going to have her certified?"

Paul noted the sudden indignation in his brother-in-law's
voice. "There is no question of that. She will give it to me
willingly."

"You think so?" James looked skeptical. He paused, then he
shook his head. "Thanks for the offer, Paul, but I'm not interested in buying Duncairn. I wouldn't do that to Clare, and
besides, I'm not about to throw that kind of money into any
property, whether it has oil or not. Nor am I sure anyway that
I necessarily want to stand around and watch them put nodding donkeys all over the headland."

Paul gave him a withering look. "I didn't see you as sentimental."

"No?" James raised an eyebrow. "Perhaps you forget that
I'm a Scot too, Paul. Aunt Margaret left the place to Clare
because she thought I wouldn't appreciate it fully. Perhaps
she was right, I don't know. But I wouldn't have sold it. I may
be a businessman, but to see Duncairn raped would hurt
even me. I won't go so far as to try to stop you selling; no one
could ignore the kind of offer you've had, but I won't stand
and watch."

Paul inclined his head slightly. "Fair enough. We understand one another, I think."

James looked him in the eye. "Indeed we do," he said
slowly. "Indeed we do."

Rex Cummin sat down on the white leather sofa and pulled
the telephone toward him. Mary was out, and the apartment
was quiet. His suitcases still lay humped together in a heap in
the entranceway where he had dropped them as he came

through the front door. It took him only a few moments to be connected with Alec Mitchison in Edinburgh.

"I've received a letter from Mr. Paul Royland, the owner's husband." The crisp Scots voice, crackling with energy, came down the wire. "He says that Mrs. Royland is unwell and he is handling her affairs. I gather he may be prepared to discuss matters."

Rex sat forward eagerly, his knuckles white on the receiver. "What did he say exactly?"

"He says he would be prepared to meet you, that's all."

"That's enough." Rex took a deep breath. "Set it up, will you? In London or Edinburgh. Wherever he wants. You'll be there, of course."

There was a pause at the other end of the line. When the voice resumed it was heavy with disapproval. "You wish to reveal your identity so early in the negotiations, Mr. Cummin? I would have thought that a grave mistake."

Rex could feel the sweat breaking out on his forehead. The supercilious Scotsman was right, of course, but he couldn't wait. Not now. There wasn't time. He took a deep breath.

"I feel sure," he said slowly, "that Mr. Royland and I can meet as private individuals. I will not mention my company's identity at this stage. I will allow him to think that I am interested in developing the hotel." He knew Mitchison didn't think he could pull it off; the man probably thought Royland knew about Sigma already. If so, so be it. They would negotiate with all the cards on the table. And he meant *all* the cards. As he put the phone down, he had already decided to find out all there was to know about Paul Royland. And he meant all. He was going to leave nothing to chance.

Behind him the door opened and his wife appeared, laden with shopping bags. "Rex! I didn't expect you. Is something wrong?" His wife's radar was finely tuned.

"Nothing, honey, nothing. They're a load of old women back there in the States, that's all. The drop in the price of oil is scaring the shit out of them."

"And they don't want to invest anymore in Europe?"

He shrugged. "They haven't said yes or no. They're hesitating and while they hesitate, someone else is going to get his goddamn hands on Duncairn." He walked over to the bar and reached for a bottle of bourbon. "Except they're not. The Royland woman's husband has written to Mitchison. He's prepared to talk. She's ill apparently."

Mary sat down slowly, unbuttoning her white raincoat. She kicked off her shoes with a groan. "Poor woman." She glanced at her husband and frowned. "Go easy on that stuff, honey, you know what the doctor said."

"That doctor is a fool." Rex refused to meet her eye. "I guess he thinks I'm getting old. They all think I'm getting old." He drained the glass and slammed it down on the bar.

"Were there problems in Houston, Rex?" Mary asked gently.

"Nothing I can't handle." He hooked his finger into the knot of his tie and loosened it slowly. "I'll be flying up to Aberdeen tomorrow, and as soon as Mitchison can arrange it I'll meet with Royland and get this deal tied up. Then perhaps that would be a good time to think about planning our retirement, what do you say?" He turned away from her before he could see the alarm in her eyes.

The roses glowed in the misty morning sunshine as Clare reached up to cut them from the back wall, then put them gingerly into her basket one by one. She swore as a thorn pricked her.

Paul had driven straight to the office when he returned from Bucksters on Monday morning so she hadn't seen him until yesterday evening, when he had returned at about seven.

"David and Gillian missed you," he said curtly as he walked in. "I explained that you were unwell."

"Was it a good party?" She smiled at him tentatively, trying to gauge his mood.

"Their parties are always amusing." He walked across to the sideboard and began to rummage in it for his whiskey. "May I ask what you did all weekend?"

"Nothing. You told them the truth, as it happens. I wasn't feeling well." She knew she sounded defensive.

"I see. Clare, I've been thinking." He poured two double whiskies, neat, and handed her one. "I think perhaps you should go away for a holiday. A couple of months in the sun would do you good."

She shook her head. "Perhaps after Christmas; I don't want to go away now."

"Why not?"

"I want to go up to Scotland. I have to sort out one or two things." There was a moment of silence.

When he spoke his voice was grim. "May I ask what sort of things?"

"Duncairn, for one." She looked him straight in the eye. "I want to discuss the future with Jack Grant. There are repairs that need doing as soon as possible to the hotel."

"I see. And where is the money going to come from?"

"I am sure I can find it. I still have money of my own, Paul."

"Yes, and I know exactly how much. How far do you think that will go?"

"Far enough for the time being."

"Clare! You're crazy. You might as well stand on the edge of that damn cliff and tear up the money, note by note, and throw it into the sea. No one in their right mind would contemplate pouring money into that hotel."

"Except the man who wants to buy it. You wouldn't object to his throwing his money away, I take it?" She tried to keep her voice steady.

"He doesn't want the hotel, Clare. He wants the oil."

"Well, he's not getting it." She clenched her fists. "I thought I would go up north later this week."

"We have a dinner party on Saturday, if you remember."

"Early next week, then. I've made my mind up, Paul."

He slept in the spare room, and he had left for the office before she was awake.

Thoughtfully she reached up to clip another rose, sniffing it absentmindedly before she dropped it into her basket. Since Zak's visit she had not left the house.

The meditation ended, she had waited for his verdict. Cautiously he had discussed what had happened. He had tried to dissuade her from doing it again. Then he had left her. But he had promised to return.

She took the roses into the kitchen and put them carefully into a porcelain vase, glancing up at the clock as she did so. Zak was coming back that afternoon before he returned to Cambridge, but she still had most of the morning to get through. She had already spent two days fighting the longing to retreat into her dream world. She wanted so much to know what was happening to Isobel. Isobel who had become pregnant so easily and who wanted so desperately to lose her child. Clare shivered. Surely her curiosity was natural? Morbid, perhaps, perverse even, but not sinister. It couldn't mean that already Isobel was gaining some kind of hold over her. Could it? Perhaps Zak was right, that already she preferred the past of her dreams to the present. She shook her head slowly. She had to get out of the house. That at least would distract her until he came.

"Paul Royland." Neil sat on the edge of the desk reading from the typed notes in front of him. "Age thirty-eight. Eton and Oxford—I knew that—we were at the same college, though he was a couple of years ahead of me. Career in the City. Coutts; Lombards; from 1981 a partner in Beattie Cameron; now a director of BCWP. Married in 1981 to Clare Gordon, daughter of the Honorable Alec Gordon who died in 1962." He threw the notes down on the desk. "Paul Royland!" he repeated in disgust. "The bastard tried to talk me down in the Union once. Then he tried to get me banned."

"I didn't know you were at Oxford." Kathleen Reardon, the folk singer, was standing watching him, her coat on, her bag already slung from her shoulder. Four years older than Neil, she looked ten years younger. "Quite the gentleman yourself, aren't you?" The soft Belfast accent was mocking.

Neil stood up. He went across to her and put his hands on her shoulders. "There are a lot of things about me you don't know."

"And a lot I do." She narrowed her light-blue eyes. "I know you're a chauvinist bastard; I know Mr. and Mrs. Royland have gotten up your nose; I know if the poor bugger went to

Eton you'll be ready to string him up from a lamppost, and I know you promised to buy me some supper and if we sit here much longer, every food outlet in Edinburgh will be locked and barred and bolted and the sun will rise over my poor bleached empty bones!"

Neil chuckled. "I always forget what an amazing appetite you have." He reached to turn off the light. "I'm going up to Duncairn again," he said as they left the office and turned out into the cold Grassmarket, the huge bulk of the castle walls looming high behind them in the dark. "I want to get this campaign off the ground before the Roylands know what has hit them, and before Sigma realizes its interest in the place is out in the open. We've got the edge on them, but only for a very short time." He pushed his hands deep into the pockets of his jacket. "Earthwatch is mounting a huge campaign against onshore drilling, and in today's climate with oil prices at rock bottom, we should be able to win. I'm going to use Duncairn to spearhead our campaign in Scotland."

Kathleen glanced at him curiously. "Just because you hate this Royland man and his wife so much?"

"No, Kath, you're wrong. Scotland and her environment are what matter to me. Those are the most important things in the world." Neil smiled. "You should know me well enough by now to know that."

Two days later Neil was back at Duncairn. He climbed on a bar stool and leaned on the counter, a glass of malt whiskey clasped reverently between his hands. "Have you heard anything from your new owner yet, Jack?"

Jack Grant had run the Duncairn Hotel for twenty years now. He had moved there from Aberdeen after his wife died, full of ideas to renovate the place and make it popular. Margaret Gordon had initially given him the money to improve the fabric of the building, a Victorian gray granite pile, built from the stones of the old castle itself, but his plans to modernize it had met with a veto. No new bar with piped music; no large notice on the main road to bring in the passing trade. She wanted the place to remain a haven of peace for the people who knew it. She was not interested in making a

profit, and slowly Jack had come around to her way of thinking and he had come to love this rugged piece of headland
with its ever-changing skies. The only solace to his former
ambition, the only extravagance he permitted himself now,
was the excellence of his menu, which was slowly gaining a
reputation throughout northeastern Scotland. There were
few evenings in the summer when the restaurant wasn't full,
and often on weekends the guests would stay a night or two
in the faded splendor of the baronial rooms. But now, in
October, the hotel was all but empty.

He ran the place with a minimum of staff. Mollie Fraser
and her daughter, Catriona, actually lived in the hotel, helping him in the kitchen and looking after the occasional
guests. In the summer two or three women came up from the
village to help, glad of any extra work. But apart from that
they coped. He and Mollie had an understanding. They were
comfortable.

Behind Neil the room was empty. From the low, broad
windows, he could see the top of the remaining tower of the
castle, the stone, yellowed with lichen, rising above the trees.
Even from here he could hear the soft soughing of the waves
below the cliffs.

Grant shrugged. "Not a word. Mrs. Royland came up here
in June shortly after old Miss Gordon died." He sniffed. "She
used to come up here a lot as a lass, wee Clare Gordon. A cute
little thing, she was, but now she's married to an Englishman
she hasn't time for us anymore."

"Do you think she'll sell the place?" Neil dropped the
question casually into the conversation.

"Never. It's in her blood. Even if she doesn't come back,
she'd not sell."

"She's had an offer for it."

Grant looked him straight in the eye, suddenly suspicious.
"How come you know so much about it?"

"I work for Earthwatch. I don't want to see this coast
spoiled by onshore drilling, and I don't want to see this hotel
closed. Your whisky is too good!"

Ignoring the compliment, Grant pulled himself up onto a

stool his side of the bar and leaned forward. "Are you saying there's oil at Duncairn?"

Neil nodded.

"And you think Clare Royland will sell up?"

"She's been offered a hell of a lot of money, Jack."

"I still can't believe she'd sell." Grant shook his head. "It would be right out of character."

"What if her husband wanted her to? He's not interested in Scotland."

"As to that, I don't know. I've not seen him more than once."

"We're going to fight the oil, Jack. Are you with us?" Neil watched him closely.

"Oh, aye, I'm with you. I'm too old to change to the fast-food and fast-women market. Leave that to the boys in Aberdeen."

"Even if it means fighting Clare Royland?"

"She won't sell."

Neil scowled. "I wish I had your faith in her."

Grant sat for a moment, lost in thought. "Surely it doesn't matter who owns the land if there's oil there. The bastards will take it anyway." Unprompted, he reached for Neil's glass and refilled it.

"Maybe not, but if the oil company already owns the land it wants to drill we have far less chance of winning. If, on the other hand, it has belonged to the same family for generations—"

"For seven hundred and fifty years."

"That long?" Neil said dryly. "And if we can shame Clare Royland into opposing any drilling, then we'll get public opinion on our side. The English public, the public in Edinburgh and Glasgow, theirs is the support we need. That and the fact that rare plants and animals and birds live here on these cliffs, with the real threat of environmental pollution— it would all give us a working chance of saving this place."

He walked around the castle again later, watching as the mists slowly crept landward across the sea. The stones were silent in the cold sunlight; no echoes this time. He pictured Clare as he had seen her, her hair blowing in the wind, her

high-heeled shoes sinking into the grass. Strangely she had
looked at home, he realized now; decadent and beautiful,
like her castle. If only she had kicked off those damn fool
shoes he might even have felt some sympathy for her. He
frowned. Was Kathleen right? Had it become a personal vendetta?

Kathleen had stayed in Edinburgh. She was booked to sing
at a club for the week and, anyway, he hadn't wanted her up
here with him. Somehow she always came between him and
the scenery. Not intentionally, but as a distraction, a discor-
dant note, in the tranquility of a landscape of which he felt
completely a part. For all her ethnic clothes and other-
worldly manner she was a city animal—a beautiful black-
haired panther of a woman, who would be as out of place
here at Duncairn as a bird of paradise on a grouse moor.

He climbed up into the tower and stared out to sea, feeling
the strange throbbing power of the wind and waves in his
very soul. Dear God, he had to save this place!

Instinctively Clare knew she had to go to Duncairn. There
she would find the answer to all her questions. Perhaps. She
longed to be there, to feel the wind on her face, to hear the
sea birds, to taste the North Sea spray on her lips. There she
would find peace.

She never gave a thought to the menace of the oil. As far as
she was concerned it was over, settled by her letter to Alec
Mitchison.

On Thursday she called Jack Grant. "I'll come up to Duncairn next week. If you could give me a room for a few days,
perhaps we can discuss the position, sort out our plans for the
future."

He could hardly refuse to have her, but after she had hung
up he sat thoughtfully gazing at the phone. Had she imagined it, or had there been suspicion and hostility in his voice?
She shrugged. She had always liked Jack Grant when she was
a child, and the thought of him there at the hotel when she
went back to the castle was reassuring. And she had to go to
the castle. That much she knew.

* * *

They had asked six guests to dinner on Saturday night. Sir Duncan and Lady Beattie, George Pierce, who had been senior partner of Westlake Pierce, with his wife Susan, Henry Firbank and Diane Warboys.

Diane was sitting on the window seat, her legs crossed, dressed in a tight black skirt, slit to the thigh, with a lace camisole beneath her black silk jacket. With her shoulder-length blond hair she looked dramatic and very sexy. Henry could not take his eyes off her. She had eyes only for Paul.

As Paul poured the rest of the guests their drinks and handed them around, Clare stood by the fire with Henry. Dragging his gaze away from Diane, he gave her a conspiratorial grin. "How are you?"

"All right. Thank you for coming over the other night."

Henry threw a quick glance toward Paul. "It was a pleasure. I hope you haven't had any more turns like that one in the elevator."

For a fraction of a second she hesitated, then she smiled. "I haven't been in any more elevators. It's usually possible to avoid them, thank goodness."

"I heard about your terrible experience, my dear." Lady Beattie's sharp ears had picked up their conversation. "I am so terribly sorry. Duncan has told the elevator company to come and check every single nut and bolt on the wretched things."

Henry grinned. "I don't think it was the machinery, Lady Beattie. There was a short power failure, I understand."

"Whatever it was"—Clare managed a bright social smile—"I shan't go near the wretched things again. Next time I have to go to the conference suite I shall take crampons and a pick and climb the outside of the building."

"What a riveting thought." Henry applauded. "If ever you need an anchorman, Clare, don't hesitate to ask me."

Amid the general laughter Clare saw Paul turn and look speculatively at his partner. There was something in his expression that made her shiver.

Diane moved forward from the window seat and sat down next to Paul, her glass dangling from red-painted fingertips.

In the office she wore black too, but sober, high-necked black, and her hair was usually drawn back into a tight slim bun, held with a velvet ribbon. She eased her position imperceptibly so her thigh was touching Paul's. "One should never allow one's life to be run by phobias," she said into the silence. "Have you ever thought of seeing a psychiatrist, Clare?"

Clare swallowed. She glanced at Paul. There was a slight smile on his lips. "No, Diane." She managed a quiet dignified laugh. "I have never felt sufficiently mad. Not yet."

"Oh, I didn't mean—"

"Of course she didn't," George Pierce broke in. "I expect Diane was thinking of psychotherapy. Everyone is into that these days, aren't they? Making people stroke spiders—that sort of thing!"

In the corner of the room Sir Duncan Beattie emptied his glass and held it out for a refill. He had been watching Paul closely, a speculative frown on his face. "Aversion therapy, I believe it's called," he said. "There are many ways of trying to cure phobias, and I suspect claustrophobia is one of the commonest. I must confess I dislike those elevators myself." He gave Clare a kind smile as Paul got up to take his glass.

Clare smiled back. She had seen Diane edging closer to Paul on the sofa and she had seen Paul's seeming indifference. She sighed. It was going to be a strained evening. A few minutes later she excused herself so that she could go downstairs to put the finishing touches to the food.

Isobel was waiting in the shadows in the corner of the room.

Chapter Seven

Mairi stared at her young mistress suspiciously. "What are you doing there all by yourself, and so quiet, my lady?" She wondered for a moment if Isobel had been crying.

The girl turned away sharply. "I shall ride again this afternoon, Mairi. Tell Hugh to bring a fresh horse."

Mairi scowled. "My lady, don't do it. You're just exhausting yourself. It'll not help."

"It will." Isobel put her hands on the almost imperceptible swell of her stomach. "It has to." She gritted her teeth. "A fresh horse, please, Mairi."

They no longer stopped her leaving the castle. A countess, with her retinue, might ride where she willed, it appeared, once she carried her lord's heir in her belly. And ride she did, galloping across the moors, regardless of the weather, until her horse was exhausted and her followers gasping. She jumped the animal over burns and gullies, and returned home aching and exhausted at dusk day after day. But still the baby inside her grew.

It filled her with horror and disgust; she could not bear to think that anything of Lord Buchan's could be growing inside her, that any part of him could become a part of her. Besides that, she was terrified of even the idea of childbirth. It was one of the few things of which she was truly afraid. The fear went back to when she was four years old and her brother Duncan was born.

She remembered the time vividly—a few beautiful days at the beginning of September in the year 1289 that would remain in her mind forever as a time of blood and terror.

Joanna de Clare had shown herself to be possessed of an uncertain temper in the last few months of her pregnancy, and she had made it quite clear that her high-spirited daughter should be kept as much out of her way as possible in this, the smallest of the earl's castles where they were all forced to share the same restricted living space, as they waited for the earl's return.

Only the old harper sitting in the corner did not seem to notice the strained atmosphere in the room. His long, frail fingers stroked the harp strings soothingly, but his eyes were fixed on the embrasure where his mistress stood silhouetted in the bright evening light. Joanna had noticed his gaze. It disturbed her to see his eyes, which had been completely blind for so long, fixed unerringly on her face.

"Isobel! Come here and show me what you've got," she called out suddenly, sitting down on the narrow stone seat. The child paused in her play, uncertain, but then as the gentle reassuring sounds of the harp continued, she rose and, gathering something up in her arms, danced with it across the floor, out of a last small patch of sunlight near the fire, across the darkening room and back into the mellow light near her mother. She dropped a slightly unsteady curtsey and held out her arms to let a tiny kitten fall on the waiting lap.

Drowsy in the heat of the fire, Joanna, lost in a dream, was brought back to the present only when the kitten, stretching, began energetically to knead at her knees, its claws hooked into her gown. She caught hold of it impatiently and threw it onto the floor, where it landed on its feet, spitting with fright and indignation. Isobel had been standing watching her mother's face with wide-eyed intensity, but now she fell on her knees beside the kitten and gathered the tiny creature up in her arms. She had looked up at her mother, her eyes blazing with uncontrollable temper, although she had said nothing, and Joanna did not notice the child's anger. She had risen from her seat and was gazing from the window once more, lost in thoughts of her husband's return.

Mairi had not, however, missed that look in Isobel's eyes. Leading her charge back to the fire, she shook her head sadly. There was temper there that must be curbed for Isobel's own sake. She had seen too many signs of it over the three years she had had charge of the child.

Mairi had first come to Isobel from a village high in the mountains of Mar. The Earl of Fife's grandmother, who was now Countess of Mar, had found the girl and arranged that she come to Joanna's service. She was a quiet, introspective young woman, clever at relating, with wide eyes and expressive gestures, the hair-raising tales of her own mountains, with their attendant ghosts and demons, sprites and fairies, and Isobel had absorbed them all.

The boy began lighting the torches with a brand from the fire. They flared wickedly for a moment as each caught, then settled to a steady flame. Joanna turned from her place at the window at last and went back to her seat near the fire.

"My lady, there are riders coming." The boy had been drawing the heavy shutters across the window. Joanna looked up, trying to steady the sudden excitement in her heart.

"Let us hope they are here before darkness comes," she said as calmly as she could. It was some time, however, before the sound of hasty footsteps came up to them from below.

Pulling Isobel to her, Mairi waited. Joanna had risen from her chair at the sound, her cheeks pale and her breath coming sharply as two men appeared at the top of the stairs. They wore the livery of the Earl of Fife, but their clothes were torn and spattered with dried mud and dust.

One, the taller of the two, stopped abruptly and remained by the door, awkwardly fingering his sword hilt. The other strode straight to where Joanna stood and went down on one knee before her.

"My lady, I have dreadful news." The man made a visible effort to collect himself and then paused again, uncertain how to continue.

"You bring word from the earl my husband?" she prompted.

He winced as if she had struck him. "My lady, we were riding toward Brechin. It was growing dark, and the men were tired. The earl wanted to reach the burgh before dusk. My lady, we were ambushed." His voice was scarcely audible as he continued with a rush. "There were so many of them, hiding by the roadside. We stood no chance, my lady! We shouted at them! There must have been a mistake." He was appealing to her now. "They were lying in wait for someone else. It was twilight and hard to see. We shouted, my lady! They were the earl's kinsmen, my lady! They wore the livery of the Abernethys. We fought them off as best we could, my lady, but two of our comrades were killed and . . . and . . ."

"And how, sir, does it happen that you are still alive? Did you flee from aiding my lord to save your own skin?" Joanna almost spat the words at him.

The man looked up with indignation. "The moment he was dead they fled, my lady. We could not follow in the darkness. And we could not leave . . . we could not leave him lying there."

She stood looking down on him in silence.

"The body is being conveyed to the abbey of Coupar Angus, my lady countess." The man by the door spoke at last. "We shall be pleased to escort you there at daybreak."

Requiem aeternam dona ei. Domine.

The mournful voices echoed back and forth, high in the shadowy vaults of stone in the abbey chapel across the garth. To Isobel in the guest house, it was the sound of doom.

Joanna had gone into premature labor on seeing the mutilated body of her husband. Her moans had continued all night. The next morning, as the monks began to sing their requiem, the first of her screams echoed around the small square building.

Isobel cowered back, her small face white, her eyes enormous. The woman with her glanced at the child. "Outside, my lady. Go outside and play." She ushered her toward the door. "Go on, quickly. I must go to your mother."

But Isobel hadn't gone. Cautiously she had followed, creeping toward the door of the small guest chamber where Joanna had been lodged, and there, unnoticed by the panicking, frantic women, she saw and heard it all.

In numb, terrified silence, she stared into the room. She

saw and smelled the blood; only this blood wasn't black and clotted like that which had stiffened on her father's embroidered tunic. It was red and alive. It soaked the sheets and covered the women's arms, and it seemed to pour from her mother's body endlessly as again and again Joanna screamed.

And then the baby came. Her brother. Duncan. Her father's heir. The new Earl of Fife. A tiny, bloodstained, ugly doll, the cord still hanging from his belly as someone held him up. And they were pleased. Even her mother, exhausted as she was, was smiling now through her tears, holding out her arms for the boy.

Isobel turned away. After tiptoeing toward the room where she had slept some of the night, she crawled under the covers of one of the beds and began to cry.

It was Mairi who had told her that she need never have a baby of her own; Mairi who had promised there were ways for women to stop it from happening and that if need be she would show her how; Mairi—who now said it was God's will —who had dragged the child Isobel back almost from the edge of madness that September day.

Isobel looked at her now reproachfully and wondered if she remembered those days too. She caught Mairi's eye and held it, and knew that she did. It was Mairi who, shamefaced, turned away.

"May I ask what has happened to our dinner?"

Paul's voice cut through the silence like a knife.

Clare stared at him blankly, then, horrified, she rose to her feet. She was seated alone at the dining table. The candles she remembered just having lighted had burned down more than an inch; the room was full of the smell of cooking.

"Paul! I'm sorry. I . . . I must have fallen asleep."

"Indeed you must." He gave a grim smile. "I warned you you would be too tired if you did everything yourself."

"It's not that—"

"No?"

He knew what she had been doing. Her eyes had been shut, but her whole posture, though relaxed, had been attentive, alert, as if she were listening to something far away. He wondered momentarily why Sarah Collins found it so alarming. Clare was daydreaming, that was all, but was it normal to sit daydreaming for nearly an hour when you had six important guests upstairs? He thought not.

"Is the food spoiled?" he asked coldly.

Clare shook her head. "The casserole needed another half hour anyway."

"I see. But you didn't think to return to your guests. They bore you, I suppose."

Clare could feel herself coloring. "You know that's not true, Paul. I just sat down for a moment to . . . think—"

"To think!" Paul repeated the words, his tone deliberately insulting. "And may I ask what you were thinking about so hard that you gave every appearance of being asleep?"

"You were watching me?"

He could see she was uncomfortable.

"I watched you." His eyes narrowed slightly.

Clare turned away from him abruptly. "If you want to know, I was thinking about babies. Childbirth." She gave an involuntary shiver.

"Clare, I have told you to stop dwelling on that." The sudden twinge of guilt made him angry.

"One can't just stop, Paul. Not after all you and I have been through in the last few months." Clare realized suddenly that they were at cross purposes.

"You have to, otherwise you will make yourself ill."

Ill. Was that it? Was that what was happening to her? She had not sat down to meditate. She had not summoned Isobel. She had constructed no ashram to frame a meditation. The dream had come unbidden, a nightmare of blood and fear and pain to put an end forever to her own special little fantasy of a beautiful sterile birth with a tiny, powdered, pink-and-white baby as the end product. She took a deep breath, trying desperately to master her sudden cold fear. "Shouldn't one of us go back upstairs?"

"Both of us, Clare." Paul took her arm. "Are you sure the food is all right?"

She nodded, dragging her mind back fully to the present.

"I'll put the starters on the table, if you'd like to bring the others down."

"Are you sure you feel well enough?" Paul asked grudgingly.

"Of course. No one will know anything. I promise." She forced herself to smile. "Go on, Paul. Fetch them now."

"A crisis, dear?" Lady Beattie smiled at her graciously as she led the other guests into the room a few moments later. "You should have called me. I'm an old hand at coping with disasters." She was peering around the room as if expecting to find evidence of calamity pushed under the table.

"It must be a frightful bore when your staff let you down." Diane's drawl cut the air like a knife. "Paul was saying that your cook is stuck down in the country."

"She's not stuck." Clare took her place at the table with a smile. "I told her not to come. It was hardly necessary for her to make the effort for a small dinner party like this." She was aware of the scandalized expression on Paul's face and felt a sudden surge of triumph. "And there wasn't any crisis. I was just putting the finishing touches to one or two things."

She had seen Henry's gaze go to the candles, already burning, translucent with heat, then back to her and she knew that he had guessed. She refused to catch his eye.

Kathleen leaned on the bar, watching Neil with narrowed eyes. She was drinking tomato juice. The Cramond Inn was packed. He was standing near her, a glass of whisky in his hand, lost in thought, then he glanced at his watch.

"She's not coming." She sat down on a bar stool near him.

"She will."

Kathleen raised an eyebrow. "It's too big a risk for her. Anyway, why should she? You know enough."

"I don't know enough!" Neil slammed his hand down on the bar. "All I know is that Clare Royland turned down the first offer. I have to know what happened when she received the next one."

"Does her reaction affect the campaign then?"

"Of course it affects the campaign. Are we on the side of the owners, fighting the oil moguls and the government, or

are we against private individuals exploiting the environment to enrich their own purses?" He was speaking quietly
but his voice was passionately intense. "The whole angle of
this campaign is going to depend on what Sandra has to say."

"They might not have heard anything yet."

"They've heard. She told me that much on the phone."

Kathleen gave a slow smile. "You want her to accept that
offer, don't you? You want to fight this beautiful Mrs. Royland." She narrowed her eyes again, catlike. "Don't let her
get to you too much, Neil." Raising her hand to his cheek for
a moment, she flexed her fingers, then stroked his face for a
fraction of a second with her nails. "You mustn't lose the cool
impersonality for which you're so famous."

Neil stepped back slightly. "I won't." He was visibly irritated. He turned his back on her and surveyed the crowds in
the room. Sandra MacKay had arrived while they were talking and was standing nervously just inside the door.

"I'm sorry. I took a wrong turn." She greeted him anxiously. "I'm not used to driving on my own. Can we go outside? I don't like pubs."

Neil opened the door for her and ushered her outside
without a word. The parking lot was cold and very silent after
the noise of the pub. It was slightly foggy. "Wouldn't you
rather I bought you a drink?" He was wondering why she had
chosen to meet there if she didn't like pubs.

She shook her head. "I was thinking that none of my mum's
friends would go somewhere like that, but I might be recognized by anyone—one of Mr. Mitchison's or Mr. Archer's
clients. I'd forgotten that that is the sort of place they would
go on a Saturday night—"

"Let's walk down to the river. No one will see us there."
Neil pushed his hands down into the pockets of his jacket,
with a quick shiver of excitement. Her air of frightened con-
spiracy was contagious.

They stood in silence at the end of the causeway, which led
out toward the sleeping hump of Cramond Island. The re-
ceding tide had left darker patches in the darkness where the
mudflats glistened. Lights showed every now and then from
the towns strung along the distant coast of Fife, then the mist

would drift back and they would disappear, only to reappear, strafed into whiteness by the monotonous lighthouse beam out in the Forth. Neil could hear the quiet confidential chatter of birds in the distance.

Slowly they walked up the River Almond and stared across into the darkness of the Dalmeny woods. Water was lapping gently below the sea wall.

"I'm sorry to be so silly," she said after a moment. "But my job means a lot to me."

"Your job is safe, Sandra," Neil said firmly. "You have my word. No one will see us here." Behind them the village was empty and deserted, the black-and-white houses of the winding street and the quay floodlit by streetlamps that showed the wet reflection on the road. Somewhere in the distance a dog barked.

She moved closer to him. "Mr. Mitchison had a letter back from Mr. Royland. Apparently his wife is ill, but he is interested in the offer, and"—she glanced over her shoulder—"Mr. Mitchison has set up a meeting between Mr. Cummin and Mr. Royland."

Neil let out a soundless whistle. "I knew it! When are they meeting?"

"Next Friday. I typed out the letter confirming it yesterday. They're going to meet for dinner in London."

In the darkness Neil was staring out across the cold water. "Do you by any chance know where they're meeting?"

"Yes."

He smiled. "Good," he said.

Casta was ecstatic. Yelping with excitement, she leapt around Clare as her mistress climbed out of the car on Sunday morning. The fog was still thick and the fields around the house were dank and silent.

Without a word Paul went to the rear of the car to find their suitcases.

"Paul—" Clare followed him.

"No, Clare. I will need you in London." He didn't even bother to look at her. "It's not convenient for you to go to Scotland at the moment. I'm sorry."

"It would only be for a few days." She could hear herself pleading and she despised herself for it. She felt trapped.

"No!" He slammed down the trunk lid. "God knows, Clare, I'd have thought after last night's fiasco you would have wanted to make amends. Sonja Beattie was scandalized by your behavior."

Clare stooped to give the dog a hug, hiding a half smile in the golden fur. "I don't think she was at all," she said defiantly. "I think she was amused. Anyway, why call it a fiasco? They didn't know what happened. And the food was good; the wine was good; there were no awkward silences. In fact" —she straightened and looked at him—"I think it was a successful dinner party all around. You should be pleased." She turned and walked into the house.

Paul's eldest brother was waiting in the drawing room. Sarah Collins had lighted the fire and the room smelled richly of the old dry apple boughs she had thrown into the large open fireplace. There were new bowls of chrysanthemums and Michaelmas daisies, beautiful among the silver frames of the photographs on the tables scattered around the room.

After throwing her jacket down on the sofa, Clare went straight to the fire and knelt before it, holding out her hands. "How are you, David? Where's Gillian?" She did not wait to kiss her brother-in-law or take his hand.

Sir David Royland put down the business section of the *Sunday Times* and stood up. He was a tall man, like his brothers, his hair a uniform gray. He wore a dilapidated cashmere sweater over baggy corduroys, and his feet were clad only in socks. The Member of Parliament for the Stour Valley was off duty. He put his cup down on the low coffee table and then straightened again, looking at her closely. "I'm fine, my dear. And so is Gillian. She thought she'd take it easy this morning, with the baby so imminent. Where is Paul?"

She shrugged. "He'll be here in a minute."

"We were sorry not to see you at the party last week." He paused. "I hope you're feeling better. Wouldn't you be more comfortable in a chair, my dear?"

Clare moved closer to the fire. "I'm fine, thank you. For

God's sake, sit down, David. Don't hover! You've come to see Paul, I suppose?" She looked up at him suddenly.

"I did, as a matter of fact." He studied her face, noticing the signs of strain, and he frowned.

Clare always made him feel uneasy. He found her extremely attractive, he had to admit, and yet she irritated him and put him on the defensive, mocking him and all he stood for from behind those innocent gray eyes. He knew she found him pompous and she teased him openly, especially about his recent knighthood. He wished he could dismiss her as a silly young woman of whom he could take no notice. But he couldn't. Whenever she was in the room with him he found himself drawn toward her. Also he respected her brain —something his own wife appeared to be able to do without —and he found himself wondering, often, how she and Paul conducted their sex life. He had frequently suspected his brother of being totally uninterested in sex. For this vivacious, beautiful woman to see anything in Paul at all was a conundrum upon which he pondered with a frequency for which he despised himself.

He sat down on a chair near her and leaned forward, his elbows on his knees, his chin cupped in his hands. Whatever he felt about Clare, he had never before found himself feeling sorry for her, but now suddenly there was a wistfulness in her face that made him feel strangely protective.

"Paul has asked me whether I would be prepared to break the children's trust fund." He looked thoughtfully into the fire. "I take it that was your idea?"

"My idea?" Clare sat back on her heels and looked up at him. "I don't know what you're talking about."

"Don't you?" He looked both surprised and pained. "Paul feels that Father's will, because it was so heavily weighted toward his grandchildren, actual and potential, is grossly unfair. My children and Geoffrey's and Em's will inherit the bulk of Father's estate when they grow up." He glanced at her. "Paul feels we should split up the money so that he can take a quarter."

Clare rose to her feet. "And you think that is my idea?"

David hesitated, scrutinizing her face. "I thought it might

be. It seems strange that Paul should suddenly want the money, but I see I'm wrong."

Clare bent to pick up a log from the basket and threw it into the fire, watching the flames lick around it. "He wants it because he knows he will never have any children to inherit anything, at least not as long as he's married to me." She clenched her fists. "But no doubt he told you that. Perhaps he feels this is just compensation for having a barren wife. It is his share of the inheritance, I suppose, so why shouldn't he have it?"

"Exactly." Behind them Paul had appeared in the doorway. "So, is that why you've come, David? To give me your decision?"

He strode into the room and leaned against the oak chest near the door, his folded arms concealing his agitation. "Have you and Geoff talked it over?" His voice was heavy.

"Geoffrey is away at some conference." David adopted a soothing tone that managed to sound patronizing. "But I'm sure we'll be able to agree about this when he gets back."

"And how much do you suppose you will be able to spare me after your deliberations?"

"That is rather up to the four of us, as trustees, and to the accountants, don't you think?" David said dryly. "If you feel you are entitled to a particular percentage, you'd better say so. The money you're talking about is at the moment to be divided equally among the children when they reach the age of eighteen, with a capital sum remaining to give each of them a small income and to cover any late arrivals." He gave a tight smile. "We four are supposed to have had our share when Father died, remember?"

"Of course I remember." Paul turned away sharply. He went across to the window and stared out at the mist. The chestnut trees were dripping dankly on the lawn, their golden leaves mud-colored without the sun.

His brother was watching him closely through narrowed eyes. "Well, if you still want to go ahead with this, I suggest we call a meeting of the trustees to discuss it." He stood up. "I'll ring Geoff tonight and see if he's back. I think I should tell you, Paul, that Gillian and I are not very happy about this."

"I'm sure you're not!" Paul didn't look around. "Your bloody kids get the lion's share."

"They will get an equal amount each." David was tight-lipped as he strode toward the door. "I'm sorry Paul is putting you through all this, Clare." As he opened the door he glanced back at her. She was still standing by the fire, her face set. "You deserve better, my dear."

Clare watched until her brother-in-law's old Bentley had disappeared up the drive, then she turned to Paul.

"Why didn't you tell me you wanted to break the trust?"

He left the window and threw himself down with a sigh into the chair his brother had just vacated. "There is nothing to tell as yet. But Geoffrey will agree with me because it's the Christian thing to do, and Em will agree because it's fair." He gave a grim smile.

Clare bit her lip, trying to fight down the guilt and unhappiness that was threatening to swamp her. She was watching him closely, and she realized suddenly through her misery that the strained transparency of the skin around his eyes and the loss of weight in his usually solid face had not just happened in the last few days. His concern about money, and his bad temper, had been going on now for months. Since the end of June when they had learned that she would not inherit any money from Margaret Gordon. Yet Paul was a rich man —both from his father's money, which, as David had pointed out, had been considerable, and through his investments. She frowned. "Are you worried about money for some reason, Paul?" she asked wearily. "Nothing has gone wrong in the City, has it?"

"Gone wrong?" He stared into the fire. "Of course not. Did it look as if anything were wrong last night?"

"No."

"Well, then." He closed his eyes. "There is nothing to worry about, is there?"

The helicopter hovered for several minutes over the field, then it circled the castle, the huge rotor blades fanning the

branches of rowan and birch, parting the grasses until they
bent and streamed like water. On the cliffs the birds flew up
in clouds, screaming, their cries drowned by the roar of the
engine.

Rex Cummin leaned forward, staring down, his eyes fixed
on the pile of gray stone that had been the tower of Duncairn. He had a notepad on his knee and there was a pen in
his hand, but he made no attempt to write. Out at sea the fog
banks were a pearly white, obliterating the horizon, but inland the ground was bathed in sunshine. His eyes gleamed.
Far below the sleeping rock, below the matted bracken and
heather and dry grass, there was oil. He knew it in his bones.

In the hotel Jack Grant stood at the office window watching as the helicopter circled. He frowned, noting the logo
painted on its side, then he reached for the phone and dialed
the number Neil had given him.

He consulted his notes. "Does the Greek letter *sigma*
mean anything to you?" he asked as the line connected.

In Edinburgh Neil cursed.

⊰⊱ *Chapter Eight* ⊰⊱

The offices of Sigma Exploration were on the third and fourth floors of a glass-fronted building overlooking the Thames at Westminster. Sitting at his desk, in the deeply carpeted, luxurious executive suite, Rex Cummin could look across the river toward the Houses of Parliament. It still gave him something of a thrill, after three years, to see the silhouette of the Victoria Tower and Big Ben against the clear duck-egg glow of the early-morning London sky.

He was sitting at his desk now, and in front of him on the blotter was a closely typed report. He picked it up and read it again slowly. He was smiling.

> . . . Beattie Cameron Westlake Pierce . . . rumors about undercapitalization . . . insider dealing . . . possible investigation by the Stock Exchange Council. . . . Paul Royland's name mentioned in the press, on each occasion unfavorably. . . . directors in internal squabble over funding. . . . Sir Duncan Beattie defends Royland to colleagues over Beattie Committee controversy. . . . M.P.'s brother suspected in collusion in funding scandal. . . .

Rex's face creased into a contented smile. He picked up the phone.

"Leonie, honey, would you fix up a lunch with Diane Warboys for me? It must be before Friday. You'll find her number in the file under BCWP in Coleman Street, oh, and honey, would you send some flowers to Mrs. Clare Royland? I have her address here, and I'll give you a note to go with those." He chuckled as he put down the receiver.

He lay back in his chair and, tapping his teeth with his

pencil, he picked up the report again. At last things were beginning to go his way.

"Would you like me to get anything for you when I'm in Ipswich this afternoon, Mrs. Royland?" Sarah appeared in the doorway of the drawing room so suddenly that Clare jumped.

She pushed back the pile of unopened letters on her writing desk—the invitations to charity events, the pleas for money, at least two demands that she join fund-raising committees—she didn't have to open them to know what they were—and glanced out of the window at the hazy garden. The sun was just breaking through the mist, shimmering on the copper and russet leaves of the chestnuts in the drive. Clare sighed. She stretched her arms up above her head. "You know, it's so beautiful today, I think I might come with you. I could do with a change of scene."

Sarah frowned. "It wouldn't really be very easy, Mrs. Royland. I . . ." She hesitated. "I've so many different things to do. But I'd be happy to pick anything up for you."

Clare bit her lip, trying not to feel rejected, trying to fight down the feeling of desolation that threatened to overwhelm her. Paul had left for London that morning before it was light. He had slept in her bed, but he hadn't touched her. If Sarah went out and left her in the house alone, the loneliness would return and with it the need to fill the emptiness with daydreams. She stood up. She would go too. She must. Suddenly she was afraid, terrified of the silent rooms. She turned to follow Sarah into the hall, but as she reached the door, the phone rang. With a pleading glance at Sarah's departing form she turned back and picked it up.

"Clare? It's Chloe. My dear, I had to call you. What on earth have you been getting up to?" Her sister-in-law sounded breathless with excitement.

Clare sat down again, making a determined effort to steady herself, her fingers once more, automatically, idly, turning over the letters on the desk. Even without the sound of car tires on the gravel outside she had known Sarah would take the chance to go without her. Her heart sank. Another afternoon alone in the house, and probably a whole evening after it, and then the night, all to be gotten through somehow. She sighed, fighting back the fear.

"Clare, are you there?" Chloe sounded indignant. "I shouldn't tell you, but Geoffrey is praying for you!"

"Praying for me?" Clare's attention snapped back to the phone.

"He's desperately worried about you and I thought I'd better warn you; he's going to come up and see you."

"What on earth for?" Indignantly Clare stood up. She shuffled all the envelopes into the waste bin and stood staring out at the grass where a blackbird was standing, head cocked to one side, intently watching a patch of daisies. "If it's to do with my inability to have a baby, it's a bit late for prayers." She couldn't keep the bitterness out of her voice. "Unless one believes in miracles."

"Oh, Clare." For a moment Chloe was silent. "My dear, I was so sorry to hear about that, and it's never too late to pray about something so important, but that wasn't what I meant." She sounded deflated.

"What then?" Clare picked up the phone and walked to the French doors. She pushed them open and stepped out onto the terrace. The sun was warm on her head, the garden still.

"Emma came to see us last weekend, just before Geoff went off to his conference. She came to talk about her and Pete. You know they're having problems with their marriage because Peter is away so much. Well, Geoff took her off into his study and"—Chloe's voice took on a hollow ring supposed to denote awe—"they talked for ages."

"So?"

"They talked about *you.*"

"Me?"

"It took me hours to wangle it out of him later. Clare, you must be doing something truly dreadful! Emma only mentioned it casually at first. Geoff said she didn't seem worried. He said she didn't realize what you were up to. So, what are you doing? Are you sticking pins in wax figures, by any chance?" There was a breathless pause.

"I see." Clare smiled wryly. "Oh, it's far worse than that." It was hard to resist the temptation to tease her credulous sister-in-law. "In fact, I doubt if you should even risk talking to me! The telephone wires might go white-hot and burn you." She walked restlessly back into the house, the phone in one hand and the receiver in the other, trailing the long cord behind her. Damn Emma. Who else had she told? "Tell Geoff not to bother coming, Chloe. I'm beyond redemption. I'm unrepentant and probably dangerous."

"You must talk to Geoffrey, Clare." Chloe's voice had lost its lightness. "Please. He genuinely wants to help you."

"I told you, tell him not to come. Tell him to mind his own business." Clare took a deep breath. "I'm sorry, I shouldn't have said that. It's just that there are too many people breathing down my neck at the moment, Chloe, and I don't need it. Whatever problems I've got I have to sort them out myself. Look, I've got to go." Suddenly she couldn't bear to talk any longer. "I'll see you in London soon. We'll have lunch. Okay?"

The moment she put the phone down it rang again. "Clare, I shall need you in London on the first of November. Would you put it on your calendar? Dinner with the Beatties." Paul's voice was uncompromisingly brusque.

"So, they've forgiven me, have they? And until the first, Paul—won't you be *needing* me until then?" She emphasized the word sarcastically.

"Clare." His tone was warning.

"That is, by my count, Paul, nineteen days. One could go around the world comfortably in nineteen days. I can have a fortnight in Scotland and still be back easily—"

"No, Clare! I said *no!*"

"Just how do you intend to stop me, Paul?" To her annoyance she found her voice was shaking. "I'm not your property; you don't own me."

"Clare." Paul took a deep breath, clearly audible over the phone. "Darling, you've misunderstood me. I do need you there." He enunciated the words slowly as if she were a halfwit. "Look, I'll be home tomorrow night. We'll talk then. I—" He hesitated. "I have a surprise for you."

"Really?" Clare raised an eyebrow. "To have you home midweek would be surprise enough." She felt surprisingly cheerful suddenly. For once she had had the last word. And she was right. He didn't own her. She was not a prisoner. There was nothing to stop her from leaving. Her car had been left in London because she had driven back with Paul in the Range Rover, but there were trains and taxis. She wasn't locked in and spied on like poor Isobel. She stood up. To plan her escape would give her something to do today. She could find out train times, plan connections, arrange to rent a car when she got to Aberdeen; and in the meantime there was always Isobel.

If there was some threat in Isobel's appearance, it was being perceived by others, not herself. She had been afraid when Isobel appeared suddenly and uninvited during the dinner party in London, but that had been because it had taken her by surprise. Now, when she thought about it, she could see what had happened. She had been tired. Her mind had been distracted. She had sat down with the specific intention of relaxing for a few moments, and she had lighted candles. Her brain had misinterpreted the signs, that was all. There was nothing sinister in it. To Clare, Isobel was a friend —a companion, a part of herself. Why should she let other people make her afraid of summoning the past? What possible harm, logically, could there be in a dream?

It was as if a tremendous weight had been lifted from her mind. There was nothing wrong in daydreaming! Her mistake had been to tell people about it! Everyone had their secret dreams and memories; she was no different from them. Except that she had talked about them. In the future she would make sure that she kept them to herself!

Buoyed up with sudden resolution, Clare ran up to her bedroom. After carefully closing the door, she pulled open the drawer in her dressing table where she kept her candles.

Lord Buchan had returned. He stood staring at his wife, his eyes fixed on her face. "So, my lady, I am told you are riding dangerously long distances each day for no reason. May I know why?"

Isobel could feel the heat rising in her cheeks. She turned away from him. "I feel trapped here, my lord, and bored. I need the air; I need to ride!"

His eyes strayed thoughtfully to her stomach where her mantle hid the slight swell of the five-month child that all her efforts had failed to dislodge.

"Then your desire for air must be quelled," he said sternly. "There is enough air to be had in walking the walls. The ground outside is too dangerous for riding now." He glanced at the heavy wooden screens over the windows. Behind them thick snow fell slowly and relentlessly, muffling the sluggish movement of the waves beneath the cliffs, smothering the ground, drifting into the rough angles of the castle walls. "No one should ride while this weather lasts." He sat down heavily on the edge of a carved oak kist. "As well we reached Duncairn before the tracks here became impassable. I did not expect such thick snow on the coast; inland the passes are already closed. There will be no more fighting until the spring." He paused. "I have brought visitors for you from Ellon. Our niece Alice is here, with her father. You must come down to greet her."

In spite of herself Isobel smiled. "I will, gladly." Even Alice's company would be better than none while she pondered ways to rid herself of her child.

Lord Buchan saw the smile, and for a moment he glimpsed his wife's loneliness. He seldom thought of her as a person. The vast Buchan lands were still ably administered by his energetic mother, so to him Isobel was merely a dynastic necessity, a woman to whom he was married for political reasons; a woman who was there solely to provide him with an heir. What she did when he was away was of no concern to him, save where it touched his honor or his child. "I told her you needed company. You should not be alone over the next few months." He frowned. "She will help organize your household and see to it that you do not grow bored. It will be pleasant for you to have a woman to talk to while you spin and weave and make clothes for the child."

Isobel clenched her fists. "I do not enjoy spinning and weaving, my lord. I shall go mad if I am forced to sit and listen to women's gossip at the loom. I cannot bear being cooped up like some poor broody hen!" She began to pace the floor. "I would rather hear the conversation of men!"

Lord Buchan gave a grim smile. "Then you will be pleased to hear, no doubt, that your great-uncle, Macduff of Fife, is here also."

The great hall was crowded. Lord Buchan's followers and those of Macduff overflowed the hall out into the snowy courtyard. Alice Comyn, the daughter of Lord Buchan's brother, Alexander, was standing, still swathed in heavy furs, her hands outstretched to the blazing fire.

She offered a cold cheek to Isobel. "We thought we'd be cut off on the road through the mountains. My father's horse went into a snowdrift up to its belly. It took two others to pull it out!" She took Isobel's hands in hers. "How are you, Aunt?" Her eyes sparkled irrepressibly. Isobel was two years her junior. "Uncle John tells me you need company. You must be so excited, carrying his baby!"

Isobel smiled wanly, liking the young woman in spite of the ineptness of this last remark. She remembered Alice as a pert, sneaky girl, constantly creeping into corners to whisper with the pages, but now she seemed changed. Isobel sensed sympathy and warmth in the girl to which she instantly responded. She drew her niece nearer to the fire. "Your own marriage is arranged, I hear," she said softly.

Alice nodded eagerly. "I am to marry Sir Henry Beaumont." She shook her head wistfully. "I long to have babies of my own."

"It is not something to look forward to!" The words slipped out before Isobel could stop them. "To know that something is growing inside you, taking you over, possessing you! Something which is going to tear you apart and perhaps kill you so that it can take life of its own!" She shuddered.

Alice stared at her, horrified. "You don't really believe that?"

Behind them the hall was noisy and hot from the flaring torches and the huge fire, heaped high with driftwood from the bay, which was fanned by the constant draft from the doors behind the screens.

Isobel stood motionless, looking at her. Alice was her husband's niece—his spy. "No," she said shortly. "Of course I don't really believe it. If women believed that, there would be no more children." She put her hand on her stomach where she could feel a faint uneasy fluttering. Lord Buchan's child had quickened.

Alexander Comyn, two years younger than his brother, was watching his daughter and Isobel with curiosity. He was a tall, vigorous man, of uncertain temper, but for the moment he was content. The warmth of the fire was finding its way into his bones and a servant was approaching him with a jug of wine. He looked at Isobel closely. She seemed pinched and thin, unhappy, but there was no doubt the girl was with child. Thoughtfully he stroked his cheek. His only comfort at his own failure to sire a son—two daughters were all his wife had given him—was the fact that his elder brother had no heir. Now this late marriage with Isobel of Fife seemed likely to give John the son he desired. He scowled.

"So, will Edward of England winter in Flanders?" His brother was at his elbow.

Sir Alexander Comyn nodded grudgingly. "I doubt if he'll move before the spring. We'll have time to plan our campaign with Wallace."

"You support him wholeheartedly now, then?" From his stance near the fire Macduff of Fife stepped forward. He strode over to his great-niece and embraced her. He was a slight, wizened man, his hair grizzled, stiff and glittering still with clotted sleet that had not yet melted in the heat of the fire. "Isobel, child, how are you?" He kissed her on the top of her head. "Are you well?" His narrowed eyes surveyed her face intently. She was no longer the carefree child with the delightful giggle whom he remembered as being so like her spirited mother. He frowned, then he turned back to the Comyns. "You recognize now how much Scotland needs the Wallace."

"It appears he is the leader that we lack while our king is a prisoner elsewhere," Alexander acknowledged. "He more than proved himself at Stirling Bridge." At last the boy with the wine had reached him. He seized the proffered goblet and, draining it, held it out for a refill. "It seems that all the factions within our kingdom will follow him. Even the Bruces seem prepared to support him."

Lord Buchan's gaze went thoughtfully to his wife's face. "Robert Bruce still broods over his grandfather's claim to the throne—a claim that his father seems singularly ill suited to pursue. I trust neither of them."

"Nor I, entirely. But for Scotland's good, Comyn and Bruce must run in harness, and as long as Lord Annandale lives, his son's pretensions are curbed. Even he sees that his father could never rule this country. He will not support a Balliol king, but while Balliol is out of the country, then he will fight for Scotland." He threw himself down into a chair beside the long table. "So, brother." He changed the subject abruptly. "You are to have an heir in the spring, I see." He chuckled. "I didn't think you'd tame that little wildcat of yours. She looks too thin. You must see she eats well this winter."

Lord Buchan sighed. He sat down stiffly next to his brother, stretching his long legs out in front of him. "I trust your daughter will calm her down. I am weary of fighting each time I speak to her."

His brother threw back his head and laughed. "So, you are henpecked, brother, and those scars come from your wife's claws, not an English pike as we all thought! I'm surprised you managed to bed her at all!" Pleased with his joke, he stood up and walked over to where Isobel stood near the fire. He threw his arm around her shoulders.

She shrank away distastefully, but he did not release her. "So, sweetheart. How are you? Is my little sister-in-law well?"

"Thank you, Sir Alexander, I am well." Her voice was cold.

"Good, because we are going to need your good offices in the spring, when negotiations resume among the lords of Scotland. We must bring them together if we are to eradicate the threat of England's suzerainty once and for all. And you have influence with some of our more recalcitrant leaders, I hear. The Earl of Carrick for one." He raised his eyebrow suggestively.

Isobel stiffened. "You are mistaken, Sir Alexander. I have

no influence over Lord Carrick. I have not seen him for a long time."

She was very conscious suddenly of her husband, still sitting at the table, looking in their direction, and she wondered if he had heard his brother's comment over the shouting and laughter in the hall behind them. There was a speculative frown on his face. As she watched he stood up and walked over to join them.

"So, has my wife agreed to talk to Lord Carrick?"

Isobel's heart sank. "I have told Sir Alexander I have no influence over my cousin," she said defiantly. "I do not see him anymore."

"While he was fighting on the side of the English"—Lord Buchan's voice was silky—"it would have been inappropriate for you to have done so, to say the least."

The color flared in Isobel's cheeks. "You yourself swore allegiance to King Edward not so long since, my lord!"

"We have all been guilty at some time of bending before the wind," Macduff put in hastily from his position near the fire. "What matters is that we should all now put Scotland's liberty before our personal ambitions and quarrels and free her of the hated yoke of England for good. And to do that we must put our differences behind us. Sir Alexander is right. Bruce and Comyn must fight on the same side."

Did that mean that she would see Robert again? Later, in the bedchamber, Isobel allowed herself to think about the possibility. For months she had gleaned small pieces of information about his whereabouts and at last heard the devastating news that he had come into King Edward's peace and fought for the English rather than support the Comyns and John Balliol. It was hard to believe that his hatred of the Comyns was greater than his love for Scotland, and however much she tried she found it impossible to justify his actions. But even though he had betrayed Scotland she had still prayed for him and desperately hoped that somehow one day she would see him again. Sometimes she thought it was her dreams of Robert that kept her sane.

With a sigh she glanced around the room. Alice was sitting near her, her spindle lying in her lap. Her attendants too were there, clustered around the fire. Some of the driftwood that had come ashore had been brought up to the tower room and it crackled noisily, sending strange green and blue lights leaping up the huge chimney, a change from the calm glow of peat. Wood was usually far too valuable to burn. Dreamily Isobel allowed Mairi to help her out of her clothes and into the fur-trimmed bed gown in which she slept.

The woman was gently combing out Isobel's long curling hair when the door opened and Lord Buchan walked in. There was sudden silence among the women. Mairi's hands fell to her sides as she saw the disgust and fear chasing one another across her young mistress's face, before Isobel concealed her feelings with a look of wary blankness.

Lord Buchan was drunk. "Leave us." His eyes were fixed on his wife's, but his command was unmistakably directed at the others in the room. One by one the women hastily gathered up their spinning and sewing and scuttled toward the door. Only Alice stood her ground.

"It was good of you to come to wish us good night, Uncle," she said firmly. "I am going to share Aunt Isobel's bed tonight. I knew you would want to remain in the hall with my father."

Isobel's eyes were fixed on those of her husband. She had gone completely cold.

"I said out." Lord Buchan did not even look at Alice. His brother's joke had touched a raw nerve and he had spent the last hour, as he drank moodily in the great hall below, allowing it to fester. Alice glanced at Isobel apologetically and edged slowly toward the door in her turn. Her aunt had not moved.

"So, at last my wife and I are alone." Lord Buchan moved slowly toward her. "I trust you will make it clear to your clucking attendants that I intend to sleep here in the lord's bedchamber as long as I remain at Duncairn."

"You must not touch me, my lord!" Isobel found her voice at last. "It—it might harm the child."

"Nonsense. Women can accommodate a man till their bellies are too big to get near them, and even then there are ways and means!" He laughed coarsely. "It seems to me that

you are always trying to keep me from your bed. You have to
learn to give pleasure to your husband, my dear. Your body
was made to please men. You must learn how to use it. Take
off that hideous robe and let me see this belly of yours."

"No!" Isobel stepped back sharply. "You mustn't touch me.
Please—haven't I done my duty enough?"

"Your duty is to please me."

He cornered her near the high curtained bed. He pulled
open her robe, pushed it back off her shoulders, and stared
down. The slim child's body had gone. Since he had seen her
last she had become a woman indeed. Her breasts were full
and heavy, her stomach, boyishly flat before, was rounded,
her hips defined. He felt a wave of intense desire shoot
through him.

"So. You think to keep me at arm's length till you are
delivered of my son!" He spoke thickly as he pulled her to
him. "Think again, sweetheart. I find you more beautiful now
than ever before." He dropped his head to her breast, grabbing for the nipple with his teeth.

Isobel caught her breath with pain. Desperately she pulled
at his hair, trying to dislodge him, and, finally managing it,
she pushed him violently away from her and dodged out of
reach. Her eyes were dark with temper. "Curse you, John
Comyn! Don't you touch me again! Don't you so much as lay
a finger on me or I shall kill this child. By the gods I swear I
shall kill this child and you will never have a son!"

She could feel the wall behind her, cold beneath its tapes-
try hanging, and she pressed her hands against it, her eyes
fixed on her husband's face. "Leave me! Leave me, now."

He had gone white. For a moment he stood completely
still, staring at her, then he stepped toward her. His voice was
very quiet. "Sorceress! Witch! Don't you ever threaten me
again!" He caught her by the shoulders. "I knew the devil
would claim you for his own one day! Be thankful there was
no one here to hear your evil tongue, my lady. Be very
thankful indeed." He shook her, then quite deliberately he
released her and hit her across the face. Her head snapped
back against the wall and she sagged forward for a moment,
stunned, but already he had grabbed her arms and pushed

her upright again, his eyes hard. "Did you hear me? You are my wife, madam. In the eyes of God and in the eyes of men and at the command of the king, you are my wife, and you will obey me."

Still stunned, she tried to push her hair out of her eyes. The side of her face was a throbbing mass of pain.

"At the command of our king!" She forced herself to stand upright, her voice mocking. "Toom Tabard. The King of Nowhere. The king without a country. He is not our king. Our true king would never have given me to you!"

"Ah, the father of the handsome Earl of Carrick!" Lord Buchan raised his hand again. "How sad that you could not marry Sir Robert, my dear. How sad that you must be forced to love and honor and obey the husband you have."

She dodged the next blow, trying to push past him, but he caught her easily. Pain exploded in her head as he hit her again. Blind with fury and tears of agony, she clawed at his face, trying to free her wrist from his grip, then as she felt him raising his hand for another blow she sank her teeth into his fingers.

With a growl of rage he tried to pull free, pushing her away from him with every ounce of strength he had. Unable to save herself, she was thrown sprawling across the high oak coffer that stood at the end of the bed. The iron-bound corner caught her in the stomach with the pain of a turning sword blade. With a scream she staggered to her feet, clutching at her belly, and as deep in her womb the blood began to flow, she collapsed at his feet.

Sarah Collins turned into the driveway and parked beneath the stag-headed oak. She turned off the engine and sat still for a moment staring at the front of the house. No lights showed and the curtains were undrawn. She frowned. Mrs. Royland usually turned on the outside lights if she was going to be out late. Stiffly she climbed out of the car. The mist was thickening rapidly. She couldn't see the lights of the village across the fields. The garden was very quiet.

She felt guilty about leaving Clare alone in the house, but she hadn't wanted to spend the afternoon with her. Acutely aware that sides were being drawn up in some domestic battle, and instinctively knowing that it would be Mr. Royland who would prevail when the time came, she didn't want him to think she was in any way on Clare's side. She valued her job too much. After reaching into the back of the car for her handbag and the two bags holding her afternoon's shopping, she closed the door and began to walk across the gravel.

The front door was unlocked. She switched on the lights and drew the curtains. "Mrs. Royland?" she called, suddenly nervous.

Quick footsteps crossed the landing and Casta ran down the stairs, tail wagging. The sight of the dog reassured her. "Where's your mistress?" She bent and patted the thick fur.

Deep down inside, she knew. She glanced around again uncertainly, and then she made her way into the drawing room. After closing the full-length curtains over the dark windows, she put a match to the already laid fire. She would put on the kettle and then she would go upstairs.

Casta followed her up, keeping close at her heels. On the broad-galleried landing Sarah hesitated. The dog had stopped, hackles raised. She growled slightly and Sarah looked down. She swallowed nervously. At the end of the hall Clare's door was standing ajar. From where she stood on the landing Sarah could see the pale glow of the candlelight.

The pain grew in waves, flowing through Isobel's body, carrying her to the edge of unconsciousness and then drawing her back. The room was hot; sweat poured from her and grew chill as she began to shiver. She was conscious of people all around her: hushed voices, hands holding hers, cool scented clothes on her face. Mairi was there, and Alice. Someone was piling more wood on the fire. She clutched at a hand, moaning as the pain came again.

Mairi was bending over her, her lips moving. *"A Mhuire mhathair!* It's what you wanted, *eudail.* Be brave. It's nearly over. The child is dead. You're losing it now. It's what you wanted, *Iseabail, eudail . . .* It's what you wanted!"

When it was over she slept. The bleeding had not stopped. Around her the women glanced at one another with pale faces. Nearby the tiny body, wrapped in the silk standard of the Earl of Buchan, lay in a basket. With the soil frozen they could not bury it; no one dared to throw it on the fire. No one as yet had dared to tell the earl. The fetus had been male.

When at last he was informed of what had happened Lord Buchan, white with fury, made his way back up to his wife's bedchamber.

"Murderess! Sorceress! You killed my child!" He bent over the bed, his face twisted with rage.

"No!" Isobel stared up at him in terror. "It was you—"

"This entire household knows what you've been doing, my lady. Riding at all hours, swallowing potions to rid yourself of it." He towered over her, his eyes blazing. "In this very room you boasted of what you intended to do! And now you have achieved it. You have murdered my son. By right you should die."

She shook her head desperately, too weak to rise from the pillows. "I didn't . . . I didn't kill him . . . I didn't . . ."

"Brother—" Sir Alexander had followed the earl up the winding stair. He put his hand on Lord Buchan's shoulder. "Leave it now. Nothing will mend the harm that's done." He eyed the vicious bruises on Isobel's temple and cheek grimly. "There will be other sons. I'm sure your wife will take better care of herself next time."

Lord Buchan was breathing deeply, the heavy blue mantle he wore falling across the bed. The brooch on his shoulder caught the candlelight in a cold glitter.

Weak from loss of blood, Isobel was barely conscious. Around her the room was full of shadows. Dimly she knew that Mairi was there. She felt herself raised and feebly sipped the decoction of bramble, acrimony, and horsetail in wine that was held to her mouth, then slowly as another wave of pain overwhelmed her the darkness closed over her again.

Mairi stared up at the earl, her expression carefully veiled. "She must sleep now, my lord. She has lost much blood."

"Please, Father." Alice appeared out of the shadows. "Take my uncle away. If we are to save Aunt Isobel's life she must have quiet."

Lord Buchan moved back from the high bed. His face was grim. With one last glance down at his wife's pale, bruised face he turned on his heel and strode toward the door, his spurs ringing on the stone flags beneath the dried heather.

Sir Alexander followed him and the two women were left alone with Isobel.

Alice glanced at Mairi. "Will she live?"

Mairi was fumbling in the bodice of her gown. She produced a necklace of dried rowan berries strung on a red thread. Carefully she bound it around Isobel's throat. "St. Bride and the Blessed Virgin willing," she said. "She bleeds still. Look." She indicated the stain, spreading on the sheet below the covers.

"She did want to get rid of the child, didn't she?" Alice gently took hold of Isobel's hand. "That is mortal sin."

"Sin against the earl, perhaps." Mairi pushed the pewter wine jug back into the embers to warm it. "My mistress deserves better than him."

Alice looked shocked. "My uncle is one of the greatest earls in Scotland."

"He's too old for her." Mairi was unrepentant. "And too hard. She's like a wild bird, my little lady. She needs gentle handling. A true mate for her would be proud of her spirit, not try and crush it. Here, let me change her linen—"

Sickened at the sight of the blood, Alice turned away to the fire. She shivered. "Is it true she loved Lord Carrick, do you think?"

Mairi frowned. Deftly packing the moss-filled strips of linen beneath her mistress's hips, she glanced up at Alice suspiciously. "She's been faithful to her husband. That I know."

"That's because he's had her watched." Alice squatted in front of the fire, holding out her hands to it. "He brought me here to watch her too. He's afraid of her, Mairi. I saw that just now. He can't understand her, or control her, save by force."

Mairi was pulling the covers over Isobel once more. "She needs friends, not people to spy on her," she commented tartly.

"And I am her friend." Alice climbed back to her feet and came back to the bed. "But how can I make her realize it?"

"Friendship has to be earned." Mairi tightened her lips. "And proved. I'll sit with her now, mistress, if you wish to go and rest."

Alice hesitated. "You'll call me if anything happens?"

"Aye. I'll call you."

Mairi sat unmoving for a long time in the silent, empty chamber, her eyes not leaving Isobel's face. Only when the candles on the coffer near her began to smoke and gutter into pools of grease did she stir. Stiffly she rose and went to sit on a stool before the fire, her eyes fixed on the flames.

Macduff visited Isobel later, sitting at her bedside, holding her hands in his. She moved a little, recognizing him in the light of the single candle that burned on the table at the far side of the room.

He smiled. "Courage, lass." His deeply lined face was gentle.

"Lord Buchan will kill me," she whispered.

He shook his head slowly. "He knows he shouldn't have struck you, and there will be other babies soon enough. You must submit to him, lass. No more arguments in the great hall; no more political statements in front of his men. You deserved to be chastized for that."

"Chastized!" She raised her hand painfully to her face. "Is that what you call it?"

"Aye. Chastized." He sighed. "You'll have time to recover, Isobel. We'll be away as soon as the weather breaks. There is much to discuss with the lords of Scotland." He looked down at her, and the name of Lord Carrick hung for a moment in the air between them, unspoken.

"Just so long as you take my husband away," she whispered at last.

He smiled. "We'll take him away, lass. Never fear."

* * *

But the snow did not relax its grip. Weeks passed. Slowly
Isobel's young body mended and once more Lord Buchan
began to think about his young wife.

⊱ *Chapter Nine* ⊱

The hand on her shoulder was hesitant. "Mrs. Royland? I'm sorry to disturb you—"

Around her the room was dark save for the candlelight. The undrawn curtains showed a starless night, opaque with fog.

Clare stared up at Sarah blankly.

"I'm sorry, but Lady Royland is downstairs." Sarah glanced around nervously, then switched on the table lamp and went to close the curtains. "I wasn't sure if I should interrupt your meditation. I hope you don't mind, only she's been here half an hour . . ." She was aware of the dog sitting, ears flattened, in the doorway. Abruptly Casta bounded into the room, tail wagging. Sarah breathed a sigh of relief. The atmosphere had cleared.

Slowly Clare stood up. She looked dazed. For a moment she stood staring down at the candle, then she stooped and blew out the flame. "Who did you say was here?" she asked hesitantly, turning to Sarah at last. In the lamplight her face was pale.

"Lady Royland." Sarah was watching her surreptitiously. "I've given her a glass of sherry and settled her in the drawing room."

Gillian was dressed in voluminous fuchsia-colored dungarees. She came straight to the point. "I think it is downright dishonest of Paul to try to break the children's trust. I couldn't believe it when David told me what was going on."

Clare sat down opposite her. She felt strangely dissociated. "I didn't know about it either," she said wearily. "But it is fair, if you think about it. If we can never have children."

"Fair!" Gillian exclaimed. "Paul had his share! This is for the kids!" She moved sideways on the sofa, easing her weight with a groan. "Don't tell me now that Paul is not worried about money. He must be if he's prepared to take the cash from a baby's piggy bank!"

Clare smiled. "Hardly that, Gill."

"As good as." Gillian was breathing heavily. "So, if he's not worried, why does he want the money? And don't tell me it's just a principle, because I don't believe it."

Clare gave a deep sigh. She stood up restlessly. "To be absolutely honest, I think he must need the money. He wants me to sell Duncairn too."

"And are you going to?"

Clare shook her head. "No." She paused uncomfortably. "I'm not being disloyal. It's just that he demands I sell it, without telling me why he wants the money, and Duncairn isn't just another asset to be bought and sold like so many shares. It's part of me." She gave an embarrassed smile. "Does that sound very sentimental?"

"I don't see why you shouldn't be sentimental." Gillian sounded comfortably practical. "I think Paul has been having things too much his way. It's time we all said no. I take it you and he had a row last week, and that's why you didn't come to the party?"

Clare nodded ruefully. "I'm sorry. I just couldn't face a whole weekend with him."

Gillian sighed. "I can't say I blame you. Impossible man! I can't think how you can stay married to him." She laughed. "No, don't tell me. No doubt he has hidden charms." She reached for her sherry glass. "But seriously, Clare. David is worried about him. You don't think he's done anything foolish in the City, do you? He hasn't been speculating and losing millions?"

"I am sure we'd have heard if it was anything like that." Clare smiled unhappily.

Gillian sniffed. "Well, you'd better warn him. David can't have the Royland name involved in any scandals."

"I thought our dear member of parliament was involved with environmental issues. He's got no interests in the City, surely." Clare stooped and threw a log on the fire.

"Only the shares of his father's that they all got. Nothing

else. And of course he's declared his interests there. But his reputation has to be protected. If there were the slightest whiff of dishonesty in the family, it could be disastrous for his career."

"Well, there isn't." Clare flared up suddenly. "So stop being so bloody self-righteous! Why doesn't he stop worrying about Paul and worry about the environment instead? Places like Duncairn, for instance. I've had an offer to buy it from an oil company. They want to destroy that beautiful place!"

"You've actually had an offer?" Gillian echoed. "You mean there's oil there? No wonder Paul wants you to sell it!"

"I told them there was no question of selling, ever." Clare hesitated. "They can't make me, can they?"

"I don't think so. But I have an awful feeling the oil isn't yours. The government can take it anytime it likes, can't it?" Gillian grimaced. "I'll ask David if you like. He'll know."

"They never wrote back after I turned down their offer, so I hoped the matter was closed."

Gillian stood up with a groan and put her hand to her back. "Well, I hope for your sake it is. I must go. I'm terrified I'm going to drop this child on someone's carpet. It's due any second, and they come so quickly. . . ." She smiled smugly. "Take care of yourself, Clare. Don't let Paul bully you. And tell him to forget about the trust. Okay?"

Geoffrey Royland arrived at ten o'clock the following morning at the wheel of a dusty Audi. He was wearing his dog collar, with a rumpled rust-colored sweater. Following Clare into the cold drawing room, he glanced around as she set the tray of coffee on the table.

"I'm sorry the fire's not lighted. Sarah went shopping for me early and she must have forgotten. It'll warm up in here soon." She handed him a cup, then, glancing out of the windows at the garden that was still swathed in damp mist, she reached for the matches and knelt before the fire. "I suppose you've come about the trust as well. I had Gillian here yesterday." She sat back and watched as the flame flared on the firelighter and spread to the rest of the kindling, licking along the twigs and across the bark of the apple logs. Behind her

her brother-in-law stood, coffee cup in hand, and stared down at her thoughtfully.

"I was passing on my way up to Norwich, actually," he said after a pause. "I thought it would be nice to look in and see how you were. I'm not here about the trust."

"Good, because it's got nothing to do with me. You and David and Paul can fight it out among you."

He studied her for a moment. She was looking particularly attractive in a flared emerald-green skirt and green-and-black sweater. He had always thought her a good-looking woman, particularly her eyes. There was something especially appealing about her eyes. But he was shocked to see how tired and strained she seemed.

"I was so sorry, Clare, to hear about the results of the tests." He sat down and balanced his cup on his knee. "Chloe told me. I hope you don't mind." He saw her knuckles whiten on the poker as she stirred the fire and he paused for a moment, waiting for her to speak. When she didn't he went on gently. "Have you and Paul discussed adoption?"

"We haven't discussed anything much lately." She put the poker down, but she stayed where she was, staring into the fire with her back to him. "I'm just glad all the tests and things are over."

"You're not going to seek a second opinion then?"

"No." She tightened her lips.

"I see." He paused again, then he went on, choosing his words with care. "And are you going to go on with your study of yoga?"

"How did you know I was studying yoga?" Slowly Clare stood up. When she turned to face him she remembered Chloe's call and she smiled impishly. "Of course. Emma told you, didn't she?"

"She mentioned it, yes." Geoffrey looked down at his cup. "My dear, I don't want you to think I'm interfering, but I was a little concerned when I heard what you were doing. Can we talk about it?"

"That sounds very portentous, Geoffrey." She sat down opposite him. "Does the Church of England disapprove of yoga?"

"Yoga is often misunderstood, Clare. Practitioners of it tend to emphasize the fact that it is just a method of exercising and relaxing one's body. They play down the fact, either intentionally or because they do not know it, that it is also a spiritual exercise, designed to bring about changes in one's whole psyche, and that if one does it properly it can open and expose one's mind and soul and leave them very vulnerable." He smiled ruefully. "Does that sound very pompous?"

She nodded. "I'm afraid it does rather. A far cry from the classes they give in the village hall here."

"But you didn't learn it in the village hall, did you?" He put down his coffee cup. "I gather the man who taught you has also taught something about meditation."

"Which again comes highly recommended in every book you pick up these days. It's the panacea of the eighties." She frowned. "It's not dangerous, Geoffrey."

He scowled. "Tell me about these visions you see."

"You mean the ones with the horns and the cloven hooves and the tail with a point on the end?"

Outside, the sun was fighting its way out of the mist. A ray of sunlight crept slowly across the carpet and stopped at her feet.

He didn't laugh. For a long moment he watched her intently, then at last he looked away. "You think it's all a joke?"

"No." She shook her head. "It's not a joke. Not to me—but it is when you take it so seriously."

"Tell me what happens. Do these people appear to you as apparitions?"

"They appear as people, in my head. They are daydreams. Imaginary. Nothing to do with you."

"But they are not daydreams, are they? You are summoning them."

"Imagining, summoning. What's the difference? It is not as if anyone else can see them. At least . . ." She stopped in midsentence. She was staring at the dog, who was lying head on paws near the door. She sometimes thought that Casta had seen them. And so perhaps had Zak. She shivered suddenly.

Geoffrey was watching her closely. He frowned. "Please let

me help you, Clare," he said. His voice was uncharacteristically gentle. "Please. I can get rid of them for you."

She stared at him. "Get rid of them?"

"These people who are tormenting you."

"They are not tormenting me! And I don't want to get rid of them!" Her indignation flared again. "I care about them, Geoff. Isobel is like another me. I want to know all about her. I want to dream about her, or conjure up her shade or whatever it is I'm doing. She belongs at Duncairn. She's part of my history; she's part of me. She's living again through me. And I intend to go on summoning her to me, even if it does put my soul in jeopardy!" She took a deep breath. "What sort of life do you think I lead here, Geoff? What do you think I do all day?" She sat down near him. "I'm young; I'm energetic; I'm intelligent. I can't have children, so I'm not spending my time with my family. I have a housekeeper to look after the house. My husband doesn't want me to work—and up to now I haven't been able to face the hassle of fighting with him about it. He doesn't want me with him all the time either. I spent a lot of time raising money for charity when we were first married—but he resented even that time I wasn't with him. I have no friends around here. A lot of acquaintances, but no one I could call a friend. I wanted to go up to Scotland to see my mother and to go to Duncairn—but he wouldn't even let me do that! So, what the hell am I supposed to do all day?" Her voice had risen passionately. "I took up yoga, Geoffrey, to try to learn calmness, to reduce stress, to try to have a baby. It appears that is never going to happen, but I have grown to enjoy yoga and meditation, to rely on it, if you like. It makes me feel good and it gives me a prop when I need one. I am beginning to fight my way out of this morass of boredom and indecision. I am beginning to question what the point of it all is. And because of that, I am beginning to make sense of my life." She paused and smiled at him. "I've always had dreams, Geoff. I've always been haunted by the past. That is nothing new. What is new is that I've learned to call it up at will, and learn from it."

"You must see, my dear, that what we are talking about has gone beyond daydreaming. You are not some sort of female

Walter Mitty. You are lighting candles and invoking the spirits of the dead. And they are, as you have found, only too eager to communicate. It is dangerous, Clare."

In the long silence that followed as they stared at each other they both heard the scrunch of car tires on the gravel outside the house.

Clare shivered again. She swallowed. "That will be Sarah coming back. I think you'd better go, Geoff."

Slowly Geoffrey stood up. "Of course." He reached out and took her hands. "Please think about what I've said, Clare. I beg you. And feel you can call me at any time. If you're lonely, come and see us. Chloe is very fond of you. We both are. And I'll have a chat with Paul. He must be made to realize that you need something to occupy you—"

"Don't you say a word to Paul!" She was angry suddenly. "I am quite capable of talking to my own husband. Keep out of it, Geoffrey. I'm working things out my own way." In the distance the doorbell pealed. "Now, go. Please go. Sarah must have forgotten her key—" She almost ran into the hall.

Outside there was a florist's van. There was no sign of Sarah or her car. A young woman was standing on the gravel, staring up at the house front, a cellophane sheaf of flowers in her arms.

"Mrs. Royland?"

Clare carried the flowers back into the drawing room where Geoffrey was still standing awkwardly in front of the fire. He smiled as she laid the flowers down on the coffee table. "It looks as if someone loves you after all." He watched as she unpinned the note that came with them.

After tearing open the envelope, Clare read the carefully written message and her face went white.

> So sorry to hear you are ill, but delighted you have reconsidered the sale of Duncairn. Look forward to meeting you when you are recovered. Very best wishes. Rex Cummin.

The sea was churning restlessly over the rocks at the foot of the cliffs. Neil walked to the place where the wall had fallen and peered down into the dark. A gentle south wind touched his cheek with cold fingers. Above, the sky was ablaze with stars.

"It's very quiet, isn't it?" Behind him Kathleen glanced nervously down over his shoulders toward the white luminescence that was the sea curdling on the rocks far below. She turned and walked back toward the keep, feeling the chill of the dew soaking into her shoes. "What a spooky place. Where is the oil? Right under the castle?"

Neil hadn't moved. Hands in pockets, he hunched his shoulders. "It's very deep. It would cost a lot to drill here."

"But not a fraction as much as it costs to drill under the North Sea, presumably." She paused. "I like your Mr. Grant at the hotel. You've got an ally there." After walking back to him, she took his arm. "We didn't need to come up here, Neil."

"I needed to." He turned to go with her. "This place is special, Kath. Can't you feel it? It represents everything that Scotland stands for. A castle high on a cliff; a castle that has stood here for eight hundred years; a place where they fought for Scotland's independence. A place where men and women died to save Scotland's resources for herself."

Kathleen shivered. In spite of herself she glanced over her shoulder. Ever since they had walked out into the darkness after dinner she had had the feeling they were being watched. "Scotland didn't have many resources. Not until the oil came," she said gently.

"Scotland has always had resources. Her people, her learning, her pride and independence . . ."

Kathleen grinned ruefully. "So, do I gather if it were a Scots oil company you wouldn't feel so bad about their bid?"

"No. Even then we would fight. The environmental threat is too great. Imagine it, Kath. A hundred-foot drilling rig here, on the cliffs. It would be sacrilege!" He pushed his hands deep in his pockets. "But an *American* oil company— run by people who know nothing of Scotland—who have never even been here! That is scandalous."

"Jack Grant said they'd been up here at the weekend."

"Oh yes, another surveyor, no doubt. I don't expect Cummin has ever been here, or his U.S. directors. The people in charge of wrecking places invariably live thousands of miles away."

High above them the tower rose black against the luminous sky, the broken walls jagged and irregular in front of the stars. Where was Clare Royland? Why wasn't she there, fighting?

"Neil—" Kathleen was beside him again.

"Go back to the hotel, Kath, please. I need to think." There was a long silence. He could feel her eyes on his face in the darkness.

Then she shrugged. "Okay. I'll see you later. Don't fall over the edge, now."

He watched as her figure faded into the darkness, then he turned back toward the castle. How could Clare Royland even contemplate selling? How could she betray her roots, her heritage like this? Couldn't she feel it when she came there—the pull? The tie that held the sons and daughters of Scotland to the land? He pictured her yet again with her expensive car and her rich, beautiful clothes, and he frowned as somewhere a bird let out a long, mournful cry. He and Clare Royland were going to have to meet. . . .

"So, how are you enjoying working in a man's world, honey?" Rex smiled at Diane Warboys as she sat opposite him in the pink alcove at Corney and Barrow. "As challenging as you hoped?"

"It's not strictly a man's world anymore, Rex. But it is challenging, yes, and I'm enjoying it enormously." She leaned back in her chair and looked at him hard. It had been nearly ten years since she had seen her godfather last. Then he had been based in Houston, and she had called to see them one vacation when she was at school. He was still an extraordinarily handsome man, tanned, silver-haired, with a smile that could charm a bird out of a tree, but he was tired, she could see it in his eyes. "How are you and Mary?" She smiled at him fondly. "I had no idea you were based in London now."

"We're just fine." Rex sighed. "Getting older. But that's to be expected, I suppose."

She laughed. "You old fraud. You don't look a day over forty."

"Well, I'm quite a bit older than that, honey." His face was sober for a moment. "A lot more than that. But let's talk about you. What is it like, working for BCWP? Are they good people?"

"The best. Well, almost. We were number two last year."

Rex frowned. "So, there's no truth in the rumors that they're undercapitalized?"

Diane raised an eyebrow. "My, we have been doing our homework." She grinned. "No truth at all. The firm is solid. There were one or two shaky moments when they first set up, but not anymore."

"I came across the name of one of your directors the other day." He glanced up at her under his eyebrows. "Paul Royland." He noticed the slight coloring of her cheeks and he frowned. "Do you know him at all well?"

"I had dinner with him and his wife last weekend, actually." Diane eyed him cautiously. "Why do you want to know?"

"Just curious to know what kind of people my goddaughter is working for." He grinned. "Is he a good businessman, do you reckon?"

"I don't know." She glanced away. "He's on the banking side, so I don't see a lot of him."

"You just said you had dinner with him, Diane." His voice was softly wheedling. "You must know him quite well to have done that."

"I was taken, by one of his co-directors. Henry Firbank. We go out from time to time."

"I see." Rex leaned forward and steepled his fingers over his glass. "I see. So tell me, from what you know of him, would you say Paul Royland would be a good man to do business with?"

Diane frowned. "Is that what you're thinking of doing? Raising money through BCWP?"

"Possibly. But I was thinking on a more personal level. I want to know if he's sound." His voice had sharpened.

She looked down. "So. This isn't just a social lunch. You've asked me here for a reason. I might have guessed. You don't change, do you? Well, the answer is I don't know. There have been rumors." She glanced up at him, uncomfortable now with his questions. "I shouldn't tell you any of this, Rex."

"It won't go any further, honey." He reached over the table and took her hand. "But I need to know."

"Well." She hesitated again. "Henry would never say anything, he's too loyal, but I know Paul's sister, Emma, quite well, and she's let slip a few things. Her husband is on the Far East desk, and she has no idea of how to keep tactful silence concerning things he's told her about the office." She smiled fondly. "And, of course, Peter only tells her because she is Paul's sister! Peter thinks that there may be trouble about the Hannington takeover, when the price dropped after they had the strike. Do you remember? The shares shot up and there were screams of insider dealing. Then the takeover fell through. I suspect Paul lost a lot of money over that deal. I think he can be less than shrewd sometimes."

"But you like him anyway." Rex raised an eyebrow.

"Is it that obvious?"

"Only to me. I've known you too long. So, what about his wife?"

Diane sighed. "Clare is rich and stunningly beautiful. I would never stand a chance."

"You too are stunningly beautiful, my Diane." He smiled at her, raising his glass. "Do you like her?"

Diane shrugged. "I'm not sure, to be honest. She's strange. A bit vague."

"And what is his sister like, apart from garrulous?"

"Nice. You'd get on well with her."

"And is she close to her brother?" He made the question casual.

Diane laughed. "She can't stand him. Poor Emma. Like Clare, she's not really a City wife. Neither of them fits in. They don't know what to talk about."

"And yet you get on with her."

"Perhaps that's because I'm different too." She grinned. "I'm a woman and I'm American. That makes me an outsider in the City as well. Why are you showing such an interest in the Roylands, Rex? Are you sure it's just business?"

"I'm interested in you, honey. That's all. I want to know all about you. It's been too long since we've seen you. I tell you what. Why don't you bring your boyfriend—Henry, did you say he was called?—to dinner one evening? Mary would be thrilled with that. . . ."

"What the hell do I do, James?" Clare's knuckles were white on the receiver. She had dialed her brother's number before Geoffrey's car had vanished down the drive.

"Sell, Clare. You'd be crazy not to. They don't have to buy, you know. They could just apply for a license to drill. And there would be nothing you could do about it. The oil isn't yours, Sis.

"What do you mean, it isn't mine?"

"Oil belongs to the country, Clare. They can take it, whatever you say. My guess is that this company wants the land and the hotel to ease the hassle. But they'll get the oil if the government grants them a license."

"I don't believe you!"

"It's true, Clare."

"Have you been talking to Paul about this?"

"He asked me about Duncairn. He can't understand why you didn't want to sell."

"So he decided to sell over my head! That's what it sounds like."

"Well, he can't do that, so don't panic. No one can force you to sell, or sell without your consent. Married women's property act and all that!"

She took a deep breath, trying to calm herself. "You are sure?"

"Paul must have told him you were ill as an excuse to start negotiating on your behalf. All you have to do is call this man and deny it."

"I can't. I threw away the letter. I can't remember the solicitor's name. . . ."

James looked heavenward. "Ask the florist, Clare, but I think you'll find that the firm is called Sigma."

* * *

Rex phoned her back as soon as he got back to his office.
"Mrs. Royland. How are you?" He sat down at his desk and
leaned back, staring out at the murky sky.

"I'm very well, Mr. Cummin. Thank you for the flowers,
but they weren't necessary. And I'm afraid you are under a
misapprehension. I have not changed my mind about selling
Duncairn. It is not and never will be for sale. And if my
husband has led you to believe that he is empowered to act
on my behalf, he is misleading you. He has no authority to act
for me. None at all." She could feel the receiver slipping in
her hand. "Please leave us alone, Mr. Cummin. There is no
oil at Duncairn."

"Ah. There, my dear lady, you are wrong. There is oil
there."

"Then leave it there. This country doesn't need any more
oil."

"There is always demand for oil, Mrs. Royland." He leaned
forward on the desk, easing his weight on the chair. "Why
don't you and I meet? I'd like to explain things to you, tell you
our schedule, put your mind at rest. I could show you my
plans for the hotel and the castle. I think you'd like what I
have in mind. I'm a Scot by descent, Mrs. Royland. I care
about that castle as much as you do."

"I doubt that." Clare bit her lips. The threat of this unknown man, and his offer to buy Duncairn, had suddenly
become real again.

"Perhaps I should explain." She could hear the sudden
pride in his voice. "I can trace my roots back to the family
who owned Duncairn once a long time ago. Comyn, they
were called. It is my ancestral home, Mrs. Royland, in a
manner of speaking. So I care very much about what happens to it. I would spend money on it."

Clare was speechless.

"Are you there, Mrs. Royland? Obviously Sigma doesn't
need to own the land. We'll get the XL—that is, a license to
test drill. But I want Duncairn to get the credit it deserves. I
want it to become the European headquarters for Sigma. I

want to raise that castle back to its former glory. I want to rebuild Duncairn Castle, Mrs. Royland."

"No!" It came out as an anguished whisper. "No, Mr. Cummin. Never. I won't sell to you or anyone." Her hands were shaking violently. "You and I have nothing to say to one another, Mr. Cummin. Nothing!"

She slammed down the receiver. Then she picked it up again and called Paul. "Don't you ever, ever, try that again! I may not be in London, I may spend half my life in a dream, as you put it, but believe me, if you try negotiating with that man again I will hear about it and I will stop you. Believe me, I will stop you!"

That night the house was full of people, waiting in the shadows.

The long summer night never grew entirely dark. Isobel, standing on the battlements in the deeper black of the shadows, caught her breath as a man appeared at the head of the stair. She had known he would come. Silently she slipped from the concealment of the walls and stepped forward into the bright starlight.

"You can see the campfires of the English from up here," she whispered.

He frowned. "Not for long. We'll drive Edward from Scotland for good this time." She saw the gleam of his teeth as he smiled down at her. "So, why does Lady Buchan want to speak to me so urgently?"

"Can't you guess? I never see you alone anymore." She tried not to sound petulant. "Robert, I know you loved your Isabella of Mar, but she is dead." Lord Buchan had told her. Before they left Duncairn the news had come and he had laughed at Isobel's white, shocked face, and then he had told her she was to accompany him south. "You are free!"

"And you are not." Robert's voice was harsh. "This cannot be, Isobel." He turned away from her abruptly and leaned with his elbows on the battlements. Below, in the luminous darkness, the scent of wild honeysuckle drifted up from the hedgerows on the night wind; she heard the grating of his armor as he shifted his weight. "Lord Buchan must send you

north," he went on, without looking at her. "It is too dangerous here. I have given orders that all the women are to be
moved on at first light." Staring out into the darkness he went
on, almost talking to himself. "Everywhere our spies are telling us that Edward is leading a huge army against us from
England. We knew he would when he returned from Flanders. We should have been more prepared. I am afraid we
have been too confident. To rid Scotland forever of the English threat, we have to defeat him again, decisively, on every front. We have to chase him away for good."

"And I must go north, away from the fighting, and I shall
not see you again for months perhaps—" She wanted to
reach out and touch him, but something in the angle of his
shoulders beneath their heavy mail stopped her.

"You must not see me at all, Isobel. Sweet Jesus! Do you
realize what you do to me when you talk like this! There can
be no love between us. You belong to Buchan!" His fists
clenched convulsively on the stone wall. "Don't you understand? My love is for this country. Scotland is my mistress,
Isobel. For her I will fight, and for her I will die, if I must, but
first I will be her king!"

"Then why are you leaving to march west? Why do you not
march eastward toward Falkirk with my husband, to meet up
with Wallace?" Hurt by his rejection, there was only one way
to retaliate—by reproaching him for turning his back on the
battle they both knew was coming.

"Because I will not fight for Balliol, Isobel. And Wallace
fights in his name. I support Wallace. It was I who knighted
him. But he rules this land as guardian for John Balliol. Oh, I
too will fight the English, make no mistake about that. But in
my lands, in the west, among my people."

"If you fight the English, you must fight in the name of
Scotland's king."

Robert snorted. "Toom Tabard! A puppet! A cipher! A
nothing in exile. What kind of king is that for a proud nation?" He sighed. "But you are right, of course. I shall be
fighting outwardly in his name. This whole war has been one
of shifting loyalties and ideals. We all have to tread a path
between loyalty and expedience, between honor and com-

mon sense, between idealism and what is right for this particular moment. A woman wouldn't understand."

"No." She shook her head sadly. "A woman would put loyalty before all else and be prepared to die for it."

He turned to her at last. For a long time he stared down into her face. Then he shook his head grimly. "A woman like you perhaps, my Isobel. Please God you never have to put your loyalty to the test. Scotland needs her men and women alive." He glanced out into the strange half darkness of the northern summer night again. "And above all she needs a strong king. That is what we have to work for. That is what her people need." He smiled suddenly. "I long for the day when your husband kisses my hand."

"I doubt if he will ever do that, Robert. I suspect he would rather die than acknowledge you his king." She stared past him into the distance and she shivered. "Dawn is near. I suppose I must go down." She took a step nearer him. "For what it's worth, you shall have my allegiance, when the time comes."

"And I shall value it." He caught her hands. "Take care, my love. Don't allow yourself to fall into danger."

"Nor you, my lord."

For a moment she thought he would kiss her, but he turned back to his watching, staring out again at the tiny specks of fire in the hills to the south that showed where the armies of the English were gathering.

"Where have you been, madam?" Lord Buchan was waiting for her in the chamber she had been allocated with her serving women. Fully armed but for his helm, just as Robert had been, he was an imposing figure in the light of the single flare that burned in the sconce near the door.

"I went up to the wall walk for some air. It is so hot down here, my lord," she answered listlessly. The room was full of the stink of stale cooking that had drifted up from the hall below. The floor coverings were unchanged and the hangings musty.

"You leave for the north at first light. That will give you air enough." He began to fumble with his surcoat and hauberk.

"Boy! Thomas! Blast you," he bellowed toward the door. "Come and help me with my harness! I want you back in Buchan, Isobel; I want you to tour the castles. With my followers away and my mother ill, they need to be closely overseen. Make sure the stewards are not cheating me. I want full storerooms this winter." He groaned with relief as the heavy mail hauberk was lifted over his head and the padded gambeson unfastened. He waved Thomas aside when all his armor had been removed. "Enough. Leave us alone." He waited until the heavy door was pulled shut before he turned back to her. "And I want the cradle full as well. It is six months since you miscarried my child." His lips tightened grimly. "And still there is none to replace it."

Macduff and Sir Alexander had between them deflected his anger from her as she lay hovering between life and death after she had lost the baby. His fury and his fear had been tempered by his guilt; he knew his blows had led to her injuries and to the loss of the baby, but his suspicions had not gone. They festered and grew every time he caught sight of his wife's wild beauty and her persistently slim figure. Somehow she was deliberately avoiding the pregnancy that was her duty, and in doing so she was defying both him and God. Deep down his anger was hardening.

Isobel felt herself grow cold beneath his gaze in the heat of the fetid room. Dozens of times he had taken her since that fated day in the winter when her prayers had been answered and her baby had died. Twice her courses had been late, and she had prayed and drunk potions of the dangerous savine, which had made her retch and vomit and cramped her stomach, and the Blessed Virgin had saved her. It was not something she wanted to do again; each time she sipped the bitter mixture she knew she was endangering her own life.

"Do you not intend to keep vigil in the chapel, my lord, before the battle?" Her mouth had gone dry.

"The battle won't be for days. First we have to join forces with Wallace and his men." He tightened the belt around his waist. "God knows, it is humiliating to follow a man who is not even a nobleman, but he is a good soldier, I grant him that. And Guardian of the Realm. And we must wait for him.

Without him we stand no chance against old Longshanks and his army." He sat down wearily on the coffer by the wall and watched her. His patience with her was gone. No longer did he try to cajole her or win her friendship. There was very little talk between them, save over the running of the household and the Buchan estates. Even there she disappointed him. She had little interest in the duties of a countess; none of her loyalty and family pride had been diverted from her own family to that of her husband. And yet his servants liked her. He heard nothing but good of her. His stewards and constables were competent in their jobs and protected their young mistress from her husband's wrath. Chatelaines and housekeepers supervised the duties that should have been hers. There was only one duty she could not be spared.

She watched, frozen with dislike as her husband, clad now in his loose robe, helped himself, as always before he bedded her, from a jug of wine on the table by the door. He took no pleasure in the raping of his wife.

Slowly, almost in a dream, she pulled off the fillet and silken net that held her hair in place and let her mantle fall in the dry, dusty heather. "Shall I call my maid to unlace me, my lord?" she asked meekly. She knew by now she could never fight him. Whatever had to be done must be done later, after he had gone.

He turned and looked at her over the rim of his goblet. Abruptly he set it down. "Come here. You have no need of a maid."

Behind them the flare sizzled and spat in the sconce, adding to the heat of the room. She could smell the animal sweat on him as he spun her around and began to pull open the laces that held her gown closed. As the blue fabric rustled to her knees he turned her to face him again. He pulled open the neck of her shift and, thrusting his hands in, he grasped her breasts.

She gritted her teeth, her eyes fixed on the wall beyond him as his mouth traveled down her neck and on toward the soft, shrinking nipple.

She heard herself gasp as he pushed her onto the high bed, but that was the only sound she made. Her pride would not let her cry out as he thrust into her. Instead she was thinking of the moon. At the first quarter her courses would come—in only four days' time—and they would wash away his unwanted seed. There would be no need this time of the bitter, life-threatening potions. Her eyes fixed on the darkness beyond the window, she bit her lips and lay, cold and uninvolved, a marble statue in her misery as the sweating, heaving body possessed hers.

The attack came at dawn. The sudden violent shouts and yells, the clash of iron on steel, the scream of a man, cut off short, and then at last the deafening clanging of the bell from the watchman on the walls. Lord Buchan woke from his deep sleep and raised himself from his wife's inert body.

"God in heaven, what's that?" He did not wait for an answer. After leaping naked from the bed, he was already in his tunic when his men came to arm him.

"It is the English, my lord! They cut down our patrols!" The man gabbled as he tried frantically to lift the heavy mail. "The ladies were getting ready to leave in the bailey—" He glanced, embarrassed, at the pale, naked woman in the bed, sitting clutching a crumpled sheet to her breasts.

Lord Buchan followed the man's gaze. "Get dressed!" he shouted at her angrily. "You should have been gone an hour since." Outside the narrow window the sky was already showing streaks of gold. He had meant only to bed her, try yet again to get a child on her, and leave her. Cursing his wife and his own exhaustion, he snatched the embroidered surcoat with its emblazoned wheat sheaf from Thomas and pulled it on. Then he was gone, walking awkwardly in his heavy armor as he ducked through the door and began to descend the winding stairs, followed by his men.

Isobel slipped from the bed and, pulling off the sheet, wound it around her. She ran to the window and peered out. Below in the bailey all was chaos as men and horses milled around beneath the hail of arrows that descended from beyond the wall. From where she stood, high in the keep, she could see over the wall to the enemy who surrounded the castle on every side. She wasn't afraid. The clash of swords and shouts of the men exhilarated her. She felt a sudden tremor of excitement that caught with her breath in her throat.

"My lady!" Mairi's voice was angry and frightened. *"Dè tha thu 'dèanamh?* Come away from the window! Do you want an arrow through your head!"

Reluctantly Isobel turned and stepped down from the embrasure. She was laughing. "They don't appear to have many marksmen there. I see no signs of King Edward's Welshmen. It's only a small band on their way to join the main army."

Mairi stared at her. "Blessed Mother! You are enjoying it!" Her mistress's face was alive with excitement.

Isobel laughed again. "I wish I had been born a man! To learn how to use a bow and a sword, to ride out into battle and fight for my country! Oh, Mairi! I was born the wrong sex!"

"I think you were, indeed, my lady." Mairi was holding out her lady's shift. She noted without comment the bruises that always followed a night with the earl.

"Are we to be besieged?" Isobel turned to allow Mairi to lace up her gown.

Mairi shrugged. "Lord Carrick was directing operations earlier. He said that they were only marauders. He said our men would break out and chase them off before any reinforcements came to help them. And as soon as they do that we must leave. The horses are ready, my lady, to take us north to Perth—" She broke off at the sound of a step on the stair.

Robert, fully armed, stood in the doorway.

"Lady Buchan? Why are you not below with the other women?"

She saw his eyes on her long, wild hair, as yet unbraided, and she saw him swallow as he glanced beyond her to the tumbled bed.

"I am almost ready, Lord Carrick." Meekly she lowered her eyes.

"Be ready now, madam. As soon as we have created a diversion I want the women away. You. Leave us." He gave the order to Mairi curtly. She curtseyed and with a glance at Isobel ran from the room.

Robert stepped forward. "You must go. But for God's sake be careful. The countryside is alive with English soldiers."

"I'll be all right." She bit her lip. "And God go with you." Lightly she put her hands on the cold steel of his shoulders and, standing on tiptoe, she kissed him on the lips. "Take care, my love. Take care. I couldn't bear it if anything happened to you."

"Nothing will." Almost unwillingly he encircled her waist with his arm. "Noting will, my Isobel. I intend to drive these devils from this land. Now go. Quickly." His kiss was hard and lingering. Then he pushed her away. "Don't wait to put up your hair." For a moment a trace of grim humor showed in his eyes as he looked down at her, so much a tomboy still, for all she was the wife of a powerful earl. "Take a mantle and go. Now." His voice was curt. "See to it that the other ladies are mounted and ready to leave at once." And he was gone.

Isobel closed her eyes for a moment. She took a deep breath, trying desperately to steady herself, then, obediently she picked up her mantle and flung it around her shoulders. Throwing a veil over her hair, she ran down the stairs after him and into the great hall, but already he was gone, striding out among his men as they gathered in the shelter of the outer wall. She stared after him for a moment, then the heavy door of the keep swung to and hid him from sight.

"So, my lady." Her husband had appeared suddenly behind her. "Lord Carrick will lead the counterattack." His eyes were fixed on her face. "And I am to lead the remainder of our men to escort you ladies north before joining Sir William Wallace." He smiled coldly. "I trust you said your farewells. It will be a long time before you return south."

Chapter Ten

"I hope your husband won't mind my taking you out like this, Mrs. Cassidy." Rex ushered Emma through the door of the theater. "It was just such a coincidence that I had a spare ticket for this show and was wondering who to take. Mary was so angry that she couldn't come, and then Diane told me how much you wanted to see it." He helped her off with her coat as they found their seats in the dress circle.

It had taken his secretary a morning's strenuous telephoning to get the tickets, and then at an exorbitant price.

Emma was looking around. "I still can't believe my luck." She glanced at him. He was a tall, distinguished-looking man with a tanned, permanently youthful face belied by the shock of white hair. And he was extremely attractive. She made up her mind to enjoy herself.

By the intermission she was aware that tickets to a show such as this were not something Rex Cummin would have normally come by.

"You're bored stiff!" she accused as the lights came up.

"Hey, come on." Sheepishly he stifled a yawn. "I guess I'm tired, that's all."

"I thought Americans never got tired." She was teasing.

"You're right. A little food will do me good."

He took her to a French restaurant in Knightsbridge. Sitting opposite each other, they both watched in silence as the waiter poured their wine. After he had gone, Rex picked up his glass. "To us. I hope we can do this again."

Emma smiled. "It's been fun." She looked at him quizzically. "Tell me. How long have you known Diane?"

"Since she was born. My wife and her mother knew each other as kids."

"And you are in the financial world too?"

"No." He hesitated. "I'm in oil."

"Oil?" She seemed intrigued but not suspicious.

He gauged her reaction carefully. "Sigma Exploration. You've probably heard of us."

Emma shrugged. "I'm afraid I don't know much about the oil business. I expect Peter knows you."

Rex nodded. "I'm sure he's heard of us." He glanced up at her casually. "And of course your brother Paul will have. I'll probably be meeting with him in the next few days. Is he as nice as you?" He tried to keep the question light, humorous. He must not let her see how every nerve was strained for her answer.

Emma laughed. "He's not nearly so beautiful as I, of course, but I expect he's much cleverer, and they tell me he's very good at his job. I don't know if anyone would call him nice, though."

He was surprised at the sudden bitterness in her voice. "Well, I guess I'll find out soon enough." He changed the subject swiftly. There would be plenty of time to ask her about Paul and Clare Royland later. He had the rest of the evening to bring up the subject again.

"I thought we might go on to a nightclub," he said at last as they finished their coffee. "Would you like that?"

Emma's eyes sparkled. "I'd love to. It's ages since I went anywhere exciting. Peter hates anything of that sort."

They had talked of every subject under the sun except the Roylands, even of his beloved Scotland, and somehow without mentioning Duncairn by name, of his ancestry, of which he was so proud, of the eight-hundred-year link the genealogists had dug up with the country's past, of his passion for its heritage, and of his secret dream, unknown even by Mary, to own one day a piece of Scotland for himself. And she talked about Julia and Peter and her gallery, confiding in him as if she had known him all her life.

Rex intrigued her. He was a strange mixture. A mature, sophisticated man, slightly exotic, much traveled; the kind of person who assimilates a little of the best of every culture by which he is touched and metabolizes it within himself into a stimulating mix of wit and intellect. And yet, at the same time, he had an adventurous, boyish streak and a monumental enthusiasm that was enormously attractive. She felt herself respond alarmingly to his charm.

He took her to Tramp and ordered them champagne, lifting his hand in greeting as a party of compatriots inched their way between the tables toward the far side of the room.

On the dance floor she was slim and vibrant and exciting in his arms, her dark eyes still darting here and there, excitedly taking in the setting as the crowds pushed them closer together. Scarcely knowing he did it, he found his lips seeking hers.

She drew back abruptly. "No." Her smile was still friendly, but he could sense the sudden wall behind it. Cursing himself for an old fool, he grimaced. "Can't blame a man for trying." He raised his hands in a gesture of helplessness. "I'm sorry."

"I'm married, Rex, and so are you." Emma's gaze was very direct. "While your wife is away and Peter is in Singapore we can enjoy ourselves together, but no sex, I'm sorry."

"You sure are a frank young lady."

She smiled a little wryly. "It's better that way, don't you think? It saves you wasting time."

"I'm not wasting time, Emma. I've had more fun tonight than I've had in years." He realized suddenly that he had meant it, and it was only a long time later, after he had dropped her off in Kew and directed the taxi back toward Eaton Square, that he realized he had not asked her about Paul again.

"You knew she was prone to these abstracted states when you married her?" Geoffrey stared at his brother in disbelief. "Why in God's name did you never mention them before?"

Paul leaned back in the leather arm chair. "They never struck me as sinister before."

"And how long has she been doing it deliberately using these meditation techniques?"

"Several months, as far as I know. The housekeeper spotted it first. Mrs. Collins seems to find the whole thing very frightening."

"And she is right to. Clare has to be stopped, Paul. I asked you to come over because I went to see her a couple of days ago, did she tell you?" Geoffrey sat forward, his hands clasped on the desk before him. "No. I thought she might not. I spoke to her at some length and I suspect she is dabbling in all kinds of dangerous fields. I had the distinct feeling she was afraid."

Paul looked around his brother's comfortable study. The faded chintz curtains had been drawn against the cold, clear evening and a fire blazed in the grate. "I had thought of a psychiatrist for Clare," he said slowly, "but John Stanford doesn't think it's necessary. He thinks that she will get used to the idea of being childless. He thinks she will get over the disappointment quite quickly and that if she doesn't, then we should think of adoption." He shrugged, surprised how easily he could talk about it now, surprised at how he had convinced even himself that it was Clare who was unable to have a child. "In the meantime he has recommended a complete rest."

Geoffrey was watching him closely. "You know, I don't think that's such a good idea at all. She is too much alone, Paul. The last thing she needs is a rest. She needs to be busy. On her own admission she has been thrown on her own resources too often."

"Well, I'm going to solve the problem by sending her away." Paul stood up restlessly. He walked to the fireplace and kicked at the glowing coke. "I'm sending her on a cruise."

"Alone?"

"Well, I can't go." Paul picked up the poker, his voice defensive. "My calendar is full for the next six months. Besides, I'm sure she'd rather go without me."

"Couldn't you send someone with her?" Geoffrey said mildly. "Emma, perhaps, or your Mrs. Collins?"

"Sarah Collins?" Paul's voice cracked into a laugh. "Do you think I've got the money to send my housekeeper on a cruise?"

Geoffrey stroked his cheek thoughtfully, watching Paul in silence.

"When are you sending her away?" he asked at last.

"Soon."

"And does she know about this great treat that lies in store for her?" Geoffrey narrowed his eyes.

"I've told her I have a surprise arranged for her."

"It'll certainly be that. And if she doesn't wish to go?"

Paul closed his eyes. By then the sale of Duncairn would have been arranged, and after that he didn't care what happened to her. "Then she will have to see an expert—a psychiatrist—a psychotherapist—I don't know." He shrugged evasively.

Geoffrey shook his head. "No, Paul. That's not what she needs. She needs company; she needs people around her all the time, and she needs spiritual protection. For God's sake, man, don't you see what is happening to her?"

"She's obsessed with the past—"

"No. It's more than that. This woman, Isobel. She is using Clare. She is taking her over, Paul. I'm sure of it."

Paul stared at him. "You aren't serious? You mean Clare is possessed?"

"If that's the way you want to put it, yes. She is possessed. Through her meditation, through these other practices, she has learned to open her mind to the powers of darkness." Since talking to Emma, and then to Clare herself, Geoffrey had been reading hard and talking to several of his colleagues. He was extremely worried. "You have to take this very seriously, Paul."

"You mean Isobel is evil?" Paul stressed the word sarcastically.

"I believe she is a spirit who is not at rest. She is using your wife as a means of communicating with the world."

"What you are saying is that Clare is a medium—"

"No, it is more than that. She needs spiritual protection!"

"Well then, give it to her. When she comes back, exorcise her or something. Not that I expect this Isobel creature will follow her to the Mediterranean. . . ."

Geoffrey sighed. "What will you do if Clare doesn't want to go to the Mediterranean, Paul?" He sat down opposite his brother.

Paul considered. "I don't know. But she will go. I'll see to it that she goes. She always does what I tell her."

Clare was standing in the garden staring up at the sky. It was a brilliant clear night and very cold. She pushed her hands deep into the pockets of her coat and shivered as the first slight flattening appeared at the edge of the radiant full moon. Behind her the kitchen door opened.

"Are you warm enough, Mrs. Royland?" Sarah peered out into the darkness.

"Yes, thanks." Clare's eyes hadn't left the moon. "Aren't you going to come and watch? An eclipse of the full moon is a bit special. It's full of portent, somehow."

Sarah shivered. "I'll pop out and see how it's going when I've got the supper on." She closed the door firmly.

Clare smiled ruefully. Another black mark. Another sign that she was on the way to perdition.

Already the shadow was cutting into the moon's side—a strange, malignant growing scar on the cold, impervious silver. Pulling her collar up around her neck, she stepped down off the terrace and began to wander over the wet grass. The night was completely silent. No owls; no bats that she could see or hear. No rustlings or squeakings from the flower beds. Perhaps all the wildlife too was standing in silent awe at the devastation going on in the sky. She shivered again. As the eclipse progressed it brought with it a strange sadness, a feeling of empty desolation. The whole thing took about an hour. By the time the moon had disappeared and the sky was black, she was shaking violently with the cold, and there were tears in her eyes.

She had woken herself deliberately after the last trance, cold and cramped after sitting cross-legged so long. The candle had almost burned down. She had stood up as she blew it out. There was still a little light in the sky, and she had stood for a moment at the window staring out at the gray garden. Beyond the beech hedge she could see the mist beginning to creep in across the fields. Resolutely she had drawn the curtains and switched on the light, then she stood staring at herself in the mirror.

She had thought for a long time about the rapes, the cold-blooded mating of a man with a frightened, unwilling young woman in order to conceive a child. Had it been so different, Isobel's ordeal at the hands of the Earl of Buchan, from her own when she and Paul had been trying so hard for a baby?

Was that it? Was her dramatic vision of the past a product of her own mind, glamorizing and making more frightening her own impersonal ordeal at the hands of the doctors, to make the whole experience more bearable? Was she fantasizing uncontrollably to compensate for her own inability to have a child? Was her vivid consciousness of Isobel's pain and hatred and fear merely a psychodrama reflecting her own emotions?

She found herself thinking completely calmly about Paul. He had not slept with her since the results had come from the doctor. It was as if, now that there was no possibility of a child, there was no reason for sex. He had lost interest, and for the first time she realized calmly and rationally that he was not in love with her. Perhaps he never had been. Was she still in love with him? Her mind sidestepped the question; if she was not in love with Paul, why was she still married to him?

Shivering, she had turned away from the mirror, feeling very bleak. In her dream Isobel refused to have a child. Did this mean she, Clare, was subconsciously trying to pretend that childlessness was her choice? Was she, even in her dreams, fooling herself into the belief that she could get pregnant still, if she wanted?

She'd turned as the door was pushed open and Casta appeared in the room, her tail wagging apologetically, her eyes pleading. The dog pushed her nose into Claire's hand and whined quietly until Clare squatted beside her and put her arms around her neck. It was strange the way Casta disappeared when she meditated—almost as if she were afraid. Why should she do that? And why, if it were her own dream, had Aunt Margaret had it too? Was Isobel after all a spirit, or a memory, echoing down the years in the genetic memory banks of the family? Was it perhaps merely that this was the inheritance of women? The burden they all carried through the millennia. The curse of Eve. She had buried her face in the dog's fur, and suddenly she had found that she was crying.

Almost at once the darkness was over. A faint silver rim was reappearing on the far side of the moon. The eclipse was passing. She walked back slowly toward the house and pushed open the back door. She was pulling off her boots as Sarah went to answer the phone.

"It's Mrs. Cassidy," she said as she handed the receiver over. The kitchen was warm and steamy; Clare could smell some kind of casserole in the oven.

"Hi, Emma. How are you?" She tried to make her voice cheerful.

"I'm pretty fed up, if you must know." Emma sounded unusually depressed. "I had to call someone."

"What is it?" Clare, the phone in one hand, wriggled free of her coat. She frowned, trying to shake off her own black mood. Behind her Sarah had tactfully left the room.

"Peter's back."

"But surely, you should be pleased."

"Yes. I should." Emma sniffed miserably. "But he's going away again, almost at once."

"Oh, Emma. I'm sorry. That's beastly."

"Yes." There was a long silence, then Emma went on, her voice a little brighter. "Do you want to hear some gossip?"

"Why not? Who are we going to talk about?" Clare tried to make herself sound cheerful.

"Me, actually." Emma suddenly gave a rueful laugh. "I seem to have found myself another man. If I want him." The last sentence was spoken almost in a whisper.

For a moment Clare, stunned into silence, didn't reply.

"Are you horrified?"

"Horrified? No. I'm impressed. Who is he? What is he like? Have I met him?"

"Ah, all that is classified information. All I can tell you is that he is sexy; he's quite old—mid-fifties, I should say. And he's an American."

"Emma, you sly old thing! How long have you know him?"
Clare was intrigued.

There was a slight pause. "Does forever sound corny?" she
answered at last.

"Absolutely awful." Clare laughed. "When are you seeing
him again?"

"I don't know. He's going up to Scotland next week. He
said he'd call me when he got back. I wasn't going to see him
again, Clare, but Peter will be away. . . ." Her voice trailed
into silence. "He's been away about six months this year so
far, and I'm fed up. I'm lonely. I know I should be able to
cope. I have Julia; I have the gallery. I'm very lucky. But I
need something else."

"I know." Clare's voice was bleak. "And for you the something else is American and alluring."

How strange that Emma too should be lonely. Two lonely
women with such different ways of dealing with their loneliness.

Paul had been watching the eclipse from the embank-
ment. Walking slowly up away from Westminster Bridge,
dazzled by the streetlights and the cars, he had stared upward with almost unwilling fascination as the moon slowly
died. He was thinking about Clare. He didn't like himself for
what he was about to do, but there was no room for sentiment in business. Or guilt.

He stood for a moment just inside the door of the restaurant in Long Acre, ostensibly taking his time as he extricated
himself from his overcoat and handed it over. Scanning the
seated diners, he instinctively picked out Rex at once. Ten
minutes late himself after his long, slow walk through the
cold streets, he had known the American would be there
early. He studied the half-averted face, trying to read the
man's character, trying to establish a base from which he
could find an advantage.

Slowly he followed the maître d'hôtel toward the table. For
a moment the two men looked at each other, one standing,
one seated, appraising each other in silence. Paul stood for a
moment longer than necessary, then he held out his hand.

"Mr. Cummin?

Rex did not rise. "I hope you're not going to waste my time, Royland. As you didn't cancel, I assume your wife has changed her mind and that you really do have her authority to negotiate this time."

Paul frowned as he seated himself at the table. "I told you in my letter—"

"Your wife called me. She said no way was she selling and that you were not empowered to act for her." He waved away the waiter who was hovering with the menus. "Unless I have some assurance that she has changed her mind—"

"My wife is ill—"

"Not according to her." Rex's eyes were fixed on Paul's face.

"Emotionally ill." Paul looked away. "May I ask when she called you?"

"Monday."

Paul thought fast for a moment, then he leaned forward, elbows on the table. "I can explain. Why don't we order an aperitif and discuss this? I think you and I want the same result from this meeting, and I believe we have something to build on."

Rex raised an eyebrow. "Okay. We'll discuss it." He clicked his fingers at the waiter. "Bourbon on the rocks."

"The same," Paul ordered hastily. His chest was feeling tight, his stomach churning uncomfortably. Surreptitiously he wiped his hands on the napkin out of sight beneath the tablecloth that covered his knees.

"Let me put my cards on the table." He took a deep breath. "As you have probably gathered, my wife is emotionally attached to the land you want. It has been in her family for hundreds of years. Any offer that was made for it would have to compensate us fully for that emotional attachment."

"My existing offer already does that." Rex picked up his glass as soon as it was put before him. "The market value on that hotel is half what I am offering, and I'm giving over the odds per acre for the land as well."

Paul could feel himself sweating. "But we are talking oil, are we not?"

Rex inclined his head. "Ownership of the land does not confer ownership of the mineral rights, as I'm sure you know." He leaned forward. "We get a drilling license, and all we have to pay you as owner is compensation for loss of amenity and rent for the space taken up by the installations. That would be peanuts compared with what I'm offering you."

"So why?" Paul was suddenly suspicious. "Why, if you don't need to own the land, are you so keen to buy?"

Rex smiled. "I'll be straight with you. It gives us the advantage over the other companies if bids go to tender when the Department of Environment hands out the sectors in the next licensing round."

"So, it's worth a lot to you, to own the land."

An ancient Cummin castle. The seat of his ancestors. A romantic ruin. A dream. Rex clenched his fists. "It's worth what I offered. No more." He drained his glass. His heart was beating very fast.

"What if another company does bid for the land?"

"They won't. No one else has been surveying that sector. I expect Sigma to be the only bidder."

"But you said—"

"I said *if*, Mr. Royland. I'm only hedging my bets. I don't need to buy. But take my word for it, oil is going to be extricated from that headland whatever happens. Whether you make money from it is up to you and your wife."

Paul looked grim. "My wife will be going away shortly. By the time she has left she will have given me power of attorney to act for her in her absence, but I shall do so only if I feel the money is sufficient compensation for the loss she is going to suffer. You had better leave the offer with me, Mr. Cummin. I have to go to Zurich for five days—" He had tried to get out of the trip every way he knew. To leave now in the middle of everything was disaster, but old Beattie was adamant.

He glanced at Cummin and saw a flicker of alarm on the man's face. It gave him a second's cautious elation. Perhaps Zurich wasn't such a disaster after all. He smiled coolly. "I must ask you not to contact my wife while I'm away. If you

wish to get in touch with me, I shall be at the Baur au Lac
Hotel."

If only he was a poker player. He had a feeling Cummin
probably was. And he didn't like the way the man had suddenly smiled. He was a good-looking bastard—rich, assured,
perhaps twenty years older but, being American, probably
ten times fitter. Defensively he picked up the menu. "Shall
we order?"

In the far corner of the room three other diners were
ordering too. Soberly they chose food and wine, then leaned
together and talked again. Only now and then, cautiously,
did Neil glance across at Paul and Rex. He was too far away to
hear what the two men were saying, but he didn't need to.
The course of the meeting had been easy to follow. The
initial suspicion, the hostility, the cautious overtures, and
now the conspiratorial bonhomie as the two men toasted one
another in glass after glass of top-price claret. So the deal was
on. Earthwatch, with the help of the nation's press, was going
to fight Sigma and the oil lobby for all it was worth, and in the
process it was going to tear Clare Royland apart.

Clare lay back in the bed and stretched luxuriantly. She
still loved Sunday mornings more than any other time. It was
the only day she allowed Sarah to bring her breakfast in bed
with the papers and she reveled in it. Casta lay on the floor
asleep.

With Paul in Zurich she felt more relaxed than she had at
any time lately. She was free to plan, and for once her plans
could be her own. She had awoken with the realization that
the thing she had feared for so long had happened. The time
for togetherness was over and she wasn't afraid. It was as if
she had been liberated. Without him she was free. There was
nothing she couldn't do; nowhere she couldn't go, at least for
a little while. She felt wonderfully free and happy.

On the carpet by the window Casta stirred uneasily. She
raised her head and looked toward the bed with a little
whine. On the back of her golden ruff the hair was beginning
to stand on end. Clare didn't notice, but she frowned. The

room seemed to have grown cold. She shifted uneasily under the soft quilt, glancing toward the window. It was closed, yet she could feel the draft distinctly playing across her face and arms, and somewhere in the distance she could hear the sea.

She jerked upright, her mouth suddenly dry with fright. "No," she whispered. "No! I didn't summon you!"

The *Sunday Times* and the *Observer* slid from the bed onto the carpet.

Casta leapt to her feet and ran for the door, her ears flat against her head, her tail pressed down between her legs as desperately Clare hung on to reality, her hands clenched into the fabric of the bedclothes as she scrambled to her knees. "No! Not now. Leave me alone. . . ."

She could see the mist swirling in the corners of the room and the fire flickering in the great fireplace of Slains Castle. It was hot now, stuffy and airless, and she could smell the bruised heather on the floor and see the shadowy figures moving to and fro in front of the windows—her bedroom windows. In terror she shrank back against the pillows, shaking her head, desperately trying to drive them away, but slowly the images were growing stronger. Then she saw Isobel.

Her eyes were full of tears. She stared up at the Earl of Buchan as he stood over her, not wanting to believe what he told her. Her Uncle Macduff was dead; the Scots had suffered a terrible defeat at Falkirk at the hands of the English cavalry and massed archers, and Scotland was in disarray.

"He was a brave man, my dear. We shall miss him at the head of the men of Fife."

She looked away, not wanting him to see the desolation that had swept over her, and she murmured a prayer for the soul of her uncle, who had shown her so much kindness in these later lonely years. Near her Alice Comyn sat at her embroidery, and she felt comforted suddenly by the other's presence. In the months since her miscarriage the two young women had become friends. She no longer looked on Alice as her husband's spy.

She looked up wearily as her husband threw off his dusty

mantle and unbuckled his sword belt, laying the long sword on the table near her. He beckoned forward a page with a bowl of water and a towel and splashed some of the dust from his face. Then he called for wine.

"Great-grandmother will be heartbroken," she said sadly. "Macduff was always her favorite son. So, what of Scotland now?" She watched him drink. "Have we lost all? What will the English do next?"

"Edward won't follow up the victory, if my guess is right," he said slowly. "The English have no food; the land is burned, the stock long gone, as happened before when Edward was forced to pay me compensation for what he did to Buchan when I came into his peace." He paused thoughtfully. "And his generals are restless. My guess is they will not press north. They have gone west now, following the Bruce and his men, but I doubt if they will consolidate any attack they make there. The men of Carrick should be able to hold them off."

Still upset and shaken after the news of Macduff's death, Isobel felt herself go completely cold. "But has no one gone to help them? Do you leave Lord Carrick to fight the whole might of England alone?" She saw Alice look up warningly, but she ignored her, the words tumbling out as she rose to her feet. "Why didn't anyone go after them? Why have you come back here? The fight isn't finished! For the love of God, did King Edward alarm you so much you had to come and lick your wounds in the north and leave others to throw out the English invaders?"

There was a moment's horrified silence. The page, returning with more wine, froze in his tracks. Slowly Alice stood up, the embroidery silks falling unnoticed from her lap. The servants and men-at-arms in the hall, sensing something of the atmosphere, stopped whatever they were doing and stared, first at the earl, then at his countess as she stood before him, hands clenched, eyes blazing, her beautiful face pale with anger.

"Well, my lord?" Oblivious of the watching faces, she swept past him, taking the jug from the page with a shaking hand. "Here, let me refill your goblet. Wine will no doubt restore your courage—"

He took the jug from her before he hit her, a blow that sent her reeling across the floor. His face taut with anger, he drank deeply. Then, tossing the jug back to the page, he strode toward his wife and caught her arm.

"No one—no one has ever called me coward," he said, his voice deceptively calm. "I returned north with other lords of the realm to plan the future and to elect new Guardians. Lord Carrick"—his voice was acid—"will undoubtedly be one of them. He has more than proved his worth. He does not need your championship of him. Sir William Wallace has failed us; he cannot continue as Guardian of Scotland, even in John Balliol's name. The task belongs with men of high rank. No mere gentleman, however fine a soldier he may be, can rule Scotland. In the meantime, your task, wife, is to serve and support your husband, not"—he paused, his breath hissing between his teeth—"accuse him of cowardice."

"I spoke too hastily, my lord. Forgive me." Fear and anger, as so often, vied with each other as she faced him.

"You did indeed."

Each time he saw her he found her more to his taste, this strange rebellious child bride who was now a woman. The trouble in the winter had matured her, both physically and mentally, even though it seemed to have hardened her resolve to fight him. Again he felt the faint stirring of desire as he looked at her, and the new respect. He knew she was afraid of him—he was a large man, still in his prime, and yet she refused to be cowed. She had proved that now and before Falkirk. She was a woman of courage and intelligence; she would make a good mother for his heir. He frowned. It was many months now since she had lost the child, and still there was no sign that she was breeding again. He crossed himself suddenly as he looked at her, unaware that every pair of eyes in the great hall of Slains Castle saw him do it, and read the thought that again and again crossed his mind. His wife was a sorceress and using her art against him.

He shook away the thought. Two nights he could spare at Slains before riding inland to Mar, to break the news, among other things, to Countess Eleyne of the death of her son, Macduff, two nights to get his wife pregnant and dissuade her from further attempts to avoid the destiny for which every married woman was intended.

Slains, like so many of the Buchan castles, was never free of the sound of the sea. That night was one of violent storm. In the darkness the never-ending waves thundered up the lines of cliffs, reverberating against the hollow rocks, casting spray high in the air as a violent summer storm and a southeasterly gale hurled itself at the east coast of Scotland. Time and again the sky was split open by the forked shafts of lightning, to be followed by crack upon crack of thunder. The lookouts cowered behind the walls, straining their eyes against the dark, while in the hall men huddled around the huge fire, banked up despite the heat and hissing as the heavy rain fell five stories through the long chimney.

Isobel had told the boy to leave the windows unshuttered. She stood watching the rain on the stone sill, not flinching as the lightning sliced into the boiling waves below, turning the sea an eldritch green. There was no fire in the hearth in the earl's chamber; two of the sconces had blown out. Only the candles remained, sheltered by the hangings of the great bed. The storm was exhilarating.

The room was empty; she had dismissed her attendants an hour before as the storm began. Slowly she pulled off her headdress and unpinned the long braids from her head, undoing them slowly and methodically, her eyes on the sea, feeling the wind lift her loosened hair about her shoulders. She shrugged off her gown and let it slide to the floor. The air was cool on her hot skin as she stood staring out of the window in the pale linen shift. Almost without realizing it she allowed that too to fall, and stood naked in the embrasure, her hand on the carved stone, not flinching as another crack of thunder reverberated across the cliffs and echoed inland.

On the deep sill, soaked with rain, stood a small jar. In it was an ointment of honey and beeswax and salt, thrice blessed beneath the moon. Mairi had made it for her; Mairi who had brought her, an hour before, the precious water in which a red-hot iron from the forge had been dropped.

"Drink it, my lady. The savine from the south is finished, but this will make you barren without making you ill as the

savine did," she whispered, glancing over her shoulder to
make sure that no one overheard. Isobel did not hesitate. She
drank the water and gave Mairi the goblet, then Mairi had
reached into the pocket of her apron. "Before your lord
comes," she whispered, "you must place this ointment inside
yourself. He'll not guess if you do it quickly without him
seeing. If the iron water fails, this will protect you, *Iseabail,
ma chridhe.*"

Throwing open the door, Lord Buchan caught his breath at
the sight of his wife, silhouetted against the flickering sky
beyond the window. He stood watching her for a moment,
conscious of the chill that had touched his spine. Again the
lightning flickered and he saw her white skin take on a blue,
ethereal glow. She didn't move. All her attention was fixed
on some point far out at sea. If she heard her husband she
gave no sign. Beside her the jar was empty.

He stared at the angle of her shoulders, the line of her
spine, the soft curve of her buttocks, shadowed by the pale
flickering candlelight behind her, and, slowly, despising himself for doing it, once more he made the sign of the cross.

Abruptly he stepped into the room and hurled the door
shut behind him. She didn't move. Only the slight whitening
of her knuckles on the stone beside the window showed she
knew he was there.

For a moment the moon showed behind the streaming
clouds. It was full, low in the east above the black jumble of
the heaving water. Isobel stared at it, feeling the gentle
touch of its light on her body, then as the cloud thickened
again and darkness cloaked the sea, she turned and faced her
husband.

❦ Chapter Eleven ❦

Clare wasn't sure what had brought her back to the present. One minute she was there in the dark, shadowed room at Slains and the next she was looking around her own sun-filled bedroom. The figures had gone, the past had retreated, and she was alone again. Slowly she climbed out of bed. Her body was tense and excited, her heart thumping painfully beneath her ribs as she walked in her nightdress to the window and pushed it open. She leaned out, taking deep breaths of the fresh cold air, feeling it cool her burning face and body beneath the thin silk. She was trembling violently. Why? Why had it happened? She had not done any yoga; she had not meditated. She had had no candle, no thought of Isobel. She had been thinking of Duncairn, admittedly, but in the present, not the past. She swallowed hard. Dear God! Was Geoffrey right? Was she possessed?

Her knuckles whitened on the windowsill. Had this happened to Aunt Margaret too? She put her head in her hands, then slowly she straightened. If it had happened to Aunt Margaret then it wasn't just her; she was not mad; she hadn't courted some kind of evil. Isobel was part of her family, as much a part of her inheritance as was Duncairn. She was returning for a reason. There had to be a reason. Clare bit her lip. What reason could this woman, dead now for nearly seven hundred years, have for haunting her descendents? Why was she returning again and again to tell her story?

Slowly she forced herself to get dressed. Fawn corduroys, a thick sweater against the cold wind, then she brushed her hair hard, almost as if she were trying to clear her head by the fierce wielding of the hairbrush. She ran downstairs to the kitchen and made herself a cup of coffee. Then she called

Casta. "We'll go for a walk across the fields as soon as I've had my coffee," she whispered. "Then Sarah will be back from church and we needn't be alone."

The wind was whisking leaves across the gravel, tossing the branches of the trees to and fro as she walked across the drive toward the gate. The roar and rustle of the leaves completely masked the sound of the car driving slowly toward her up the drive. It drew to a halt near her and the driver sat still for a moment staring at her. Slowly Neil opened his door and climbed out.

"Mrs. Royland?" He made it sound like a question, though he had recognized her at once. He eyed the slacks, the heavy sweater, the brogues. Even in country clothes, her hair tangled by the wind and with the bare minimum of makeup, she looked elegant. He could feel his resentment welling up again.

The decision to drive home via Suffolk had come to him suddenly, in his hotel room after the dinner at Long Acre with his two London colleagues. Even as he drove through Dedham and found the turn that led to Great Headham he had not made the decision to go in. He just wanted to look at the house and see for himself what kind of extravagant life the Roylands led, trying to justify his irrational dislike of Clare.

From the lane all he had been able to see was the long drive, the cluster of warm red roofs, the old peg tiles glowing beneath the blustery sunshine, and the trees around the front of the house and on the lawns that surrounded it. Almost without realizing it he had turned the Land-Rover in through the gates. And then he had seen her.

"My name is Neil Forbes." He held out his hand to her formally. "I wonder if I could speak to you for a few minutes?" His voice was coldly polite.

Ordering the dog to be quiet, she shook his hand warily. "We've met before, haven't we?" she said slowly. "I don't quite remember where—"

"At Duncairn. We didn't meet, but I was there."

"Of course. You were at the castle." She remembered him

clearly now. He had watched her, intruded on her privacy, and Isobel's. . . .

She pushed her hands deep into her pockets. She didn't want to speak to him; she didn't want to speak to anyone yet. Isobel was still too much with her. The memory of that moon-lit room and the naked, defiant woman still overwhelmed her, and in a strange way it still excited her. "I'm sorry, Mr. Forbes, but it is not a very good time. As you see, I am just going out."

"It'll only take a few minutes, Mrs. Royland. And it is important." He folded his arms. The sexy bitch had been in bed with someone. He could see it in her eyes, in the glow on her face. And it hadn't been her husband. Paul Royland was in Zurich. "I think you'd want to hear what it is I have to say to you." The slight undercurrent of threat in his tone was obvious. "It is about Duncairn."

Clare studied him coolly. "What about Duncairn?" She was on the defensive now, wondering if he was from the oil company, or if he was somehow connected with Paul. In either case she had no wish to speak to him.

"You have been offered a very large sum of money for the estate, Mrs. Royland. I should be interested to know just how long it took you to accept." His voice was heavy with scorn. "I can't believe you need the money that badly." He glanced disparagingly over his shoulder at the beautiful old house. "Did you think at all about the repercussions on the people in the village up there? Did you consider the environmental ramifications that the development of the area will bring? Did you think about Jack Grant at the hotel? Or the castle? Or the birds and the plants and the other wildlife? Did you, Mrs. Royland?" He took a step nearer to her.

Clare, for a moment so astonished by his attack that she didn't answer, was suddenly furious. "What I do is none of your business, Mr. Forbes! How dare you! It is none of your business at all! Please leave! I assure you I don't need a stranger to point out my responsibilities at Duncairn!" She was white with anger.

"Someone obviously has to, Mrs. Royland!"

"No! No one has to! Least of all a complete stranger. Please leave, Mr. Forbes, or I shall call the police!"

He put his hands into his pockets. "I am here to warn you, Mrs. Royland. Scotland has always suffered from absentee English landlords. They don't care for the country; they don't love the land. All they care about is the amount of money they can make out of it—"

"I am a Scot, Mr. Forbes—"

"No, Mrs. Royland, you are English. English in your heart and your methods; married to an Englishman. English to the core!" He meant it an insult, as only a nationalist Scot can mean it. "And now Duncairn doesn't want you. You do not belong there and it has never belonged to you. Keep away, Mrs. Royland. Allow the people who love the place to fight for it."

Even as he said it, he knew he was wrong. She belonged there. The day he saw her the echoes had reached out to her, not to him. He had felt them, yes, but they had spoken to her.

They stared at each other angrily for a moment, the leaves whirling around their feet as the wind got up again. Casta gave a quiet throaty growl as she sat at Clare's feet.

Neal took a deep breath. "I am sorry, but this is something I feel very strongly about."

"So do I, I assure you." She was trying very hard to steady herself. "As it happens I am going up to Scotland within the next day or two."

"Don't bother. You'll only be in our way."

"Our way?" Clare gasped. "Who exactly is *our*?" She was furiously indignant. "What the hell do you mean?"

"Earthwatch. We shall be coordinating the opposition to onshore oil prospecting and drilling throughout the east coast of Scotland. We intend to fight Sigma all the way."

She frowned, trying to collect her wits. "How exactly do you know so much about all this?"

"We have our methods." He swung around with a exclamation of disgust as another car turned into the drive. Following his gaze, Clare saw Sir David Royland's old Bentley turn in between the gates in the distance. Slowly it began to make its way toward them.

With relief she turned to Neil. "I think you'd better go. That is my husband's brother, and I don't want any trouble."

"I don't intend to make trouble, Mrs. Royland. Not here." Neil looked grave. "However, as you have visitors I shall leave. I can't expect support from pseudo environmentalists like Sir David any more than from you—"

"You know my brother-in-law?" Behind them the Bentley drew to a halt beneath the trees.

"By reputation. New jobs for rural areas—that's his ticket, isn't it? Very praiseworthy until you discover that the jobs are for newcomers and the people who have lived in the area for centuries are excluded from his concern." Neil climbed into his battered Land-Rover. "I'm glad I've met you at last, Mrs. Royland. I don't suppose there will be any need for us to meet again. I suggest if you want to avoid any unpleasantness you keep away from Duncairn from now on." After slamming his car door, he turned on the ignition and reversed violently, sending the gravel flying from beneath the wheels before he drove without a backward glance down the drive.

"Your visitor seemed in quite a hurry." Gillian heaved herself out of the passenger seat. "I hope we haven't driven him away."

Clare gave a rueful grimace. She found she was trembling. "You did, actually, and I'm very grateful. He was some kind of environmental campaigner. He seemed to think I'd sold Duncairn and he didn't like it. I think he was threatening me. Come in. Sarah will be back from church soon."

Gillian said, "We'd love to scrounge a cup of coffee, Clare, darling, if that's all right. We're having lunch with David's agent and his wife, so we thought we'd pop in. Just in case you were lonely, with Paul away in Zurich."

"Paul and I had a bit of a chat," David went on as they followed Clare indoors, "just before he left yesterday. We talked about the trust and other family matters, and he asked us to look in on you, to make sure you were all right."

"It was kind of you to come." Clare led them into the drawing room.

"He's worried about you, Clare," Gillian put in. She lowered herself cautiously into a chair. "You're too much alone here. You rattle around in this great house."

"I have Mrs. Collins." Clare was on the defensive now.

Through the window she could see Sarah walking slowly up the drive. "I'm not alone, I can assure you. Besides, I enjoy my own company. Look, Sarah's just got back. I'll go and ask her to make us some coffee—"

"No. You talk to Gillian. I'll go." David was on his feet again almost as soon as he had sat down.

Gillian and Clare sat and looked at each other as the door closed.

"Did they settle matters about the trust?" she asked at last.

Gillian shrugged. "God knows. I think Paul is being a bit crass about that."

"I think the whole idea is stupid. I wish he'd never brought it up." Restlessly Clare stood up. "Excuse me. I think I'll go and check that coffee is on its way, as you're in a hurry."

The kitchen door was half open. From the shadowed hall Clare could see Sarah standing near the table. Behind her on the stove she could see the chicken in its roasting dish. Clare wasn't sure what made her stop and listen; perhaps it was the same uneasy suspicion that had driven her from the drawing room.

"You do understand, Mrs. Collins, I would never normally ask anyone questions like this." She could hear her brother-in-law's voice at its most confidential and reassuring. "But we are all so concerned for her state of mind. My brother has been enormously grateful for the way you've kept an eye on Mrs. Royland." He paused. From where Clare was standing he was out of sight, behind the door. "Tell me, is she still having these strange turns of hers? What exactly does she do?" David asked quietly.

"She sits on the floor, with this lighted candle in front of her, and oh, sir, I'm so afraid sometimes, it's all I can do not to give in my notice and go. I can't bear being in the same house with her, and that's the truth. If Mr. Royland hadn't begged me to stay—"

"But what do you see?" David persisted quietly.

"Spirits!" Sarah said darkly. "Shadows. Ghosts, moving in the darkness around her."

In the hall Clare gasped. She felt suddenly very sick.

"You are quite sure of this?" Even without seeing his face she could hear the skepticism in David's voice.

She saw Sarah color. "If you don't believe me, you ask Mr. Royland. He's seen her do it. He told me. In the London house. And look at the dog! Animals always know. There's evil in this house, Sir David. Evil!"

Clare leaned against the wall, pressing her burning face against the cool wooden paneling.

"It's good of you to stay, my dear. Mr. Royland is deeply grateful. He is relying on you to look after her while he's away, but he is seeking expert help. There is nothing for you to worry about in the meantime, I promise you—"

He broke off as Clare marched into the kitchen. Her face was white, but somehow she kept her voice steady as she looked from one to the other of them. "So, where is this coffee? Don't forget you're in a hurry, David." She smiled at Sarah as brightly as she could. "Gillian and I thought you must have run off together!"

"What do you mean by lying to Sir David about me?" Clare asked Sarah after Gillian and David finally left. "How can you tell him those wicked things?"

Putting down her wooden spoon, Sarah turned. Her face was white. "I never tell lies!"

"You told him you'd spied on me. Oh, I believe that! But you said you'd seen things!"

"I did see things." Two bright pink patches appeared on Sarah's cheeks. "I told him the truth! What you're doing is evil, Mrs. Royland. If it wasn't for Mr. Royland I wouldn't stay here another minute!"

"Then don't."

"No." Sarah was shaking her head. "No. No. I can't leave. I have to stay. I have to try to help you. I've been praying for you." There were tears in her eyes. "Please let me stay—" She broke off as the door opened and Casta nosed her way into the kitchen.

Clare stared down at the dog, then she dropped to her

knees and put her arms around Casta's neck, burying her face in the thick fur. Casta wagged her tail and licked Clare's hand.

"Was she really afraid?" Clare looked up at Sarah suddenly.

Sarah nodded. "Animals always know, Mrs. Royland."

"Don't leave me, Sarah. Please." Suddenly Clare's anger had gone. It was replaced by fear. She could feel herself beginning to shake. "I shan't be doing it anymore. None of it. No yoga. No meditation. It was really only daydreaming, you know. I wasn't doing anything terrible. It was just something to fill the emptiness. . . ."

Sarah's face softened. "You should do that with real people, Mrs. Royland." Embarrassed by the sudden intimacy, she turned back to the stove and, picking up the wooden spoon, she began restlessly to stir the gravy. "Mr. Royland has been very worried about you, you know."

"I'm sure he has." Clare's voice was dry. "Well, there is no need for him to be worried now. It is finished."

"She said she could *see* the people, Zak!" Clare came straight to the point. She had barely looked at the bright, sparsely furnished room with its view across the Cam. "Don't you see, she said she could see *them!*"

She had hardly slept the night before, and when she had, the nightmare had returned: the eyes, the bars, the terrible, all-embracing fear. She had called Zak at half past seven and set off for Cambridge only half an hour later.

"Zak, you didn't say they were *real*. That other people could see them!" Her voice was unsteady.

He replied slowly, considering every word. "I don't believe I really saw anything physical, and I very much doubt if your Mrs. Collins did either. My guess is that she was making it up—trying to impress; saying something she knew would shock your brother-in-law. Perhaps she had been exaggerating when she talked about it to your husband, and she couldn't retract what she'd said."

"You said before that you thought I might be creating thought forms," Clare said wearily.

"I still believe that." He was watching her face, noting the pale, drawn expression, the dark rings beneath her eyes.

"But aren't they things that no one else can ever see?"

Zak frowned uneasily. "I'm not saying it's not possible for other people to see them," he said cautiously. "People can and do create tangible thought forms by the sheer power of their imagination. But I have always believed that when people claim they've seen independent entities, what they have seen actually comes from telepathy rather than physical manifestation—" He hesitated. "But I've read about it happening. I've read about people creating creatures of such power that they can exist on their own."

"And would those creatures be able to return on their own without invitation?" Clare asked softly.

"Without invitation?" Zak echoed.

"Yesterday, Zak, it happened to me without my summoning them, and it is the second time it has happened." She paused. "My brother-in-law, who is a vicar in the Church of England, thinks they're spirits. He thinks I've raised the spirits of the dead."

Zak swallowed nervously. He was out of his depth. "Yes," he said at last, "that is possible." He ran his fingers through his hair.

"I feel tied to Isobel. She's part of me. She's haunting me, Zak. What am I going to do?"

"What does your husband think about all this, Clare?" he asked quietly.

"He thinks I'm going mad," she whispered. "He doesn't understand. He won't even try. I'm not sure he even loves me anymore."

"Ah." He paused for a moment, then tentatively he looked up. "Do you still love him?" He was clutching suddenly at the obvious, the Freudian explanation for her dreams. "If you're feeling trapped, Clare, and your life is unhappy and lonely," he went on, "perhaps the thing to do is to change it. Radically. Perhaps you should leave him for a while. If you loved him, Clare, you would go to him, trust him, let him help you," he continued thoughtfully. He stood up abruptly and caught her hands. "Clare, you need to rethink your whole life. All your problems. The dreams, the meditations, the visions, the emptiness, they are all part of some dead-end alley you have wandered up; part of the dream of marriage and babies and husbands that you've been living in too long. Those dreams tell it all. You are trapped. You want to break free. You *have* to break free."

"I do love Paul," she said at last.

"Do you? Do you really?" Zak looked at her searchingly. Abruptly he released her hands. "Okay. You love him. Then stay with him. Go to London. Go to Zurich or wherever it is he is. Stick with him. Follow him. Don't be alone. But don't bury your personality in his. Be yourself. Be strong."

"And that will stop the dreams?"

"It will if you really want to stop them." He wished he felt more certain. "You have to find the strength to fight them, Clare. No more meditation. That path is not for you. You have to find the answers through activity, not passivity. And you must get rid of that castle to keep yourself safe from Isobel. If someone wants to buy it, sell. Then create something real with the money."

"Sell?" she echoed.

"You have to. If you cling to that, you cling to the past and to the dreams, don't you see?"

"No, Zak," she said, "I don't. I can't do that. Never. I'll never give it up."

The meeting with John Carstairs of Carstairs Boothroyd had lasted less than an hour soon after Paul returned from Zurich. The young man was so excited he was barely able to sit still in Paul's office. Paul, behind his desk, watched him speculatively. At the far side of the room Henry was impassive. The takeover, if it happened, would make Carstairs's fortune, and he had asked BCWP to advise his company.

Paul shifted sideways behind his desk. "We'll schedule a meeting with the full board," he said at last. "But I don't see any problems." And Henry had nodded in agreement.

In the quiet office of the old Cameron Beattie building that afternoon, Paul glanced at his watch. It was just after three. Slowly he reached for his direct-line phone and began to dial.

Stephen Caroway, at Magnet Charles Plimsoll, was an old friend. He asked no questions as he wrote down the order for Carstairs Boothroyd shares that Paul gave him and automatically noted the time. "You want these New Time, for payment at the end of the next account, old boy, and to be sold as and when, right?"

"They'll triple before settlement date." Paul's mouth had gone dry.

Caroway smiled. "I don't doubt it. The profit to the usual account?"

"If you please. And lunch on me, next week. Okay?"

"Screw lunch! I'll take a case of Bollinger when the time comes." Caroway hung up.

It was Thursday, October 23. If the gamble came off, Paul stood to make a fortune.

Doug Warner, a tall, fair Texan in his late forties, grinned at Rex. "You win some, you lose some. This one, I think, you win. I had a word in the right ear at the department, Rex. There aren't any other applications in that sector as yet. Could be you'll be unopposed. Unless they say no in Houston."

Rex slammed his fist on the table. "You leave Houston to me. We're going to walk into this well, Doug, and it's a good one. I can feel it, in my bones. Royland is going to sell." He narrowed his eyes. "And I'm going to shift the European headquarters up there."

Doug gaped at him. "To Duncairn? What in God's name for?"

"Prestige, Doug. That's what for. The hotel can come down. We'll put up an admin building there. Airstrip—everything. And rebuild the castle. Sigma is going places, Doug!"

"Do they know all about this in Houston?" Doug asked.

"Some." Rex was guarded. "As much as they need to know." He smiled. "It's the right place, Doug. It has all the ingredients. A rich oil strike on company-owned land with space to develop, space for a railhead, new roads, collecting tanks, plant, a refinery, everything!"

"You haven't begun test drilling, yet. We haven't even got the XL—"

"We'll get it. No problem. I've had a word with the man at the D.O.E. too. There is no opposition to the idea in principle, and if there are no other applications we'll walk in at the next round. Then all we have to do is convince the local planners."

"And we'll own the land by then."

Rex nodded. "I've got Mitchison working on the contracts already. I've told him we're running to a deadline. Royland has until next Wednesday, and he's running scared. He'll sell."

"Or what?" Doug stretched out in a leather easy chair. He was watching Rex with amusement. He had never seen his usually phlegmatic boss so animated.

"Or he'll wish he had agreed before Wednesday." Rex gave an easy smile. "I didn't like Royland. Too smooth. Too conceited. Too anxious. I like his sister." He paused thoughtfully. "I even like the sound of his wife. Now, she's a real fighter." He stood, his head slightly to one side. "I'd sure like to meet her one day—show her what I intend to do with that ruin."

"I reckon you're keener on owning that castle than actually striking oil, my friend," Doug said, amused.

Rex threw back his head and laughed. "Just as long as you don't say that to the boys in Houston. I don't want them to know too much about this deal till we've signed all the contracts."

Doug hauled himself to his feet. "How much are you paying for the land?"

Rex looked down at the desk. "The final figure isn't agreed to yet. Royland is going to take less than I offered. He's afraid I'm going to back out." He smiled again. "He thinks he can push me up, but he's wrong. I know one or two things about Mr. Paul Royland, and he is going to pay me to keep quiet about them!"

Paul arrived back at Bucksters on Friday night. Clare was in the drawing room, sitting on the rug in front of the fire, listening to some music. Casta lay beside her, deeply asleep.

For a moment Paul stood looking down at them, his face expressionless. The market had dropped fifty points at close of dealing. It would go up, of course, and the Carstairs Booth-royd shares would soar next week, but still, the knowledge that he was £10,000 down so soon had made him very edgy. He smiled at his wife. "How are you, darling?"

Clare jumped to her feet. "Oh, Paul, I have missed you." She put her arms around his neck and almost shyly kissed him, on the cheek. Talking to Zak about leaving Paul, facing the real possibility, she had backed away from the thought. "I'm glad you're home."

He gave a tight half smile. "I've brought you a present from Switzerland." He reached into his breast pocket and pulled out an envelope. "A peace offering. I've been less than understanding lately, Clare. I'm sorry." He handed it to her awkwardly.

Clare stared up at him, weak with relief. He was the old generous Paul.

He was standing watching her, waiting for her to open the package. Slowly she pulled the flap up and extricated a fold of tissue. Inside it was a wafer-thin gold watch.

"Oh, Paul, it's beautiful!"

"Put it on. See how it looks."

She slipped it onto her wrist and held it up, staring at it in delight, then she turned back to him and put her arms around his neck again. "Oh, Paul, thank you. It's been so awful, quarreling all the time."

He frowned, drawing back slightly. "We've both been un-der a lot of strain. I suggest we put our differences behind us and plan for the future." He sat down on the sofa near the fire. "Pour me a sherry, darling, and listen. I've had nearly a week to think and there are some things I want to say. Now. While they're fresh in my mind."

Clare poured two glasses of sherry and then subsided onto the rug again, hugging her knees.

"This has been a difficult year for us both," Paul said. "All those tests; finding out we could never have a baby; your Aunt Margaret's death; and then the will. On top of all we have had worries at the office." He looked at Clare, who was listening to him intently. "BCWP has had a bad few months; the merger didn't happen without some problems. The directors all put a lot of our own money into the firm to try to put things right. That is why I'm in need of some funds. That is why I feel it is right to claim money from the trust, and why it would help me beyond all belief if we could sell Duncairn." When the shares went up, if they went up enough, perhaps he would back out of the sale. Give her back her castle. But until he was sure, he had to go on, had to cover himself. There was too much at stake to stop now. "No—" He raised his hand as she moved uneasily on the rug. "No, Clare. Let me talk. I've thought about it very hard. Hear me out. What I suggest is this. We sell Duncairn to Sigma, then I shall buy you another estate in Scotland—probably a great deal more beautiful, but a tenth of the price. I can't say fairer than that."

"No." Clare clenched her teeth. "Paul, I'm sorry. No. Duncairn isn't just an estate in Scotland to me. Surely to God you've realized that by now?"

His face was white and strained. She saw that there was a thin film of sweat over his forehead. "I need the money, Clare."

She shook her head miserably. "I'm sorry, but no."

Paul took a deep breath. He leaned sideways to take up the briefcase he had dropped by the sofa when he came in. "Okay. I understand. We'll drop the subject." His hands were shaking slightly. "But look at these anyway. I've had a couple of Edinburgh agents send some details of sporting and farm properties in the north." He pulled out a sheaf of glossy brochures.

"No, Paul. I'm sorry, but no." She buried her face in her arms.

He smiled thinly, throwing the leaflets down on the coffee table. "Okay, darling, okay. Don't get upset. We'll forget the whole thing. Let's not talk about it anymore. Look, I have another present for you. Something to cheer you up. Here." He extricated a folder from the flap of the briefcase and tossed it at her feet.

"Paul, please—"

"Open it, darling. The surprise I promised you."

She opened it cautiously and pulled out the contents.

He smiled. "Six weeks in the Greek islands with a quick flight over to see the pyramids. You deserve it, darling. To get you away from the horrible winter weather, to take your mind off things."

Clare was staring at the ticket in her hand. She looked from it to Paul and back. "I don't understand."

"It's a holiday, darling. A cruise. So you can rest and get your strength back."

"Oh, Paul!" She had scrambled to her feet. "Do you think I'm that naive? Come on. Give me credit for a little intelligence, please." She threw the ticket into his lap. "For a moment I thought you cared. I really thought you cared about me. Do you think I can't see what you want to do? With me out of the country, you'd find a way to sell Duncairn over my head!"

Emma, Peter, and Julia had arrived at Bucksters on Saturday morning. Almost at once Julia disappeared with Casta across the fields.

Clare went straight to the point. "Paul's gone into Dedham. He'll be back soon." No need to tell them about the long cold silences, the almost frightening atmosphere in the house last night, or about the nightmare that had ripped her out of her sleep, to wake, screaming and alone. Paul must have heard her, but he hadn't come. "He still wants to sell Duncairn. I can't make him change his mind." She turned to Peter. "Is it true he had to put a lot of his own money into the firm?"

Peter shifted uncomfortably on the sofa beside his wife. "It could be, I suppose, Clare. I don't know."

"He says BCWP is in trouble and he's lost it."

Peter frowned. "That doesn't sound right. As far as I know we're doing well. We showed a good profit on the first year. Clare—" He hesitated. "If you were to ask me my opinion, I should think very carefully and get some independent advice about whether or not you sell that old place. And, if there are any problems at the office, it is important you keep any money you have or make from a sale in your own name. We

are a limited-liability company, so a wife's property, separate
and in her own name, should be completely safeguarded."
He moved sideways slightly, obviously uncomfortable with
the conversation. "Do you have a good solicitor, Clare? And
an accountant?"

Clare shrugged. "Paul has—"

"You. You personally."

"No. All our affairs are handled together by Paul's people."

Peter frowned. "Then may I suggest you find yourself an
independent advisor? If Paul is in trouble financially, there is
no need for you to be dragged in. And there is a huge amount
of money at stake with the deal over Duncairn. You cannot
afford to make mistakes."

As Clare stood watching the bath fill that night, the bedroom behind her remained empty, the bed immaculate beneath the white lace cover. There was no sign of Paul.

He had never been a passionate lover; kind, considerate as
far as it went, yes, but always detached, never sorry, she
suspected, if she was too tired or too depressed for sex, and by
evening she often was depressed. He'd be buried in his papers or on the phone to his colleagues long after she was
exhausted and longing for sleep. She would wait, hoping this
time she might—might what? Tempt him? Entice him to
fling his papers over his shoulder and drag her into his arms?
She enjoyed sex but instinctively she knew there must be
more. There had to be more. Paul was the only man she had
ever slept with. Sometimes she wondered if she had really
slept with him at all.

She lay for a long time in the bath, listening to the howl of
the wind outside among the chimneys, then slowly she got
out and dried herself. She massaged some scented body oil
into her skin, slowly working it into her arms and legs, over
her breasts and thighs. Then, walking naked across the soft
carpet of her bedroom, she pulled open a drawer. Inside
were several silk nightgowns. Slowly she pulled them out—
black, coffee, deep red, midnight blue, all trimmed with lace,
soft and sensuous beneath her hand. She close the red one
and drew it slowly over her head. The silk was cold and soft

like water, as it fell to the floor, caressing her skin. She could feel it against her nipples, which hardened responsively to its touch.

Barefoot, she tiptoed down the stairs toward Paul's study. The central heating had gone off for the night and the house was cold. Outside the landing window she could hear the wind roaring in the branches of the horse chestnuts in the drive, tearing off the last of the six-fingered leaves. It was a clear night. Already the lawns beneath the stars were silvered with frost in spite of the wind. She put her hand tentatively on the latch of the door and listened. Inside the room all was silent.

She could feel the skirt of the nightdress stirring slightly in the draft, the silk whispering against her legs. Taking a deep breath, she raised the latch and opened the door.

The room was in darkness save for the lamp, which threw a pool of bright light over the desk where Paul was sitting. There were no papers before him, just an empty blotter, the blotting paper crimson in the lamplight.

He looked up at her blankly.

"I'm sorry, Paul. Are you working?" she asked tentatively.

"I am." He stared at her expressionlessly, his hands lying on the desk in front of him.

She swallowed nervously. "I wondered if you were coming to bed?"

"Later. I'll sleep in one of the spare rooms so as not to disturb you."

She felt a sharp pang of disappointment. "Paul, I'm sorry—"

"So am I." Sitting where he was on the edge of the bright pool of lamplight he could barely see her in the darkness by the door. If he noticed the nightgown, he gave no sign. "Good night, Clare."

Wordlessly she turned away.

Paul sighed. He glanced down at the blotter and slid from beneath it the page of figures at which he had been staring when he heard her opening the door. If the market went up sharply over the next ten days there was a good chance of recovering most of his losses, and if the Carstairs Boothroyd shares doubled he could really come out smiling. However, to be sure, he needed the money from Duncairn.

Back in the bedroom, Clare stood for a moment leaning against the door. The old house was never completely silent. The timbers creaked in the wind, the trees outside moaned, and the radiator ticked once or twice as it grew cold. She was utterly alone. Even Casta had deserted her, preferring to stay with Julia and the promise of midnight biscuits high in the attic bedroom. The house might have other people in it, but her bedroom and her bed were empty.

Her hand was on the key before she realized it, locking the door against the silence. With only the slightest hesitation she went to the drawer and took out a candle. After lighting it, she turned off the bedside lamp and stood for a moment staring at the single flame, her skin prickling with fear. The darkness of the shadows in the corners of the room seemed suddenly very threatening, but she hesitated only a moment, then slowly and deliberately she walked around the candle in a circle; she raised her right hand and made the sign of the cross in the air, then she sank to her knees before the flame.

Chapter Twelve

Alice was standing, her hand on the door handle, staring at Isobel who was sitting on a stool by the table. "You don't want it!" she repeated, her voice husky with shock.

"No. I don't want it." Isobel stood up wearily. "Have you not realized yet, Alice, that I do not want a child! The last thing I need is a charm to bring one! Keep it. If ever you marry your Sir Henry you may have need of it yourself." She picked up the small leather pouch from the table and pressed it back into Alice's hand.

"B-but I had thought you prayed for a child," Alice stammered. "It is four years since you miscarried; I thought you were desperate to conceive."

. Isobel gave a hollow laugh. "Oh, Alice, dear. If you only knew! No, I am not desperate to conceive. I thank the gods daily that I am barren."

"And the potions? The potions Mairi makes for you—they ensure your barrenness?" Alice's eyes rounded in horror. "I thought they were to help you bear a child! Isobel, what if Uncle John should find out!"

"He'll never find out." Isobel shivered. He had her watched now, day and night. She knew that. He was losing patience with her. Perhaps he even suspected what she did. Only his preoccupation with the war had saved her. From what she wasn't sure.

Here at Scone they were together more than she liked, sharing this dark bedchamber in the sprawling, ruined palace burned by King Edward three years before and now only partly rebuilt.

The conference of loyal Scottish lords had dragged on. They still met in the name of King John Balliol, and now he was free of his imprisonment, but he was an exile in France. Still Scotland had no real leader. And still the Bruces and the Comyns feuded.

The previous autumn Robert Bruce, Earl of Carrick, had led the defense of southwestern Scotland against the English, but by the time a truce was finally declared at the end of January, when the winter weather set in at last and made further fighting impossible, he had made up his mind. Patriotism could not be served by reestablishing John Balliol on the throne. For the time being he would, as far as the world was concerned, stop fighting in the name of King John Balliol and come into Edward of England's peace.

Lord Buchan had seemed almost unsurprised when Robert broke the news at Scone. "I have always mistrusted him. He's a timeserver and a traitor at heart." He stormed into the chamber with scarcely a glance at Alice, who quietly slipped out of the door behind him and left him alone with Isobel.

Isobel went back to her seat. The name of Robert Bruce still had the power to make her mouth go dry with longing and her heart beat faster at the thought that he was nearby, possibly under the same roof at that very moment.

"He thinks only of his English lands and protecting them!" Lord Buchan walked restlessly to the window and leaned against the ornate stone sill. Behind him the sunlight threw a pattern of colors onto his mantle through the stained glass. "We need his support for Scotland, goddamn it! Loath though I am to admit it, he is a good general. The men follow him. This feud with the Comyns is crazy! It will destroy Scotland."

"You speak as though the feud were of his making. Can you not understand that he will not accept John Balliol as his king?" Wearily Isobel looked up at him. She sighed. "He believes that his father should be king."

"Ah, yes. Could I have forgotten that I speak to the Bruces' greatest champion!" Buchan's face twisted into an ugly smile. "Lord Carrick's father. A weak fool! And no one knows it better than Lord Carrick himself. In all seriousness he cannot expect Scotland to support any claims for that one!"

"But Scotland would follow Lord Carrick himself."

"Would she indeed?" Lord Buchan looked down at her

grimly. "Well, she will not get the chance, particularly if he declares himself Edward's man. If ever you do see him alone, madam, and I think it unlikely that you will"—he gave a cruel smile—"I suggest you use whatever influence you have over him to persuade him to follow John Balliol, or he will find himself branded a traitor when the war resumes. Scotland will not forgive another lapse of loyalty." He pushed himself upright. "I go now to speak with Badenoch and my brother and de Soules in the council chamber. I suggest you stay here and pray that Lord Carrick sees the error of his decision before it is too late!"

She sat for several minutes in the small shadowy chamber after he had left, using the silence to compose herself. It was so rare to find herself alone and unwatched. Slowly she stood and walked across to the window. The room was in one of the few corners of the palace to have escaped King Edward's wrath. It still had its glass windows, its carved oak ceiling, its embroidered hangings. The room was full of warm color, beautiful in its way. Normally she would have enjoyed it, run her fingers over the hangings, tracing the pictures, reveling in the stories they told, but today they made her feel hot and trapped in a long-dead world. How could Robert betray Scotland again? Suddenly making up her mind, she turned and ran to the door.

With both hands on the heavy ring handle she dragged it open. One of Lord Buchan's men lounged outside. He stood to attention.

Fixing him with a haughty stare, she commanded him to follow her. He did so unquestioningly, escorting her through the passages and courtyards of the old building, parts of it rubble now, part being rebuilt by order of the Guardians of the Realm in the name of their exiled king.

She walked on purposefully, looking, or so she told herself, for Alice.

Lord Carrick, business over for the day, was practicing in the makeshift lists at the side of the north park, riding at the quintain with his brother Nigel and his friend James Douglas, watched by quite a crowd. Alice was among them.

Isobel joined her silently. "Is your uncle here?" she whispered.

Alice looked surprised. "No. He's closeted with John de Soules and some of the others in the palace. I came to watch the practice for the tournament." She smiled at Isobel. "Have you decided who you are going to give your favors to tomorrow?"

Isobel glanced in spite of herself at the group of horsemen gathered at the far end of the ground. Robert, mounted on a gray stallion, had removed his helm. He held it beneath his arm as he joked with his companions, resting easily in the high saddle as the horse shifted restlessly beneath him. Near him an esquire held his lance. Isobel looked away, her heart thumping. It was the first time she had seen him for many months.

"I doubt if I shall be asked," she said with a wistful smile. "It is for you unmarried ladies to bestow such gifts on the clamoring knights."

Alice giggled. "But even a married lady may have a champion, and I think I know who yours will be. His eyes have been on you since you arrived."

Isobel started guiltily. "I can't think who you could possibly mean—"

"No?" Alice looked back at the men on the field. Pages had brought refreshments and some of the knights had now dismounted. Robert, however, still sat his horse. As both women watched he bent to take the goblet that was being passed to him and then raised it in a gallant toast in their direction before throwing back his head and quaffing the wine.

"Can you still not guess?" Alice whispered at her elbow. "There can be few on this field who can't."

Isobel could feel her face coloring violently. "You do talk nonsense, Alice." She turned abruptly back toward the palace. "I came to look for my husband. As he is not here, I shall return to our room. You may remain with the lady Alice." She flung the instruction over her shoulder at the man at her heels. Without waiting for him to protest, she began to walk quickly away.

Robert saw her leave. He caught up with her in a shaded

garth, surrounded by partly dismantled cloisters behind the ruined abbey. They were alone.

"Isobel—" He caught her hands. "I could not believe that at last Buchan had brought you with him. I see you so seldom now." In spite of himself he found he thought of her often, and yearned for her too. He missed fighting with her! He missed her wit and her courage, her beauty and the passion he sensed simmering below the surface whenever they were together. The thought of her with Buchan was something to which he had sternly to close his mind. "There is so little time," he went on. "I leave tomorrow after the tournament for my lands in England."

Isobel disengaged her hands reluctantly. "I heard. You are going to betray us, Robert—"

"No!" She heard the agony in his voice. "No, my dear. What I am going to do, I do for Scotland. It is not right to allow the men of Scotland to die year after year to keep a puppet on the throne, and I cannot stand by and see it continue. I have fought at their side; I have seen my own men die for that cause. Scotland can be free only under her rightful king." His eyes were burning with zeal.

"Your father?" Isobel said bitterly. "No one will support your father. The country mocks him. Who will ever forget how your mother threw him across her saddle and abducted him—"

"That was a lie!" Robert was white with fury. "Have you lived so long with the Comyns that you would believe malicious gossip like that?" He turned away from her. "But you are right," he went on suddenly. "The country will not fight for my father, and he would not want them to. He doesn't have fire in his belly as grandfather had." He paused. "But they will fight for me, Isobel. One day they will fight for me, and I will win!" He swung back to her and caught her shoulders. "You must believe that, sweetheart. You must. I leave for England tomorrow, but my heart will remain here. I have plans, friends—" He looked around hastily, his eyes scanning the shadowy corners where the new-budding herbs were slowly forcing their way through the tumbled rubble toward the spring sun. "God's blood! I shouldn't tell you, Buchan's wife, but always you have been a daughter of Fife first and his wife only second, and I know you above all others can keep secrets. Trust me, Isobel. Remember, whatever happens, whatever I appear to do, I keep faith with Scotland."

"I do trust you," she whispered. She was trembling slightly. "When shall I see you again?"

He shrugged. "Maybe not for some time." He hesitated, staring down into her face. "Dear God, Isobel, if only you were my wife. What battles I could win with you beside me." He could have bitten off his tongue; he had never meant to let her hear those words.

"I am beside you, Robert!" Suddenly she could bear it no longer. She threw her arms around his neck, clinging to him. He had removed his mail, but he still wore the padded gambeson over his tunic. Burying her face in it, she bit back her sobs. "Each time I see you it is worse. I want you so much—"

"Isobel—" Gently he took her wrists, trying to push her away, but she clung harder. "I could be at your side, Robert. I would ride with you. I could come to England with you; anywhere. Please—" Her veil was pulled from her head as his arms slid around her slim waist and he saw the dark shimmer of her hair. The heavy braids were coming unfastened. "Let me come with you, please."

Her lips were close to his, her wild, dark eyes beseeching. He could feel the longing sweeping over him, the urgent desire flooding through his veins. Half of him wanted to hurl her away from him, stride back through the archway into the sunlit world of men. The other half wanted to push her down onto the soft new grass among the stones and make her his own at last.

Feeling his uncertainty, Isobel gave a little sob. Raising her face to his, she pressed her lips against his, closing her eyes. They stood together for a long time unmoving, then slowly Robert's hand moved to the neckline of her gown beneath the saffron mantle. As his fingers found her breast Isobel felt a wild surge of excitement. With a little moan of pleasure she pressed herself against him, kissing him passionately, feeling her lips tracing the outline of his nose and eyes and his cheeks. As he stooped, his mouth against her throat, she gave a small animal cry, her legs weak beneath her, oblivious of the danger, oblivious of everything save her need for this man. He would have taken her there, on the grass, in the open, as forgetful of the danger as she was had not the abbey bell behind them suddenly begun to ring a slow mournful summons through the afternoon sunshine. It was the hour of nones.

With a groan he drew away from her. "Holy Virgin! I was forgetting. Forgive me, Isobel. My love for you blotted out everything else! Forgive me."

For a moment she didn't move, stunned by the suddenness of his move, then, dazed, she closed the neck of her gown and pulled her mantle tightly around her once more. "What did you forget, Lord Carrick?" She meant to sound carefree, amused, but her voice was still husky with passion. The words caressed him, and she saw him shiver. She hugged herself exultantly. Behind them the bell rang on, summoning the remaining brothers into the ruined abbey.

"I forgot you cannot be mine!" His voice was harsh. "It is as well I leave tomorrow, or I might have to tell Buchan to lock you away from me." He gave a wry smile. "He'd do it happily too, I think." He raised his hand to her hair for a moment, then let it fall again.

Behind them a figure was standing in the shadowy archway. Robert stepped away from her abruptly and the figure vanished, but not before Isobel had seen it too. She clenched her fists with a tremor of panic, fighting the longing that swept over her as he moved away from her, and with as much dignity as she could muster she drew back. There was a physical pain somewhere beneath her ribs that made it hard for her to breathe, and she found that she was fighting back her tears. "Must you go?"

"You saw. Someone was there."

"It was no one. Please, Robert—"

"No, my love. I have to go. This was madness, you know it as well as I."

"Madness?" She stared at him for a moment, blindly, then without another word she turned away from him and fled back through the arch into the bright courtyard. Behind her the abbey bell stopped ringing.

The palace was full of people. Her head low, her veil drawn across her face, she hastened back toward the Buchan quarters, not noticing the slight figure who watched her, slipping out of sight into a doorway as she passed.

Mairi was in the bedchamber waiting for her with three of her other women. There was no sign of Alice.

"Lord Buchan is looking for you, my lady," Mairi said in a whisper as Isobel slipped into the room.

"So?" Isobel stared around, half blind in the darkness of the room after the bright sunlight outdoors. She pulled off her veil, conscious that her hair was in disarray beneath it. Seeing Mairi's raised eyebrows, she blushed. "Find a comb, if you please, instead of standing there staring. I was at the lists, and it is windy." Her voice was unaccustomedly harsh.

"Of course, my lady." Mairi rummaged in the coffer at the end of the bed. She jumped as the door swung open and stood back with a curtsey, the comb in her hand, as Lord Buchan appeared on the threshold.

"Leave us." He gestured the four waiting women toward the door with his thumb, then he turned to his wife. "Did you give Lord Carrick my message?"

Isobel could feel her face burning. "No, my lord. I haven't spoken to him—"

"Don't tell me you haven't been with him, madam. You were seen." He pulled off his gauntlets and unpinned his mantle, flinging it down over a joint stool near him. "You fawn and cling to him like a common whore! Were the circumstances different I would kill Lord Carrick for what he did today, but he can wait. As matters stand, perhaps I shall kill you."

Isobel went white. "My lord! I only said good-bye to him. He is my cousin—there was no dishonor."

"No dishonor? When you allow your cousin to fondle your breasts and you kiss him like a drab! You have a strange idea of honor." He gave a cynical laugh. "Were you trying to dissuade him from his new marriage? You thought perhaps to be a widow soon with your games of poisons, and available for him yourself?"

"His new marriage?" Isobel echoed faintly, not even noticing the implied accusation as the shock of his words sank in. "Lord Carrick is to marry again?"

"Did you expect him to stay single? He needs sons, just as I do." He emphasized the words deliberately. "Oh yes, to seal his newfound friendship with the King of England, he is to marry Lord Ulster's daughter. Richard de Burgh is one of Edward's closest followers, and his daughter, as I'm sure you have heard, is reputed to be one of the most beautiful women in Ireland." He waited a moment, allowing the information to sink in. "Surely he told you his plan? He is riding tomorrow to meet his bride."

Somehow she managed to control her face. He must not see how hurt and angry she was. He must not have the satisfaction of knowing how much she was in pain. After walking slowly to the coffer, she picked up the comb Mairi had thrown down, and slowly she began to draw it through her tangled hair. Her face was white and her hand shaking as she dragged it through the half-unraveled braids. "What Lord Carrick does is of no concern to me," she said at last. "He had no reason to tell me. We merely exchanged farewells."

"Farewells indeed." He gave a cruel smile. "I intend to see to it that you do not see him ever again. Tomorrow at dawn you will return to Buchan, and you will remain there."

"But, my lord, the tournament—"

"You are not going to the tournament. Do you expect me to watch my wife give her favors on the field to Lord Carrick in front of all the people of Scotland? Do you expect me to watch her fix her eyes on him, cheering when he wins and going so prettily pale when he loses? Do you expect me to hear myself called cuckold before the whole world?" He was speaking very quietly. "No tournament, Isobel. You go back north under guard and you remain there." He turned and picked up his mantle again. "And don't try to leave this room until it is time to set out. I am going to place a man-at-arms at the door."

She stood quite still for a few seconds after he left, stunned, then, picking up a hooded cloak, she flew to the door and pulled it open. He had not locked it, and to her relief there was no one there yet. In his hurry and his anger he had come to their room without an escort, and now he had to go to look for one of his men to stand guard over his wife.

Without thought of the consequences, she ran out into the courtyard and toward the lodgings where she knew she would find Lord Carrick's quarters.

He was standing in his room, dressed only in his tunic and hose, dictating a letter to a clerk while his servants busied themselves with his belongings.

There was a gasp of astonishment as she flung back her hood. "Go! I have to speak to Lord Carrick alone!" she commanded.

Without a word the men dropped what they were doing and fled.

Robert's face had darkened. "Are you out of your mind? To come here, like this, to my chamber? Isobel, for the love of the Holy Virgin, go! Now. Quickly! I'll call my men back—"

"No!" She stood with her back against the door, her hands outstretched as if to hold it shut. "Tell me it's not true. Tell me you're not going to marry the lady Elizabeth!"

"I see!" He scowled. "So that's what this is all about. Who told you?"

"My husband told me. Tell me it's not true!"

"It is true." He was becoming impatient. "I have to marry again. It is five years since my Isabella died. My daughter needs a mother and I need sons."

"And is it true she's beautiful?" Her voice had risen in her despair.

"Yes." He gave a boyish smile. "She's beautiful."

"More beautiful than I?"

Robert shook his finger at her. "Such a vain question, my love. She is different. She is burnished copper, you are black, glittering coal. You are as beautiful as each other. I make no distinction in degree!"

She could see he was teasing her and it hurt. "But you chose to marry her."

"Isobel. You are married to another. Besides, we are within the prohibited degree. Your mother was niece to my grand-mother. Even if you were free we could not marry without dispensation. But you are not free. Our love is forbidden by God and the church, and forbidden by man. You must forget me." He came toward her and, reaching past her, took hold of the door handle. "Leave. Quickly. I have to try to find my men and stop them from talking. Your husband must not find out you were here." Gently he pulled her hood back up over her hair. "Go, Isobel, now."

She stared at him, her eyes brimming with tears. For a moment neither of them moved, then she turned and ran from the chamber.

She did not go back to the Buchan rooms. Instead she walked out toward the deserted lists. The wind was soft. It lifted her hood and stirred her hair, cooling her hot face. Beneath her gown her body was cold. She was shivering. In the shadow of the hedge there was a clump of gillyflowers clinging to a pile of old stones, and she stood staring at the sweet-smelling orange and yellow blossoms, trying to blink away her tears. The field, which so recently had been crowded and noisy as the men practiced at the quintain, was completely silent.

She knew they would come for her. She knew her husband's patience was exhausted, but she didn't care. She was numb. Had she, in her heart, prayed for Lord Buchan to die, so she might marry Robert? Did she feel betrayed because she had thought he would wait until she were free, as she would have waited for him, forever? She had never allowed the hope conscious form—or had she? She had dreamed. She had dreamed of freedom, of love, love with the lean, muscular frame of Robert of Carrick, never the knotted, scarred body of her husband. And she had dreamed of passion and of tenderness, not of cold-blooded rape.

Three figures were making their way toward her across the field. Two men-at-arms and one of her husband's knights. She could see the golden wheat sheaves on their surcoats in the sun.

Slowly she turned toward them, her fists clenched, her

head high. Every nerve and muscle in her body was tensed to run, but she would not flee. She was the Countess of Buchan, daughter of the ancient House of Duff. And never again would she let anyone see her cry.

David and Gillian Royland lived in an elegant Georgian manor house on the far side of Great Headham from Bucksters. Surrounded by acres of newly plowed, hedgeless fields, the house, with its neat gardens and manicured lawns, seemed desolate and isolated in the dusk as Paul drove up the long, treeless drive with its post-and-rail fencing. The house front was in darkness save for three identical uncurtained rectangles of light on the first floor. The senior Roylands were taking tea in the drawing room.

Paul sat down on the very edge of one of Gillian's matching armchairs. "I've come about Clare."

David and Gillian exchanged glances. She turned. "Is what your housekeeper told David the truth, Paul?"

"Sarah wouldn't have lied to you."

"Then, God help you, Clare needs to see a psychiatrist! I can't believe it of her!"

"But Clare has always had an unstable side, in my opinion, Paul," David said. "Her whole attitude is iconoclastic."

"You only say that because she makes fun of your title, darling," Gillian put in. "After all, her grandfather's went back centuries."

Neil's apartment on the top floor of the restored tenement on the Canongate in Edinburgh's Royal Mile looked out over the Calton Hill and beyond it toward the Forth. Kathleen was standing at the window, eating yogurt out of a carton. Behind her the apartment was deserted. Neil was, she presumed, as always, at the office, even if it was a Sunday. How could she have imagined he would be anywhere else? She glanced around. Books and records overflowed the shelves on every wall. The old sofa, battered, the springs broken, was covered with a brightly colored rug. Like his office, it was the perfect reflection of his personality. Every corner betrayed his love of Scotland, his love of nature and of music, his lack of interest in creature comforts. She sighed and walked through into the kitchen. It was meticulously tidy, but the facilities were minimal.

After heaving her suitcase onto the double bed in Neil's bedroom she opened it, first taking out a pack of cards wrapped in a black silk scarf. The dresses she had worn for the concert in Belfast were crumpled now and shapeless. She tossed them onto a chair and then, catching sight of herself in the mirror on his chest of drawers, she stopped. She despised makeup, but she used it more and more now to hide the sudden transparency of the skin around her eyes, the shadows, the lurking thickness in her jawline. She drew her hair tentatively around her face. Her hair was still glorious— glossy, long, thick, and black. She smiled. A hairdresser for a tint was something she would have despised two years ago. So much older than Neil, she had to be very, very careful.

She glanced down idly at a pile of papers on the chest of drawers. Topmost was the information on Paul Royland. On the second page his two addresses were listed. Someone had underlined the second, in Suffolk, and written in pencil: *CR spends most of her time here.*

CR. Clare Royland.

"Hello! When did you get back?" Neil had come in without her hearing him.

Kathleen turnèd to face him with a forced smile. "Only about half an hour ago. I was going to give you a call. I thought you'd be in the office."

Neil gave her a perfunctory kiss. "I was. So, how was Belfast?"

"It was all right. Did you go to London?"

He nodded.

"And did you see Paul Royland?"

"Only from a distance. We didn't speak. He didn't recognize me."

"From what I hear on the news, the oil lobby is backing down on prospecting new sites these days. These people will be withdrawing their offer for Duncairn any day now."

Neil frowned. "No. You're wrong. Sadly, it's the easy-access onshore sites that are in no doubt at all. It is comparatively so cheap to extract the oil."

"You went to see her, didn't you?" She couldn't stop herself; the words were out before she had realized it.

Neil frowned. She could tell instantly she had irritated him with the question.

"If you mean Clare Royland, the answer is yes, I went to see her. Briefly." Turning away, he stood with his back to her, hands in pockets, staring out at Calton Hill.

"What was she like?" She couldn't resist asking.

"Arrogant." He hunched his shoulders uncompromisingly. "She ordered me off her land."

Kathleen's lips twitched imperceptibly. "And did you go?"

"Of course."

"Forget her, Neil. She's not worth it. This whole thing is going to blow over. You should be concentrating on real concerns like pollution and the disposal of nuclear waste. You're letting this Duncairn business distract you from where you're really needed."

She threw herself down on the bed. "I've got a gig in London next week. Are you going to come down with me?"

"I wish you wouldn't call them gigs!" Neil didn't turn. "It makes you sound like a cheap pop star."

"I'm a folk singer, Neil."

"And a damn good one." He sounded irritated. "You don't take yourself seriously enough. You have class. You should exploit it."

Kathleen raised an eyebrow. "So class is important to you suddenly, is it?"

Neil turned at last. He looked at her gravely. "Don't knock it, Kath."

"That cow has really got to you, hasn't she! But you still intend to shoot her down in flames, I hope."

"I haven't changed my mind."

Emma was sitting on Clare's bed. "Paul says he's going back to town this evening," she said cautiously. "Things aren't going too well, are they?"

Clare shook her head.

"Why don't you come up to London tonight, with us?"

"I don't want to, Em. I think it's better if Paul and I see as little of each other as possible for a bit."

"So, are you still going to Scotland?" After kicking her shoes off, Emma lay back on the lace bedspread.

Clare shrugged. "Of course. I'm just not sure when."

"You haven't let that man scare you off!" Emma sat upright indignantly. "Clare! It's none of his business. Duncairn is yours."

"I know." Clare sighed again. "I have to be here anyway for a couple of things this week, and Paul and I have a dinner in town on Saturday. Once that is all over, there's nothing on my calendar for a week or so. I think I'll go home for a bit then. Mummy says Archie will be away for ten days, so it would be a good time to go. I can't stand it when he's at Airdlie."

"Will you tell Paul where you're going?" Emma was watching her closely, her arm bent to support the back of her neck so she could peer at Clare across the room.

"I don't know. I expect so. He can hardly stop me from going to my mother's, can he?"

They were both silent for a moment.

"He went to see David and Gillian this afternoon, on his own," Emma went on cautiously.

"I know. He's obsessed with that trust business."

"Has he lost money in the stock market? Peter thinks he must have."

Clare shrugged again. "He's put money in the firm, apparently. He says they're having trouble. . . ."

Emma frowned. "BCWP isn't having problems, Clare."

"Are you sure? Pete may not have wanted to tell you."

"No." A look of pain crossed Emma's face. "No. You're right. He might not have. He hardly talks to me these days at all, as I'm sure you've noticed. And when we do it's trivia, or about Julia."

"Does he know about this other man?" Clare asked quietly.

Emma smiled. "He's not another man. Not like that." She looked away. "He's just a nice person who's fun to go out with."

"So you're seeing him again?"

"I expect so."

"When Peter's away?"

"Probably."

They looked at each other for a minute, then Clare gave a rueful smile. "You're lucky."

Emma's eyes widened. "I thought you adored Paul!"

"So did I." Uncomfortable, Clare stood up. She turned and glanced out of the window toward the gravel drive where Peter had appeared in the dusk with Julia and Casta. She could see the cold, blustery wind lifting Julia's hair on the collar of her parka. For a moment she watched them in silence, then she pulled the heavy curtains across the windows, blotting out the darkness. "But he's changed, Em. He's changed completely. Sometimes—" She hesitated. "Sometimes he frightens me."

Paul left Bucksters at six, throwing his briefcase and suits into the back of the green Jaguar. Half an hour later the Cassidys too were on their way.

In the drawing room Clare looked at a sketch Julia had done for her. Bright and cheerful, it lay on the coffee table, flamboyantly signed across the bottom "Julia Victoria Cassidy."

There are ways of helping you to conceive a child! Alice's voice was so distinct she looked around, startled. *I know some spells; I'll tell you, if you like.*

A log crackled and subsided in the hearth, sending a shower of sparks up the chimney. She was alone.

Sitting down abruptly on the sofa, Clare put her head in her hands.

There are many things you can do. Bathe in mare's milk, wish on a child-getting stone, carry bistort and an acorn and hang a necklace of pine cones around your neck.

Was the voice in her head or in the room? In panic Clare folded her arms over her head, pressing her elbows against her ears, trying to block it out.

Lady's mantle and the juice of sage and roots of ginger rubbed to powder. They will all help you. Wear your necklace

*of cones, and give your husband a stone of beryl to reawaken
his love. . . . It works, it always works. . . .*

The voice faded to silence. For a long time Clare sat unmoving, then slowly she lifted her head and looked around
the room.

A long time later she stood up, her movements slow and
dazed, rubbing her hands against her cheeks as she went
almost unwillingly to her writing desk. She pulled open one
of the little drawers and took out a small box. Inside, wrapped
in cotton wool, was a ring. It had been her father's. She stared
at the huge flat-cut stone with its engraved crest, then
slipped it on her finger, raising it to the lamplight, where the
pinkish red shone dully on her hand. Someone had told her
once that it was a beryl.

Slowly she rehearsed Alice's list of remedies in her mind.
Most of them would be easy to find. Pine cones, ginger, sage.
Such simple things. Did she seriously think they would help?
What of the other things? Mare's milk? Bistort? What was
bistort? And where would she find a child-getting stone?

After shutting the drawer, she sat down again by the fire,
staring at the ring. If only she could ask Alice herself. But
another visit to the past would have to come later, when
Sarah was safely in bed and the house, outside her own
locked door, was in darkness. She did not intend to be caught
at her meditation again.

Paul let himself into the house on Camden Hill with a sigh.
He switched on the lights and drew the curtains in the drawing room before going straight to the drinks cupboard and
pouring himself a hefty half tumbler of malt whisky. He put
his attaché case on the sofa beside him and opened it. The
contract note lay on the top.

He did not touch the papers. He drained his glass, then he
topped it up again. The knock at the front door caught him
halfway across the room with the bottle in his hand. Cursing
softly, he put it down.

"Hi." Diane Warboys was standing on the doorstep. "I
hope you don't mind my knocking, Paul, but I saw your light
on as I drove past, and I suddenly remembered we hadn't

discussed the plans for my Brussels trip. I did want to talk to you about it."

Paul stared at her, trying to focus his mind. Reluctantly he stood back and allowed her to precede him into the living room. "I've only just got back from Suffolk. You'll have to forgive me. Would you like a drink?"

Diane nodded. She glanced around, noting the suitcase in the middle of the floor and the attaché case open on the sofa. With a smile she accepted the glass of neat malt whisky. "Clare's upstairs, is she? I don't want to intrude—"

"Clare is still in Suffolk." He frowned. "Look, I don't want to hurry you, but I have quite a bit of work to do this evening.

"Of course. Oh, Paul, I am sorry, it was thoughtless of me to drop in like this." She paused as an idea struck her. "Look, if you're on your own, why don't you let me go downstairs and rustle you up some supper. I saw where Clare keeps things when I was here the other evening. It's the least I could do after disturbing you, and it would let you get on."

She stepped a little closer to him. He could smell her perfume, mingled with the whisky. Distastefully he moved away.

"No, Diane. Thanks, but I've been eating all weekend. I don't want any food. As for the plans for your trip, my secretary will be handling all those arrangements. Perhaps you could have a word with her in the morning." He turned away.

Diane sat down. She glanced down into his open briefcase, and her eyes widened as she stared at the document lying there. From where she was, she could see that the contract note came from Magnet Charles Plimsoll.

Behind her Paul turned. He put down his glass with a thump on the table and walked over to her, pushing the lid of the case closed. "Diane, I hate to hurry you, but—"

"Then don't. Don't hurry me." She stood up slowly. She was very close to him as he stood, his hand on the lid of his briefcase. "Why don't we work later?" she whispered. The undiluted malt whisky had gone straight to her head. "Let's have another drink and relax now, shall we?" Her hand crept up the front of his pullover. He could feel her nails plucking at the strands of blue wool somewhere near his shoulder. Her face was very close to his. "You must be exhausted after your long drive," she went on, her voice husky. "Let me fix you another drink—"

Paul stepped sharply away from her. "I think you'd better go," he said curtly. "I have a great deal to do."

"I could help you—"

"No!" Irritation snapped through the superficial politeness of his tone. He picked up her coat and held it out to her. "I'll see you at the office in the morning."

Diane colored. "Sure. I get the message. No dice. Fair enough." She snatched the coat from him. "It was worth a try, don't you think?"

Paul could have lightened the moment with a smile; perhaps saved her face a little with a compliment. He did neither. After ushering her out, he closed the door behind her with a sigh of relief, then he went back to his case. He pulled back the lid and stared inside. Dear God, the contract note was on the top! Had she seen it? She would know that BCWP was handling the Carstairs Boothroyd takeover. And she would realize he was dealing on inside information. Sweat broke out on the back of his neck as he stood staring down at the sheet of paper. Suddenly his hands were shaking.

Rex opened the front door himself. He was in his shirt sleeves.

"Hello, Uncle Rex." Diane stepped inside. "Can I cadge a drink?" She smiled at Mary who was sitting by the window, sewing in the light of the spotlight trained on a bowl of green plants just behind her shoulder. Diane sat down and then turned back to Rex. "Do you remember you were asking me about Paul Royland? The bastard just tried to make a pass at me." She was already slightly drunk as she took a gulp from the glass Mary passed her.

Rex looked quizzical as he stretched out once more in his chair. A copy of the *Wall Street Journal* lay crumpled at his feet. "I thought that would have pleased you, honey," he said calmly.

She shook her head, coloring slightly. "He's an attractive

man and I admit I did like him but this was horrible." She almost believed it herself already. "I went to his house to give him some important papers. He was working there alone because Clare's in Suffolk still, and he asked me in and—" She took a deep, dramatic breath. "Well, never mind. It's over. You remember, you were asking if he was a good business-man, Rex? Well, he isn't. He's completely screwed himself." She gave a bitter laugh. "He's about to go down about three-quarters of a million on the Carstairs Boothroyd issue. He must have bought them after he heard that they were being taken over, and I happen to know the deal fell through on Friday night." She paused and gave him an impish smile. "He hasn't paid for them yet!"

Rex stood up. His whole body was suddenly taut with ex-citement. "Are you sure?" Irrelevantly it flashed through his mind that now he wouldn't need to see Emma Cassidy again.

Diane nodded. "I saw the contract note in his case. He's got to find that money by settlement day, and I think he is al-ready badly down on the Hannington deal. A lot of people lost over that, and I'm pretty sure Paul was one of them." She had seen the excitement in her godfather's face. It boded ill for Paul and that pleased her. He was going to regret turning her down. He was going to regret it bitterly.

She finished her drink and stood up unsteadily. "I must go. I'm sorry to drop in like this. To be honest, I was a bit shaken and I knew you were close."

Mary kissed her. "My dear, are you sure you're all right?" She eyed Diane's pale face and bright, almost feverish eyes in concern. She had smelled the alcohol on the girl's breath as soon as she had set foot in the room, and she knew the only reason for the visit had been revenge. She glanced at her husband whose face was alight with satisfaction, and she shook her head sadly.

"Before you go, Diane, honey." Rex tapped her arm. "Would you give me Paul Royland's home telephone num-ber? In fact, give me both his phone numbers, if you will." He was tense with excitement.

Diane smiled. "Of course, Uncle Rex. As it happens I know them both by heart."

Chapter Thirteen

Kathleen, bleary-eyed, staggered out of bed and followed Neil into the kitchen the next morning. He looked at her thoughtfully as she hunted for a cigarette.

"I'm going up to Aberdeen. Jim Campbell and I are drawing up a schedule of protest meetings about onshore oil prospecting. We're calling a press conference, demanding a public hearing, lobbying the planning committees, perhaps organizing one or two publicity stunts—making sure we get as much press coverage as possible to get public opinion on our side."

Kathleen stared out of the window, her eyes narrowed. "Is this onshore oil in general, or Duncairn in particular?"

"Both." Neil sat at the kitchen table. "Have you any bookings this week?"

She nodded. "Four days here, then a week in London. I might go back to my place, Neil, while I'm doing that. I'll only annoy you by coming in every morning at dawn, and if you're going to be away some of the time anyway—"

"Good idea." Neil was absently thumbing through a pile of papers. "I'm going to the office early. What are you going to do today?"

She could tell he wasn't interested. "I'm going back to bed."

"Great." He grinned up at her suddenly. "Sorry I can't join you, but I've got to get to work."

"I'm sorry too, Neil." She forced herself to smile back, but inside she felt a shiver of fear. She had been away a week, but he hadn't fallen on her when she came back. In fact, they had not made love for a month. And now another week or two would go by. She went into the bedroom and slammed the

door. Her suitcase lay open on the floor. She drew out the
cards and, climbing onto the bed, sat there cross-legged,
setting out the spread on the rumpled blankets in front of
her.

One by one she examined the cards. The two of cups reversed meant quarrels and misunderstandings and separa-
tion, and next to it the seven of swords presaged a journey
and a permanent move. She bit her lip. As always *she* was
there. The other woman. This time she was the Queen of
Swords. She swept the cards together in a heap and sat for a
moment staring down at the pile of disordered pictures, then
she reached into her dressing-gown pocket and pulled out a
folded piece of paper. It was a page torn from an old maga-
zine. As she unfolded it, she stared down. Her hands had
begun to shake.

> Among the guest at the funeral of the Hon. Margaret Gordon
> was Mrs. Paul Royland, great-niece of the deceased.

She had folded and unfolded the page so often now that
the paper had cracked and discolored, now on the point of
disintegration. The blurred photograph showed Clare, elegant in a black coat with a black fur hat on her head. The
unhappiness in her face captured by the photographer could
not hide the beauty of her features or the fineness of her
bones.

Kathleen sat staring down at the picture for several minutes, then, scrunching it up in her fist, she hurled it across the
room. "God rot the bloody bitch!" she whispered under her
breath. She scrambled to her feet and stubbed her cigarette
out angrily in a saucer on the bedside table. She stood for a
moment staring toward the window, her face contorted with
pain, then she turned back to the bed and hurled herself
facedown onto it, burying her face in the pillow.

Paul met Rex for a breakfast meeting at the Savoy. While
the waiter poured his coffee, he sat back, unfolding his napkin with exaggerated care. Inside, his pulse was racing. "We
have a reached a decision. My wife has agreed to sell." He

could feel the sweat running down his back. "I will have the necessary documents by the end of the week."

"Make it Thursday at the latest." Rex suppressed the wave of excitement that shot through him. "I have to fly to the States on Friday. I want a legal entitlement to take with me."

Paul closed his eyes. "You shall have it."

Rex smiled. "I'm glad you made her see sense. I know you can use the money." He shifted slightly in his seat, leaning with his elbow on the table. "You've gone down for quite a lot, I hear." His tone was casual.

Paul stared at him. "I'm not sure I know what you mean," he said stiffly.

"No?" Rex smiled. "Carstairs Boothroyd. I gather the deal is off. The shares will plummet today. Anyone in heavily is going to lose a packet." He helped himself to a slice of toast and began to scrape a thin film of marmalade onto it; no butter.

Paul winced at the sound.

"It might have been a good deal," Rex went on thoughtfully. "But young Carstairs was not the man to see it through. There is no confidence in him in the City. I'm surprised you didn't know."

Paul looked up. His hands were shaking. "What the hell are you suggesting?"

"Nothing, Paul, nothing at all." He used Paul's Christian name with a long, slow drawl to it. "Let's just hope you can get yourself out of this mess before anyone starts putting two and two together and wondering if you were using inside knowledge." He laughed. "If you were, it should have been a little more thorough, shouldn't it!" He suddenly looked up and held Paul's gaze. His face was hard. "Thursday, Royland, or the deal's off!"

Clare was sitting at her desk in the drawing room at Bucksters. She stared dispiritedly at the pile of letters in front of her. No real letters. No fifteen-page effusions from friends, no notes from anyone she cared about. Her life was empty, useless, and flat. What good was she to anyone? If she had been able to have a baby, things might have been different.

She would have had a purpose then, a reason for living. She would have had someone to love her. . . .

Miserably she reached for the phone.

Archie Macleod answered. "I will fetch your mother for you, Clare." She could hear the coldness in his voice. "How are you?"

"Fine, thank you. I'm fine." She forced herself to smile at the wall.

There was a long pause, then she heard the receiver being picked up. "Clare, darling, how are you?" her mother asked.

"I'm all right." Clare steadied her voice with an effort. "Mummy, can I come up and see you?"

There was a pause. Clare knew her mother was speaking to Archie. "We are a little busy at the moment, darling. Perhaps later—that would be lovely. . . ."

"Good. Yes." Clare's eyes filled with tears again. "I'll call you soon, then, okay?"

"Do that, darling. Love to Paul."

Clare stared at the receiver blankly. Her mother had hung up; they had exchanged no more than a couple of sentences.

She stood up abruptly. "Casta!" She glanced at the fire. The fresh crackling logs were only just getting warm. She could see the white heart of the flame that was the firelighter. But no Casta. Suddenly panicking, she pulled open the door and ran out into the hall. The house felt very empty. "Casta?" Her voice echoed up the black oak staircase and around the galleried landing. "Casta?" She ran toward the kitchen and flung open the door. The light was off and the room was silent save for the tick of the old clock in the corner. No lights at all, and the stove was only gently warm. "Sarah?" Clare looked around frantically, her voice rising in desperation. "Sarah, where are you?"

But she already knew. The car was gone from its customary position in the side yard; Sarah's basket wasn't in its usual place near the door, and Casta's leash had disappeared from its hook. They must have driven into Dedham or Colchester, leaving her alone.

Clare felt miserable. She must talk to someone. Slowly she went into the drawing room and picked up the phone, dial-

ing Emma with a shaking hand. The phone rang on and on in
the silence.

Clare stood, the receiver pressed against her ear, staring
out at the rain. The bright Michaelmas daisies in the bed
outside the windows were turning into brown knots on the
end of their stems.

She counted ten slow rings, then she hung up. For a moment she sat staring down at the phone, then wearily she
stood up and went back to the fire. She knelt in front of it to
throw on another apple log before staring into the flames.

In the twentieth century she was alone and depressed and
it was raining. In the thirteenth it was sunny. Without warning, Isobel had returned.

Isobel had offered no resistance when she was led back to
her room, nor when her husband ordered an escort to take
her, by force if necessary, to Ellon, up the long road through
the eastern flatlands toward the windswept, sea-bounded
northeastern fastness that was Buchan. She swathed her face
in her veil and rode, shoulders back, head erect, at the head
of her husband's men. Two women had accompanied her,
Mairi and one of the Buchan ladies, Meg. She had not seen
Alice again.

Ellon Castle, the administrative seat of the earldom, rose in
the bright sunlight on the banks of the river Ythan, the dowager's standard flying from the highest tower as Isobel reined
in her tired horse at last. Behind her the escort of men-at-
arms halted. She lifted her veil, staring toward the teeming
burgh that clung around the castle in the small encircling
fields of new green corn, feeling the warmth of the afternoon
sun on her face.

She stood for several minutes, her horse hanging its head
from exhaustion after the long ride. The men around her
made no move to hurry her; the officers of her husband's
household had mixed views on their countess. The constable
of Duncairn thought her a spoiled child; the steward of the
vast Buchan estates was deeply sympathetic to her; she was
universally popular among the servants and lesser folk. The
chaplains of the various castles, and her husband's youngest

brother, the priest, Master William Comyn, detested her. She was that thing most despised by the church, a beautiful and disobedient wife; she had failed to provide her husband with an heir and wherever she went men's heads turned, attracted by her unconscious allure, her slim, elegant figure, her natural vivacity, and her bold eyes. They all knew she hated and feared her husband; many of them knew she loved another.

Master William was waiting with the Dowager Countess of Buchan in the great hall of Ellon Castle when Isobel at last urged her horse in over the bridge and dismounted wearily in the courtyard. She kissed them both dutifully, her heart sinking at the set expression on their faces.

Master William curtly dismissed her attendants and then everyone else in the hall. Within minutes it was completely empty save for the three of them. A thin, tall man, he resembled his brother only in the dark, hirsute Buchan coloring. His face had a cruel asceticism that showed no tolerance of others. There was a letter in his hand.

"Your husband has written to me about you, my lady," he began without preamble. "What he says disturbs me beyond measure." He threw the parchment down on the table. "He asks me, with the help of our mother"—he bowed sparely in the direction of the dowager—"to supervise your stay in Buchan and see to it that these matters are investigated in the greatest detail."

Isobel stared at him. Her mouth had gone dry. She felt herself swaying slightly, overcome with weariness after the long ride, but somehow she managed to remain upright. "I don't know what you mean!" She forced some asperity into her voice. "What matters?" She stepped forward and snatched up the letter, unfolding it with shaking fingers.

It was written in her husband's own hand, sealed with his private seal. She read it with mounting horror. He had accused her to his brother of sorcery and witchcraft; of procuring the death of her baby and avoiding conception by mortal sin. It also accused her of the intention to commit adultery, and of the committing of that sin in her heart and in her body with an unnamed man in the palace of Scone where the act had been witnessed. She read the letter slowly, aware of the two sets of eyes fixed on her face. Her chest was tight with panic, her stomach turning over with fear. The crabbed black script blurred and jumped before her eyes. Desperately she fought to control her features as at last she refolded the letter and threw it down.

"My lord and husband was drunk when he wrote this," she said flatly. "I deny absolutely everything of which he accuses me. If he believed me capable of killing my child, why has he waited so long to accuse me? You cannot believe it!"

Master William walked slowly away from her, toward the end of the dais. He folded his arms deliberately inside the sleeves of his fur-trimmed gown, then he turned and walked back. "I do believe it. In your latter actions, madam, your behavior has been neither secret nor even discreet, and as to the other, infinitely graver matter of the death of your unborn child, your husband first made his suspicions clear at the very time that you miscarried. Perhaps he waited, in his love and mercy, in the hope that you might show signs of repentance and the desire to rectify the terrible deed in providing him with another son, but that too you decided to avoid with yet another sin."

"You have shamed the House of Buchan!" Elizabeth de Quincy hissed suddenly. She sat down heavily at the head of the long table and rested her hands, fists clenched, on the scrubbed oak boards. "I thought marriage would change you, Isobel. I thought John could tame you and make you into a good and virtuous wife. I was wrong." She shook her head slowly. "He has been too lenient with you, hoping to win your trust and affection. More fool he!" Her voice was laden with venom. "We will not make the same mistake."

"Indeed not." William's voice was silky. "Mother Church, in her wisdom, has ways of dealing with women such as yourself. Harsh ways, perhaps, but we must all accept punishment if it is for the good of our immortal souls." He smiled at her suddenly, then his eyes hardened again. "The woman from Mar. It was she who taught you the ways of sorcery, I understand. She who procured for you the articles you needed for your spells? Your accomplice? She shall be questioned about her role in this affair."

"No!" Isobel was shaking her head. "No, you're wrong!" She was frantic with fear, but already Master William had shouted for the guard and she found two men-at-arms at her elbow. "Mairi knows nothing," she cried desperately. "All she has taught me are a few simple remedies for the flux. She is no sorceress! For pity's sake, you do not believe that?"

But Master William had turned away.

She rattled the door desperately, but it was still locked fast. There was no sound outside the chamber. Looking out across the castle walls and over the heather-thatched roofs of Ellon toward the southern hills, Isobel could feel her fear turning back to anger. How dare they lock her up! She, the Countess of Buchan, in her husband's castle. She had been brought no food and nothing to drink. There was no sign of Mairi, which frightened her. Isobel was certain of the woman's total loyalty. She would never betray her—and yet something in Master William's implacable expression had terrified her. If only Mairi would come and they could talk.

Twice more she paced up and down the small chamber, then she went back to the window. She was high up in the keep, under the roof, and there were no sounds from below. No sounds at all, as the long spring afternoon drew on. In the end, exhausted, she threw herself down on the floor, sitting against the wall, her arms wrapped miserably around her knees, her eyes closed. She was desperately afraid for Mairi.

They came for her at dusk the following day as the golden glow of sunset turned to a deep misty green across the land. She was escorted back into the great hall, which was illumined with a hundred flaring torches. On the dais sat a line of grim-faced men, at the center of the line, Master William. There was no sign of the dowager. Isobel stopped, looking around, her stomach churning with fear, but the men on either side of her pushed her on. The unusual silence, the expressions on their faces, the layout of the chairs and stools, so they all sat facing her in a semicircle as she was led to the center of the hall, all filled her with apprehension. The man on her right halted her at last with a restraining hand on her arm.

Isobel stared at her brother-in-law, hoping her fear did not show. Slowly he stood up.

"Lady Buchan, as you know, grave charges have been laid against you by your husband. It has fallen to me, in my capacity within the church, to inquire into these charges and make judgment as to whether or not you are guilty. Specifically you are charged that by the use of sorcery you procured the death of your unborn son and that you have since that time used the blackest of arts to prevent the conception of another child, to ensnare men, and to endanger the life of your husband."

"That's not true!" Isobel burst out desperately. "For the love of the Holy Virgin, I swear to you, it is not true!" She shook off the restraining hand of the man at her side and took a step forward.

Her mind spun and dodged desperately, but nothing could change the fact that it *was* true. She had practiced the magical arts. She had made spells, used the herbs the way Mairi had taught her, but how could they know? How, when she had been so careful? She steadied herself desperately, her eyes fixed on her brother-in-law's hard face.

"I have done nothing that was wrong!" She repeated.

"We have a witness against you, my lady." William's voice was triumphant now. He turned his head toward the door and nodded sharply. "Bring her in," he called. He looked back at Isobel, folding his arms, and he waited in silence.

The eyes of every person in the crowded hall were directed toward the door as it was pushed open and two of the Buchan men-at-arms appeared. Between them they were dragging a woman. They brought her to the edge of the semicircle of seats and pushed her down onto her knees where she knelt gibbering with fear. It was Mairi.

Isobel gasped. She made as if to step toward the other woman, but at once hands grabbed her arms and she was held where she was. "In the name of God, what have you done to her?" she screamed.

Mairi's face was a mass of swollen, bleeding bruises. Her

hands were wrapped in dirty clouts soaked in blood. Her gown was torn to the waist. Even huddled as she was Isobel could see the cruel bite marks of the pincers on her breasts.

She thought she was going to faint. She could feel the room beginning to spin. Her body was soaked with sweat beneath her shift. Desperately she tried to free herself from the hands that were holding her so that she could go to Mairi, but they gripped her firmly. She was powerless to move.

"Mairi . . ." she whispered. "Mairi . . ." It was all she could manage to say.

William stepped toward the edge of the dais. He looked down dispassionately at the broken woman. "I want you to repeat what you said to your interrogators," he said slowly. "I want you to repeat every word."

For a moment the silence in the huge echoing hall was absolute, then with an enormous effort Mairi raised her head. "It was her," she said. Her voice was barely recognizable as she lifted the bloody lump of rags that was her hand and pointed at Isobel. *"A thighhearna bheannaichte! A Mhuire mhàthair!* It was her fault. She told me the things to get. She told me she wanted to kill the bairn. She hated her husband. She wanted him dead so she could marry Lord Carrick!" Her mouth was bleeding. Where her two front teeth had been there were two gaping black holes in her gums. Her words were so muffled they were barely comprehensible. "It was her, *Iseabail* . . ." She waved her swathed hand with an effort. "It was her!" She was sobbing pathetically now. For one moment her eyes, swollen and bloodshot, met Isobel's enormous, terrified ones, then she collapsed moaning into the dried heather that covered the floor. Blood and spittle were drooling from her mouth.

"No!" Isobel whispered. *"No!"* She was slowly shaking her head. "No. . . ."

"Yes, my lady." William's voice was strident over the prostrate body between them.

"You've tortured her," Isobel accused desperately. "She was forced to say those things—"

"She spoke freely and at length to the men who questioned

her," William answered coldly. "God sees to it that the truth emerges in the end."

"God!" Isobel stared at him wildly. "God would not do this! God would not allow such vile cruelty, such bestiality!" And yet, even as she spoke the words, she knew that he would. After all, it happened all the time.

William was smiling. "Allow me to be the interpreter of Our Lord's intentions, madam," he retorted. "Our Lord, whom, I believe, you do not recognize. You invoke the goddess in your prayers. Many have heard you. That is heresy." His eyes glittered.

"No," she whispered. She was mortally afraid. "No. That's not true. I swear it—by Our Lord's Blood! By the love of the Holy Virgin!"

"Enough, my lady!" William held up his hand. "For the sake of your immortal soul you must be purged of your heresy."

"No!" She was struggling desperately now, but the two men held her with ease.

"At dawn," he went on, "your servant will burn—" He broke off as Mairi raised her head. Her eyes had suddenly focused.

"No! *Obh obh!*" she screamed. "You said if I confessed I would be spared—"

"I said you would be saved." William looked down at her without expression. "Your soul will be saved. Purged by the blessed fire—"

Mairi was struggling to stand, but her legs would not support her. Frantically she was trying to drag herself away, but her broken body would not obey her.

Isobel pulled desperately against the men who held her, but it was no use. She was forced to stand as, at a nod from William, Mairi's guards seized her arms and half dragged, half carried the woman away.

William did not even bother to look after her. He waited until the sound of her desperate screams were muffled by the closing of the heavy oak doors, his eyes fixed on Isobel's face.

At last he spoke. "Do you wish me to hear your confession before I pass judgment on you?"

Isobel stared at him. She was beyond fear. "Do you intend
to burn me too then, Master William?" Her voice was cold,
heavy with scorn. It seemed to be coming from someone else,
someone outside herself. "Does my husband know the powers you have taken for yourself—the power of a bishop at
least?"

He gave a slight smile. "He knows, my lady." He turned
and, walking back to his seat, slowly sat down. "This is an
ecclesiastical court, madam. I sit here with the authority of
the church and of the bishop. It is your husband's men who
will burn that wretch tomorrow, not mine. But it is my jurisdiction that decided her fate and it is my jurisdiction that will
decide yours." He folded his arms. "You will not burn. We will
bring you back to the church, my lady, and we will bring you
back to obedience to your husband. I believe a long and
bitter penance will show you the error of your ways. Tonight
you will spend in the chapel here, praying for your soul and
for the soul of the woman who is to die because of you." He
paused, letting the word sink in. "Then tomorrow you will be
taken to the castle of Dundarg, at the northern edge of
Buchan, and there you will serve your penance until such
time as my brother or I feel you are sufficiently repentant."
He nodded curtly to the men on either side of her and at
once they began to drag her from the hall.

The dowager was waiting in an anteroom near the chapel.
With her were two of her serving women and two menser-
vants. She was deaf to Isobel's pleas. Her face sour with dislike, she ordered the two men to hold Isobel while the
women removed her gown. They took her headdress and
veil and her shoes and stockings, leaving her shivering in
nothing but her shift, then they led her to the chapel.

At the door Master William was waiting. In his hands was a
wooden cross on a leather thong. Solemnly he hung it around
her neck. Isobel pulled away from him sharply.

"You are not a holy man, William Comyn. You are evil,
vindictive, and vengeful," she cried. She took hold of the
cross and pulled it off. "This is not the symbol of forgiveness
and mercy. It means vengeance and torture!"

She flung it away from her, and there was a gasp from the

men and women around her. William gestured to one of his attendants to pick up the cross. He stood for a moment staring down at it, then he looked up at her.

"It seems we must save you in spite of yourself, my lady," he said softly. "Fetch a cord!" he ordered curtly. "Bind her wrists behind her."

The dowager frowned, but she said nothing as one of the priests tied Isobel's hands behind her back. When it was done William stepped forward once more and hung the cross around her neck a second time. He looked down at her and she thought she saw him repress a smile before he turned and led the way into the chapel.

It was lighted by only four candles. Two burned on the altar, another by the reserved sacrament, and a small light flickered before the statue of the Virgin. As the priests and men-at-arms filed into the chapel behind them, the light from the torches they carried lighted the chapel suddenly, making the shadows leap and contort over the high painted walls, filling the place with harsh moving shapes.

In front of the altar William stopped and genuflected, then he turned to Isobel. "We shall leave you here to contemplate your sins," he said. "There will be a guard on the door, so do not attempt to leave."

The sound of the door closing died in the echoes and the candles dipped and flickered. Isobel stood without moving as the shadows regrouped and steadied. Above the altar the figure on the high carved crucifix seemed to writhe, the hands and feet straining against the reddened wooden nails that held them in place. She stared up at it in terror.

The cord that bound her wrists was firmly knotted. The man who had tied it had not pulled it cruelly tight, but however much she tried she could not free herself. Slowly she backed against the wall, staring terrified at the shadows. The chapel seemed to be full of accusing eyes. Beneath the shift she was naked and she was shivering violently. The flagstones were icy beneath her bare feet. Outside the huge Gothic arch of the window the sky was black. Staring up at it, she thought with another pang of fear of the dawn, and at last she began to pray.

She didn't sleep. Sometimes she prayed, sometimes she walked up and down, feeling the weight of the wooden cross banging against her breasts. One by one the candles went out. As the last one guttered and flickered out, leaving the chapel in total darkness, she sat down on the altar steps, leaning against the fluted granite pillar, and slowly the tears began to slide from beneath her lids as she tried in vain to tuck her frozen feet beneath the hem of her shift. When she looked toward the window again she could see a faint grayness behind the colored glass.

It was almost daylight when they came to collect her. She was led, bound and barefoot as she was, outside the castle wall and down toward the meadow beside the broad, fast-flowing river. There the stake had been prepared.

Mairi, when they carried her to the stake and tied her there, was barely conscious of what was happening. Pain and fear had numbed her until she was floating in and out of consciousness. She did not see them piling the faggots and bundles of dried heather around her torn skirts, nor feel the heavy roughness of the wood against her legs. She wasn't aware of her bruised breasts naked before the silent staring crowd, nor did she see Isobel.

High above, the small mackerel clouds were tinged pink in the brilliant blue of the sky. Rooks were cawing in the beech trees around the castle, and the light was coming to the meadows and to the sandy dunes along the river, touching the gorse with gold. The air was cold and fresh.

Standing next to Mairi, the executioner, a burning brand in his hand, waited for the signal from the black-robed priest. He might have turned her over to the secular authority of his brother for the execution of the punishment, but William Comyn intended to direct its every moment himself. And he wanted to watch Isobel's face. She was white as a sheet. Her shift of fine lace-trimmed lawn, cut low at the neck, gave her no protection against the chill of the early morning or against the eyes of the curious people of Ellon. Where the hem trailed in the long grass with its haze of speedwell it was transparent with moisture, clinging to her legs. His eyes moved speculatively to the swell of her breasts with the heavy wooden cross hung on the rough leather thong and he smiled. Her hands were still tied behind her back.

He nodded abruptly to the man with the brand who pushed it at once into the faggots at Mairi's feet. William saw Isobel catch her breath in agony. Her face was white.

As the smoke began to rise and spread the people standing too near the fire moved away sharply. Mairi, too weak to struggle, had begun to sob in terror as a man climbed swiftly onto the unlighted faggots behind her. Quickly and silently he fitted a noose around her neck. The church in its mercy had decided she should be strangled before the flames could reach her.

Clare came to herself screaming. After scrambling to her feet, she ran to the windows and flung them open, then plunged out onto the terrace. It had begun to rain. The garden smelled of wet earth and dead leaves, and there was a sudden cold bite to the wind. She staggered to the low wall that bounded the terrace and sat down on it, pushing her hair out of her eyes. She was trembling all over. She closed her eyes and lifted her face, feeling the cold wet rain cleansing it, running down her cheeks, soaking her hair. Beneath her hands as she clung to the stone she felt the crawling tendrils of scarlet creeper. She shredded them and then stared uncomprehendingly down at the handful of crushed red leaves in her lap. Indoors the telephone had begun to ring.

Paul was standing at his desk, staring as usual out of the window as he held the receiver to his ear, frowning. Behind him Henry was sitting in the leather armchair, ankle on knee, a folder of papers in his lap. Paul drummed his fingers impatiently on the desktop. It was the fourth time he had called. At last Clare picked up the receiver her end.

"Clare?" Paul frowned. "Where the hell have you been? I've been trying to call you for half an hour! Look, are you going to be in tomorrow morning? I've asked Henry to drop by with some papers for you to sign. The accountant needs them back as soon as possible."

Clare was clutching the receiver so tightly in her wet

hands that her knuckles were white. She was dripping all over the carpet. Behind her the windows still stood open, and the rain was pouring down, splashing into the room off the terrace. "Of course."

"He'll be in a hurry." He slammed down the phone. She had sounded vague and withdrawn. Lonely. He should have told her to come to London to buy a new dress for the chairman of the Stock Exchange's party on Saturday. He should have asked her how she was. Instead all he had felt on hearing her voice had been blind rage that her stubbornness was putting his career at risk. It was her fault, entirely her fault. Without her stupidity and selfishness he wouldn't have needed to gamble on Carstairs and his damned takeover in the first place. Without her refusal to sell Duncairn he could have paid off his debts and had change to invest. He ran a finger uneasily around the inside of his collar. He had lain awake all night thinking about Clare and the money. The time of persuasion was over. She had to be forced to sell.

The solution, when it came to him, had been staggeringly simple. He would trick her into signing over everything to him. If Henry took the papers down she would suspect nothing. He knew Clare. She wouldn't bother to read them. He had a wad of tax forms for her anyway. One more would go unnoticed, particularly if she was sufficiently distracted. And he knew Henry. Henry Firbank would give his right arm to sleep with his wife. Well, perhaps he was about to get lucky.

Chapter Fourteen

Henry arrived at Bucksters at ten forty-five. It was a bright, blustery day, the brilliant golds and russets of the trees flaming against a vivid, cloud-streaked sky. Clare met him at the door. She was wearing an emerald-green cowl-necked sweater and a full, calf-length skirt that emphasized her slimness. Her eyes were shadowed and she looked very pale.

"Would you like to walk around the garden for a bit? You must be fed up with sitting in the car." It was as if she could not bear to be inside the house another minute. Without waiting for his answer she came out onto the gravel, leaving the front door open behind her.

Obediently Henry put down his briefcase and followed her onto the grass. She wasn't wearing a coat. The wind caught her hair, tossing it wildly, and flicked her skirt, showing a froth of white lace beneath it. Henry licked his lips.

She had had the nightmare again that night. The fear; the desperate attempts to escape; the eyes peering at her. She had awakened at five in the morning, her nightgown drenched with perspiration and, shaking, had groped her way to the window and pushed it open. It hadn't been a cold night. The wind was fresh and salty as if it had come straight from the sea, and she had sat there on the window seat watching the day creep imperceptibly over the fields. She was terrified that now she was awake Isobel would come back to her. She had no wish to return to that violent, terrifying world, ever. As dawn broke at last, crimson and green streaked with copper, she had realized with another pang of fear that she had at least four hours to wait until Henry arrived.

"It is beautiful out here." Henry followed her toward the

beech hedge that hid the pool. "You and Paul are lucky to have such a lovely home."

"Yes, aren't we." Her smile was artificial, brittle; unlike her.

Henry felt a wave of compassion. "You look tired, Clare. Is everything all right?" He took her arm gently and to his dismay he saw there were tears in her eyes.

She shook her head. "I didn't sleep well, that's all. Take no notice." Gently she pulled away from him. "It's good of you to drop in with the things for me to sign. Paul is always pushing great sheaves of papers at me and they always seem to be urgent." She smiled wanly. "We'd best go inside."

She knelt in her favorite position before the fire with the brown manila envelope Henry had taken from his briefcase. Inside were about a dozen sheets of closely typed or printed paper. Clare glanced at the top one and pulled a face. "From our accountant. He's always wanting me to sign boring forms." She unscrewed the cap of her fountain pen and signed with a flourish.

Henry, sipping coffee, watched her from the sofa. When she reached the third document he frowned. "Don't you ever read them to see what you're signing?" he asked, reaching for a biscuit from the plate on the table near him.

Clare shrugged. "Not usually. They're so boring. Paul just marks the places."

"You should, you know." Henry shifted uncomfortably in his seat.

"Do you know what these are?" She looked up at him.

"Of course not. The envelope was sealed. It's just that no one should ever sign anything without reading it carefully." He grinned wryly. "Sorry, am I being boring?"

"I suppose you are right." Making a face, she drew her legs up beneath her and began to skim through the sheaf of papers. One document near the bottom of the pile consisted of a cover sheet on which was marked a space for her signature. Beneath it, also marked by Paul with pencil crosses, were spaces for the signatures of two witnesses—Henry and Sarah Collins. Putting down the rest of the pile with a frown, Clare opened the document and began to read.

Henry saw her face whiten as she read the two closely typed pages. She came to the end at last and looked up. She appeared stunned. "So, you couldn't bring yourself to go through with it!" she cried. "What stopped you?"

Henry clambered to his feet, his own face white. "I don't know what you mean—"

"Don't you? Look at this! I would have signed it!" She held out the folded paper to him and shook it in front of his nose.

Henry caught it with difficulty and began to read. In it the signatory—Clare—made over all her property and the administration of all her affairs, voluntarily, to her husband, now and for the foreseeable future. Signed, witnessed, and dated, it would have had the weight of a legal document.

Henry read it again, slowly, feeling himself going cold all over. Carefully he put it down and retrieved his coffee cup. He did not look at Clare. "I didn't know what was in the envelope. Paul just said they were important papers from your accountant. I thought it was a bit odd, asking me to do it, but I always like seeing you. I suppose he knows that. . . ." His voice trailed away.

"You know what this would have done?" She jumped to her feet. "It would have given Duncairn to Paul. It would have allowed him to sell it! He was trying to trick me!" Her voice shook. "I would have signed it, Henry. Why? Why does he want the money so badly?"

Henry swallowed. "I think he's in bad trouble, Clare." He could not bear to see her strained expression. Business loyalty was one thing, but this was quite another. Paul was behaving like a complete shit. "He's in over his head on a deal. It went bad and now settlement day is coming up. I shouldn't tell you this. I don't suppose he even knows I know. He owes a great deal of money, and I think he may have gambled again on some other shares using inside knowledge of a takeover that was being planned, and now they've gone down too. I suspect he needs to raise a lot of cash by early next month." He paused. "I'm sorry, Clare."

"Are you talking about insider trading?" She stared at him. "He could go to prison for that!"

Henry nodded grimly. "He's not been very clever about it;

I think quite a few people have guessed, and now that the deal has fallen through he's trying to raise money all over the place. He'll be in real trouble unless he can find the cash. Maybe—" He hesitated. "Maybe, Clare, you should bail him out." He looked away, unable to bear the sudden bewildered pain on her face. "It might be his only hope."

"To sell Duncairn?" she echoed. "But why? Why did he do it? We had so much money. He didn't need more. What about his shares in the firm? He said BCWP was in trouble. He said he's lost money there—"

Henry shook his head. "Our first-year profits after the merger weren't as good as we'd hoped, but things are okay now. His shares in the firm are all right."

"Then he could sell those."

Henry nodded slowly. "He could, but that would be the end of his career in the City."

Clare swallowed. Her mind was desperately darting back and forth, trying to find a way out. "And if I sell Duncairn, will that save his career?"

There was a long silence. Henry shrugged. "That depends how much it would bring, exactly how much he has lost, and how many people know about the way he's been setting up these deals."

Clare stared at him white-lipped. "You mean he might still be caught? Still go to prison, even if he has the money?"

"There's been too much scandal, Clare. Too many cases of insider trading in the last few years. The authorities won't let anyone get away with it now."

"Why didn't he tell me?"

"I don't suppose he wanted to worry you—"

"Worry me! I have been going through hell these last few weeks, knowing he wanted Duncairn sold and not under-standing why, knowing everything was going wrong be-tween us. I thought it was the fact that I couldn't have a baby—" Her voice broke suddenly and she turned away.

Henry put out his hand toward her, then lowered it again helplessly. "Clare, my dear—"

"He's put everything I care about in jeopardy!" she burst out suddenly. "Everything! I can't sell Duncairn! I can't!"

"You may have to, Clare." His voice was gentle. "He doesn't have anything else."

"But he does!" She spun around suddenly. "He still has the Royland shares. He must have. He can't sell them without offering them to his brothers and Emma first, and I know he hasn't done that. When his grandfather's firm went public they all got founder shares. They are worth about two million."

Henry sat down. "Then there's no problem about the money. If he's careful he could get himself out of that particular corner without touching your money!"

Clare closed her eyes. She was so pale her skin was almost transparent. Henry wanted very badly to go to her, to take her in his arms and hold her. Clenching his fists, he forced himself to stay where he was.

"You'd better sign the other papers," he said.

She nodded. After sitting down on a chair near him, she read each one of the papers and carefully signed them. The other document she folded up and put into her pocket before standing up. "Take the rest back to him, Henry. Don't say anything. For your own sake, keep out of it. I'm coming up to London tomorrow. If he wants to scream and shout, he can do it to me."

She watched as he put his briefcase on the backseat of his BMW. He kissed her lightly on the cheek, then he climbed in. He did not trust himself to look back.

Mary Cummin stared out of the condo window and sighed. She had become used to the view across Eaton Square with its majestic trees and the white-painted Georgian houses on the far side. Each time she crossed the Atlantic now it took a little longer to adjust. Was that advancing age? she wondered. She turned her back on the window and stood instead in front of the mirror, smoothing her white skirt down over her narrow hips. Her hair was glossy and immaculate, her face taut and youthful. She looked far less than her fifty-six years.

She glanced at the tiny diamond-studded watch on her

wrist and frowned. Rex was late. The meeting with the bosses at Sigma must be running over.

He came back at nine. She could smell the liquor on his breath. Rex threw himself down on the couch. His tie was already loose.

"They've screwed me, Mary! After all the fucking years I've put in, they've screwed me."

Mary sat down near him, shocked as much by the unaccustomed language as by the damp pallor of his skin. "What do you mean, hon?" Her voice came out as a whisper.

"They've kicked me out. Shown me the door. Fired me. Told me to take early retirement."

"Early retirement?" she whispered. "From Sigma?"

He nodded.

"Not go back to London?"

"No."

She stared at him, shocked into silence. No more London. No more apartment in Eaton Square. She bit her lip. She had dreamed for so long about the house on Martha's Vineyard: lovely, old, white-painted weatherboard, pretty yard, nice neighbors—oh, she could picture it clearly. But not yet. She wasn't ready for retirement yet.

They both sat for a while, each wrapped in his own misery, then at last Rex hauled himself to his feet. He reached for the decanter of bourbon and poured out two hefty measures.

She looked up blindly. "Why, Rex?"

"Because I've been ill. Because they say I've lost my grip. Because Doug and those bastards in the London office have been plotting against me. Because the price of oil is dropping and they don't need a full board executive over there, and if they do it is going to be Doug Warner, not an old has-been like me!" He drank the bourbon in one gulp. "They've vetoed any onshore prospecting in Britain next year. The applications for licenses are going to be withdrawn."

"You mean they won't be trying to buy Duncairn?"

"Nope." After setting down the glass with a bang on the table, he tore off his tie and threw it down. "Some other company will step in there and clean up."

"Paul Royland will be upset." Mary found a tissue and

dabbed delicately at her eyes. "He sounded like he needed the money."

"He sure did." Rex stood for a moment in front of the window. He parted the blind with his fingers and peered out into the darkness. "There's oil there, Mary. I know it. I've been in this business too long not to play a hunch like this. All those years out in the field before they put me behind a desk. I know. It's like tingling in the fingertips. I can feel it. There, under the ground. Godamn it! Those stupid crazy bastards are going to lose the best strike there's been in years!" He picked up the decanter again and refilled his glass before going back to the window.

"Will you get any money from Sigma?" Mary asked slowly. The whiskey was going to her head, but not so much she couldn't begin to think of practicalities.

"Oh, sure. A pay-off to ease their consciences, and a pension." He sighed. "And a month to go back, hand over to Doug, pack up the apartment, then that's it. After forty years in the business all I get is a kick in the ass!"

Mary stood up unsteadily. "It means we'll get time together at last, honey. We'll be able to buy the place we've always dreamed of on the Vineyard. Get some traveling in to places we always wanted to go while we're still young enough. Places where there isn't oil." She tried a not very successful smile.

Rex was gazing into the bottom on the glass. He didn't appear to have heard her. He dropped the blind and slowly turned back toward her. Like a man in a dream, he went to his briefcase, opened it, and took out his calculator. The blurriness had vanished from his face. Mary watched him through a haze of misery as he tapped numbers into the little machine.

"What is it?" she whispered.

He didn't answer. He sat down abruptly and pulled a sheet of paper toward him, jotting down a column of figures. Suddenly he was smiling as he pulled the telephone toward him.

"Who are you phoning, Rex?" Mary picked up the decanter and refilled her own glass.

He ignored her. He was already dialing. "Royland, is that

you? I'll be back in London on the sixth." He paused as Paul spoke on the other end of the line. Then slowly he smiled. "Good, but not good enough. The offer just went down by ten thousand. And if we don't sign on the sixth then it will go down again, my friend." He slammed down the phone.

"Rex?" His wife turned to face him, glass in hand. "What offer? What in hell are you talking about?"

"Duncairn." Rex pushed the sheet of paper in her face. "My ancestral home. I'm going to buy it myself!"

The bar at the Duncairn Hotel was packed. Neil looked around with some satisfaction as he climbed up on the stool, which raised him head and shoulders above everyone there, and lifted his hands in a gesture that eventually produced enough quiet for him to make himself heard.

"Ladies and gentlemen. First, I want to thank Jack Grant for letting us use the hotel for this meeting. It seemed the right place because here, more than anywhere, the changes that oil would bring to Duncairn would be felt." He looked around. He had their attention now. "As you know, there have been strong rumors that Sigma Exploration, one of the American-based companies operating out of London and Aberdeen, has made an offer to buy Duncairn—the hotel, the bay, the village, the castle. I myself went down to England a couple of weeks ago and spoke to Clare Royland, and she confirmed that an offer has indeed been made." He paused. The faces around him showed consternation, anger, polite interest, concern. It was his job now to see that every man, woman, and child at Duncairn felt the same thing: the absolute commitment to fight.

"Many of you knew Margaret Gordon personally. I know she came here often; she involved herself with Duncairn's affairs even though she didn't actually live here. She loved this place. Would she have wanted it sold?"

He loved this part. Speaking to an audience, cajoling them, winning them, whipping them into a frenzy, even this small taciturn group, fishermen mostly and their wives, a couple of farmers, one or two newcomers who had settled in the bay.

"The Gordons lived in the castle for four hundred years

until the English government dismantled it after the rebellion in '45, and after that they stayed here in their hearts." Neil kept his voice even. He knew just how to appeal to their patriotism, the Anglophobia that was so easily stirred in the Scots heart. "They never stopped loving this place. They kept faith with their ancestors. Margaret Gordon was as loyal as any of them!"

There was a growl of assent around him and he saw them nodding. Behind the bar Jack Grant was leaning against the wall, his arms folded.

"But Margaret Gordon made one mistake," Neil went on gravely. "She left the estate to her great-niece, Clare. Oh, as a child Clare came here often. She loved it here. She felt the ties that have bound her ancestors to this land for nearly a thousand years. But then she went away. She married an Englishman." He paused for effect. "She left Scotland and she forgot Duncairn. Margaret Gordon thought the inheritance would be safe with Clare Royland. But she was wrong; it was not safe." He looked around. "She has agreed to sell!"

There was a stunned silence, then a roar of dissent from the people crowded around him. Neil let the noise continue for a few minutes, then he raised his hand.

"It is true, my friends. I'm sorry. Now, you may wonder where I come into all this. I am here for two reasons. One is that I, like you, love this place." He paused. "I used to come here as a child; I went on coming here as a student." He grinned at them conspiratorially. "I used to camp on the cliffs and watch the birds, and on several occasions when I was doing that I met Margaret Gordon. The second reason is that now I am the Scots director of Earthwatch—the environmental group that is going to coordinate the fight against Sigma, the fight in which every one of us here tonight is going to take part." He paused as a ragged round of applause and cheering broke out, then he went on. "Now, I know that the first argument Sigma will produce will be that the oil will bring jobs and money to the area." He paused again. "I think we have all lived with oil in Scotland for long enough now to know that the people who get the jobs are not necessarily the ones who live here. The benefits the directors of Sigma will talk about are not the benefits that we here will feel. Only two lots of people will make money from the oil here: Sigma and the government in England. And only one individual will grow rich. And that is Clare Royland!" He took a deep breath in the silence that followed that statement, letting it sink in. Once he was sure it had, he went on. "And now—" He smiled at them again, the same special conspiratorial smile that seemed personally directed at everyone in the room. "Now I am going to open this preliminary meeting to the floor. Any thoughts or ideas you have that can help us in our fight are more than welcome, and to help inspiration the bar is now open and the drinks are on Earthwatch!"

He stepped down from the stool amid even more rousing cheers as Jack Grant unfolded his arms and stepped forward.

It was after eleven when the last person when home. Neil let himself out of the side door of the hotel and walked slowly down the gravel drive toward the brake of trees that sheltered it from the sea. Behind the trees sprawled the ruins of the castle.

It was a cold blustery night, very dark. There was no moon, and only one or two stars appeared between the threatening clouds. Neil found his way almost by instinct toward the castle and stood, his hand on the crumbling stone of the seaward wall, listening to the deafening crash of the waves on the beach. Every now and then he could see the white foam on a rolling breaker exploding in the darkness below him. The air was sharp with salt; the ground seemed to tremble beneath his feet with the power of the sea, the ground with its dark, hidden reserves of oil.

He sat down on the wall, the collar of his jacket pulled up around his face, his hair whipping around his ears, feeling specks of spray stinging his skin. The first round had been played, the first shots fired across Sigma's bows. He stared thoughtfully into the dark. The money would be a lure to the locals, he was under no illusions about that. They were hard realists. They might love Duncairn but they lived here. They knew the poverty that could come with a poor fishing season. They were not sentimental. He had to appeal to a deeper, more atavistic instinct than sentiment. Sentiment would do for the people of Edinburgh and Glasgow, for the readers of the English newspapers, and for himself.

He ran his hand over the cold stones with their wet film of spray. They belonged to Clare Royland and she belonged to them. Why, oh why, could she not feel it too?

There had been no word from Paul last night and none this morning before Clare and Sarah had set out for London.

She was sitting before the dressing table combing her hair when she heard the front door slam, then the murmur of Paul's voice as he spoke to Sarah. It was a full ten minutes before he came upstairs. He stood for a moment looking at her, then, after slowly taking off his jacket, he proceeded to hang it up in the closet.

"I hear the traffic was bad coming into town."

Clare swallowed. "It was heavy," she agreed cautiously.

"Chloe phoned last night," he said after a long silence. "She wants to meet you for lunch tomorrow. I told her you would unless she heard to the contrary tonight." He disappeared into the bathroom and she heard the water running into the basin.

She had been breathing deeply, expecting any moment a tirade of abuse. This cold politeness was more than she could bear. She stood up and went to the door. Paul was washing his face. Looking at his broad back and heavy shoulders, she felt an unaccustomed shiver of distaste. "Aren't you going to say anything about the document?" she said defiantly.

He paused for a moment over the basin, then he went on sluicing water over his face and neck. "What is there to say?"

"You tried to trick me into signing it!"

He straightened and groped for a towel. "In what way did I try to trick you?"

"You hoped I'd sign it without reading it!"

He scanned her face slowly. "If you are foolish enough to sign things without reading them, Clare, then you must expect occasionally to sign things that surprise you." He permitted himself a tight, humorless smile. "The surprise in this case seems to have been avoided." He pushed past her and pulled a clean shirt out of the drawer.

"You don't even bother to deny it?"

"Why should I deny it?"

She stared at him in silence. There was a cold hardness about him that frightened her.

"Paul, is it true you've lost money in the City?"

"Did Henry tell you that?"

"No. No, not Henry. Is it true?"

"I have to find a large sum of money by settlement day, certainly."

"When is settlement day?"

"The seventh." He spoke curtly.

"And if you don't pay then?"

"I will probably be able to get some extra time, but not much."

"And then? What happens then? Are you in real trouble, Paul? Is it true you've been insider trading?"

He looked at her with withering contempt. "Clare, you don't even know what that means! You know nothing about the City—"

"I know enough, Paul." To her surprise she felt completely calm. "I also know that you could cover yourself by selling the Royland shares. There is no need to sell Duncairn."

She was watching his face in the mirror as he stood with his back to her tying his tie and she saw the muscles around his jaw tighten. His face was white. "I cannot sell the Royland shares, Clare."

"Why not?"

He turned to face her. "Because there is a condition that I have to offer them to Geoffrey and David before putting them on the open market."

"So?" She sat down on the bed.

"Do you think for one moment I would let them know I am in need of money?"

"They already know. You've been trying to break the children's trust, remember?"

"The children!" He spat out the word. "Of course. The children. All the Royland grandchildren."

Clare clenched her fists. "Paul, please—"

"Please? Please what? You can't give me children, and you

won't give me Duncairn." He swung around to face her. "You are useless, Clare! A barren wife with no loyalty!" He turned back to the mirror.

Clare stared at him. "That is not true." She felt completely cold.

"Isn't it?" He peered at himself in the reflection. His handsome face was pale and expressionless. He turned back to her. "If you're ready we'll go down. Sarah has cooked us dinner and there is just time for a drink first."

Clare looked up at him in disbelief. "I'm not hungry."

"Then you must force yourself to eat. There is no need for Sarah to be upset. We will not discuss this any further." He looked at her thoughtfully for a moment. "You have been under a great deal of strain in the past few weeks. It's beginning to show. I think perhaps you should see a doctor."

Clare stood up. "I don't want to see any more doctors, ever. I'm perfectly all right."

He smiled. "Are you?"

They dined in almost total silence. After dinner Clare excused herself and went upstairs to the bedroom. For a long time she sat on the end of the bed, staring into the distance, clenching her fists. She could not bear the atmosphere downstairs; she did not want to be near Paul, yet up here, alone, she was afraid.

Isobel was near her, she was sure of it. She glanced around the room apprehensively. She did not want her; did not want to see what terrible things were happening in the past—did not want again to smell the burning flesh, see the cruel faces of the ogling crowd. Exhausted and trembling, she climbed into bed. Eventually, sleep came and neither Paul nor Isobel appeared.

Chapter Fifteen

Mary refused to go back to London with him.

"You're crazy! Do you know that? All our savings, Rex! What about the house on Martha's Vineyard?" There had been tears in her eyes when she said it. "What about our plans?"

"Screw our plans!" He was drinking heavily again, every now and then doubling up in pain as he clutched at his stomach where the ulcer throbbed and burned. "This is special, Mary! The ancient castle of the Comyns—my ancestors, for Chrissake!"

"Your ancestors!" Mary's voice was scornful. A daughter of the *Mayflower* herself, with a pedigree to prove it, she sounded pitying. "You and your Scottish ancestors, Rex! All the genealogists said to you was that the name Cummin *could* have come from Comyn! That's all, Rex!"

"I'm a direct descendant, Mary!" He pressed his stomach uncomfortably. "And I'll prove it. The genealogists are getting there—"

"Getting where? They've managed to go back barely a hundred and fifty years! There's another four hundred or so missing!" Usually she encouraged him with his dream, supporting his quest for his roots, massaging his ego with remarks about his aristocratic bearing. The sudden acid hurt and astonished him.

"They know my family came over from Scotland—"

"So did about a quarter of the population of North America!" she retorted tartly. She was not going to grant him even an ounce of hope. "If you go ahead with this, Rex, I'm leaving you."

He had stared at her. "Mary, honey—"

"I mean it, Rex. I'm not going to Scotland."

"But you'd love it."

"I would hate it." She said it with great energy. "Be realistic, for heaven's sake. You are talking about a ruin! A few old walls on a cliff in the coldest part of Europe! To rebuild your castle would cost millions of dollars, and you still couldn't do anything about the climate!" She shivered ostentatiously in spite of the carefully controlled seventy degrees in their apartment building—no higher, no lower, whatever the season.

Rex walked into the bathroom and found his bottle of Maalox in the cabinet. "I'm not going to change my mind, Mary. I'm going to buy it! It'll be all right, you'll see."

"I won't see, Rex. I won't be there to see." She said it so quietly that in the bathroom he didn't hear her.

Alone in the London house, with Sarah and Casta out visiting Sarah's sister, Clare paced through the rooms, fighting her loneliness and fear. She did not want to go back into the past again; she would not meditate.

When she heard the crash of the door closing in the empty house she looked up, startled, thinking it must have come from upstairs. But it was an oak door, a heavy door—the door of the chapel at Dundarg.

She had not looked for Isobel; Isobel had come looking for her.

At first Isobel hadn't minded the hair shirt. She wanted to suffer; she wanted to atone. The long ride north in the hot sun, bareback on the bony horse, her head uncovered, her flesh naked beneath the harsh prickling shift they had made her wear: She deserved it all. She could feel the perspiration trickling down between her shoulder blades, the raw itching bumps where the fleas had bitten her, the sharp agonizing pricks as they went on biting. Through every town and village she was paraded slowly, the earl's wife, the repentant sorceress, conscious of hundreds of eyes watching her. Some onlookers were pitying, some jeered.

They rode on north, through the Forest of Deer, then

followed the Ugie Water, skirting the foot of the Mormond Hill. Isobel was scarcely conscious of the watching eyes by then. Her mind was numb, her body a fiery mass of sores. Every step of the horse dragged the rough cloth across her back and shoulders again, and when at long last they reached Dundarg they had to help her dismount. Master William Comyn stood before her and looked her up and down. There was a glint of satisfaction in his eyes as he met her gaze. "The Lord will look with mercy on your contrition," he said.

Isobel straightened. For a moment the rebellion returned —the urge to retort, the longing to spit in his eye—then it retreated again. She would not give him the excuse to use force on her again. She would not give him the pleasure of binding her wrists—for it had given him pleasure, of that she was sure.

Stiffly she walked before him into the shadowy keep. It was cold inside, after the heat of the sun. She shivered gratefully, welcoming even the ache of her bare feet on the flagstones beneath the coarse heather that was strewn over them.

In the chapel of St. Drostan, musty with cold incense, she knelt obediently before the altar, unaware that she was alone. The attendants who had followed her from Ellon had dispersed. In the bailey the knight who had headed the escort pulled off his helm and handed it to his esquire. He stooped over the horse trough, reached for a dipper, and poured scoop after scoop of water over his head.

The door of the chapel opened and closed softly as Master William entered the dark sanctuary. He walked silently on sandaled feet to stand behind Isobel. In his hand there was a leather-thonged scourge.

Lifting her face from her hands, Isobel glanced at it, then raised her eyes to his with undisguised scorn. "So. Do you intend to whip me as well in the name of your God?"

William glance at her disdainfully. "That is your husband's duty, my lady." He genuflected before the altar and laid the scourge reverently on it. "The penance I have laid on you calls for the mortification of the flesh. It calls for the lesson of obedience. Here, at Dundarg, at the very edge of my brother's demesne, where you will find there are no distractions, you will suffer and you will pray. Sir Donald Comyn will remain here to guard you with his detachment of men— men, my lady, whom your husband can ill spare in this time of trial for Scotland. Master David, the chaplain here, will oversee your spiritual needs, and two sisters from the abbey have arrived already to attend you. I must return south at once."

Isobel gripped her hands together as she knelt on the chancel steps, trying to hide the elation that swept over her. She could feel her brother-in-law's eyes on her face but she had no clue as to his feelings; his expression was completely bland. She knew she was ugly and dirty in the stinking, itching garment he had forced her to wear; her feet were bare and bleeding from the stops they had made on the journey between towns and villages where she had been forced to seek out what moments of privacy she could to relieve herself. She did not guess that he was trying to master an unaccustomed surge of desire as he stared at her slim body and shapely legs and fine ankles with the narrow torn feet, ill concealed by the ugly shirt. He raised his eyes thoughtfully to her tired face with the wild tangle of black hair and swallowed hard. She had seen his lust as he held the scourge. He had indeed intended to use it on her himself, but he had seen the danger in time. He would leave that duty to the sisters. He bowed stiffly toward her. "I shall leave you to your prayers. Later you will be taken to your chamber."

As the door crashed shut behind him she rose painfully to her feet, fighting off the longing to tear off the filthy shirt and press herself naked on the cold stone flags to try to ease the rawness of her skin. To be found naked in the house of God would convince them finally of her depravity and bring her, like Mairi, to the stake.

Sir Donald Comyn watched Master William leave Dundarg with unconcealed relief. As soon as the priest's horses were out of sight he turned to the chapel. As he pushed open the heavy door and peered into the darkness, he thought for a moment she had gone, then he saw her standing near the altar.

"My lady? Master William has gone. Shall I show you to the solar?"

She turned to him and he saw the relief on her pale face; he also saw the pain she had in walking as she stepped toward him.

The small solar, high in the keep, had two arched windows that looked south over the windswept valley. The two nuns were waiting there for her, sitting talking quietly in one of the window embrasures. They rose as Isobel came in. The elder, a tall, thin woman with a gaunt pale face, smiled. "Lady Buchan?" She held out her hands kindly. "We arrived this morning after Master William sent messengers to the abbey. This is Sister Julian and I am Sister Eleanor. We will be happy to serve you."

Isobel had hoped to be alone, to have the chance of stripping off the hated shirt, but she greeted the two sisters with a tired smile. Sister Julian was younger and prettier than her companion, but her face had a hardness that Isobel found disturbing.

"Master William sent us instructions for your care." Sister Julian's words, though polite, were spoken with an edge of sharp authority. "The hair shirt is to be worn for forty days, and for each of those days you will suffer the penitential scourge. If you cannot bring yourself to inflict it on yourself, as we do, then one of us will do it for you." Her eyes were hard.

Even at night she was not to be alone. She stretched out, still wearing the hated shirt, on a low board bed in the corner of the room. Nearby the two nuns, who removed their gowns and veils but were still clothed in their shifts, also slept.

Only in the chapel was she permitted to undress; there before the altar the hair shirt was pulled down to her waist so that her back, raw and bleeding from the bites and sores of the fleas and lice, could be further lacerated by the leather thongs of the scourge, wielded with a strange mixture of compassion and enthusiasm by Sister Eleanor. When it was over she helped Isobel on with her shirt again, only once lightly touching her back. Isobel did not see the strange expression on her face.

Ten days after she arrived Sister Julian fell ill. Isobel was woken in the night by the sound of the woman retching. Eleanor, groping for the flint in the darkness, was trying to light the candle.

Isobel sat up. She was tired all the time now, prevented from sleeping properly by the constant pain, but wearily she dragged her aching body from her bed and made her way across to the nuns. "What is it, sister?"

"Hush." Sister Eleanor raised her hand. She was stroking Julian's damp forehead. "She is feverish. Go back to your bed, my lady. I shall take care of her."

All night the woman vomited and groaned, but by dawn she had at last fallen into a restless sleep. With one long look at the pale, exhausted face Sister Eleanor beckoned Isobel outside onto the stone stair. "We'll leave her to rest, my lady," she whispered. "Sleep is the best cure for what ails her."

In the narrow bailey, still shadowed behind the perimeter walls of the small castle, it was very cold and light was still dim. Only the high walls of the keep were bathed in sunlight. Automatically Isobel turned toward the heather-thatched lean-to kitchen against the wall. Her fast meant she could eat first thing, when she was given some bread and some water from the spring; after that she was allowed no more food until dusk.

As she turned away Eleanor touched her shoulder. "Sir Donald is in the great hall. He wishes to speak to you," she whispered. She was smiling.

Isobel stared at her. For a moment she hesitated, then, slowly, she returned the smile.

Sir Donald was standing before the fire. On the table near him stood a huge bowl of hot, steaming meal made into brose.

Near it stood a jug of cream and a goblet of Gascon wine.

"My lady." He bowed to her formally. "While Sister Julian is unwell, it might be a good idea to eat a proper meal or two." He winked at her. "Here." He reached out toward her, a silver spoon in his hand. "Sit down, lass, and start eating!"

Isobel stared at him. Then she looked at Sister Eleanor.

The nun smiled and nodded encouragingly. "Go on, my dear. I'll not tell Master William. It's Julian who writes long letters to him every evening, not I."

Isobel did not wait for a second invitation. Her stomach was crying out for hot food. After picking up one of the carved wooden bowls from the table, she scooped herself a helping of the rich, spicy brose and began to eat. Only when she had finished and drunk the wine did she turn back to Sir Donald. She smiled. "That was most welcome, Sir Knight. Thank you. Do I take it that you do not write regular letters to my husband either?"

He grinned. "Indeed not, my lady. At least, when I do they are about the castle and its garrison. I do not presume to comment on your ladyship's affairs." He stood up abruptly. "Now, if you will excuse me, I have things to do." He smiled at the two women. "The gates of the castle will be open for a few hours while the hay is brought up from the fields. If you wish to walk by the sea for a while you will be undisturbed."

When he had gone Isobel turned to the nun at her side. "Walk by the sea? What does he mean? What about my penance?" Her voice was bitter.

Eleanor shook her head. "You've done enough penance for the moment, my dear. Sister Julian will never know if you miss a day or two." She smiled wryly. "I think we can be certain she will be tied to her bed for a while yet." She looked down innocently, tucking her hands into her broad black sleeves.

Isobel stared at her. "You made her ill," she whispered. "You gave her something to make her sick!"

"Nothing so very bad, I assure you. It will not harm her." The nun's aquiline face was alight with humor suddenly. "Just bad enough to keep her in her bed for a while and give us a holiday, that's all!"

It was late summer when the Earl of Buchan arrived with his retinue. He greeted his wife in the solar where she sat alone waiting for him. In the great hall he had given the two nuns letters for their abbess and gold for her abbey, then he had dismissed them. In spite of Eleanor's timid plea, he did not consider it necessary for either of them to bid his wife farewell. Among the retinue he had brought with him were four ladies, picked by Alice, to serve Isobel, and with them chests of linen and gowns.

Her penance, he announced without preamble, was over.

The last weeks had not been so bad. For forty days she had had to wear the shirt and submit to the scourge. After that the nuns had dressed her in a simple black gown like their own habits and covered her hair with a black veil. Her fast was over and she could eat again; the scourging was over; the long hours of prayer in the chapel were reduced by half. Now she was allowed again to ride with the sisters at her side and to turn her hand to spinning and embroidery as the long summer evenings stretched out toward autumn.

When her husband at last appeared Isobel rose to her feet and curtseyed low as he walked into the room. She was very frightened.

He looked her up and down. "So. Your lesson is learned, I trust." He gave her a grim smile. "You will find that clothes for you have been taken to the earl's chamber, and new ladies await you there. If you will change into something more befitting a countess, we shall dine together in the great hall."

Her new ladies bathed her in a tub of rose water, then dried her still-scarred skin with soft towels. They put on her a shift of cool rich silk and over it a fine linen gown of sapphire blue and over that a scarlet tunic. Then she sat down on a stool while one of them brushed and braided her hair.

It was the job Mairi had performed a thousand times. For a moment she thought she would betray herself as the choking sobs rose in her throat. She clenched her fists and closed her eyes against the tears.

Gentle hands touched her shoulders. "It's all right, my lady." The girl whose name she did not even know smiled.

Lord Buchan was grim-faced at the table. "The situation in France is critical. King Philip has been defeated by a rabble in Flanders near the town of Courtrai, and I hear he is so weak now he is going to have to make an alliance with Edward of England. If he does, it is imperative that Scotland is included in any treaty they make. A delegation led by de Soules and myself is leaving at once to go to France, to put the case before the French king." He waved aside the hovering servants with their steaming bowls of rich venison stew and platters of salmon and chicken stuffed with ground pine kernels. "Philip is a friend to our King John, who is now living in comfort on his own estates in Picardy. He recognizes him as our king, but he must not be allowed to forget his commitment to Scotland as a whole."

Isobel, sitting quietly at her husband's side, glanced around the shadowy hall. The sun, low now in the west, threw only the slimmest of lights through the narrow windows. Already the pages were lighting the candle branches and the flares. The room was unbearably hot and stuffy. "When do you leave, my lord?" She tried to keep the relief out of her voice. An ambassadorial trip to France would mean her husband would be away for weeks, perhaps months.

"Soon. King Edward is going to give us safe conduct, it seems. Perhaps he too is anxious for peace at last. We ride for Perth tomorrow; we shall sail within weeks, I hope."

"And I, my lord? Am I to stay here?" She kept her voice low, aware of Sir Donald sitting beside her, his elbows on the table among the trenchers and goblets. He was idly cutting his gravy-soaked wheaten bread into squares with his dagger and throwing the pieces to the hound that lay beneath the table at his feet.

"You?" Lord Buchan turned to her with a look of scornful amusement. "You think while I am away to chase after Lord Carrick again, perhaps? Didn't you know that he is now married to Lord Ulster's daughter and confirmed as a traitor to Scotland's cause?"

He was watching her closely. Isobel held her breath, not allowing a muscle to flicker in her face as she met his eye. "So I believe," she said. "What Lord Carrick does, my lord, is of no interest to me." She managed to keep the defiance out of her voice. "My only concern now is to serve you, my husband." Meekly she lowered her eyes. Below the linen napkin on her lap her fists were clenched so tightly together her knuckles cracked.

On her knees before the altar in the chapel of St. Drostan, who had built his cell upon the promontory of Dundarg hundreds of years before the first Comyn keep was built there, she had in the long weeks of the summer begun to pray. There she had prayed for the soul of her beloved Mairi and there she had vowed to forget Robert the Bruce, Earl of Carrick, with his handsome, easy charm. She could never win against her husband. Her only hope of an even tolerable existence would be to make up her mind to obey him—even to wheedle him a little if she could. Now she forced herself to smile at him, and she saw with a small flicker of hope the answering widening of his eyes.

He stared at her. The months of hardship and fasting had made his wife intolerably thin—but her face with its fine nose and mouth and high cheekbones was more beautiful than ever. The suffering had changed her. She had grown calmer, more controlled, and, in his eyes, infinitely more interesting. He felt a sudden wave of desire. "Eat." He beckoned the food forward again. "You're a bagful of bones. Then we'll go to bed." He didn't meet her eye, not wanting to see the fear and loathing he knew would be there.

Isobel picked up her spoon with a shaking hand. "I'm glad to see you, husband," she said in a whisper.

She had already gathered the herbs she needed against this day. There would be no child this month. Almost cheerfully she began to eat.

"Good." He dropped his knife and put his arm around her shoulders awkwardly. "Because we will be seeing a great deal of one another from now on. I have decided to take you with me to Paris, to see the King of France!"

Henry Firbank raised his glass in a slow, heartfelt toast. "Here's to your husband. It was very gracious of him to let me take you out to dinner."

Clare, wearing a deep-blue silk dress, with sapphires at her ears and throat, was looking exceptionally beautiful and far happier than when he had seen her the week before.

It was three days since that last vision of Isobel, and since then she had had no dreams and no visitations from the past, spontaneous or otherwise. She had not felt threatened in any way, and so she was much more calm. Even Paul had been bearable! She had had time to think and to plan.

"Paul has been in a strange mood these last few days." She clinked glasses with Henry with a smile. "When I came down to London on Thursday I was terrified he'd do something awful when he found out I'd torn up that document."

"And did he?" Henry tried hard to make the inquiry sound casual.

She shook her head. "We had words, but not too bad. Then he became terribly civilized, even solicitous. He bought me these"—her hands strayed to her throat—"to wear to the party on Saturday."

Henry resisted the urge to stretch out to touch them. "I thought money was a problem," he said.

"Apparently not now." She smiled. "And he hasn't mentioned Duncairn again. We went out for lunch with friends of his on Sunday and that was fine as well, and then yesterday when he found out he had such a late meeting in the City he suggested this dinner tonight to make up for it."

"And now he's unavoidably detained at the last moment so you have to put up with me as understudy." Henry grinned ruefully. "I'm sorry."

"I'm not." She touched his hand lightly. "I can't think of anyone I'd rather have dinner with."

"Really?" For a moment he allowed the eagerness to show.

"Really." She picked up her fork again. "How is Diane? I haven't seen her since you both came to dinner."

"And you went into a trance before the hors d'oeuvres." Henry chuckled "She's fine. Okay. Nice lady."

"But not special?" She looked at him sympathetically.

"There's only one special woman for me, Clare." He stared ruefully down into his glass.

There was an awkward silence. "Paul oughtn't to have asked you to take me out tonight, Henry. It isn't fair," she said quietly after a moment.

"No, he oughtn't." Henry's fingers whitened on the glass.

"He knows damn well how I feel about you. He's thrown it at me often enough!"

She stared at him. "Paul knows?"

"He knows. He also knows you'd never be unfaithful to him. I wish I could prove him wrong, the bastard!"

Clare looked away unhappily. "We shouldn't be talking like this. And we shouldn't meet again. Not alone. It isn't fair to you." She crumpled her napkin between her fingers. "Look, Henry, there's something you ought to know." She fixed her gaze on the creased linen, studying it with concentration. "I'm going away next weekend—back home to Scotland, and I'm not telling Paul." She bit her lip. "I'm just going. Leaving him."

"You mean you're going for good?" Henry put down his knife and fork abruptly. He was surprised how much her news shook him.

She shrugged. "I don't know. Maybe. My stepfather is going to be away for a few weeks and Mummy called last night. She doesn't dare ask us home when he's there. He hates James and me." She gave a dry laugh. "He must hate us even more now that James owns the house he lives in. Anyway, with her there on her own I can talk to her and think. Get things straight in my mind about the future."

"Any chance I could be part of it?" He pulled a face, trying to keep the question light.

She shook her head apologetically, knowing she was hurting him. "You stick to Diane. She's perfect for you. I'm much too bitter and twisted." She smiled, but he noticed the smile didn't quite reach her eyes.

"Are you going to visit Duncairn while you're in Scotland?" He changed the subject abruptly.

"I don't know." She shook her head. "Maybe. Maybe I'll go up there and chase Neil Forbes off my land."

"Neil Forbes?" Henry looked puzzled.

"An objectionable man who tried to tell me what I should and shouldn't do with Duncairn." She gave up trying to eat and pushed her plate aside. Neil Forbes's image had returned to plague her again and again since his visit to Bucksters. Even the thought of him made her angry.

Henry noted the sudden color in her pale face and the sparkle in her eyes. Thoughtfully he leaned back in his chair.

"I'd like to be there when you catch him."

She laughed. "I might even sell tickets."

"I think Paul's hoping you'll give him a chance to exonerate himself." He gave a weak smile. "He asked me to take you back to the office after we'd finished here. He's got yet another present for you, apparently."

"At the office?" Clare stared at him.

"Yes. I've orders to deliver you back to BCWP at eleven o'clock on the dot. And he will be waiting with champagne ready in his office."

She frowned, suddenly apprehensive. "You're coming too?"

He glanced at her sharply. "Of course. If you want me to."

James had arrived at the Campden Hill house just as Sarah was going out for the evening. Saying he'd wait for Clare, he closed the door behind her, then he turned and walked back into the drawing room and helped himself to some of Paul's whisky.

He wandered around the room and idly, he pulled open a drawer of the desk. After shuffling through the contents he closed it and pulled open another. He read through a couple of letters and threw them down. He wasn't entirely sure what he was looking for—anything about Paul's finances, or Duncairn, he supposed—while he had the chance.

He had been thinking about Paul's offer to sell Duncairn to him, and the more he thought about it, the more it made sense. His initial reaction had been stupid and sentimental; his second and third thoughts had been far more complicated. After all, it was possible that Clare would agree to sell to him, and she might agree to do so for far less than Paul was asking. She might even agree to swap the land for one of the farms, or even for Airdlie. Once Duncairn was his, then he could sell it to Sigma himself. After putting down his glass, he began systematically to search the house.

It was upstairs in the master bedroom, in the bottom drawer of a Regency walnut chest of drawers, hidden behind a pile of silk nightdresses, that he found the candles. Half a dozen tall, silver candles wrapped in a black silk scarf. He unwrapped them and lined them up neatly on the pale-green carpet, staring at them thoughtfully. With them in the drawer was a stubby candle holder, some incense sticks, and a small bottle of oil. He opened the bottle and sniffed its contents cautiously. It was scented: spicy and sweet and rather exotic.

Casta was sitting in the doorway watching him intently. James glanced at her. "Are these the candles your mum uses to summon the spirits?" The dog put her head on one side. "Of course they are." He picked one up and weighed it in his hand. "These are special, magic candles." The dinner party candles were in the sideboard with the napkins and table mats. He had seen them downstairs.

As the doorbell rang Casta leapt up and hurtled downstairs, barking.

Emma stared at James in astonishment as he opened the door. "I thought there was no one in except the dog. Where's Clare?"

"Out for dinner, apparently." James stood back to let her in. "I came in to wait, but now I don't know. She might be hours. Can I give you some of Paul's Scotch?"

"Please." Emma took off her raincoat and hung it in the hall. "I wanted to talk to Clare. Apparently she had lunch with Chloe last week and she scared the pants off her. I wanted to know exactly what she said." She giggled suddenly.

"I thought the sainted Chloe was unscareable." James did not like his brother-in-law's relations.

"She was going on about witches and spirits and Satan."

He laughed uncomfortably. "And Chloe believed her, did she?"

"I think so. You can never quite tell with Chloe, but Geoffrey's taken it very seriously. I gather he's now talking about consulting his bishop." She sobered. "James, what do you think about all this stuff she's involved in? Does she really believe in it?"

"Yes."

"And do you think it's true?"

James shrugged. "Probably."

"You don't think it could hurt her in any way, do you? One hears such frightening stories about people being possessed by evil spirits."

"I don't think Isobel was evil." James sat down thoughtfully. "She was just a very unhappy woman, that's all. Clare's been obsessed by her for years."

"Obsession is a psychological condition, James—"

"Clare is not mad, Emma." James spoke unusually forcefully. "And if Paul is telling people she is, he's a liar!"

❦ Chapter Sixteen ❦

The security men at BCWP were expecting them. As the taxi drew up outside the building, they unlocked the doors and let them in.

"Mr. Royland is in his office, Mr. Firbank."

"Come on." Henry took Clare's hand.

Together they walked up the broad flight of stairs that led from the huge hall, lighted now not by the vast chandelier but only by the low-watt courtesy light on the reception desk. The landing was in darkness.

Outside Paul's door, Henry paused. "Okay?" he whispered.

Clare nodded. It was idiotic to feel nervous.

Henry didn't knock. After throwing open the door, he ushered Clare in. "Here we are, right on time!"

Paul was sitting in one of the leather armchairs near the fireplace. Beside him on a low table stood an ice bucket with a bottle of Bollinger and three glasses. On the desk by the window lay a sheaf of red roses.

He rose slowly. "Clare, darling." He kissed her gently on the mouth. It was a slow, lingering kiss, and Clare felt a strange clutch of excitement in her stomach. "Come on, Henry. Do the honors." He waved at the champagne.

Paul helped her off with her coat, the luxurious wild mink he had given her for her twenty-eighth birthday, and threw it on a chair. Then he turned to the desk. "These are for you, my darling. To make up." He picked up the flowers and thrust them into Clare's arms.

She stared at them. "Paul, they're lovely—"

"I've been a bastard these last few weeks, I know." Paul put his arm around her. "Say you forgive me?"

"Of course I forgive you." She stared up at him. Relief was making her feel weak at the knees.

"Here you are." Henry had poured the champagne. He glanced at Clare, trying to keep his face cheerful. "I'm beginning to feel that I'm the proverbial gooseberry here. I'll drink your health quickly then I think I'll leave. You don't mind?"

Clare looked up at Paul's face. He was smiling, but there was a slight sheen of perspiration on his forehead. For a second she hesitated, then she shook her head. "Of course I don't mind. Thank you, Henry, for a lovely evening."

"My pleasure." Henry drank his half glass of champagne rather too quickly, then he put the glass down and turned to the door. "Be good! Remember the security boys! I'll see you in the morning, Paul."

As the door closed behind him, Paul picked the bottle out of the ice and refilled Clare's glass. "Nice chap, Henry. Useful sort of man to have around. He's in love with you, you know." He sounded amused.

Clare swallowed. "I don't think so. Not really. He's very fond of Diane."

"Diane?" Paul raised an eyebrow. "Then he's a fool. The woman is a whore." He thrust the bottle back into the bucket with a noise like splintering glass. "Anyway, she's his problem, not ours." He smiled. "Drink up, then we'll go home. We don't want to shock those guards, do we!" He ran his finger slowly up her arm.

Clare sipped her champagne. She was feeling slightly lightheaded. The office was full of the scent of roses.

Slowly Paul walked around the room, turning off the lights one by one, until only the table lamp by the chair was left on. The room was very silent. "I told the guards it was our anniversary," he murmured. "You'd forgotten, hadn't you? We met on the fourth of November."

Clare put down her glass carefully. "So we did. I was sixteen. You'd come to school to see Emma and you agreed to stay for the fireworks party."

"Remember, remember the fifth of November," he said slowly. "The day I fell in love." He put his arms around her and kissed her again. His mouth tasted antiseptic, as if he had just gargled. "Before we go I want to show you something."

Clare smiled uneasily. "Paul darling, let's just go home—"

"It won't take long. Come on. Bring the flowers." He reached into his desk, picked up an envelope, and tucked it into his inside pocket. Then, after gathering her coat over his arm, he turned off the light. In the sudden darkness a dim shadowy twilight from the streetlamps outside lighted the room, filtering around the edges of the heavy blinds. By its light he guided her to a door on the far side of the room and opened it. The corridor outside led through into the new offices. Off it led a passage, which took them to a private elevator. Paul pressed the button on the wall. "I want you to come up and see the view. It's a beautiful night now. The rain has gone and the whole city is glowing in the starlight."

"No, Paul, please. Let's go home." Clare hung back, every sense warning her to run.

The elevator doors slid back without a sound and stayed open as Paul stood, his finger on the button.

"You're not afraid. Not with me here?" He ran his fingers over her shoulders. "There's more champagne upstairs, Clare, and candlelight. We can make love on the roof of the world. Come." Taking her hand gently, he stepped into the elevator and she had no alternative but reluctantly to follow him. As they both turned to face the door he fitted a security card into a slot and pressed the top button.

Clare buried her face in the roses' blooms as the steel doors slid shut, and she held her breath as with a slight bump the elevator began its upward journey.

Paul stopped it between the twelfth and thirteenth floors and removed the card. He slipped it into his breast pocket and leaned against the wall, folding his arms over her mink. He was smiling.

"This, I think, is as good a place as any to have our little conversation, don't you?" he said.

Clare stared at him in disbelief, clutching convulsively at the roses.

"All I want, my darling, is your signature on this document." He reached into his pocket for the envelope. "Oh yes,

I kept a copy. Henry and Sarah can 'witness' it tomorrow. The important thing is for you to sign it. Now." He glanced at his watch. "It is almost exactly midnight. The witching hour. And on the thirteenth floor. Most appropriate, don't you think? We have the rest of the night, if necessary. I told the security men we didn't want to be disturbed, and they won't check this elevator."

Clare closed her eyes, trying desperately to fight back the rising waves of panic. "Paul, please—"

He was taking a gold-plated ballpoint pen out of his pocket. After dropping her coat on the thickly carpeted floor, he slowly extricated the papers from the envelope.

It was growing hot and Clare's arms tightened convulsively on the roses. She could feel the thorns tearing her skin through the cellophane. "I won't sign!" Defiantly she backed into the corner, feeling the walls of the elevator cold through the thin silk of her dress. "Please, Paul, this is ridiculous!" She had begun to tremble. Her mouth had gone dry and her breathing was coming in short, shallow gasps. Desperately she tried to remember the techniques Zak had taught her.

Breathe slowly. Count. Think of the ashram. Think of Duncairn in the sun. Think of the sea whispering gently at the foot of the cliffs. Think of the wind whispering in the spicy, fragrant branches of the old pines. Count. Count slowly. You have nothing to fear but fear itself. Paul can't keep you here forever. He is a big man. He will need oxygen before you do. He doesn't want to die. Soon he will begin to gasp and feel the need for oxygen. . . . Soon he will want to open the doors. . . .

She raised her eyes desperately to his. He was smiling. Beads of perspiration stood out on his brow and his face was slightly flushed, but otherwise he was calm. Slowly he held out the paper and pen to her.

"Sign, Clare."

"No." Blood was running down her wrist from the rose thorns, but she didn't notice. "I'm not going to sign it." She clenched her teeth. "You will run out of air long before I do, Paul."

The walls were beginning to spin.

"I don't think so." He smiled. "After all, I'm not panicking, am I? Sign, Clare. Then it will all be over. Here—" He tore the roses out of her arms and threw them to the floor with the coat, staring in distaste at the bloody scratches on her arms. Seizing her hand, he folded her fingers around his pen. "Sign, you stupid bitch!" His voice was thick. "Sign!" Suddenly he was beside himself with anger and fear.

"No." He barely heard her whisper.

"Sign!" He laughed desperately. "Look at you. Terrified of shadows; a madwoman, living in the past! What kind of wife do you think you are, Clare? Useless! Certifiable! And, by God, I'll have you certified! There won't be a doctor in the country who would let you walk free after what I tell them about you, not with Geoffrey as my witness. You thought it a joke, did you, telling Geoffrey all about your little games. Raising the devil! Summoning the spirits! Black masses on the lawn! No joke, Clare. No joke at all. Not when the evidence is corroborated by Sir David Royland, M.P."

She barely heard him. She could see the eyes, the bars; the elevator walls came and went; voices echoed in her head; jeers. She could feel the wings flapping desperately around her head, and she didn't even know if they were her own. . . . Suddenly she couldn't breathe. The light in the elevator grew dim; there was a roaring, rushing sound in her ears then all went black. With a strangled cry she crumpled at Paul's feet.

He stood looking down at her dispassionately. "Stupid, stupid woman! I tried to help you!" He hardly knew what he was saying. "If you'd signed it would have been all right. Now I've got to hand you over to them. I won't be able to save you." He felt in his pocket for the security card and, after slowly slotting it into place, pressed the button for the ground floor. It was stiflingly hot. As the elevator began to move he pulled out his handkerchief and wiped his forehead.

Clare opened her eyes slowly. She was lying sprawled in a chair in Paul's office. In the dim light of the desk lamp she could see him standing by the window. He had raised the blind and was staring out into the street. There was a glass in his hand.

She must have made some movement for he turned. "When you feel well enough we'll get a taxi home," he said quietly. His voice was quite normal again.

"I'm well enough now." With an effort she pulled herself upright in the chair.

"Then I'll tell one of the men at the desk to phone for one." He put down his glass. For a moment he stood looking down at her, then he turned and walked out of the room.

Clare closed her eyes. Her head was splitting. She couldn't think. She didn't want to think. She couldn't face the implications of what had happened, and she felt sick and very frightened.

When Paul returned she rose shakily to her feet and began to walk toward the door. Her face was white as a sheet as he picked up her coat and put it over her shoulders, then he handed her the roses. "I'll not give the cleaners the pleasure of seeing them in the bin," he said curtly. "Take them."

The drawing-room light was on when they got home. There was a note on the table.

> Sorry to have missed you. Will call tomorrow. Hope you had a nice evening. Sorry about the whisky but Em was here as well.
> James

Paul threw down the note and picked up his decanter. It was empty.

Behind him Clare walked slowly up the stairs. Automaton-like she took off her coat and hung it in the closet. She dropped the roses on the dressing table and began to run a bath. They had not exchanged one single word in the taxi.

She was already in bed, pretending to be asleep, when Paul came upstairs. Only when she felt his weight on the edge of the bed did her eyes fly open. He pulled back the covers and climbed in beside her. "We don't want you having nightmares alone, do we?" he said grimly.

Clare shrank away from him. "I'm tired, Paul," she said sharply.

He smiled. "Afraid I'm going to jump on you? You think stubborn stupidity and hysteria turn me on?" Leaning toward her, he hooked his finger around the thin strap of her nightdress and flicked it contemptuously off her shoulder. "Perhaps they do. Making love to an insane woman might just be exciting, but then again, perhaps not." He lay back on the pillows.

Clare turned her back on him. She could feel a slow anger burning through her fear, but her terror of the man next to her was the stronger. She was afraid to move, afraid to get out of bed in case it angered him again. Tensely she lay beside him, listening to him breathing evenly beside her. It was a long time before she realized he was asleep.

She closed her eyes, feeling tears of anger and frustration and exhaustion running down her face and into the pillow, listening as a car drove noisily down the silent street outside. The curtains weren't properly closed and she could see a streetlight, blurred behind the rain-streaked glass. She fixed her eyes on it miserably, wishing it were morning. Even Paul's claim that the evening had cleared and that there were stars had been a lie.

Dream, child. Don't you trust yourself to dream?
Aunt Margaret's voice was loud in the room.
Command the dream and the nightmare will be finished. Follow Isobel, Clare. Follow her. Fight. . . .
Restlessly Clare stirred on the bed.

"I have a message from the Earl of Carrick." The small, wizened man bent close to her. His wrinkled, nut-brown face was alight with humor. "Does the Lady Buchan want it?"

Isobel glanced over her shoulder. The rabbit warren of buildings that clustered around the Palais de la Cité was always crowded, always bustling, always noisy. She beckoned him into a corner out of earshot of her two attendants, who were watching the antics of a street musician with his dancing bear. "Of course I want it!"

Lord Buchan was yet again with de Soules, Bishop Lamberton of St. Andrews, and Matthew Crambeth, Bishop of

Dunkeld, in the audience chamber at the palace with King Philip and his advisers.

"A small reward, perhaps, for my care of the document?" He was watching her intently.

There were a great many Scots in Paris at the moment, hangers-on with the Scots delegation, messengers, servants. She hesitated, then she felt at her shoulder for the gold-and-enamel pin fastened there. "Here. You'll have to sell it; it might be recognized otherwise. It's worth several sous."

The man took the brooch and held it up to the light. "Would the beautiful countess wear anything but gold? I shall trust you, my lady. Here." He groped in his scrip and produced a folded letter. The seal was intact. As he thrust it into her hands he glanced over his shoulder, then with a wink, he was gone.

Isobel clutched the letter, her heart beating fast. It was inscribed in Robert's own hand. She had heard nothing from him since his marriage to Elizabeth de Burgh. No messages, no letters, no news save of his treachery to Scotland.

It was eighteen months now since she had sailed with the Scots delegation to France. Ever since their arrival they had been living in one guest house after another in Paris and in Picardy near the château where John Balliol, still titular King of Scots, lived in frustrated exile.

Their mission had failed—when the treaty between England and France had been signed at last, it had not included Scotland. But in spite of that the Scots had still been optimistic. King Philip of France had promised that they would eventually be part of the settlement, and to achieve that end the delegation had waited on in France. But King Edward had renewed his attacks on Scotland, and the news had become increasingly dire. By February Scotland was defeated once more.

The delegates were dismayed. Storms in the Channel had delayed further news, and it was not until the letters from the north came at last that they heard the outcome of the parliament that had met at St. Andrews. John Comyn, who had been left in Scotland as the Guardian of the Realm, had demanded that the rights and freedoms of Scotland be preserved. Edward, statesmanlike and for once coolheaded about his northern neighbor, had apparently agreed, but only after demanding allegiance and fines and terms of exile for the leading Scots who had opposed him. For the Earl and Countess of Buchan it meant that they would stay in France. Their diplomatic mission ended, they were now in exile; the earldom and their lands were confiscated.

Now they were back in Paris again, camped in the Abbey de St. Germain, which was convenient to the King of France's two favored residences, the Château du Louvre and the Palais on the Ile de la Cité. They had not given up hope of being able to influence the French king in their favor, and in the meantime all they could do was wait.

After tucking the letter into her gown, Isobel pulled her cloak around her cautiously. First she must attend Queen Joan and while away an hour or two with their hostess, mindful ever of the need to stay in favor with King Philip's wife, then she could return to the guest house. There, in one of the small chambers of ease let into the walls of the old building, she would be able to make use of one of the only places to find privacy in this crowded city and at last she could read his letter.

She read it and read it again, holding it up to the light of the narrow window where the last scarlet streaks of sunlight still hung above the mellow roofs of the abbey, turning the clouds to green and gold as they raced across a sky torn to ribbons by the strength of the March gale.

The man who bears this letter I would trust with my life and yours—nevertheless burn this at once lest it fall into the wrong hands. He will carry your reply and serve you as you wish. . . .

Desperately she scanned the letter for terms of endearment, for inquiries as to her health and happiness; there were none. His questions were all about the delegation; about King Philip and his true feelings about Scotland and the treaty with King Edward; and finally about the opinions of her

husband and his fellow delegates regarding the course events
had taken over the last few months.

He was asking her to spy for him.

Slowly she walked back into the main room of the guest
house and out into the abbey gardens. She stood for a while
watching two of the brothers, their sleeves folded up to their
elbows, raking rose prunings into a pile. As they kindled
them into a bonfire she stepped forward and dropped the
letter onto it, watching it shrivel and curl in a haze of wisped
blue smoke.

Once she would have betrayed her husband without a
second's thought, but the long months in France had matured her. She had realized that what he did, he did for the
sake of Scotland. She still hated and feared him, but she had
watched and listened and learned to respect him too. He was
an able statesman and an intelligent man, sincere in his belief
that what he did was for the good of his country and his king,
his cousin John Balliol. On only two matters was he irrational
and prone to fly into ungovernable rages: Isobel's failure to
give him an heir and the Earl of Carrick.

Never again had Isobel trusted anyone with the secret of
her concoctions or allowed anyone to hear her prayers. She
gathered her herbs in secret, sometimes after dark in the
lonely monastery gardens, sometimes covertly collecting
them on their stops on the long rides through the French
countryside between châteaux. Month after month she repeated her spells and curtseyed to the moon and prayed to
the Queen of Heaven alone and in secret, and month after
month her prayers had been answered as her womb was
washed clean of her husband's seed.

During the daytime she saw little of Lord Buchan. At first
she had been overwhelmed by the crowded busy life of the
delegation, homesick and miserable in Paris, longing for the
moors and the cliffs and seas of home, but slowly she had
grown used to the life. She had no friends—she trusted no
one—but she had no enemies either. She was popular among
both Scots and French for her beauty and her small kind-
nesses to anyone who crossed her path. Most of the delegation knew of her maid's death as a heretic and of Isobel's long

weeks of penance; none spoke of it. They were sorry for her and respected her unbowed spirit. No one ever whispered now of Robert the Bruce.

Robert's messenger sought Isobel out once more the next day after mass in the Sainte Chapelle. Slyly he beckoned her into an alley below the soaring buttresses. She glanced around, but her ladies were gossiping among themselves, enjoying the unexpected soft spring sunshine after a week of storms.

"I have nothing for you," she whispered to him. "Tell Lord Carrick I will not betray Scotland. His allegiance may have changed, mine has not!"

The man's eyebrows seemed to shoot up into his hairline. "It is because Lord Carrick knows your allegiance to be unswerving, my lady, that he asks your help. Do you think he does not feel the same?" The man's whisper was indignant.

"He has sworn allegiance to Edward of England!" She could not keep the scorn from her voice.

"So has nearly every noble in Scotland at some time or another," he said with slow deliberation. "And there have been many these last few weeks. So, my lady, did you, when it was expedient. And so might you again." His eyes were intense.

She took a deep breath. "You know a lot about me."

He smiled. "My lord speaks of you sometimes."

"He does?" She could not keep the eagerness from her voice.

"He admires you, my lady. He finds you courageous and astute." He was watching her closely. "He believed you would understand that he too works for Scotland. The time is not yet right for him to show his intentions openly. When it is, he will act."

Behind them a crowd of court ladies swathed in brilliant silks and velvets appeared, chattering and giggling as they hurried toward the river. Isobel pulled her velvet hood nervously around her face.

"Trust him, my lady," the voice whispered again. "Help him. He needs to know the way the wind blows." He ran his fingers through the air expressively. "One day he will be your

king, my lady." The intelligent eyes had not once left her
face; the lilting voice was almost crooning. "Believe in him."
He moved closer to her. "When he wrote that letter to you he
was waiting for his sick father's death. On my way to embark
for France the messenger caught up with me. Lord Annandale is finally dead, my lady. Robert Bruce, Lord of Carrick, is
now our rightful king."

Isobel caught her breath sharply. "So. It has happened at
last. He has waited a long time for this."

"Aye." The man's eyes were glittering. "And knowing this,
will you help him?"

Isobel walked away from him slowly toward the low wall at
the end of the alley. It bordered some steps that led down to
the Seine. She leaned on the stone, her eyes fixed on the
glitter of water. He followed her, still hovering behind her.
Any moment her ladies would join her.

She bit her lip. "Please tell Lord Carrick that he has my
friendship," she said guardedly, "And that when he is
crowned king he will have my allegiance. But I dare not
betray my husband. Like Lord Carrick himself, I have to
move with time and tide."

He raised an eyebrow. "Time and tide, madam, will bring
you home to Scotland soon." He drew himself up suddenly.
"If you change your mind, I lodge in the château. Ask for
Gilbert of Annandale. Most people know me. May I at least
take your good wishes to my lord?"

Isobel smiled. "He knows he has those always."

Below the wall a flock of swans was swimming majestically
upriver, stemming the ripples made by the gusty wind. She
glanced up, but he had gone. She was alone beside the river
as a heavy shower swept across the towers and spires of the
Sainte Chapelle and drenched her velvet cloak.

In May Edward laid siege to Stirling Castle, the last garrison in Scotland to hold out against him, and in May he agreed
to restore to the Earl of Buchan his earldom and all its rights
and lands and give him safe conduct to return to Scotland on
condition that he come into his peace with a personal oath of
loyalty.

"Do you mean to pay allegiance to him?" Isobel was standing with her husband in the audience chamber in the king's château.

"I am of no use to anyone if I stay here," he retorted, angry at her implied criticism. "The important thing now is to get the administration organized and persuade Edward to allow John Balliol back into his kingdom."

"He will never do that." Isobel was watching with half an eye a band of musicians settling themselves on stools in a corner. They were picking up their instruments and gently tuning them.

"Edward is a clever man. He does what is just." Lord Buchan shrugged. "It appears he is to pardon most who stood out against him, as he has agreed to pardon us. All seem to have at least a hope of some kind of restitution save Sir William Wallace, whom he seems determined never to forgive for his rebellion."

"Poor Sir William." Isobel dodged as a small child hurtled passed them toward the musicians. "He was a true patriot. Have they captured him?"

Her husband shrugged. "I think not. No doubt Lord Carrick will hunt him down in time. I hear he is organizing the siege of Stirling at the moment, but once that is over no doubt he will spare some men for Sir William." His voice was full of bitterness.

Isobel turned away sharply. She would not rise to his taunts, and anyway, she could not justify Robert's actions even if she wanted to. If the news was true and he was not only now in Edward's peace, but also one of the besiegers, then she could neither understand nor forgive him.

"Give orders to the household to pack our things," Lord Buchan said abruptly. "Now that our exile is over we can ride for the coast as soon as we have made our farewells."

"Yes, my lord." She was half elated, half afraid.

He glanced down at her suddenly and smiled wearily. "Perhaps a return to Scotland will help you to conceive at last."

She looked away quickly. "Perhaps it will," she said quietly. "Perhaps it will, my lord."

It took them six long weeks to return to Scotland. Isobel

enjoyed the journey. Her husband, distracted by meetings
with the people through whose lands they passed and then
by the arduous sea journey with its complete lack of privacy,
left her completely alone. She loved the sea. From a small
child she had never for long been out of the sound of the
waves, first in Fife, on the edge of the Forth, and then from
the age of four in one or other of the remote clifftop castles of
Buchan. Now she spent hours at a time on deck, clutching the
rail below the billowing straining sails, her eyes narrowed
against the glare of the sun on the water. She was dreaming
about Scotland and Scotland's future king.

There were no guards now, no orders as to her behavior.
She resumed her position as mistress of her husband's lands
without opposition. Almost at once he had left her alone,
riding to join his colleagues in Perth, so it was easy for her to
ride forth from Buchan that summer with an escort of men,
ostensibly to visit her great-grandmother at Kildrummy Castle. At her side rode Gilbert of Annandale.

There were no obstructions, no problems. Eleyne, Dowager Countess of Mar, was waiting for her in the south-facing
solar in the Snow Tower. At the age of eighty-two she was still
as erect and graceful in her movements as a woman half her
age. She almost ran to greet Isobel, hugging her, and then
pulled her down to sit beside her on the cushioned seat in the
window embrasure. "It has been so long, child! Come, tell me
about France. . . ."

They talked about Scotland, about Isobel's trip to the court
of France, about the loss of her baby, and about the death of
Mairi, who had come from Mar. It was a relief for Isobel to
speak to someone she could wholeheartedly love and trust,
and she found herself weeping into her great-grandmother's
lap, Robert temporarily forgotten.

Eleyne listened, trying to hide her distress at Isobel's unhappiness, and comforted her and distracted her with stories
of Isobel's mother, at last remarried and living in England.
Not once did she speak of the granddaughter of her marriage
into the house of Mar, Isabella, who had married Robert
Bruce, nor did she mention Robert himself.

They talked for a long time, and at last Isobel remembered the reason for her visit. She hesitated, torn between her love and respect for the old lady and her longing to see Robert again. Eleyne had made no mention of the fact that he was at Kildrummy, and yet he must be. Gilbert had promised her. . . .

Almost reluctantly she stood up, and took the old lady's hand. "You must be tired, Great-Grandmama. Shall I leave you awhile to rest?"

Eleyne smiled. "I think that would be nice, my child. I shall see you in the great hall later." She looked at Isobel's face and tried to quell the feeling of unease that filled her suddenly. But there was no putting it off. Isobel's fate was already written in the flames. She sighed. "There is someone else here, I believe, who would like to talk to you about France." She looked grave for a moment, raising her gnarled fingers to Isobel's cheek. "Take care, my darling. Remember your husband."

Isobel frowned, feeling the color rising in her face. Did everyone know then how much she still yearned for Robert? She kissed the old lady's cheek and hesitated just for a moment, seeing the expression in her great-grandmother's eyes. Then she almost ran from the room.

Robert was standing before the window when she was at last shown into his presence after a seemingly interminable walk through the long passages and circular corridors that linked the towers of the castle. He was reading through a pile of letters. He turned with a smile as she entered. "So. My lady Buchan. It is good to see you again." He paused as the esquire who had shown her into the room bowed and withdrew, and they were alone.

For a moment she stood without moving, almost breathless now that she was near him at last. Then, going to him, she knelt on the strewn heather at his feet. Taking his hand, she touched it to her lips. "So, now you are truly my rightful king," she whispered.

Robert looked down at her gravely. "Not yet, my love. Not in name, nor yet in power, but one day soon. One day!" He smacked his hands together then, realizing that she was still on her knees, he turned back to her and gently raised her to her feet. "So, what is it, my dear? Why did you want to see me so urgently? It wasn't easy to spare the time to ride north to Kildrummy. Do you have information for me of the delegation, or of the Scots parliament at Scone?"

Isobel shook her head. She looked away from him, suddenly abashed. "I have no information. I just wanted to see you. To be with you again."

Neither of them mentioned the last time they had met, nor the precipitate way Isobel had been escorted from Scone, but for a moment the memory hung between them.

He frowned. Uncomfortably he turned away from her. "I had heard that you were reconciled with your husband, Isobel. I had hoped you would tell me about King Philip's views—"

"You still want me for a spy!" She was angry. "Is that all I am to you now? A voice from the Comyn camp? An ear at the keyhole when my husband talks!"

"You said you owed me your loyalty," he said gently.

"I do!" Furiously she paced across the small room and then back again, her long skirts scattering the dried heather stems. She stopped and collected herself with a deep breath. "I'm sorry. You do have my loyalty, you know you do. And if it helps I will tell you all I know." She smiled wryly. "If you have time to listen, or does your new wife insist you return to her side every evening at dusk?" She turned away, cursing her sharp tongue and trying to hide the sudden misery in her face. No one had mentioned whether Elizabeth had ridden north with him.

Robert walked over to her and catching her shoulders turned her to face him. "My wife is entitled to my presence, Isobel. And to my respect."

"And your love?" She looked at him desperately. Her pride and her longing were tearing her in two. She could not, would not, throw herself at him if he did not want her.

He was watching her, his handsome face shadowed as he stood with his back to the narrow window. Outside there was a sudden shouting and the clatter of hooves on cobbles as a horse, frightened by the hiss of iron in water, bolted from outside the blacksmith's shed. Neither of them heard it.

"She has my deepest respect and affection, Isobel. She is entitled to that. And she has my daughter's love. That means a lot to me."

"Isabella of Mar's daughter!" Isobel pulled her hands away from him, ashamed of the jealousy she still felt at the mention of his first wife's name.

"*My* daughter." His voice was stern.

She closed her eyes. Her whole body ached with longing for this man's touch. She took a deep breath "I am glad, for little Marjorie's sake," she said.

There was a soft chuckle from Robert. "You are a very bad liar, Isobel," he said softly. "You always were. I can read your face like a book."

She opened her eyes wide. "Then does what you read there horrify you?"

He stepped toward her again and put his hands on her shoulders. "It horrifies me that you should risk so much for me."

"I would risk everything for you," she whispered. She stood on tiptoe to kiss his bearded cheek.

His eyes narrowed; she felt his hands tighten on her shoulders. There was a long pause. Her heart was beating very fast.

"What of your husband?" he asked at last.

"He will never know." She reached up to slide her arms around his neck. "I have loved you since I was a child," she whispered. "I would have been yours. If I can never be your wife, at least let me be your love."

He frowned at her bluntness as his arms tightened about her. "You risk more than you realize—"

She buried her face in his tunic. "I know. I am risking my life. But I have to. I love you more than life, don't you understand?" Her voice was full of pain. "Please, please, make love to me, Robert." Her pride had lost. The words came out slowly, weighted with longing.

For a moment longer he hesitated, fighting his conscience, but the feel of the woman, so eager and so lovely in his arms, was more than any man could resist. He seemed to have needed her, to have longed for her, forever. He was drowning in her gaze, lost.

After releasing her, he strode toward the door and slid the bolt, then he turned back to her. "There can be no going back, Isobel. What we do here can never be undone."

"I know." It was a whisper.

Already he was unfastening his belt. He laid it with his sword across a stool then he began to pull at the lacings that held his tunic closed.

His hands on her body were firm and strong as he pushed her gown and kirtle from her shoulders, letting them fall to the heather, a heap of rustling scarlet silk. Then he pulled off her shift. For a moment he stared at her, then slowly he drew her against him, pressing her slim pale body against his own as he wound his hands into her hair, pulling her head back, kissing her with increasing ferocity as instinctively her body arched to meet his.

With a sudden explosion of happiness she threw her arms around him, clawing at his back. He laughed, burying his face in her hair. Dropping to his knees, he pulled her with him, his mouth against her breasts as he pushed her down beneath him on the sharp heather stems, possessing her body with mouth and hands, holding her prisoner as she writhed at his touch. She could hear herself sobbing as she thrust her hips toward him and he laughed softly, holding her wrists pinioned for a moment to prevent her tearing at his back. His inhibitions had gone, his notions of chivalry, his sense of honor toward his new wife, the memory of his gentle Isabella, even the knowledge that the wrath of the Comyns, if her husband ever found out, would destroy her and bring down his secret cause, all were forgotten as he drowned in the wild beauty of the woman beneath him. With a shout of triumph he entered her, rolling with her in the heather, feeling the wiry, dusty stems tearing at his body as she wound her legs about his hips, fighting him now, her hands in his hair, her spine arched like a bow as with a shrill animal scream she felt her body explode into his. Again and again he plunged into her, then at last, exhausted, he lay beside her on the heather, his hand still possessively across her thighs.

She sat up slowly, trembling violently. Her body was singing; for the first time in her life she felt complete and ecstatically happy as she gazed ahead of her in silence, hugging her knees, feeling the chill of perspiration on her blazing body. Slowly she pushed her damp hair off her face.

Outside, the bailey was silent. In the heat of the afternoon men and animals were dozing in the shade.

Robert rolled toward her and put his hand on her back. Slowly he ran his finger down her spine. His eyes narrowed suddenly and he sat up. "Are these the marks of a whip?"

Isobel leaned contentedly toward him. "The scourge was part of my penance."

"You did that to yourself?" He stared at her, awed.

She shook her head. "I refused. The sisters did it, at Dundarg."

"Dear God!" He touched the scars on her back with gentle fingers.

"It's over, Robert. I want to forget it." She knelt up and put her arms around his neck again, nuzzling his ear.

"Like the hair shirt and the prayers?" He looked at her quizzically.

"The nuns were kind in their way." She didn't want to think about it, not now. She must not think of Mairi anymore. She could not bear to think of Mairi, not now. "One of the sisters took me down to the sea to bathe my wounds," she rushed on. "We went in near the rocks below the castle. I took off my shift and swam naked."

"Did you indeed." He raised his eyebrows, amused. "And how many of the garrison saw you?"

"None." She was indignant. "Afterward we lay to dry ourselves on the sand at the foot of the cliffs. Sister Eleanor put salve on my wounds." She frowned suddenly. "She . . . she touched me as a man would . . . here, and here. . . ." Her hand strayed toward her legs.

Robert's eyes narrowed with amusement again. "A follower of Sappho, your nun. And did you enjoy her attentions, my dear? Did she make you cry out in ecstasy as I did?" He pulled her suddenly across his knees.

"Certainly not!" Isobel's eyes flashed with indignation. "It was wrong! I didn't let her—"

"That is because you are a man's woman." Robert buried his face between her breasts. "I'd like to have seen you with your nun, my dear." He bit her gently, just above the sharp angle of her collar bone, holding her as she tried to wriggle away. He laughed as she struggled with fury to be free, and he pushed her over onto her back again.

When he had finished this time she lay quite still, too exhausted to move, her slim body curved into the heather, her hair tangled in the dried brown stems. Robert stood up and slipped on his tunic and hose. He took a checked woolen plaid from a hook on the wall and tucked it gently around her, then he pushed her hair back from her face.

"Rest for two minutes, love, then you must dress. I fear the whole castle knows what we're about in here."

She looked at him dreamily. "I'm too tired and too happy to move." Her body felt heavy and languid.

"Two minutes," he repeated threateningly. He moved back to the desk and picked up the letters he had been working on when she had been shown into the room. In two minutes he had forgotten she was there.

An hour or so later she awoke. He was still working. Wearily she stood up and pulled on her kirtle and dress, piled her hair up beneath her veil, and dragged her mantle around her shoulders. Then she walked over to him and, putting her arms around him, she kissed the back of his neck.

She slept alone in one of the guest chambers in the Snow Tower that night after dining at the high table in the great hall, seated between Robert and the Countess Eleyne. There had been no sign of Robert's wife.

It was dawn when the door opened and Robert slid into the shadowy room. His hands were cold on her warm body, heavy with sleep, exciting, rousing her, his mouth on her eyelids, her hair, her throat where the mark of his bite showed as a purple bruise.

When they lay quiet at last he raised himself on his elbow. "I must go away today," he whispered.

"Away?" She stared at him sleepily.

He nodded. "And you must go back to your husband." Seeing the expression on her face, he smiled grimly and kissed her firmly on the lips. "You cannot stay here, Isobel, you must see that. For Scotland's sake you have to go back. People will know I was here, and he will guess you came to see me. Open war between me and your husband would be disaster now."

Wriggling away from him, she sat up abruptly and stared at him in desperation. "You can't send me back. You can't!"

"I can, Isobel, and I must."

"I won't go."

"Then I shall have you taken back by force. Oh, my love, don't you see?"

"No!" She jumped from the bed, dragging a sheet with her to wrap around her. "No, I don't see! We love each other! We belong together. We have always belonged together! You have to let me stay. Your wife isn't here. She won't know—"

"Isobel, everyone in this castle knows you are here. The people of Mar are my people, and loyal, but one cannot burden this household with this sort of secret. Human nature is too frail. Someone will tell Buchan."

"But I will leave him. I will stay with you—"

"No, Isobel." His mouth closed in a hard line. "I have a wife. She has the connections to help my cause; she is faithful to me; she is good for my daughter, and one day she will be my queen."

Isobel went white. "And I? What am I?"

"You are a wild, beautiful creature from the farthest corner of my realm." He stood up and put his arms around her again, his eyes burning as they looked into hers. "You are the woman I love." He put his hand under her chin and raised her lips to meet his. "You are part of this land, Isobel, your spirit is part of the sea and the mountains and the wind and the rain, the wildness that is my kingdom. And I love you! One day, perhaps, we can be together, but not now. Now I have a kingdom to win, and you, if you are loyal to me, must obey me."

He caught her wrists and pulled her to him. The linen sheet fell to the floor and there was nothing between their bodies in the predawn cold of the room.

She struggled to be free of him. "But I want to stay! I can fight with you!" She knew she sounded like a child, pleading. "You can't send me away!"

"I must, my love." He kissed the top of her head gently. "I shall send for you when I am crowned. To follow tradition I need your brother, the Earl of Fife, to come from England to place the crown on my head, and I will need you to support him."

"Without the Earl of Fife you cannot be king!" Her eyes were blazing with pride again.

"Oh, I will be king and with no one's permission, but I should like to honor the old customs." He smiled grimly. "The proxy John Balliol used to place himself on the throne did not help his cause at all, so I shall insist on a descendant of the House of Duff to do the honors." He grinned. "And when I am king"—he kissed her hard on the mouth—"no one shall question who I take to my bed. Now, dress. I shall have your escort summoned to take you home to Buchan." He was still holding her wrists. "That is a command, Isobel."

Furiously she struggled to be free of him. "What if I refuse to go?"

"Then you will be taken by force." He released her abruptly. "Please, my love. Do as I ask. We will be together soon, I promise." After turning away from her, he pulled on his tunic and began to buckle his belt.

She was putting on her pale silk shift when suddenly he caught her in his arms again. "You will take care, my love. If there were only a way I could keep you with me, I would—"

"I know." She swallowed her misery as best she could.

"Don't provoke your husband, Isobel." Suddenly he was terribly afraid for her. "Obey him, love. We both know we were betrayed before, and we both know that your maid paid

with her life for our moments together at Scone. Remember
her—"

Her eyes were on his. "I will never forget her."

He nodded grimly. "Then go now. And pray you haven't
been missed."

Chapter Seventeen

Emma answered the door to Henry and ushered him in. "It was sweet of you to come. I know this is a bloody thing to ask anyone: to get involved in someone else's family crisis! But we need advice." She pulled him into the sitting room where Peter was sitting reading the paper. The two men greeted one another laconically and Peter moved toward the tray of bottles on the sideboard.

"Have a drink, Henry."

"Thanks, I think I will. We've had a hard day today. Paul wasn't in the office and the old man was in a foul mood."

"Not in?" Emma frowned. "Where was he?"

"Nobody knows, apparently."

Glancing at her husband, Emma sat down. "Well, it's Paul I want to talk about. We're all family and you are as good as." She leaned down and gave him a quick kiss on the cheek. "It's for Clare's sake. We're worried about her."

Henry sipped his drink slowly. "She seemed all right when I took her out to dinner last night," he said cautiously.

"Really all right?" Emma sat down next to him.

Henry shrugged. "Happy enough. Paul had just given her some beautiful sapphires."

"Sapphires!" Peter stared at him. "I thought Paul was supposed to be in money trouble."

There was a moment's silence, then Henry sighed. "Yes," he said. "That's what I thought too."

"She hasn't changed her mind about Duncairn?" Emma glanced from her husband to Henry and back. "She can't have. She wouldn't!"

"No, she wouldn't." Henry drained his glass and put it down. He looked at her uncomfortably. "But Paul is still very anxious to make her change her mind; or he was last week."

He wondered for a moment whether to tell them about his visit to Suffolk. After a moment or two he decided not to. If Clare had wanted Emma to know, no doubt she would have told her. "I don't know whether he is still of the same mind, but he's under pressure from two sides to sell. He certainly needs the money, I think we all agree about that, and there is no doubt that he is under a lot of pressure over Duncairn from Cummin at Sigma."

"Cummin?" Emma frowned at the name.

He nodded. "Rex Cummin, the president of Sigma UK, the oil conglomerate that wants Duncairn."

Emma stood up abruptly. She had gone white.

"What is it, Em?" Peter was looking at her hard. "Do you know this man Cummin?"

Emma poured herself another drink. There was a slight chinking noise as the gin bottle hit the rim of her glass. For a moment she didn't answer, then she turned and gave him a tight smile.

"I do know him, yes. The bastard! He is Diane Warboys's godfather or something. She introduced us because he had a spare ticket for a show I wanted to see when you were away." She took a deep, shaky breath. "He asked me about Paul and Clare." Her voice died away to a whisper. "He asked me about them a lot. I thought he was just being friendly."

There was a long silence.

"How many times have you seen him?" Peter spoke at last. He didn't look at her.

Henry gazed down into his glass, deeply embarrassed.

"How often, Em?" Peter repeated quickly.

"Only three times. For goodness sake, Peter, there's nothing in it. He's married. He just wanted to go to the same show. We had interests in common. He's a very cultured man—"

"Which I'm not, I suppose."

"You're just not very often here, Peter."

"I never knew Di was his goddaughter," Henry put in quietly. "I've talked to her about Clare and Paul's problems, I'm afraid. Just a bit. After she and I had dinner there once and things were a bit strained. I had to give her some sort of explanation. . . ." His voice died away.

"So between you and my wife," Peter said slowly, "you have told this man Cummin everything he needs to know. That Paul is desperate for money and that if he puts enough pressure on him Paul is going to find some way of getting Clare to agree to sell Duncairn."

Emma put her head in her hands. "You make Rex sound so ruthless."

"He didn't get to his position in an international oil corporation without being ruthless," Henry said gently. "He also has a lot of charm." He stood up and walked around the room for a minute or two, then he sat down again. "Something happened last week. I wasn't going to tell you. I didn't think it was any of my business, but now, well, perhaps you ought to know. Paul tried to trick Clare into signing away everything she owns. He'd had some kind of agreement drawn up giving himself complete control of her affairs.

Emma's face tightened in disgust. "She didn't sign it!"

"She would have." Henry looked at them both with concern. "If I hadn't stopped her. She was going through a pile of documents, just signing them. It was I who told her to read them first. Paul obviously knows her well. He'd counted on her not bothering."

"Was he furious?" Emma's eyes were fixed on his face.

"I think he was. And what's more, I think she's a bit afraid of him. She told me that she was thinking of leaving him, you know."

"Leaving him?" Emma echoed. She paused, then after a moment's thought she shrugged. "I can't say I'm surprised. My brother is cold, calculating, and sadistic. I know him of old. I don't really know how she's stuck it out so long."

"Oh, come on," Peter was growing more and more uncomfortable. "You're making him out to be some kind of fiend. He's not that bad."

"He is, believe me. If Clare is defying him, he's quite likely to get—" She stopped in midsentence.

"To get what?" Peter was gave a scornful laugh. "Come on, Em. You're becoming melodramatic!"

"Am I?" Emma stared at her feet. "There is a lot at stake. Paul's future. His job. His reputation, if all the rumors are true. His life-style. What chance does Clare have against what he's got to lose? And God help her if he ever found out she was going to leave him. He'd be furious. I think we should warn her just how much pressure he is under. I don't think she has any idea—"

There was a moment's silence. "I took her back to his office last night and left her alone with him there. At midnight," Henry said slowly.

Emma stood up. She looked at them both for a moment, then she walked toward the telephone. "I'm going to call Clare," she said. "I know I'm being melodramatic and I know it's probably silly, but I'd like to make sure she's all right."

The two men watched as she dialed the number.

In the house in Campden Hill the telephone rang on in the silence. The place was empty.

Paul sat down heavily in Geoffrey's leather armchair. His face was haggard and he looked ten years older than his brother. "I'm glad Chloe's out. I wanted to talk to you alone. I've been walking around all day. Something terrible has happened." He flung himself back in the chair and closed his eyes.

Geoffrey eyed him gravely. "You'd better tell me."

Paul nodded. "It's Clare. She needs help, Geoffrey. Real help. Things have got out of hand."

Geoffrey sat down in his own chair behind the desk and folded his hands on the blotter. He was shocked by his brother's face. Paul's exhaustion and distress were obvious.

"You'd better tell me what has been happening," he said slowly.

For a moment Paul did not reply. He stared down at the carpet between his feet, thinking hard. He had to get his story right. "Clare is going out of her mind, Geoff," he said at last. "She has begun hallucinating, accusing me of things." He frowned. "Threatening to tell people that I've tried to harm her, and she's been doing strange things in the garden.

At midnight. Lighting candles in the shelter of the hedge—raising her arms and sort of chanting, invoking spirits."

Geoffrey was watching him closely. "You've seen her?"

Paul nodded. "I was too far away to hear what she was saying or to see anything." He hesitated. "If there *was* anything to see. Is this for real, Geoffrey? Is she really raising the spirits of the dead, or is it all in her mind?"

Geoffrey sighed. "I had hoped and prayed that she would stop all this before it went too far. So often people begin these things so innocently—yoga, meditation. . . ." He frowned. "Everyone is being urged to do it. I see it all the time in newspapers and magazines, and it fills me with worry. People are being taught without realizing it to open themselves up on a spiritual level, and in so many cases there is nothing there to fill the space they have created. So then comes the interest in the occult and the dabbling in the black arts. Satan waits and watches all the time, ready. And once he has won someone for himself, he won't give up without a struggle."

Paul's expression was grave. "What can you do?"

Geoffrey rubbed his face with his hands wearily. "I shall talk to her again. And I shall pray for her, of course."

"You must be able to do more than that! For heaven's sake, Geoff! She is irrational, hysterical at times! I think she's all right, she's calm, and she seems terribly sane, and then suddenly she comes out with something completely mad. Some of the things she says are truly insane, Geoff. She will probably tell you things about me! She thinks I'm trying to harm her! You mustn't believe anything she tells you—" Paul was becoming agitated. "You know that she has these hallucinations, and nightmares, and conjures up this woman from the past. Sarah will back me up. Dear God, Geoffrey! You know I'm not a religious man. I confess I've never had any time for your mumbo jumbo up to now, but this is something else. It gives me the creeps. You've got to help her." He paused for a moment. "I think she needs locking up. For her own safety."

"Locking up?" Geoffrey looked up, shocked.

Paul nodded slowly. "Some kind of private nursing home, perhaps. Somewhere where they will take care of her."

"Have you spoken to your own doctor about this, Paul?" Geoffrey was frowning.

Paul nodded. "He said she needs to get away, to have a complete break, but she won't go. Not voluntarily. She is too obsessed with this Isobel. Geoffrey—" He stood up suddenly. "This is just between us, isn't it? This story must not get out. Imagine the field day the press would have if they got hold of it. This has to be kept quiet. You must see that. The Royland name—David's career. Mine—yours! Can you imagine the headlines? *'Sister-in-law of MP and South London Vicar in Black Magic Scandal!'* " He shuddered.

"No. You're right. I do see that," Geoffrey agreed cautiously.

"People are beginning to talk, Geoff." Paul leaned across the desk toward his brother. "She's got to be put away somewhere where she can be no danger to herself or to anyone else."

"Paul." Geoffrey stood up slowly and put his hand heavily on Paul's shoulder. "This doesn't have anything at all to do with your desire to control Clare's affairs, does it? I'm not suggesting you're making any of this up. I have seen and spoken to her myself, so I do know her state of mind, but this desire to get her out of the way—"

"Is for her own safety." Paul walked away from him and stood with his back to the empty grate. Geoffrey was not reacting in quite the way he had intended. He controlled his anger with an effort. "She has a knife. A jeweled dagger. God knows where she got it from. I took it away from her, but she went berserk. She was insanely angry, so I gave it back to her. Now she has it hidden. She could hurt herself, even kill herself, Geoff." He wasn't sure where the idea for the dagger had come from. It seemed inspired. And it worked. Geoffrey was appalled.

"Dear God! Where is she now?"

"At home in Campden Hill. At least she was when I left her," Paul said.

Geoffrey stood with his back to the window, his hands clasped behind him. "Leave it with me, Paul. I will go over to see her now, this evening."

* * *

Clare had lain still without moving for a long time after she woke that morning. She could feel Paul stirring at her side. Desperately she closed her eyes, trying to keep her breathing even so he wouldn't guess she was awake. She could sense that he was lying staring up at the dark ceiling, just as she had been doing for the last hour since she had come suddenly and completely out of her dream. One moment she had been there, with Robert and Isobel, as the dawn light filtered into the shadowy room at Kildrummy, and the next she was lying wide awake in London on a sheet damp with perspiration, her heart pounding, her stomach churning. Then as the shock of the awakening subsided she found her body was still aroused, alive, tingling with anticipation. Unconsciously her hands had strayed to her own breasts as she lay there, staring up into the darkness.

Beside her Paul suddenly sat up. For a moment he didn't move and she tensed, pressing her face into the pillow, holding her breath. She felt his weight shift then he climbed out of the bed. A moment later the bathroom light went on. She hunched over, her back to the door, clutching her pillow miserably as the past receded completely and the memory of all that had happened the night before came flooding back and with it the realization that her marriage was over. After what Paul had done to her last night she never wanted to see or speak to him again.

She tensed as he came back into the bedroom, clenching her eyelids tighter, but he did not approach the bed. She could hear the faint sounds as he pulled on his clothes, then the noise of the bedroom door opening and closing and then silence.

She did not move for a long time. Only when she heard the front door bang downstairs did she at last climb slowly out of bed. After going to the window, she lifted the corner of the curtain and peered out into the darkness of the early morning. She could see Paul walking slowly down the hill beneath the streetlights, his broad shoulders hunched against the rain. He was carrying his briefcase.

It took her five minutes to shower and dress. She glanced

around the room as she threw her suitcase on the bed. Her party clothes, her silk dresses, she would not need. All she wanted were sweaters and trousers, a skirt, her boots. The rest of her clothes were at Bucksters—she would collect them some other time. She threw in her makeup and a couple of dresses and that was all. Her sapphires and the slim gold watch she left where she had dropped them the night before, on the shelf above the towel rail in the bathroom.

After leaving the suitcase in the hall, she ran down to the kitchen. Casta was lying under the kitchen table, nose on paws. She got up and stretched as Clare appeared, her tail wagging.

Clare knelt down and hugged her. "Breakfast, darling, then we're going to Scotland." The dog licked her face.

Clare was shaking from lack of sleep. She heated the coffee and cut herself a piece of bread, glancing at the kitchen clock. She had told Sarah not to come back until the evening, but one could never tell with that woman. If she had what she called "words" with her sister, she might arrive back any second.

She spread honey on the bread with trembling hands and then forced herself to sit down on the bar stool to eat it. She had a seven-hour drive ahead of her and she had to gather every bit of strength before she set out. Ten minutes later she and Casta were on their way.

"She's taken her suitcase and her coat and the dog. And she left her keys behind. She put them back through the letter box." Sarah's voice on the telephone was anxious.

"I see." Paul sounded suddenly flat. "Well, there is nothing we can do tonight. I'll see you in the morning. I'm going to spend the night here at the office."

He slept in a chair, waking frequently, gnawing at his problems. Where was Clare, and what was she saying to people? He turned restlessly, trying to make himself more comfortable. Would anyone believe her if she told them what had happened in the elevator? Geoffrey wouldn't. Of that he was fairly certain. But what about the others? What about Emma? He chewed the inside of his cheek. Emma would believe Clare. Emma would believe anything of him. Unless he destroyed Clare's credibility totally and for good, he was finished. He glanced in the semidarkness across at his desk where the calendar stood. So short a time to go until settlement day, and then, unless he could pay, he was finished.

It was just after eight the next morning when, returning from a trip to the washroom to shave and change his shirt, he noticed the envelope that had been put on his desk while he was out of the room. He stood staring down at it with a frown while in the corner behind him the computer screen flashed quietly with the morning's prices.

He sat down and picked the envelope up from the blotter. For a moment he just looked at it, then at last he tore it open. Inside was a clipping from *Private Eye*. Attached to it was a note from Sir Duncan Beattie. "Don't know if you saw this," it said. "I should like your comments."

The short piece was to the point:

> Rumors in the City of yet another foul up as leading financier gets his calculations wrong. Again. For Rent signs are appearing on strongboxes all over Switzerland. Pollo Royfield, director of one of the megaconglomerates, must be shaking in his shoes. Watch this space.

Paul screwed the cutting into a little ball and hurled it across the room. Diane Warboys! He could never prove it, of course. But it had to be her. Who else knew? The bitch! The disloyal, vindictive bitch! He would see to it personally that her career in the City went no further.

What the hell was he going to tell Sir Duncan? Sweating suddenly, he picked up his attaché case and clicked back the locks.

Among the sheaf of papers was a copy of his father's will. He walked with it to the window and read through it slowly yet again, the paper trembling slightly in his hand. He already knew what it said. The Royland shares were to be divided evenly among the four children. Then the sentence that trapped him: "If at any time any of the four should wish to sell their share in the company, they may do so only if they first offer the shares to the other three severally or together. At that point it is my wish that that person offers up all the rest of the shares and dividends bequeathed by me to them in this will. To sell a holding in the family company means he or she is desperate for money or no longer interested in Royland International and its holdings. Either way he or she will need to liquidate." He could still hear his father's voice dictating the succinct words and imagine the haughty, stubborn face behind them.

He could never tell David he had to sell the Royland shares; and he would not admit to anyone, ever, that he had already liquidated the rest of his holdings. He was trapped.

He folded the document back to the first page and threw it down on the desk. Damn and blast Clare!

He picked up the will and threw it back into the briefcase. A copy of his own was there in the folder too, and a copy of Clare's. Idly he picked hers up. They had made them together, four years before. In it, apart from small legacies to all her nephews and nieces, she had left the bulk of her property to him. There was no mention of Duncairn as a separate package. She had been confident then that she would have a baby, an heir to the Gordon estates, so she had had no thoughts of leaving it to James, who in those days anyway was still without any sense of family—the reason that Aunt Margaret has not left Duncairn to him in the first place. His interest in the past had begun and ended with the battles of Robert the Bruce, something Margaret Gordon had quickly spotted. It had not displeased her. He would come to it in the end, as Alec, his father, had done, and in the meantime Clare would be the right caretaker for the place. It had always been the women who had loved Duncairn.

Paul read it through again, then slowly he put it back in his briefcase, his face impassive. He had an appointment with Rex Cummin at four o'clock.

Clare had stopped the night before at a motel near Bishop Auckland, too tired to drive farther. She bought a can opener at a village store, with a dog bowl and some cans of dog food, and some ham and bread for herself. Once they had settled in she and Casta had a picnic together in the motel room, sitting on the floor in front of the TV.

For a while she watched, then, tired and her sandwich finished, she turned off the program and threw the window open. The night air smelled glorious after the long days in London and the drive in the car. It was soft and rich and intoxicating as she leaned on the windowsill, feeling her elbows cold and damp on the mossy bricks.

In the garden behind the reception area in the main house there were a lot of people milling around. She could hear laughter and talking, and children's shouts, and she could just see the flickering light crystals from the sparklers the children were holding. Suddenly there was a cheer. A sheet of flame shot upward and she saw the whole garden lighted for a moment in flickering orange lights as a huge bonfire, built in the motel's kitchen garden, burst into life. For one moment she saw the face of the effigy, strapped to an old wooden chair on the top of the fire—an impassive, round, expressionless face—then a cloud of thick smoke swept down across the garden and blocked everything from sight.

Clare turned slowly away from the window and sat down on the floor, putting her arms around Casta's neck. Her eyes were full of tears. For a moment the reality of the scene had been vivid. The figure, the fire, the staring, shouting crowds. "If only they knew, Casta," she whispered. "If only they knew what it was really like." She shivered.

After standing up slowly, she closed the window and drew the curtains. She tidied up the empty food bowl and the paper bags, had a shower and washed her hair, then, wearing nothing but a bathrobe, she pulled back the bedspread. Perhaps she could do some yoga to ease the stiffness in her shoulders after the long drive.

Behind her Casta whined.

Clare turned and stared at her. The dog was trembling. Outside in the garden a volley of deafening explosions rang out. Relieved, Clare found she was smiling. "Casta! You fraud. You're not afraid of the bangs? You're supposed to be a gun dog!" She bent and rumpled the dog's ruff affectionately.

Casta backed away from her, her hackles raised.

Clare frowned. The room was cold. She glanced at the window, but she knew she had closed it properly. The curtains hung still with no sign of a draft. Biting her lip, she looked back at Casta. The dog was growling now. As Clare watched she jumped, with a little whine, onto the bed, pressing herself backward against the headboard. She was staring into the middle of the room, her eyes tracking back and forth across the empty space as if she could see something there.

Clare backed toward the bed too. She was suddenly very frightened; her mouth had gone dry. The lights were on; the white-painted walls were stark, decorated with bright prints of wildflowers. There were no shadows here. It was the fireworks, that was all. They had unnerved the dog, just as the fire itself had unnerved her.

She sat down on the bed, groping behind her for the TV remote control, which she had dropped onto the quilt. She snapped it on and clicked up the sound, filling the room with the voice of the newscaster.

Behind her Casta was trembling. Suddenly the dog threw herself off the bed and ran to the door, scratching at it frantically, trying to get out of the room.

Watching her, Clare could feel her heart beginning to jump wildly under her ribs. She glanced at her suitcase, lying open on the floor by the dressing table. In it were her candles —the beautiful candles she had bought to summon Isobel, and with them the oil Zak had told her about. She had gone to the shop whose address he had given her, a shop that sold crystal balls and incense and books on all the esoteric arts, and there, feeling embarrassed and slightly foolish, she had bought the magic oil. "You use it to anoint the candles, like this." He had shown her how. "And yourself, on the forehead and heart and palms, like this, to keep away any evil spirits." He had smiled. "Just in case your brother-in-law is right. Just in case. . . ."

She had bought the oil, but she had never used it. It seemed so silly and superstitious. And she had never used the new beautiful silver candles either.

The suitcase was a few feet from her. She had only to stand up, find the small bottle, and open it.

But she couldn't move.

Desperately she raised the volume on the TV again, the remote control clutched in her hand. "Please go away. I don't want to know what happened to you. Please. . . ." Her voice was shaking as she spoke out loud, the sound lost beneath the measured tones of the newscaster booming around the small room. "Leave me alone. Please. . . ."

❦ Chapter Eighteen ❦

"Lord Buchan is in Perth, my lady," the man said, handing Isobel the letter. "He commands you to join him there without delay."

Gilbert of Annandale had guided her back to Buchan without mishap, but at Duncairn she had found the messenger waiting. A silk scarf wound about her throat to hide the purple bruise left by Robert's teeth, Isobel took the letter reluctantly and she shivered.

Her body still glowed from Robert's touch; every nerve and every sinew seemed to have come alive. The countryside seemed brighter, the huge, overpowering hills beneath the purple heat haze seemed more beautiful, the flowers in the long, whispering grasses beside the tracks were glowing like jeweled enamels. Once, on the ride back, she had started singing. Gilbert had glanced at her from his thin, raw-boned horse, and grinned, but he said nothing. He knew the effect his master had on the ladies. Let her think she was the only one, poor lass. She was by far the most beautiful. Then he had sighed. She was also the most dangerous.

Turning from the messenger, Isobel unfolded the letter and read her husband's curt message. She was commanded to join him in Perth and from thence they were to ride south to England.

Her hand shook as she read the brief lines. To England, when at last Robert was back in Scotland! How could she bear to be parted from him now?

But there was no choice, and with a heavy heart she obeyed. She organized the household of the earl for travel. Turning her back on Buchan, she rode south, her bruise now hidden beneath an elegant fine linen wimple, at the head of an escort of his men.

The Earl and Countess of Buchan arrived at their estates at Whitwick in Leicestershire in early August, and it was there that the summons came to attend the court of King Edward. The English parliament would meet in the second week of September, and Buchan, as one of the representatives of the land—no longer the kingdom—of Scotland, was to be there. But for some reason Edward had decided that he required Lord Buchan's presence at Westminster a month early.

They arrived in London on Sunday, August 22. It was hot and crowded, the narrow stinking streets noisy as they rode at last out toward Westminster. Nervously Isobel edged her horse nearer to her husband's, conscious as never before that these people were the enemies of Scotland. The crowds were restless, volatile, excited, surging around their horses, sharp eyes watching the wheat sheaves of Buchan on the surcoats of the retainers, questioning, exchanging insults with their escort. Beside Isobel one of the knights loosened his sword in its sheath with a rattle. Nerves were tense.

"What is it? Why are they so hostile?" Isobel asked her neighbor.

He shrugged. "The Scots are not popular in England, my lady. Did you think we would be?" He grinned humorlessly.

They rode slowly out across the marshy ground that separated the City of London from Westminster and clattered across one of the bridges that led across the Tyburn and onto the Isle of Thorns. There the palace and the Abbey of Westminster huddled together amid a crowd of houses and spreading streets on the muddy tidal banks of the broad river Thames.

King Edward received them in one of the small painted rooms in the palace. He had aged visibly since Isobel had first seen him at Duncairn, and he looked very tired. As she knelt to kiss his hand she glanced up at the gray, lined face. His eyes were unchanged. They studied her shrewdly. "Lady Buchan. Welcome to England." His fingers as she touched them with her lips were ice cold.

Silently she rose and stepped back to her husband's side, but he was still speaking to her. "Your brother, madam, is here at Westminster." The king's lip curled. "You will no doubt wish to see him while you are here. He is a member of my son's household. I do not entertain my son's friends however hard he tries to persuade me, as no doubt you have heard, but I have no doubt you will find young Fife somewhere around. We are overrun with Scots, it seems." He pulled his velvet mantle around his shoulders more tightly, shivering in spite of the hot airlessness of the room, then he turned to Lord Buchan. "You will have heard, no doubt, that Sir William Wallace has been captured at last and is being brought to London." He glanced sharply back at Isobel, hearing her quick intake of breath. "Indeed, madam. The rebellious traitor and outlaw." He smiled humorlessly. "He is being held tonight at the house of William de Leyre then tomorrow he will be brought out here to Westminster to stand trial. You will no doubt be glad to hear we have at last apprehended such an evil man, my lord." The king eyed Lord Buchan closely.

Isobel felt her husband shift uncomfortably from foot to foot as he stood beside her. "Indeed, Your Grace."

"He will die, of course," Edward went on. "I do not permit opposition and treachery, particularly from small men. You can hear the crowds." He raised his hand to the leaded window, and it was just possible to hear the muted roar of the rabble who were roaming the tracks between Westminster and the Palace of the Savoy.

"You were merciful, Your Grace, to others of the Scottish army," Lord Buchan put in uncomfortably.

"And I pardoned them. Yes, even you." Edward's thin lips parted in another smile. "You did what you no doubt thought was right at the time, Lord Buchan, but you saw the error of your ways and came into my peace. This . . . this upstart knight has persisted in his opposition to me for too long. When I might have given quarter he rejected it, so now he must pay for his temerity." He stood up abruptly and went to stand close to the fire that smoldered fitfully in the small grate. Two of his attendants rushed to his side, but he waved them away.

"Take heed of what happens to Wallace, my lord," he went

on slowly. "And see to it that there is no more rebellion in Scotland." He turned away.

Lord Buchan bowed. "Indeed, Your Grace," he murmured. "I shall take heed."

"You attend our parliament soon, I think?" Edward addressed him without turning around.

"There are ten Scots representatives coming, Your Grace."

"With twenty good Englishmen, to draw up a new constitution for the land of Scotland." The king smiled unpleasantly. "Just so. We shall talk again, my lord, once this affair with Wallace is settled, about the obedience of the Scots." He looked at Isobel again suddenly. "You seem pale, Lady Buchan. Can it be that you feel sorry for this leader of the rebels?"

"Sir William is a brave man, Your Grace," Isobel said clearly. "And he is no traitor to you. He is a Scotsman born. He has never paid allegiance to the King of England."

"Unlike you, my lady, if my memory serves me right." The sallow face was pinched. She could feel his eyes boring into her skull. Nervously she straightened her shoulders.

"I did what I had to, Your Grace," she murmured defiantly.

His mouth twisted into a half smile. "Against your will, it seems. Can it be that your wife too is a rebel at heart, Lord Buchan?"

"Indeed not, Your Grace." Behind her Lord Buchan's face had gone first white and then red. "She is an ignorant woman, Your Grace, and very foolish. She doesn't know what she is saying."

There was a long silence as Edward scrutinized Isobel's face, and she looked away, suddenly terribly afraid. At last he spoke. "I think you underestimate your wife, Lord Buchan," he said slowly.

Isobel's brother found her later in the quarters the Buchans had been assigned in a distant wing of the palace. The Earl of Fife was a tall, slim boy of sixteen, very like his father and head and shoulders taller than his sister. Isobel felt her heart miss a beat as he came into the room that they were using as a solar. They were all there: the same color hair, the same hard gray eyes, the same negligent charm she remembered so faintly in her father all those long years ago. "So, my big sister. How are you?" He kissed her hand and then gave her a quick peck on the cheek.

"I am well, Duncan." Isobel eyed him critically. She had last seen her brother as a screaming, red-faced baby. Now he was a court dandy. Her eyes rose slowly from the ornate spurs and exquisite embroidered shoes to the parti-colored hose, the padded doublet emblazoned with the arms of Fife, with rows of buttons on the sleeves from wrists to elbows, and the jeweled dagger at his belt. His hair was cut and rolled in the most modern fashion.

"I hear you are a friend of Prince Edward," she said at last. She sat down on a carved stool.

Duncan smiled. "I am in his household certainly. As no doubt you have heard his highness is not in favor with his father; his highness's friends even less so. So, I follow the prince. I find life at the English court amusing."

Isobel scrutinized his face. He was still a carefree child. Like a child he caught her hand suddenly. "Come on, let us walk a bit. I shall show you around. You must see everything there is to see while you are here. Would you like to see the great hall where the Wallace will be tried tomorrow?"

Isobel's eyes widened. "You make it sound like some kind of show."

"And so it will be. The best thing that has happened in months!"

Scandalized, she clutched his arm. "Duncan! Do you realize what you are saying? Sir William fought for our country! For our freedom from . . . from . . ." She glanced around. "From England, and King Edward." She dropped her voice to a whisper.

Duncan was horrified. "For the love of the Holy Virgin, don't say such things!" He looked over his shoulder in terror. "His grace is overlord of Scotland. Anyone who fights him is a traitor—"

"Duncan, how can you say such a thing! You, the Earl of Fife!"

"Of course I can say it. You don't understand, sister." Testily he shook off her arm. "Come on." He changed the subject quickly. "Do you want to see the sights of Westminster or not?"

Slowly she followed him through a maze of passages and courtyards to the great hall of Westminster where they slipped in unnoticed among the crowds of workmen who were putting up benches for the forthcoming trial. On the dais the chairs of judges were already in place. Isobel stood and looked up in awe at the vast beamed roof where sunbeams strayed among the oak timbers and shadows played on the distant painted decoration. Even in Paris she had not seen such a great hall as this. Two men pushed past her, carrying trestles, and for a moment she and her brother were separated. She looked around wildly, then she saw him, a colorful caricature of a figure, hand on hip, leaning against the wall. There was a supercilious curl to his lip.

After finding her way back to his side, she looked at him challengingly. "When are you coming back to Scotland, Duncan?"

"Scotland?" He looked horrified. "Not for a long time, I hope! This is the center of the world, Isobel! This is where I want to be! When the king dies—" He lowered his voice with a hasty look around him. "When the old man dies, Prince Edward will be king and then I shall be in a position of influence."

"You?" Isobel couldn't keep the scorn from her voice. "You are only a boy!"

"Prince Edward likes boys!" Duncan stared at her defiantly.

Isobel gasped. "Holy Mother of God!" she whispered. "Are the rumors true, then, about Edward of Caernarvon?"

"What rumors?" Duncan raised an eyebrow. He smirked archly at his sister. "How shocked the Countess of Buchan looks!"

Isobel had gone pale. She began to walk back toward the door. "I have to go back to our rooms—"

"Oh, come on!" Duncan was suddenly contrite. "I didn't mean anything. We're friends, that's all. He's not that many

years older than I!" He stared at her anxiously, a little boy
suddenly, for all his towering stature.

Isobel frowned. "Well—"

"Oh, please, come on. I'll take you to see the shrine of St.
Edward." He caught her hand again. "The abbey is so close.
Come, I'll show you! It is more beautiful than anything
you've got in Scotland, I'll wager!"

Outside, the air was thick with dust. They threaded their
way back through the noisy, crowded alleys and courtyards
until they came to the great Abbey of St. Peter, where an
endless stream of pilgrims lined up to enter and pay homage
at the shrine of St. Edward the Confessor. Standing in the
porch, out of the blinding sunlight, Duncan once more
caught her hand. He gave her a wry smile. "I didn't mean to
shock you, Isobel," he said in a whisper. "I'm not one of
Edward's boys. Not like that. I'm no catamite." He glanced
down at his dusty embroidered toes. "In fact"—he looked up
again, suddenly all smiles—"I am betrothed. To Marie de
Monthermer, daughter of our cousin Gilbert's guardian. We
shall marry next year when the dispensation comes through
from the Holy Father, if Lady Gloucester agrees."

All around them there were booths, displaying souvenirs of
the shrine, tiny vials of holy water, pieces of the true cross,
fragments of St. Thomas's cloak and of his shinbone, gold
medallions, miniature reliquaries, beads, and pilgrim badges.
At one of the stalls Duncan bought candles for himself and his
sister, to offer before the shrine, and with them a gold-and-
enamel brooch, which he pinned carefully to her mantle. All
around them the vendors were crying their wares until they
were hoarse, each one vying with the others for the pilgrims'
custom as the weary travelers, many of them sporting the
traditional staff and scrip and cloak, lined up in the sun.

Once they reached the pass door in the huge carved oak
doors at last, Duncan dived in front of her into the glowing
darkness of the abbey. From behind the screens they could
hear the monks singing the office, the sound of their voices
rising and falling in the echoes. The air was heavy with incense and the smell of candle wax. Moving slowly in the
broad untidy line of pilgrims, they made their way eastward

toward the shrine. Isobel glanced around her. The abbey was indeed beautiful, the towering pillars, in the new French Gothic style, soaring heavenward, the creamy stone painted and gilded in a myriad of colors by the armies of decorators brought in by King Edward's father, Henry III, the windows glowing with their pictures in colored glass.

Around them were crowds of tired, sweating pilgrims dressed in a variety of clothes, from the gorgeous costly fashion such as Duncan wore, to rags and pilgrim cloaks. The pilgrims, many of them ill, had come to seek the saint's aid, and they shuffled slowly forward. Immediately in front of them was a band of black-cloaked men, their sandaled feet scuffing across the painted tiles on the floor.

In the chapel of the shrine, with all its memorabilia of the saint, Isobel, like every pilgrim before her, stopped and stared at the beauty of the place and at the shrine itself, with its carved and gilded superstructure over the tomb, and high above it the shadowy carvings of the roof. The crowds did not allow her to stop for long. Once again the line moved forward, and she, like her brother and every person who entered the place, lighted her candle and put it with the thousands of others around the shrine. Then she knelt before it and crossed herself, whispering a prayer before the saint. Then almost too soon they were moving on, Duncan at her side, with always around them the soaring voices of the monks in the body of the abbey behind the carved rood screen.

Near an altar in a niche at the east end of the chapel Duncan stopped. He crossed himself reverently and then caught at Isobel's sleeve, pulling her into the shadows. For a moment the brother and sister stood, quietly watching the shuffling crowd of pilgrims move past them and out into the main body of the church again. At their feet the sunlight threw a pattern of glowing color from the stained-glass window above their heads onto a patch of stone flags, as yet untiled. "There is something here I want to show you," Duncan whispered. "Come."

He drew her quietly into a corner of the chapel. "There. Look." The crowds shielded them, the shuffling feet, the whispers, the sounds of coughing from the sick who had come to pray for health. Duncan pointed. "See. Edward's coronation chair."

Isobel looked. The carved and gilded oak chair standing on a step in the shadows was painted with birds and exotic animals and luxuriant foliage. It was rich and very beautiful. Beside it stood two of the king's men-at-arms in royal livery. "See," Duncan murmured. "In its base."

Isobel stared into the shadows. A candle flared and dripped nearby, and in the sudden wildly flickering light she saw the great stone set into the chair's base.

For a moment she didn't understand. She frowned, seeing the warm candlelight nudging at the rough sandstone, catching the slight sparkle in the stone. Beside the chair one of the men-at-arms, seeing her gaze, straightened, bringing his lance to the ground with a sharp crack.

"It is Scotland's Stone of Destiny from Scone," Duncan whispered. "I remember when the king had it brought here to the abbey four years ago. He had the chair made specially to hold it. It cost him a hundred shillings." He gave a quick smile. "Prince Edward will be crowned on it."

"A King of England, on Scotland's most sacred stone!" Isobel was horrified. Suddenly she clutched her bother's arm. "Not you! They would not use you to place the king on the throne? It is your right to crown Scotland's king! Scotland's, Duncan! Edward will never be king of Scotland!"

"Then who?" Duncan, embarrassed by the stare of the guards, pulled his sister back into the shadows again.

"Robert. The Earl of Carrick. He is our true king."

"Lord Carrick?" Duncan looked doubtful. "Are you sure? His brother Edward is one of the prince's household here. I know him well. Lord Carrick is in the king's peace, Isobel. In fact, he is working closely with the king. I've seen him here at Westminster."

"Only because it is not the right time!" Isobel retorted indignantly. "One day he will free Scotland!"

Duncan shrugged. "Wallace said *he* would free Scotland, and look what's going to happen to him."

"Sir William isn't the king. He isn't even an earl," Isobel replied slowly. "He is a brave man, but that is not enough."

"Well, if your Robert is crowned king of Scots, it will be without me." Duncan shrugged again. "Someone will have to stand in for the Earl of Fife, like they did when Balliol was crowned. I have to stay in England whether I want to or not."

"But you won't crown Edward?" Isobel caught his hand in anxiety. "Swear you won't crown Edward."

Duncan laughed uncomfortably. "Of course I won't. The archbishop will crown him."

Isobel turned back to the carved chair. She stepped closer, staring in awe at the stone, her brother suddenly forgotten. She could sense its power, sense the sleeping strength of its magic. She moved closer again. With an exclamation the guards stood to attention. One drew his sword, the sound of the metal scraping against its scabbard, echoing among the vaulted arches of the abbey. Around them people stopped and stared, and there was a frisson of fear among the crowd, who hurried on past, not wanting to know what was happening, not wanting to be involved. Duncan gasped. "Come away," he whispered in anguish. "Isobel, come away! Oh God, I shouldn't have shown you!"

She ignored him. Fixing the man with a haughty stare, she pushed aside the flat of the sword blade with her bare hand. "Do you think I'm going to put your pretty stone in my pouch and steal it away?" she asked him imperiously. "All I want to do is touch it." She gave him a pleading smile, then as the man hesitated she fell on her knees before the chair and put her hands on the stone.

It was icy cold, but it was alive. She could feel it in her hands. She closed her eyes, willing the magic of it into her body, feeling the tingling in her palms and fingertips. For a moment she forgot where she was, in the shadowy abbey with a soldier of King Edward of England standing over her with a drawn sword. Instead she seemed to see around her the trees, the hills of Scotland, feel the gentle wind on her hair, the soft rain on her face, and sense the sacred presence of the ancient gods around her. Then someone was pulling at her arm.

Duncan, in an agony of fear, was trying to drag her to her feet. "I'm sorry; I'm sorry!" he kept saying over and over to the guards. "My sister is not well. Don't hurt her. I'll take her away. I'm sorry. . . ."

Behind them a knight of the king's bodyguard had appeared, his spurs ringing on the stone flags as he strode toward them.

"I think you should take the lady away, my lord." The man spoke kindly, recognizing the boy as one of the young nobles from the prince's household. He nodded at the guard, who sheathed his weapon with a rattle.

Slowly Isobel rose to her feet. She looked around her, dazed, as Duncan put his arm around her shoulders. "Come on," he hissed, and before she could protest he had dragged her away. They left the abbey in silence.

Outside once more in the hot sunshine Isobel smiled. "It let me feel its power," she whispered. "Duncan, I felt it. It gave it to me!"

Duncan swallowed. He eyed his sister nervously. "You shouldn't have touched it."

"I had to. Don't you see? If you cannot crown the king, I must! I am a child of the earls of Fife, just as you are. I will crown him when the time comes! And I will give him the power from the stone. I have it in my hands." She held out her hands, palms up, in front of her, and they both stared at them in awe.

Duncan looked around, frightened. "You're talking treason, Isobel."

"No." She shook her head. "I am talking loyalty, to our true king."

She barely slept that night, tossing and turning in the huge curtained bed at her husband's side, and when she did she was racked with nightmares. It was dawn before she slept properly at last, so worn out she did not hear her husband wake when his attendants came to dress him.

The earl, with one look at his wife's tousled, exhausted face asleep on the pillow beside him, rose without waking her. For a long time he stood looking down at her, and then he leaned across the bed and gently he touched her flushed cheek. She roused such strange emotions in him, this strange, wild, beautiful woman to whom he was married. He knew she respected and feared him now. She would never risk crossing him again, but she would never love him either. In fact, he suspected that something like hate lurked below her meek, obedient demeanor. And always that reckless courage—courage that would speak out even before King Edward without thought of the consequences. He sighed, suddenly feeling old. What exactly were his feelings for her? He owned her, and at least on the surface, he had tamed her, and perhaps now and then between the rages and the anger he felt something like affection for her, even a strange possessive sort of love. One thing was certain. If she ever betrayed him he would not let her live.

He dressed quietly and, with one final look at his wife as she lay ensnared in her unhappy dreams, he left the room without disturbing her, ordering her ladies to let her sleep.

When Duncan came they turned him away, and he went without a murmur to find his friends, jostling with them to watch Sir William Wallace, crowned with a mocking wreath of laurel, brought in chains to the great hall of Westminster. He did not give Isobel another thought; it certainly did not cross his mind that he would never see her again.

Isobel awoke just before noon, stretching out in the bed. The painted glass windows let shafts of colored light play across the rush-strewn floor and touched the tapestries that hung on the wall. Idly she stared at the vivid pictures of kings and queens and unicorns and lions. Her head ached.

The palace was unusually silent. When at last she dragged herself to her feet and pulled on a loose linen robe, she was still alone. She rang the little bell standing on a coffer near her. No one came. Opening the door, she stared out into the dark passageway. That too was empty.

Frowning, she went back into the room. After splashing water from a basin on a side table over her face to try to dispel her headache, she bundled her heavy hair into a netted headdress and began to pull on her shift and gown and kirtle.

It was very hot in the silent room. Already she could feel

the perspiration breaking out between her shoulder blades and under her arms. She found a bottle of rose water in one of her boxes and, unstoppering it, splashed it on her neck and forehead. Then, ready at last, she set out to find Duncan.

The entire palace of Westminster seemed deserted. Cautiously she peered into room after room, taking care to keep well away from the king's own apartments. On the south side of the palace the windows looked down over the riverbanks where the shining mud, exposed by the low tide, was stinking in the sun. Flocks of birds picked over the debris that had collected at the edge of the tide. They were the only sign of life. Even the usual procession of boats and ferries was missing. Then at last, in the distance, as she made her way toward the courtyard at the center of the palace, she heard something, the distant but unmistakable sound of a vast crowd of people.

The entire population of London and Westminster and the surrounding villages appeared to have gathered outside Westminster Hall. The streets around the palace and the abbey and the bare ground beyond the twin outlets of the river that surrounded the Isle of Thorns were clogged with people—citizens, nobility, peasants, beggars, all shoulder to shoulder, craning to see Sir William Wallace leave the place of his trial. The doors of the hall were still closed as Isobel hesitantly opened the door in the palace wall and slipped outside to stand alone on the steps beyond it, peering out across the courtyard with its seething mass of bodies. Within seconds others had joined her on her unlooked-for vantage point, and she found she could not turn back. She was hemmed in on every side.

Desperately she tried to fight her way back into the palace, trying to find a guard to help her, but at that moment the huge double doors of the hall began to open and with a predatory roar the crowd surged forward. She found herself carried with her unlooked-for companions to the edge of the steps.

The verdict had been a forgone conclusion. The Scot was guilty. There had never been any doubt of that. This had been only a mockery of a trial. And now the people heard what they wanted: the sentence; the reward, as they bayed for the Scotsman's blood.

The words of the sentence echoed back and forth across the tide of humanity with the sound of waves crashing against the rocks. He was to be drawn, then hanged, disemboweled, and decapitated, and then his body would be quartered. His head was to be displayed on London Bridge and the quarters of his carcass to be sent to Newcastle, Berwick, Perth, and the scene of his greatest victory, Stirling. A shudder passed across the crowd, and as Sir William was at last brought out of the hall there was, for a split second, a moment of almost awed silence before the savage yelling started again.

Desperately Isobel tried to turn away, but she was trapped. She saw him for a moment, standing upright and proud in spite of his chains, the laurel wreath still on his head, then the crowd closed around him and he disappeared from sight.

Two horses were being brought through the tight pack of people. She saw them halted at the spot where Wallace had disappeared. Then slowly the horses were being turned and she saw them moving with difficulty back toward her through the crowd.

They passed the steps where Isobel stood, two men at the head of each horse as they were half led, half dragged at a walk through the press of humanity, sidestepping nervously, tossing their heads, their eyes rolling in terror. Behind them they drew a hurdle to which Sir William had been strapped, his wrists already bloody, his face covered in spittle. For one second Isobel gazed down horrified at the man who had tried to save Scotland, a man she had met on several occasions, a man who had tried to console her for the death of her uncle by telling her of his bravery on the battlefield, a man whose bluff sincerity had impressed her, a man who did not deserve to die—as no one deserved to die—with the horror and brutality that had been arranged for him. Then he was gone, the crowds closing around him again, following him on that last agonizing journey to the place of execution at Smithfield. The mocking crown of laurel was now adorning the ears of one of the horses dragging him to his death.

Freed at last, as the crowd surged after him, Isobel turned back into the palace, blind with tears. She groped her way along passage after passage, crossing rooms and courts she had never seen before, completely lost, trying desperately not to imagine the horrors that lay ahead for the man on the hurdle. Once she bumped into someone and she stopped, turning blindly away, not even seeing the surprised look on the face of the tall, handsome man who stood back to let her pass. He turned thoughtfully to watch her as she fled, and Isobel never knew that the hands that had steadied her for a fraction of a second were those of Edward of Caernarvon.

The Earl of Buchan was sitting at a table in their rooms. He stared at her coldly as she came in and then rose to his feet. "So, you could not resist going to see."

The eyes she raised to his were still full of tears. "I didn't mean to. I saw him. I saw him being dragged away."

"God rest his soul." Buchan crossed himself perfunctorily. "You would do well to remember what happens to those who cross the King of England." He threw himself back into the carved chair once more and reached for another of the letters piled before him, more moved himself than he was prepared to admit by the happenings of the morning.

He flicked open the seal with the point of his dagger and unfolded the letter. As he began slowly to read Isobel turned away. She had her hand on the ring handle of the door when the exclamation of fury from behind her made her turn back to him. Lord Buchan had risen to his feet, his face white, the letter still clutched in his fist.

He looked up at her slowly and the expression in his eyes made her blood run cold.

"W-what is it? What has happened?" she stammered.

He stepped forward, the parchment still in his hand, and held it out to her. "Is this true?" He shook it under her nose. "Is this true? That you went from Duncairn to Kildrummy and that you saw Lord Carrick there?" After throwing down the letter, he seized her wrist. "Well? Is it true, madam?" He dragged her away from the door. "Why should I receive a letter here, telling me this if it isn't true?" He was still holding her tightly. "Do you know what this kind, informative, anonymous person says? No, of course you don't. You haven't read the letter. Then I shall tell you. He says that you slept with the Earl of Carrick. He says you slept with Robert the Bruce and that fifty men and women at Kildrummy can bear witness to the fact." He dropped her hand abruptly. "If this is true, Isobel, before God and the Holy Virgin, I will see that you pay with your life for the dishonor of my name!"

Stephen Caroway had been on the phone to Paul every day. "Christ, Paul! Why didn't you wait until you knew about those shares for sure? Of all the crazy, ill-informed, bungling—" Words had failed him. "There has got to be some price support from somewhere, surely? There must be someone else coming in!" He had lost a small fortune before he had managed to sell his own shares. He had not managed to find a market for any of Paul's.

Nobody else had come in. The shares had continued to slide and there was no evidence of any buying interest in the market.

It was Thursday morning when Paul called him back—the day before settlement day, and the shares had already fallen a further ten percent. "You're going to have to give me more time, Steve. The money is on its way, but I can't find it for tomorrow. You'll have to carry my settlement over into the next account."

Stephen ran his fingers through his hair, a feeling of deep unease building within him as he began to consider the implications of a major default. He hesitated before posing the next question, his throat growing increasingly dry. "Can you give me any indication as to how you intend raising the money if we can't find a buyer?"

"No!" Paul snapped. "I'll have the money by the end of the next account on the twenty-first. That is all you need to know. You've got to give me until then."

That gave him fourteen more days.

"You know, I was really pleased when they cancelled the gig." Kathleen sat back in the Neil's Land-Rover and stared out of the window as they drove north out of Aberdeen. "The club was damaged by fire, so their insurance will pay me anyway. It was nice you could meet me at the station. I didn't fancy paying a taxi to take me up to Duncairn."

Neil was staring through the windshield wipers. He said nothing.

"You didn't mind me coming up to be with you?" She was babbling and she knew it. She groped in the bag at her feet for her cigarettes.

"Of course not." For the first time Neil glanced at her. He grinned. "Things are going well up here. We're trying to get a date organized for the public inquiry, so we've been busy. We're going to have to bring in a lot of people from outside."

"You mean the poor bastards who actually live at Duncairn would love to see oil there?" She struck a match, defiantly aware of his disapproving glance, and lighted her cigarette, inhaling deeply. After winding down the window a quarter of an inch, she pushed out the dead match. "Oh, Christ! That's me, littering the road! Sorry." She took another drag at the cigarette.

"You look tired." Neil changed gear as they approached a traffic circle. He smiled at her gently. "Has it been a tough week?"

"Three one-nighters. I hate them. What I want is a good long engagement to set me up. In London or Newcastle or somewhere. I read my cards before I left," she went on suddenly.

Neil shook his head. "I wish you wouldn't do that. You know there are periods when I think you are probably quite normal, then you slip back again. So, what did they say? Are we going to win?"

She pushed a strand of black hair back from her eyes and blew smoke at the roof of the Land-Rover. She hadn't asked the cards about the campaign at Duncairn. She had asked them about her future with Neil, and she had not liked what they said. There had been a predominance of swords in the spread and there was no sign of the Queen of Pentacles, her own special card. Instead there was another woman.

"I can stay up here with you for a few days if you like." She turned sideways on the seat to face him, easing the seat belt on her shoulder.

"Good." He was concentrating on the road. The shower was becoming heavier; hailstones rattled on the glass. "It looks as if winter is on its way at last. We'll have to get our first meeting in before the snows start."

"They haven't definitely got the license to test drill yet, have they?" she asked, throwing out the stub of the cigarette.

Neil frowned. "Not yet." He forced himself to smile across at her. "Jack Grant will be glad of some female company at the hotel. In fact, perhaps we can use you to bring in some customers. Are you ready to sing for your supper?"

"If I must." She gave a thin smile. "I hoped you'd be glad of some female company too."

"Of course." He patted her knee briefly. "Look over there, at the sea. It's looking pretty rough. You are sure you wouldn't rather have flown south with the swallows for the weekend?"

Across the fields to their right they could see the thin line of the beach. The sea beyond it was gray and angry, whipped into white, the clouds so low and heavy they seemed to be part of it.

It took half an hour to cover the twenty or so miles to Duncairn, and by then Kathleen had smoked four cigarettes. As he parked in front of the hotel Neil gave an inward sigh. She was taut, defensive, suspicious, and he wasn't looking forward to a weekend with her, almost alone at the hotel. Kathleen belonged to the city. She needed people to make her sparkle. As he watched her climb out of the car, her hair torn back by the strength of the wind, he found himself thinking, not for the first time, how ill she fitted into this wild, rugged place.

He picked up her suitcase and carried it in, closing the door behind her, leaning all his weight against it to shut out the wind. "Come on. I'll show you our room."

They climbed the broad oak staircase to the first floor, aware the whole time of the drumming of the wind around the huge old house. Neil's room was the last one on the left of the corridor. It faced the castle and, beyond it, the sea.

He put Kathleen's suitcase down beside the huge Edwardian wardrobe. "The bathroom is through there. If you want to settle in, I'll meet you in the bar later."

In the corridor outside he paused and took a deep breath. Poor Kath. By Sunday evening she would be out of her mind with boredom.

Jack was somewhere in the kitchen. In the bar Neil helped himself to a large malt whisky, then he walked over to the windows and stared out gloomily. The sunny intervals of the morning had gone. The sky was deep lowering gray and, as the wind swung inexorably around to the north, the rain had turned first to hail and now to sleet. The stand of trees that bordered the small rough lawn bent before the wind; behind it he could see the gray stone of the castle keep dark with rain.

"So, where is the glamorous lady?" Jack Grant walked into the bar and glanced around.

Neil turned from the window. "She's just settling in. She'll be down in a minute. What is the weather forecast?"

"Winter." Grant brought the whisky bottle over and topped up Neil's glass before pouring one for himself. "The temperature is going to drop over the next couple of days." He looked gloomily out of the window. "The barometer is falling fast. I doubt we'll get many people to a meeting."

Neil grimaced. "It's a pity it's this time of year, but we'll do it, don't you worry; we'll get people in if I have to bus them up from Edinburgh."

"You might have to." Grant threw himself into a worn armchair. "The locals are beginning to think onshore oil might be a hell of a better way to earn a living than fishing the North Sea holes."

Neil shook his head. "Jobs for the locals is a blind, Jack. You know that. And you've got to help me convince them. Sigma will bring in heavy labor from down south to build the pipeline and they'll bring in their own employees to run things."

"And meanwhile your birds and flowers are more important than oil anyway." There was no irony in Grant's voice, only mild resignation.

"We've got to use every argument we can, Jack. People, environment, conservation. The lot."

"Aye." Grant leaned back in his chair and closed his eyes wearily. "You'll not do it, you know. They always win."

"Never!" Neil punched him on the shoulder. "Here. Let me give you another drink, then you can start preparing a gourmet meal to put the lady in a good mood!"

"If she ever puts in an appearance." Grant stood up slowly.

Both men were late for their appointment. Paul arrived first and ordered himself a large whisky. He was already sweating.

Rex stood for a moment in the doorway of the smoking room at the club, staring at him as he waited to hand over his immaculate camel-hair coat. Paul did not look up.

They did not make small talk. After ordering himself a Perrier with lemon and ice, Rex stared pointedly at Paul's glass, already nearly empty, and waited for him to speak first.

Paul took a deep breath. "How much time do I have to complete the deal?"

"None." Rex's voice was flat. "Sigma has withdrawn its offer."

Paul went white. His fingers closed convulsively around the glass. "You can't do that!" He shut his eyes, not wanting to see the handsome cold face opposite him. "You've made a legal offer."

"Which your wife turned down."

"Well, she's changed her mind, and I have her power of attorney." Paul looked him straight in the eye.

"Indeed." Rex met his gaze evenly. "Well, it may be that we can do business if you still want to sell." He paused. He had recognized Paul's panic, seen his desperation, and he knew enough about his man now to gauge the situation to a T.

He smiled coldly. "Only this time the price has come down. If you can deal within two weeks, I'll take the land myself, at agricultural value, which is all it's worth. There will be no drilling now. Oil prices have dropped too far to make even onshore exploration viable."

"That's not true." Paul stood up. "The OPEC agreement—"

"Means nothing, Mr. Royland. Sit down, man. The whole goddamn room is looking at you." Rex pushed his own chair back from the low table uncomfortably. He reached into his inside pocket as Paul sat down again. "I have the valuation of the Duncairn estates that Mitchison had drawn up for me here. Now, I am prepared to offer more than that—to cover the value of the hotel and the ruin—" He paused, trying to conceal his excitement. "It is less than Sigma was prepared to offer, but I am willing to split the difference. That is my figure." He pushed the piece of paper toward Paul. "And that is final. It will cover your debts."

Paul was staring down at the document. Abruptly he looked up. "What do you know about my debts?" His face was white with anger. It wouldn't cover them, not by a long way. But it would help.

"Enough. Shall we say I know enough about them and your business methods to spoil your cozy reputation in the City." Rex met his gaze coldly. "If you accept my offer there would of course be no need for me to say a word to a soul." He smiled. "So, do we have a deal?"

Paul's hands were shaking visibly. "That is blackmail," he said furiously.

Rex smiled. He said nothing, waiting.

There was a long silence. "All right," Paul whispered at last. "I agree."

Rex nodded slowly, trying to hide his elation. "Good. I'll get my solicitors to contact yours."

Paul nodded, trying to recover his composure. "I'll have the power of attorney by the time they are ready."

Sharply Rex looked up. "I thought you said you had it."

"I have. I have. It's just the final formalities," Paul said hurriedly. "Clare has agreed to the sale. She's going away. As you know she was ill. She has to rest. . . ."

Rex scanned his face thoughtfully. "Just so long as there is no delay," he said at last.

Paul's face was grim. The new settlement day was only

thirteen days away now. He did not have until the end of the month.

Paul left the club without finishing his drink.

The sun was reflecting on the puddles in the gutter; damp leaves lay thick on the pavement, their brilliant colors muddied and dirtied by a thousand passing feet. If Clare were dead there would be no problem. If she had died, there in the elevator. . . . Angrily Paul shook his head. What kind of a man was he turning into, for Christ's sake? He didn't need her dead, but she had to be found and she had to be forced to agree to the sale. She had to. He had called the house—both houses—again and again that morning but Sarah Collins had not seen her in London and there had been no reply from Bucksters. She had disappeared.

In the end Paul called Airdlie. Wherever she was she would almost certainly go there in the end. And he had to forestall her.

Archie Macleod answered. "Clare's not here, Paul. Why? Have you lost her?"

Grimly Paul told Archie the story he had worked out: that Clare had become involved with a satanic cult; that she was trying to give away all her possessions to its leader. That Archie must beware.

"If she turns up, Archie, you've got to keep her there. For all our sakes as well as her own. Then call me, and I'll fly straight up. I know what to do. She's ill, Archie. Ill in her mind. You've got to take care."

Chapter Nineteen

The Jaguar hurtled northward over the long switchback of the A68. All around there was nothing but heather, brown and matted, covering the misty distances of the Cheviot hills, which were empty of life as far as the eye could see. Clare lowered the window until her hair was blowing wildly across her face. She was exhilarated and, suddenly, happy again.

The night before, watching Isobel trapped in the web of her husband's anger, she had suddenly become aware of the sound of the television blaring around the room, the sound beating at her ears, and over it a furious knocking on the door. Dazed, she had looked around. Casta was lying flattened under the bed, trembling. Clare staggered to her feet stiffly and switched off the TV, relieved at the sudden tangible silence as she went to the door. The woman outside was red-faced with fury. "Can you turn that damn TV off and keep it off! Some of us have been trying to get to sleep!" she screamed at Clare.

Clare pushed her hair back from her face, confused. "I'm sorry. I didn't realize it was so loud. I must have fallen asleep—"

"Asleep! The woman stared at her. "With that noise even the dead couldn't sleep!" And she turned and flounced down the corridor, disappearing into a room two doors up, slamming the door behind her.

As Clare stood staring after her Casta began to whimper.

"Casta!" She crouched down and hugged the dog, burying her face in the animal's fur. "They've gone. They've gone, darling. They've gone. There's nothing to be afraid of anymore." There were tears on her cheeks as she wound her fingers into the dog's collar.

The hotel bedroom was hot and stuffy. As she threw open
the window, she couldn't imagine how she had ever thought
it cold. She turned and looked around the room, half expecting for one terrified moment to see the figures of the earl and
his wife waiting in the corner, but they really had gone. After
locking the bedroom door, Clare climbed into the bed, still
wrapped in her bathrobe, and patted the pillow beside her.
The dog jumped up with alacrity and licked her face. "What
am I going to do, Castie?" Clare murmured. She could feel
the cool breeze now from the window, lowering the temperature of the room. "I didn't want her to come. I didn't want it
to happen. She's haunting me." Every light in the room was
on.

She lay back, her arms around the dog's neck, and tried to
sleep, but the first pale glow had begun to show in the sky
behind the stand of dying elms on the edge of the road
outside the hotel before she nodded at last into an uneasy
doze.

It was early afternoon when she reached the Forth Bridge.
The water of the firth was white-topped, whipped into spin-
drift by the wind, and as she waited to pay her toll she
watched a yacht sail close-hauled out of Queensferry, heel
over steeply, and cream into the thick green water below the
twin bridges. She paid her toll at last and drove slowly across
and then onto the throughway, glancing eastward with a
shudder toward the high chimneys and flares at Mossmorran.
Was that what they wanted to do to Duncairn? Bring to yet
more of the quiet countryside of Buchan the roar of the flares
and the nights that were never dark?

The countryside was brilliant now in the sunshine, the
clouds still racing across the sky, their shadows streaming
black along the ground. Clare felt for her sunglasses in the
glove compartment as she swung the heavy Jaguar around
the circle at the end of the throughway and headed up the
A9 toward Dunkeld. She had made up her mind. She was
going to Airdlie. There, at least for the time being, she would
be safe from Paul. She had to go home.

Between Perth and Dunkeld Clare turned off the main

road. She drove up a long narrow lane and then brought the
car to a halt at the end of a ride on the edge of a hillside forest.
Pulling on her Burberry, she climbed out of the car. Casta
rushed ahead of her up the track, her plumed tail waving as
slowly Clare began to climb, her boots sinking into the soft
pine needles.

Now that she was so near home her nerve had begun to
fail. Her mother had as good as told her not to come. Her
stepfather loathed her. Aunt Margaret wasn't there anymore. The house belonged to James, and it was the first place
Paul would think of looking if he wanted to follow her. So
why was she going there?

She raised the collar of her raincoat against the increasingly sharp wind and pushed her hands firmly into her pockets, feeling the crunch of pine cones beneath her feet as she
stepped off the muddy track and onto an outcrop of rock. The
air was sharp with resin. Ahead of her she could see the
hillside, still here and there splashed purple with late
heather. The sun was dazzling after the dark shadowy track
of the firebreak between the trees.

Where did she belong? She had no one and nowhere to go.
Even at Duncairn Jack Grant had made it clear that he did
not want her at the hotel, thanks to that interfering man from
Earthwatch.

Stepping out of the shadow of the trees, she glanced
around her at the panorama of rolling Perthshire hills, patch-
work-colored in the sunlight, cloaked on their lower flanks by
the dark-green scented spruce. Following Casta, she picked
her way through the heather to an outcrop of sun-warmed
rock and sat down, feeling the wind tugging at her hair. With
a yelp of excitement Casta disappeared over the shoulder of
the hill on the trail of some rabbits. Far below she could just
see the green metallic glint where the car was half hidden by
the trees. She was completely alone.

Wishing passionately she could stay there forever, relaxed,
safe, hidden from the world, Clare stooped, and, picking up a
stone from the mossy grass at her feet, tossed it idly into the
heather. In the distance she could hear the warbling call of a
curlew and nearby the sharp metallic note of a stonechat.

This was the country where Isobel had been happy, the country of her birth. Clare frowned, pushing the thought of Isobel away. She shivered as the wind tugged at her raincoat.

Don't you want to know what happened? Don't you want to know what my husband did?

The words spun out of the air, almost lost in the sound of the wind in the heather and the trees behind her.

Clare swallowed, glancing around. "No! I don't want to know. Leave me alone. Please!" She put her hands to her head, tugging at her hair, shaking her head. "Leave me alone. Leave me alone!"

She scrambled to her feet, groping in her pocket for the magic oil. With shaking hands she unscrewed the top and slopped some of the oil onto her hand. A little spilled onto her Burberry and she saw the dark stain spreading on the pale fabric.

"Go away! Keep away from me! I don't want to know. Please. . . ."

She backed away from the rocks, smearing the oil across her forehead, holding the bottle in front of her like a talisman.

Don't you want to know what happened? Don't you want to know . . . ?

The voice was stronger now, inside her head. Insistent. Desperate. Pleading.

Isobel had turned away from her husband, her mind numb with fear, her nerves already stretched to breaking point by the sight of the man on the hurdle and the baying crowd around him.

"Well, madam, have you lost your tongue?" Lord Buchan was immediately behind her. "Do you not have a reply to these charges?"

Isobel turned slowly to face him. "Would you believe me if I denied it?" she said. She felt completely calm. She gazed up into his face and the sudden absence of fear disconcerted him.

"No," he said slowly. "I wouldn't believe you. You have sinned with this man a thousand times in your heart, which makes you guilty in the eyes of God. Now you have sinned with your body and you are guilty in the eyes of the world."

She expected him to hit her. She almost wanted him to hit her. Then at least his vengeance would have begun. This sudden icy calm was more frightening than anything she had ever seen.

Thoughtfully he turned from her. "Lord Carrick is a friend of the king at present. He is a powerful influence here at court. I do not wish to jeopardize Scotland's position in the coming parliament by fighting him openly. Not yet. You are not worth it." The disdain in his voice was cutting. "But one day I shall kill him." The words were spoken with a venom so quiet she wondered if she had heard them aright.

He turned back to her and his face was once more taut with anger. "But you are a different matter. It seems you do not learn by your mistakes. My mother said she feared you were untamable. It appears she was right." He sat down heavily once more with a deep sigh. "Was your maid's death not warning enough for you? Are you not afraid to die at the stake as she did?"

In spite of herself Isobel gasped. "You cannot mean to have me burned?" she cried. "I've done nothing to deserve that!"

Buchan smiled. "Not even ensnared a nobleman of Scotland by your spells? Not even made mockery of your marriage vows and defied God and the Holy Church? Not even, once again, resorted to magic to prevent the conception of a child?" His voice dropped to a hiss.

Isobel went white. He couldn't know that! No one could know that. "Th-that's not true," she stammered. "None of that is true."

"No?" He gave a cold smile. "So, you deny throwing a web of enchantment around the Bruce? I'll warrant he wants none of you. And why"—he sat forward suddenly—"have you not conceived a child unless you have avoided it by sorcery?"

"That is God's will," she whispered.

"I think it is more the will of the devil." He stood up. "It is my intention, madam, to see you never get the chance to see the Bruce again. Or Scotland, since so much temptation lurks there." He paused, his eyes on her face, and he gave a tight smile at the sudden pain he saw there. "I have no time for you at present. The affairs of Scotland are pressing and I have to stay here at Westminster. While I am here I will decide what to do with you, but it seems to me that if I need an heir I must be free to remarry." He was still watching her thoughtfully. "In the meanwhile I will see to it that you do not—ever —have the chance to betray your vows to me again." He turned and left the room, turning the key in the lock behind him.

Isobel sank onto a stool. Her knees were trembling and she felt very sick. Slowly the afternoon passed and it began to grow dark. There were no fresh candles in the room and suddenly it was cold. Huddling on the window seat, Isobel could see little through the leaded colored glass. She was hungry and very frightened.

It was pitch dark when the door was unlocked. Her husband stood outside, a flare in his hand. "Come," he ordered curtly. Isobel rose stiffly to her feet.

He took her to their bedchamber. After bolting the door, he thrust the flare into a bracket on the wall, then he turned to her. "An escort awaits to take you back to Whitwick where you will remain a prisoner until I decide what best to do with you, but before you leave there is something I must do."

It was a long time since he had beaten her. He struck her repeatedly with the flat of his hand until, barely conscious, she collapsed onto the bed. Somehow her pride sustained her and she managed to bite back her screams, but she was scarcely aware of what was happening as at last he began to pull off her clothes, ripping her gown and kirtle from her back and tearing her shift in two, waiting with some shrinking part of herself for the rape that she knew would follow.

Somewhere in the distance she heard him laugh as she huddled away from him, her eyes closed, her arms wrapped around her aching body, too dazed and bruised to react even when she heard the rattle of metal. He pulled her back toward him and she felt the cold iron around her waist, then the cruel tongue of metal between her thighs and heard the snap of the lock. "That, madam, will ensure you are never unfaithful to me again," he whispered. Then he caught her arm and pulled her to her feet. "Now get dressed."

She rode in a litter, thrown uncomfortably from side to side as the horses sped north through the darkness, their way lighted by the streaming flares of the armed escort. It grew light and they stopped for food and water at St. Albans. Isobel refused to eat. In agony from the bruises and welts on her body and desperately conscious of the vicious, cruel manacle clamped to her body beneath her torn shift, she lay dazed in the litter for the whole of the long journey north.

At Whitwick she was carried to the bedchamber by her husband's steward. There, alone in the great curtained bed, still fully clothed, she allowed herself to cry.

She expected to die. Each meal as it was brought to her was suspect. He would have ordered her to die by poison there, far away from London, then he would be free to marry again. At first she refused to eat, but her hunger forced her to try the food, and to her surprise it was good. She was not kept locked up. There was no more punishment. Far away in London Lord Buchan was distracted by affairs of state. For the time being he had put his wife out of his mind.

Life at Whitwick was ordered and calm. They heard little news. The men and women of the household were wrapped up in their own affairs, and they had no interest in Lord Buchan's except where they touched them personally. Isobel's wounds healed, her natural resilience returned, and she found herself slowly falling into the pattern of life at the manor as the long autumn days shortened and grew cold.

It had been made very clear to her that although she was not locked up, she was nevertheless a prisoner. She was not to ride—that anyway, she realized in rueful embarrassment, would have been too uncomfortable to contemplate. She was not allowed to walk beyond the immediate gardens of the manor with their ordered beds of herbs and the rose bower the steward's wife had made over the years for her own pleasure, and even there she was never alone. There was nothing for it but to wait and occupy her time as best she could, and to dream. At first her daydreams were all of escape; she would picture herself riding through the heather, or standing on the cliffs of Buchan, listening to the sea. She had not thought it possible to miss the sea so much: the smell, the sound, the vitality of the wind and spray, the power of the waves. The forest and fields of Leicestershire were gentle and the air was soft, the people so very different from the rugged loyal men and women of her northern home.

She filled her time with sewing and taught herself to weave; she sat spinning in the evenings with the steward's wife and the three ladies who served them, and by the light of the candles she read. There were three books at the manor: a book of hours, a book of psalms, and an exquisitely illuminated copy of *Le Roman de la Rose*, which Isobel herself had brought and left there on one of her previous visits.

The first soft snowflakes were falling from the sky when she had her only visitor. Alice, now married to Sir Henry Beaumont, rode into the manor courtyard with an entourage of men and horses at the beginning of December.

"Aunt Isobel?" She kissed Isobel cautiously, as if doubtful of her reception. "How are you?" Her nose was pink with cold, her figure very obviously pregnant. "Uncle John said I could come and visit you."

Isobel raised an eyebrow. "I had thought he'd forgotten I existed," she said with a rueful smile. "In fact, I hoped he'd forgotten I existed." She gave Alice a hug. "Come in, my dear. I am so very glad to see you."

They sat together by the roaring fire in the solar while her ladies mulled them some wine.

"So. You are expecting a baby!" Isobel took her niece's cold hands. "When will it be born?"

"In the spring." Alice hugged her again. "It's going to be a boy, I know it." She eyed Isobel critically. "You have grown so thin. Have you been ill?"

Isobel smiled ruefully. "No. Not ill. Just lonely and bored."

"Uncle John wouldn't tell me why he'd had you sent here." She glanced away. "Is he still angry with you?"

"Still angry?" Isobel gave a hollow laugh. "You could say so, my dear. But let's not talk about me."

"No. We must." Alice glanced over her shoulder at the women by the hearth, then she rose and took Isobel's hand, leading her to the window embrasure. They could both feel the wind beating against the polished horn screens that served in some of the windows in this old manor house instead of glass. "What happened? What did you do?"

"Something bad enough."

"Before, when Uncle John sent you to Dundarg to do that dreadful penance . . ." Alice bit her lip. "Aunt Isobel . . . it was I who betrayed you. I was stupid and self-righteous and I wanted Uncle John to be pleased with me so he would help to arrange my marriage with Henry. I told him I'd seen you with Lord Carrick in the garth. I didn't realize. I didn't know he would be so angry. I just thought he would rebuke you. I'm sorry. Oh, I'm so sorry." She was crying suddenly, kneading her skirt between her fingers.

Isobel stared at her, her face pale. She took a deep breath, as if she were about to say something, but she changed her mind. She turned away. "Oh, Alice," was all she said.

"Can you ever forgive me?"

"I don't know." She felt completely stunned. "And are you here to spy on me again?"

"No." Alice shook her head violently. "No, I swear it! If I can ever make it up to you, I will. Oh, please, Isobel, forgive me." She caught Isobel's hands. "Please. And tell me why you are here. Perhaps this time I can help."

"I am here because I was spied on again, it seems." Isobel's voice was flat. "Someone sent your uncle a letter saying I had been seen with Lord Carrick in the summer."

"And was it true?" Alice spoke in a whisper.

Isobel smiled. "I don't think I should tell you that, should I?"

Alice glanced away. "I am not a spy." She had heard the rumors. Everyone at Westminster had heard the whisper that the Countess of Buchan had been unfaithful to her husband with the Earl of Carrick. They had waited with baited breath for Robert to put in an appearance at Westminster when the parliament met in the autumn, but he seemed content to stay in Scotland and he had never appeared. And Isobel, banished into Leicestershire, had not been there to confirm or deny the rumors.

"Please. Let me be your friend." Alice turned back to her. "Please. Let me make it up to you somehow."

Isobel gave a wan smile. "Just your being here is enough, Alice dear. I have been so lonely."

"Can we talk later, in bed?" Alice whispered, with a glance at the women by the fire as the warm rich scent of wine and herbs began to percolate through the room.

It was the custom for relatives and guests of the same sex sometimes to share the great bed if the man of the house was away, and after a moment's hesitation Isobel nodded. "We'll talk later," she said.

So, that night, Alice, cheerfully naked in spite of her bulky belly, jumped onto the high bed and held back the covers for Isobel to join her.

Isobel eased herself onto the mattress, still wearing her long linen shift. She could not bear Alice to see the iron belt that still, in spite of her thinness, so cruelly clamped her flesh. But Alice had guessed. She touched Isobel's waist gently in the darkness and then hugged her close. "Did Uncle John do that?" she whispered.

Isobel nodded. "I was unfaithful."

Alice's eyes widened in the darkness. "So, it is true. You do love Lord Carrick?" They were both speaking very softly, conscious that beyond the bed curtains one of the serving women was sleeping on a truckle bed by the fire.

"Yes. I love him." What was the point of denying it?

"Dear God!" Alice's whisper was explosive. "Who gave men the right to treat us like this? We become their possessions, their property!" She lay back on the pillows and thumped the sheet with her fist. "We cease to exist as people!" She raised herself onto her elbow and looked at Isobel in the darkness. "Does he plan to leave you like this forever?"

"I think he plans to kill me." Isobel's answer was barely audible.

"What?"

"He wants to marry again—marry a woman who can give him a child."

"But you could—"

"No."

There was a long silence. Beyond the curtains they could hear the fire hissing softly in the hearth. The truckle bed creaked and groaned as the sleeping woman moved, and at last there was the sound of a soft snore.

Alice put her hands up to touch Isobel's face in the darkness.

"Would you get rid of that belt if you could?"

Isobel stared up toward the dark curtains. "Of course I would. But my lord and husband holds the only key."

"It could be cut off." Alice's words were so quiet Isobel could scarcely hear them.

"How? There is no one here who would help me."

Alice smiled quietly. "I think I know someone who would do it. For you. But do you dare? What will Uncle John do when he finds out?"

"I told you, he will probably kill me." Isobel eased herself uncomfortably beneath the warm covers. "But then he will probably do that anyway. I'm prepared to take the risk." Her heart was beginning to beat with slow, steadily mounting excitement. For the first time in many weeks she allowed herself to feel a suspicion of hope.

Alice squeezed her hand. "Leave it with me. I'll see if I can arrange something."

The something was a six-foot young man in the livery of Sir Henry Beaumont.

He came into the bedchamber the following evening lugging a trug full of blacksmiths tools. "Do you remember Hugh, the farrier's son from Duncairn?" Alice asked with a giggle. "He helped you once before."

Isobel stared. "Hugh?"

"Aye, my lady. And ready to serve you again." He smiled, his brown eyes merry in the tanned face.

The soft lilt of the Buchan accent brought tears to Isobel's eyes. "Hugh? Are you to be forever releasing me from my imprisonment?" In her embarrassment she laughed and caught his hands.

"As often as you like, my lady. I'll be happy to serve you." He glanced up shyly, his eyes alight with humor.

Firmly Alice moved to the door and drew the bolt across.

"Now, we haven't much time. I've explained the situation to Hugh and he says he can cut you free. Come and lie down." Bustling nervously, Alice arranged the bed covers modestly over Isobel's body so only the broad iron belt around her waist and the lock that fastened it was visible.

Hugh rummaged among his tools then she felt the weight of his knee on the feather mattress beside her.

It seemed an eternity before with a grunt of satisfaction he freed the lock and she felt the heavy metal slide away. In a moment he had gathered it up with his tools. He turned his back tactfully while Isobel regained her feet and smoothed down her gown.

"How can I ever thank you?" she asked. "I have no money."

"There is no need of money. Just let me stay in your service when Lady Beaumont leaves." He smiled broadly. "She has agreed."

The Earl of Buchan arrived unannounced at Whitwick a month later, two weeks after Alice, amid many tears, had left. Isobel waited, heart in mouth, for him to send for her, but the summons never came. He spent six hours at the manor, checked his stables and the men he had left on his Leicestershire estates, then he left, riding north for Scotland with only three men as his escort. He spoke to Isobel when she appeared in the hall just before he left, curtly and with obvious dislike, for less than five minutes; neither touching her nor inquiring after her health.

In London the Earl of Carrick had at last appeared for a while that autumn, and was high, it seemed, in King Edward's favor. Lord Buchan was going to have to bide his time if he still valued Scotland's peace above his own personal, mortal grudge. Isobel's fate would be decided soon, but not yet, not if he wanted to avoid offending Robert Bruce and through him, perhaps, the king of England.

Behind him as he rode north the snow was sweeping up from the south, soft, blanketing drifts engulfing the countryside and blocking the roads. It was to last several weeks.

Christmas came and went and here and there the first

snowdrops pushed through the melting ice. Conscious of an easing in the attitude of those around her and secure in the fact that her husband was hundreds of miles away, Isobel began slowly to increase the distance she roamed from the manor, and, always careful to ask the steward or one of his officers to go with her, she began to ride again. Slowly her confidence returned and with it the courage to plan her escape.

The servants at the manor liked her, her husband's men liked her, and the people in the village liked her. They seemed to have forgotten she was their prisoner; to them she was the lady of the manor and more and more a trusted friend. She promised herself that as soon as the roads opened and her plans were complete, with Hugh's aid she would run away. Somewhere in Scotland there would be a hiding place for her, and somehow she would persuade Robert to accept her and acknowledge his love.

However, in the first week in February, before she had the chance to put her plans into effect, Lord Buchan returned, and with him a huge entourage of men and horses, on his way south once more to see the king. Once more he greeted her distantly and did not try to touch her. He took to his bed, so one of her ladies told her, the widow of one of his knights.

He remained, this time, for several days, and for every moment of them she waited in terror lest he find out that she was free of his chains. But he never came near her, and at last it dawned on her that he wanted her to beg: to beg to have the belt removed, to beg to allow her to go back to Scotland. From that moment on, her fear of what he would do when he found out that she was already free was almost extinguished by the secret triumph of knowing that she would never beg him for anything again.

It was a wet, monochrome day with the clouds low on the hills and the trees leaning before the thrashing gale when a sweating horseman clattered into the courtyard and threw himself from his mount. He pushed his way through to the great hall of the manor, almost collapsing with exhaustion, and went down on one knee before the earl.

"My lord, news from Scotland!" He shook his head, trying

to catch his breath. "Your cousin, the Red Comyn, my lord, has been murdered!"

A puff of ragged smoke blew back down the wide chimney and filled the hall with acrid fumes.

Buchan stood up, his face white. "Murdered!" He stepped forward and caught the man by the shoulder, shaking him. "Murdered, you say? By whom? What happened, man?" He seized the unfortunate messenger by the ear and hauled him to his feet.

The man gave a yelp of pain. "By Lord Carrick, my lord! Lord Carrick stabbed him! They quarreled, in Greyfriars Kirk in Dumfries, and Lord Carrick killed him there, by the high altar! It was murder, my lord, and the most foul sacrilege."

There was a horrified silence in the hall. Isobel, who had been sitting stitching delicate rich designs into the piece of velvet she was embroidering in a corner near a branch of candles well out of sight of her husband, rose unsteadily to her feet, the silver and gold threads with which she had been working falling unnoticed into a pool of wax on the table. She had gone cold all over.

"Are you sure of this?" Lord Buchan hissed at the man. He let go of his ear abruptly and the man collapsed sobbing onto his knees.

"Aye, my lord. Quite sure. The whole of Scotland is talking of it!"

Buchan turned slowly toward his wife. "So, now at last we know where we stand. You see what has become of your Robert Bruce?" He had not raised his voice, but in the intense silence in the low-ceilinged hall she heard every word. He smiled almost triumphantly. "He has shown his hand at last. He is nothing but a sacrilegious murderer!"

His eyes narrowed. With Robert Bruce so abruptly severing himself from King Edward's peace, there would be no need to step warily any longer; there would be no need to pretend an alliance with the man he hated more than any other man on earth, and there would be no need anymore to keep his adulterous wife alive.

Her eyes holding his, Isobel read his mind as clearly as if he had spoken out loud. She found her breath coming in short quick gasps and a pain like a stitch gripped her side, but before she could move or speak, the messenger went on.

"There is more, my lord. Lord Carrick has declared himself King of Scots! Already he had taken Dumfries when I left, and by now he probably has other towns. The people of Scotland are rising to his support on every side!"

With an oath Buchan picked up his sword, which had been lying near him on the table, and dragged it from its scabbard. He lifted it high above his head with both hands then brought it down, point first into the oak bench near him, and left it quivering there for a moment before wrenching it free. "By Our Lady, I have sworn to kill that man, and now I shall do it! By Christ and all the saints, in the name of King John Balliol I shall do it!" His face had gone puce. He turned back to Isobel. "The people of Scotland may be rising but you, madam, will not be there. With the Bruce alive or dead, you will not be there! Take her, and lock her up!" He shouted the order to the steward. "And keep her here until I return. I shall deal with her then!"

Within an hour he had set off at a gallop, not toward Scotland but south toward Westminster and King Edward, taking a small escort of men and leaving the rest to guard his wife and await his orders for the march north.

Isobel was beside herself. Tears and pleas and angry commands to release her were ignored by the steward. Isobel was forced to pace the small room where she was imprisoned. No more news came. From the window she could see that the bulk of her husband's men and horses were still at Whitwick. She did not know where the earl had gone, or that King Edward, on being told what had happened at Dumfries, had at first refused to believe it of his trusted servant, Robert, Earl of Carrick, and wasted precious time waiting for confirmation of his treason.

Down in the courtyard rumor was rife. The majority of the earl's men were Scots; they were drawn from his wide estates across the length and breadth of Scotland and many, while loyal to the earl, were far from easy with the present situation with Scotland as England's vassal. The thought of a native-born king, a descendant of the old kings of Scotland, grandson of old Robert Bruce, the claimant who had represented the senior male line of descent from King David, was intriguing and, to many of them, infuriated by having to march side by side with the hated English, exciting.

The unrest came to a head the day Isobel was released from her chamber in the manor. The steward, with no further orders from the earl, succumbed at last to her pleading and unlocked the door.

Initially she was uncharacteristically cautious. She had to take care. She had to escape, but with the manor alive with her husband's men it would be difficult.

She had reckoned without the aid of Hugh the smith. He found her almost at once as she stood in the courtyard, staring up at the lowering sky. The wind was so strong she could hardly stand.

"Greetings, lady!" Suddenly he was at her side, his hair blowing crazily across his eyes. "Do you need a horse again?"

She smiled, for the first time, it seemed to her, in weeks. "I need the best you can find me, Hugh, and shod for a long journey."

"Are we going to the King of Scots?" His words were torn from his lips.

"We?" She found she was laughing.

He nodded. "You and I and, if I guess right, half your husband's men."

She could not believe it; within an hour the steward and the few knights who remained loyal to the earl were under arrest, and the rest of the men were armed and ready. In an agony of impatience Isobel mounted the huge gray stallion Hugh had led up for her—one of her husband's favorite war horses—and gathered up the heavy gilded rein as the men assembled around her in the screaming wind, pennants flying, horses outfitted in the heraldic colors of Buchan, azure and gold, their manes and tails whipping viciously as the intensity of the storm increased.

The men were going to support their rightful king. They were following her, and they were bringing weapons and horses, but she was bringing as well something far more important. She was bringing herself as representative of the ancient House of Fife, for, without her, and in the absence of her brother, King Robert could not be properly crowned.

Sitting with her back against an outcrop of rock, Clare found she was shivering violently. The wind and rain were real, but the horses were gone. Across the broad valley she could see the sunlight slanting over the fields, but here, above the woods, the sky was black. She could feel the rain sliding down her neck; her corduroys were soaked and her feet in her green boots were very cold. Casta was sitting beneath a tree about fifty yards away, watching her reproachfully, her ears flattened against her head.

Dear God, it had happened again! Without warning and without her own volition Isobel had imposed herself upon her, possessing her mind, oblivious of anything save the need to tell her story. Clare put her face in her hands. She was shaking uncontrollably. "What am I going to do?" she whispered. "What am I going to do?" On her lap lay the small glass bottle of magic oil, half spilled before she had jammed the lid back on. She picked it up, brushing the tears out of her eyes, and stared at it. It hadn't worked. The oil was useless—a superstitious farce. Angrily she crushed the bottle in her hand and the thin glass cracked and splintered. She threw it down with an exclamation, looking in disgust at the line of cuts that had appeared on her oily palm and the shards glittering in the rain around her feet. Scrambling up, she looked around for Casta, then she dropped to her knees, sniffing miserably, trying to pick up the glass. With shaking hands she picked up the pieces and hid them carefully in a deep crevice in the rocks, then she stood up. Her happiness, her sense of freedom had gone. She was still strangely exhilarated, but it was a spurious exhilaration: It belonged to Isobel and to her band of mounted knights with their huge, powerful horses and the flying banners in the gale of long ago. It had nothing to do with this windswept hillside and the lonely, terrified woman who was being haunted by the past.

After pulling up the collar of her Burberry around her ears, she pushed her hands deep into her pockets and turned toward the trees. She whistled to Casta, who came at once. So the shadows had withdrawn. But for how long?

By the time she had reached the car, the shower had passed. Sunshine was raising clouds of steam from the tarmac as she backed out onto the road and turned north once more. She was still shivering uncontrollably. The sun was low in the sky now, throwing slanting shadows across the hills, and on the dark side of the mountains the night was moving in.

When at last she turned in at the gates to Airdlie and began to travel up the long, winding drive between banks of dripping rhododendrons Clare's spirits fell even further. Her mother had told her not to come while Archie was there; neither of them were going to be pleased to see her. She shouldn't have come. From the misery and uncertainty of living with Paul she had fled almost deliberately to the sour disapproval of her stepfather. But where else could she go?

The car drew up at last under the stately cedar tree outside Airdlie's front door. It was a huge, mainly Victorian house in the Scottish baronial style, with an original sixteenth-century wing at the north end, complete with tower. Now in the wet evening light it looked forbidding in the extreme.

For a moment she did not move, then slowly she pushed open the car door and climbed out. Beside her the front lawns ran down gently to the broad, rain-pitted waters of the Tay. She stood staring at the river, feeling the cold rain on her already damp shoulders as behind her the front door opened.

Chapter Twenty

"You didn't call me back, honey." Rex looked around his office with a slight shiver as he watched the wet sleet slide down the huge picture windows. Across the Thames he could see the light on at the top of Big Ben. The House of Commons was sitting. The triple clusters of streetlights on Westminster Bridge cast ethereal reflections on the wet road. "I've called you three times."

Already the filing cabinets were empty; the in-box on his desk held only a letter to the agent who dealt with the assignment of the company apartments. In a week or two this would no longer be his office and he would no longer have a home in London.

"I'm sorry, Rex." Emma's voice was frosty. "I've been busy."

"Has your husband left for the Far East?"

"Yes." Her sigh was clearly audible. "He's gone."

"Then why didn't you call? You sound as though you could do with some cheering up."

"I could. Damn it, Rex! Why didn't you tell me the truth! Why did you lie to me?" Sitting on the floor in the drawing room in Kew, Emma banged on the carpet with her fist. "I liked you, you bastard! I thought we had things in common! I liked talking to you!" To her fury she felt near to tears.

There was a short pause the other end of the line. "So. You've found out about Duncairn."

"Did you imagine I wouldn't find out?" Angrily she pushed her hair back from her face.

"I guess not." He liked her too much to blow it by lying to her now. "Look, I'll be straight with you, Emma. I got to know you deliberately. I admit it. It seemed too good a chance to pass up. I wanted Duncairn and I wanted it at any

349

price. But as it happens, you didn't tell me anything I couldn't have found out from others. Paul Royland's affairs seem pretty widely known. Anyway, he and I have come to an understanding."

"You have?"

"Yup. I owe Paul Royland and Duncairn a big debt of thanks, Emma. Without them, I wouldn't have had the chance to know you. And right now that is the most important thing in my life."

And he would get even with Mary. If she thought he was going to go crawling back to her, she was wrong. When she wanted to, then she could come to him. At Duncairn. Until then he needed some intelligent and attractive company.

"I don't quite believe you," Emma said.

"Please, Emma, come to dinner with me."

"No." Emma's face was a picture of misery. "I can't leave Julia."

"Okay." Rex drummed his fingers on the desk. "I'll take you both to lunch tomorrow. Your husband can't object to that, can he?" He was at his most persuasive.

"Well."

He heard the hesitation in her voice and hammered his advantage home at once. "I'll pick you up in Kew at twelve, okay? Listen, honey, I've got to go to a meeting. If you change your mind, call Leonie, my secretary." He put the receiver down quickly before she had time to speak. He was fairly sure she wouldn't call, but not entirely certain. That was part of her attraction. She was an unpredictable lady.

It had taken Archie Macleod a long time to tell his wife Antonia about Paul's call. He had spent hours thinking about it, trying to reconcile his antipathy toward Clare and his respect for his son-in-law with the deep common sense that told him Paul was completely mad.

It was the evening of the call, as Antonia had finished getting ready for bed, before he went into her bedroom and sat down uneasily on the velvet-covered Victorian nursing chair by her small open fire. Antonia had just climbed into the old-fashioned high bed, still dressed in her pink ribbon-

trimmed dressing gown. Recognizing the signs that a serious
discussion was about to take place, she set down the well-
thumbed Georgette Heyer novel and took off her glasses.
"What's the problem, Archie?" she asked as she hauled herself up higher on the pillows.

"Trouble, old girl," he said slowly. And he told her exactly
what Paul had said.

Antonia had not said a word until he stopped speaking,
then there was a long silence. She was staring out of the half-
drawn curtains at the black reflecting glass of the windows.
Outside it was pitch dark and very quiet.

"What do you think?" Archie asked tentatively at last.

"I think, as you do, that Paul has gone completely mad."

Archie was gnawing his thumbnail. "They must have had a
fight, do you think?"

"They are always fighting." For a moment Antonia
frowned. "Clare has called me twice lately. She did sound
unhappy."

"You don't think this business of not being able to have a
baby could possibly have unhinged her?" He stared hard at
his feet, waiting for the explosion he knew would follow.

Antonia swung her legs purposefully to the floor. "You are
not telling me you believe what he told you?" She took a
deep breath, which enlarged her already ample rosebud-
covered bosom by several inches.

"No, dear, of course not, but Clare has always been a little
fey." He looked up cautiously. To his surprise he saw a small
doubtful frown between his wife's eyes.

The following morning before Clare set out from her
motel in Northumberland Archie had left the house. He
drove the Volvo to Edinburgh where he visited his solicitor
before going on to the manse of a suburban church where he
spent an hour closeted with the minister, an old school
friend. Finally before he set off back to Dunkeld he called at a
shop on the Mound and bought a six-inch-high ivory crucifix.
Holding it cautiously in its paper bag between finger and
thumb as if afraid it might bite, and feeling just a little foolish,
he went back to the car and locked the paper bag in solitary

splendor in the back. When he got home he had told Antonia he had spent the morning in Perth.

Now he sat in uneasy silence clutching his own glass of neat whisky while his wife and stepdaughter exchanged uncomfortable small talk. He was watching Clare surreptitiously. She had lost a lot of weight since he had seen her last; she was thin as a rail, with dark circles under her eyes. She was a looker, Clare, like her mother used to be, but there was definitely something wild about her—the part of her that he had always resented, the part she had from her father. Cautiously he watched her eyes as she fondled their dogs. They were sensitive, expressive eyes, reflecting her every mood, shadowed by long lashes as her concentration was for the moment fixed on the animals. All three were around her now, vying for the touch of her hands, pushing against her knees, grinning stupidly at her. He had always trusted the dogs' judgment. They knew. He took a deep sip of whisky, reassured. Then he nearly choked. He had just remembered about witches and their familiars.

They ate together in the high-ceilinged, cold dining room. Clare, making her long drive the excuse, went to her room directly afterward. The atmosphere in the dining room had chilled her. Her parents were more than usually edgy and ill at ease, and she was too uncomfortable to go with them back into the drawing room for coffee.

Her bedroom was exactly as she had left it last time, exactly as it had been when she was fifteen. It was a huge room on the west side of the house looking out over the river. She closed the door behind her and looked around fondly. So many treasures and memories: her teddy bears, four of them in varying degrees of tattiness, lined up on the bed, her pictures, her dressing table with the silver-backed hairbrushes Aunt Margaret had given her on her sixteenth birthday. There were faded photographs under the glass of the table, mostly of James and her father and various generations of dogs. There were still two torn posters on the wall: the Royal House of Scotland, and the clans and their tartans; and between them the Landseer oil sketch of the ruins of Duncairn Castle with a stag in the foreground.

Slowly she knelt in front of the hearth and put a match to the fire that was laid there. The house had had central heating for ten years now, but it didn't seem to make much difference to the huge chilly rooms. She loved having a fire in her bedroom; it seemed so right and comfortable. After undressing slowly, she climbed into bed and lay staring at the merrily crackling flames. Outside she could hear two owls calling to one another sharply in a tall Scots pine.

She awoke screaming as the bars closed around her. The eyes were closer tonight, the faces uglier, the terror more real than ever before.

She lay for a long time, too afraid to open her eyes, clutching at the sheets. The room was ice cold, the fire long-ago dead. There was a sheen of damp on the top of the bedclothes. For a moment she didn't know where she was and she was terrified that when she opened her eyes it would be real. She whispered Casta's name in the dark, but Casta didn't come. She was downstairs with the other dogs. Reaching out in the darkness, Clare's hand closed around a cold soft fabric paw. It was one of her teddy bears. She sat up in the freezing room and gazed around, dazed, then slowly she lay back again against the pillows. Somewhere far away one of the owls hooted.

When she woke again it was daylight. She climbed, aching, out of bed and went to stare out of the window at the gardens. The blustery winds of the day before had torn most of the last of the leaves from the trees on the far side of the river; they lay a crisp blanket of color on the ground. There was a suspiciously frosty sheen on the grass below the pines, but the sun was out and the sky was an intense steady blue. She shivered violently, putting her hand tentatively on the radiator. She had already guessed that it would be stone cold. After putting on her corduroys, a silk shirt, and two sweaters, she made her way downstairs.

Her mother was in the kitchen. She looked as if she hadn't slept a wink. "Good morning, darling. Would you like some coffee?" She didn't ask if Clare had slept well, and Clare wondered briefly if she had heard her screams. When she was a child her mother had stopped coming to comfort her after her nightmares soon after she had married Archie, leaving Clare to cry herself to sleep. Archie had forbidden her to go to her daughter and Antonia had not dared then, at the start of their marriage, disobey him. It was one of the first ways Archie had shown his resentment of his stepchildren.

Antonia gestured toward the stove where a coffeepot was warming. "Archie has taken the dogs for a walk."

Clare helped herself to coffee and sat down at the long pine table. The kitchen was the only warm place in the house.

"Is something wrong, Mummy?" She poured some cream from the heavy earthenware jug.

"No, darling, of course not." Antonia turned away sharply.

Clare looked up. "I know you told me not to come till Archie was away, but I had nowhere else to go. I've left Paul."

For a moment there was silence, then slowly Antonia turned. "Left him," she echoed. "For good?"

Clare shrugged. "Well, for the time being, anyway."

"Oh, Clare!" Her mother sat down opposite her. "Paul is such a nice man. What has gone wrong?"

Clare smiled sadly. "Perhaps he isn't such a nice man as we thought. Anyway, I'd like to stay if you'd let me. Until I sort something out."

"Of course. You can stay as long as you like." Impulsively Antonia put her hand on Clare's.

"Will Archie be furious?" Clare met her mother's eyes steadily.

"Probably." Antonia shrugged. "I'll deal with him. Have you told James all this?"

"I haven't seen James for ages. You know him. He thinks Paul is the cat's whiskers, so I would hardly confide in him."

"I suppose not." Her mother grimaced. "Poor Clare, has it been awful?"

Clare nodded. She stood up abruptly. "Damn Archie. I need my dog to go out. Where has he taken them?"

Antonia shrugged. "I've no idea. I should avoid him if I

were you, darling. If you want a walk go toward the village. He never takes them near the road."

Clare didn't see her stepfather again until that evening. It was as they were sitting again in the formal dining room, the three dogs lying under the long table, that he cleared his throat. He put down his knife and fork, his salmon almost untouched. "Clare, I think you should know your husband called us."

Clare looked up. "I thought he must have," she said.

Her mother was clutching her fork as if her life depended on it, stabbing randomly at a piece of crumbling fish. "Clare, I don't believe a word of what he said," she burst out defiantly.

"No more do I, I think." Archie reached for his glass of wine. "But he did say some strange things, Clare, and your mother and I have the right to know whether there is any truth in them."

Clare took a deep breath. "What did he say?"

"He said you hadn't been well, darling," Antonia said firmly. "That's all. He says you've been under a lot of strain."

"He said," Archie went on, frowning, "that you have become involved in some kind of black magic cult."

"Black magic?" Clare echoed. She felt a sudden shiver run down her spine. So, the stupid story had come full circle. "What rubbish! I have taken some yoga lessons from a man I met in Cambridge, that's all."

"He said you were involved with some strange people," Archie continued as if she hadn't spoken. "Strange, evil people who consort with the devil." He swallowed, his eyes shifting in spite of himself to the sideboard where he had left the cross, wrapped in an old spotted cravat.

"That's not true," Clare cried. "For God's sake! You don't believe him? Mummy! You don't believe this, do you? There is nothing strange or evil about Zak! Paul is angry because I've left him. He is trying to get even with me, to discredit me. Surely you can see that?" So that they wouldn't believe her if she told them what had happened in the elevator. It was so obvious what he was doing. She took a deep breath. He needn't have worried, she would never tell anyone about that.

Casta, hearing her mistress's agitated voice, got up and came and put her head on Clare's knees.

"Tell me you don't believe him!" Clare looked at them both in turn.

"Well, I don't." Antonia took a defiant mouthful of food. "Come on, Archie, neither do you. And your supper is getting cold."

Archie glared from one woman to the other. He was not sure what to do next. On the one hand, he was extremely relieved that he had brought it all out into the open and Clare had not turned on him with sulphur and brimstone. On the other hand, he kept hearing Paul's words again: *She is clever at hiding the truth. . . . Don't trust her. . . . She will deny it. . . .*

He shrugged. "Well, I'm glad to hear there's nothing in it," he said at last. He gave an embarrassed smile.

"Does Paul know I'm here?" Clare was looking straight at him.

"No, dear, he called before you arrived," Antonia answered.

"Does he?" Clare's eyes were fixed on her stepfather's face.

He nodded defensively. "I called him today. He has a right to know where you are, Clare. He *is* your husband."

"Is he coming up here?" Clare clenched her fists.

"He said he would fly up tomorrow." Archie didn't dare look at his wife.

"You know why he's doing all this, don't you?" Clare flung her napkin aside and stood up. "This is all because there is oil at Duncairn, and I've been offered a lot of money for it. I refused to sell, and he is furious."

"Oil? At Duncairn?" Her mother's mouth had fallen open in astonishment. "Don't be ridiculous."

"Oh, it's true, and Paul needs the money. He needs a lot of money." Clare's voice had risen in desperation. "He could sell his shares in the family firm, but he won't. He wants my money to pay his debts and I refused." Her anger had brought a touch of color to her face. "I will never sell Duncairn!"

There was an astonished silence. "Paul can't have any debts!" her mother said at last. Her glance at Archie was full of doubt. "Paul is a very rich man, darling."

"I should know, I am his wife." Clare walked across to the fireplace. She put her hand up to the high mantelpiece and rested her head on it. "What is he going to do when he gets here? Try to persuade me to sell again? Twist my arm? Try to make you change my mind?"

There was an awkward silence. "I think he wants you to go back to London with him," Archie said at last.

"No. I've told you. I've left him, and I'm not waiting here to have yet another argument with him! I'll never go back to London with him. And if he's coming here, then I won't stay here another minute."

Clare ran up to her room, deaf to the protests of her parents. She threw her clothes back into her suitcase, grabbed her fur coat from the closet, and put on her Burberry. The undrawn curtains showed a crescent moon low in the sky above the river between the trees. She could feel the chill off the glass. It was a very cold night. With one longing look around the room she walked out, snapping off the light, and lugged her suitcase down the broad flight of stairs, Casta following.

The headlights lighted up the long rhododendron-lined drive, showing a sparkle of frost already on the rough tarmac. Clare slowed cautiously as she turned out onto the road, feeling the car wheels chassé sideways slightly on some hidden ice. Only her mother had been in the hall to say goodbye. Clare had not told her where she was going. She glanced at the car clock. It was nine-fifteen. If she made good time she should be at Duncairn in about three hours or so.

She turned east toward Blairgowrie, pushing the car as fast as she dared on the narrow, winding road. She caught glimpses of water, reflecting in the moonlight on the right, then the car swept on, plunging between woods of pine and beech and thick clumps of rhododendron. Every now and again the road climbed onto barren moor and the lights caught patches of gorse at the road side. There the sparkle of frost was thickest.

It was just after ten when the rabbit leapt off the verge and stood for a moment, blinded, in her headlights. Automatically and without thought of the consequences she slammed on her brakes. The car spun out of control across the road, plowed up the verge, and slewed into a rutted field.

For a moment Clare didn't move. She was faint with shock. She closed her eyes, trying to steady her breathing, feeling her legs dissolving as the adrenaline coursed unpleasantly through her.

There was a whimper from the backseat. Clare released her seat belt and turned stiffly, aware suddenly that her arm and shoulder were throbbing painfully. Casta had been thrown down and wedged into the narrow gap between the seat on which she had been asleep and the back of Clare's. Whining and panting, she scrabbled her way off the floor, ripping great grooves into the upholstery with her claws. She seemed to be unhurt. Relieved, Clare turned back and, pushing open the door, climbed out.

The moon was hovering on the horizon, almost gone, the car headlights cocked up in the air by the angle at which they had stopped. All around, the countryside was deserted and completely silent. They were about twenty feet from the road.

Still shaking, Clare walked slowly around the car, trying to see what damage had been done. There was a dent on one wing and a long scratch on the driver's door, otherwise there seemed to be nothing much amiss. Stiffly she climbed back in and tried to restart the engine, but the wheels wouldn't grip. One of them was completely off the ground. Without help there was no way she could move. Sobbing with shock and cold and misery, she climbed out and looked around again. The moon had gone, sliding out of sight almost as she watched. Icy starlight lighted the fields and beyond them the moor. As far as the eye could see there were no houses anywhere; no lights. They hadn't passed a house for more than two miles. Shivering violently, she climbed back into the car and tried to think.

Someone would come, surely. It wasn't so late.

But nobody came. The road remained deserted.

Twice she started the engine to warm the car, hugging Casta, the fur coat draped around them both. Her immediate instinct had been to get out of the car and start walking, but she wasn't sure where she was exactly. In the dark and without a map she might be miles from help of any kind. Desperately she tried to picture the road, but it was months since she had driven up there, and she couldn't remember where the next farm or village was. From the high field she could see for what seemed like miles in the starlight. The road stretched away a lonely ribbon in both directions, completely deserted.

Slowly her eyes began to close. She thought briefly about the candles in her suitcase in the trunk. Should she light them to keep her warm? Beside her Casta stirred restlessly. She flattened her ears and growled softly in her throat. Condensation had misted the windows. Outside, the fields were lonely and very still.

"What is it, love? There's no one there." Clare rubbed at the windshield with the heel of her hand and peered out. Under the starlight the ground was suddenly full of shadows. Clare's hand tightened convulsively on the dog's collar.

"She won't hurt you, darling," she whispered into the dog's ear. "She's not real. She's part of me. She's part of my dreams." She had begun to shake with fear.

The temperature was dropping fast as the icy night air began to penetrate the car. Clare buried her face in the dog's neck. "Help me, darling. Help me to make her go away! I'm going to save Duncairn for her. Isn't that enough?" She was sobbing out loud.

With a growl Casta wrenched herself free of Clare's arms and hurled herself across the passenger seat into the back of the car. The condensation had closed across the windows again, trapping them in the darkness. The only sound was the frightened panting of the dog.

Clare lifted her head. A pattern was forming slowly in the condensation on the windshield. Backlit by the starlight, she could see the flowers and whorls as the ice came. And behind them she could see the horses, eyes red, manes and tails streaming, as Isobel led the men of Buchan north across the Perthshire moors.

The horses were exhausted after the long miles on the snow-covered Cheviots beneath livid skies, thundering across moors where the snows had gone and only the blackened heather stems remained, galloping till their flanks were black with sweat and their nostrils flared scarlet, screaming for air.

Isobel was frantic. She had to reach Robert. She had to be there for his coronation. Gossip roared across the land like a fire in the heather. The Scots had risen at last, the English were being routed on every side. Word had gone around, the fiery cross was traveling the length and breadth of the nation and the people were bidden to Scone, the traditional sacred place of crowning.

The King of Scots was to be crowned there without delay. "But not without me. I have to be there. He can't be crowned until I get there. I have to be there." Isobel murmured the words again and again in her head like a prayer.

Her hair was loose beneath her hood, her face streaked with dirt. Her gown clung to her, soaked with sweat beneath her cloak.

Again and again she glanced behind, terrified she was going to see her husband's horses in pursuit, but the horizon to the south, purple and heavy with storm, stayed empty. She allowed neither men nor horses time to rest, driven by her desperate need to reach Robert before it was too late.

On they rode, north toward Perth and then at last, on the twenty-sixth day of March, they arrived at Scone. From far away they could see the crowds even though it was nearly dark for already the flares and fires had been lighted, and by their light they could see the tents, the horses, the banners in the chill wind, and above them all the royal lion of Scotland, a burnished flag against a bruised sky, flying proudly over the partly dismantled Abbey of Scone.

Isobel slid from her horse at last after threading her way through the shouting crowds, her eyes on the standard, her men around her. She was unaware of her wild hair and ragged, dirty clothes as she saw a lone figure walking toward her through the shouting, singing crowds. Gilbert of Annandale stopped short a few feet from her.

"He is crowned, my lady. Yesterday. By the Bishop of St. Andrews in the abbey."

She stared at him. "No. No! That can't be! He can't be crowned!"

"He was, my lady. He is now our king. There were three bishops and two abbots in the abbey, my lady. He is crowned beyond all doubt."

"No!" She pushed past him. "That cannot be! He cannot be crowned without me. Where is he? I have to see him! Without me he cannot be king! Without the Earl of Fife's blessing his crowning will not be valid. He knows that. I have to see him!"

"He is feasting, my lady—" Gilbert called after her, but already she had pushed past him, her heart heavy with despair.

With the men of Buchan behind her, she ran toward the hall where Robert and his followers were at table. Torches and candles threw a thousand flaring lights about the great hall of Scone Palace. The noise was deafening and the heat intense. The hall was packed to the doors. For a moment she stood staring across the crowds, then she saw him.

At the table on the dais Robert sat in splendor dressed in rich robes, a gold crown upon his head, and beside him sat his queen, Elizabeth, her red hair gleaming beneath a veil of silk and a circlet of gold. At the high table with him were his brothers, one of his sisters, his daughter Marjorie, and some of his closest friends and supporters, among them Lord Atholl, and the Earl of Lennox, the lord of Menteith, and close to Robert his ward and nephew, Donald, the young Earl of Mar. She could see the bishops there and the two abbots with them.

At first no one noticed the newcomers in the doorway, then as table after table spotted the upright pale figure in the mud-plastered fur, silence began to fall over the hall.

Slowly she began to walk toward the dais, pushing back the hood from her hair, feeling her soaking skirts catching in the soft-scented herbs that were strewn between the tables. At the top table conversation faltered to a halt and at last Robert looked up and saw her. Slowly he rose to his feet.

In complete silence she approached the high table and walked around it. In front of Robert she stopped at last and knelt.

"Your Grace, I bring you the allegiance of the House of Duff. I bring my brother's greeting, and his blessing, and I claim the right, in his stead, to set you on the throne of Scotland." Her voice carried clearly around the entire hall.

Robert stretched out his two hands to hers and clasped them for a moment, then he smiled. "Your allegiance I accept, and gladly, Lady Buchan. But I am already crowned."

"Sire!" Behind him Bishop Lamberton clambered to his feet. The old man stared fiercely down at the kneeling exhausted woman, his blue eyes intense. "The Countess of Buchan brings you the seal of tradition. The ancient right of the earls of Fife to enthrone the king is not to be denied."

Robert turned. "Would you have me crowned twice, my Lord Bishop?"

There was a guffaw from behind him. "Why not! By God, that would be a splendid start to your reign, Robert!" Lord Atholl stood up too. "Of course she must enthrone you!"

"But where?" Next to him the Earl of Menteith was shaking his head. "The earls of Fife have always enthroned our kings upon the Stone of Destiny, and that has gone with so much else to England."

Isobel straightened. "I have the power of the stone in my hands," she said, her voice so quiet it was almost a whisper. "I went to St. Edward's shrine at Westminster, and I laid my hands upon it, where it lies in the chair Edward of England has had carved to hold it prisoner, and I prayed for its power so that I could pass it on to you, my king. And the stone gave me its blessing. I felt its power!"

There was a moment of total silence. Robert, who was still clasping her hands, let go of them abruptly.

Slowly she stood up and she raised them before her. Every eye in the great hall was riveted to her fingertips.

Bishop Lamberton swallowed. He glanced at his colleague,

Bishop Wishart. "This is part of the sacred inheritance of
Scotland," he said at last, his voice hushed with reverence.

The other nodded. "We should ask the countess to perform
the ceremony without delay. Tomorrow. It will be Palm Sunday." The old man's face was solemn. "Thus may our king,
Robert, enter his kingdom twice, and in the steps of Our
Lord."

The awed silence that followed Wishart's words was bro-
ken by a muffled snort from Elizabeth, at Robert's side.
"These are the games of children!" she murmured audibly.
"Do you seriously expect this woman to crown you again?
Surely one such farce is enough!" She pulled her mantle of
rich furs around her, her green eyes fixed on Isobel's face.

For once Isobel did not react. The horrified intake of
breath from those at the table who had heard the words of
their new queen was enough. She dropped her gaze modestly to the floor. "I am here to serve my king if he desires it,"
she said.

"And he does desire it!" Robert took her hand again with a
gallant bow. "Tomorrow, my lady, you shall enthrone me in
the ancient manner upon the sacred hill outside the abbey,
before the people of Scotland." He gave a small smile. "Tell
me, my lady, does the Earl of Buchan know what you are
doing?"

Isobel bit her lip. "I have no doubt that by now he knows,
sire." She glanced up at him suddenly. "I hope this time you
won't tell me to go back to him."

He shook his head. "Not this time, my lady. This time I
shall keep you with me." His words were spoken so quietly
no one heard them but Isobel.

Beside them Elizabeth scowled. Pushing back her heavy
chair, she stood up. "My lord, it is time for us to retire," she
said sharply. She had not heard their words, but like everyone close to them she had seen the sudden tender intimacy
between them.

Robert glanced at her. "It is too soon, madam. Please sit
down," he said curtly. "All of you, sit down and make a place
for Lady Buchan. It seems our celebrations are after all only
half over!"

That night Isobel could not sleep and, tired though she was, she paced the floor of her chamber in the palace for hours after she had withdrawn exhausted from the noisy hall. The touch of Robert's hands, his eyes, his whispered words, the thought of him, here beneath the same roof, all set her heart lurching beneath her ribs.

At last she pulled off her clothes and lay down, but it was no use. She got up almost at once and dragged a fur-trimmed gown out of one of the two boxes she had brought with her. Pulling it on over her chilly nakedness and knotting a girdle around her waist, she went to the door at last, and listened. After easing it quietly open, she crept out of the chamber. The passages of the palace were drafty and ill lighted. At every corner there were men-at-arms. She felt their eyes follow her as she tiptoed down the long winding stair toward the royal chapel. She must not think of him as a man. Not today. Now he was her king, and she was here to perform a sacred act. Before the altar in the chapel she would kneel and try to compose her thoughts.

The chapel was in darkness, save for the ever-burning sanctuary light that showed up the newly painted walls and the carved and gilded cross above the altar. Crossing herself, she knelt before the crucifix, staring up at its outline in the dim light, and fervently she began to pray. The gods who had blessed the Stone of Scone and sanctified it had walked this sacred spot a thousand years before Christ and they were here still, even in this chapel, to give their blessing to the new King of Scots.

"Isobel?"

Her name was whispered so softly she thought it part of the silent echoes. For a moment she didn't move, then, startled, she scrambled to her feet. There was a movement from a faldstool at the side of the altar, and she saw a figure materialize out of the darkness.

"Robert?" Her heart thumped uneasily as he approached her. "What are you doing here?" He was dressed only in a simple tunic. He had laid aside his robes and crown.

He smiled. "I came to keep vigil as I did the night before I was given my spurs. See." He nodded toward the altar and she realized for the first time that a naked sword lay on the altar cloth. "I came here yesterday before my crowning and I have come again to pray and keep vigil before my enthronement. I need all the strength that my prayers can give me."

"It will be a hard task winning Scotland back from the English," she said quietly.

The simple words conveyed clearly just how much he had to accomplish. For a moment they were both silent, contemplating the immensity of the undertaking upon which he had embarked.

"No, it won't be easy. But I shall do it," he said at last. "I have God and the right behind me." He spoke softly, but his voice was very certain. He caught her hands suddenly. "I am glad you came to me. I wanted you to be here. I wanted you to be the one to enthrone me."

They stared at each other. In the semidarkness their mutual longing was tangible.

Isobel drew away. "Not tonight," she whispered. "Tonight you belong to Scotland. Later you will belong to me." She smiled up at him and, falling on her knees, she kissed his hand. "Good night, Your Grace. May the gods be with you always. I shall leave you to your vigil now."

Rising, she turned away and silently she let herself out of the chapel.

The following day dawned fine. The sky was a vivid cold blue, torn with racing puffy clouds. Clusters of early daffodils danced in the wind and air was sharp and clear. In the distance the mountains still showed their caps of snow. On the Moot Hill, outside the abbey, on the sacred place of enthronement they had placed another stone, a lump of granite carved from the living rock of Scotland. The bishops blessed the stone and sprinkled it with holy water, then they anointed it with oil. In England the king himself was anointed, but here, in Scotland, where the ceremony was more ancient and more primitive, the crowning and the enthronement of the king were the more important acts. When the men of God had finished, Isobel knelt before the stone and placed her hands upon it, willing into it the power and the magic that she had felt flow through her in the shrine of St. Edward the Confessor. Around her the watching crowds fell silent. There was a breathless hush.

Rising, she stood back for a moment, looking beyond the palace and the abbey and the forests that surrounded it toward the distant hills. She was dressed now in velvets and rich furs, her kirtle trimmed with silk embroidery, and on her head was a diadem of Scottish silver found for her among what survived of the royal regalia, so carefully hidden through the wars by the bishop of Glasgow. Every eye was on her now.

She drew herself up and, taking a deep breath, she turned toward her king. After stepping toward him proudly, she took his hand and led him to the stone, covered now by cloth of gold. After he was seated on it she placed the crown upon his head once more, and all the people who were watching, crowded dozens deep around the strange flat-topped man-made hill that was the most sacred place in Scotland, roared their approval and their assent until the echoes rang.

Several paces from Robert stood his queen, dressed in blue and scarlet and gold. She was frowning. "This is asinine," she hissed at the Earl of Atholl, standing at her side. "We shall be king and queen for the summer if we are lucky! Robert cannot defeat Edward of England. No one can!"

The earl, who had been watching the scene attentively, glanced at her with a scowl. "This king will reign for longer than a summer, madam. Be sure of that!" he retorted tartly. He wasn't the only one that day to compare the beautiful dark Countess of Buchan, with her wild silver eyes and her passionate loyalty, to the icy golden queen and find the latter wanting.

The new King of Scots summoned the Countess of Buchan to his presence that evening as the sun set in a blaze of crimson and black behind the western hills. He was standing alone in one of the antechambers, staring out across the forests, his face lighted by the dying sun.

"Isobel! We have only a moment before I have to meet my counselors. I just wanted the chance to tell you that I was proud of you today." He stepped toward her into the shadowy room. "Scotland will remember you forever."

She smiled. "And so, I hope, will Scotland's king."

He smiled. "Isobel." He was suddenly very serious. "I am under no illusions about what lies ahead. Nor must you be. If you follow me there will be hardship and danger. My family already knows it and they have chosen to support me. Will you do the same?"

"Do you really have to ask?" She smiled at him. "I will follow you to the edge of the world if you ask me, my love." She put her arms around his neck, and, standing on tiptoe, she reached up to kiss him.

He gathered her into his arms hungrily. "Dear God, Isobel, but I want you! It will be so hard having you near me. I'm not sure I am going to be strong enough to bear it—"

"You won't have to bear it, Your Grace." Her lips were on his neck, his ears, his throat, and then again claiming his mouth. "I shall be there every time you summon me. I am yours to command. You will find a way."

"I'll have to find a way, my love," he murmured into her hair. "God, but I want you now!"

Behind them the door opened suddenly and fell back against the wall with a crash. Elizabeth de Burgh, the Queen of Scots, stood there. She was smiling. "So, the private conference his grace is engaged in, and which his fawning subjects are so anxious I should not disturb, is with the daughter of the Duffs, a murderess and a witch by all accounts." She folded her arms as Isobel drew guiltily away from Robert. "What have you to say, my lord? Or has she bewitched you as well?"

Robert eyed his wife coldly. "If she has, madam, it was a long time ago. I have known my cousin of Fife since she was a child."

"And loved her as a cousin, no doubt." Elizabeth's voice was sarcastic. She moved away from the door. "As well it is nothing more." She gave Isobel an acid-sweet smile, "Because I shall see to it she never has the chance to be alone with you again, my Lord!"

* * *

The tractor had stopped right in front of the car. A man climbed slowly down from the cab and walked toward it, a flashlight in his hand. Casta, who had been trembling in the backseat of the Jaguar, began to bark sharply and Clare started violently. She could still see the shadowy room, the three motionless figures, the streaming candles, but she could also see the outline of the windshield, opaque with frost, and beyond it the cautious wavering beam of the flashlight.

Desperately she pulled herself together, trying to regain some kind of a grip on reality. With numb fingers she groped for the ignition key and turned on the power, then she fumbled on the dashboard to find the lights. The powerful headlights flooded the field, bathing the tractor in a silver spotlight. She tried to lower the window, but it was frozen solid. Putting her whole weight against it, in sudden panic, she pushed open the door.

"Hello?" A voice greeted her at once. "Are you all right? I saw the car there, from the road!"

"I skidded!" Clare climbed out stiffly, gasping at the cold. She winced at the pain from her bruised shoulder. "And I couldn't get back on the road. I don't think the car's damaged but it is stuck. Can you help me?"

It took him half an hour in the icy wind to attach the rope and gently ease the Jaguar back onto the road. Then, having given all her tires a hearty kick, presumably to test their soundness, he offered Clare a drink from his Thermos. The tea had been fortified by about half a pound of sugar and a large measure of whisky. Clare gasped, her eyes watering, but it was just what she needed to kick the blood back into circulation within her veins.

She was back on the road at ten past five.

Chapter Twenty-one

Neil stirred and opened his eyes. Beside him Kathleen lay on her face, her hair spread across the pillow, her naked shoulders looking somehow very defenseless. He leaned across and drew the tumbled blankets over her before getting up and walking over to the window. Streaks of green light were illuminating the sky above the haze of rose. High up he could see a flock of white gulls, their wings stained crimson by the sun still below the horizon. With a quick glance at Kathleen he began to pull on his trousers, a shirt, two sweaters, his thick jacket. He could see the white frost on the grass now.

He let himself silently out of the hotel and, hands in pockets, made his way across the crisp grass into the teeth of the wind, toward the sunrise.

He saw the dog first. The retriever, nose down, tail wagging, exploring the stand of trees behind the hotel.

Walking briskly across the uneven frosted ground, he headed toward the castle through the first hollow cold of winter. The sky was losing its green; the crimson was spreading upward now from its intense center, where any moment the sun segment would appear above the sea, staining the waves into a vast inverted V of color.

She was sitting on a fallen lump of masonry, the fur coat wrapped tightly around her, the collar up, hugging herself against the wind, her eyes on the sunrise, her hair blowing wildly back from her face.

He stood for several moments watching her, trying to make sense of the emotions that swept over him. Hostility, resentment, anger, they were all expected, but also that strange sense of rightness; the feeling that she belonged, and something not unlike pleasure at seeing her again.

Slowly he walked up to her. The howl of the wind drowned the sound of his steps sighing through the ice-crisped grass. He stopped behind her.

"Good morning, Mrs. Royland."

She jumped violently. "Mr. Forbes!"

She remembered his name at once, he noticed. She didn't have to grope for it. But then perhaps she had been expecting to see him up there.

For a moment they were both silent, staring out across the cliffs toward the sea as the first small rim of the crimson sun appeared, an intense unwatchable center to the flaming sky. Below them the sea was crashing onto the rocks, the white foam luminous on the black water.

Neil tore his eyes away from the sunrise and glanced back toward the road. Was that the green Jag parked in the shadows beyond the castle walls?

Clare hadn't moved. "Are you here on behalf of Earthwatch, Mr. Forbes?"

"I'm here to watch the sunrise." He rather enjoyed putting her down.

She said nothing. Slowly she stood up. She gave him a quick dismissive glance, then she walked slowly away from him toward the arched doorway that had once been the entrance to the chapel. It was very still there out of the wind where the grass was neatly mown. Clare glanced around. The atmosphere was heavy, unnaturally cold. It seemed to be giving off waves of unhappiness.

Almost without realizing he had done it, Neil followed her. He looked around frowning, feeling the strangeness around them. It was as if she triggered something in the ancient stones each time she came here. He shivered.

"I hope you haven't come up here to make trouble, Mrs. Royland. I warned you about local reaction to your plans," he said, trying to shrug off the feeling of foreboding that had descended on him.

"You know nothing about my plans," she retorted. She turned to face him. "Are you aware that you are standing on private property, Mr. Forbes? Duncairn still belongs to me, you know."

"I have permission to be here. From Jack. Your tenant." He put his hands in his jacket pockets.

"Then I must tell him not to be so prodigal with his favors."

Her face was beginning to take on some color; sparks of anger were animating her eyes. She had forgotten what a good-looking man he was. Somehow it made her resent him more.

Neil smiled coldly. "Do that." In spite of his intense dislike of the woman, there was something about her that intrigued him—the contrasts in her: the sophistication, the expensive coat, the stylish haircut, the upper-class English accent, all so much at odds with her windswept wildness and whatever demon had brought her here to sit on a clifftop at sunrise on the coldest morning of the year so far. In spite of her anger she was slightly abstracted still, as if listening to something faraway in her head, her face strangely enigmatic in its beauty. He watched her curiously, realizing with a sudden flash of anger that she no longer even knew he was there. She and her castle were bound in some strange communion that did not include him.

Behind them the sky was changing. High up the clouds were turning pink, racing inland from the sea, while the whole sun now rested on the rim of the world.

"How could you sell it!" The words were rung out of him before he could stop himself.

She stared at him. "I told you, I haven't sold it."

"No. But you are about to. Dear God! Does money mean so much to you?"

"No. It doesn't." Clare's temper flared. "Mr. Forbes, please get off my land!"

From high in the keep a gull took up the wild pitch of her voice and echoed it, its cry ringing from the stones.

Clare did not watch him as he turned and left the chapel. She walked across to the broken window arch and, leaning against it, stared out to sea, once more trapped in her own world.

Isobel was there. Around her the air was electric, the shadows beyond the new cold sunlight opaque. Distantly she heard the yelping echo of the bird's cry as it soared on the wind. With a sob she clenched her fists, pressing her forehead against the stone, wishing now she had not sent Neil Forbes away. Isobel came to her only when she was alone.

Beyond the walls Casta gave a shrill bark and Clare looked up.

The grass was wet where the sun had touched the frost and she could see the dog running zigzag across the meadow, leaving a trail of blackness in the silver. A beam of sunlight pierced the window near her and the shadows drew back. After pushing herself away from the wall, she began to walk out toward the dog. She had fought Isobel and won.

Twenty minutes later she drove up to the front of the Duncairn Hotel. She opened the front door and walked in, smelling the early-morning scents of furniture polish and coffee and a newly lighted driftwood fire. It was very quiet.

"Jack? Jack, are you there?" She walked stiffly across the cavernous entrance hall and put her head around the door of the restaurant. One table was laid for breakfast. For two. The others were bare. She tried the bar and then the office. All were empty, then suddenly Jack Grant appeared behind her.

"Mrs. Royland?" His voice was far from friendly. "No need to ask what you are doing here so early, I suppose."

"That's right, Jack. I'd like some breakfast, please."

"I meant, I suppose you've come to give us all our notice."

Clare sighed. "Oh, Jack! Have you been listening to that man Forbes? Look, please. Listen to my side of the story. He doesn't know what he is talking about. Give me some breakfast, and I'll explain the situation." She was too tired for this.

"I'm sorry, I'm not serving breakfast." He turned away.

For a moment Clare stood still, shaken, then slowly she walked out into the wind. "No one seems to want me here, Casta," she said quietly as she climbed into the car. For a moment she put her head back against the headrest and closed her eyes.

She drove the few hundred yards back down the winding drive and then pulled off into the trees near the castle again. She had come to see Duncairn, after all: the family home, Isobel's home, not the hotel. Any tryst she had to keep was there among the shadows, not in the bright lights of an unwelcoming hotel.

Paul arrived at Airdlie just after nine. When he found out that Clare had gone, he was furious.

"For pity's sake, Archie! Couldn't you tell the state she was in! Hallucinating! Having nightmares! On the point of a nervous breakdown! I told you she'd fool you. For God's sake, where is she?"

"Calm down, Paul." Antonia put a cup of coffee and a slice of shortbread on a plate on the table next to him. "You seem far closer to a nervous breakdown than Clare."

Paul took a deep breath, aware suddenly that his hands were shaking. "I'm sorry, Antonia. It's just that I've been living with it for so long. Listen, if you don't believe me, call my brother. Geoffrey has talked to her. He was the first one to realize the danger she is in."

"You really believe this yourself, don't you?" Archie was sitting in his favorite chair by the fire, his feet up on the coffee table. He was wearing fawn plus fours and an old lovat tweed jacket. His favorite clothes gave him confidence; Paul always made him feel uneasy.

"Oh, yes, I believe it. And so will you, if you're honest with yourselves." Paul paused. "Think back. Don't you remember her doing odd things in her childhood? Daydreaming? Living in the past? Talking to imaginary people? I can remember you and Aunt Margaret telling me about it, for God's sake! And now it's developed into all this. Dear God! I wish it wasn't true, but it is!" He leaned back wearily in his chair. "I wish to God it wasn't." His sudden defeated tone was far more convincing than his anger had been.

"She said she'd spend the night at a hotel and call me. I don't know where she's gone," Antonia said softly. "But if we find her, can we take our own minister to talk to her?"

Paul frowned. Just in time he stopped himself from leaping to his feet and forbidding it. "Of course you can, only for pity's sake speak to Geoffrey first. The sight of a man of God could trigger something off. She's very volatile. You've no idea how careful we have to be." He leaned forward, elbows on knees.

"I'll tell you what we have to do. We have to bring her back here and keep her here. She mustn't, above all, be allowed to escape and go back to her friends in Suffolk. We must keep her here, under lock and key, if necessary." He glanced at them quickly, gauging their reaction. So far, so good. His plan, such as it was, was working.

"Geoffrey has promised to come and see her up here, and so will our own doctor if he has to. The main point is to keep her away from this man Zak and his followers. I only hope we can keep her quiet and unhysterical. I have some tranquilizers I can give her if necessary." He had wheedled them out of John Stanford for himself.

"Oh, Paul, no." Antonia was shocked.

"Only if I have to, believe me. And in the meantime, there is another problem." He paused. He had to get it right—the right tone, the right amount of concern. He mustn't seem too anxious. "She is threatening to make over all her property, everything she owns, to Zak de Sallis." He glanced up at his father-in-law under his eyebrows, shrewdly judging his reaction. "I know you will agree that can't be allowed to happen. So I must have power of attorney."

"Oh, poor Clare!" Antonia was weeping discreetly into a pink Kleenex. "And she told us you wanted Duncairn because there was oil there. Oil! Can you imagine! She will be all right, won't she?"

Paul smiled. "Of course she will," he said. Everything was working for him. He had trapped them with the three sacred cows that people of their background worshiped: the church, the medical profession, and the sanctity of property. "Now the only thing is to find her before she harms herself."

"Duncairn," Archie said.

"Of course," Antonia said. "She always goes there when she's miserable. Why don't I call that nice Mr. Grant?"

"No!" Paul put his hand on her arm. "No, Antonia, don't phone. If she thinks we're on to her she'll run, and that is the last thing we want. I'll drive over to Duncairn myself. If she's there I'll bring her back."

"I'll come with you, my boy." Archie straightened his shoulders.

Paul shook his head. "No. I'll manage better on my own."

With her parents on his side he would have Clare exactly where he wanted her. Either she would sign Duncairn over to him voluntarily or he would get power of attorney, with the help of Geoffrey and David and her parents, and John Stanford, if he could persuade him, and he would keep her out of the way until it was too late for her to do anything to save Duncairn.

Rex picked Emma and Julia up at twelve o'clock exactly.

"Am I forgiven for the way I engineered our first meeting?" When Rex had booked the table at the Compleat Angler, he had ordered champagne on ice to be waiting for them.

Emma frowned. "It was a bloody thing to do! You were spying on my brother."

"As it happened there was no need. And that means the other times we met were because I wanted to see you."

Emma stopped herself from smiling back with an effort. She glanced at him surreptitiously. The bastard wasn't going to charm her that easily. He was looking pale and tired, but he was still one of the most attractive and exciting men she had ever met.

"What has happened about Duncairn?"

"Your brother has agreed to sell."

Emma stared at him. "But it isn't Paul's to sell."

"No, I know that, but his wife has agreed, and anyway I gather he has control of her affairs since her illness."

Emma frowned. "Clare is not ill, Rex."

"Yes, she is. Aunty Clare has gone mad." Julia looked up from her glass. The bubbles were making her wrinkle her nose. "Uncle Paul told Daddy."

"That's not true!" Emma stared at her daughter furiously. "Were you listening at the door?"

"No, of course not! Everyone knows, Mummy. Aunt Chloe has discussed it with Piers and Ruth. They told me last week when we went over to the rectory. I think it's rather exciting!

She sleepwalks or something and has fits and screams in elevators."

"Holy shit!" Rex looked alarmed. "Is this true?"

"No," Emma said firmly. "The bit about elevators is, because she suffers from claustrophobia, but she is not mad and she is perfectly capable of handling her own affairs. Look, Rex. I'd better tell you the whole story." She glanced helplessly at Julia. "And you'd better listen too, so you know the truth instead of this awful gossip." Briefly she outlined Clare's interest in meditation and the story of her daydreams. "That is all it is. She is not mad or possessed, just obsessed by the past. But Paul—" She hesitated. "Well, you obviously know my brother. He is single-minded and devious and he wants the money for Duncairn. He is furious that Clare doesn't want to sell, and he's putting pressure on her to do so. I think that's why he's telling everyone she is ill."

Rex looked thoughtful. "Paul Royland is about to go bankrupt. He'll be ruined without that money. So, for your family's sake, it might be a good thing if I did buy Duncairn. It might make your sister-in-law sad to part with it, but it would make her an awful lot sadder to see her husband in jail for insider trading and bankrupted into the bargain."

Emma clutched the stem of her glass. "Oh, Rex!"

"Believe me, Emma. I'm probably the only chance he's got." Rex let his hand touch hers for a second. "So, if you have any clout with your sister-in-law, you use it. If she refuses to help her husband, she could be condemning him to several years in prison."

"I don't know if I can persuade her," Emma said, agonized.

Rex shrugged. "Then leave it to me. Now, to change the subject: Let's talk about us and make the first really important decision of the day. What are we going to eat for lunch?"

Stiff and cold, Clare stood up. It had turned into a beautiful day, bright and blustery and very cold. She realized she had been sitting staring out to sea on the cold wall too long. She was faint with hunger and her arm and shoulder were throbbing with pain.

She frowned. She could see the smoke from the hotel chim-

neys streaming up behind the trees, tattered and shredded
by the wind. Why on earth had she not explained to Jack her
true position? Why hadn't she told Neil Forbes? Stupid pride,
that was the reason. She felt they should have believed her;
they should automatically have trusted her. But they hadn't,
and now Forbes had no doubt turned everyone against her.

Stretching painfully, she whistled to Casta and set off purposefully across the grass. She would go back to the hotel, put
Jack in the picture, and see Neil Forbes and swallow her
pride and explain to him as well.

Jack was in the restaurant supervising the laying of the
luncheon tables. They usually ended up with a dozen or so
visitors on a Saturday at this time of year, because their
reputation was spreading, and however bad the weather
people usually managed to get there. He still prided himself
on his food, even if the restaurant would soon be closed.

He straightened as she walked in.

"Is Neil Forbes here?" she said as firmly as she could. "I'd
like to speak to him. I think there are one or two things I
should make clear to you both."

Jack raised an eyebrow. For a moment she thought he was
going to refuse, but he said nothing. He walked through to
the office and called Neil's room. He did not go back to her.

Neil and Kathleen found her in the bar, standing staring
out of the window. She was still wearing her coat. For a
moment she and Kathleen gazed at each other. Kathleen felt
a warning prickle creep up her spine. The woman was beautiful, young, elegant. Oh God, and rich! She narrowed her
eyes, glancing at Neil. His face was closed and uncompromis-
ing.

"Mrs. Royland?"

Clare turned to him from the window with an uncertain
smile. "I want to talk to you."

"All right." He inclined his head.

"Alone."

"All right. Kath, if you will excuse us, Mrs. Royland and I
can talk in the lounge. You have a drink. I won't be long."

Not even seeing the look of venomous anger that crossed
Kathleen's face, he led the way into the small residents'

lounge and, closing the door behind them, leaned against it, waiting for her to speak.

She swallowed, appalled suddenly to find herself near to tears. He had folded his arms, his eyes on her face. "I had to talk to you again."

"Mrs. Royland. We belong to different worlds. Mine is a caring one." His expression was very hard. "When it comes to talking, I very much doubt if we speak the same language." He knew he was being hard on her; he could see she was upset but somehow he wanted to go on punishing her.

"Why don't you let me explain?" she cried. "Why do you hate me so much? You know nothing about me!"

"Mrs. Royland, I assure you—"

"Clare. My name is Clare." She could feel her hands shaking.

He raised an eyebrow. "How nice." His tone was sarcastic. "Then, Clare, let me assure you that I have no reason to hate you personally. After all, I hardly know you. What I hate is everything you stand for."

"And what do I stand for?" She stared at him.

He gave a short laugh. "The uncaring face of capitalism."

"Uncaring?" she echoed. Walking across to the window, she stood with her back to him and took a deep breath. "I'm sorry I was rude to you this morning. I had an accident in my car and had been out all night."

Neil frowned. "Were you hurt?"

She shook her head. "Just a few bruises and some wounded dignity, that's all." She managed a bleak smile. "I shouldn't have ordered you off my land." She took another deep, unsteady breath. "We're on the same side, Mr. Forbes. When I told you I had not sold Duncairn, I meant it. I have turned down Sigma's offer. I never even considered it."

He looked at her incredulously. "Then why in God's name didn't you say so?"

She shrugged. "You put my back up, I suppose. You assumed the worst and called me names."

"I called you names?"

"Yes, you did, Mr. Forbes, you called me English." She gave a wry grimace.

He burst out laughing. "And the insult hurt! I'm sorry. I retract every word of it. Look, Mrs. Royland—Clare—I'm sorry. I've obviously jumped to the wrong conclusion about you. Perhaps I should explain. I don't know you, but I do know your husband—or at least, I did some years ago. We were at the same college, and although I was a couple of years behind him we had occasion to cross swords once or twice."

To his surprise she had gone pale. "You know Paul?"

He nodded. "He must have changed a lot if he's prepared to pass up an offer such as Sigma has made."

"He hasn't changed." Her bitter words were so quiet he hardly heard them. Suddenly she was desperately trying not to cry; she groped in her pocket for a handkerchief.

"Hey, come on—" Touched by her distress, he stepped toward her and reached out involuntarily.

Her throat was aching; there was a weight of tears somewhere in her chest. Blindly, scarcely realizing what she was doing, she went to him, desperate for any kind of comfort. She clung to him desperately, her face buried in his shoulder, overwhelmed by the reassurance of being held by another human being. He was warm and solid and his arms around her were very strong.

He was surprised how frail she felt, even wearing the thick coat. He scowled down at the soft dark fur but managed to restrain himself from commenting. Now was not the moment to tell her she had blood on her back. Instead he patted it awkwardly in the region of her shoulder blades. "I gather he is still a bastard," he said gently. To his surprise, he found he wanted to go on holding her. She felt right in his arms.

She nodded, still clinging to him.

"And he's putting pressure on you to sell?"

She nodded again. She felt a sudden shock as her body became aware of his, so close to hers, and at the recognition that flowed through her. She pulled away. "I'm sorry. I don't know what's the matter with me. Please, forgive me."

"Don't be silly," he said gruffly. He pulled himself together swiftly. "Let's discuss this over a cup of coffee."

She smiled at him wanly. "Can you persuade Jack to give me one? He refused to serve me."

"I'm afraid that's my fault. If you'd only told me!" He turned to the door and pulled it open. Jack was waiting in the bar with Kathleen. "Jack! I've misjudged Mrs. Royland. I jumped to the wrong conclusion about her. Can you get her some coffee, then we can have a council of war."

Behind Jack, Kathleen was peering at them. She eyed Clare suspiciously.

"You mean she is not going to sell?" Jack's face was dour. "Or did they not offer enough money yet?"

"They offered more money than I'd ever dreamed of." Clare gave a weary smile. "I turned them down."

"Well, good for you!" Kathleen's tone was sarcastic. "Didn't you need any more for the moment?"

Clare glanced at Kathleen but said nothing. Still huddled in her coat, she walked over to the window overlooking the front of the hotel and stood, hands deep in her pockets, staring out. "Paul will follow me here," she said.

"He can't force you to sell." Neil folded his arms.

"No." She sounded bleak.

"Are you running away from him?" he asked cautiously after a moment.

"Yes, I suppose I am."

Behind them Jack placed a tray with a pot of coffee and four cups and a plate of biscuits onto a low table.

"The thing is, he needs the money, and I think he will stop at nothing to get it."

"You make him sound like a dangerous man," Kathleen said mockingly.

"He is." Neil's soft voice made Jack and Kathleen halt in their tracks. "Don't sneer, Kath. Remember, I know Paul Royland of old."

Clare shivered. "What am I to do?"

"Keep on running, dear," Kathleen said with a smile. "That's what I'd do in your shoes. He wouldn't know where to follow you after Duncairn."

Neil shook his head. "She can't run for the rest of her life."

"Your aunt wouldn't have run at all," Jack put in. "She'd have stood and fought."

And so would Isobel. The unspoken thought was suddenly in Clare's mind.

Neil was watching her face. "I don't think Clare is the same kind of person her aunt was," he said.

He saw the color flare into her cheeks. "Meaning you think I'm a coward?"

"No." He smiled. "But maybe you've lived in the south too long. You would prefer to negotiate your way out of trouble."

"You can't negotiate with Paul," Clare said flatly. "Not even you, with all your native Scots cunning, could do that."

Jack was watching Clare closely. The color had drained from her face again. She looked exhausted and near collapse. He felt a sudden wave of compassion. He had always been fond of wee Clare. Her new image as traitor and absentee landlord had never really seemed to fit her. Margaret Gordon would never have left her Duncairn if there had been any doubt about Clare's fitness to own the place. "Why don't I find you a room, lass," he broke in impatiently. "You look as though you could do with a sleep. You'll have had a long drive, I'm thinking. If your husband turns up, we'll send him on his way."

"Can you do that for me?" The relief in her eyes was obvious to them all.

"Give me your car keys. I'll hide that gas guzzler of yours in one of the garages at the back of the hotel." Neil put down his coffee cup. "We'll talk some more when you are rested. Jack is right. You should have a sleep. You look as if you are about to collapse."

The room Jack gave her looked east toward the castle. It was a large room, next to Kathleen and Neil's, with two tall windows, a double bed, a mahogany chest of drawers, and two vast wardrobes. Casta, who had followed Clare upstairs, lay down contentedly on the carpet between the windows as Clare sat down on the bed to pull off her boots and trousers. Then, too tired to undress further, she threw herself back onto the bed and dragged the covers up over her. In spite of the terrible ache in her shoulder she was asleep within two minutes.

Paul walked into the Duncairn Castle Hotel at three-fifteen. Jack Grant was in the office. He recognized Paul at once.

"Mr. Royland. How nice to see you again."

Paul smiled tautly. "And you. Is my wife here, Grant?"

"Your wife?" Jack looked blank. "I've not seen her for a long time, Mr. Royland."

"Are you sure? She was on her way here."

Slowly Jack shook his head. "We've had quite a lot of visitors here today, with the sunshine, but I'd have seen her if she looked in."

Paul swore under her breath. Then he went to the window. "I suppose she would have gone to the castle, if she had come here. I'll go over and see."

The castle was deserted. Paul walked into the courtyard and stopped, looking around. The clouds had reached him now and they were carrying sleet. The first shower slanted in from the sea and across the stone walls, soaking into his jacket. Below the cliffs the sea was plunging angrily onto the rocks, sucking at the shingle and swirling in among the weed. He shuddered. What did Clare see in this godforsaken place? If it had been his, he would have paid someone to take it off his hands!

He walked around slowly, peering into the chapel, the tower, around the curtain walls, searching, expecting every moment to see her huddled figure against the stone. Twenty minutes later he strode back into the hotel.

Neil was standing with his back to the fire in the hall reading the *Scotsman.* He lowered it as Paul came in. Jack was nowhere to be seen.

Neil nodded. "Jack Grant told me you were here, Royland. It's been a long time."

Paul stared at him, for a moment at a loss, then his eyes narrowed in recognition. "Forbes! I heard you had involved yourself in our affairs."

Neil grinned humorlessly. "Earthwatch is opposing the

granting of prospecting licenses on this and several other sites on mainland Scotland, yes."

"Sigma will get the license." Paul peeled off his sodden jacket. "The government lobby for onshore oil is too strong."

"We'll see," Neil said amiably. He eyed Paul. "Do I hear you have lost your wife?"

Paul's jaw tightened imperceptibly. "We were to meet here. Apparently she hasn't arrived."

"Oh, she arrived." Neil folded the newspaper and put it down on the table in the middle of the hall. "She never mentioned that she was meeting you here, though. She must have forgotten." He grinned. "She has gone on north. She mentioned that she was going to stay with a friend in Fraserburgh."

"Fraserburgh?" Paul stared at him.

Neil nodded emphatically.

"The only person she knows in Fraserburgh is old Jeannie Campbell," Paul went on thoughtfully.

"Then that must be where she has gone." Neil was standing with his back to the fire, feeling the comforting warmth of the burning driftwood. He put his hands behind his back and rubbed them together, trying to curb his dislike of the man facing him.

Paul frowned. For a moment he hesitated, then he swung back toward the door, shrugging his wet jacket back on. "I'll go after her." He paused and glared at Neil, not even trying to hide his animosity. "We'll meet again, Forbes, if you continue to oppose my plans for this place. You can't stop progress, you know. No one can."

Neil narrowed his eyes. "The campaign I'm organizing would stop World War III. You won't know what has hit you, Royland, if you tangle with Earthwatch. Believe me." He kept a grip on his temper with difficulty. "You just look at the papers next week if you don't believe me." He smiled, turned away, then over his shoulder he added, "We'll see how the public likes the idea of rich City tycoon Paul Royland selling his wife's inheritance to make yet more money out of the environment. I hope you find your missing wife, Royland." His tone was mocking.

Paul smiled grimly. "Oh, I'll find her," he said. "Make no mistake about that." A moment later he was gone.

"Did she tell you she knew someone in Fraserburgh?" Kathleen was standing at the foot of the stairs.

Neil nodded. "Pity it wasn't Wick," he said sourly. "It would have taken him a lot longer to find out she wasn't there."

Kathleen put her arm through his. "What are you going to do about her?"

Neil glanced down at her. "You don't like her, do you?"

"No." It was better to be honest. "There is something odd about her." Kathleen shivered ostentatiously. "Something unlucky. She is bound up with this place, but in a bad way. I don't like it."

"Is this more of your famous second sight?" Neil teased. "If you ask me, there is nothing unlucky about that lady that wouldn't be cured by ditching that bastard, Royland."

"He will never let her go."

"He won't have any choice, if she divorces him."

"She's not going to divorce him." Kathleen crouched before the fire and held out her hands. "She's trapped in that marriage. I saw it in the cards."

"Oh, my God!" Neil looked heavenward. "You haven't brought those damn things with you?"

Kathleen scowled. "They go where I go. Where is she, anyway? Is she still asleep?"

"I suppose so. She looked exhausted. If she is not awake by the time Jack starts serving dinner, someone can go and wake her up and tell her that her husband has gone north. That should please her."

"If he believed you." Kathleen was staring into the flames.

Clare opened her eyes and stared up into the darkness. For a moment she couldn't think where she was, then she heard the sea. Panic shot through her. For a moment she lay rigid, her heart pounding with fear, then slowly she sat up. She groped for the switch on the bedside light. It was the same sea, the sea that haunted her dreams and visions, but this time it was real.

She took a deep breath as the light came on and she saw the black reflections that were the windows of the room. Behind them the wind whistled against the glass. The sea, a hundred yards away below the cliffs, was pounding against the coastline, booming in the caves along the coast, reverberating through the castle, across the brittle winter grass and around the hotel. The room was full of sound.

She climbed stiffly out of bed. Her shoulder was throbbing painfully and her head ached. She glanced at her watch. It was six-thirty. She gritted her teeth, and, going from one window to the other, with an effort she pulled the heavy old curtains across, trying to block out the sound of the waves.

She went through into the bathroom and drew the curtains in there too. It had once been a dressing room, and was much too big and drafty really for a bathroom, although the cracked linoleum had now been replaced by carpet, and a light had been put above the basin to give it some semblance of twentieth-century comfort. The bath was huge and old, with four clawed legs. She turned on the taps. The water that swirled down onto the stark whiteness of the new enamel was peaty brown. She glanced up, alarmed, as the lights flickered, but they steadied at once. Jack had installed a generator, she remembered, comforted, which would cut in if the wind brought the power lines down.

After automatically locking the door, she pulled the switch that turned on the electric bar heater on the wall and slowly she took off her sweater and shirt. A shower of hail hurled itself at the window, the rattle of ice on the glass clearly audible above the sound of the running water. She shivered, waiting for the bath to fill, then painfully she climbed in and lay back in the comforting warmth, feeling it soothing her bruised shoulder. The lights flickered again.

In the bedroom Casta growled gently in her throat and then went back to sleep.

Chapter Twenty-two

"I've phoned up to Mrs. Roy-
land's room as you asked me." Jack put his head around the
door of the bar where Kathleen and Neil were having a drink
before dinner. "There's no reply. Do you reckon I should go
up and see if she's all right?"

"No need." Neil was on his feet at once. "I was going up to
get some notes anyway. I'll give her a knock as I go past."

He knocked twice on Clare's door. The dog barked at once,
but she did not reply. Cautiously he turned the handle. The
bedroom door opened and he peered in. The room was
lighted only by the bedside lamp. He could see the covers
rumpled where she had slept, but there was no sign of her.

"Where is your mistress, dog?" Neil looked doubtfully at
the bathroom door. "Is she all right, do you think?"

Going over to the door, he knocked. There was no reply.
Behind him the lights flickered again. Beyond the window he
could hear the wind and the hail lashing the side of the
building.

He knocked again. "Clare? Are you all right?"

Beside him the dog whined, its hackles on end.

Neil looked down at it, then he tried the bathroom door. It
was locked. He knocked more urgently this time, thundering
on the wooden paneling. "Clare! Clare, can you hear me?"

Suppose she had passed out? She had made light of the car
crash, but he had seen the size of the dent in the XJS's fender.
He put his shoulder to the door and with one sharp thrust
pushed it open with a splintering sound as the small bolt
wrenched free of its screws.

In spite of the electric fire high on the wall the room was
ice cold. He shivered involuntarily, looking around. Clare

387

was lying in the bath, her eyes closed, the water lapping gently around her breasts. She was as white as a sheet.

"Christ!" Neil stared at her for a fraction of a second, then he strode toward the bath. Seizing her shoulders, he pulled her into a sitting position, shaking her so that her head fell forward, a curtain of dark hair tumbling over her face. Her skin was clammy and very cold.

"Clare? Clare! Are you all right!" He shook her again, leaning forward to pull out the plug and release the water. She had been within inches of slipping under in the long, old-fashioned bath.

Clare's eyes opened. For a moment she stared at him completely blankly, then she looked around in confusion and she frowned. She could see Isobel, swathed in her cloak, standing talking to a group of armed men. In the darkness their faces were shadowy, concerned. The wind was catching their hair and clothes, tearing the manes and tails of the horses near them. Robert was there too, fading now, his handsome face strained and angry. He opened his mouth as if he were about to say something, but he was growing more insubstantial every second, disappearing before her eyes. She was trying to reach out toward them when she was shaken again, hard, and stunned by a slap on the face. The figures disappeared abruptly.

She gasped. Her eyes snapped into focus and she began to shiver violently.

"Here, wrap this around you." Neil snatched the bath towel off the radiator and put it around her shoulders. "Now, stand up. Here, let me help you out."

She couldn't stand. Neil stooped and lifted her out of the bath as she clutched the towel around her frantically, staring puzzled at the light above the mirror, which was faintly flickering. "What's happened? What are you doing here?"

"I was afraid you might have had an accident, so I broke the bolt on the door. Just as well. You were asleep in the bath. You might have drowned!"

She stared at him and he wondered suddenly if she remembered who he was.

"You hit me?" Indignation was beginning to surface.

"Yes." He grinned. "I'm sorry. I couldn't wake you. I was afraid you had concussion or something."

Clare was still confused. "And you hit me, to cure my concussion?"

Slowly, as the warmth returned to her chilled body, her position was dawning on her and she was beginning to realize what had happened. She could feel her face coloring with embarrassment as she clutched the towel more closely around her. "You had absolutely no business breaking in like that, Mr. Forbes. I was perfectly all right!"

"It didn't look that way to me. Another ten minutes and you would have died of cold. It was freezing in here." He stared up at the fire, puzzled. The room with its radiator and electric fire seemed perfectly warm now.

"Rubbish! I was dozing, that was all. I resent your intrusion." Clutching the towel to her, she walked past him into the bedroom. "Now, please go."

"Clare Royland is a spoiled child!" Neil said with feeling when he was once again downstairs. "The sooner she's out of this hotel, the better."

Kathleen smiled. "Do I gather she didn't welcome your visit?"

"Not exactly." He threw himself down in his chair and reached for his whisky.

"Was she grateful that you got rid of her husband for her?"

Neil stared at her. Then suddenly he laughed. "I forgot to mention him," he said.

Paul reappeared exactly two hours later. He strode into the bar. Neil and Kathleen were sitting by the blazing fire. They were the only people there.

"Clare didn't go to Fraserburgh," he said curtly. "She only knows one person there and she hadn't seen her. She's here."

"Rubbish, man." Neil eyed him with dislike. "Why should she be here?" For a moment he had been tempted to tell Paul exactly where she was, but something had stopped him. Probably the fact that however much he disliked Clare Royland his hatred of her husband was ten times greater.

"She's here somewhere. She's tied to this place. It haunts her. It's got some kind of hold over her."

"This hotel?" Neil smiled. "Why should this hotel haunt her?"

Paul shook his head. He eyed the other man with undisguised disdain. "The castle, not the hotel. The place obsesses her. It has sent her out of her mind."

Kathleen looked at him sharply. "You mean your wife is mad?"

Paul looked her up and down. "Yes, I mean my wife is mad," he said at last. "And she is the only one who doesn't know it."

He turned abruptly on his heel and walked out of the bar.

Clare had been in bed when Catriona brought up her tray. She stared at the soup and the light salad, realizing suddenly how desperately hungry she was. "Who ordered this?" she asked with a wan smile at the girl.

"Mr. Forbes. He said you were too tired to come down." Catriona smiled shyly as she laid the tray across Clare's knees. "Will there be anything else you'd be wanting?"

Clare shook her head. "No, thank you. This will be lovely."

"There is a candle there on the side with matches if the lights go," Catriona went on. "The electricity is quite likely to fail in this gale and the generator's acting up today. Now, just you phone down if you want anything else." She glanced around the room, pretending not to notice the dog lying quietly thumping her tail by the window.

Clare smiled at Casta as the door closed. "She disapproves of dogs in the bedrooms, like her mother," she said. "Poor darling. It's not been much of a day for you. I'll get dressed after I've had this. We'll go down and I'll get them to find something for your supper, then we'll walk over to the castle and give you a bit of a run." She picked up the spoon and began to sip the soup.

Outside, the hail clattered against the window. She could hear the rhythm of the sea crashing in below the cliffs. She shivered. So, Neil Forbes had ordered her supper. She had to admit she was glad he had. With every mouthful she felt stronger.

She lay back against the pillows thinking about him. She hadn't met anyone like Neil Forbes before. He was an intense man, consumed with passion for his cause, ruthless, of that she had no doubt, bigoted, strong. A good man to have on your side, a bad enemy. And which was he? She wasn't sure she knew. She thought he had believed her when she said she wasn't selling; but he still despised her. She was still the enemy—rich, landed, and probably still English in his eyes. He had seen her naked; dragged her out of the bath, touched her, held her! The only man save Paul ever to have done that, and almost worse, he had seen her in a dream. Even though she was alone she found she was blushing suddenly, and her anger returned.

The food finished, she pushed the tray to the bottom of the bed and picked up the glass that had come with it. Cautiously she sniffed it. Neat malt whisky. She smiled. "Well, thanks for that, at least, Mr. Forbes," she murmured out loud, and she raised her glass in a toast toward the door.

The lights of the hotel flickered and went off for a moment, then they came on again. Clare noticed a movement in the corner of the room. "Five minutes, Casta." She lay back on the pillows, sipping the whisky. It was warm in the bed, beneath the old-fashioned eiderdown, warm and safe. The light flicked on and off again, and then it dimmed. In another minute it would probably go off altogether and then it would be too dark to find the matches, and she didn't want to be alone in the dark. She forced herself out of the bed, ran to the candle, and brought it back to the bedside table. After lighting it, she slid back under the eiderdown. The flame had scarcely steadied when the lights dimmed and died. At once she heard the chuntering of the generator from the cellar in the distance. It coughed twice and then it fell silent. Somewhere a door banged as Jack Grant, flashlight in hand, set out to do battle with the alternative fount of power. Clare lay back on the pillows and looked at a room that was changed and softened by the candlelight, and filled with shadows. She picked up her whisky and sipped it, suddenly uneasy. Again

the slight movement, a shadow no more, against the curtain.
It wasn't Casta. She stared, her fingers tightening on the
glass.

With a howl of fear Casta dived under the bed and lay
there trembling, pressed against the wall.

"Isobel?"

She didn't realize she had breathed the name out loud.

Clare caught her breath. First in the bath and now here,
uninvited, not wanted. "No, please. Not again," she whispered. "What is it you want with me? Why do you keep
coming back?" She strained her eyes against the shadows.

There was nothing there. Nothing but a deeper shadow in
the fold of the curtain.

"Oh, God, I'm going mad!" She finished the whisky with a
gulp.

There was complete silence in the room now, save for the
sounds of the sea and the wind, which were part of the fabric
of the stones with which the hotel had been built—stones
that had once been part of the castle itself.

She never noticed when she dropped the glass. It smashed
on the thin rug and the shards of splintered glass lay glittering in the candlelight.

Isobel was alone with Robert at last. His men liked her; she
was popular for her beauty and her courage and because the
king loved her. And because he loved her they helped her to
be with him. Elizabeth was cold; she was open in her dispar-
agement of her husband's efforts and she was haughty with
his followers.

By tacit agreement time and space was found for the lovers
to be together.

She massaged his neck gently, her cool fingers kneading
the flesh where his mail had rubbed. "The people love you.
They will follow you wherever you lead."

"And will you follow wherever I lead, my Isobel?" He
reached up and caught a handful of her hair, pulling her face
down to his.

"You know I will," she whispered. She gave him a lingering
kiss.

He pulled her toward him on the bed. "I have to fight the main English army soon. I don't like the idea of Marjorie and my sisters and you being here, so close to the danger."

"None of us would be anywhere else. Surely you have no doubts, my Lord?" Her gray eyes mocked him.

"None." For a moment his face sobered. "Scotland depends on me for her freedom. I will make her a nation again."

"And your women will applaud you from the edge of the battlefield. Even her grace, your queen, in spite of her daily doubts." Isobel rolled away from him. "She is only here because I am, you know. She doesn't trust you with me."

"She is here because she is my wife." His lips tightened. "And you will not speak against her." He caught her wrist and pulled her back to face him. "She is a good and faithful wife to me."

"And you, Your Highness, are a bad and unfaithful husband!" She reached up and put her arms around his neck. "But I saw you first."

"Cat!" He kissed her again but she pushed him away.

"Robert, are you never afraid?"

"When Isobel of Fife has put the crown of Scotland on my head? How could I be afraid?"

She frowned. "Don't make fun of me." She sat up suddenly, her long hair covering her breasts. "King Edward is a vengeful, vindictive man." She shivered. "And he is a powerful king."

"And he is an invader, Isobel." He frowned. "What he did to Sir William Wallace still haunts you, doesn't it?"

She drew up her knees, hugging them thoughtfully beneath the sheet. "Doesn't it you?"

Robert shrugged. "He was a brave man, and Scotland will revere him always, but he was a soldier, Isobel. He knew what would happen if he was caught after he refused to come into Edward's peace."

"Does that make it all right?" She buried her face in her knees, refusing to recognize the terror that crept up on her sometimes, swamping her without warning, as she thought of what could happen to the man she loved.

"Edward would say he was following the law." Robert groped for her hand and squeezed it, recognizing her fear and admiring her for the way she controlled it. "He is above all else a lawyer. Nevertheless, I believe he was being vindictive and vicious. He could have tempered his judgment with mercy and he chose not to."

"Because Sir William defied him." She swallowed. "As you are defying him now."

Robert gave a dry laugh. "It is a slightly different circumstance, my love. Sir William was a soldier, albeit a good one. I am a king."

"A month or so ago you were Edward's man." She looked at him, her clear gray eyes holding his steadily.

"Things were different then." He smiled grimly. "You had not yet made me king."

She shivered. "I hope I never see King Edward again. I don't suppose he would approve of what I did."

Robert glanced at her sharply, then he pulled her to him again. "You never will see him again, my love. I shall see to that."

There had been no time for a parliament after the coronation, no time for talk. Scotland had to be mobilized and fast. Robert marched southwest back to his own lands where support for him was strongest, and with him went his family and supporters. Isobel entered passionately into the campaign. She was delirious with excitement, reveling in her freedom, severed at last from her union with the Earl of Buchan, and irrevocably so. She would never see him again. There could be no going back.

Inevitably she was one of the queen's household, but she was able to avoid Elizabeth much of the time. She grew very fond of Robert's sister, Christian, the widow of the last Earl of Mar who was her great-grandmother's son, and so had been her kinsman. Christian was now the wife of Robert's friend Sir Christopher Seton, and she found she liked her enormously, as she did Robert's other sister Mary, and his little daughter, Marjorie. For the first time in her life she would have been completely happy had it not been for the situation in which they now found themselves.

They were traveling constantly and tensions were high. News from central Scotland and the southeast was bad. King Edward had not been idle for long. At first unable to credit that Bruce, whom he had thought loyal, had risen against him, he had swiftly turned the full force of his attention to quelling the rebellion, and now the English were sweeping all before them. Aymer de Valence, Earl of Pembroke, the dead Comyn's brother-in-law, had been appointed to retake Scotland, and order went out that no quarter be given throughout the length and breadth of the land. Men, women, even children who supported the rebellion were to be put to the sword.

Robert and his followers became increasingly worried. Spring was turning toward summer. Robert knew that he had to turn the tide and drive the English out soon or it would be too late. News came that Bishop Lamberton and Bishop Wishart had both been captured and sent south in chains. The news was shattering to Robert and his followers. Isobel saw the lines on Robert's face deepen. There were streaks of silver in his hair.

Increasingly worried about the vulnerability of his family, he took them all with him when he marched north toward Mar. He left them all there in safety, Isobel included, in the Earl of Mar's great castle of Kildrummy in the keeping of his brother Nigel. In vain she pleaded with him to stay with him, but he was adamant. He wanted no women with him now. As he marched out of Kildrummy at dawn, three days after arriving there, Isobel suspected he had already forgotten she existed.

Even though her beloved great-grandmother was still there in her private apartments within the Snow Tower at Kildrummy, Isobel had no intention of staying there. Without Robert's presence the queen found many subtle ways to make her life a misery, ways that Sir Nigel could neither see nor prevent, had he known about them. Isobel put up with it for a couple of weeks, then she planned her escape. A company of men from Mar were marching south to reinforce Robert's armies in central Scotland. It was comparatively easy to join them, after a whispered farewell to Eleyne, ac-

companied by the ever-faithful Hugh. And it was wonderful
again to find herself at the head of a company of soldiers,
buoyed up with the thrill of riding fast, heading breathlessly
into danger and to Robert's side.

Robert had decided that the confrontation had to come at
Perth where Aymer de Valence now held the town for King
Edward. As night fell on June 18, Robert's men fell back from
the walls to bivouac in the woods on the banks of the river
Almond, easing off their armor in the hot June night, their
weapons at their sides, their campfires springing up in the
nightlong twilight of midsummer. Six miles to the east Perth
lay in semidarkness, the walls patrolled by Valence's men,
lights and fires extinguished. The town seemed to be sleeping.

Isobel left her horse at the lines and went toward the place
where the king and his men were talking outside the makeshift tent that was the center of his operations. Overhead, in
the darkness, she could see the standard of Scotland, limp in
the still night air. She stopped, half hidden by the shadows,
not wanting to interrupt, afraid now that she was there that
he would be angry with her for coming. She saw one or two of
the men glance up and notice her and she saw them smile,
but Robert had his back half turned toward her and went on
talking.

With him were his most trusted followers—his brother
Edward, the earls of Lennox, Atholl, and Menteith, James the
Stewart, and James Douglas.

Around them, spread out in the woods, most of their men
were settling down for the night, although some had set off in
parties to forage for food and others, seeking more comfortable sleeping quarters than the woods, were moving farther
afield into outlying farms and cottages. They expected no
attacks; the guards were, unbelievably, minimal.

Robert pored over the map on the makeshift table in front
of him. He stabbed at Perth on the parchment with his fore-
finger. "Lord Pembroke is not one to skulk behind walls. He
may not have come out to fight today, but he will accept my
challenge and meet us tomorrow, you mark my words. He

will not be able to resist our invitation for a full-scale battle, with my kingdom as a prize!"

"The heat must have made him sleepy today." The Stewart wiped his hand across his forehead with a scowl. He had noticed Isobel now in the shadows, and he grinned. "The English aren't used to our Scottish summers." There was a growl of laughter at the joke.

Robert smiled grimly. "He'll like our Scottish summers even less when we drum him out of the country on the run." He straightened and moved the stones that were holding the map flat, allowing it to roll up with a snap. The candle flickered on the table. "If God be with us, sirs, we shall hold the last key to Scotland by tomorrow and be on our way to driving out this invader for good."

He walked out of the circle of light into the shadows on the far side of the circle of men. "I suggest you get some sleep if you can in this accursed heat, my lords."

He had noticed the small stone chapel as night fell. As he made his way toward it, Isobel followed him. One or two of his companions made to go too, but the Stewart raised his hand and stopped them. Only Isobel went on.

In the darkness the chapel was deserted, standing in a clearing in the center of a stand of ancient oaks. Slowly Robert pushed open the door. The interior was in total darkness. Leaving the door wide so that the luminous starlight filtered in, he walked toward the altar, a lump of rough stone with a carved Celtic cross upon it. After crossing himself, he laid his sword on the ground before it. Then he knelt. His earlier optimism and resolve had faltered as dusk fell. Behind him he could hear the quiet talk of his men and the occasional shout of laughter. From far away, beyond the campfires, a lone voice was singing a soft ballad to the plaintive accompaniment of a fiddle. His men trusted him. They had absolute faith in his cause.

"Lord Christ and Our Lady, St. Fillan and all the blessed saints be with us in the battle tomorrow."

He stared up at the narrow window with its outline clearly visible in the starlight, wondering whose chapel this was and why it had been built here in the middle of nowhere. "Preserve Scotland from her enemies, and give your protection to her people in their hour of need."

Behind him there was a sound in the doorway. Seizing his sword, he leapt to his feet.

"I'm sorry. I didn't mean to interrupt your prayers." Isobel stood in the darkness by the door.

Robert closed his eyes briefly as he lowered the sword and laid it before the altar once more. "I might have run you through!"

"I'm sorry." For once she was humble. "I shouldn't be here."

"No, you shouldn't! How did you get here? I gave orders for Nigel to keep you with the queen safe in the north!"

"I followed you with a company of men from Mar who have joined your flag." She took a step nearer to him in the darkness. "I had to be with you, Robert. Please, don't send me away." Her voice broke suddenly. "It's going to be a very big battle tomorrow, isn't it?"

Robert laughed grimly. "Big enough. Pembroke has Mowbray and Umphraville with him and they have a strong force there, in St. John's town. But we have a strong force here at Methven. And right is on our side."

"And God fights on the side of the right." She gave a small smile.

"God, my dear, favors the strongest, it's as simple as that." Robert spoke with unusual cynicism. He turned and, picking up his sword, led the way slowly out of the chapel.

Around them the oaks formed a clearing, allowing the sky to illuminate the ground. Somewhere a blackbird, disturbed in its sleep, fluttered shrieking out of the undergrowth.

Robert stood gazing down at the ground. "I committed sacrilege, Isobel. I spilled blood in the house of God when I slew Comyn." He stared up into the dark canopy of leaves. "Can God still be with me after that?"

"Pembroke's men have done a great deal worse," she replied quietly. "They have raised the dragon flag and give no quarter, even to men of God." She shuddered.

"True." He smiled suddenly. "So, we are all in an equal state of sin. I shall have to put my faith in God and trust that he knows which side is right and must prevail." He was holding his sword in both hands, digging the point into the soft loam of the track. Behind them, beneath the trees, two of his men were waiting. Ostentatiously they had turned their backs. Robert smiled.

He caught Isobel to him and kissed her lightly on the forehead. "Go now, my love. You cannot stay here. I want you to ride back to Kildrummy now, tonight. I will send two men with you. I dare not spare more. Go back to the queen and stay with her. That must be your penance for seducing a married man!" He kissed her again.

"Robert. I want to stay. Please, let me stay."

She was in an agony of fear suddenly. The excitement she had felt before the skirmishes in the west had gone; the excitement of her ride south had dissipated. All she felt was a heavy leaden weight of dread. She could sense his preoccupation—the burden he carried on his shoulders—and it frightened her. She put her arms up around his neck. "Robert, what if—"

But he stopped her, his fingers over her mouth. "There must be no ifs, Isobel. Now go. And obey me."

She released him abruptly. "Please—"

"I have commanded you to leave Methven, Isobel." He spoke with the full weight of royal authority.

"I'm sorry." Blinking back her tears, she dropped a deep curtsey. "God save Your Grace!" She turned without another word and fled blindly into the shadows.

Robert beckoned one of the figures from beneath the trees. "Go with her, James. Send two of your most trusted men to take her back to Kildrummy." He watched for a moment as his friend too disappeared into the darkness, then he turned back into the chapel and knelt once more before the altar.

She heard afterward what happened. It was just after midnight and the encampment was fast asleep when the Earl of Pembroke, scorning the chivalrous challenge to fight the following day that Robert had made and he had accepted, crept out of Perth in the starlight and attacked the unsuspecting Scots.

The silence of the wood in the mist was abruptly rent with

shouts and screams as men and horses hurtled in among the trees. The sleeping soldiers, grabbing desperately for their dew-wet armor, were cut down where they stood, still groping bleary-eyed for the swords that had lain beside them on the ground.

Bruce's followers fought bravely with their king, and the battle was fierce in the strange half-light of the summer night, but they were outnumbered. As Bruce's men died around him he fought more and more fiercely himself, but to no avail. Their feet slipping in the blood beneath the trees, the loyal Scots were slowly beaten back.

As dawn broke Isobel, with two of the Stewart's men, was riding north across the mountains into Mar. She had ordered Hugh to stay as near the king as possible, as she could not, and he had agreed with alacrity and remained. Her heart too was still with Robert, and her hands on the reins were cold with fear in spite of the heat of the night. Her sixth sense told her something was wrong.

Twice she halted her sweating horse, wanting to turn back, but the men had their orders. The Countess of Buchan was to go back to the queen at Kildrummy. The king wanted her in a place of safety, so to a place of safety she would go.

The third time she stopped, however, she was adamant. She reined in the horse and turned it defiantly. "Would you turn your backs on your king when he needs you most?" she challenged them. Something in her wild eyes and desperate voice persuaded them. All three horses turned and slowly they began to retrace their steps toward Methven.

At Robert's side Sir Thomas Randolph was overpowered and dragged away, a prisoner. One by one men dropped and died on the blood-soaked grass, the faithful Hugh among them. As dawn finally came to the devastated wood, and the sun rose, first in a mist of pearl, then in a blaze of crimson across the sky, the carnage was terrible to see. The king and the Earl of Pembroke had fought hand to hand. Two horses had died beneath Robert as he saw his friends captured and killed, but still he fought on, exhausted though he was, his sword arm never failing, until at last he was forced to recognize the inevitable. To save the lives of those who remained he must flee from the field and recoup his strength in safety.

With his army dead, scattered, or captured, the king fled into the dawn with some five hundred men out of the thousands who had been with him, and he vanished into the hills.

Behind him the King of England's army began methodically to search for survivors.

Neil was standing by the bed in the leaping shadows of the candlelight. Again the room was ice cold. Slowly he brought his hand up before Clare's face and moved it up and down. Her eyes were open; she blinked slightly, but her gaze was turned inward; she wasn't looking at anything in the room. He glanced at the dog. It was cowering in the corner again as it had before, staring into the distance, but at a very definite point in the room. He watched as its head moved slowly, tracking someone or something Neil couldn't see.

"Christ!" He could feel his own hackles rising like the dog's. Abruptly he caught hold of Clare's shoulders and began to shake her.

"What the hell is the matter with you, Clare? You're at it again, for God's sake. Wake up!"

As Clare's eyes moved vaguely to his face he shook her again. "What are you, some kind of lunatic? Wake up!"

Clutching her negligee around her, Clare scrambled to her knees on the bed, in a state of shock, still seeing the blood, hearing the screams of the wounded men and horses, still present, at least in her mind, on the battlefield. She stared at Neil disoriented and confused.

"Oh, God, no!" She was shaking her head. "So many dead. . . ." She was sobbing now as she stared at him, still not recognizing him as slowly the dream began to fade.

Neil watched her, frowning, as gradually her face cleared and he saw her focus on him. Behind them the room was gradually growing warmer again.

"What are you doing in here?" she cried at last, upset and angry. "Get out! How dare you barge in like this! Get out!" Her hair fell across her eyes and she pushed it back frantically. "What is it with you? Are you some kind of peeping Tom or something?"

"You should lock the door if you don't want people coming in," he retorted.

"Catriona must have left it unlocked. She must have taken my tray when I was asleep," she said defensively. The tray had vanished, so someone else had come in and seen her without her realizing they were there. She shivered.

"Asleep! That's what you call it!" Neil snorted. "It didn't look like sleep to me!"

"Look, Neil, I'd like you to leave this room," she said. "If you won't, I'll call for help."

"It's all right. I'm going." Neil moved toward the door. He glanced back at her. She was beautiful, this wild, aristocratic, rich woman, in her pale silk negligee with her bare feet and her disordered hair. And she was mad. Just as Paul Royland had said.

He took a deep breath. "I came up to tell you that your husband is here."

"Paul?" Her face drained of color. "Oh, God! Does he know I'm here?"

"Not for sure; he went to Fraserburgh as I told him, but he came back and he seems convinced you are here somewhere. At the moment he is outside wandering out by the castle, but he's sure you are around. And"—he put his hand on the door knob—"he seems convinced you're mad. I must say that on present evidence I'd be inclined to agree with him."

In the icy darkness Paul was standing at the edge of the cliffs, his hands in his pockets, his collar pulled up around his ears. The sea was pounding on the rocks below, shaking the ground beneath his feet. Salt spray mingled with the sleet on his face, chilling his skin. He shivered. She had to be there somewhere. He turned his back on the sea and stared up at the castle in the thick darkness. The wind screamed around the old keep, howling in the crevices of the walls, flattening the dried grass and thistles into tangled mats. It was a bleak, ugly, terrifying place. What in God's name would any sane person see in it? Clare was nowhere to be seen. He made his way back to the hotel.

In the cellars of the hotel, built among the foundations of the ruined outer walls of the castle, Jack Grant, with a wrench and an oil can, was doing battle with a twenty-year-old generator in a pool of candlelight. He took a flashlight from his pocket.

Paul walked across the cobbled yard toward the garages and stables. One by one he pulled open the doors and peered in. None was locked. Clare's Jaguar was in the third he looked at. He stood for a moment, staring at it with a tight smile of triumph. The key was in the ignition. Lying on the passenger seat was Casta's leash. He put it into his jacket pocket before turning toward the black bulk of the hotel and making his way silently toward the back door.

He tiptoed past the kitchen where the two maids, Catriona and Kirsty, were giggling in the candlelight. He let himself into the empty corridor that ran the length of the hotel. Walking quickly in the flashlight beam, he let himself cautiously into the front reception hall. The fire had died to embers and the hall was deserted. He could hear the murmur of voices from the bar where Neil and Kathleen were sitting in the light of several flickering candelabra, finishing their coffee.

On tiptoe Paul sprinted for the staircase and made his way up to the first floor, wincing as the steps creaked loudly beneath his weight.

Upstairs the broad corridor ran the whole depth of the house from east to west. Ten doors led off it, five on each side. Paul stopped. He didn't want to walk into the wrong door and advertise his presence. Cautiously he made his way forward.

He stopped and listened outside each door. All he could hear was the howl of the wind and the drumming of the hail on the window at the end of the landing.

Very cautiously he gave a low whistle. Almost at once he heard a sharp excited bark coming from one of the rooms at the far end of the corridor.

In six strides he was there. The door was locked. He

thumped on it with his fist. "Clare! Open this door or I'll break it down," he hissed. He waited. "Clare, did you hear me? I'll smash this door down. I know you're there. *Clare!*" He banged again, louder this time.

Casta was still barking, scratching the door. Seconds later it opened. Clare, still dressed in the negligee, stood there in the flickering candlelight.

"Go away, Paul. I don't want to talk to you. I don't even want to see you."

"I can imagine." Paul pushed past her into the room and closed the door, turning the key. "Get dressed. I'm taking you back to Airdlie."

Clare sat down on the edge of the bed. "No, Paul. I'm not going with you. We're finished. I want a divorce."

Paul smiled. "A divorce? My dear, you're not well enough to go through a divorce! You must get better first. You need me." He glanced down at the dog who was sitting at his feet looking uneasily from him to Clare and back, and he groped in his pocket for the leash. He slipped it over Casta's neck and pulled it up short, forcing the dog to stand behind his knee. "Get dressed, Clare, please. Now."

Clare could feel the anger rising in her throat. Once she would have obeyed him without question. But not now. Now she felt only hatred and resentment as she looked at him. After what he had done to her in that elevator she would never trust him again. "I am not going to be bullied by you anymore, Paul. Please get out of here. This is my hotel. I'm staying here and so is Casta. Let her go." She was surprised at the strength in her voice.

Paul glanced down with a sneer, then he gave the choke chain a vicious tug. It wrenched the dog up onto her hind legs and she let out a pitiful yelp.

"Paul!" Clare flung herself at him, trying to get the leather handle on the chain out of his hand. "Let her go, you bastard! You're strangling her!"

"I said get dressed." Paul gave Clare a push that sent her reeling across the room. "Get dressed now, or this damn dog will suffer."

Clare glanced desperately at the door, but it was locked

and the key was in Paul's pocket. "This is crazy, Paul! I don't understand you."

Casta let out another pitiful whimper.

"No, you don't." Paul slackened the chain slightly. "And you don't seem to realize that I'm not the crazy one, my darling. You are." He gave a cold smile. "If you don't hurry up, I'm going to have to take you as you are. I'm sure you don't want me to carry you through the hotel in your night-dress, and I'm sure you don't want your parents to see you like that either. It will only reinforce their view that you are out of your mind!"

"Paul, they're not going to believe that."

"They already do." He took a deep breath. "Get dressed, Clare. You're wasting time."

"I'm not coming—"

The dog cried out in pain as Paul wrenched the choke chain tight again, lifting her almost off her feet.

"Get dressed, Clare."

For a moment she hesitated in anguish. One more yelp from Casta persuaded her. "All right," she cried. "I'll dress, but only if you let her go."

Paul smiled but he loosened his hold on the dog slightly.

With trembling fingers she zipped up her corduroys and buttoned her shirt, pulled on her thick dark-blue sweater, then her boots.

"Pack your things," he said.

She hesitated, then she obeyed him, putting her nightdress and spare clothes into the overnight bag she had brought up from the car, tossing her cosmetic purse and washing things after them. Paul picked up the bag. He was still holding Casta's chain very short.

Paul took the coat out of her arms. "Put your coat on," he said. "It's cold out there."

They walked quickly the length of the landing and then on down the stairs.

The hall was still empty; the sound of quiet talk and laughter came from the bar. The door was now closed.

Clare glanced at Paul. She took a deep breath and turned toward it, but he had anticipated her move. He caught her arm and pulled her violently against him. "One sound and I'll put my hand over your mouth. I mean it, Clare. You are coming with me." With a hard push he propelled her into the passage that led to the back of the building.

As he hustled her at a run past the kitchens and out into the yard, she realized for the first time exactly how immensely strong he was. She tried to stop and duck free of his hands but he kept hold of her easily. He pulled open the garage and, after dragging open the car door, he threw her suitcase into the back. He pulled the seat forward so the dog could jump in after it, then he pushed Clare into the passenger seat and slammed the door.

Chapter Twenty-three

Neil stood up and wandered over to the window. Lifting the curtain, he peered out into the sleet. Paul's rental car was still standing on the gravel in front of the hotel. He glanced at his watch and frowned. The man had been outside for over an hour now.

He turned back to Kathleen, who was sitting at the bar, and put his glass down beside her. "Get the landlord to give me another, Kath, when he comes up from the cellar. I'm just going upstairs for a minute."

"Keeping an eye on the beautiful Clare?" Kathleen couldn't keep the acid out of her voice.

Neil frowned. "I might just make sure she's all right, yes. Her husband has been here for rather a long time."

As he spoke there was a distant roar of life from the generator. The lights came on, dimmed, then flared brightly again, flooding the room with harsh color after the subtlety of the candlelight.

Neil ran upstairs and made his way along the corridor. Clare's door was ajar. Cautiously he pushed it open and peered in. The room was empty, her belongings gone. He walked in and looked around. He could still smell the faintest trace of her perfume on the air. The candle was still alight by the bed. He walked over and extinguished it between finger and thumb. Had Paul found her or had she run away? There was no trace of her, no forgotten shoes, no sign of the dog. Apart from the disturbed bed there was no sign that she had ever been there.

Back downstairs, he said to Jack, "Mrs. Royland's gone. She's taken all her stuff."

"Aye. I saw them leave about twenty minutes ago." Jack was draping a dishcloth over the beer handles on the bar.

"She was with her husband?" Neil frowned.

"Aye. All lovey-dovey they were too. They didn't look as if there had ever been anything wrong. He had his arms around her and rushed her out through the rain to her car. So much for hiding it! I think our Clare was spinning a bit of a yarn about her husband."

"God!" Neil slammed his fists into his pockets. "And I trusted her. I nearly told her our plans for the meeting."

Jack glanced at him from under raised eyebrows. "So, she took you in, did she?"

"Didn't she you?"

"Aye, I suppose so." Jack nodded. He sighed. "Pity. I always liked the lassie. And she seemed so genuine."

In their room Kathleen was sitting in front of the mirror brushing her hair.

Neil said, "I just can't believe she'd go with him. Not after all she said."

"Perhaps she didn't know what she was saying. He did say she was mad." She stood up and slipped out of her dress.

"Did she look mad to you?" Neil scowled. He hadn't even glanced at the black lace teddy and garters.

Something about the way he said it puzzled her. "Why? Did she to you?" she asked. She went over and sat on the bed beside him. "What is it?"

Neil shrugged. "She was behaving oddly. Each time I spoke to her she seemed to be somewhere else; watching something that wasn't there."

Kathleen felt the skin on the nape of her neck prickle. Three times now the nine of swords had appeared in the spread. Pain and suffering. Imprisonment and despair. Nightmares and premonitions. But for whom?

"Perhaps her husband is right, then," she whispered. Gently she put her hand inside his shirt. "Perhaps she is mad. Anyway, we're well rid of her. If I'm to be stuck in a storm on the edge of nowhere with the man I love, I'd much rather not have Lady Macbeth in the room next door."

Emma was at the vicarage at eight the next morning. It was Sunday and Geoffrey was in church.

"Paul's followed Clare up to Scotland," Emma said. "He's in trouble over money." She hesitated. "Chloe, I think it is a case of sell Duncairn, or he will go to prison!" She sat down across from Chloe at the scrubbed pine kitchen table.

"Prison?" Chloe echoed.

Emma nodded.

"Does Clare realize it is that bad?"

"I don't know." Emma shrugged helplessly. "We've got to make her understand; we've got to make her sell, Chloe."

"What about the family shares?" Chloe was suddenly practical. "Surely he's got some, like you and Geoff and David? Why doesn't he sell those? They're worth a bundle."

Emma shrugged. "Perhaps they've already gone."

They were silent for a moment. "Paul came to see Geoff last week," Chloe said at last. "Geoff was very worried afterward. Speak of the devil—"

They both looked up as the door banged. There were heavy footsteps in the hall above, and then the sound of someone running downstairs. Geoffrey greeted his sister with a kiss. "Can I have some breakfast, dear, please? I'm starving."

"I'll make you some toast." Chloe stood up. "Emma is here about Paul and Clare, Geoff."

Geoffrey frowned. "Poor, poor Clare. I have to help her. Paul is genuinely very, very worried, you know." He leaned forward, his elbows on the table. "I know you have both talked to her, and I know neither of you is inclined to take what she's doing seriously, but things appear to have deteriorated badly. Paul has actually watched her at these practices of hers—invoking spirits."

His wife and sister both stared at him, stunned. Behind them the toast under the grill turned black. "She began innocently enough, experimenting with the trance state," he went on. "I understand that, just as I understand the unhappiness that led her to experiment in the first place, but she wasn't told how to protect herself. She opened her mind and allowed something evil to possess her."

"Doesn't it occur to you, Geoff, that Paul could be lying

about all this?" Emma said slowly. "Clare isn't raising the dead! For God's sake, you don't believe him?"

"I did wonder at first, I must admit." Geoffrey rubbed his hand across his face. "But things he told me, things she told me herself—"

"I thought she was teasing you, Geoff."

"Whether to test me or to taunt me, I don't know, but she was afraid, Emma, really afraid." He sighed. "I have prayed again and again for help. I don't know what to do." He stood up, rubbing his hands together helplessly. "I have decided to go to see the bishop and talk to him about her. There are special teams of people within the diocese who know how to deal with things like this. Specially trained people. Exorcists—"

"You are not serious!" Emma interrupted.

"I have never been more so."

"You can't! You can't exorcise her! That is grotesque! Paul is a cynical, lying bastard. You should know that as well as I do, damn it! He wants Clare broken so he can sell Duncairn over her head! Oh, God, can't you see?"

"No, Emma. You're wrong. You are not being fair to Paul." Geoffrey put in wearily. "He is thinking of Clare. He wants what is best for her, believe me."

"He wants what is best for himself, Geoff. Money to stop him from going to prison."

Geoffrey sat down heavily, staring from his wife to his sister and back. "Prison!" he repeated at last.

"Yes." Briefly Emma related what Rex had told her.

"I'll talk to David. If it's true that Paul has already sold the family shares, then he's in breach of the trust and we can't help him. If he hasn't, then maybe we can do something. But this has nothing to do with Clare's state of mind, Emma, believe me. Her danger is very real." He stood up. "I want to talk to her doctor; perhaps get a psychiatrist to see her. I won't just act on Paul's story. I shall investigate every possible explanation for what is happening to her, I promise. Look, I've got to go. We'll talk later. Come to the service with Chloe, Emma, and then come back to lunch afterward—"

Emma shook her head slowly. "I can't Geoff, I'm sorry."

She caught her brother's hands. "Promise you won't go to the bishop. Not yet. Please."

Geoffrey kissed her on the cheek. "The bishop is a wise man, Em. He will advise me. I don't know what to do for the best, and I have to do something. Believe me."

"If you do, you are falling for Paul's trick. He wants Clare so confused she doesn't know what's happening to Duncairn."

"That's an appalling accusation to make!"

"Yes." Emma stared at him, her eyes blazing suddenly. "It is, isn't it? I think he is prepared to buy himself out of trouble with Clare's sanity. That's the kind of man our brother is!"

It was nearly two in the morning when the green Jaguar nosed its way up the drive toward Airdlie. It drew up on the graveled area in front of the steps and Paul switched off the engine. A light was on in the hall. He could see it through the colored glass above the front door.

Beside him Clare sat hunched in the passenger seat, her eyes closed.

"I don't suppose your parents are still awake, but no doubt the door is open." Paul climbed out of the car.

The sleet had stopped and the wind was less strong inland; the temperature had dropped several degrees and a sheen of ice was forming over the puddles on the drive.

Followed by Casta, Clare climbed stiffly out of the car and walked toward the front door. She was shivering. Paul pulled her suitcase out of the car. He was immediately behind her as she pushed open the front door.

The hall, as usual, smelled faintly of lavender furniture wax and dogs.

"I suggest you go straight to bed." Paul closed the door behind him. "I'll take this upstairs for you."

Somewhere at the rear of the house they could hear Archie's dogs barking. Slowly Clare began to climb the stairs. She was suddenly so weary she could hardly walk. Paul followed her to her bedroom—her own, not the spare room she shared with Paul on the few occasions they had stayed at the house together—and he opened the door for her, turned on the light, and dropped her suitcase just inside. Then he stood back. "Sleep well, my dear. We'll talk in the morning."

In the drawing room he poured himself a large double whisky, then he picked up the phone.

Sir David Royland took several minutes to answer it. "For the love of Mike, Paul, do you know what time it is?"

"Of course I do. I haven't been to bed yet. I've been driving halfway around Scotland." Paul took a sip of whisky. "Listen, David, there's trouble coming. Neil Forbes of Earthwatch is up at Duncairn and he's well stuck in there. I know him of old. He has a reputation second to none for stirring up trouble, and he's already on to the press about Sigma's interest. You've got to knock the story on the head before it gets off the ground."

"What do you mean, knock the story on the head? Why? What on earth has it got to do with me?"

"Oh, for God's sake, David!" Paul was impatient. "My name is Royland, and as far as Forbes is concerned, I'm the bad guy in this story. He's going to milk it for all it's worth. You think the press is going to overlook the small matter of my being your brother—you, an MP?"

"Development in the area will mean jobs," David said calmly. "That's my interest, Paul. Jobs."

"Jobs for whom?" Paul stood up and reached toward the sofa table for the whisky bottle. "Not for locals, David, and not for long. All that will happen is that the fishermen will have yet more to complain of. Believe me, you've got to keep Forbes away from the press."

"I can't do that, Paul." David sighed. "Unfortunately it is the kind of story that Fleet Street loves, and there is not a damn thing we can do about it, old boy. I suggest you grin and bear it. No doubt counting the money you get for the land will compensate you for the aggravation. I take it you have persuaded Clare to sell?"

"Oh, yes." Paul nodded grimly. "I've persuaded her to sell." He put down the phone, flung himself into the chair, and drained the whisky glass.

Christ! What if the campaign succeeded? What if Cummin withdrew his offer? He could feel the sweat standing out between his shoulder blades. He had thirteen days to close the deal.

Neil and Kathleen were back in Edinburgh by ten-thirty next morning. The Grassmarket office was cold and damp. As he lighted the gas fire, Neil glanced out of the back window across the small yard toward the black granite cliff. High above them the castle was a dark silhouette against the blue, blustery sky.

Kathleen shivered. "Do you really have to work on a Sunday?"

Neil nodded grimly. "Go back to the apartment if you like. I'm going to be here all day. This campaign is taking off tomorrow. I'm going to nail that bastard Royland. There won't be a paper in Britain that isn't going to make his greed a lead story!" He smiled grimly. "If you want to make yourself useful, my love, you get the coffee going. I'm got some phone calls to make."

"What about Clare Royland? Are you going to nail her as well?"

"She went back to him, didn't she?" Neil's hand tightened on the receiver.

"She did indeed." Kathleen smiled. "He's an attractive man, Paul Royland." She glanced around. "She never meant a word of all that protestation of innocence, did she? She intended to sell out all the time."

He opened his notebook, looking for the campaign phone numbers. "Well, she's going to wish she'd never been born when I've finished with her!" he said. "Paul Royland is just an English shit. She is a traitor to her country!"

Clare had not slept. She had lain in bed, tossing and turning, afraid to close her eyes for too long in case the nightmares returned. Outside, the night was very quiet. She dozed uneasily for a while, Casta on the bed next to her in the cold room, then abruptly she was awake again. She groped for the clock on her bedside table, but it had stopped. She had no idea what time it was. She lay still a moment listening. The house was totally silent. It was still dark but some sixth sense told her it was nearly dawn. She rose quietly and dressed, then she tiptoed to the door and opened it a crack. A cold nose touched her hand.

"Come on, Casta. Let's get out of here," she whispered.

Her shoes in her hand, she crept down the long hall, past her parents' bedrooms and down the broad flights of the oak staircase. The dog's paws padded silently after her. The front hall was dark save for a lamp burning on the chest next to a huge bowl of Michaelmas daisies. After slipping on her shoes, she opened the glass inner door of the vestibule. Beyond it the air was ice cold. Above the front door she could see the sky faintly outlined in the glass panel. The stars were brilliant. She put her hand on the door handle and cautiously turned it and pulled. Casta whined with excitement and scrabbled at the oak paneling.

"It's locked." The voice behind her made her jump violently. "And the key is in my pocket."

"Paul!" She turned to face him, her heart thumping with fright. "Well, open it then. Casta wants to go out."

"The dog can go out. Not you." Silhouetted against the lamp, he looked very large. He had spent what remained of the night on one of the sofas in the drawing room; from there he could see the front hall and the stairs.

Upstairs, doors opened. Her parents appeared at the top of the stairs and peered over the bannisters. Antonia's face was very white.

"When did you get back?" Archie strode past his wife and began to descend the stairs, his red striped pajamas swathed in a tightly belted camel dressing gown. At the bottom of the stairs he stopped. He peered past Paul into the shadowy vestibule. "Clare? Come in, my dear. Your mother is going to get us all some breakfast."

"I want to take my dog for a walk first." Clare kept her voice even with difficulty.

"I'll take her out in ten minutes with the others. No problem." Archie gave a falsely hearty smile. "Do come in and shut that door. The hall is getting cold."

Reluctantly Clare stepped back into the hall. She looked

up at her mother who was halfway down the stairs, clutching the bannister for support.

All four sat down at the kitchen table. "Look," Clare said, "I don't know what Paul has been telling you, but I warned you something like this was going to happen. As far as I'm concerned, our marriage is over. He knows it, and I know it. I'm not going back with him and I am not staying under the same roof with him here." She looked at them all in turn.

Paul cleared his throat. "Clare, darling, I have brought you back here for your own good. It is important you are with people who love you and want the best for you at this time."

"At what time? What do you mean?"

"While you get better."

"Better?" Clare stood up angrily. "Paul, there is nothing wrong with me!"

"I'm afraid there is, darling. Please, don't be foolish about this. It will be so much easier if you cooperate."

"Cooperate? By doing what? Selling Duncairn? That is what this is all about, isn't it? You want me to sell up and get you out of trouble in the City!"

Paul raised his hands in exasperation. "You see?" He turned to his father-in-law. "She doesn't even recognize her problems. Archie, Antonia, you have to help me help her. Her sanity depends on it!"

"Paul dear, are you sure you know what you are saying?" Antonia stood up uncomfortably. She walked over to Clare and put her arms around her daughter's shoulders awkwardly.

"Quite sure." Paul's face was a picture of concern.

"There is nothing wrong with me!" Clare moved away from her mother, irritated. "This is crazy! What are you going to do?" Her voice rose in panic.

"Help you, darling. Help you to get rid of the nightmares, the spirits, all the unhappiness that is ruining your life. Make you happy again." Paul fixed his eyes on her face. "That's all."

"That's all?" Her voice rose hysterically. "Everyone has nightmares, Paul, and a lot of people meditate. It doesn't mean they need to see a psychiatrist! I don't need help. I'm fine. I just want some peace. I don't want to live with you anymore."

"No one is talking about psychiatrists, Clare darling, and you can live with us, here." Antonia had pushed her hands deep into her dressing-gown pockets. "We'll take care of you while Paul sorts everything out. You mustn't worry."

"Geoff is going to come up to talk to you, Clare. He can help you. He knows about these things." Paul gave her a paternal smile.

Clare turned on him. "Geoff? I don't want to see Geoff! With his platitudes and his holier-than-thou interference. I refuse to see him! In fact, I won't be here because I am leaving straight after breakfast."

"You see?" Paul said in an undertone. "You see what I mean?" He glanced at Archie. "An almost pathological fear of the church. Darling." He turned back to Clare. "Geoff can help you."

"Like hell he can!" Clare stood up and moved purposefully toward the door. "I don't think I am even staying for breakfast. I'm leaving now. May I have the key to the front door?"

"No." Paul moved very fast. He reached the kitchen door before her and stood with his back to it. "You're not going anywhere. You will stay here till Geoff arrives."

"And how are you going to stop me from going?" Clare was standing in the middle of the kitchen floor. She had gone white. She was fighting back little waves of panic. This could not be happening.

"I'll lock you up if necessary, Clare." Paul folded his arms. "Please be sensible. There is no need for any of this."

"I don't believe I'm hearing this!" Clare glanced wildly from her mother to her stepfather and back. "Are you going to stand there and let him threaten me like this?"

"Clare, darling," Antonia cried. "We love you, you must believe that—"

"And so we have to do what is best for you," Archie finished for her.

"Sit down, Clare." Paul stepped away from the door. He pulled out a chair for her.

"For your own safety we have decided you must stay indoors, Clare. Once Geoff has arrived he will tell us what must be done to help you."

"You intend to keep me here as a prisoner!" Clare stared at him.

"Rubbish. We'd just like you to stay indoors until you are recovered. Now, if you will excuse me, I must make some phone calls to London. If I could use your study, Archie?"

As soon as he had gone Clare leapt to her feet. "Mummy! Archie! You don't believe him? For God's sake, you can't believe him!"

Archie scowled. "Sit down, Clare. You are lucky you have a husband who cares so much about you. In his place I'd have packed you off to an asylum. We brought you up to be a God-fearing Christian! What will people say if this ever comes out? Black masses, for God's sake!" He shuddered.

"Is that what he's told you?"

"It's no more than the truth, Clare." Paul had appeared in the doorway. "I wanted to spare your parents all this heartache, but by coming to Scotland you have involved them. I can watch her now, Archie, if you want to go out with the dogs."

Clare followed her father into the hall and stood watching as he turned toward the back of the house. With a pang she saw Casta follow him, tail wagging as he whistled her after him. She turned and walked into the drawing room, which was flooded with cold early-morning sunlight, then she swung to face Paul who had followed her. "You bastard! What good do you think this is going to do?"

He smiled. "It's going to make you change your mind about selling Duncairn."

"Never."

"We'll see. You may not feel claustrophobic now, in the daylight, in a big house, but it will build slowly, and the more upset you get, the more your parents will be convinced about your instability."

"You're out of your mind, Paul!"

"No. Desperate perhaps." He folded his arms. "If you want to be free of me, Clare, all you have to do is give me power of attorney over your affairs. Once this business is all over I shall give you a divorce and you need never see me again."

"I will never give you power of attorney."

"As you wish. Then I shall take it. I think you'll find that if an MP, a doctor, and a minister of the church all swear to your insanity, it will be comparatively easy for me to get it, with or without your cooperation."

"They wouldn't—"

"Ah, but they would. You see, they are all desperately concerned about you, Clare. They all know about your visions and the strange things you have been up to. You have told Geoff about them yourself, after all. And David has spoken to someone who actually saw you conjuring ghosts out of the air." He smiled. "They all care about you, darling. They only want to do what is best for you, and it is best if you have no worries at the moment."

"I don't believe you. They wouldn't!" Clare was really frightened. "You can't keep me here! You can't guard every door and window all the time. What happens when you have to go back to London?"

"I'm not going until Wednesday." He smiled. "I'll have what I want by then."

"And if I sign, then what happens? Do I have a miraculous cure?"

"That's up to Geoff. Your soul is his department. After all, Clare, I'm not making any of this up, am I? You can't deny what you have been doing."

Clare turned away, her face white. "But what I'm doing isn't bad. There's nothing wrong with it!"

"Then Geoff will no doubt give you a clean bill of health." He smiled. "Personally, I think you are possessed."

"No." She shook her head desperately.

Paul folded his arms. "What about the beautiful Isobel, then? She just comes along for a chat when you're lonely, is that it? Grow up, Clare, and face the facts! You need help. You've needed help for a very long time!"

The day seemed endless to Clare. As Paul had promised, every door was locked, and she was never allowed to be alone for a moment. Either Paul or Archie followed her wherever she went. Antonia did not reappear. Outside the cold rain showers swept in across the hills from the east, splattered against the windows, and disappeared as swiftly as they had come, leaving the gardens brilliant with cold, blustery sunshine.

Archie cooked a roast beef for lunch and the three of them sat around in the cold dining room in silence, picking at their plates. Tea and supper were the same. Clare watched and waited patiently, trying to force herself to relax, trying to keep calm, determined Paul would not see her nerves beginning to fray. She had worked out what she was going to do. It was so obvious, and it would be easy once everyone had gone to bed. As a child she had climbed often from her bedroom window, edging along the parapet and scrambling down the sloping roof to the old apple tree, and she was sure she could do it again. But she had to wait. She must not seem too eager. She must not let Paul suspect. It was just after nine when at last she stood up. "I may as well go to bed," she said. "I'm exhausted and my shoulder hurts."

"Good idea." Paul stood up too.

"There's no need for you to come!" She had snapped at him without thinking, forgetting her resolution to be calm.

"Oh, I think I'll come." Paul smiled at her mockingly. "Is everything ready for her, Archie?" He turned to his father-in-law.

Archie nodded uncomfortably and subsided once more onto the sofa before the fire. He sat hunched with his back to them as Paul opened the door for his wife and followed her out into the hall.

"There is no need for you to come up, Paul." At the foot of the stairs Clare stopped. She spoke through clenched teeth. As the time for her escape came closer she was getting more and more nervous.

"Oh, but there is, darling." He strode up the stairs beside her and accompanied her along the landing.

She had reached out to open her bedroom door when he took her by the arm. "Not here. Not tonight. We thought you might be more comfortable somewhere else."

Clare froze. She clung to the door handle. "What do you mean, somewhere else?"

"I'll show you." He tightened his grip on her arm and he began to force her along the landing. At the north end of the corridor there was another staircase, leading up to what had been Aunt Margaret's rooms in the old tower. Paul smiled. "We thought you would be happier up here. Archie has brought all your things up for you. It has the advantage of a bathroom of its own and windows you can't climb out of." He was dragging her now, up the narrow stairs, his hand around her wrist. She tried desperately to pull away, fighting him, her shoulder a mass of pain, but he was very strong. His fingers bit into her arm. "I don't want to hurt you, Clare, believe me," he muttered through clenched teeth. "Just remember, to get out of here, all you have to do is sign. It's all so easy." He pushed open the door at the top of the stairs and, flicking on the lights, propelled her inside. She just had time to see that a new shiny bolt had been screwed onto the outside of the door below the key before Paul banged the door behind her and she heard the key turn. Then the bolt slid home.

She looked around in despair, still hardly able to believe what was happening to her.

Aunt Margaret had loved this room. It was large, almost circular, built into the first floor of the sixteenth-century tower around which Victorian Airdlie had been built. Like most buildings of its date, its windows were small, set deep into the thick walls, and they were high above the ground. There was no possibility of anyone escaping through them. The bathroom was built into what had been a storeroom next door and beside it, behind a thick oak door, a spiral staircase led up to the room Margaret had originally used as a bedroom before she grew too old to climb the stairs. The room Clare stood in now had in those early years been a living room, giving the old lady a self-contained suite in the house. Directly above it was another room that she had used as a studio, painting competent and very attractive surrealist watercolors until her eyes had failed her. Above the studio a staircase led up onto the roof of the tower, with its battlements and the flagpole where James used to raise the Gordon standard when they were children.

Cautiously Clare tried the upper staircase door. It opened. She ran up the dark, cold, winding stairs, groping for the light switch at the top, and she peered into her aunt's former bedroom. It was empty save for the huge wooden frame of the bed, which had been built up there and could never be moved. There were no curtains now, no carpets, not even a shade on the light bulb, and there was no heat. The room was bitterly cold. She did not bother to go up the next flight. That room would be empty too, filled with the memories of the sunlit days when a younger Margaret had painted in the quiet stone room, the air sharp with the smell of turpentine and linseed oil. There was no point in going up on the roof. There would be no escape that way.

After turning off the light, Clare made her way back downstairs to the room that was still furnished. Her suitcases, she saw now, stood beside the four-poster bed. Her old woolly dressing gown, from behind her bedroom door, was laid across a chair.

She went to the door and tried the handle, but it was still locked as she had known it would be. Paul had not been joking when he brought her up there, he had been deadly serious. She shivered again. She went over to one of the windows and looked out. The night was completely black. All she could see was her own white face, gaunt in the reflection, peering back at her. She drew the curtains sharply and stared around the room, overwhelmed with despair. She was a prisoner—a real prisoner in her own home! She sat down on the bed, realizing suddenly that there were tears on her cheeks. She was exhausted, aching, and very frightened.

It was a beautiful room. The four-poster bed, the table, the chairs, the coffers, all were carved out of ancient black oak, softened and cushioned by warm blue velvets and old worn brocades. The carpet was Aubusson; she had always wondered why her mother hadn't taken it downstairs to show it off, but perhaps she hadn't dared. This was still very much Margaret Gordon's room and always would be. But Margaret Gordon wasn't there. Clare had never felt more alone.

She stood up restlessly, drying her tears, and began to pace the floor. Her moment of self-pity over, she was once more frustrated, angry, and very tense. Too tense even to have given a thought to Isobel. She was too preoccupied with her own worries.

And she didn't feel claustrophobic, not yet. It was a large room, a room she had always loved, and she was very much aware of the two large echoing rooms upstairs, with above them the roof and the sky. She was not hemmed in. Not caged. Her mind shied away from the thought quickly and she frowned. The situation was beyond belief. If she told anyone what had happened she doubted if they would believe her. Probably that was what Paul was counting on. She thought of Emma suddenly, and her eyes filled with tears again. If only Emma were there. She could imagine Emma's voice: *My God, how bizarre! How Gothic! You mean he locked you up?* One day they would laugh about this together, but not now, not yet. She shivered violently.

Again and again she pushed at the door, rattling the latch, but it held absolutely solid. Beyond it the house lay in total silence. She had no way of knowing what the time was. For the hundredth time she cursed the fact that she had left her watch behind in London—such a feeble, useless gesture of defiance. It felt late, but then she was desperately tired. Wearily she got up at last and went into the little bathroom. It was a gesture to normality to run a bath and change into her nightdress. When she came back into the bedroom it was growing cold. The radiator was still warm, but outside when she peered through the curtains she could see the silver moonlight streaming across the tops of the fir trees. They glittered with frost.

She climbed into the bed at last and sat there, hugging her knees. The bookshelves were empty. Antonia must have taken all Margaret's books downstairs. There was no radio or television. Only one book remained in the room, lying on the bedside table next to the lamp. Clare stretched out to reach it; it was a brand-new Bible. She threw it down on the bedspread with a shaky little laugh, then with a frown she picked it up again. Perhaps it would help to keep the nightmares at bay.

She had to sleep. She was so tired she could hardly keep her eyes open—and yet she was afraid. Afraid of the nightmares that would come, she was certain, as soon as she closed her eyes. Afraid of Isobel, who would come when she wanted to, whether Clare closed them or not. She hated the silence, the shadows. Huddling beneath the blankets, Clare hugged the Bible to her.

She had only been asleep for a few minutes, or so it seemed, when she was woken abruptly by the sound of the bolt on the door sliding back. She sat up, her heart pounding as the door opened, hoping Antonia or Archie had relented and decided to release her.

It was Paul. He came into the room and locked the door behind him, dropping the key into the pocket of his silk dressing gown. He stopped for a moment in the middle of the floor.

"How nice to know one's wife is bound to be there waiting for one. How dutiful." He began to undo his dressing-gown sash.

"Go away, Paul." Clare felt suddenly very frightened. She lay down, turning her back on him. "I don't know how you have the gall to come up here." She pulled the blankets around her. Her mouth had gone dry and she felt sick with fear.

He laughed quietly. "And so loving. It's a long time since you and I made love, Clare."

"And we're not going to again. Ever." Clare clutched the blankets tightly.

"No? It was you who came to me, that night at Bucksters, with your silk nightgown and your perfume, oh so seductive. You wanted it then, didn't you?" His tone was mocking.

"Well, I don't want it now!" Clare buried her face in the pillows. Behind her Paul sat down on the edge of the wide bed. He pulled the key out of his pocket and slipped it under the corner of the high mattress, then he took off his dressing gown. Letting it fall to the floor, he turned out the light and climbed into the bed beside her.

His hands on her breasts were very cold. Clare threw herself toward the edge of the bed, but he held her easily, pulling her back and pinning her to the sheets with the weight of his body. "A little marital indulgence would be good for us both, don't you think?" he murmured, dragging at her nightdress. He didn't try to kiss her. Instead he buried his face between her breasts and with a shock of pain she felt his teeth closing on her skin. For a while she struggled to throw him off, then she lay still. He was too heavy for her to shift him, and anyway Paul's lovemaking never went on for very long. All she had to do was endure it, then he would go away. She closed her eyes in the darkness and gritted her teeth.

"Do you make love to the devil, like the witches of old?" He was murmuring in her ear now, his hands hard on her breasts. "Is that what happens in the garden at home, when you summon your spirits? Do your lovers come to you with horns? Or in the shape of animals perhaps?" He forced his thigh between her legs.

"Oh, God!" Disgusted, she tried once more frantically to wriggle away from him. "Is that what it takes to turn you on, Paul?" She was crying now. He could feel the warm wetness of her tears on the pillow under his face, and the fact that she was crying pleased him. Suddenly he wanted to hurt her; he wanted her to suffer the way he had suffered when he had learned he could never father a child. He grabbed a handful of her hair and pulled her face toward his own. "Witch!" he said. He liked the sound of the word. "Witch!" The witch who had stolen his virility. He could feel her thighs pinned beneath his, as she struggled to avoid him. She could struggle all she liked; she wouldn't be able to prevent him from entering her when he was ready.

Except that he was not ready. Not yet.

He laughed out loud. "You know, I almost believe it myself. A wife possessed by the devil. It sounds exciting, doesn't it?" He caught her wrists and held them above her head, pressed into the pillows. "Your parents believe me, you know. They believe every word, and they're determined to save your soul!"

He laughed again.

He wanted her, he wanted to pin her to the bed and screw her till she screamed for mercy, but still he wasn't ready. He wasn't hard and she must know it. Perhaps she knew he could never be a father. Perhaps she had guessed it wasn't her fault they would never have a child. Coldly he looked down at her, seeing nothing of her face in the darkness, feeling with his mouth her hair tangled across her eyes. He had to possess her; he had to show her he was her master.

She was lying still now, not bothering to struggle, and he knew that she had realized that he was impotent; that she despised him; that she was probably laughing at him even now.

He rolled off her and lay still, his face in the pillow.

Wide-eyed in the dark, Clare dared not move. She wasn't sure what had happened. Had the thought of her consorting with devils put him off? Cautiously she edged away from him.

She lay still a long time, waiting for him to move or speak. He did neither. Then at last she heard his breathing grow steady and regular and she guessed he must be asleep. Cautiously she crept out of bed, shrugging her nightdress back into place. She found his dressing gown on the floor, and, holding her breath, she began to grope in the pocket for the key to the door. It wasn't there. She patted the floor around her desperately, wondering if it had fallen out. In the darkness she could see nothing and she dared not turn on the light. Falling on her knees, she ran her hands over the floor in wider and wider circles, feeling the edge of the carpet and the boards beneath it under the bed, rubbing her hands over it again and again until her fingers were sore.

She couldn't find it. After a long time she gave up. For a moment she thought she would cry again, but somehow she stopped herself. Wearily she climbed to her feet and for a moment she stood looking down in the darkness toward the place where her husband lay. Then slowly, shivering with cold, she felt her way across the room. She found the door to the tower and opened it. She slipped through and pulled it shut behind her, then groped her way upstairs. It was very cold. She didn't put on the light. Thin beams of silver moonlight lay across the floor. She could hear the wind moaning softly in the trees outside.

She walked to the center of the room and sat down cross-legged in a patch of moonlight. The broad old oak floorboards were bitterly cold. She looked up at the moon through the narrow window and she raised her hands in invitation. "Come to me," she whispered. "Isobel, come!"

In the bedroom below Paul began to cry.

Chapter Twenty-four

Nigel Bruce was standing in the solar of the Snow Tower in the great fortress of Kildrummy Castle, staring out of the window toward the west. Behind him the new Queen of Scots was pacing the floor, a letter in her hand. "My father says I should go to him," she said slowly. "He says there can be no hope for Robert."

Nigel clenched his fists. "As far as we know my brother is still free. He will not fail us!" He turned to her. "And I should be with him, not here!" He waved his arm helplessly to encompass the room.

"We should all be with him." Isobel was sitting in the window embrasure on the far side of the solar. Outside she could see the long shoulder of a hill shrouded in black storm cloud. It was very hot.

Fleeing soldiers had saved her life after the battle of Methven, meeting her and her two escorts in the hills near Perth.

At first she and her companions had not believed them. They had listened incredulously to the story of the defeat and of Robert's flight into the hills. Isobel was in despair at their tale, and more anxious than ever to get back to Methven, but her escort would take no chances. Already doubtful about the wisdom of turning back in the first place, they halted as the exhausted soldiers moved on, and debated what to do.

Duncan and Malcolm were the Stewart's most trusted servants. They had been guarding their charge with almost frenzied weariness, well aware that she was their king's sweetheart, and now they were more conscious than ever that they must take no chances with her safety, so when, in the distance, they saw a party of armed men scouring the glens, their minds were made up. Even from their hiding place they could recognize the distinctive device of argent and azure bars, with an orle of martlets gules on the shields of the men of the Earl of Pembroke. The sight made Isobel more frantic than ever, but it convinced Duncan and Malcolm that they must turn back.

When they tried to go north again, however, their retreat was cut off; every track and path seemed to be patrolled by marauding bands of English soldiers, and they found themselves doubling back again and again as they tried to head away from Perth. Each night Isobel lay wrapped in her cloak on the ground trying to sleep while nearby the two men talked quietly, huddled against the dew-wet chill of the summer nights. Not once did they dare to light a fire.

In the end they had managed to turn east, following the tracks that led into the heart of the high mountains, secret paths known only to the deer and rabbit as the mists closed over the mountaintops. But even there they had seen parties of armed men searching for the scattered survivors of Methven, and several times they passed burned-out farmsteads, the ground still smoldering, where men who had supported the Bruce had lived. The vengeance of the English was swift and brutal. The women and children who had lived on the farms were already dead or captured or scattered. In the first few days they never saw anyone other than the distant enemy alive.

Their horses were exhausted, their own shoes already worn to holes from leading their mounts on the steep, uneven ground, their clothes in rags as they circled in the rough terrain day after day, trying to break through toward Kildrummy. Duncan and Malcolm took it in turns to scout. They skirted around hamlets and villages, everywhere hearing the same stories of the revenge that had been exacted on the king's followers who had been captured, and, shuddering with horror, they turned north again. It was days later when, exhausted and dejected, they at last returned to Kildrummy and found they were the first to bring news of Robert's defeat to his queen and his family. None of them wanted to believe that Robert's courageous thousands could have melted away until there were but a few hundred left. The small garrison waited desperately for more news. None came. The mountains of Mar, shrouded in the haze of a summer heat wave, were empty and silent. Their king had vanished into the hills of the west. All they could do was wait.

Then at last letters came from the south—one from the Earl of Ulster for the queen, and others giving further news of the atrocities being carried out by the soldiers of the English on the people of Scotland. They confirmed that the dragon banner had been raised. No quarter was being given; even the women and children of the king were not to be spared if they were caught. Rape and murder would go unpunished if perpetrated on the family and friends of the outlaw king.

Elizabeth de Burgh shivered. She looked down again at her father's letter and then at her husband's brother. "My father says I should go to him, but my place is with Robert," she said at last.

"But Robert said you should stay here." Nigel was impressed by her courage. As he had got to know her better he had begun to admire, if not to like, his brother's wife. She did not approve of what Robert had done, but she was prepared to stand by him because he was her husband, and he thought highly of that kind of loyalty. He himself was in an agony of indecision. He wanted desperately to go to his brother's side, as he felt sure their other brothers, Thomas and Alexander, would have done by now, but Robert's orders had been clear. Nigel was to keep the women out of harm's way at Kildrummy.

He smiled reluctantly at the queen. "You will all be safest here." Then he glanced at his sisters.

Christian was sitting by herself on a low stool, a spindle in her hand. She had spun nothing; the carded wool lay untouched in a basket by her feet as she sat, preoccupied, staring into space. This great castle had been her home until the death of her husband, Gratney, and it had been the scene of much happiness. Now it was the seat of her son, Donald, who until his majority would be his uncle Robert's ward. Now she was the wife of another man, Christopher Seton. Perhaps already she was a widow again. Christopher, one of Robert's

most trusted friends, had been captured after Methven, that
much they had heard in one of the letters. Surreptitiously
Christian wiped away a tear. She was as proud as all the
Bruces. She would not add to Nigel's problems by weeping
and wailing in her worry.

Mary was more cheerful. The man she loved, Neil Campbell, was still with Robert as far as they knew, and as far as
they knew neither man had been wounded. Surely they
would have heard if Robert and those close to him had been
hurt.

Isobel, sitting a little apart from the others, bit her lip in
frustration. Although the king's sisters had made her welcome, and the Princess Marjorie openly adored her, the
queen's enmity was always there. In the presence of the royal
ladies she tried to stay in the background, tried to maintain a
tact that was foreign to her and difficult to keep up. She
wanted to jump to her feet, throw herself at Nigel Bruce,
drag him to his horse if necessary, and force him to take them
to Robert. She knew how much he wanted to go to his
brother and she knew it wouldn't take much to persuade
him, but she managed to keep silent, comforted by the
thought that Eleyne of Mar, upstairs in her own solar, knew
how she felt, Eleyne who had so much patience herself. So
she did nothing, sitting staring out of the window, her hands
in her lap, waiting for the queen to decide what to do.

The decision was made for them. Gilbert of Annandale
arrived with two companions late one night. Their horses
were exhausted and one of the men was hurt. Gilbert was
grim-faced. "The king is in hiding in Drumalban; he has
decided it would be best if you all joined him there." He was
speaking to Nigel, but his glance swept the ladies who were
standing anxiously around them. His gaze rested on Isobel for
a moment and he frowned again. "The Earl of Pembroke is
set on capturing the royal family, Sir Nigel, and no quarter is
to be given. I don't have to tell you the danger. The king feels
he can give you all more protection in the hills to the west.
He has his men there, and much support. We should set out at
once."

Nigel nodded, his face lightening. "At last! I have been a

nursemaid for too long!" He bit his lip and bowed hastily toward the queen. "Forgive me—I did not mean . . . It is just that I want to be with Robert! I want to see some fighting!"

Gilbert grinned. "You'll see enough fighting soon enough, Sir Nigel, have no fear. More than you want, no doubt." He sighed. Later he took Nigel on one side and talked to him alone for a long time. When he had finished Nigel's face was very serious.

They left a small garrison at Kildrummy, and with them the Dowager Countess of Mar, who refused to budge. "I am too old," she said when they tried to persuade her to leave. "I'll be all right. No one is interested in an old woman. You go on, and God go with you." So at dawn the next day the party of horsemen set off southwestward. From Strathdon they would head through the hills toward Braemar and then into the mountains of Atholl, keeping to the lonely tracks where the sun blazed down on the tightly budded heather.

The hills were shrouded in a haze as the horses picked their way through the glens. Once or twice overhead Isobel could hear the eerie scream of a golden eagle as it circled, a glittering lookout high above them. The air was sharp with heather and sweet with the scent of pine.

Nigel rode up beside her, his horse lathering. "Gilbert thinks Robert will ride to meet us on the banks of Loch Tay."

Isobel smiled across at him, her heart giving a little jump of happiness. "I can't wait to see him and be sure he is all right." She was very fond of Nigel. He was a younger, slimmer version of Robert, gentler, lacking his brother's ruthlessness, with dreamy eyes and a kindness that touched her heart. She glanced ahead, to where the queen was riding beside her little stepdaughter. "Queen Elizabeth will be glad to see her husband."

"And he her." He grinned. "But not half so glad, I suspect, as he will be to see you."

Isobel blushed. "Where will we go? Do you know?"

Nigel shrugged. "Gilbert says Robert doesn't have many men. Many who weren't killed or captured fled. He has to gather his strength once more. The losses after Methven were terrible, far worse than we imagined." He glanced over his shoulder to where his sisters rode at the back of the file. "Gilbert said they have news of Christopher. I've not said anything to Christian yet. He's dead."

"Dead?" Isobel stared at him. "But we had heard he was captured—" She stopped, her heart in her mouth. "They killed him?"

Nigel nodded. Sir Christopher Seton, the king's brother-in-law, had been castrated and then disemboweled—a signal to them all of the kind of treatment they could expect if they were taken. He shuddered beneath his mail. He had told Gilbert to keep the details of Christopher's death to himself. There was no point in distressing the women yet. They would no doubt hear soon enough. He forced himself to smile at Isobel again. She was vivacious, excited, looking forward to whatever was to come, not realizing in her innocence what could lie ahead for them all. He wanted to spare her too for as long as possible. She was very beautiful as she rode beside him, her dark hair escaping from her veil, her face already dusted with gold by the fierce summer sun. Not for the first time he found himself envying his brother his easy way with women and the string of mistresses he managed to maintain around the country. Of them all he found the Countess of Buchan the most attractive, and he suspected she was the one that Robert found the hardest to put out of his mind.

He glanced up as the fierce yelping cry of the eagle sounded closer. It was very loud in the breathless air. Beneath him his horse sidestepped nervously. He looked around. He had posted outriders on both sides of the column. There were scouts ahead of them and behind, and yet still he felt uneasy. The responsibility for the women was a heavy one, and he felt it deeply.

That night they camped in a lonely glen, the women sleeping wrapped in their cloaks near a broad brook that threaded through soft grass and clouds of meadowsweet, lulling them to sleep with its quiet murmur. It was a warm night, the moon high and soft, its light spilling across the ground, casting shadows over the scree on the mountainside. Nearby the horses were grazing peacefully, with two men on watch beside them.

Isobel lay awake, gazing up at the sky. In spite of her exhaustion after the long days of riding, and the nervous tension that beset them all, she was lost in daydreams. Soon she would see Robert again. This time he had sent for her—asked especially for her, so Gilbert had told her with a wink—and somehow they would find a way to be alone together.

She scarcely heard the rattle of stones on the loose scree up the glen and for a moment she did not react to the sound at all, then abruptly she sat up, her heart thumping with fear. She glanced at the guards. Neither of them appeared to have heard anything. They were talking quietly in the moonlight, their backs turned toward the horses. The horses had heard something though. Isobel saw a dozen heads turned, ears pricked. One or two were moving nervously backward, pulling against their halters. She looked around. The other women were all asleep, huddled on the dew-damp ground, Mary cuddled up with Marjorie in her arms. Nigel was lying with his back to them, his arm beneath his head, his sword beside him on the ground. Beyond him the men of their escort were all silent and motionless in the moonlight. She swallowed nervously and glanced back toward the horses. They were still uneasy. All around them the glen lay deserted, the outline of the mountains clear against the luminous sky.

Somewhere far away on the high moors a curlew called.

"Nigel!" Her whisper was no more than a faint echo of the silence. "Nigel!" Slowly she began to edge toward him. "Nigel, I think there is someone out there."

He stirred, then all at once he was awake, his hand on the hilt of his sword, every nerve straining as he lay still, holding his breath. A moment later a man was standing over him, the tip of his sword resting against his throat. Around them shadowy figures had sprung up everywhere seemingly out of the heather and grass. Every man of their escort was covered. The whole maneuver had been carried out in complete silence.

"So, this is how you guard my queen and her ladies!" Robert removed the sword from his brother's throat and plunged it into the ground beside him, leaving it standing quivering in the soft grass. "I could have killed you, brother! And every man and woman here!" Robert was furiously angry. "Are you out of your mind to sleep like this in the open with no guards!"

Nigel had scrambled to his feet. "I did post guards—"

"And they were worse than useless. For the love of the Holy Virgin, don't you realize this country is alive with enemies? Enemies who would give anything to take any one of the people here in your care!"

Everyone was awake now. With a little cry of joy Mary scrambled to her feet. Beside her Marjorie was rubbing her eyes, staring around in the darkness in confusion. Moments later she spotted her father and with a shriek of excitement threw herself toward him. "Papa—"

Robert looked down at her. For a moment he didn't move, his face very grave, then he bent and swept her up into the air. "So, my little princess is camping in the mountains like a soldier!" He gave her a quick kiss on the head and then put her down.

Behind her Isobel was still sitting on her cloak in the shadows. She hadn't moved. As the king embraced his wife and then his sisters, she found that she was trembling.

"Lady Buchan?" Suddenly he was standing over her. "Are you all right?"

She looked up. His face was grim. There was no pleasure in his eyes at seeing her.

"I am all right, sire," she said. Slowly she climbed to her feet. He did not touch her and she was conscious of eyes watching them on every side. "I am glad to see you." She looked away from his face to the ground, sensing the despair that for a moment overwhelmed him.

"And I you, Lady Buchan." Already he had turned away to his brother. "Mount your party. We must move on at once before it is light. There are men in these hills who support Edward of England, and we are not strong enough yet for a confrontation."

"Where are we going?" Nigel had recovered from his

shock and humilition. He stood beside his brother proudly now.

"West. Out of reach of our enemies. Perhaps to the Macdonalds of Islay, perhaps even to Ireland. We must recoup our strength and gather our scattered supporters, then we can hit back." Robert's face was hard. "And this time we cannot fail." He turned away abruptly and again Isobel felt the uncertainty sweep over him—the weight of sadness for his dead friends and the suffering that his fight for freedom must bring to Scotland. She ached to reach out and touch him, to tell him that she understood—but she didn't move. It was little Marjorie who crept forward again and for an instant slipped her small fist into her father's hand.

By dawn they were five miles farther west, at the end of Loch Tay. The mountains were black against the clear dawn sky, the water shrouded in mist. All was silence, save for the soft tread of the horses' feet on the peat tracks. The air smelled cool and sweet. Robert rode at the head of the column of men with his brother beside him. Behind them came the men of Mar and then the women huddled together, silent with exhaustion and apprehension. The rear was brought up by the men Robert had brought with him to meet them.

Beside the track the water beneath the mist was silent. Once a fish jumped, the silver body visible for a moment in a ray of thin sunlight above the cream of drifting mist, then it was gone. The splash seemed audible for miles.

As the sun rose the mist evaporated, leaving the loch a brilliant blue beneath the sky. It was going to be another hot day.

"Where shall we stop?" Nigel glanced at his brother. "The ladies haven't slept. They must be exhausted." Behind him men and women were riding in a daze, their horses following one another automatically now. Marjorie, long since too exhausted to sit a horse on her own, was asleep on the saddle in front of one of Robert's companions, safe within the circle of the man's arms.

Robert glanced around. "There. There's a sheltered bay where we can rest and eat. Then we must go on to join up with the others."

"How many are there left, Robert?" Nigel glanced across at his brother. He had lowered his voice.

The king shrugged. "Perhaps five hundred, perhaps more. Not enough." His face was grim.

"But God is on our side."

"Is he?" Robert eased himself in his saddle.

"Can you doubt it?" Nigel was horrified. "You still worry about the murder of Red Comyn?" He frowned, upset by his brother's unaccustomed moment of doubt.

"It was sacrilege to kill a man in the house of God!" Robert dismounted in the shingly cove, with its sheltering headland, and gave the sign for the others to follow suit. They were all tired now, exhausted by the long days in the saddle under the hot sun and by the fear of being followed.

Pleased by the respite, the women gathered at the far end of the cove, washing their faces in the cold water of the loch, and eating some of the oatmeal cakes, all the food they had left, before huddling up to sleep, wrapped in their cloaks.

Isobel could not sleep. Her head ached and her limbs were stiff but her mind was racing in circles. It would not let her rest. Giving up the attempt, she stood up. Tiptoeing away from the others, she gathered up her dusty skirts and scrambled up onto some rocks to sit, her back against the slim trunk of a rowan tree, gazing out across the loch.

It was a long time before Robert joined her.

"You must not blame Nigel for last night. We didn't know Pembroke's men were so close," she said as he sat down beside her. She had kicked off her thin, worn shoes and he could see her slim feet brown with dust. She wore no stockings.

"Not knowing is no excuse," he replied sharply, lying back on the short grass. "He should have guessed. He should have taken no risks. You could have all been slaughtered!"

"Then thank the blessed Lord it was you and not Lord Pembroke." She smiled down at him. "God is on your side, Robert."

"You think so." He brushed away a fly from his face, smiling, his eyes tight shut against the sun.

"I know so." She leaned over and, picking some of the

small white flowers from the saxifrage that scrambled through the fine grass, dropped them onto his face.

He brushed them aside, then opened his eyes and reached up toward her. "Are all the others asleep?"

She nodded.

He pulled her down toward him and kissed her gently, then he let her go again, putting his arm across his eyes. "I shall go back. When my men are rested and regrouped we will find Pembroke and chase him from Scotland forever." She saw his fists clench. "Then and only then will this country be safe and free." A breeze stirred the leaves and the small hard yellow berries of the rowan above their heads. She couldn't see his face because of his sleeve. She ached with love for him and she was very frightened.

For a long time they remained silent. Isobel stared out across the water, watching as an osprey plummeted into the water out in the center of the loch, emerging seconds later with a pike clasped in its talons. It was very hot, even in the flecked shade of the tree.

"Robert." Her voice was very quiet. "Robert—I love you."

He did not answer. Exhausted, he had at last fallen asleep.

The remnant of Robert's men was waiting at the head of Strathfillan, camped near the ancient shrine to the saint. It was one of two churches dedicated to St. Fillan in these mountains, a small stone chapel with, beside it, a cluster of huts and buildings where the monks who served the saint lived. As the king's party appeared the Dewar of Coigreach, the custodian of the saint, came out to greet him. At his side was the Abbot of Inchaffray.

"Welcome, my son." Abbot Maurice had been at the coronation, but after it had returned to his lonely mountain abbey.

Robert knelt to receive his blessing.

"We have found food for your men, and we shall find more for your companions." The abbot smiled. "You and your ladies will be welcome to use the guest house, small though it is."

Robert thanked him, but he was frowning. "Why are you here, my lord abbot?"

For a moment Maurice hesitated, then he smiled. "I have come to be God's instrument in your absolution, my son. Sir James Douglas came to me and told me how heavily your crime of sacrilegious murder hangs upon you. If you confess your sin before God and beg forgiveness and absolution, it will be granted to you."

Robert frowned. "Is it possible that God could forgive such a deed?"

"God is merciful, my son, and with the intercession here of his blessed servant Fillan, he will hear your prayers."

Robert smiled. "Then I shall accept your offer gratefully." He stepped toward the chapel eagerly, but James Douglas, who had been listening at his side with a frown, put his hand on Robert's shoulder.

"Tomorrow, Robert, in the open, before all your men. It will reassure them and give them courage, give them the strength to fight again."

Abbot Maurice nodded approvingly. "He is right, Your Grace. This must be done openly, so all Scotland knows about it. It will remove any lingering doubts your men may have—any hint even that God does not support your cause."

Robert smiled, for the first time, it seemed to him, in weeks. "You are right. I shall beg God's forgiveness before the world."

"Good." The abbot beamed. "And now you may eat and rest, here in the guest house. It is small but it is all we have to offer our king and his ladies to rest in."

He beckoned to the Dewar who with a solemn bow ushered the king and those with him toward the small stone tower beside the shrine.

Robert was sitting at a table in the upper chamber of the lonely tower house alone, when Nigel knocked on the door that evening. He pushed it open and peered in, frowning to see his brother gazing into space, the ink on the quill in his hand long since dried. The room was very quiet in the twilight.

"I have a visitor for you, Your Highness," he said with a wink.

Robert looked up wearily and sighed. He smiled at his brother ruefully. "I'd rather have wine than visitors, if you can find any."

"I think under the circumstances both might be in order." Nigel pulled the door open and ushered Isobel in. "The rest of the ladies have gone to the chapel. Later I shall distract them and give you as long as I can. . . ."

She stood before him, still barefoot, her kirtle torn and stained with blaeberries, her hair tangled on her shoulders, her face tanned by the fierce Highland sun. For a moment they stared at each other in silence, then Robert stood up.

She curtseyed to the ground. "Your brother thought you might like some company for a while, Your Grace."

He smiled. In two strides he was beside her. After aiming a kick at the door to close it, he dragged her into his arms.

They didn't hear Nigel knock or see him push a jug of rough wine around the door with two wooden bowls to drink from. They did not hear him close the door behind him or know that he had posted a guard at the foot of the stairs, nor did they see him gallantly lead the queen outside later with the Princess Marjorie and walk with them beside the river, where the king's sisters were already taking advantage of the cool evening air. He checked the fishing lines that had been laid out among the reeds and led them farther and farther away from the tower as the long twilight stretched out into the luminous night.

They had two hours together, two hours when they forgot the war, the dead, the prisoners, the long summer night, and Robert's queen, complaining bitterly of the midges as she walked beside Sir Nigel. They forgot the past and the danger to come, locked in the passion and the longing that flooded through them. Then at last they lay together on the heap of plaids and furs that had served them as a bed.

"Where are we going next?" Isobel stretched out, her head on his chest, her slim body cradled in his arms.

Robert kissed the top of her head. "To the west—perhaps

even to Ireland. We'll gather our strength there, to fight back in the spring."

"You will fight back?" She shifted slightly so she could see his face in the twilight. "You won't let Scotland down?" She was thinking of his oath to Edward.

"Of course I'm going to fight!" He clenched his jaws together. "Methven was a setback, a disaster—" He frowned. "But it was not the end. It was the beginning. Those men must not have died in vain."

"How long will it take to get to safety?" She pushed her long hair back from her face, snuggling against him.

He shrugged. "We are safe as soon as we are with friends. We must avoid fighting again too soon. The men are tired and disheartened, they are in no state to fight again. Not yet. But, God willing, once we are among friends we can stop and regroup our forces and plan a new campaign. I will not be defeated."

"Why do you have to wait until the spring?"

He laughed. "So impatient, my love? I must, then I'll drive Edward out of Scotland forever. I'll chase out every man who has supported him and I shall be king in reality as well as in name." Gently he pushed her away and sat up. "Scotland will rally again beneath the lion banner, and the fiery cross will be carried from glen to glen in my name. We shall win, my love. We shall win."

For a moment neither of them reacted to the faint knock, then reluctantly Robert stood up. He dragged on his tunic and, walking over to the door, pulled it open a crack.

"Sir Nigel and the queen have returned, Your Grace." The warning was whispered through the crack. "They are below."

Robert swore quietly under his breath. He pushed the door closed and turned to Isobel. "I have to go, my darling." He buckled on his belt and, picking up his mantle, he fastened it on his shoulder with the circular cairngorm brooch he so often wore, the brooch his Isobella of Mar had given him before she died. He dropped on one knee beside her. "We travel on tomorrow after the abbot has given me his absolution. I pray God will give us time together again soon, my love." Gently he reached out and touched her breast. "Our time together must always be stolen. May the blessed Virgin and St. Fillan guard you and watch over you. Now, dress quickly." He smiled again, his teeth white in the darkness. "It would not do for you to emerge naked from an audience with your king." He took her face in his hands and kissed it, then he was gone.

The next morning his men were assembled early before the shrine of the saint. The fine weather had gone at last, and a pall of mist shrouded the mountains. Steady rain was falling as the king, bareheaded and barefoot, knelt before the abbot and made his confession for all to hear, receiving the absolution, which was given in ringing tones that echoed across the valley. Soon afterward Robert assembled his men and they began to move on, northwest up Strathfillan. It was a straggled band of men-at-arms and knights, the tired, disheveled, sad remnant of a proud army, although now newly reassured and pleased by the abbot's blessing on them all. In their midst were the queen's ladies, mounted, and rested at last after their night in the comparative security of the guest house. They followed the course of the river up the broad glen, glancing now and then at the shrouded mountains in the distance on either side, the sound of the horses' hooves and the chink of their harnesses masking the patter of the soft rain on the surface of the river.

Isobel eased herself in the saddle wearily, her eyes always seeking for Robert among the men ahead. The rain was cold, soaking into her clothes, sliding down her cheeks like tears. She was uneasy, her exhilaration gone. There was a strange prickling of the skin at the back of her neck. Again and again she looked around into the cold wet mist, feeling eyes upon them, but the distances were silent, shrouded in white. Even the eagles were quiet.

They were passing a small loch now, on their left as they approached the head of the glen where the mountains pressed closer. Ahead the track led between the low foothills of the pass. There, waiting in the mist, crouching behind boulders and scattered trees, were almost a thousand men, half naked in their kilts, armed with swords and Lochaber axes. As Isobel saw them she screamed, her terror echoing in her own ears. Then she screamed again.

Only it wasn't Isobel, it was Clare, Clare who had seen the ambush long before any of the men in Robert's train, Clare, who from hundreds of years away, from the vantage point of her dream, had seen the trap and was trying to warn them. But they couldn't hear her. They rode on, straight toward the pass, Isobel with them.

Again Clare tried to shout a warning, but her voice wouldn't come. However hard she tried to make herself heard, the room remained full of silence, as slowly the figures of Robert's army disappeared into the mist.

Stiff and cold, she looked into the darkness, afraid, trying to call them back, but it was no use. The vision had gone. Something had distracted her, sent the shadowy figures back into the past, riding toward their fate, leaving her lost and shaking, on her knees in the middle of the floor. The moon had vanished and the silver streak of moonlight had crawled away from her toward the wall.

"So, that's how it's done." Paul's voice from the shadows made her jump violently. "No spirits, no devils, just the dream of a madwoman who sits in the moonlight, the tears pouring down her face." His tone was mocking.

"How long have you been standing there?" Clare knelt without moving. She didn't even look at him.

"Half an hour at least." He was wearing his dressing gown again, tightly belted, and leaning against the wall beyond the slice of moonlight. Somewhere in the garden two owls were hunting, their sharp cries echoing through the frosty silence.

"What time is it?" Her voice was flat, defeated.

Paul smiled. "It's after three."

"So late?" She was still dazed.

He smiled. "There is still plenty of time to go back. Why don't you—go and find your Isobel again—all the ghosts who haunt you? I enjoy watching." He folded his arms.

"There is nothing to watch, Paul." She scrambled to her feet, shaking with cold.

"Nothing to watch? You cry, you smile, you laugh, you

scream—your eyes follow them as they walk around the room." Paul shuddered. "God almighty, woman. And you claim you are not mad!"

She looked at him, but his face was dark, out of the moonlight, and she couldn't see his expression.

Hesitantly she moved toward the door. "I'm going to bed," she said. "Please go away, Paul. Leave me alone." Her voice was flat.

He made no move as she put her hand on the handle and pulled the door open. Slowly she walked down the dark narrow stairs into the bedroom. The light on the side table was on, throwing shadows on the walls. Clare glanced at the door to the rest of the house, wondering for a moment if he had unlocked it. Something told her he hadn't. Slowly she went to the bed and climbed in, shaking with cold.

Paul had followed her down and for a moment he stood staring at her. She looked at him sullenly, not wanting him to see her sudden fear, but he made no move toward her. Instead he walked over to the door, the key in his hand.

"Sweet dreams, my love," he said as he unlocked it. "You might as well live in your dreams—you're no damn good to anyone in reality."

She sat without moving as the door closed and she heard first the key and then the bolt on the outside. It was a long time before she closed her eyes. She felt completely empty.

Rex glanced at the pile of newspapers on Emma's kitchen table and shrugged. "We have a publicity problem, it seems."

Emma had phoned him as soon as she had dropped Julia off at school. If it had been anyone else he would have told them to make an appointment in a week's time—he didn't appreciate being commanded anywhere, but for Emma he had cancelled two meetings and a lunch and grabbed a cab.

He sat down heavily in Emma's pine kitchen and shuffled through the newspapers. Neil Forbes's story had made the front page in four nationals, it was an inside lead in three more.

" 'Scots heiress sells her birthright,' " he read out loud. " 'Scandal of oil rigs at more British beauty spots.' " He glanced at Emma. "Who is this man Forbes? He should try and get his facts right. Sigma has withdrawn their application for a license."

"What!" Emma stared at him. "Why? What happened?"

"The price of oil happened. They don't want to invest any more money in British exploration at the moment." He took a deep breath. "And I'm leaving Sigma." He had tried so hard to tell her when they had met at the weekend, but somehow he couldn't. It hurt too much.

"Does Paul know?" Emma folded the papers up and put them in a neat pile.

"Sure. And he knows that I still want to buy Duncairn."

"Why?"

"To restore the castle. To save it when they do take the oil. If Sigma doesn't get that license someone else will. There is oil there, make no mistake about that. If I own the castle I'll know what to do to make sure the place isn't harmed."

"But can you pay as much as an oil company, Rex?" she said at last.

"Nothing like as much. That's Paul Royland's bad luck. But I will still pay enough to bail him out."

"And by buying Duncairn do you think you can save it?"

"I just don't know, Emma. But I can hope."

He glanced down at the paper again. "This bastard is making much of the fact that it is Clare Royland's family seat. Perhaps I should tell them that my family lived there a long time before hers."

Emma frowned. "Is that honestly true?"

"The Comyns were one of the great families of Scotland. The earls of Buchan." He smiled modestly.

"Buchan?" Emma stared. "Like her Isobel? Then you must be related to Clare! You should be on the same side! Does she know that it is you who wants to buy the place, not Sigma?"

"I don't know. That brother of yours is dealing with everything. He seems to think his wife is incapable of handling her own affairs—"

"But that's not so."

"Well, whatever the situation, Paul Royland is the only one I've been talking to."

"These environmentalists have got it in for Paul," Emma said quietly. " 'City Fat Cat Wants More and More.' Poor Paul."

Rex glanced at her. "You didn't call me here to show me these, did you, Emma?" he asked gently.

Emma shrugged. "Oh, I knew you must have seen them." She stood up. "I've been thinking about Paul." She looked down, flipping through the pile of papers again absentmind-edly. "I'm afraid. I know my brother. He is ruthless." She bit her lip. "You've offered him the way out of his financial mess. You said that if he doesn't pay this debt he could go to prison."

Rex nodded. He leaned forward and caught Emma's hand. "That's right, so there is no problem. Your brother is going to be okay."

"No. You don't understand." Emma snatched her hand away. "For all this to happen he has to force Clare to sell Duncairn. *Force* her, Rex! Paul is capable of anything. He might hurt her if it was the only way to get his hands on the estate. He might even kill her, don't you see?" Her voice had risen sharply. She turned away and leaned against the wall, her eyes shut.

"Oh, come on, Emma." Rex was staring at her as he stood up. "That doesn't make sense. No man is going to kill his wife over a piece of land, not even for the kind of bucks I'm offering. Besides, he needs that money fast. If he waited to inherit the place it would take him months and months to clear up all the inheritance taxes and things like that."

Emma shook her head stubbornly. "If he were to inherit it, he could get a loan against it."

Rex studied her face. "Emma," he said softly. "Are you seriously telling me that your brother is capable of murder?"

She sniffed, groping in her pocket for a handkerchief. "I think he could be, and you're the only person who could stop it from happening."

"What the hell can I do about it?"

"You can withdraw your offer to buy the land."

"I can't do that."

"You can!" She came and sat down opposite him. "You can,

Rex. We're not talking about multimillion-dollar corporations anymore. The oil doesn't come into it, does it? You say they'll get the license one day anyway. But you don't have to buy it. You can change your mind." Lightly she put her hands over his. "Please, Rex. Please. Withdraw your offer." After standing up suddenly, she ran around the table and slipped her arms around his neck. "Please."

Rex reached up and stroked her hair. He was in a turmoil of conflicting emotions. He had Royland where he wanted him: desperate. He could preempt Sigma and rub its nose in the shit when the strike eventually came up. He had won. And yet this slip of a woman was trying to wheedle him into throwing over the deal. The touch of her body, young and vibrant, round in all the right places, pressing against his, so different from Mary's with her brittle, designer-slim hips, struck chords he thought he had lost touch with long ago. She was beautiful, sexy, trusting, and spunky. And now she had shown herself vulnerable too.

He stood up and folded his arms around her. "Emma."

"Please, Rex. Withdraw your offer." She was looking at him, her lips near his.

He knew she felt it too: the attraction, the longing. They were both lonely; they had found each other when they both needed someone badly. The differences in age did not matter. He smiled triumphantly into her hair. Now she wanted something from him, something he had it in his power to grant if she could persuade him. . . .

Slowly he brought his mouth down on hers. It was a gentle kiss, sensitive and full of carefully controlled passion. "Oh, Emma," he breathed. "You're so lovely."

For a moment she went on clinging to him. His kiss had made her go weak at the knees, and she was appalled to find how badly she wanted him. She pushed him away gently. She wasn't going to trade favors. "You know it won't work, Rex," she said sadly. "We're both married."

"Does that matter so much?" He reached for her again. "Neither of them would ever know—"

"No, Rex." She spoke sharply. "I'm not going to bed with you to try to persuade you to withdraw your deal. That's what you thought, didn't you? Well, you're wrong! I'm not like that."

"I know that." He shrugged. "The two things aren't related. We want each other—"

"Maybe we do." Her voice was very quiet. "But I am not going to bed with you, Rex. You'd better go. I'm sorry. You've got the wrong idea about me."

"That's not true, Emma. You're special. Very special. What I decide to do about Duncairn has nothing to do with us—I'll think about that, okay, but that's all I'll promise." He paused. She was asking a great deal of him. A very great deal. "I think you're wrong about your brother," he said slowly. "For what it's worth, I think he's a weak character. He hasn't got the courage to kill anyone. He's a bully, that's for sure, but he would never hurt Clare. He hasn't got the guts."

Chapter Twenty-five

Paul had found a message from Rex waiting for him when he got back to London. He was to meet him at the Ritz. Rex looked Paul up and down with new interest. There was a slight family likeness to Emma—the dark coloring, the square shoulders, the determined chin, but where she was small and pretty, he was tall and muscular, or had been before the slight flabbiness and the relaxed skin at the throat and below the eyes had betrayed him. They stood eyeing each other.

"So. Do you have your wife's authority?" Rex asked.

Paul took a sip from his brandy. "I'll have it by next week."

"No use." Rex shook his head. "I'm not waiting any longer. If you can't get her witnessed signature by"—he glanced at his watch—"by this time tomorrow, the deal is off."

"What do you mean, off?" Paul had gone white.

"I'm going back to the States, Mr. Royland. All my affairs in this country have been settled except for this one. There is no more time."

It was a calculated risk. When he set off for the Ritz that morning he still hadn't decided what to do about Duncairn. He wanted it. He wanted it as he had never wanted anything before, and yet in the back of his mind lurked the fear that Emma might be right—that this man might indeed be capable of murder. Was he prepared to put Clare's life at risk for Duncairn's sake? He eyed Paul again.

"There has to be more time. You can't back out now, man!" Paul grabbed his arm. "Look, give me two more days. My wife is in Scotland. I'll fly up and get her signature—"

"How?" Rex narrowed his eyes for a moment. He could feel Paul's desperation now; feel the unbalanced power of

449

the man's sudden panic. No wonder Emma was frightened for her sister-in-law.

"Your wife has made it very clear, it seems to me, that she doesn't want to sell Duncairn, and never will," he went on. "You have had weeks to persuade her. I don't think you're going to manage it in another twenty-four hours." He glanced down at his Rolex again. "I think you ought to admit defeat." He smiled. "I told you I had certain information that I would divulge if you didn't manage to get the contracts drawn up for me—" He paused. Paul's gaze was on his face, a rabbit before a weasel, paralyzed with fear. Rex felt a quick rush of triumph. "At present"—he paused again, for maximum effect—"I have decided to sit on that information. No doubt it will all come out anyway when you fail to pay up your debts on settlement day." He put his glass down on a table nearby. "But for your wife's sake, I shall say nothing. She has, it seems to me, enough to bear, being married to a bastard like you."

Back in his office, Paul was seething. He poured his third glass of whisky and began pacing up and down the carpet. It was Clare's fault! If she hadn't prevaricated and fought him and lied! If she had given him some loyalty as a wife should! The cold, stupid, mad bitch! He drained his glass, then he called his solicitor. "Ken, I'm coming back to you about the papers over my wife's committal when the doctors and others have seen her again. But now I want you to make a statement to the press refuting the garbage Forbes talked about the family on Monday." He was breathing heavily through his nose. "Tell him Clare Royland is not selling Duncairn. There has never been any question of it. And tell them Forbes is an ignorant troublemaker. Clare confirms that the site has absolutely no interest whatsoever ecologically or archaeologically. It's just a cold, barren cliff and a third-rate hotel with nothing to offer visitors but an east wind straight from Siberia, and what is more no one, repeat, no one has made an offer to buy the place. Got that? Oh, for God's sake, Ken, word it any way you like, but get Forbes off my back!" He slammed down the phone, then he went back to the whisky bottle for the fourth time. He had been summoned to appear before Sir Duncan and the members of the full board in half an hour.

Geoffrey was very thoughtful after his return from seeing the bishop. He sat down opposite his wife in the comfortable, shabby sitting room of the vicarage and, leaning forward, took her hand.

"I told him everything—including your doubts." He smiled. "And the fact that you think she is making it all up. We discussed her for a long time, and we prayed together. He is rather of the opinion that we are right to be afraid for her." He paused. "Chloe dear, he has left it to me to decide what to do. I am going to celebrate a Eucharist for her and I am going to talk to the bishop's special committee about her, but he has given me permission to conduct a ceremony of exorcism myself if I feel that that is the only thing to do that could possibly help her."

Chloe stared at him. "An exorcism? You're not serious! Geoffrey, for God's sake!"

"Yes, my darling, for God's sake." He looked very grave. "Please believe me, I do know what I'm talking about. I wouldn't enter into this lightly—and I may never do it. I shall have to talk to her and to everyone around her again and again before I decide, but I have the bishop's approval to go ahead if I feel that it is the only course that will help her." He stood up, frowning. "Believe me, I have thought about this hard, Chloe. It is not something I want to do. It is not something I am qualified to do."

"Then don't do it. For God's sake don't do it, Geoff."

"I'm sorry, Chloe, I must." He shook his head. "I'm going to discuss it again with Paul. I know he wants me to see her again, and if necessary sign this paper giving him power of attorney while she is ill. She is certainty not capable of making rational decisions at the moment. No—" He held up his hand. "I know what you're going to say. I shan't sign anything that will harm Clare or allow Paul to misuse her assets in any way. I'm not stupid. I shall see Clare either when she returns south or, if necessary, I shall go up to Perthshire. I would like it to be as soon as possible, but the moment must be right."

Antonia followed Clare into Archie's study. "Who are you calling, dear?" she asked nervously as Clare sat down at her father's desk and picked up the phone. "I don't think you ought to—"

"I'm calling Neil Forbes." Clare began to dial. She had found the number of Earthwatch in the directory after she saw Paul's statement in the paper her father had hidden in the boot room.

She drummed her fingers on the desk. If Paul had issued a public statement two days ago that they were not selling Duncairn, why was she still a prisoner? She would take that one up with Archie when he came in.

Neil was about to go out to lunch. "Why, Mrs. Royland! Surprise, surprise!" His voice was acid. "I didn't expect to hear from you again after your solicitor's oh-so-public vilification of me and my organization."

Kenneth Beaumont's carefully phrased answers to Neil's original attack had lost none of Paul's venom, for all that the libelous content had been removed.

"They are not my solicitors, Mr. Forbes," Clare said desperately. "They are my husband's. I did not say any of that. None of it. I know Duncairn is special. I know it is ecologically very sensitive. I know the castle is a historic monument. I love Duncairn. I would never say any of those things."

"Then why allow statements like that to be put out in your name?"

"I didn't know about it. Paul is in London. I only saw it today. My husband doesn't speak for me."

"No?" Neil gave a short laugh. "Well, it hardly matters, does it? You're not selling, that's the main thing. That much is true, I take it?"

"I told you that at the hotel."

"Ah yes, before you ran away into the night with your husband."

"I didn't go with him willingly, Mr. Forbes."

"Of course not." His tone was sarcastic. "I don't see much

point in this conversation, Mrs. Royland. Our quarrel is not with you now. Earthwatch is going to direct its campaign against the issuing of prospecting licenses in sites of special interest like Duncairn. Because this case has had so much publicity, we will center the battle in Scotland there, separately from but in close consultation with the similar campaigns going on in the south of England. If you care about Duncairn, Mrs. Royland, you would be there with us."

"I do care," Clare said wearily.

"But duty to your husband keeps you at his side? Of course." Neil's tone was mocking. "I understand perfectly."

"You don't understand at all." Clare's voice fell to a whisper.

"To support us would be to contradict his statement about us. What more is there to be said?"

"I want to support you—" Clare said desperately.

"So what is stopping you, Mrs. Royland?" Neil hung up.

"What indeed?" Clare put the phone down. Her hands were shaking. She put her head in her arms on the desktop.

"Oh, Clare, darling." Antonia went over to her and patted her anxiously on the shoulder. "You must not upset yourself like this—"

"Please, Mummy, let me go." Clare groped for her mother's hand. "Please. I'm sure Paul would say it was all right."

Antonia shook her head unhappily. "It is for your own good, darling. Besides, the best thing is for you to stay here quietly until Paul has sorted everything out. Did I tell you James is coming up for a week's shooting? He called last night."

Clare raised an eyebrow. "James? So he's in on it too, is he?"

"He's coming to shoot, Clare." Her mother sighed in exasperation. "But maybe he will be able to help us."

"James?" Clare walked over to the window and stared out at the bleak garden. "Why should James know anything about it? He'll just think you and Archie have gone completely off your heads."

"Perhaps he will." Antonia gave a wan smile. She hadn't dared to tell her daughter that Paul had arranged for Sarah

Collins to fly north and help them watch her, or that she would be arriving that afternoon.

Sir David Royland had picked up Geoffrey in central London before driving out to Kensington. They both stood in the drawing room of the Campden Hill house while Paul poured them a drink, then all three men sat down. Paul was on edge. The meeting at the office had been awful. They all knew. He had been suspended from the board, pending an internal inquiry, and asked not to go into Coleman Street for the next few days. It had been suggested that he develop an expedient case of flu for the time being. On top of that had come his elder brother's phone call announcing his visit this evening with Geoffrey.

"I think you should know, Paul, that we talked with Emma this evening, and she has given us permission to act in her name as well as our own," David said slowly. He took a sip from his glass. "We want to know the exact situation. Are the rumors true? Are you about to go bankrupt?"

"It looks like it. I shan't be able to meet a settlement charge."

"How much?"

"A little under two million."

"Good God, Paul! Are you out of your mind?"

"It was a gamble—a certainty, I thought. If it had come off, no one would have been the wiser."

"Until next time," Geoffrey put in. "Look, Paul, have you still got your shares in father's company?"

Paul stood up. The veins in his temples were distended and throbbing. "Of course."

"Then the three of us will take them off your hands. David and I will take a third of them each, and David is going to chip in with the rest to buy a third for Emma. That keeps it all in the family, as the trust lays down. That will clear your debt and leave you some over for any other obligations you may have. It will also take the worry off Clare's shoulders." He frowned. "She must be protected from any outside stress at the moment at all cost."

David was nodding. "It's the best way, old chap. Then,

when things get better, you can buy them back. This keeps it all in the family the way Dad would have wanted, and it leaves the children's trust fund untouched." He glanced at Geoffrey.

"The children's trust fund!" Paul echoed. "With one more little Royland to benefit, I gather." He gave a bitter laugh. "I haven't congratulated you on the birth of your new son yet, have I, David?" He threw himself back in his chair with a sigh.

"Cheer up, Paul, old chap," Geoffrey put in awkwardly. "This puts everything right. No more problems. No one will ever know. It could have happened to anyone."

Paul was staring out into the dead, dark garden through the undrawn curtains. No one would ever know—as long as Rex Cummin kept quiet, and Diane Warboys, and as long as the board of BCWP closed ranks and kept silent and united against any questions that might be asked about insider trading. "Of course it could have happened to anyone," he repeated dully. "But it didn't, did it? It happened to me."

The next morning he called the president-elect of Sigma International in London and offered him first refusal of the lands of Duncairn at a knockdown price. "Once the environmental lobby is silenced, which it will be once the licenses are confirmed, you'll be laughing. I just thought I'd tell you the property is still on the market in case you want to apply again before the applications close." He hung up. He might have lost his holdings in the family firm, but he hadn't lost everything. With the money from Duncairn he would buy into a new issue, recoup his losses tenfold, and buy back the shares within three months.

And Duncairn had to go. After what Clare had done to him, he was going to make her pay. He was going to make her pay with Duncairn, and with her sanity.

He sat down at his desk, staring at the opposite wall. Locked alone in that tower, tormented by ghosts, how long would she last? Either she would break or she would throw herself off the top of the tower in a frenzy of claustrophobic terror.

* * *

Sarah Collins adored Airdlie on sight. She had seen photographs of the house before, but the reality met every romantic notion she held of the baronial Scottish hall: the huge drafty rooms, the pointed Victorian roofs, the stained glass, the wrought iron, and there at one corner the genuine sixteenth-century tower with its flagpole—the tower where Clare was held prisoner.

Clare was sitting in the library, her feet up on the sofa, reading, when Antonia brought Sarah in at last. "Clare darling, look who has arrived. Mrs. Collins come to give us all a hand." Antonia was looking distinctly nervous.

Clare's face had lost weight. She looked gaunt and tired. Sarah smiled. "Mrs. Royland. It's good to see you."

"Hello, Sarah. Did Paul send you?" Clare swung her feet to the floor.

Sarah, who had been half expecting to find Clare in chains, was almost disappointed to note the sheer stockings and the Gucci sandals.

"He thought perhaps your mother and father could do with a bit of help with you being here and your brother coming tomorrow." Sarah smiled uncertainly.

"What a kind thought." Clare did not try to hide the sarcasm in her tone. "Where is he?"

"Mr. Royland? In London. We've closed up Bucksters for a while."

"I think I'll make some tea," Antonia put in hastily with a glance at Clare. "Please, sit down—Sarah—" She had hesitated, wondering whether to use the woman's first name or to be more formal.

Sarah sat down with alacrity, facing Clare. Within ten minutes she felt as if she had been there forever.

James was enjoying himself. Airdlie was his, even if his parents did live there. He loved the house, the gardens, the river, and the moors. Not for long, mind you. More than a week and he'd probably be as mad as poor old Clare, but out on the hill with his stepfather and the guns and the dogs he was deliriously happy. It was such a change from the City, and he was glad to be out of the City for a while. The press comment about Paul and Clare and the rumors about Paul were all becoming a bit embarrassing.

Sitting at the breakfast table, he opened his copy of *The Times*. Opposite him his mother, neatly dressed and coiffed, was ladling out the porridge.

"Oh, God, there's another bit about Duncairn here." James folded back the paper. "Earthwatch has held a public meeting there to protest against onshore oil drilling on sites of special scientific interest. Where is Archie's *Scotsman*? That will probably have more about it."

"Don't let Clare see it, for goodness sake." Antonia put a bowl down in front of him. "She's furious enough with that Forbes man as it is."

"Here it is. On the front page." James had rescued the *Scotsman* from his stepfather's chair. "Oh, God!" He read on in silence.

"What does it say?" Antonia glanced at the door in agitation in case Clare appeared.

In spite of Sarah's meticulous relaying of Paul's instructions that Clare was to be watched and guarded at all times, Archie had decreed, with one glance at his wife's thunderous face, that just keeping her in the house was sufficient restraint for the time being, and Clare had been released from her room as usual as soon as she awoke that morning.

"They've got hold of some story that Clare wanted to contest Aunt Margaret's will!" James read incredulously. "That Duncairn was not enough for her and she wanted money too. Is that true?" He turned to his mother in indignation.

"No, of course it's not true." Antonia was visibly distressed. "Really, that man is impossible! How could he even suggest such a thing?"

"Paul will probably sue him this time." James put down the paper and turned to his porridge, shamelessly spooning sugar into his bowl. "Meanwhile, what on earth are you going to do with Clare? You can't keep her here forever. The whole thing is ludicrous."

"I know." Antonia looked up at him unhappily.

"Then why do it? Surely to God you're not afraid of Paul?

There's nothing wrong with her, you know. Or nothing a day or two in the fresh air wouldn't cure. Paul is a sadistic bastard, if you ask me, and Archie's no better. And the dreadful Mrs. C! God, she was bad enough in the south! Here she's like a female Visigoth! It's bloody bad luck on Clare."

"What is?" Clare came in, closely followed by Sarah Collins. Clare was wearing some old jeans and a sloppy green jersey that James vaguely recognized as one of his old ones. Her face was pale and unmade up, her hair longer and straighter than he remembered it. It dawned on him for the first time to his surprise that his sister was a very beautiful woman.

"Keeping you cooped up inside," James answered. He stood up and pulled out a chair for her, ignoring Sarah, who sat down at the far end of the table. "Why don't you come up on the hill with us?"

"Why not indeed?" Clare tightened her lips. "I suggest you ask our stepfather."

"I have." James shrugged.

"And he told you the lies Paul told him." Clare picked up the paper. She glanced at it halfheartedly, then she stiffened. "There's a bit about Duncairn here. They've held a meeting there."

James exchanged glances with his mother.

"It's Mr. Forbes again I'm afraid, dear," Antonia put in. "I'm sure Paul will deal with him. You mustn't let it worry you."

"Worry me!" Clare stared at her. "Did you see what he said about me?"

She couldn't use the phone again. Four times she tried, but on each occasion either her mother or Sarah came in. She had no intention of speaking to Neil Forbes with either of them listening. What she had to say to him was for his ears only. She was hurt and angry. She had told him the truth and he had ignored it; he was turning his campaign into a vendetta against her personally. Furiously pacing the floor, she began to chew her thumbnail. She had to get to Duncairn.

Only there would she be able to clear her name and fight Paul, but first she had to get out and take one of the cars.

The nights had been the worst. Three times she had had the nightmare. She had awakened each time, crying and trembling, aching for Casta who would have comforted her, but Casta had been banished to the gun room with her stepfather's dogs and she was alone. Between the dreams she fought Isobel. Oh yes, she wanted desperately to know what had happened when Robert led his men into the ambush, but she was afraid now that if she allowed Isobel back it would make Paul's accusations true. What if her mother or stepfather came in while she was away in the past, as Paul had done? What if they saw her?

Miserably she distracted herself, taking piles of books to bed with her, fighting sleep and fighting Isobel, and growing more and more exhausted. Isobel was there, she was certain of it, trying to reach her, trying to tell her what happened from behind some thin veil in her mind, as desperate to contact her as she was to avoid being contacted.

Each night she lay in bed, watching the streaks of moonlight crossing the old tower room, and each night she wondered if Margaret too had lain there watching; if she too had seen Isobel—perhaps from that same bed. The thought comforted her marginally. If Aunt Margaret had seen Isobel and knew her story, Aunt Margaret who was undeniably sane, surely it could not be so bad to want to know what had happened all those centuries ago?

When Isobel finally won, that was the excuse Clare had used to herself. Somehow it made it seem as if it were her own considered, free decision. She waited, relieved that the struggle within herself was over, pacing up and down to keep herself awake until two in the morning—she had borrowed an old wristwatch of her mother's now—and then at last she sank to the floor, and, raising her arms, she looked into the shadows and let the past sweep her up in its story once more.

Isobel found herself clinging to Mary, the two women separated from the others suddenly by a riderless horse, its ears back, its high saddle soaked in blood, the huge hooves throwing up clods of mud as it thundered past. Mary fell back with a shriek, her fingers slipping on the coarse wet stems of heather. Isobel, falling on her knees beside her, put her arms around her, sheltering her as best she could behind a mound of gorse.

"Where's Robert? For God's sake, where is Robert!" Mary was sobbing with shock.

Isobel shook her head in despair. There was no sign of the queen or Marjorie. In the mist all they could do was listen to the sounds of shouting, the screams and the clash of blade on blade. Once or twice they saw shadowy figures battling out of the murk. Each time they fled farther back down the glen, away from the noise of battle, and each time the battle followed them, as relentlessly the king's small, desperate army was beaten back. The fighting was hard and bloody, their enemy not English but men from the Highlands, men of the Lord of Lorne.

The women, herded in panic to the back of the line, watched in horror, helpless as the clouds settled over the bloody scene, the rain slanting down, turning the swiftly reddening ground to mud. Somewhere a horse screamed; it crashed to the ground, its windpipe severed. Its rider fell, saved himself, slipped, and went down, a broadsword through his ribs in the vulnerable gap in his mail beneath his arm.

Then at last they saw Robert. Sword in hand he hacked his way back toward them, beside him two men, unrecognizable for the blood running down their faces, and with them was the queen and Christian, with little Marjorie. "Back," Robert yelled into the mist. "Back. Save the women." He gestured behind him along the glen with his sword arm. "Jettison everything that slows us down and retreat, back into the mountains. Hurry!"

The small lochan was beside them now, black beneath the mist, the waters deep and still. One by one the men hurled their heavier weapons in, together with the few coffers that remained on the milling horses—then they turned and fled along the glen, urging the women with them, while Robert stood, shoulder to shoulder with the remnants of his army, protecting them, fending off their pursuers.

He glanced at Nigel who fought at his right hand. "Go with the women!" he shouted breathlessly. "Back to Loch Dochart. There is a castle on the island. Get them across to it. They'll be safe there. Hurry, man! We'll defend your rear!" He whirled as another onslaught hurtled toward them out of the mist.

The weather saved them, the low clouds rolling over the ground, touching the heather and grass with soft, thick mist that wrapped them around and sheltered the weary, injured party as they trailed, exhausted, south into Glen Dochart. Robert and his band of surviving fighting men were behind them all the way. They followed the track up the eastern side of the loch this time, a narrow path, close to the still water. There Robert halted the exhausted men who were still unhurt, drawing them up across a path so narrow it could scarcely take two horses abreast, where the granite cliffs came down almost to the water's edge. He was prepared to hold the position while his brother led the others on until they reached safety. In the center of the loch, on a small island, stood the castle, its murky shape seeming to dissolve and reform in the mist as they watched. Summoning all his strength, Nigel shouted across the water, his voice echoing off the tower.

The bedraggled party on the shore watched as two men pushed a boat into the water and climbed in, rowing slowly and steadily toward them across the rain-pocked water. "The lord of Glendochart is away from home," one of them called as they reached the shore. He scrambled to his feet, dropping his oars, and leapt into the shallow water near them. He glanced around doubtfully at the disheveled band of men and women.

"He would not grudge us shelter, man." Sir Nigel had already waded out into the water and grabbed the gunwale of the boat. "Take us to the castle and give us shelter, for pity's sake. I have women here, and wounded men! Your king's wife and child—"

The boatman stared at the huddled figures, obviously uncertain, glancing back at his companion who still sat in the bow of the boat. It was the companion who nodded. "Aye, let them come. I'm sure Sir Patrick would give them shelter were he here."

Isobel was in the first boatload, sitting in the stern huddled beside Robert's queen, both women acutely conscious of the closeness of the black water as the laden boat labored slowly back toward the castle. Isobel bit her lip, her anguished thoughts still with Robert, though her eyes were fixed, mesmerized, upon the thick weeds parting like tresses around them as the water slid passed. A patch of mist cleared suddenly and, looking up, she could see the far shore of the loch, thick with oak and alder, silent beneath the high ridge of mountain that sheltered the glen to the east. To the west the towering shoulder of Ben More was lost in clouds.

Their boat labored on slowly to the jerky oar strokes through the shallow, peaty water. In front of them two wounded men lay moaning, their blood seeping out onto the bottom boards to mingle with the loch water as it swilled about their feet.

It took twelve trips to ferry everyone across to the castle.

The wounded were laid in rows on the floor of the main hall of the tower. It was hot and crowded, lighted by hundreds of rush lights and a few smoking flares, full of the stench of blood and sweat and fear. Isobel and Mary worked tirelessly among the wounded. In the distance they could see Christian struggling to tie a blood-soaked bandage around a man's eyes as he screamed and fought her, covering her in his blood. Only the queen, standing pressed against the wall, her arms around the king's daughter, watched and did nothing. The little girl was sobbing in terror. Isobel spared them only one glance—then she turned back to the man she was tending.

Suddenly Robert was there in the doorway. She saw his gaze going from woman to woman, visibly counting heads, and she saw him sigh with relief. His right arm was stained to the elbow with the blood of his enemies. At his shoulder stood the Earl of Atholl and Sir Neil Campbell, both near collapse with exhaustion. She saw Sir Neil search frantically for a glimpse of Mary among the survivors. He found her, and she saw his face relax into a weary smile.

Behind them Sir James Douglas staggered into the hall. He threw himself down onto the ground beside two other wounded men, and she saw that he was trying to staunch a vicious sword slash on his arm with a strip of rag. Leaving the man she was tending with a gentle encouraging smile, she went and knelt beside Sir James and took the cloth from his hand.

"Let me, Sir James." She tore another strip from her ragged cloak and bound it tightly around his arm.

He grinned at her through gritted teeth. "They nearly did for us there, my lady." He glanced up at Robert who was standing near them, leaning on his sword. The king's face was gray. He had lost his cloak, with its precious brooch, and his mail was split open down his left arm from shoulder to wrist.

Isobel scrambled to her feet. "Robert! You are hurt!" she cried. Her voice was shaking. Beneath the split, tortuous rings of the mail she could see the torn tunic and the jagged angry rip in the flesh.

"Leave it!" His voice was curt. "Help the badly wounded. And you, madam, leave the child. You help them too." He addressed his queen who was standing, her arm still around Marjorie, frozen in a daze of fear and horror.

By daylight eleven of the men in the hall were dead. Some dozen others were critically wounded. Of the five hundred or so men who had ridden the morning before up Strathfillan, less than two hundred were still with them, defeated by the thousand men John Macdougall had led across the mountains to intercept the Bruce and his men at Dalrigh. Robert had grimaced at the irony of the name when he heard it. *Dail Righ*, the King's Meadow. What fate had ordained that they meet there, to be totally and completely defeated and humiliated? But at least he and his women and a number of his friends had escaped.

Sir Nigel and the women did not know how close he had been to death, when, pursued by three of Lorne's men the night before, on the narrow path above Loch Dochart, he had been cornered and had survived only after a desperate hand-to-hand fight during which the three men, a father and his two sons, so the story was told later among Bruce's men, were all killed by the king single-handed. In the fight he had lost his cloak and the precious brooch that held it in place, a brooch that later the Macdougalls were to produce and treasure as a relic of the battle, but he had escaped with his life.

By dawn the king had spent two hours already in discussion with Douglas, Campbell, Lord Atholl, and Nigel Bruce as to what to do next. The men of Loch Dochart were uneasy, obviously unhappy with their illustrious but unlucky guests, and Robert suspected that their lord, Patrick of Glendochart, still unaccountably absent from his castle, might well have been the man who had betrayed their presence in the mountains to John of Lorne. For the time being he put the thought from his mind. One day he would find out the truth, and if the rumor had any substance, the lords of Glendochart would be punished for their treason. Now he had too many things to think about to worry about them.

He and his men could stay in the castle safely no longer, that much was certain. A temporary respite, it could also easily become a trap. As dawn broke he called the remnants of his friends together, his face heavy with grief and anger, and surveyed them.

"We cannot continue traveling together," he said, anguished by their exhausted, agonized loyalty as they looked to him for leadership. "We must split up, for all our safety. Nigel, you and Lord Atholl must take the queen and the other ladies with the wounded and what remain of our horses back to Kildrummy. I should never have brought you west! You would have been safer there. Wait for us there, or travel on north, whichever you think is best. Aim to get to Norway —to our sister, Isabel." Their sister had married the king of Norway and, though now a widow, would undoubtedly help them. "The rest of us will go on toward the coast—protect your retreat and then, God willing, regroup and join you later. Then"—he smiled wearily—"then we will fight back!"

The men and women of Robert's party gathered at last on the eastern shore of the loch, reunited with the surviving horses, which had been left to fend for themselves overnight.

High up on the ridge their lookouts saw nothing in the distance save wisps of mist as the sun dried out the heather, and far away on a distant skyline a herd of deer, silhouetted for a moment against the limpid blue of the sky. The enemy was long gone back into their northern glens.

At last they were ready, the wounded mounted, some tied to their saddles to stop them from falling off, the queen on a scarred gray gelding, the king's sisters and Isobel riding on some of the nervous war horses that had survived the battle.

Isobel looked down at Robert, who was standing with his men, those who would continue on foot through the mountains, leading their enemies away to allow them the chance of safety.

"Robert—" It was a whisper. No one heard. No one saw her desperate hand outstretched toward him. The king had not glanced her way.

But he was thinking of her. He touched Nigel's arm. "Take care of them, Nigel, my queen and my child."

"I will, sir. With my life." Nigel punched him gently between the shoulder blades.

"And my Isobel. See she is safe, Nigel. For me."

Nigel nodded without a word. Suddenly he couldn't speak. He gave his brother a quick, hard hug and turned away so that Robert wouldn't see his tears.

Chapter Twenty-six

"Our Father who art in heaven, hallowed be thy name . . ."

The quiet words filled the room, agitated, urgent, swirling in the silence. Clare opened her eyes. Her face was wet with tears, her hands clenched so tightly her nails had cut little welts into her palms.

The room was almost dark. In one corner a lamp was burning, and in the chair near it Sarah Collins was sitting. Again and again she was repeating the words of the Lord's Prayer, mechanically, desperately, not letting the silence in. The room was full of fear and sadness. Its atmosphere was palpable, surrounding Clare in an almost visible cloud.

Clare's face was white and dazed. She looked around for a moment, confused and lost, and for a moment Sarah was too afraid to move.

If only Isobel had gone with him. If only he had allowed her to stay at his side as he longed. If only he had not sent her away.

Margaret Gordon's voice was clear in the room between them. Clare stared at Sarah, her eyes enormous in her pale face. "What did you say?" she whispered. Slowly she stood up.

There was a small worn Bible clutched in Sarah's hand.

"Sweet Savior protect us; guard and preserve this woman," Sarah muttered. "Sweet Lord, be with us here—" She took a deep breath. "Clare? Clare, my dear? Are you all right?" Her voice was barely audible.

If only Isobel had gone with him. If only . . .

* * *

The voice was fainter now, farther away. Clare looked around wildly. "Aunt Margaret?" she called. "Aunt Margaret? Where are you? Come back! Please!" Suddenly she was sobbing.

Sarah could feel a cold draft playing up and down her spine. She clutched her Bible to her, gazing into the shadows. "What was it?" She gasped. "Who was it?"

Clare shook her head. "She's right," she whispered. "She shouldn't have left him. If he had let them stay together she would have been safe. . . ."

Sarah looked around again wildly. The room was very cold. It was nearly half past three in the morning.

She didn't know what had made her get up, put on her dressing gown, and pad along in the dark, by the light of her small flashlight, to the tower. Cautiously she had unlocked Clare's door, and after listening for several minutes on the staircase outside, she had pushed it open. The room had been silent, and she peered in, expecting to see Clare in bed asleep. Finding her kneeling in the middle of the floor in the light of the single lamp filled Sarah with fear, but she had forced herself to go into the room, her hand firmly on the Bible in her dressing-gown pocket. The moonlight was bright beyond the curtains, illuminating the square of the window. Outside, the garden was as bright as day. On the hills in the distance there was a sprinkling of snow.

Clare's eyes were closed, but she was kneeling upright, and Sarah could see her eyes behind her eyelids moving rapidly from side to side. Her breath was coming in short tight gasps, her skin pale and slightly damp in the lamplight. Sarah was very frightened. She didn't dare wake her, and she didn't dare leave her, so, forcing herself to sit down in the chair, she had begun to pray. She felt inadequate; unable to cope with the situation. Her mind had blanked, suggesting nothing but the one repeated prayer. She wanted to make some sign, whisper some formula that would release Clare from her suffering, but no words would come. All she could do was clutch her Bible to her own heart, which was suddenly full of pity as well as fear, and recite again and again and again the words she had learned at her mother's knee.

Cautiously she touched Clare's shoulder. "It's all right. You're safe now," she whispered hesitantly. On impulse she put her arms around Clare and hugged her. "You're safe now," she repeated. "She's gone."

Clare's body was ice cold; she was trembling violently. For a moment she clung to Sarah, then she collapsed onto the chair that Sarah had vacated. "Oh, God help me!" she whispered. "I'm so afraid." She could still feel the misery and fear in the room like a real presence. "Did you hear her? Did you hear Aunt Margaret?"

Sarah shrugged. She didn't know what to say. Had the words just been in her head or had they rung out in the room? Now she wasn't sure. She crouched down beside Clare and took her hands, chafing them gently in her own. "God will help you, my dear. I know He will."

"She appeared to Aunt Margaret too, you know." Clare went on so quietly Sarah could hardly hear the words. "It's not just me. I'm not going mad—"

"Of course you're not." Sarah clasped her hands tighter. "No one thinks you're going mad—"

"Paul does."

Sarah shook her head. "Not in his heart," she said, suddenly realizing it was the truth. "He doesn't really believe it for one moment." She raised Clare's hand to her cheek and held it there for a moment. It was a strangely maternal gesture. "Clare, my dear, you must get away from here. I've been as bad as the rest of them, believing it was best for your own good to force you into some sort of confrontation, but this is all centered here, where your aunt lived." She shuddered. "To keep you here is foolish."

"Then you'll help me get away?" Clare's face had focused abruptly. She sat forward eagerly. "I have to get out of here, I have to! I must get hold of a car somehow—"

Sarah nodded slowly. She acknowledged for the first time her increasing unease about Paul's behavior. "Your mother has asked me to drive into Perth for her one day this week, and she is going to lend me her car. Somehow I'll arrange it so you can take it, while your father and your brother are out on the hill. I promise, I will help you. . . ."

Emma was standing in front of the desk in her gallery on Kew Green, her face red with fury. "Yes, I talked him out of buying Duncairn. And why not? I care about Clare. She's my friend and I am not going to stand by and watch you destroy her. I don't know why you are making such a fuss. We've bought your shares, haven't we? You're off the hook in the City?"

"You betrayed me." Paul was white with anger. "You betrayed me to that man Cummin. You! My own sister!"

"What I did, I did for Clare!"

"Are you having an affair with him?" Paul was studying her face.

Emma froze. She had gone very pale. "No," she said bleakly. "No, I'm not. I love my husband."

"You tramp!" There was a sneer on Paul's face as he looked up at her. "He'll find out, you know. Peter will find out! People talk in the City."

"There is nothing to talk about, Paul!" Emma glared at him. She was shivering suddenly in spite of the warmth of the room.

"I've some news for you, Emma. I don't like being outsmarted by you or anyone else, and I don't intend to be made a public laughingstock. I am going ahead with the sale anyway. Duncairn is still going to Sigma—behind Cummin's back." He lifted his briefcase onto her desk and, opening it, took out a manila envelope. Inside were three sets of papers. He passed one across the desk. "Look."

Emma looked down. The document was notarized and witnessed. It gave Paul power of attorney over Clare's affairs and made over to him unconditionally all her property in Scotland, giving him specific permission to sell it as and when he saw fit. At the bottom of each page was Clare's signature.

Emma stared at it. Then she looked up at her brother, shocked. "I don't believe it. She wouldn't! Clare wouldn't do it. What have you done to her?"

He took the paper back and slid it into his case, then he

laughed out loud. "Nothing. Nothing that needed Clare's presence. All that took was a good eye and a steady hand."

"You forged her signature?" Emma was speechless for a second. "You can't!"

"I already have." Paul smiled. "It fooled you, and it fooled our bank manager. I showed it to him this morning."

Emma gasped at his conceit and complacency in telling her. "You won't get away with it. I shan't let you. I'll tell everyone—"

He laughed coldly. "You would too, you little bitch. Let me tell you something, Emma. If ever I do use this, you will keep quiet about it, do you hear me? If you are as fond of Clare as you claim, you will keep very, very quiet about it."

"Why? What would you do if I didn't?" She looked him in the eye angrily.

"I could make life very unpleasant for Clare. It is not pleasant being insane; being locked away in some asylum—and that is where she will end up if I don't get your and her cooperation. I am going to give her the chance to help me voluntarily. One more chance, that's all. If she doesn't I shall use this." He tapped the lid of his briefcase. "If Clare denies signing it, Geoffrey and our family doctor are going to have her committed." He smiled triumphantly. "My wife is insane, Emma, however much you might like to deny it to yourself. At times she is lucid, I fully acknowledge that—she was, for instance, when she signed these." He smiled again. "Alas, her periods of sanity are growing shorter and shorter." He was watching his sister's face closely, "I intend going north to Airdlie tomorrow or the next day. I shall bring her back to Bucksters, and then Geoffrey is going to spend some time with her. He is actually planning on doing an exorcism!" He contained his laughter with difficulty. "Once he has signed the correct documents we are going to keep her somewhere quiet and safe until all the excitement over Duncairn is forgotten. I shan't be cruel. Once it is all over, I shall bother her no more. She can divorce me if she wants. I shan't care. Our marriage is a childless farce in any case. But if she makes a fuss and denies signing anything, she is going to find herself in a padded cell. And we both know how much she would hate being locked up."

Emma was white to the lips. "You are the one who is insane, Paul!"

He shook his head. "I don't think so."

"You are! None of this will work! None of it." She leaned toward him, her hands on the desk. "Paul, you have got to give up. You don't need the money! You don't need Duncairn!"

"Oh, but I do. Besides, it is better for Clare to be rid of it. It is Duncairn that is haunting her." For a second his voice was sincere.

Emma shook her head. "Paul. No. I can't let you do this. I can't!"

"Don't try to stop me, Emma." Paul walked around the desk and caught her arm. "The only one who will get hurt if you do is Clare. And Peter, of course. Think how upset he would be if he found out that you were having an affair."

Emma waited until he had left the gallery, then she grabbed the phone. Her hands were shaking. She had to warn Clare what Paul was up to and that he was on his way back.

At Airdlie, Antonia answered the phone.

"This is Emma Cassidy. How is Clare?"

In the drafty hall Antonia glanced up the stairs. Clare was still in her room. "She's all right, thank you, Emma. She's very well. Enjoying her holiday. Her brother is here too, you know."

"Is he?" Emma paused. She hadn't realized that James was in Scotland. "Could I speak to Clare, please, if it's not too much trouble?"

"I'm sorry, my dear. Clare is out today." Antonia bit her lip. It made her hot and uncomfortable when she lied.

"Oh, I see." Emma was clearly taken aback. "Then please, could you ask her to call me as soon as she gets back. It's very, very important."

"Of course." Antonia grimaced as she put down the phone. She had always disliked Emma. The girl was wild and unprincipled. She had been a bad influence on Clare at school, always getting her into trouble, and nothing appeared to have changed now that she was an adult. There was no way she was going to let Clare talk to her if she could help it.

That evening while Sarah was helping Antonia in the kitchen, Clare managed to reach the phone. James and her stepfather were in the gun room. The dogs were sprawled in front of the drawing-room fire. She picked up the receiver carefully so it shouldn't make a noise and dialed.

"Zak? Oh, thank God!" She was almost sobbing with relief. "I thought you might be in the States still. I need to see you. Please, you're the only person who can help me."

"Clare. Where are you? What's happened?" Zak frowned, knowing his own voice sounded reluctant, hearing the fear in hers.

"I'm in Scotland. I'll be in Edinburgh by the end of the week. Please, Zak. I know it's a lot to ask, but can you come there? I'll pay your train fare, anything. Look, contact me at—" She racked her brains for a moment. "At Earthwatch. They are somewhere in the Grassmarket. Please, Zak. Don't let me down."

She didn't wait for him to reply. Gently she tipped the receiver back into its cradle. It fell back silently and she breathed again.

Clare flung on her clothes, threw a few things into her big shoulder bag, and grabbed the coat Sarah pushed at her. "Bless you, Sarah."

She was barely outside the gate when she realized the gas gauge was nearly at zero. She drove straight to the garage and waited, trying to hide her impatience as the car was filled, listening to the friendly chatter of the pump attendant. He had known her and her family for years.

Tell him you are going north. Tell him you're going to Duncairn. Put them off the trail.

"Where's the dog, then? I thought you two were insepara-ble!" he said as she fumbled in her purse for her credit card. He took it from her and headed toward his office. The comment, thrown casually, nearly threw her. She was missing

Casta desperately. "She's on the hill with my father, being a real gun dog," she managed to reply. "She's on holiday, like me!" She waited in an increasing agony of impatience as he hunted for his slide machine below the counter. At last he found it. "Well, you have enough gas to get you halfway across Scotland now." He grinned at her as he handed her card back with the credit slip. It was a question.

"I'm going over to Duncairn," she said firmly. "I'll be staying at the hotel for a few weeks, I expect. . . ."

But the road she took led south toward Perth. From there she took the M90 toward Edinburgh and now she was thinking only about Zak. Please let him be there, and let him find a way of helping. Otherwise she didn't know what she was going to do. . . .

She found a parking place in the Grassmarket quite easily. For a long time she sat there at the wheel of the car, staring up at the castle silhouetted against a black and threatening sky. She was shaking with exhaustion as the succession of sleepless nights caught up with her and suffering from the tension of her escape and the fast, nervous drive down from Dunkeld. Now the anticlimax hit her. She had arrived in Edinburgh. No one knew where she was. She was safe. And she wasn't sure what to do next.

She must try to find the office of Earthwatch to see if Zak had made contact.

She found it fairly easily. Neil Forbes was seated alone in the office, poring over a desk full of papers. For a moment he stared at her blankly, then he rose to his feet. "Mrs. Royland?" he said in disbelief. "This is an unexpected pleasure!" His voice was cold.

Hurt and angry at his tone, she launched straight into her counterattack, her anger and resentment of him returning with full force. "Why did you call a meeting at Duncairn without telling me? And why did you tell the papers all those lies about me?"

"If they were lies, which I beg to doubt, your husband fielded them skillfully enough!" He did not smile. He came around the desk and leaning against it, folded his arms. "So, Mrs. Royland, why have you come here?"

She gritted her teeth. "I gave this address to a friend as a place to find me. Zak de Sallis. Has he been here?" She could not hide her anxiety.

Neil raised an eyebrow. "No, he hasn't been here, and I would prefer it if you did not use this place as either a mail drop or a rendezvous for your lovers, Mrs. Royland."

"He's not my lover!" Clare replied hotly.

"Of course, I had forgotten. You are now fully reconciled with your husband."

"I have left my husband." Clare looked him straight in the eye. "I should be grateful if you would inform the press of my exact position over Duncairn, Mr. Forbes. I am the sole owner of the property. I, not Paul, and I do not intend to sell it! We did not at any time query my great-aunt's will, and I was delighted with my share of the bequest. You may also tell whatever branch of the newspapers that may be interested that I wholeheartedly support the Earthwatch campaign and that I shall be helping you if I can be of any use. And, for the record, I shall be seeking a divorce from my husband."

Neil whistled. "That sounds like a declaration of war!"

Clare gave a tight smile. "I think that is what it is." She sat down abruptly on the chair by the door. "Will you help me?" She couldn't hide the slight tremor in her voice.

Neil's gaze was fixed thoughtfully on her face. Without any makeup her pale skin had a translucent quality he found very appealing. "In what way?" he said cautiously.

"I think Paul will try to find me again."

"What if he does? He can't force you to go with him."

"He did last time." She looked away from his face, then quietly she told him what had happened at Duncairn.

Neil listened in silence, his face darkening. "Where are you staying in Edinburgh?"

She shrugged. "I wanted to avoid the hotels. That's the first place he'll look for me. I don't want to stay with friends either, for the same reason. I thought perhaps I'd try a bed and breakfast."

"There is always my place." He had said it without thinking, then he realized that he meant it. Why not?

"But your friend might object." Clare too spoke without first thinking that her words implied acceptance.

Neil shook his head. "Kath is going off to a gig in London for the weekend." He pushed himself to his feet. "I tell you what. We'll go over there now and get my spare key for you. Then we'll go out for dinner later and draft a statement for the press tomorrow. How does that sound?"

His apartment intrigued her; the rooftop views, the evidence of music and books everywhere, the untidiness, the well-equipped but shabby, ill-stocked kitchen. It was very obviously a man's apartment. There were few signs of Kathleen there. There was also no evidence of a spare room.

Neil pushed open the door to the bedroom. "You can sleep in here. I'll sleep on the sofa."

Clare frowned. "I'm putting you to an awful lot of trouble."

"Not at all. Hang on. I'll find you some clean sheets." He smiled. "Paul won't ever find you here."

She returned the smile uncomfortably. "No, I don't suppose he will."

"How did you get to Edinburgh?" His voice was gentle.

"I stole my parents' car."

"And where is it now?"

"Outside your office, on a meter."

Neil glanced heavenward. "Bloody hell, woman! Anyone can see you're no good at being devious. I tell you what. We'll dump it somewhere tonight, then you can put the keys in the mail to your parents. As long as you keep it, they can locate you through the police."

"The police!" Her face went white.

"If they really want to find you, all they have to do is report it stolen."

Clare bit her lip. Abruptly she sat down on the end of the bed. "Oh, God! What am I going to do?"

He sat down beside her. "You are serious about leaving Paul? Absolutely sure?"

She nodded.

"There will be no going back once we go into print."

"I am sure."

"Okay. I had to check." He turned to her and, putting his hands on her shoulders, gave her a little shake. "Why did you ever marry the bastard?"

"I don't know." Her eyes flooded with tears and she looked away from him, embarrassed, desperately groping in her pocket for a handkerchief. "I thought I loved him, I suppose—"

"But you didn't?"

She shook her head mutely.

"And now you love someone else?"

Again she shook her head.

"Then what opened your eyes?"

"Seeing what it is like to be really in love, and seeing what he's prepared to do to me. He's never loved me. Not for a single moment."

"Seeing what it's like to be in love?" He frowned. "You mean someone you know is in love?"

She bit her lip, and slowly she nodded. "Yes. Someone I know is in love."

Someone whose feelings she could share and watch and feel as if they were her own.

She looked up at him wearily. "I'm afraid of Paul." The words were out before she could stop them.

Neil swore under his breath. Impulsively he pulled her to him, his arm around her shoulders. "There's no need to be anymore. With a bit of luck you need never see the bastard again!"

Her face, wet with tears, was close to his. He could smell her perfume—the perfume he remembered from Duncairn, the smell of the cool fragrance on her hair and her skin.

Suddenly he realized how much he wanted her; how much he had wanted her since the first moment he had set eyes on her. Slowly he leaned toward her and kissed her on the mouth. She didn't move. She sat absolutely still, every muscle taut, her eyes closed as if she were terrified even to breathe. He frowned, then gently he tried again, this time putting his arms around her properly, drawing her close to him. Her mouth opened almost unwillingly beneath his, but still she didn't struggle, nor did she try to push him away as he eased her gently back onto the bed. He kissed her face exploratively, gently probing, touching her eyelids and nose with his lips and tongue, running his fingers through her hair and down the line of her neck. Then slowly he began to fumble with the zipper of her dress.

She lay still, not daring to move, her emotions in complete conflict. Half of her wanted to run, the other half wanted him to hold her, to make love to her, to make her feel wanted and alive. She felt him ease the straps of her bra off her shoulders, then his hands were on her breasts and she gasped as a knife-edged flicker of excitement shot through her.

"I think we've been promising ourselves this for a long time," he murmured. He ducked his head to let his lips find her nipples.

She opened her eyes as he sought out her mouth again, and suddenly she found herself clinging to him. She dug her nails into his shoulders, pulling him against her, thrusting her hips toward his, for the first time in her life driven by a strange, blind, frantic desire. She forgot where she was; she forgot who she was; she forgot she hardly knew this man and that for the time she had known him she had disliked him intensely. All she knew was that she wanted him as she had never wanted anything or anyone in her life before.

It was over as quickly as it had started. Clare turned away from him, drawing her knees up toward her stomach defensively. She was shaking like a leaf.

"Hey, what's the matter? It was good, wasn't it?" Neil said.

She nodded miserably.

"So, why are you crying?"

"I don't know." Slowly she dragged herself upright. "Where's the bathroom?"

Neil was sitting at the kitchen table when she came out at last. He had opened a bottle of wine. He pushed a glass toward her. "Beaujolais nouveau," he said. "You won't get vintage anything in this house. If you give me your car keys I know someone who is going across to Glasgow tonight. He'll drive your parents' car across and leave it near Queen Street

Station. With bit of luck that will put them off the scent. They'll think you've gone somewhere by train."

Clare sat down and picked up the glass. "Thank you." Her voice was flat. "Do you want me to find somewhere else to stay?"

He shrugged. "It's up to you."

"I'd like to stay here." She was terrified suddenly of being alone.

"Stay here then, but don't expect bloody kid gloves."

She gave a watery smile. "I won't."

"You still want me to put out a statement to the press?"

She nodded. "Nothing's changed."

"No?" He looked at her closely. Then he stood up. "No, perhaps you're right. Nothing has changed." He picked up his jacket from the back of the chair. "Right. I'll take your car over to Patrick right now. You might as well stay here and tidy up. Make up the bed for yourself." The slightest inflection on the word yourself told her exactly where she stood and she colored slightly. "I'll be back later," he went on. "Then we can go up the road for a tandoori."

He was holding out his hand for the keys as Clare fumbled in the pocket of her coat when the front door of the apartment opened. Kathleen stood staring at them for a full twenty seconds before she stepped inside and slammed it behind her.

"So," she said. "Bloody Neil Forbes! I tell you I'm going to be away a couple of nights and you can't wait, can you, you lousy shit!" The cards had warned her: the tower. Twice— and then again the priestess—the woman with the psychic eyes.

Kathleen stood staring at them, her hands in the pockets of her heavy camel coat.

"Kath—" Neil's tone was warning.

"Kath—" She echoed, mocking. "Oh, Kath, you're not going to make a fuss, Kath! You would never have known, Kath! Don't be a spoilsport, Kath . . . !" She walked over to the bedroom door and stared in. The bed was still rumpled where they had lain; the clean blue bed sheets had fallen, still folded, to the floor.

Neil put on his jacket. "If you don't like it, you know what you can do." He pulled open the front door. "I'll see you later." His tone was as bored and curt as when he had addressed Clare.

"Neil—" Clare suddenly realized he was going to leave her alone with Kathleen—but already the door had banged behind him and they could hear his footsteps running down the long flights of worn stone steps to the windswept Canongate below.

Kathleen gave a cold smile. "Typical man! Running out on the mess," she said. "Are you planning on moving in, because if you are, don't bother. I'll get him back."

Clare sat down at the table. She snatched up her glass. "I'm only staying a couple of days, until I find somewhere else." Her hands were shaking again.

Kathleen looked down at her coldly. "You'd better make that someone else as well."

"There's nothing between us." Clare couldn't look at her.

"No?" Kathleen gave a sneering laugh. "Do you think I don't know when two people have been screwing? It's written all over your faces."

Clare blushed. "It . . . it didn't mean anything."

"No!" Kathleen's face was hard. "I don't suppose it did! Well, keep it that way. Quite a triumph for Neil, to lay someone like you, considering how much he loathes you." She walked over to the desk, pulled open a drawer, and took out an envelope. In it was her train ticket, the reason she had to come back to the apartment before walking down to Waverley. She pushed it into the pocket of her skirt. "I'll be back on Monday," she said. "Enjoy him while you've got him."

Clare stared at the door for a long time after Kathleen had left, then slowly she walked back into the bedroom. She felt sick and degraded. She stood staring down at the bed. She had never slept with anyone but Paul before. What had possessed her to do such a thing? Neil had made no secret that he despised what she stood for; he had promised her nothing. He was probably at this moment crowing over his victory with his friends in a pub somewhere. . . . And yet he had given her something. His hands on her body had released something she had never known she possessed. She had felt passion and hunger for a man for the first time in her life. Her lovemaking with Paul had been a shadow of this. She sat down on the bed and put her hand on the rumpled sheets where Neil had lain, slowly becoming aware of the fact that her body was still glowing and satisfied, awakened for the first time in her life. This was how it had been for Isobel. This was the feeling that she had been willing to throw away everything for—that and love. She frowned. Neil had asked her if she had ever loved Paul. She had never loved anyone at all. Not as Isobel had loved Robert. . . .

When Neil returned she was still there, lying on the bed, her eyes closed, her arm across her face.

He stood looking down at her. "Are you all right?"

She nodded silently.

"Your car is on its way to Glasgow, and the keys will be mailed back to your mother from there."

"Thank you." She felt the bed sag as he sat down next to her. He pulled her arm away from her face. "I take it you sent Kath on her way?"

Clare turned away from him. "She left, but not without having the last word."

"That sounds like Kathleen." He laughed quietly. "So, did you manage to stand up for yourself?"

Slowly she sat up. "You make it sound like some sort of test."

"Maybe." He folded his arms, looking at her hard. "Every time I've seen you, you've been running away from something. Even that first time at Duncairn. I don't know what from, but you were running then, and then that time in Suffolk, I could see it in your eyes, and again at the hotel the other day. And it's not just Paul Royland you're running away from, is it?"

She swung her legs to the floor and sat there, hugging her arms around herself miserably. "I don't know who else it would be."

"Yourself, perhaps. Can I give you a piece of advice? Trite, perhaps, but I think good advice, nevertheless. If you stop running from yourself, you'd find you didn't have to run away from other people anymore. I don't think the real you is a passive victim of circumstance. I think she's a fighter. And I think she took the first step in that fight right here on this bed." His face was very serious, then suddenly he grinned. "End of lecture. Are you hungry?"

She nodded with a faint smile. "Neil." It was the first time she had called him by his first name. "Will you answer one question?"

"What?"

"Do you loathe and despise me?"

"That's two questions."

"No. Be serious. I want to know."

"No and no. Satisfied?"

"I don't believe you."

"Then why ask? Come on, let's go and get something to eat. We have a manifesto to draw up, remember? The Clare Royland unilateral declaration of independence. Don't worry about what other people are thinking about you, Clare. The important thing is to know what you think about yourself."

Zak walked slowly up the Grassmarket, staring around him. He had never been to Edinburgh before and the sheer rugged beauty of the place had taken his breath away. So few cities lived up to their postcard images, but this one did. The presence of that great brooding castle on its rock, hanging over the city; the sense of history echoing from every wall of every street. He glanced down at the piece of paper in his hand. Earthwatch. It sounded good.

He found the office in the end, right beneath the soaring walls of the castle. It was closed. He tried the door twice, then with a shrug he walked away. He'd have to find himself somewhere to stay, then try again in the morning.

He began to climb the steps up Castle Wynd toward the esplanade. The place was getting under his skin. Edinburgh. Scotland. Suddenly he was beginning to understand Clare better. The echoes were everywhere; for a sensitive they would be overwhelming. And he had unlocked that sensitivity for her. Before he had come along she had had her dreams and her nightmares and her phobias, but now, now the thin skin that separated past from present had somehow been breached and she was standing right in the way of the flood of memories that was pouring through the hole. That was why he had to come. Not because he could help her, but because he felt somehow to blame.

That evening after Neil said good night, Clare went alone to his bedroom. She went over to the window, and drew back the curtains. Silently she pulled up the bottom half of the window and leaned on the sill with her elbows, feeling the icy wind touch her hot skin. She could smell the bitter salt of the Forth and, beyond it, carried on the wind, the chill of ice from the distant hills. Shuddering, she closed the window and crawled into the bed. She was very, very tired and she forgot to be afraid.

This time the nightmare was slightly different. There was a rime of frost on the bars, and the faces behind the eyes were muffled against the cold. She could feel the ache of it through her bones, dulling the terror, cocooning the despair as she huddled back into the shadows, seeing the snowflakes drift toward her through the bars.

Neil heard her sobbing as he sat writing late at the kitchen table. For a while he sat there frowning, then at last he stood up and cautiously opened the bedroom door. He turned on a lamp and stood looking down at her. She was asleep, the tears running down her face and into the pillow as she turned restlessly from side to side, her face contorted with fear. He sat down on the edge of the bed and was reaching out to take her hand when she began to scream.

Chapter Twenty-seven

"But he has managed to pay every penny of the debt!" Henry leaned forward in his chair in his anxiety. It was settlement day: November 21.

Behind the huge partners' desk Sir Duncan Beattie shook his head sadly. "I know, old chap, I know, but it's out of my hands. I did what I could, but Paul has been a fool." He tightened his lips. "He should have known better. He dealt on insider information and everyone in the City seems to know about it, and now the Department of Trade and Industry inspectors has asked for my cooperation over an inquiry." He stood up and paced up and down the floor a couple of times. "We have to think of BCWP. If we try to protect him, we implicate ourselves. Caroway at MSP is already involved." He shook his head sadly. "I'm not allowing Paul to come back, Henry. I'm going to ask for his resignation."

"No!" Henry was white. "You can't do that. It will crucify him!"

"I can and I will." Sir Duncan sat down again slowly. He suddenly felt very old. He and Paul's father had known each other for over thirty years, and he had always been very fond of the three Royland boys. They had done so well for themselves—David and Geoffrey—Geoffrey a slow starter, but now firmly in line for preferment, according to a friend of his at the club who was a colleague of Geoffrey's bishop. And now this! He sighed. "I know you're fond of Clare and Paul, Henry, and I know this is going to be hard for you, but I want you to avoid them for a bit. The less contact there is between members of the board and Paul as long as the investigation is going on, the better."

"Have the police been called in?" Henry could barely put the question into words.

Sir Duncan nodded. "I gather a preliminary report has been sent to the fraud squad."

"Hell!" Henry banged the palms of his hands together in anguish. "Is there nothing we can do?"

"Nothing," Sir Duncan said firmly. "I do not want BCWP involved. The firm's entire reputation is at stake, and I am not going to take the chance. Not for one man."

"What about plea bargaining? It's been done before."

Sir Duncan smiled wearily. "You have to have something to bargain with, Henry. You find something, and I'll see the information gets to the right quarter, but I can't think of anything Paul has done that would be usable, can you?"

Henry thought too. If Paul had ever given large sums to charity he had certainly never broadcast the fact, and being Paul he would have seen to it that everyone would have known if he had done anything like that. No, privately he thought it unlikely that Paul had done anything that would tell in his favor. Clare did a lot for charity, but enough to help Paul now? You needed to have given millions for it to carry any weight.

He was still thoughtful when he walked back down to his office. He could call Clare and ask her, of course. It would be a legitimate reason for contacting her behind Paul's back and making sure she was all right. And he did have the Airdlie number. Perhaps he could even go up there and see her. . . .

"I don't know where she is. I'm sorry." Antonia's voice was firm. "She's not staying here anymore."

"Not staying there?" Henry frowned. "But I have to find her. If you could tell me where—"

"I'm sorry." Antonia put the phone down and looked at Sarah. "That was one of Paul's colleagues. Paul doesn't believe me that she's gone! He has asked someone else to call and check!"

Sarah raised an eyebrow. "Perhaps he thought we were so cowed by his threats we would find her and drag her back!" she said tartly. Now that she had found an ally in Clare's mother, she felt far braver about Paul. She had confided in

Antonia in the end about her role in Clare's escape, and both women had been vastly relieved to find they had someone they could talk to; someone who understood their doubts. They had spent a long time huddled together trying to decide what to tell Archie when he finally came home.

In spite of all their mutual confidences, however, there was one thing Antonia had not told Sarah, even now. She had said nothing to anyone about the crucifix she had found wrapped in one of Archie's silk scarves, pushed to the back of the sideboard in the dining room.

When Archie and James reappeared that evening, James had cheered at the news that Clare had gone.

"You realize she has probably gone straight to this man de Sallis! How did she escape?" Archie looked from one woman to the other furiously. "How?"

"It was one of those things, dear. This isn't a prison. We couldn't have kept her here forever," Antonia said firmly.

"Especially since there is nothing wrong with her," James said. "Nothing at all."

"Except that now she has shown herself to be a common thief as well as everything else," Archie said acidly. "It seems to have slipped your attention that we are all trapped here without a car now." He was so angry that he began to sputter.

James glanced at his mother. He had been the angriest when he discovered that Paul had taken the keys of the green Jaguar back to London with him, but now the situation struck him as rather humorous. Antonia was staring down at the carpet, and for a second James thought he detected a quiver at the corner of her mouth. She looked up and caught his eye. "I told you it was a pity you didn't bring your Porsche, James," she said slowly, and to his amazement she winked.

He cornered her on her own in the kitchen later. "Why do you put up with him, Mother?"

"He's my husband, James."

James looked heavenward. "More fool you. He doesn't really believe all this about Clare?"

"A lot of it is true, dear." She sat down and put her elbows on the kitchen table. "The nightmares, the daydreams—she's always had them. Margaret warned me so often that this might happen one day. She fought it herself, right up to the end, you know. . . ." Her voice trailed away.

James stared at her. "She saw Isobel as well?"

"Oh, yes. I'm sure she did."

"Then it's not just Clare! Have you told Clare this?"

"Clare must know, darling. She and Margaret used to talk on their own for hours—I always wondered if your father ever saw her too, or whether it's just the women in the family. . . ." She smiled at James anxiously. "She's never appeared to you, dear, has she?"

James paled slightly. "Never!" He shuddered.

"No." His mother shook her head. "I didn't think she had. I think it's the women she talks to . . . pleads with. . . ." She shook her head again. "Poor Clare. I want to help her, but I don't know how!"

When Clare awoke the next morning, Neil had gone. He had lain beside her, comforting her, holding her close, soothing away the dream until they had both fallen asleep. For the first time in a long time she had slept well, secure in the knowledge that he would be there when she awoke. But he wasn't. She found a note on the kitchen table.

> Wander down to the office when you feel like it and we'll have lunch. By the time you get here the die will be cast and I will have contacted the papers. N.

She smiled. Her die had been cast long since, had he but known it.

She made herself some coffee, then, after a moment's hesitation, she picked up the phone. Silently she crossed her fingers. If her father or Paul answered she would hang up. Her luck was in. James picked up the receiver in the kitchen, a piece of toast in his hand.

"James? Listen, can you talk?"

"If you mean am I alone, yes. Our aged, neurotic parents aren't up yet, and Mrs. C is also still abed. Your great escape has exhausted them all." He chuckled. "Great going, Sis. Where are you?"

"Is Paul there yet?"

"No. I gather he decided not to come until you had been rounded up. He's furious with Archie and has told him to find you or else."

Clare smiled grimly. "James, will you do something for me?"

"Anything within reason. You know me. Moderation in all things."

"I want my car and I want Casta."

"I see. Nothing much. Grand larceny and kidnapping."

In spite of herself she laughed. "Please, James. If you can't find the key there is a spare in the pocket of my blue suitcase. I'll meet you—" She hesitated, not wanting suddenly to tell him where she was.

"In Edinburgh," James put in quickly. "I don't want to know where you are, in case Paul uses thumbscrews on me, but I'm booked on a flight back to Heathrow tomorrow tea-time, so if you can find your way to Turnhouse, I'll bring your mislaid possessions with me and then leave the country before Archie realizes what I've done." He laughed. "What the hell have you done with the parents' car? They're going bonkers over it. They think you've given it to your guru to join his fleet of Rollses!"

"Oh, God!" Clare's disgust was clearly audible over the phone. "If they had only met Zak they would realize how stupid all this is. He isn't a guru. He's an academic. He hasn't got even one car, for God's sake!"

"Then where is the parental Volvo? You'd better tell me."

"It's quite safe." Clare crossed her fingers. "And the keys are in the mail to them right now."

"Thank God! If there's one scratch on it Archie will go mad. You know what he's like. So, how is freedom?"

Clare smiled. "Not bad," she said quietly. "Not bad at all."

They had a cup of coffee downstairs in the airport coffee lounge. James looked at her closely. "You look better. Not so haunted."

Clare smiled. "I am better. I'm free."

"Of the ghosts as well?"

She shrugged. She hadn't had the nightmare again. Neil hadn't mentioned it and so she had said nothing either; last night he had not made a move to sleep with her again. She had gone to bed alone, and she had slept dreamlessly and heavily, only awaking at eleven o'clock this morning to find once again that Neil had been out of the apartment for hours. About Isobel she was more cautious. It was as though a shutter had come down across her mind—a shutter she had learned to hold in place herself, which had been reinforced by the fact that every moment she had been awake and down at the Earthwatch office Neil had made her work.

"What do you mean, you've never worked?" Neil had stared at her in astonishment.

"I mean I've never had a job. I met my husband when I was still at school," she said defensively. "We married as soon as I left."

"Dear God!" For a long time Neil had stared at her, then he had set her to work at every office job he could think of. She had loved it.

James sat sideways and put his arm along the back of the seat. "One or two pieces of news you might like. I gather your sister-in-law has had her baby."

Clare closed her eyes, not expecting the pang of misery that ran through her. "Oh," she said. She made a great effort and smiled at her brother. "So, what is it?"

"A boy, I understand. A brother for Ilona, Steven, and Hal, this one to be called Marcus!" He leaned forward and touched her hand, suddenly seeing her pain and cursing himself silently. "Sorry. It was tactless to tell you."

"Don't be silly. The rest of the world isn't going to stop having babies just because I can't have them." Unconsciously she rested her hand for a moment on her slim, taut stomach.

The London flight had arrived just before Clare had entered the airport terminal building. She had not noticed Kathleen swathed in a black embroidered shawl, making her way toward the taxis, her suitcase in one hand, her guitar in the other, but Kathleen saw her and stiffened. Abandoning the row of taxis, she turned and followed Clare back into the building with a smile of triumph. So, the bitch was flying back to London.

Cautiously she followed Clare through the crowded passengers. Clare had not gone toward the check-in counters, however, but had turned instead toward the coffee lounge, and there a few minutes later she met a tall, handsome young man, very much Clare's type. Kathleen's eyes narrowed. Carefully she made her way closer, hoping the crowds would hide her, but the couple had eyes only for each other and never once looked around. They bought coffees and sat down, very close together. Two steps closer, and she would be able to hear what they were saying.

James had just lighted a cigarette. He blew the smoke into the air. "I don't see how Paul will ever find you if you keep your head down. If necessary you can take to the heather in time-honored fashion!"

Clare laughed. "That's strictly for the summer, I think. I'm a lot more comfortable than that."

"Really?" He eyed her closely.

"Really. I should have left Paul a long time ago." She touched his hand. "I hope all this doesn't make things awkward for you at the office."

"Nothing I can't cope with." James hesitated. "I don't know if you care, but he managed to pay off his debts in time. Geoff and David bought out his holding of the family shares and he was able to pay up on Friday."

Clare closed her eyes. "Thank God. That means he'll leave Duncairn alone now, and me." She opened her eyes and looked at him. "He'll have no reason to go on with this charade, James!"

"Let's hope not." James frowned. "Look, keep away from Airdlie for a while even so, Sis. He is still issuing orders to have you recaptured." He glanced up as the loudspeaker began announcing the London-bound flight and he stabbed out his cigarette. "Keep in touch, Clare. Call me, won't you, and call mother from time to time, just to let us all know you're okay. Mum's on your side really, you know, it's just that she's so dominated by the boor she's married to. Take care of yourself."

"I will." She flung her arms around his neck. "James, thank you!"

Embarrassed, he pushed her away. "Don't be silly, Sis. Look, here's the keys of your car. Casta will be going crazy waiting out there. I managed to grab your suitcase and shove as much as I could into it. I don't think anyone will miss things. I told them I was driving back to London and taking Casta and the Jag to Paul. I don't think they believed it, but they didn't say anything."

Clare scowled. "Is Mrs. C. still there?"

James nodded. "She's terrified of what Paul is going to do when he gets his hands on her and expecting to be fired, but for two pins the parents would keep her, you know. She gets on rather well with Mother. Must go." He raised his hand.

She sat for a few minutes after he had gone, then she got up and walked outside.

Kathleen was standing in the cold blustery wind, waiting for a taxi when the green Jaguar swept past. She smiled. It had taken directory inquiries only one minute to give her Paul's London number, and it had taken her only two more to give him Neil's address.

"My God, you have to be fit to live in Edinburgh!" Zak was panting as she let him into the apartment that evening. "It's nothing but stairs and stairs and more stairs, inside and out! Where else on earth would you find a sixth-floor walk-up?"

"I have to get rid of her, Zak. I have to stop Isobel's haunting me. I can't go on like this. She will drive me out of my mind. Every time she returns and the story goes on unraveling in my head, I am more and more afraid that I shan't be able to stop. That I will get stuck in her world. I can't wake myself up. Each time it has gone on and on until something from outside has interrupted her. Your protecting oil was no use. It didn't work!"

"So, you think it is a haunting?" He crossed his long legs uncomfortably.

She nodded slowly. "She comes from outside me, Zak. I'm not making her up. And I have to get rid of her!"

"And just saying that to yourself is not enough?"

She shook her head. "Even here, I find I'm afraid of her. I'm terrified she's going to come back. Oh, Zak! What am I going to do? It's as I imagine epilepsy or something like that must be: a sudden change in perception, a sudden sharpening of colors, a sudden shrinking back of this world and then that other world is there and I can't stop it; I am forced to watch; I'm trapped, until something or someone releases me."

Zak looked down at his hands. "You told me your brother-in-law was a clergyman, Clare. I think maybe you should talk to him after all."

She stared at him. "You're not serious!"

He nodded. "I've thought about you and your Isobel a lot. I wanted her to be a thought form because then I would be taking credit for her in a perverse way—thinking I had taught you so well that your visualization was strong enough to create her, but that's not it, I can see that now. She's always been with you in one way or another, hasn't she? She is a spirit, feeding on your psyche, possessing you." He paused and, seeing the fear in her face, went on hurriedly. "I mean possessing you in the sense that she won't go away when you want her to. You need professional help, Clare."

"But you are professional help! That's why I called you!"

"I'm not a psychic, Clare. Not a real one. I've faced that fact now. I'd like to be; and I know enough theory to feel maybe I can touch on the psychic experience now and then, but when I'm confronted by something like this, something way beyond me, I don't know what to do. I'm sorry. Either you must go to someone you know who can help—like your brother-in-law, who must have come across this sort of thing before—or I can try to find someone for you, but that's all I can do."

"That's all?" She looked at him in such despair and disappointment that his heart lurched.

"Clare—" He hesitated. "Look, I do know something about psychic self-defense. I can teach you things to do and get you some books to read on the subject so you can arm yourself against her. That might work." He was chewing the inside of his cheek. "She was a sorceress, your Isobel, didn't you tell me that? You have to fight her with her own weapons." He paused uncomfortably. "Have you ever tried speaking to her?"

Clare stared at him. "Only when I summoned her."

"Well, next time she comes, try it. See if she sees you as a person, see if she knows you are there. Maybe all you are tapping into is the replay of an old film, something trapped in the ether. If that is so, all you have to do is switch off the projector. The power to do that is inside you. If that's not the case—" He shrugged. "Well, you could try reasoning with her."

Clare shivered. "But that means I have to summon her again. . . ."

"Better to summon her on your terms and then dismiss her than to have her come uninvited," he said firmly.

She stood up and walked uneasily around the room. "It frightens me, Zak. The last time I summoned her she came so easily—"

"Then either deep down inside you do still want her with you, or she is a separate entity who wants to contact you."

Clare frowned. "If she comes because I want her, she should go when I don't want her; but she won't. She's too strong."

"Stronger than you?"

They stared at each other, then slowly Clare nodded. "Much stronger than I."

Zak felt himself go cold. "I don't know what else to suggest," he said helplessly. "I'm sorry."

She sat down again in silence, then at last she looked up at him. "Will you meditate with me?"

Zak looked uncomfortable. "I guess so."

"Please. Sometimes I'm so afraid I won't wake up. . . ."

He stood up. "Clare—I'm not so sure this is a good idea. Perhaps you shouldn't try until we've talked to some more people—"

He broke off as the phone began to ring, but Clare ignored it. "I want to do it with you there, Zak. I don't want it to happen when I'm alone. Please."

For a moment they were both silent, listening to the persistent ringing of the bell, then with an impatient exclamation Clare picked it up.

"Oh, Neil, it's you, I'm sorry. What?" She stared down at the table as the voice spoke in her ear. When he stopped at last she put down the receiver. She had gone white.

"Paul knows where I am," she said. Her hands had begun to shake. "Neil's girlfriend told him."

Zak raised an eyebrow. "He can't take you back to London by force, Clare."

"I wouldn't bet on that," Clare said bitterly. She sat down. "Neil is coming over now. I can't stay here anymore. I'm not prepared to risk a confrontation with Paul. I don't want to see him at all. I'm leaving."

"Now?" Zak felt slightly guilty at the overwhelming relief that swept over him.

She nodded. "Zak, you'll stay in Edinburgh for a while, won't you? Please?"

For a moment he was tempted to say no; to say he had to go back to Cambridge, but his conscience got the better of him. He nodded. "Of course I'll stay. Just for a few days. I want to see something of Scotland while I'm here."

Neil drove her to Moray Place in his Land-Rover. "So. Who was the handsome young man you were drooling all over at the airport?" He glanced at her as they pulled up at the lights at the foot of the Mound. "It was obviously not your husband."

Clare was hugging her shoulder bag on her knees. Behind them Casta was sitting in the back with the suitcase James had brought her. It was only twenty-five minutes since Neil had first phoned, but now there was no sign of her at the apartment in the Canongate. It was as if she had never been there at all.

"I wasn't drooling, that's for sure." Clare laughed. "Your Kathleen doesn't make a very good spy. That was my brother."

"I see." Neil brightened. "So, you aren't entirely alone in a world of tormentors."

"Not entirely alone, no."

"And who exactly is Zak de Sallis?" The two men had shaken hands briefly, then Zak had left, still trying to hide his relief at being able to postpone the meditation.

"Zak taught me yoga and meditation last year. He's doing a Ph.D. at Cambridge."

"Cambridge via San Francisco, or some such place, I take it?"

She laughed again. "Yes, something like that! He helped me a lot, Neil, when I was going through a bad time."

He glanced across at her. "Can you tell me about it?"

She shook her head. "Not yet. I asked him to come up here. I needed to talk to him, to help sort myself out."

Neil engaged gear, turning left into Princes Street. "You don't need any sorting out that can't be achieved by booting your husband into orbit." The wind was tearing at the trees in Princes Street Gardens. They could feel it buffeting the Land-Rover as they drove. "I'm taking you to an apartment belonging to a friend of mine. She's away for three months, so it's empty."

"Won't she mind?"

"Not as long as you don't wreck it." He gave a grim smile. "You'll be safe as long as you want to stay there." He swung the Land-Rover north and a spattering of sleet hit the windshield. "Have you decided what you're going to do, Clare?"

She didn't reply. It was only just sinking in that he was taking her across town, far away from his apartment and from Earthwatch. She would be alone again. Alone with Isobel.

She shivered. "I should have brought my car and saved you the journey." Zak was staying at the Caledonian Hotel. She could always reach him—but she had seen his expression of relief when the phone rang and interrupted them; she knew he didn't know what to do.

"It's safer where it is. You don't want it parked outside your front door. It's too easy to spot, especially with that big dent."

"I suppose so." She desperately wanted to put out her hand to touch him. Since he had made love to her that first time he hadn't made a move to touch her. Save for the tenderness he had shown when he had comforted her after her nightmare, something he had never alluded to again, he hadn't made a move in her direction.

Was it true then? Had he slept with her just to win some cheap victory over her? Did he now despise her more than ever?

He drew up at last at a house in a circle of terraced Georgian houses built around a center garden. "Here we are. I think you'll like it here. It's more your scene, I suspect, than the Canongate."

Diving into the back of the Land-Rover for her suitcase, he missed the look of misery that crossed her face. By the time she had climbed down from the passenger seat, her expression was under control.

It was a second-floor apartment, with a large, high-ceilinged living room looking out toward the gardens, with two bedrooms behind it. All were beautifully furnished—some antiques, some tasteful and very modern pieces. Between them stood some tall, glossy potted plants. Clare looked around in delight.

"It's beautiful. Who does it belong to?"

"A friend." Neil smiled. "She's a lecturer at the university. She's taking a few months' sabbatical." He slapped a walnut chest of drawers. "I may be a Philistine myself but she trusts me enough to give me a key just in case I find myself with a stranded female of impeccable taste who needs a roof."

"I see." Clare forced herself to laugh.

Neil could sense the panic building in her again. He frowned. It was better for her if she learned to stand on her own feet. She must not come to rely on him as she had obviously relied on Paul. "I have to get back now. I've got a lot of things to do," he said firmly. "Will you be all right? I have to sort out Kathleen next. She's moving out of my apartment for good."

"Oh?" Clare didn't know what to say.

"I value loyalty very highly," he went on gently. "She betrayed me when she called your husband."

"She came back early," Clare said inconsequentially.

"She came back to check up on us and to make me throw you out. There wouldn't have been room for both of you in that apartment." He sighed. He hadn't given Kathleen a thought when he had offered Clare the use of it. "She's a very jealous woman."

"I can't think why. There's nothing to be jealous of, after all, is there?" Clare straightened her shoulders. He was an attractive man, but surely the passion that had so swamped her, that had given her her first orgasm, had all been inside her head. She had been taking advantage of him as much as he had been taking advantage of her. She looked him straight in the eye. "Is there?" she repeated.

Neil raised an eyebrow. "Maybe. Maybe not." He smiled. "We'll have to see, won't we?" And with that she had to be content.

There was very little food in the kitchen. Clare poked about in the cupboards and found a jar of coffee and a couple of packages of biscuits. She made herself some black coffee and shared a few of the biscuits with Casta, then she unpacked her clothes. The apartment was silent. It felt all wrong, as if it resented her presence. It was beautiful, peaceful, and asleep until its owner returned. She wondered briefly who this unknown woman was. Another of Neil's admirers? He obviously had many. After all, he was an attractive man.

Restlessly she paced around, listening to the wind and the hail against the windows. Winter was coming with a vengeance. She turned on the TV on the counter in the kitchen to drown the sound and left it on for company as she went into the hall and fiddled with the controls of the central heating, trying to make it come on. She desperately wished Neil had stayed a bit longer. Casta had remained in the kitchen, sitting subdued in a corner. Clare stared down at the key Neil had left on the telephone table in the hall, then she reached for her coat.

The night was blustery and very cold. They walked around the streets for half an hour, then Clare turned back, defeated, smelling the bitter scent of a brewery on the wind as she opened the front door and let them back into the apartment.

It was warm now, but emptier than ever. Casta shot past her and back into the kitchen.

Clare stared around, sensing a slight change in the atmosphere.

"No," she whispered. "No, I don't want you. Go away."

She went back into the hall and looked down at the phone. She had to call Zak. She needed someone now. Crossing her fingers, she dialed the hotel, but Mr. de Sallis was neither in his room nor, when they paged him, in the restaurant or bars. "Zak! Oh, Zak!" She could feel the palms of her hands sweating.

By the time she had had a bath she knew she couldn't fight it anymore.

The silence of the apartment closed around her again at once, and with it, as she sat down slowly on the carved Regency sofa in the large drawing room, came the sound of horses' hooves, the smell of leather and horse sweat, and the heavy breathing of men and animals, crowding in around her in the immaculate, cold room.

"Please go away. I don't want to know what happened. . . ." Her voice sounded hollow and strange, as if it came from a long way away. "Please, leave me alone. Please. . . ."

Eleyne, Dowager Countess of Mar, was waiting for them in the courtyard of Kildrummy Castle. She took Isobel's face between her thin, heavily ringed fingers and kissed her, oblivious of the milling horses around them. "Thank God, you are safe! I had such terrible dreams! Where is Robert?"

Isobel shrugged, trying to blink back her tears. She couldn't speak for misery.

The castle, strong and well stocked in the fertile valley of the Don in the heart of Mar, was like home now. There they could tend the wounded properly; they could wash themselves and find clean clothes and sleep in beds after the long nights on the hard ground.

Isobel grew thin; there were dark circles beneath her eyes. She watched and waited with the others, outwardly cheerful, outwardly friendly with the queen who was less hostile, more conciliatory now that Robert wasn't there, and often she

played and talked with little Marjorie, of whom she had
grown very fond. But inside she was torn apart. Her thoughts
never left Robert; in her imagination he was tired and pale as
she had seen him last; wounded, bloodstained but unbowed;
still brave, still determined, and still every inch a king.

The huge army under Edward of Caernarvon—King Edward's son—was spotted long before it entered Strathdon,
winding purposefully into the center of Mar toward Kildrummy. At once Lord Atholl, Robert's former brother-in-
law, and Nigel Bruce called a council of war in the great hall.
"We cannot stay here. We must go on. We have to save the
women at all cost!" Atholl's face was white and strained. "We
must take them north. Robert is not going to come here now.
He must have gone west toward Ireland. We must do as he
said and go on to Norway."

"But he said he'd make his way here!" Elizabeth put in
desperately. Like all of them, she felt safe at Kildrummy.

"Not now; not with Lord Pembroke and Prince Edward
about to camp on our doorstep." Atholl frowned. "Somehow
we have to hold Kildrummy for Robert and at the same time
get you ladies away to safety, in case the worst happens." He
glanced at Nigel, who had been sitting glumly on one of the
piled sacks of corn. "What do you think we should do?"

"You're right. We have to get the ladies away. And now,
within the hour. Edward's army will be here by tomorrow.
Our informers said they were moving fast." He stood up.
"What do you say, shall we toss for it, John?" He grinned at
Atholl. "One of us will go with the ladies and one of us will
stay and hold Kildrummy for Robert." He fished a coin out of
his pouch and bounced it gently on his palm. Lord Atholl
glanced at the queen, as if doubting whether she would approve, but she made no protest. He looked back at Nigel and
nodded. "We toss for who stays then? I call heads." Every eye
in the room followed the silver coin as it spun up into the air,
catching a slanting beam from the setting sun as it flew, and
then fell to the floor. Nigel crouched over it without touching
it. He bit his lip. "I stay, it seems. So be it. I shall hold the
castle for the king." He tucked the coin back into his pouch,
his disappointment obvious.

By dusk they were ready to leave, the women and Lord Atholl with two of his best men, all wrapped in black cloaks. They were all afraid. Capture meant death, of that there was no doubt, but the women were Robert's weak point, the people who made him vulnerable. They had to escape. Kildrummy would, with any luck, hold the English army distracted for months—impregnable as it was with its huge stores of food and its deep wells—but they could not risk being trapped there. They had to reach Norway and safety.

Nigel took Isobel aside as the queen was fussing over her stepdaughter's cloak. "I promised the king I would take care of you, my lady." He gave her his boyish grin. "But as fate has decreed that I have to stay here, John will look after you instead of me. He will keep you safe for Robert. You can trust him with your life."

Isobel caught his hand. "Can't I stay here with you and Great-Grandmama?" Eleyne had once more refused to leave. "When Robert comes we can all greet him together—please. You said yourself the castle is impregnable, so there can be no danger—"

"No." Nigel glanced over his shoulder. The hall was bustling, full of men preparing for the siege. The gates and doors were already shut—all but the small postern above the deep ravine known as the Back Den, through which the escaping party would creep as soon as full darkness came. "You must go. It is imperative that you get to Norway." He was adamant.

She bit her lip. "You will take care of yourself." Impulsively she stood on tiptoe and kissed him on the cheek. Sometimes he was very like his brother—an angle of the head, an expression in the eye that tore at her heart, and, just occasionally, in his determination to be obeyed.

He squeezed her hand and then released it. "I shall hold Kildrummy for the king. Don't worry about us. There is no way the English will ever take this castle."

The great courtyard was lighted with torches as men and women scurried to and fro—people from outlying farmsteads and villages taking cover within the great walls. Leading their horses, the small band of women and Lord Atholl and his two handpicked men slipped out of the postern gate. As soon as they were through it the gate was pushed shut and they heard the heavy bolts clang home. The castle was sealed and they were outside it.

The darkness of the deep ravine was absolute, the noise of their passing muffled by the sound of the small creek pouring over the rocks. The air smelled of cool damp moss; it was cold and dank, the rocks slippery beneath the women's leather-soled shoes and the horses' hooves in the darkness. Once Isobel fell. She saved herself by clinging to her horse's neck, but her foot plunged into the icy water and she felt her ankle turn. Almost she cried out, then she felt John Atholl's hand beneath her arm and they were moving on, creeping farther and farther from the castle.

Nearby a horse whinnied in the night and Isobel's heart stopped beating. Instinctively she put her hand on her mare's nose to stop her replying and she saw the others do the same. Somewhere near them were other riders, and they had to be the enemy.

She saw Lord Atholl's face, near hers, grim in the starlight. They had left it too late; they should not have waited until dark. The enemy was already here. They could hear subdued voices now and a laugh, cut off short from somewhere behind them in the trees. The English were flanking the castle, having slipped north through the broad valley as dusk fell.

Behind them Kildrummy appeared to slumber. The castle was in darkness, the walls, patrolled by the garrison, silent as they watched and waited.

Lord Atholl glanced upward, and Isobel, following his gaze, saw the rim of the moon appearing above the trees. He looked back toward the castle. Beside him, Isobel could feel his indecision, his panic in the darkness. Somewhere close by they heard a horse's hoof strike a rock and a subdued curse from one of the men. Isobel swallowed, her mouth dry with fear. She glanced at Atholl. He shook his head imperceptibly and began to move on.

They reached the end of the ravine. Ahead of them the track sloped away across open meadows before plunging once more into the forest that covered the lower slopes of the hills. Once in the forest they could breathe again perhaps, but the meadowland in between was open and clearly visible in the starlight. Behind them the moon was growing brighter by the second as it swam above the trees on the ridge. The small band of men and women halted beneath a clump of whispering aspen and stared across the tussocky ground. There was no sign of life. The English too had taken cover. Soundlessly Lord Atholl pointed up. A mass of cloud was streaming toward them, black against the starlight. "When it covers the moon," he mouthed, "get ready to ride." Silently they all mounted, glad that the wind in the aspens and the water on the rocks masked any sounds they might make, then they all stood watching the sky as the patchy clouds blotted out the stars in their race toward the moon. In a moment they reached it and the meadow slowly disappeared into the darkness.

As silently as they could, in single file, they cantered across the meadow, holding their breath, hearing the movement of the horses through the long grasses and the thud of the hooves on the dry earth, but no one saw them. There was no warning shout, and long before the moonlight spread again across the silvered meadows they had gained the forest and were climbing steadily toward the hills.

The first attack on Kildrummy came at midnight. From their hiding place in the mountains north of the castle they watched the fires flare and heard the shouts of men and the scream of horses as the huge army launched itself upon the castle. Under cover of darkness Prince Edward's men had dragged siege engines into place, and already the huge machines were hurling rocks at the great walls. As first dawn broke Atholl and the women with him looked back at the distant gray-pink granite walls of the castle, so long secure in its pocket in the hills, and around it the tiny black figures moving to and fro, setting up tents, drawing siege engines closer, all the signs of a huge army settling in for a long siege.

Lord Atholl was tight-lipped as he stood and looked down, his eyes straining in the glare of the sunlight. He had nearly led his precious charges straight into the enemy's jaws. He murmured a prayer for Sir Nigel and the garrison of Kildrummy, then he turned his back on the castle and headed north.

He did not let them rest, even at night. Beneath the huge, red harvest moon they rode on through the mountains, threading their way northwest through the glens toward Strathspey. They forded the Spey in the heat of the midday sun, setting the horses into the broad river above a series of cataracts where the smooth granite glittered blue and rose and white beneath the torrents of water. Around them the air was fragrant with pine and soft uncut hay and wild autumn roses.

Then it was on into the higher mountains and over the empty heather moors, purple as far as the eye could see. They passed a lonely loch, set in a ring of hills. On an island in the center a castle stood sentinel in water black with wind ripples. Gulls swooped and screamed but still they dared not stop. Reining their horses toward the north, they skirted it, watching for signs of life, and headed once more toward the high forest and the mountain passes and the moors, the haunt of snipe and dotteral, deer and, on the high passes, ptarmigan and eagle.

On they went through the long hot September days. They slept on the ground, wrapped in thick plaids on the springy heather, chilled by the cold nights as summer slowly dipped toward autumn. Lord Atholl and his two male companions caught fish and once or twice stalked and shot a deer with the longbow they carried with them. They helped the women cook the flesh over their lonely campfires, keeping an eye forever on the far horizons least the thin wisps of white smoke be spotted by their enemies.

The women did not complain. The three Bruce ladies and the child rode bravely on behind Lord Atholl and Isobel, who invariably rode side by side, the two other men behind them. They all suffered. They were hungry and exhausted and afraid, their lives made misery by the midges and horseflies that plagued the moors. They were either too hot beneath the blistering sun or wet and cold beneath heavy, penetrating rain as they turned north again toward Inverness, to which they gave a wide berth, and on over the low-lying fertile ground of the Black Isle. Isobel no longer cared where they were going. So many times they had tried to break out toward the coast and every time they had been headed back inland by marauding parties of soldiers, or bands of travelers whom they did not wish to meet.

When at last they saw the welcome gleam of water in the distance it was the Dornoch Firth, gray, slate-green, red-brown in the changing light of a windy sky. There Lord Atholl halted them at last. "Maybe we can find a ship here." He smiled wearily at them. "Courage, ladies. God is good. We are in St. Duthac's country here. It may be that he will bless us and send us safely on our way to Norway." He stooped and caught Marjorie's hand as she sat on the ground, her eyes closed, her head resting wearily against the rough bark of a pine tree. "Not much farther, sweetheart, I promise."

She looked up and gave him an exhausted smile. She liked her father's friends, with their brusque kindness and gentleness. John of Atholl had carved her a doll out of an old piece of wood with the dirk he carried in his belt. She kept it wrapped in a scrap of cloth, tucked into her girdle. Surreptitiously she touched it now. It was the only thing she had to call her own.

"I'm sorry, Uncle John." She gave him a wistful smile, adult far beyond her years. "I'm a nuisance because I'm so young."

"A nuisance!" He looked at her in mock horror. "How can the charge of the princess of Scotland be a nuisance? It is an honor your Uncle Nigel and I had to fight for!" He bowed gallantly.

He glanced at the women over her head. Mary and Christian too had their eyes closed. Isobel was standing supporting herself with one hand on her horse's saddle, her eyes fixed on the broad firth beyond the ancient burgh of Tain. Across the water, streaked a deep blue now beneath the shadows of the clouds, the northern shoulders of Caithness humped into the pearly mist.

"Will we go into Tain?" Elizabeth glanced at him. She was the least tired of all of them; still upright, still clear-eyed, but her face was taut with worry.

"I'll go in on my own." Lord Atholl glanced around. "You

must all rest. We have to find somewhere you can get some food and sleep."

When he returned his face was grim. He looked from one woman to the other, still undecided whether or not to tell them what he had learned in Tain, where people had not recognized the ragged traveler wrapped in a plaid as an earl, one of the exiled rebel's closest friends, and had gossiped freely to him as he bought bread and cheese and smoked fish. He distributed the food among the others and sat watching them as they ate.

It was Isobel who questioned him first. Waiting until Marjorie had snuggled into her plaid and fallen asleep in the shelter of a clump of whin, she walked over and sank to her knees beside him. "What news, John? I can see in your face it is not good."

He shrugged, unable to keep it to himself any longer, shaking his head with misery. "Kildrummy has fallen."

"Fallen?" She stared at him white-faced. Hearing her cry, the others came and squatted beside them. "It can't have fallen!"

"They were betrayed. The blacksmith, you remember that surly bastard, Osbourne, may he rot in hell forever! He fired the corn in the great hall. The fire spread—" He shook his head, unable to go on. "The castle fell. They were all taken."

"Nigel?" Mary whispered.

He nodded. "Tain is full of it. Osbourne was killed by the English—they had promised him gold for his betrayal and the story is they gave it to him, pouring it molten down his throat." He gave a grim, humorless laugh. "They have a fine sense of irony, the English, I give them that. Nigel has been taken to King Edward." He shook his head again.

"And Great-Grandmama?" Isobel asked, her mouth dry with fear. "What has happened to her?"

He shrugged. "There was no mention of her," he said.

There were tears in all the women's eyes. Frightened, they huddled together in the shelter of the bushes as a shower of rain swept up from the firth, soaking them. Nearby Marjorie slept on, unaware.

Lord Atholl swallowed. "Prince Edward will know we

were there," he said softly. "They will already be looking for us. We must find a ship."

Twice they saw people as they made their way cautiously down toward the shore, once a party of travelers, almost as ragged as themselves, and once a group of men cutting peats on the moor. The peat cutters stopped work and watched them as they rode past, then, with a surly greeting, they bent again to their backbreaking task.

A little later they saw two horsemen standing on the crest of a rise about half a mile from them. Atholl ignored them, but the men remained, watching them carefully for some time before they turned away and rode fast toward the town.

Isobel clutched Mary's arm. "Why were they watching us? Did they recognize us?"

"How could they?" Mary had dropped the reins on her horse's neck as they rode at last down onto the shore beyond the walls of the burgh, letting her tired cob follow the horse in front. "No one up here would recognize us. They don't know where we come from."

She spoke too soon. Barely half an hour later they saw a troop of horsemen riding out of Tain. Lord Atholl stared at them, narrowing his eyes in the glare of the sun on the water as another shower sped across the firth and vanished south across the low hills. The three gold lions rampant on a scarlet ground told him all he wanted to know. He looked around wildly. There was no shelter there, no hiding place save the chapel of St. Duthac standing foursquare on its grassy hill against a wind that was whipping up the waves in the shallow sandy water of the firth.

"In there. Quickly!" He brought his hand down on the rump of Marjorie's horse, making the exhausted animal leap into a canter. "We may pass ourselves off as pilgrims."

They threw themselves from the horses outside the chapel and went inside. Out of the wind it was very silent; the thick stone walls and narrow pointed windows kept out every sound of wind and water. A dozen candles burned before the shrine.

"Who is it?" The queen touched his arm. "I couldn't see the banners—"

"Lord Ross, madam. No friend to your husband, I fear." He spoke in an undertone, but his voice seemed to fill the hush of the chapel.

"Are we safe here?" Isobel looked at him intently.

"I doubt it." He put his hand on his sword.

"No." Elizabeth shook her head. "Do not shed blood in this holy place. My husband has already committed sacrilege enough. It may be that they have not recognized us."

Behind her Christian put her arms around Marjorie and hugged her close. The echoing cry of a gull rang through the chapel as the four women, the child, and the three men waited. Elizabeth knelt before the shrine. Stooping, she kissed the cold stone of the saint's tomb. Slowly Mary and Christian followed suit.

Only Isobel was standing now. She was clutching the torn remains of her cloak around her. The chapel was chill after the blustery autumn sunshine. She could hear the horsemen now, on the shingle. They weren't hurrying. They knew their quarry could run no farther.

It was Earl William himself who entered the chapel, drawn sword in hand, bending to avoid the low archway. He stopped and straightened, giving his eyes a moment to adjust to the dim candlelight inside. Behind him two knights stood shoulder to shoulder in the doorway, blocking out the sun.

"So. My lookouts were right. I must reward them for having such sharp eyes." He smiled, then he bowed mockingly toward Elizabeth. "The so-called Queen of Scots, if I mistake not, and Lady Buchan?" He turned sharply to Isobel who stood proudly near the wall. "Who would have thought to see you here?" he went on with a chuckle. "I was speaking to your husband but a week ago."

Isobel clenched her teeth. Her skin was crawling with panic. The man was playing with them. She glanced at the others. They were all motionless, white-faced, staring at the earl as if mesmerized. Suddenly Lord Atholl made a move to draw his sword. In a second the two knights behind Lord Ross had sprung at him, and it was wrested from his hand together with his dirk.

"That's better." Lord Ross smiled. "So. Now the question is, what do I do with you?"

Elizabeth straightened. "This place is holy ground. You cannot take us from here. I claim sanctuary, in the name of Christ—"

"Whose holy name your husband did not hesitate to abuse with blood when it suited him," Ross snapped back. "Do not think you can claim sanctuary here, madam, or anywhere else in Scotland."

He made a move toward the women and Marjorie let out a little cry of fear.

"Dear God, save us!" Isobel closed her eyes, a vision of the dragon banner floating before her, the token by which any woman who supported the rebel cause could be taken and raped and murdered with impunity. Mary was standing as if stunned, so she moved to Marjorie and, putting her arms around the child, held her close. Outside they could hear the horses snorting impatiently, the chink of harness, the restless hooves on the shingle among the grass.

Ross took the queen's arm. "Outside, madam. Think yourselves lucky it was I who found you." He glanced at Isobel. "Had your husband got to you first, Lady Buchan, he would not have let you live long enough to see the sunset. As it is, it is for the King of England to decide what is to be done with you all. I shall take you to him."

Chapter Twenty-eight

Her apartment in Rothesay Place was cold and dusty. Kathleen looked around it sadly, then, dropping her two suitcases on the floor, she walked across to the window and threw it open. The taxi was just drawing away from the curb and she stood watching as it drove out of sight. So. It was over and Neil had thrown her out.

"Goddamn it, but you're a bastard, Neil Forbes! And you'll pay. I'll make you pay—and that English bitch. You can't throw me out like that!" She had known it was coming. It had been in the cards for months now. She fished in the patchwork bag she had thrown down on the table and brought out her cards, turning them over twice in her hands, feeling the familiarity of them, the comfort, the immediate sense of certainty and rightness they gave her. She could do less and less now without consulting them—they told her everything; they were confidant and advisor, friend and family. She sat down and ran her hand across the pack, spreading them facedown across the table. Then, edging one at random out of the run, she picked it up. For a moment she didn't look at it. What was she asking of the cards? Was it Neil or herself or Clare Royland she wanted to interrogate? Slowly she turned the card faceup. The tower. She stared at it blankly. The house of God or the house of the devil. The most complex of all the cards: disruption, imprisonment, disaster, and change. But for whom? Who had she been thinking about when she asked her question? She smiled grimly and stood up, walking slowly back to the window. Clare. That was the future for Clare.

Neil would soon tire of her. She was too effete, too feeble for him. He needed a woman with strength and experience

—a woman like herself. Men were so naive! Did he really think she didn't know where he had stashed Clare away! Did he really think she would let him hide her away for his own amusement just because he had thrown her out? This time when she told Paul Royland where his wife was she would see to it that he found her at once; and she would see to it that Neil never knew how he had done it! She smiled bitterly. All she had to do was find out where Paul Royland was staying.

Paul took a taxi from the airport straight to the Canongate. He stood for a moment in the windswept street, staring up at the high buildings around him, then he began the long climb to the top floor.

Neil opened the door in his shirtsleeves.

"Where is she, Forbes?" Paul was panting heavily. It put him at a disadvantage.

Neil looked at him for a moment before answering. "Nowhere you will find her." He didn't bother to pretend not to know who Paul was talking about.

For a moment Paul's face darkened, then he took a visible hold on himself. "You'd better let me in. We have to talk."

Neil hesitated. It made more sense to speak to him and find out which way his mind was working. For Clare's sake. He turned and led the way into the untidy living room, wondering briefly why he wanted to do anything for Clare's sake.

Throwing himself down in the armchair, he left Paul to stand or clear himself a space on one of the other chairs cluttered with newspapers and books.

Paul elected to stand. "I know she's in Edinburgh," he said slowly. "And she's obviously taken you in. Look, Forbes, there are one or two things I'm going to have to tell you; information I'm going to have to trust you with." He hesitated, picking his words with care. "Clare is a very vulnerable woman. She is, or should be, under the care of several professional people at the moment, a doctor and a priest among them." He glanced at Neil. "I would rather not have told you this, but I must."

Neil was watching him closely. His face was impassive.

Paul moved toward the window and stared out for a moment at the sheen of frost on Calton Hill, then he turned back to Neil. With his face in shadow, his expression was harder to read. "My wife is very unstable, Forbes, and has been since she was a child. As a child her family protected her, and when I found out what I had married"—he paused—"I protected her." It was nothing less than the truth, he realized suddenly in amazement. "Without me there, and without the backup of the people who understand her, she is a danger, both to herself and to those around her." He paused again. Neil said nothing. The silence stretched out between them and Paul found he was rubbing his cheek nervously. He was beginning to sweat in the heavy overcoat. "She is schizophrenic; she hears voices and sees visions. She began some months ago to dabble in the occult and as a direct consequence of all this she has been in some way possessed."

Neil stood up slowly. "You bastard!" he said. "Do you really expect me to believe all that?"

"You will—when you get to know her." Paul walked toward the door. "Bear in mind that you are keeping her from her friends, her family, her doctors, and her medication," he said portentously. "You have taken a very great responsibility on yourself, Forbes. God help you if anything happens to her."

Neil stood for a long time after Paul had left, just staring at the spot by the window where his visitor had been standing, then slowly he went to the telephone. It was several seconds before she answered. "Clare? I thought I'd better tell you that your husband is now in Edinburgh. He has just paid me a visit."

There was a moment's silence, then: "What did he say?" Clare sounded subdued.

"A few choice epithets on what would happen if I failed to tell him where you were. You'd better not come near the office or the apartment today in case he's still prowling around. He doesn't seem to be the kind of man to take no for an answer. I'll pick you up at lunchtime and we'll have lunch outside Edinburgh somewhere, okay?"

"Thank you."

"Are you all right? Is the apartment comfortable?"

"It's lovely."

"Did you sleep all right?"

"Oh, God! What's Paul been saying?"

He heard the sudden sharp, defensive note in her voice. "About your sleeping habits?" Neil managed a laugh. "Nothing at all. Did you expect him to?"

He picked her up at one and drove her out to the Hawes Inn. Clare was very pale. He glanced at her from time to time as he drove. She was wearing a pair of trousers and a heavy multicolor sweater this morning; they made her look less formal, more relaxed—more approachable. And completely sane.

"Did your friend Zak get into the Caley all right?"

He saw her tense. "I think so. I tried to call him last night, but he wasn't there." She was on the defensive again. "He doesn't know where I am. If he gets in touch will you tell him?" She sounded lost.

They arrived at South Queensferry and Neil backed the Land-Rover into a parking spot. The Forth glittered in the hazy sunshine. High above them a train roared across the diamond segments of the bridge. She desperately wanted him to touch her. Her whole body had suddenly become intensely aware of his.

"Why are you doing this?" They were leaning on the wall, staring down into the swirling water.

"What, exactly?" He turned his back on the Forth to watch her, his eyes narrowed in the frosty sunlight.

"Taking me out to lunch. Being nice."

He smiled. "You don't feel it's in character?"

"Kathleen told me you loathed me." Her gaze was fixed on the far shore.

He didn't answer and she closed her eyes, unprepared for the desolation that gripped her. She had expected him to deny it at once.

"I loathe what you stand for," he said at last. "A moneyed aristocracy, class privilege, the fact that you can own somewhere like Duncairn and can, with the snap of your fingers, dispose of it and the people who live there at a whim."

"But I haven't disposed of it. I turned my back on the money and remembered my responsibility to the land and to the people." She intoned the words softly like a litany.

He glanced at her. "That must be why I think there is hope for you yet." He grinned at her unexpectedly. "Why don't I buy you a drink and something to eat before you fade away completely?"

After lunch they took Casta for a walk in the Dalmeny woods. On the edge of a sheltered bay they sat down on a fallen log out of the wind. Clare had been very silent.

"Is any of what Paul told me true?" He said it very quietly as they sat with Casta, panting, between them. Both of them reached forward to fondle her ears.

Clare tensed her shoulders. "What did he tell you?"

"That you are under the care of a doctor. That you need regular medication."

"That's a lie." She took a handful of Casta's scruff and kneaded it gently.

"That you've been ill since you were a child."

"That's a lie too. There is nothing wrong with me."

"When I came in and saw you in the bath—" He was picking his words with care. "And later that evening, when you were in bed, it was as if you were in some sort of a trance."

She was staring across at the shore of Fife, hazy in the afternoon sunlight. "I was daydreaming, I expect."

"And that was all?"

"What else would it be?" Their hands met for a moment on the dog's neck. Clare closed her eyes. She desperately wanted him to leave his there, lying coolly on her fingers. For a moment he did, then slowly his hand moved away toward Casta's ears. "I suppose he told you about Geoffrey," she said. Her voice was strained.

"Who is Geoffrey?"

"My brother-in-law. He is a vicar in London. For a joke I told him I was conjuring up spirits and things. He took me literally." She gave a tight laugh. "The Roylands are all very pompous. They have no sense of humor."

"My God! And the MP as well? How many are there?"

"Three brothers and a sister, Emma. She's my friend." She said it very simply.

Neil glanced at her. "You said that as if you didn't have any others."

"I sometimes don't think I have." She shivered. "A thousand acquaintances and one friend. I'm not doing very well, am I?"

"To date, no." He laughed. "But I think you'll find you've got a lot of friends in Scotland, if you want them. People at Earthwatch, at Duncairn."

"Jack Grant used to be my friend."

"I'll put him right." Neil stopped stroking the dog. He picked up a pebble and threw it far out into the water. It made no rings in the choppy windswept tide. Casta ignored it.

He took Clare to the committee meeting that evening, introducing her simply as a new member. Afterward he dropped her at the door of the apartment in Moray Place. He made no move to get out of the Land-Rover. For a moment she hesitated; she wanted him so badly she was almost prepared to beg. She didn't understand herself. She had never felt this way before. The longing and the fear of being alone were sweeping over her, drowning her. She glanced at him, but it was too late. He smiled and, leaning across her, opened the door. "I'll see you tomorrow evening," he said.

She gave him a strained little smile back and, snapping her fingers at Casta, slid out of the car. Then she ran up the steps to the front door, fumbled for the key, and let herself in without a backward glance.

Zak looked at Neil hard, studying the rugged, weather-beaten face, sensing the sensitivity and the turmoil within. Slowly he nodded. "Yes. Clare does have problems. Nothing like her family makes out, but she needs help, without a doubt. Not the kind of thing her husband has in mind, however, that's for sure."

"And she really thinks she sees this woman, Isobel?"

"She really does see her." Zak spread his hands out on the table between them. The restaurant was very quiet. It was barely twelve. "Clare is very psychic. From the first time I met her I knew that, and I could tell she didn't have the knowledge or the confidence to deal with her own powers. I taught her to meditate. I thought it would give her insight into her own subconscious and give her control. . . ." He shrugged. "At first I thought Isobel was some kind of visible projection by her mind of this woman she seems to have been obsessed with since she was a child. Now I don't think so." He was studying Neil's face, looking for the slightest flicker of doubt or derision. Neil's expression was impassive. "Nor do I think she is reliving a previous life. This woman Isobel seems to have haunted Clare's aunt as well. She is a family obsession —and she is tied up with Duncairn Castle and with Clare's nightmares and her claustrophobia. Clare feels—lives with— Isobel's emotions all the time."

"So, you think Isobel is a ghost who haunts Clare? Or her family?" Neil frowned. Nightmares—he had seen one of those himself. Claustrophobia? Poor Clare. She hadn't even hinted at the horrors that surrounded her.

Slowly Zak nodded. "When a person is haunted like this, it is called possession," he said slowly.

Neil raised an eyebrow. "So, perhaps the good Royland vicar could help her?"

Zak shook his head. "I doubt it. It is Isobel who needs help, not Clare, and I doubt if he is the man to do it."

"Do we need a Roman Catholic priest then?" Neil ignored the waitress who placed two large square rush mats on the table and proceeded to lay their places. She threw a menu down between them and flounced off. Neither man had even glanced at her.

"Maybe." It was Zak's turn to shrug.

Neil sat back in his chair and studied his face for a moment. "May I ask what your own qualifications were to get involved in all this in the first place?"

Zak gave a rueful smile. "I'm doing a doctorate in psychology. You could say all this is within the scope of my studies— all forms of extrasensory perception have been a lifelong interest of mine."

"So you are a psychologist?"

Zak nodded.

"But not a parapsychologist. Aren't there people here at the university who can help with all this?"

"Perhaps." Zak frowned. He had already thought of that and rejected the idea. "But do you want to run the risk of what might happen if Clare's story became public property?"

"No." Neil frowned. "She couldn't take any more publicity —not the kind that would follow if this story got out."

"So, it comes back to me." Zak sighed. "And I admit, I'm out of my depth with this. I'm into meditation, spiritual progression, the individual's pathway forward—all that is part of my sphere, but Isobel. . . ." He rubbed both hands down his face wearily. "Perhaps we should contact the university. I just don't know. Clare is so vulnerable. I will stay here as long as I can—as long as Clare needs me, but I don't think I can help her anymore."

The waitress returned. Neil ordered a Scotch and Zak a mineral water. Neil picked up the rush mat in front of him and balanced it carefully on edge. "Clare seems a very lonely woman," he said cautiously.

Zak nodded. "She is. She hates her husband's world. She belongs here." He glanced toward the window. "I realize it now that I'm here. History is everywhere up here and she is part of it. Maybe that is her karma."

"Is this Isobel threatening her in some way? Is Clare in danger?"

Zak stared into his glass of water. "I wish to God I knew. I don't think so. At least, not physically." His voice died away.

"Then how?" Neil was growing impatient. "Damn it, man, you must know something about it! How do you know all this isn't just her imagination?"

Zak closed his eyes for a moment. "I don't, I suppose. I just feel it. Isobel is an external entity and she has a reason for contacting Clare, I'm sure of it. I don't know what is going to happen to Clare—but whatever it is it will happen here, in Scotland."

"How do you know?" Neil narrowed his eyes skeptically.

"I just know." Zak raised his hands helplessly. "But pushing won't help, Neil. If I knew what to do, I'd tell you! We've just got to be there when it happens."

"What about a doctor, or a psychiatrist?"

"She doesn't want to see any more doctors, and I don't blame her."

"Is there any way I can help her, if you can't? Anything I can do?"

Zak shrugged. "I don't know. Get her to talk about it if you can. The more she talks about it the better—it's all bottled up inside her. If she faces it, fights it, confronts it, that's good."

"Does Clare recognize the danger?"

"Yes. That is why she asked me to come."

Paul stood staring up at the City skyline, sniffing the heady mixture of traffic fumes and excitement that characterized the ancient narrow streets. Sir Duncan's message, relayed to the Edinburgh hotel by Penny, his secretary, had been terse, demanding that he come into the office as soon as he returned to London. Paul had caught the next flight down. He had no need to stay in Edinburgh; he had contacted a private inquiry firm up there. They would find Clare for him and then he would return.

He was glad to be back in London. His short exile had been painful. He missed the office, the pressure, the whole world of money that he lived for. He had given up his share in the family business, but his debts were paid and he was ahead. He shrugged heavily. He could recoup some of his losses fairly swiftly if he were careful. He had had a couple of tips that he was prepared to gamble on. As soon as he had spoken to Sir Duncan he would give Stephen Caroway a call, and by now he should have had a response from Doug Warner at Sigma.

As he swung through the doors in Coleman Street he smiled broadly at Baines and took the stairs two at a time, smelling with pleasure the rich lavender furniture polish and the scent of the roses on the antique table on the landing beneath the portraits. The door of his office was ajar.

Penny was standing behind his desk. "The old man said he

wanted to see you as soon as you came in. He seems anxious to speak to you. Are you feeling better?"

"Much better. Thank you." Paul smiled at her.

She looked away. "Can I go to lunch, Paul? I'm meeting someone at twelve-thirty and I'm already late. . . ." There were rumors in the office already. She didn't want to be there when he came back from his meeting with Sir Duncan.

"Of course. Take an extra half hour or so if you like." As he picked up the sheet of notes from the desk he was already reading the top one. From Dan Mackenzie in Edinburgh. It contained an address and the words: "The lady in question has been staying at the above address for several days."

He smiled and tucked the note into his wallet. It had taken the man less than twelve hours. The next memo detailed the summons from Sir Duncan, and Penny had underlined it three times. The old boy was obviously getting testy. He wondered why the urgency. The last message was from Diane Warboys. He stared at the piece of paper. Penny had, as always, meticulously noted the date and time of the phone call. November 27. Time: 10:46. Message: *Tough shit!*

Paul stared at it.

Behind him, Penny closed the door quietly as she left the room. He frowned at the paper then screwed it up and threw it into the bin, but his mood was spoiled. As he picked up the phone he felt a slight shiver of apprehension.

Sir Duncan was sitting by the window of his large, elegantly furnished office. His desk was empty of papers, the pens and pencils aligned with military precision on the maroon leather blotter. The empty office chair faced the desk squarely. Sir Duncan sat on a leather sofa by the fireplace. His face was drawn and white.

"Where have you been, Paul?" he barked as his secretary showed Paul in. "I expected you at ten."

Angry at his discomfort beneath the stony stare of his senior partner, Paul walked to the chair near him and sat down. "I'm sorry but the shuttle was delayed. I only just got back from Scotland. What is the urgency? Do we have a problem?" He gave a forced smile.

"*You* have a problem, Paul." Sir Duncan stood up slowly.

His shoulders were stooped as he walked stiffly to his desk. "I'm sorry to have to inform you that I have been officially notified that your activities are to be investigated by the fraud squad. I'm sorry, Paul, the board has no alternative but to ask for your resignation."

The public meeting had ended at just after ten, and Clare, Jack, and Neil had toasted its success in the small bar at the Duncairn Hotel. Then, as Jack built up the fire and covered it with turf Clare made her way up to bed. She bathed and brushed her hair, relaxing in the warm glow of the electric fire. Outside the stars were brilliant, lighting the gardens and trees, picking out the dark silhouette of the castle against the sky.

She heard Neil's door open and close as he went into his room across the passage. Still he had made no attempt to touch her, no suggestion that he wanted to make love to her again. They were no more than allies now in the fight to save Duncairn. She had denied her loneliness, fiercely ignoring her longing, concentrating all her energies on the Earthwatch campaign and on meeting again the people of Duncairn. Most were fishing families from the village at the foot of the cliff where the stream flowed out into the sea a couple of miles up the coast from the castle. Many had known Margaret Gordon personally and some she herself had known when she was a child.

She walked to the window and drew back the curtain to stare out at the starlight. Behind her Casta whined softly.

"Do you want to go out?" Clare glanced down at the dog, half exasperated, half eager to get out into the clear crispness of the night herself. Her head was aching slightly after the heat of the bar and the cigarette smoke and the two neat malt whiskies that had finished the evening. On impulse she pulled open the wardrobe and took out her fur coat, pulling it over her silk nightdress. She pushed her feet into her boots and opened the door to her room. The hotel was in darkness. Fumbling, she found the light switch on the landing and flooded the hall and stairs with light. On tiptoe she crept downstairs, followed by the delighted dog. Outside it was ice cold; a thick heavy dew soaked the ground. In sheltered corners the grass was crisp and white with ice; the air had a clarity that resonated in the silence. Thrusting her hands deep into the pockets of her coat, Clare walked quickly over the grass toward the break in the trees. Beyond it she could hear the sea sighing against the cliff base. The castle was very dark. The high walls cut out the starlight and the blackness within them was total.

She could see Casta zigzagging across the grass, her nose low, her plumed tail wagging excitedly as she tracked a rabbit toward the cliff's edge. The wind off the sea was cold; she drew back behind the wall of what was once the great hall and leaned against the stone.

"Can't you sleep either?" Neil's voice was very soft. Casta lifted her head and near front paw for a moment, pointing on the silvered grass, her paw marks black holes in the dew. Then, reassured, she went back on the trail of her rabbit.

Clare hadn't seen him in the shadow of the wall. Even now, with her eyes narrowed in the blackness, she could barely make him out.

"Casta wanted a walk." She spoke softly, not wanting to spoil the silent magic of the night. "And it's so beautiful out here. I couldn't bear to sleep and miss it."

"Poor Clare." His voice was very quiet, almost lost in the gentle sigh of the sea. "You've missed so much."

She had stepped toward him without realizing it, drawn by the quiet magnetism of his voice, barely able to see his face in the dark. His hands reached out for her, drawing her closer, and she felt his lips on hers with an explosion of relief. Her arms slid up around his neck as she felt his hands slip under her coat and beneath the thin silk that covered her breasts. Her gasp at the coldness of his touch was smothered by his lips.

Their lovemaking was swift and fierce, there in the sheltered angle between two ancient stone walls. Clare felt a passion and a primitive lust she had never dreamed of. Neil was far from tender. He took her hungrily, almost angrily, possessing her violently as he thrust her against the stone, and she responded with equal violence, with nails and teeth and an animal scream of fulfillment as her body responded to his.

Beyond them in the long grass Casta ignored them, intent on her own excitements.

For a moment they remained still, their bodies bathed in sweat, then slowly Neil drew away from her. He pulled her coat around her. "Let's go inside," he said. "You'll catch pneumonia otherwise."

His hand on her arm, he propelled her back across the grass. She could feel the air frosty on her burning face, the chill of her body beneath the silk. She was exhausted. All she wanted was to crawl away and sleep, but when he opened her door it was to send Casta into the bedroom with a curt command before he pulled her across the passage into his own. The curtains were open and the room was lighted by starlight. Without bothering to turn on the light he pulled off her coat and dropped it on the floor. He dragged back the bedclothes and pushed her onto his bed, covering her with sheets and blankets, then he climbed in beside her.

He ignored her feeble protests of exhaustion but now he was more gentle, more considerate, and this time she knew she had fallen in love with him.

She awoke once, at about four in the morning, to see a brilliant half moon rising above the trees, flooding the bed with silver light, and she lay sleepily still, watching it. She was still sticky and she could smell their lovemaking on her skin, but she was too tired and happy to get up. Her body was sated and content. With a sleepy smile at the moon she fell asleep again.

She was awoken by the sound of Neil moving around the room. He was already dressed. "Come on. Wake up." He pulled the covers off her naked body. "Breakfast is ready and I can hear that dog of yours crying." He picked her coat off the floor and held it out to her as a dressing gown. As she slipped her arms into it he folded his hands across her breasts and pulled her against him, nuzzling her neck, but his voice when he spoke was fierce.

"Don't ever let me see you wear this coat again, Clare. You

don't need the skins of slaughtered animals to make you beautiful."

The next afternoon she was sitting on the wall overlooking the sea, watching the gulls sweeping down below her at the foot of the cliffs. Behind her Neil was standing looking up at the crumbling masonry of the castle.

"You're going to have to do something about this stonework if you want to preserve the ruins," he said.

Clare glanced over her shoulder. The soft pinks and grays of the granite were shaded yellow and gold where the coating of lichens frosted the stone in the slanting afternoon sunlight. The castle was benign, relaxed—a happy place today.

Stretching lazily, she rose and went to stand beside him, placing her hands lightly on the stone. It was warm, almost alive beneath her touch. "I hate to change anything. I love it as it is."

Neil smiled tolerantly. "Nevertheless, the tower will fall unless the cracks are repointed. A few more winter gales and it will begin to go." He put his hand over hers on the stone. "Are you enjoying yourself up here?"

The dark rings had gone from beneath her eyes, her face had filled out, and she was laughing again.

She glanced up at him, thinking of last night, and her smile was suddenly shy. "You know I am."

"Good." He looked at her closely, then he took her hand. Moving over to the low pile of stone that had once been the western wall of the chapel, he pulled her down to sit beside him. "Did I ever tell you that I met your great-aunt once? I was camping about half a mile up the coast, bird-watching, and she came to visit me one morning. She was a wonderful old woman. She told me I was trespassing." He smiled at the memory. "Then she sat down with me in the heather in front of my tent and talked birds, and when she was leaving she told me to go to the hotel and get myself a proper breakfast." He smiled again. "You're very like her in some ways." He paused. "I think we have to talk, Clare, and I think Duncairn is the place to do it." He was gentle now, as he saw her face tighten defensively. "I want to know the truth about you—

the whole story. Not what your husband claims, not what Zak thinks, but what really happens."

At first she was evasive and resentful, but her body was still a part of his, content and at peace, trusting, and it was hard to lie to him. Besides, suddenly she wanted him to know everything.

She told it all, the truth, the theories, the dreams, the nightmares, and the fears. She told him everything she knew about Isobel and everything she knew about Duncairn. And when she had finished she was crying.

Neil put his arms around her. She was wearing the Burberry now—the mink pushed into the back of the mahogany wardrobe—and he cradled her head against his chest.

"Don't let her come between us, Neil." She looked up at him, the tears clinging to her eyelashes. "I'm not possessed."

"She won't come between us." He tightened his arms. Looking over her head into the depths of the old chapel, he frowned. She wouldn't come between them, but she was there, at Duncairn, the beautiful, tragic Countess of Buchan. And she was waiting for something. Even he could sense it.

"You have to come to terms with this, Clare. You are not possessed. I don't believe in possession." His arms held her tightly so she could not see his face, and his voice was calm. "But I do believe in obsession. It is the most powerful of emotions. You have inherited this obsession from your great-aunt as you have acknowledged. You are sensitive." He had been about to say "a sensitive"—that's what Kathleen would have said, or Zak. "You are a dreamer. You have been lonely and unhappy. You have a romantic background that many people would give their eyeteeth for." He smiled wistfully. "You have a sense of humor that, on your own admission, has got you into deep trouble with your brother-in-law, and up until now you have been a bored little rich girl." His grip tightened as she stirred in protest. "Oh, yes, you have. And now you are completely screwed up!" He smiled, holding her away from himself suddenly. "So, you're going to set yourself free. You're on the way, Clare. You've ditched Paul, which is probably the best thing you've ever done in your life. You've joined Earthwatch and made a stand for what you believe in, and you have me. All you have to do now, my love, is get free of the lady Isobel."

Clare glanced around her. "I don't know if I can, Neil. She needs me, and sometimes I think that deep down inside I must need her."

"Nonsense!" He put his hands on her shoulders and shook her. "When did you last do your crazy meditation? In Edinburgh, when you were on your own, right? The best thing to do is to see you never have time to do it again. You haven't done it here, have you?"

Twice she and Zak had tried to meditate together in the borrowed apartment and twice it had failed. Isobel had refused to come to her. Her mind had remained empty. Isobel had no wish to be dismissed. Zak had gone back to Cambridge.

"She's still here, Neil. She is here, at Duncairn! And she is inside me—"

"She is not inside you, Clare!" Suddenly he was shouting. "She is dead. She is at rest!"

"No." Clare stopped struggling and stared up into his face. "That is the whole point, Neil. Don't you see? She is not at rest!"

Rex had a spray of freesias in his hand. He thrust them at Emma with a boyish grin. "Just stick them in some water for now, Emma, then we'll get going. I've a table booked for eight-thirty and I've got a taxi waiting at the corner." He grinned. "I wasn't sure about the neighbors. . . ."

Emma had pushed the flowers, still in their cellophane, into a vase. She stood it in the sink and ran cold water into it. "I don't give a damn about the neighbors. You're so provincial, Rex! Anyway, we've nothing to hide. I told Peter I might have dinner with you while he was away." She stooped to sniff the blooms, hiding her face.

He had booked a table at Claridges. "First things first, Emma. I have told your brother I don't want the castle. I've withdrawn my offer." He ordered himself a Scotch and a white wine and soda for her.

Now that he had made the decision, he felt as if a load had

been lifted from his mind. The dream castle would have drained his personal resources to nothing—left him broke and foolish. He recognized that now. "Paul looked pretty mad."

"He would." Emma grimaced. "I'm glad. Clare will be so relieved!" She smiled at him and reached across the table to touch his hand. "Thank you, Rex. I know how much owning Duncairn meant to you."

"I think Clare is entitled to it." He sighed. "I've been reading up some more of my Scottish history. Robert Bruce took the castle away from the Comyns, you know. One day I'll trace the connections between my family and the earls of Buchan. I know it's there, but I can't prove it. Not yet." He gave a sheepish smile. "Most of it was wishful thinking, I guess." He looked at Emma. "There is still oil there, Emma. Clare will have to accept that one day soon someone is going to take it."

"But they won't take her castle."

"The Comyns' castle," he corrected her gently. "I guess not. Not unless she changes her mind and sells to someone else."

"She'll never do that. Will they hide the scars of what they do?"

"Sure they will. Eventually. No well lasts forever."

Emma picked up her glass as soon as it appeared before her. "But it won't be the same, will it? I suppose some of the romance will go. That feeling of timelessness. I felt like a complete intruder when I went up there. I didn't like it much, to be honest. That bleak landscape, those angry cliffs. I can't think why Clare loves it so passionately."

"It's in her blood." Rex frowned. "I didn't know you'd been there, Emma." For a moment he looked shocked. "How come you didn't tell me?"

She shrugged. "I only went once. Clare took me up there to stay on a holiday when we were children. I never went back."

He frowned. "Perhaps she'll let me go there for a holiday one day. Consolation prize. What do you think?"

Emma smiled. "I'm sure she would. You must meet her."

"I'd like to. So—" Rex raised his glass. "Where do we go from here, Emma?"

"We?" Emma looked down, suddenly embarrassed.

"You and I. Together or separately?" He took a gulp of neat whisky, then he added some soda to his glass. "I've screwed up all around, Emma. My career; my ambitions, such as they were; my castle; my marriage—"

There was a pause.

"I thought you said you and your wife got on well together," Emma said cautiously.

"We do. Don't misunderstand me. I just don't think we want the same things. She suddenly seems ready to retire, put on her slippers, pick up her knitting, buy that goddamn house on Martha's Vineyard!"

"And what do you want to do?"

He shrugged. "Have a passionate affair with a beautiful Englishwoman perhaps. Forget my failures and my age." He didn't look at her.

"You're not a failure, Rex, and you're not old." Emma was suddenly crisp. "And if you want a beautiful Englishwoman, I'm sure I can introduce you to one or two."

"I see." He glanced up, trying to keep the unhappiness from his face. "Peter is coming home, is that it?"

"He was always coming home, Rex." She spoke very gently, her decision made.

He sighed. "You know, you've been very good for me, Mrs. Cassidy." He spoke her name with humorous irony. "I was a selfish, single-minded bastard when I met you. I think you've found whatever there is in me that's still human."

"I'm glad." Emma suddenly pushed back her chair and stood up.

Somehow she held back her tears until she reached the ladies' room. After rushing into the cubicle, she slammed the lock and, leaning her face against the door, she began to sob.

Neil was asleep, half turned away from her, the moonlight streaming across his face while Clare lay, propped on her elbow, watching him. For the first time they had talked about themselves that night. "Are you on the pill, Clare?" He had sat down beside her on the bed, his face serious.

She had shaken her head. "I can't have children, so there's no need." She had said it calmly, without self-pity, but she saw him frown.

"Nevertheless, these days one ought to take precautions anyway." He stood up abruptly. "Neither Kath nor I have ever been the promiscuous type—you're in no danger of catching anything." He smiled. "But you should have thought of it."

She blushed. "I'm not used to this sort of thing, Neil. There's only ever been Paul."

He sat down again and she saw that he believed her. "Then I'm honored."

Somehow she managed to smile, to keep it light. "Yes, you are!"

He pulled her to him. There was no violence this time, just tenderness—the antagonism gone, and afterward he slept while she lay awake, staring up at the ceiling. She was relaxed and happy, listening to the sharp, urgent calls of the night birds in the distance.

When Isobel came, she was completely unprepared.

Chapter Twenty-nine

Christian came to stand behind Isobel at the window and looked out across the dark courtyard. The first gales had hit Scotland now, and the leaves were being torn from the trees and whipped against the walls of the abbey to lie in soggy heaps against the stone. They were both thinking about Robert, the man each loved, one as a brother, the other as a lover, the man for whom they might both have to die. Isobel closed her eyes and began silently to pray again that he at least was safe.

"What do you think is going to happen to us when we get to Edward?" Christian had long since accepted her husband's death—her anguish and sorrow for Christopher was contained now with the other sorrow that had overwhelmed her when her first husband, Gratney, had died. She was a tall, beautiful woman, very like her brother to look at. She had Robert's eyes, his coloring, and above all his bearing.

Isobel shivered and glanced back into the darkness of the room. The queen and her stepdaughter were already asleep, huddled together on the bed. Their imprisonment had brought them all close at last. The queen had lost her hauteur; her fear, and her desperate attempts to hide it, had endeared her at last to her two sisters-in-law. Only to Isobel was she still reserved, even though, night after night, they had to share a room and even a bed.

It had been a nightmare journey: long days in the saddle, surrounded by Lord Ross's escort of fifty men, followed by nights with the women locked together into a succession of chambers in towers and castles as they rode southward through Scotland. Now, at Perth, they were incarcerated in the guest house of St. John's Abbey while outside the door two English soldiers were playing dice. They could hear the roll of the bone on the flagstone floor and the silence as the men bent to look, then the roar of approval as each successive score came up.

Mary was sitting near them on the edge of the bed. "Did you hear that Edward has given orders for them to dismantle the Abbey of Scone—he is so angry that Robert was crowned there, and so determined no other Scots king ever should be, he has ordered that they remove every single stone." She was trying to fill the silence, trying to distract them.

Christian glanced at Isobel in the darkness. By the light of the stars she could see that the other woman's face was tight with fear as she stared out of the high, unshuttered window, and suddenly they were all thinking of the coronation. Edward must know that it was Isobel, the daughter of Fife, who had placed the crown on Robert's head.

She touched Isobel's hand gently, but there was nothing she could say to reassure her. Instead she talked about herself. "I am so thankful Gratney did not live to see this. It would have broken his heart."

"What about your son?" Isobel rested her head wearily against the stone embrasure. At least she had no children to worry over.

Christian shrugged. "Like your brother, he is in England now—a ward of the English court." She sighed. "Lord Ross told me he has been taken into the household of the Prince of Wales. Please God he is safe." Both women were silent for a moment. "Surely they will be spared punishment," she went on at last. "Edward would not harm them just because they are our kin, would he?"

Isobel looked back into the dark room again. They had been given no fire or candles, and the only light was from the frosty sky at the narrow window. She was thinking about Marjorie, the King of Scots' daughter—his only child and his heir. What would become of her? And what mercy could she herself expect from Edward of England who had ordered that no quarter be given to the women or children who supported the rebel king; he who had ordered that the impersonal stones of a church be dismantled because it had displeased him?

"He will have me put to death," she said at last in a whisper. "You have done no more than follow Robert—you can plead that he forced you to stay with him, all of you, and everyone knows that Elizabeth thought him a fool to proclaim himself king. It is I who went to him of my own free will and put the crown upon his head." She clenched her fists. The icy weight of terror was there all the time, lurking in the shadows. She tried not to think about it; refused to allow her mind to dwell on what would happen when they reached the King of England; tried to hope, but in her heart she knew he would sentence her to die. Her nightmare now was the method he would chose to put her to death. It haunted her every moment. Would he sentence her to hang or to burn? Would he sentence her to be drawn, like poor Sir William Wallace? In her dreams she had already felt the rope around her neck a hundred times, and another hundred she had felt the flames, and smelled the smoke and dreamed of Mairi, but Edward of England was known for his unpredictable vindictiveness. No one could guess how he would punish them in the end. She forced her mind away again, feeling the sweat break out on the palms of her hands. She wanted to squeeze her way out of the narrow, high window and jump to her freedom, to soar up toward the clear, impersonal windy sky, but she couldn't. There would be no escape. She felt her stomach begin to churn and for a moment she clung to Christian's shoulder.

Outside the door the guards let out a yell of triumph. One of them had thrown a six.

King Edward was at Lanercost, a lonely priory in the hills of Cumberland within sight of Hadrian's Wall. There the four women and the child were brought before him in October 1306.

He had dealt with hundreds of Robert's adherents already, seeing the prisoners dragged before him in the chapter house of the priory and then taken out again to face death or imprisonment. When the women in their dirty, ragged clothes were at last herded into his presence he was tired and ill tempered as he stared at them, surrounded by a silent crowd of his supporters and the royal bodyguard.

Elizabeth fell on her knees before him, and the others, taking their lead from her, followed suit. Marjorie was crying.

Edward was sitting on a raised chair with a pointed back, his gaunt frame swathed in furs against the east wind that swept across the hills. The shrewd, bright eyes were sunk now in the pallid wrinkles of his face, but they had lost none of their venom. He surveyed the women silently, scrutinizing the faces of the prisoners one by one, then he turned to one of the men standing behind him. "See, Lord Buchan, it seems we have caught your runaway wife!"

Isobel gave a gasp of fear for the first time, looking beyond the king to his companions. There, behind Edward, her husband was standing with his eyes fixed on her face. She had never seen such anger and hatred in anyone's expression before.

Edward smiled coldly. He was rubbing his thin fingers, laden with rings, together in his lap. The joints were swollen with arthritis. The cold wind made him ache all over and he had a hard, painful cough.

"So, the outlaw's women," he said at last. "Wife and mistress—" His eyes dwelt on Isobel's face for a moment. "Sisters and child." He stood up slowly, an extremely tall man, head and shoulders above many of those around him, and he took a dragging, painful step forward. He would deal with them swiftly, then he could leave the drafty chapter house and drink some mulled wine to ease the cold a little. He gave them all another cold, appraising glance. He knew exactly what he was going to do with them all.

"You, madam." He was addressing Elizabeth now. "I hear you did not approve of your husband's puny attempt to snatch himself a throne. My spies tell me you even rebuked him for it." He gave a tight smile. "And you are still, when all is said and done, the daughter of the Earl of Ulster." He paused thoughtfully. Lord Ulster was a powerful man—one he did not wish to alienate. "I am inclined, madam, to show you leniency, although I shall imprison you, of course." He turned to a clerk near him. "Madam Elizabeth is to be sent south to Burstwick in Holderness and confined there with two companions. Sober, elderly companions, I think." He turned to her again. "To help divert your thoughts to prayer and dissuade you from any ideas you may have of returning to court—mine, or your husband's." The last three words were spoken in a mocking tone that brought a smile to the faces of his followers.

His attention left Elizabeth, who was staring at him, almost faint with relief, and moved on to Christian, who was kneeling beside her, upright and tight-lipped. "Lady Christian." He gave a grim smile. "Your husband has already paid with his life for his allegiance to the outlaw. I wonder, would you have willingly followed your brother had you known what lay in store for him? Your son is my ward now." He paused again thoughtfully. Christian did not move. Her eyes rested on his face, unblinking. "I think, like your sister-in-law, you too must spend the rest of your days in prayer and meditation. Where shall I send her?" He turned to the clerk and snapped his fingers.

"You suggested a nunnery in Lincolnshire, Your Grace." The man fumbled with his notes. "Sixhills, Your Grace." The mother superior there was well known to the king and would be strict enough with the outlaw's sister. He smiled to himself. The king had, with his usual thoroughness and impeccable eye for detail, already thought out the punishment for these women. However much he made a show of deciding their fate now, he already knew what was to happen to every one of them.

Christian had closed her eyes. She too was weak with relief. There was a movement of unrest in the room, even disappointment. Was the king growing feeble at long last, to let them off so lightly? But there were more sentences to pronounce.

Edward's cold eye had moved on to Marjorie. The girl bit her lip, desperately trying to control her tears. She straightened her thin shoulders. Lady Isobel had told her that her father would expect her to be brave and behave like a princess of the Scots, no matter what happened.

"With the pretended king's child," he said portentously,

"we are dealing with a traitor." There was a sudden expectant hush in the room. Isobel could see pity in one or two of the faces near the king, but his own was like carved stone. She saw Mary's hand creep out to hold Marjorie's as the long silence drew out around them.

"The Tower of London," he said at last. "The Lady Marjorie will be taken there and held there, incarcerated in a cage." He smiled again. "So that the people of London can come and view the spawn of the traitor, Bruce." There was a gasp from the men around him. Marjorie looked up, her eyes full of tears, not understanding, but already the king had turned his attention to Mary.

"And a cage for you too, madam, I think, to curb your rebellion. I wish to make an example of you and the child. When the people see you penned like an animal they will mock and they will spit on you and they will think twice before ever they support a Bruce again—people like Neil Campbell, madam, who persists in his support of your pretended king." He fixed her with a stony stare. His spies had told him everything, of her passionate support of her brother, of her vilification of the King of England, and even of her love for a rebellious Highlander. Edward did not like the sound of Mary Bruce. "And we'll hang your cage somewhere in Scotland, I think, to remind your brother's would-be subjects that he and his family are fit only for a menagerie. Caged lions." He smiled. "Such as I brought to Scotland, to show the people what the King of England does with a lion when he holds one alive!"

The clerk was busy scribbling. The king had already given orders for the cages to be constructed. At Roxburgh this one.

Mary had gone white. She stared at Edward, transfixed, her hand still clasping Marjorie's. Isobel closed her eyes. As the king's attention moved slowly from one woman to the next, she had grown more and more afraid. To be caged like an animal was the most terrible fate she could imagine, far worse than anything she feared. Worse even than death. Death at least was over soon, and then your soul could fly free, up toward the clear blue sky.

"And now, Lady Buchan." At last Edward turned to her.

"We come to you. And in your case we have your husband
here to advise us. Lord Buchan, do you have anything to say
before we sentence your wife for high treason?"

Isobel had stopped breathing; her mind had stopped func-
tioning. Part of her was watching from some great distance as
the earl stepped forward. She saw his lips move, heard the
words spoken, echoing in the silence of her head—heresy
. . . sorcery . . . murder . . . treason . . . seduction . . .
adultery . . . the subversion of his men . . . the thieving of
his best horses. . . . The list went on and on, his hatred and
his resentment palpable, surrounding her, enfolding everyone in the room, encircling the king.

She was completely cold. On her knees on the flagstones, a
little apart from the other women, she raised her eyes at last
to look at Edward's face. His thin lips were almost colorless,
his features gaunt, the papery skin drawn tight across the
bones, the eyes deep set and black, two bright, intelligent,
cruel eyes fixed upon hers, and she knew suddenly, irrelevantly, that he too was near death.

Unexpectedly he smiled, but it was not at her. "So, what do
you suggest I do with her, my lord, to punish her for this
overlong list of crimes?"

"The death sentence, Your Grace." Lord Buchan spoke
firmly. "No less. She has to die."

Isobel closed her eyes. She clenched her hands tightly. She
must not break down; she had to be brave. Robert had always
been so proud of her bravery, and she must make Robert
proud of her now, even at the end.

The king sat down again painfully and leaned back in his
chair. "The rope," he said musingly, "or the fire?" Behind
him the clerk sighed. He already knew the sentence. He was
cold and he wanted to go out to the kitchens and find himself
some hot soup to take the ache of these cold northern moors
out of his bones.

"No." The king sat forward again slowly. "No, my lady.
Death would be too easy for the woman who put the crown
on the outlaw's head. Too easy and too quick. A cage like the
others." He smiled slightly at Isobel's gasp of fear. "A cage,
madam, to show you up as the animal you are. A cage where

everyone can see you and mock and torment you—the woman who crowned an outlaw, the woman who lay with him as a whore. You too will serve as an example to the people of this land who dare to defy me, and we will hang your cage at Berwick. You love your land of Scotland, madam, I think. I saw that when you came to me at Westminster. You'll be able to see your beloved Scotland from your cage, madam, but you will never set foot there again. Berwick belongs to England now. And you will hang there in your cage until you die."

"Clare! Clare, for God's sake, wake up!" Neil was shaking her. "Wake up! It's only a dream." He pulled her into his arms and held her tightly. The room was ice cold and he found he was shivering violently. "Clare!"

She stared at him blankly. "She was here," she said slowly. "She was here. It has happened. The cage. . . ."

His arms tightened around her. "It all happened a long time ago, Clare. It's finished."

"No, it's not finished; it's not!" She clung to him. "I can't go through it, Neil. I can't. Not the cage! I can't!" She was almost hysterical. In the distance they could hear Casta howling from the room across the landing. "She's making me go through it with her. She's forcing me to live it!"

"That's not true, Clare. It was only a dream; only your imagination. It's not real."

"Not real?" She pushed him away and scrambled out of the bed, groping for her negligee, which had slipped to the floor beside the wall. "How can you say that! She is real. She is as real as you are!" She knotted the sash around her with shaking fingers. "Dear God, what am I going to do?"

Neil swung his legs over the side of the bed and groped for his bathrobe. "Have you ever been to Berwick, Clare?" He leaned across to switch on the bedside lamp.

She stared at him. "Of course I have—"

"Really been to Berwick? To the castle, where she was held?"

"Well, no." Her face was white, her eyes huge in the lamplight.

"Would it help to go there? To face it? It's a ruin now, Clare
—far more ruined than Duncairn. There's nothing left: no
ghosts, no shadows, no echoes, just a beautiful river and a
railway bridge!" He smiled and was relieved to see an answering lightening in her eyes. "Would you like to go there?
If I come with you?"

"I don't know." She sat down on the bed with a shiver. "I
don't know that I've got the strength, Neil. I'm frightened."
She looked very frail in the thin silk negligee, her arms
crossed defensively across her breasts.

"You'll find there is nothing to be afraid of. The cage is long
gone. Everything has gone."

"I know."

"And I'll be there."

"Where is Clare?" Sir David Royland looked at Paul over
the rim of his glass.

Paul was sitting in the chair by the desk in Geoffrey's study.
He was in a foul temper. Being summoned by his brothers
like an errant schoolboy was bad enough; being lectured by
David and patronized by Geoffrey was worse, especially as
he knew he was in the wrong.

"Christ Almighty!" David had burst out as soon as the door
closed behind Chloe. In the corridor outside she stopped
dead. "What possessed you, man? Whatever happened to
honesty? To honor? To your common sense? Do you realize
you could get five years for this?" His handsome face was
contorted with fury.

Geoffrey was standing by the table, his own glass and Paul's
still in his hand. Pursing his lips he handed one of them to
Paul. "Steady on, old boy. I'm sure Paul realizes the gravity of
what he's done."

"Does he?" David was still shouting. "I doubt it! He's
dragged the entire family into the mud with him. The entire
family! Including his wife! So, where is she, Paul?"

"In Scotland." Paul's voice was flat and defiant.

"Is it true she's left you?"

Paul shrugged. It was none of their damn business.

David looked up at the ceiling. "Dear God, man! Pull yourself together. Think what it will look like to the press. Your wife walks out on you a few days before you are accused of fraud. It will emphasize your guilt, don't you see? They'll think she's done it because of that."

"So you think I'd do better to fetch her home? A madwoman, to prop up my case!" Paul leaned back in the chair, his voice heavy with sarcasm. "Come home, darling, and tell them what an honest, kind, doting husband I am!"

"It would help." David's voice was acid.

"I don't think it would necessarily be a good thing," Geoffrey put in hurriedly. "Clare is unwell—"

"Then we will see that she is cared for." David walked over to the window. He stood with his back to his brothers. "Where is she, Paul?"

"In Edinburgh." Paul drained his glass. "With her lover."

There was a moment's stunned silence. Geoffrey walked to his desk and sat down behind it. He put his head in his hands. "The press is going to have a field day."

"Who is the lover?" David had not turned. He put his empty glass down on the low sill of the bay window next to the scented geranium, embarrassed and astonished at the sudden pang of jealousy that shook him. "Do we know?"

"Yes, we know. Neil Forbes."

David swung around. "The Earthwatch man?"

"The same."

"Christ!" David hit his palm against his forehead. "And you let her go to him?"

Abruptly Paul stood up. He slammed his empty glass down on his brother's desk. "What would you suggest I should have done? Lock her up?" He paused. Now was not the moment to tell them he couldn't even do that properly. "Or should I have gone after her and dragged her back?"

"Remember Clare's state of mind, David," Geoffrey put in from his position behind the desk.

"In my view Clare is a thoroughly bored and spoiled young woman. Her neuroses are frankly unimportant compared with this catastrophe." David gave Paul a withering look.

Paul's color heightened slightly, but any reply he was going to make was forestalled by Geoffrey. "I think you and I should go and fetch her, David. I'm sure she will see the sense in returning to London while Paul is in need of her support."

"I doubt it." Paul's anger was simmering to the surface. "And if anyone fetches her, it should be me."

"You have to stay in London"—David was sharp—"to prepare your defense. Thank God father isn't alive to see what you've done to the family name." He swung around to face the door as it opened and Chloe peered into the room.

"I'm sorry to intrude." She glanced from one man to the other hastily. "But your church guild ladies are beginning to arrive, Geoff. I wasn't sure what to do with them, so I've put them in the TV room."

Geoffrey stood up. He glanced from one brother to the other. "Give us her address, Paul. David and I will go and talk to her, then if she agrees, she can come here to stay for the time being."

"May I ask who is coming to stay?" Chloe stopped on her way out of the room and looked back.

"Clare, my dear."

Chloe frowned. "Geoff! I thought we'd cleared all that up." She looked at Paul hard. "She does not need Geoff's help, Paul. There is nothing wrong with her."

Paul laughed harshly. "The ministrations of the church! Oh, but she does, Chloe! Twice over. Not only does Geoffrey have to retrieve her sanity if he can and reclaim her from whatever ghosts have possessed her, but he has to remind her now of the sanctity of the marriage vows she made in front of him when he married us and stop her from running off with the first man who is stupid enough to take her on. My wife has proved herself to be a whore; a fitting mate for a crook like me, I'm sure you'll agree!" He pushed past her and out into the hall.

He was conscious momentarily of several pairs of eyes watching from the open door of another room, then he was out in the porch. Glowering, he set off down the path. He had the car and he had Clare's address in his pocket. If Geoffrey and David thought he was going to sit back and let them get to Clare first, they had another think coming. Oh, they could have her, and welcome, and force her to dress up in a sober black dress and jacket with pearls at her throat and ears when she sat in the visitors' gallery at his trial at the Old Bailey or wherever they dragged him, but he was going to get to her first, and by the time he came to trial he would be a rich man. Rich with the money from Duncairn, because Sigma had at last come back with a yes.

The castle at Berwick upon Tweed is almost gone. Above the angle of the river, near the towering arches of Stephenson's railway bridge, there are some walls, the remains of the sixteenth-century Water Tower, and some steps, known locally as the Breakynecks. Above them a wall built by Edward I climbs almost vertically up the hill, and there more masonry rears up. Beyond it—everywhere else the castle used to be—there is the railway station, monument to a Victorian disregard for history.

Standing on the remains of the Water Tower, Neil and Clare stared south across the broad river Tweed toward the low hills of Northumberland. The tide was low and seaweed stained the shingle beaches. Out in the center of the water three swans swam majestically upstream against the current.

All the way there in the car, next to Neil, Clare had found herself wanting to touch him; she felt herself charged with excitement. Her body had been alive, a separate entity of its own, not listening to her brain. It had been conscious only of the man so close beside her behind the wheel of the old Land-Rover, not touching her, perhaps not even aware of her in the long silences as they drove south from Edinburgh down the A1. Now they were here he put his arm around her at last as they stood staring out across the river toward the south, but it was too late. The horror, the memories were closing in around her again.

She shivered. Slowly she turned and stared up the wall that climbed the steep hillside. Neil watched her.

It was a cold day; the wind was biting, carrying with it the salt smell of the sea. Behind the gray stone of the wall, smoke from the chimneys of Berwick, sweet with the scent of burning fruitwood and pine, rose and mingled, shredded, with the patchwork of torn, ragged clouds. Neil pushed his hands deep into the pockets of his jacket.

Clare turned back to the river as, high above them, the train crept cautiously across the old bridge into Berwick Station. It brought the twentieth century only momentarily into focus. Both were thinking of the past.

Neil touched the stones of the wall experimentally. They were very cold. He glanced at Clare. "How did she survive the winter?" he asked quietly. He had known the moment she was no longer conscious of him as a man.

She was staring at the bank of the river opposite. Some oystercatchers were working their way up the shingle beach, their black-and-white plumage and red beaks bright against the muddy stones. "They were going to keep her outside in the cage," she said after a moment. Sometimes she found she could remember things, things that she had not yet seen in the story, as if Isobel's memories and her own were one and the same. "Until they realized she would die. That wouldn't have done at all. They wanted her alive. So when the deep cold came, eventually they took the cage inside. But they never let her out."

"Bastards." Neil shrugged deeper into his coat. "She must have been a very brave lady."

Clare smiled. "She was. She never let them see her cry. She was a Scots noblewoman, and she never let them forget it. Even when the spring came and they took the cage and hoisted it back onto the walls, and all the people came out to see how she had fared through the winter and to taunt her because her king had not come back to rescue her."

Neil frowned. "Do you think she haunts this castle?"

Clare stared back at the high walls. For a moment she didn't say anything, then she shrugged. "I don't know. Perhaps. I think I would, in her shoes."

Privately Neil agreed. "I'm glad there's so little of the castle left. Shall we go to the hotel now?"

Clare was still staring up at the wall above them. "I'd like to climb up there first. There is a tower there, at the angle of the wall—"

"It's not the same date, Clare. The old castle has gone."

She shook her head. "Some of it was there then—this high wall down to the river—the tower we saw by the station. They were there, Neil, when she was here." She faced him, feeling the wind tug at her hair as they stood above the river. "Do you still want me to do it, Neil? Shall I sit down here, on this seat, and summon her back to Berwick?" Her voice had tightened unsteadily and Neil frowned. He didn't like the wild note he heard there.

He shook his head. "I want us to do what Zak suggested on the phone. Quietly at the hotel, tonight. I want you to try to dismiss her. Send her away. You have been to Berwick now. You've faced the castle. You've seen where it happened and it means no more to you than it does to me—an awful, tragic, romantic story, but a story. From the past. Nothing to do with today. Zak thinks, and I agree with him, that having been here your nightmares will stop and that, given determination on your part, Isobel will leave you alone."

"I hope you're right."

"I *am* right." He put his arm around her shoulders again. "You'll see. You're going to banish poor Isobel back to where she belongs—the land of shadows and dreams, and then you're going to get on with your own life."

It was St. Andrew's Night and the public rooms at the hotel were hung with flags. Neil signed the register and collected the key to their room. Casta had been left with Jack at Duncairn. "They're having a party later," he said as he guided her toward the stairs. "The receptionist said we might be a bit disturbed by the noise, but we're invited to it if we want to go. I'm sorry. I didn't realize what date it was."

Clare laughed suddenly. "Oh, Neil! The archetypal Scotsman, and you didn't think of St. Andrew! You, of all people!"

He smiled gently. "We're not in Scotland, Clare. Berwick is English for the moment, remember?"

"Yes. I remember. How could I forget?"

The room was small and painted white, with a wardrobe, a narrow double bed and a large, much-mirrored dressing table next to the window. Squeezed among the rest of the furniture were two armchairs. Through a door in the corner they could see a small bathroom with a heap of snowy towels. Near them on a low cupboard stood a kettle and a tray with cups and saucers and little packets of tea, coffee, sugar, and powdered milk. There were two wrapped wafer biscuits, two apples, and two oranges in a bowl.

Neil smiled at her. "A feast seems to be included! Will this do?"

Clare was standing looking around. "It's fine." She walked over to the window and threw it up, letting in a blast of cold, damp air. They could see over the rooftops toward the river. Neil came and stood behind her. He frowned. They could just see the outline of the Constable Tower behind the leafless trees. He put his arms around Clare. "Do you want to change? I'll take you out to dinner first if you like."

Her body was tense, unresponsive, as she shook her head. "I want to do it now. Straight away."

Neil frowned, uncomfortable now that it had come to the moment. "Doesn't it have to be dark or something?"

She laughed bitterly. "It has to be neither dark nor anything else."

"And you're sure you can do it with me here?"

She shrugged. "I don't know. I've brought the candle . . ." Her voice trailed away. "I do need you here, Neil. You won't leave me?"

"Of course I won't leave you." He took her hand. "You don't have to do it if you don't want to, Clare."

"But I do, don't you see? She's going to torment me for the rest of my life if I don't stop her—appease her—send her away—whatever I have to do to get rid of her." Her voice rose desperately. She moved away from him abruptly and sat down on the end of the bed. She felt strange, remote, still unaware of him as a man. All the sexual charge that had been between them had gone. Her body was cold, centered within itself, closed once more to every emotion but the emotions of that other woman from the past.

Silently she pulled her suitcase onto the bed and opened it. From the bottom she extricated one of the silver candles, wrapped in tissue. She took out the small candleholder and set the candle in it and put it on the bedside table, then she glanced at him for the first time. "Have you got any matches?" Her face was white and strained. Isobel had refused to come to her when Zak was there in Edinburgh. Perhaps she sensed that Clare was going to try to finish it. Perhaps she would refuse the summons again this time. She half hoped she would.

Neil shook his head grimly, then he raised his hand and touched her arm. "I saw some in the bathroom." A packet emblazoned with the hotel's name and crest lay in a small straw basket with soaps and shampoos and tissues.

He lighted the candle for her and realized that his hands were shaking. Silently he backed away and sat down on one of the chairs in the corner as Clare picked up the candle and set it on the floor. The flame flickered in the draft from the open window, and she turned and stared out for a moment. Darkness was almost on them now. Opaque, windswept, the river had gone, as had the shadows of the castle. There were no stars. Rain spattered in on the cold wind and with it the dank salt stench of the North Sea.

The room was growing dark.

Isobel did not have to be summoned. She was there. Waiting. Staring into the past and into the future.

She had been put in a underground cell beneath the castle. No one spoke to her, no one told her what was happening. Twice a day they brought her food. The place was completely dark. They did not give her a candle. There were no blankets, only a bed of musty damp heather that rustled slightly in the darkness. By the dim light that flooded in when the door opened she had time to see the dungeon—low-ceilinged and foul—then all was darkness again. They gave her a bucket to relieve herself and a jug of water to drink, that was all. She had to find both by groping in the darkness.

When the sentencing was over there had been total silence in the chapter house at Lanercost. Then Marjorie had begun to sob. At last Mary, still stunned by the king's pronouncements, had put out her arms and hugged the child to her. The crying stopped.

Edward had folded his fur mantle more closely around his

thin body. "Take them away," he said. His eyes had strayed to Isobel's white face for a moment, then he smiled. He had turned to the Earl of Buchan and he slapped him on the shoulder.

There had been no time for good-byes, no chance to speak at all. The women were separated at once and Isobel found herself locked in one of the monk's cells, alone. She was too stunned by the sentence to react.

For a long time she stood at the narrow window staring out at the bleak Cumberland moors. The heather had turned brown; it was matted and flattened by the rain. Eventually she turned away and climbed into the narrow wooden bed. Wrapping herself in the thin woolen blanket, she turned her face to the wall.

For the journey to Berwick they put chains on her wrists. "Mustn't let our little bird fly away, must we?" The man hammering them closed didn't trouble to be too accurate with his blows. She gasped with pain as the hammer slipped and she saw her wrist thicken and begin to color. They put her in a closed litter—Edward had forbidden her to ride, instinctively knowing that riding was a pleasure, a freedom, and therefore denying it.

Then the nightmare had begun.

At first when they came for her it was an enormous relief. It was a brilliant sunny day and the glare and brightness dazzled her after the darkness. The air was sharp and fresh. They made her climb to the top of one of the towers in the walls, stooping beneath the low doorway to step out onto the warm, leaded roof. There, from the ramparts overlooking the town and the bend of the river, they had hung her cage, a small wooden structure, latticed with iron, with open, barred sides so that she could be seen from every angle as the king had decreed. Only the back was closed—hanging as it was against the wall of the castle—and there there was a small enclosed cubicle, built into the ramparts, a privy for her, by order of the king. The governor of the castle was waiting for her. He swung open the door between two battlements of stone and beckoned her over. "Your lodgings are ready, lady." He gave an exaggerated bow.

Isobel stared at the cage in horror.

"No," she whispered. "No." She shook her head desperately and looked around her, but she was surrounded now with men, the castle guard, the constable of the castle, and the armorer, ready at last to strike off her chains. This man was more careful. He examined her bruised wrists with a frown and a professional shake of the head, then with a practiced stroke of mallet and chisel he had cut off the manacles. Isobel rubbed her wrists and straightened her shoulders. With a desperate attempt to cling to her pride she smiled. "So special a little house! And just for me?"

"Just for you, my lady." He didn't hurry her. They all stood, patiently waiting.

"And with such a commanding view."

She wanted to stretch; to hold out her arms to the sun. There in the cage it was shadowy, dappled with rays of light, sliced by the shadows of the bars lying across the floor.

In the distance from the wall walk she could see the brilliant blue line on the horizon that was the sea.

The men were growing impatient. She saw the governor shift his weight from one foot to the other. The sun shone on the mail at his throat and on his shoulders, blinding her. She raised her hand to her eyes.

Behind her one of the guards moved impatiently. His sword rasped against the flints of the wall.

Isobel swallowed. She would not let them push her in. She must keep her pride at all cost. She stepped toward the parapet. "I trust it is securely fastened," she managed to say. "I'd hate to fall so far."

"Never fear, my lady. That is built to last a lifetime," the governor replied grimly. He offered her his hand. Isobel felt herself grow cold. She had begun to shake all over. She took his hand, hoping he wouldn't notice how her own trembled, and stepped up toward the parapet, then she crouched to fit through the small latticed door and climbed inside. The door swung shut behind her and she saw the key turn in the lock. The governor withdrew it. For a moment he stood looking at her unsmiling, then he turned away. He had gone several steps, followed by all but two guards who remained at attention on the wall, when he turned. "I forgot to tell you, madam. Lest you get bored in your new abode, his grace the king has arranged some entertainment for you tomorrow." He gestured toward the open ground below the castle wall, then he left her.

Isobel looked around in growing panic. The cage was some six feet long and about five feet deep, securely bolted into the crenellations of the wall. Beneath her feet, under the oak floorboards, there was a dizzying drop: the height of the tower to the ground beneath. Above her head they had half roofed the cage with heather to give a meager shelter from the sun and rain. She tried cautiously to stand up and found she couldn't without crouching.

There was a shout below. She looked down. Two boys had stationed themselves in the scrub beneath the wall. One put his fingers to his mouth and whistled, then he knelt and groped around his feet. In another moment a stone whistled through the air. It struck the heather roof of the cage and fell harmlessly back to the ground; a second followed it. It fell into the cage and skittered across the floor to Isobel's feet.

"Mother of God!" She moved as far back as she could, but still they could see her. Still they could watch her fear.

The boys shouted at someone in the distance and she saw two other figures heading across the green from the town. Behind them two women, alerted by the noise and curious to see what it was that had appeared on the castle walls, made their way toward her too. Isobel watched in terror. There was nowhere to hide save the privy. Desperately she crept behind the small wooden partition and pressed herself flat against the castle wall.

Beneath the cage the crowd grew all afternoon. She could hear the shouts and catcalls, see the hail of missiles that from time to time rained down between the bars. Twice she crept out from her tiny refuge and each time she was greeted by a chorus of yells as she knelt on the cage floor, blinking in the afternoon sunlight.

All afternoon they stayed, amusing themselves at her expense. The crowd sometimes grew and sometimes thinned, but always they were there, the people of Berwick, taunting and tormenting her.

Somehow Isobel held back her tears. She mustn't give way. She must not give them the pleasure of seeing her suffering.

Slowly the sun went down in a blaze of red and gold and the shadow of the castle below the cage lengthened across the ground. The evening grew chill. One by one the people below began to leave, making their way back to their homes and firesides. By the time it was completely dark the meadow below was deserted.

Isobel was shivering violently. The wind had risen, whistling around the ramparts and through the bars. She felt her way back to the back of the cage and peered between the crenellations, through the bars of the door toward the wall walk. The guards had vanished in the darkness. The castle was silent.

She could hear her teeth chattering violently now. Behind her and below her, all around there was nothing but a void of blackness. She peered out at it, trying to force her eyes to pierce the night, but she could see nothing, and for the first time in her life she was afraid of the dark. Desperately she tried to huddle out of the wind, clutching her ragged gown and kirtle around her. Beneath her shift her legs and feet were bare.

Then someone came. A woman, tall and slim and beautifully dressed, swathed in warm furs, with behind her a page carrying a flare, a woman who in another life might have been Isobel's friend, her equal. Her arms were full of rugs. She beckoned one of the guards forward out of the darkness into the crazy tossing light of the flare. "Open the cage and give her these."

The guard did as he was bidden. In the wildly leaping shadows he fitted a key into the lock and pulled open the barred door. The bundle that was thrust through to Isobel contained two blankets and a fur-lined cloak. Isobel clutched them gratefully in the flickering light, terrified the wind might tear them from her grasp and snatch them away through the bars into the great black darkness behind her. The door was slammed shut and relocked, then the woman

stepped closer and stared in at her. She had a haughty, stern
face that showed very little compassion. Merely practicality.
If the prisoner froze to death on the first night of her exhibi-
tion, the lesson to the people of Scotland would be lost and
her punishment cut far shorter than King Edward intended.

She studied Isobel's white face in the leaping torchlight
and for a moment her hostility wavered. "I will have some
food brought for you," she said, the wind whipping the words
from her lips, "and tomorrow I will see you get some warmer
clothing."

Then she was gone and Isobel was left alone once more.

With shaking hands she fastened the cloak around her and
wrapped herself in the rugs. They were warm and comforting against the wind.

Sometime later the flare appeared again upon the wall. A
servant brought her a bowl of onion stew and a pasty; there
was a jug of wine and, best of all, a lantern. She stood the
lantern in the shelter of the privy wall, terrified it would blow
out. Behind the panels of polished horn a small tallow candle
was burning rapidly lower in a pool of smelly grease, but it
lasted long enough for her to see what she was eating. She
drank the rapidly cooling stew and ate the pasty ravenously.
Then as the candle died, she sat with her back to the castle
wall, cocooned in rugs, the jug of wine inside them with her,
drinking from it from time to time and staring out into the
black, windy night with its scattering of stars. By the time she
fell into a restless sleep the jug was empty.

The hotel room was in darkness, save for the circle of
candlelight. The woman sitting cross-legged on the floor was
pale too, dark like Isobel, with the same bone structure of the
face, but where Isobel's hair was long and matted and wild,
Clare's was shoulder length and fashionably styled and
glossy. Where Isobel was dressed in a torn, filthy gown that
had once been rich with embroidery and color but was now
bleached and stained, Clare was wearing a plain deep-red
sweater with a cowl neck and trousers. Both women had bare
feet. The eyes of both were closed, their faces calm as their
minds reached out to each other across the centuries.

Neil found he was shivering in the draft from the open window but he made no move to close it. The rain spattered onto the sill and the blowing curtains smudged and grew wet. His eyes were fixed on Clare's face. Her voice had been low, unemotional, but his skin crawled at the words she spoke in response to his hesitant, quiet questions. "Talk to her very softly and persistently," Zak had told him. "I think you'll find she will answer."

In his mind's eye he could see her, this other distant woman from the past; see her shadowy shape, the muted blaze of her eyes, the ivory shade of her skin, see the bars throwing their shadows across her face. He shook himself suddenly. Christ! She wasn't in his mind. She was real! There in the room with them. He could feel the small hairs on the back of his neck standing up. He was terribly conscious of the dark town beyond the window, of the wind playing in the castle ruins above the sweep of the river, and suddenly for one crazy moment he shared her fear of the dark. It had been this time of year, surely, that she had been brought to Berwick, perhaps a little earlier.

Somewhere in the night he heard the yelping scream of a gull and she was gone, back to the shadows, and Clare and he were alone.

"Clare!" He cleared his throat and tried again. "Clare, can you hear me?"

Below, through the floor, he could hear the steady beat of music. There was a distant whoop from the dancers.

"Clare!" His voice sharpened. "Clare?" He launched himself across the room and pulled her into his arms. Her eyes flew open and she stared at him blankly for a moment. "Neil? What's wrong?"

"You haven't done it! You haven't told her to go! You let her use you; you let her possess you, Clare!" His voice was raised in anger. "For God's sake, tell her to go!"

"I can't, Neil." She pulled away from him angrily and got up. "Don't you see? She needs me!" She went to the window and leaned out, feeling the wind and rain on her face. A few lighted windows showed as pale squares in the darkness. Beyond them the night was black. It had been black in the cage. Cold, desolate, terrifyingly black, hanging out in the darkness above the empty void.

She glanced back into the room, biting her lip. Isobel was still there somewhere, waiting for her, her loneliness tangible. Leaving the window open, she turned back to the candle. Stooping, she picked it up and held it high, watching the leaping shadows slide up the wall. "I'm listening," she whispered. "You're not alone. I'm listening."

Isobel woke with a blinding headache. The green and the town walls and beyond them the countryside and the river were lost in a thick white mist, luminous in the darkness. She was stiff and shivering and her rugs and clothes were heavy with clinging moisture. For a long time she didn't move. The wind had dropped and the world was completely silent. Somewhere in the distance she thought she could hear the gentle sighing of the sea on the rocky shingle. Slowly the mist grew pale as the darkness shrugged back toward the west. It was very cold.

They brought her bread and fruit and wine just before dawn, then once again she was alone, watching the sun rise from the sea in a blaze of red and gold as it thrust aside the clouds and the sky behind her turned to pale green.

It was not long before the crowds began gathering again. This time however their attention was divided. On the grass below the cage they were building a gallows. Isobel watched from the shadows at the back of her cage with growing sickness. As the sun blazed down and the day grew hot the people below were acting more and more wildly. It was like a fair. A man came with a pipe and around him people danced; they brought pies and ale, sitting on the grass around the gallows, amusing themselves from time to time by throwing stones at her. But today their aim was lazy and nothing reached her.

It was noon when the noise of the crowd increased tenfold, and she saw in the distance that a man was being dragged out of the town streets toward the gallows. Isobel rose to her knees and edged forward in her cage, pressing her face

against the bars. The attention of everyone below her now
was diverted from her. No one was watching her.

She could barely see the figure of the man. Surrounded by
the crowd and by his guards, he was just a puppet figure
below the gallows, being pushed upward toward the platform under the noose. Then he was standing on the platform
and she could see him more clearly. They were placing the
rope around his neck. He was a proud, upright man, not
cowed by his treatment, his hair blowing back from his face
in the wind, which had arisen again from the sea. For a
moment she tensed. He was too far away for her to see his
features, but there was something familiar about him, something agonizingly familiar—then he had turned away, facing
the sun, and she could not see him anymore. Seconds later
there was a roar from the crowd and she saw his body swinging beneath the gallows, jerking spasmodically on the end of
the hempen rope.

Isobel closed her eyes, her knuckles white on the bars.

Requiescat in pace—

Numbly her lips framed the words. "Dear Lord, have
mercy upon us; Sweet Holy Mother, pray for us, have mercy
upon us." Slowly she opened her eyes. Already they were
cutting him down, throwing the body on the ground. She saw
the flash of a sword blade, then heard again the roar of the
crowd as someone bent, seized the head by the hair, and
waved it in the air.

Miserably she turned away.

*Absolve, quaesumus, Domine, animam famuli tui ab omni
vinculo delictorum.*

She hunched back against the cold stones of the castle wall,
her arms around her knees and began silently to cry. *Requiem aeternam dona ei, Domine.*

Already the crowd was turning away, their entertainment
at an end. Once more they sought the excitement of tormenting the woman caged like an animal for their enjoy-
ment, a live target better by far when the blood lust was
roused than an inanimate body that was far beyond suffering.

Isobel barely saw them. A stone struck her on the cheek
and a small trickle of blood began to run down her face, but

in the main the missiles hurled at her fell short or had lost the impetus to hurt her by the time they reached the height of the cage. The sound of men behind her stirred her from her lethargy, however, and she slowly turned to see the constable of the castle surrounded by his men on the wall walk behind her.

"Did you enjoy our little show?" He smiled at her coldly. "So end all traitors and enemies to the king."

Isobel stared at him in silence. He would tell her now who it was, no doubt. That was what he had come to do. To watch her face. To see her suffer. She clenched her fists again.

The governor turned. He nodded to the men behind him. With them, she saw suddenly with a surge of nausea, they had a bloodstained sack. They carried it toward the wall a few yards from her cage where, she realized suddenly, an iron spike protruded vertically from the stonework.

Suddenly she knew what they were going to do. She closed her eyes.

There was a humorless chuckle from the constable. "Company for you, Lady Buchan. Just so that you don't get too lonely."

De profundis clamavi ad te, Domine . . .

She could hear the sounds: the slight scrunch of bone and gristle on iron, and then the volley of yells and whistles and catcalls from below; the feet of the governor and the guards tramping back toward the staircase; and then, from somewhere overhead, the wild yelping cry of circling gulls and already the calling of the crows.

Slowly, forcing herself to do it with every ounce of will power at her command, Isobel opened her eyes.

Impaled on the spike near her, young, handsome, the clear hazel eyes open and gazing into the distance, was the head of Nigel Bruce.

❧ Chapter Thirty ❧

By that evening Neil had taken Clare back to Duncairn, to an ecstatic welcome from Casta. The reason for the sudden departure from Edinburgh had been a phone call from Jim Campbell at Earthwatch. Paul had arrived at the office there, hot on Clare's trail. But neither Paul nor Kathleen had been in touch with Jack Grant and Neil sighed with relief as they walked into the hotel. It was like coming home.

The next morning dawned cold and wet. Catriona Fraser set the teapot on the tray and tucked the paper in beside it, then she carried it up to the double room and knocked. Clare was in bed alone.

"There's a bit about you and Mr. Forbes in the paper," she said shyly. "There's ever such a nice picture of you both at the meeting last week."

Clare slid up against the pillows, her face suddenly white. "Where?" She reached for the paper.

"Right there. On the front." Catriona passed it to her. "Will I pour your tea?" She was reluctant to leave before she had seen Clare's reaction.

"Please." Clare was staring at the item at the bottom of the page.

> As investment banker Paul Royland prepares to face serious fraud charges in the City, his wife is seen in Scotland in the company of conservationist Neil Forbes. Friends say they are inseparable. . . .

Clare dropped the paper. She threw back the bedclothes and groped for her slippers. "Where's Neil?" Her hands were shaking.

"I think he's taking the dog for a walk—"

She was grabbing her clothes already. "Thank you, Cat. I'll have breakfast downstairs, later." She dived past the astonished girl into the bathroom and began to throw on her shirt and sweater, then her jeans, fumbling with the zipper in her haste as she pulled them up over her hips.

Jack Grant was in the hotel office. She threw the paper down in front of him. "Is it true? Is my husband being charged with fraud?"

Jack nodded slowly. "So the papers say. Neil was trying to keep it from you for as long as possible. He didn't want you to worry yourself about it. The man has to face his own destiny."

Clare sat down on the wooden chair near him, her face troubled. "I should really be with him."

"Why? You've left him." Jack shuffled a bundle of invoices together and tucked them into a drawer. "You've made your decision, lassie, don't go back on it now. You'd never forgive yourself. You've a good man in Neil Forbes. Let him guide you."

"Who could have told the press we were together?"

"I certainly didn't. I talk to the press about the campaign as much as possible—we all agreed that was the right thing to do—never about things that don't concern them, and they've not asked. But all they had to do was use their eyes."

She did not refer to the newspaper article when Neil came back with Casta and neither did he. Jack told him later that she knew, and he watched her covertly, trying to see if she was upset about it, just as he watched for signs that Isobel had come with them back to Duncairn. Every now and then he still sensed a preoccupation in her that worried him, a tenseness that would grip her suddenly when she thought he wasn't looking and set her listening to some distant sound he could not hear.

Rather to Neil's surprise, there had been no further word of Paul, which had relieved him enormously, but still he felt safer with Clare away from the capital. If Paul had thought of returning to Duncairn they would all have heard about it by now, so it seemed safe to assume that he was still in Edinburgh or that he had returned to London. Tentatively Neil suggested that Clare stay at Duncairn. "I'll be back on the weekend, Clare," he reassured her. "There is no point in your coming. You stay here with Casta. The air is doing you good and there is a lot to do up here." She had put on a little weight, he noticed, and her eyes were brighter. The hunted look was less often there. And she was busy.

Besides all the work she was doing for Earthwatch she had, with a new burst of energy, begun to help Jack with the hotel as well, thinking up ideas for refurbishment in the spring, together with methods of publicizing it a little more—not too much, but enough to increase their turnover. The publicity about the oil was already bringing in the curious and the concerned; there had been twenty extra people for lunch on Saturday, and they had had hundreds of signatures added to the petition against the oil that had been left in the bar—but they needed to plan long term.

"I'll miss you." She clung to him suddenly.

"It's only for a few days. I'll come back on Friday night, I promise." Gently he pushed her away. "You have to learn to do without me, Clare. You have to learn to stand on your own two feet . . . without me and without Isobel."

She looked away. "You're right. But what if Paul does come here?"

"He won't." He said it grimly. "If he has any sense he's gone back to London to prepare his defense."

David and Geoffrey Royland sat facing Neil in the Earthwatch office as the first sleet of the year slanted down the street outside, the two large men in their heavy dark overcoats, the one with the old Etonian tie, the other wearing a dog collar, dwarfing the small office.

"It is important that we see Clare," David said in a patronizing voice. "I don't know how much our brother has explained to you, but she is in urgent need of very specialized help."

"She is getting that help." Neil stood behind his desk, a pen in his hand. He looked from one to the other with cold politeness. Their visit had been an unexpected shock. "Was there anything else?"

"Yes, by God there was!" David was suddenly angry. "We want to see her."

"I'm afraid that's not possible."

"Please, Mr. Forbes." Geoffrey had noted the hardness settling into Neil's face as David began to speak. "We really do have Clare's best interests at heart."

"Do you indeed?" Neil glanced at him. "Well, I'm sorry. All I can do is relay Clare's wishes to you. She no longer considers herself part of the Royland family. She is seeking a divorce from her husband and she does not wish to see any of you for the present. I'm sure you can respect and understand her feelings under the circumstances."

"No." David's eyes narrowed. "I'm afraid we can't, nor can we accept you—" There was a slight hesitation at the pronoun, enough to convey David's disdain. "—as her spokesman. Divorce is out of the question."

Neil kept his voice calm with difficulty. "I think that is for Clare to say."

"No. My sister-in-law is not competent to judge her own or anyone else's wishes." David's face was growing florid. "And I should point out that anyone keeping her from us could find themselves in serious trouble with the law. Abduction is a criminal offense, Mr. Forbes!"

"I have not abducted Clare." Neil was keeping a rein on his temper with difficulty. "She is a free agent."

"Clare is a very sick young woman," Geoffrey put in before his brother could reply. "Sick in her mind. You must realize that if you know her at all well. This isn't a matter merely of marital disharmony."

"Marital disharmony!" David snorted. "This man has been screwing our brother's wife! And while her mind is disturbed!"

"David—" Geoffrey's indignant reply was lost as Neil burst into laughter.

"You pompous bastard!" he shouted. "There is nothing wrong with Clare that separating her as far as possible from people like you won't fix. Get out of my office, both of you! And I advise you not to accuse me of abduction!" His eyes had narrowed dangerously. "Or the papers will hear the real story of Paul Royland and his wife and their marriage! And if you are thinking of bringing in the law, Sir David Royland"— the contempt in his voice as he used David's title was every bit as real as David's own had been—"I should think again. Having heard Clare's story—and spoken to the witnesses she can produce who have seen your precious brother's behavior towards her—my legal advisors would wipe the floor with you."

After the Roylands had left he stood for a long time at the small rear window looking up at the great rock out of which Edinburgh Castle grew. His heart was still slamming against his ribs with fury, his fists were clenched. He was very frightened. Not for himself, but for Clare. For the first time he realized fully just what she was taking on. The Royland family were now a united front. Faced with Paul's troubles they were calling in every card they possessed, and they had a great many: wealth, power, influence, the establishment background, the bland confidence of the church, the influence and respectability of Parliament, no doubt the closing ranks of the City, perhaps the aristocracy as well, for all he knew. And they all wanted Clare. He sighed. He was frightened of the emphasis they were putting on her state of mind. There was something sinister there, something he did not like at all.

He thought back suddenly to the hotel room at Berwick. The spirit of the Countess of Buchan had been in that room as surely as had Clare herself, but had Clare summoned her there, an entity from another time, or was she merely the creation of a disturbed and tortured mind? That he didn't know.

He turned away from the window sharply and picked up the phone. He had to warn Jack to hide her somehow. The Roylands had threatened to accuse him of abduction. He had no doubt at all that they would think nothing of doing it themselves.

The phone was still ringing when Jim Campbell came into the office. Under his arm was a newspaper. His face was grim. He tore off his scarf, threw it down on the chair, then he put the paper on the desk in front of Neil and thumped it with his fist. "Look."

Neil looked down at the screaming headline and suddenly he felt sick. "Sigma Oil Buys the Duncairn Estate in £1 Million Deal!" it said.

Paul was sitting in the drawing room at Airdlie, staring at the huge blazing fire as Antonia poured tea from the silver teapot.

"We were devastated when we read it in the papers, Paul," she said. "Devastated. How can they print such scandal?"

"You'll have to sue them, old boy." Archie had stuck his stockinged feet on the fender near the recumbent bodies of the two dogs.

"I'm afraid I can't." Paul took a deep breath. For a moment he had thought they were talking about Duncairn. That fool Doug Warner! By spilling the beans before everything was finalized he had put the whole deal in jeopardy. Now it was even more imperative that he find Clare, and find her before anyone else did.

No one had questioned the signatures; no one would as long as Clare kept quiet. And still he didn't know where she was!

He smiled at his parents-in-law coldly. "I was caught on a technicality. It was just bad luck; I did something everyone used to do all the time in the City, and people used to turn a blind eye to it. All I was doing was keeping my ears open. Five years ago it wouldn't have been considered wrong. Everyone did it. Sadly, some of these newcomers in the City have no idea how to turn their backs like gentlemen." He knew this would appeal to Archie.

Antonia passed him a cup. "My dear, it is simply ghastly for you. Is there nothing you can do?"

"I can get a bloody good lawyer." Paul sat back in his chair with a sigh. "Or at least the bank will. In fact, they already have. It's the least they could do for me."

"And meanwhile?" Archie sounded cautious.

"Meanwhile I'm taking some time away from the bank. Until after Christmas, so that Clare and I can sort things out.

I've missed her dreadfully." He glanced from one to the other. "You know where she is, I suppose."

He waited, his hand stirring the sugarless tea in the cup, as husband and wife looked at each other. He was holding his breath.

"She's in Edinburgh, Paul," Antonia said at last. "With this terrible animal-protection person. It's been all over the papers up here."

"It's been all over the papers everywhere," Paul said coldly. "Has she called you lately?"

Archie shook his head. "James saw her briefly after she left here." He looked embarrassed for a moment. "She hasn't bothered to call us or anything. I had to go all the way to Glasgow to collect the car. My car! She's a spoiled, thoughtless—"

"Archie!" His wife looked at him reprovingly. "She was very upset and disturbed when she was here. We've been worried sick, Paul."

Paul put down his cup. "As I have. We have to find her. My brother Geoffrey has agreed to come up here to see her; to help her, if only we can find her."

"She's not at Duncairn, is she?" Archie helped himself to one of his wife's scones. He loaded it with butter.

Paul shook his head. "I called Grant. It was the first thing I did. He said he hadn't seen her since she and Forbes went off to Berwick together."

"Berwick?" Archie looked startled. "What did they want to go to Berwick for?"

Antonia bit her lip. She was suddenly thoughtful. Berwick was where they had hung the cage. She remembered Margaret telling her—telling the children—endlessly, even after she had begged her to stop because Clare was getting obsessed by the story. . . . Margaret. It always came back to Margaret. All this was her fault. . . .

Paul was shrugging his shoulders. "God knows why Berwick! There was probably some rare lichen there that some poor soul was about to tread on and Forbes is going to lynch him for it. Anyway, he's back in Edinburgh now, I gather, but Clare is not with him. You have to help me. Please." His voice was tight with emotion suddenly. "I want to bring Clare here, not take her to some awful clinic; I want to bring her here for Geoffrey to take care of. Can I? Please?" He looked as if he were on the brink of tears. "We have to save her between us. I know a woman who works with Neil Forbes at Earthwatch. She says she can find out where Clare is. I've given her this phone number . . . I knew you wouldn't mind. . . ."

It was lonely at Duncairn after Neil had left. Suddenly the intensity of physical life was gone and Clare missed it terribly. But still she was busy. An architect had to be consulted, the plans for the hotel improvement had to be drawn up, and the campaign continued. She found herself sketching for the first time since she had left school—ideas for the hotel, layouts for leaflets, designs for posters, and when they were all done, just sketching for fun: the castle and the cliffs, the sunsets, the tortured east-coast trees. Then there was the office work—the phone calls to the printers, the mailing shots she was planning to be sent from Edinburgh. The busyness delighted her—the exhaustion, the importance of it all. She took over one of the empty bedrooms as an office and filled it rapidly with paper and envelopes, a copying machine, and even a word processor when, to her delight, Catriona shyly admitted having taken a course on how to work them in Aberdeen after she left school.

Neil hadn't come back that first weekend as he had promised. She put down the phone after his call and sat for a moment, staring into space, fighting her desolation and disappointment, then abruptly she had whistled to Casta and, shrugging on her Burberry, had walked out into the cold rain.

There was a mist over the cliffs, drifting up the wet granite ledges, dripping off the grass, hanging in chains and clusters of droplets from the spiderwebs that curtained the corners of the old stones. She touched one of the webs with a fingertip, watching as the raindrops shuddered to the ground and the threads stretched and coagulated into a sticky mat, destroying the beautiful symmetry. She felt empty and drained by her disappointment.

For the first time in days she thought of Isobel. "Where are you?" she whispered. "Are you here, or did you stay at Berwick?"

Not once since they returned had Isobel come to her; nor had the nightmare of the cage. Her relief had been mixed with an inexplicable sense of loss and the feeling that she had in some way betrayed a friend.

She glanced around at the dissolving shapes of the ruined walls in the murk, but there was no answer. Shivering, she pushed her hands farther into her coat pockets.

She had been so sure Neil would come back, so confident that he wanted her as much as she wanted him, but now her doubts flooded back. She hugged Casta closer, kneeling in the wet cold grass. Neil and Isobel. They had both deserted her, and she had never felt more alone.

She woke in the early hours of the morning, her body tense and aching, and lay there for a while, staring up at the ceiling before she realized she had been counting in her sleep. For a moment she lay still, puzzled by the feeling of exultation that filled her. She hadn't been dreaming; it was as if she had been working at some calculation, some niggling sum that refused to let her rest. For a moment longer she lay there, listening to the total enveloping silence, then suddenly she was sitting bolt upright in the dark. She groped for the light switch. The room was shadowy, cold, unnaturally quiet as she sat hunched in the bed, hugging her knees.

She was nearly three weeks overdue.

For a while she seemed to have stopped breathing. She could feel her pulse drumming urgently in her ears. Her chest was tight, her stomach churning. It was several long minutes before she could move, then she slid out of bed. She groped in her bag for her date book but she didn't need it. The years of counting, the months of tests, the rare occasions when for a day or two her hopes had been raised, had all taught her to be acutely aware of time. She carried it back to her bed and opened it, holding it directly under the shade of the bedside light. Her hands were shaking.

Neil.

That first time, with Neil, at his apartment when they had thrown themselves at each other in mutual recognition and anger. It had been her fertile period: She had marked out the days in every month in her diary; the days she would have been taking her temperature, watching and waiting, the days she and Paul had so clinically set aside for sex—

She closed the diary and put it down, then she ran her hands slowly down over her stomach. She didn't know whether to laugh or cry.

Pulling her nightdress up over her head, she walked to the old Victorian wardrobe and pulled it open. Inside the door was a mottled full-length mirror. She stared at herself. Neil had said she was putting on weight at last. Perhaps her face was fuller, less taut and aquiline than before—that was too many of Jack's Scottish breakfasts—but her stomach was as flat as ever. Her eyes traveled slowly up her body to her breasts. Were they different? She stood nearer the mirror, frowning in the dim light, feeling herself beginning to shiver violently in the cold room. Surely they were larger? She stared down and was suddenly aware that where her breasts had been white below the slowly fading line of her bikini top and brown above it, now they were laced with a faint network of blue veins.

She didn't fall asleep until the cold dawn was throwing streaks of light across the sky. No one woke her. Clare slept on, a deep, heavy, untroubled sleep.

When she awoke she stood in front of the mirror again and stared at herself for a long, long time. Daylight had put a restraint on her euphoria. She must not let herself hope, not yet. It was too soon. The change in life-style, the worry, the sudden intense swings of emotional stress, any of them could have done it. She must not tell anyone. If she was pregnant, then it was her secret; she would not even go to a doctor— there had been too many doctors. Nor would she tell Neil. It was not Neil's child, it was hers. Above all, she would not tell Paul. How strange that one of her first reactions, lying in bed in the early hours of the morning, had been to reach for the phone to tell Paul that the test had been wrong; that she could have a child. But he must never know. The baby could not be his; he and she were no longer married in any way but the legal sense, and soon she must take the first steps to finish that as well. Then she would be free.

She walked across to the window and looked out. Normally it would have been the first thing she did. Every morning she leaned from the window to sniff the glorious air, no matter how damp or cold. Today she had not thought once about the air or the window.

Outside there was a white blanket of snow across the garden. That explained the eerie silence in the night. It was as if the whole world had been made anew. Pushing open the window, she leaned out, her elbows on the granite sill, feeling the cold pure wetness of the sleet on her face.

Paul was dozing by the fire at Airdlie when Archie called him to the phone. He sat for a long time after he put the receiver down, then slowly he stood up. Kathleen had been laughing as she spoke. "It was so obvious! They haven't even tried to hide it. She went straight back to Duncairn after they returned from Berwick. She's using the place as an office, openly. They think you've given up and gone back to London."

Paul had shaken his head. "Where's Forbes?"

"Oh, he is here." Paul could hear the purr in her voice. "And he'll be here for the next couple of weeks. I've seen to that. You leave Neil Forbes to me."

She had told him she had been evicted.

"Please, Neil, for old times' sake. Let me stay, just for a few days until I find somewhere else."

By the time he came home that evening she had already brought four suitcases and two crates over to his apartment and carried them herself up the long stairs. "I'll sleep on the sofa. Clare will never know." She said it humbly, as though accepting defeat.

Neil stood looking around, trying to hide his dismay and anger. "Kath—"

"Please, Neil, don't make me beg." She had taken a long time with her makeup, chosen her clothes with meticulous care, the understated style not to her taste but she had to admit it made her look striking, even elegant. Her hair was newly tinted too and her nails manicured. She felt like a million dollars, and the feeling gave her confidence. Without knowing it she was exuding the charisma that usually only appeared when she was on stage. Unconsciously, already Neil was responding to it.

"Let me take you out to dinner to say thank you." She smiled, relaxed, easy, the tightness of her nerves hidden. No emotional blackmail, no scenes; the cards had told her what to do.

Neil was tired. He had been trying to phone back to Duncairn but there was a problem with the line. He had heard the devastation in Clare's voice when he told her he couldn't make it this weekend either. He really didn't want to feel tied and he didn't want a permanent relationship just now. He had things to do in Edinburgh—the phone had never stopped ringing since the statement from Sigma. It seemed as if only three people in the world hadn't phoned him: Doug Warner at Sigma, Paul Royland, and now Clare herself. He wondered what she was feeling as he jiggled the phone rest and dialed Duncairn again. Why hadn't she mentioned the deal? Paul must have told her. He must have got her signature somehow. Or had he tricked her? Cheated her? Used one of his unspeakable relations to twist the law somehow? Clare would not have lied. He realized now how deep and passionate her relationship with Duncairn was. He wondered suddenly if she even knew it had been sold. He frowned and dialed again, cursing. Should he go up there after all, or should he wait?

They had not gone out to dinner. He had been too tired. Instead Kathleen had cooked moussaka, just the way he liked it.

In the bathroom she was undressing. The scented bath oil she knew he liked—he had given it to her. She had bought the full-length black nightgown, trimmed with lace, at Jenners that afternoon. Her hair was loose, just slightly rumpled, her makeup still meticulous, if understated now that she had rubbed off the lipstick. Be casual; don't be obvious or loud. Ignore him while I make the toddy. Play it cool. Remember the cards.

Paul left a note for Antonia, who had driven down to the post office in Dunkeld with Sarah.

> Clare is back at Duncairn. I've gone to bring her home. Remember what we've decided. It's for her sake. Remember we all love her. P.

Archie had gone out. The house was deserted. Paul threw his coat into the car, then slowly, almost as an afterthought he walked back inside. He glanced into the drawing room then into the study. The top drawer of Archie's desk was open a couple of inches. In it he could see a ring of keys, each meticulously labeled. He pulled open the drawer and took them out.

In the gun room there was a long glass-fronted cupboard. In it were Archie's own guns, James's, Clare's father's, and several museum pieces, including two muskets that used to hang crossed above a door in the hall until the police had told Archie to lock them up. They were all there, carefully listed and locked in place. Paul stood in front of them for a moment, staring at them, then, hunching his shoulders, he selected a key from the ring in his gloved hand. After unlocking the cupboard door, he pulled it open and ran his hand lightly, almost sensually, over the regimented barrels. The beautiful Purdeys, the two Remingtons, the air guns that had for a while in his early teens been James's inseparable companions and that Antonia had disapproved of so strongly. His hand hovered over the rack and closed over the barrel of one of the hunting rifles. He unlocked the bar that held it in place and took it down, weighing it experimentally in his hand, then he turned to the safe where Archie kept the ammunition. He unlocked it, levered the two handles, and swung open the heavy door. He took a handful of 303 cartridges from the box, dropped them into the pocket of his jacket, then slammed the door and relocked it. He closed the gun cupboard, relocked the room behind him, and returned the keys to their drawer in Archie's desk. Archie would miss the rifle within hours, of course, but Paul would explain.

He put it into the back of the Range-Rover and threw a rug over it. He wasn't entirely sure himself yet why he had taken it.

Clare picked up the receiver yet again to check whether the phone was working. There was a silence, then a crackle, and suddenly the purr of an open line. She dialed the Earthwatch offices but only the answering machine replied. Next she tried Neil's apartment but there was no answer there either. She bit her lip as she put down the receiver. She hadn't spoken to him for two days.

When the phone rang later that afternoon she grabbed it, certain it would be he, but it was Emma.

"Clare? Thank God, I had to speak to someone! Can I talk?" Her voice was blurred and unhappy. "It's over between Peter and me, Clare. Our marriage is finished."

Clare was stunned. Sitting at the makeshift desk in her office overlooking the castle tower and the sea, she felt a million miles from London. With an effort she wrenched her mind away from her own problems.

"No. No. It's not Rex. It's nothing to do with him, not really." Emma sounded very distant. "He's a symptom, not a cause. Oh, Clare, what am I going to do? How am I going to tell Julia?"

"Where is Peter? Has he left you?" Clare was trying to grapple with this new crisis.

"No . . . yes." Emma was near tears. "It's all very civilized. We're not throwing things or anything. We've discussed it and we've agreed. He's going back to the Far East next week. When he's gone I'll tell Julia." There was a pause. "I'll tell her something. She sees so little of him, perhaps she'll hardly notice." Her voice was brittle with pain. "He'll be away over Christmas."

"Oh, Em." Clare was almost crying in sympathy. "What will you do? Will you go to David and Gillian as usual?"

"And end up in a house obsessed with that squawking brat? No, thank you." There was a shudder in Emma's voice. "It's not as if you and Paul will be there either. The whole family is breaking up. I'd rather stay here alone."

"You can't do that. Come here." Clare suddenly brightened. "Come here, to Duncairn, Emma! You and Julia. It would be lovely. We'll all have Christmas at the hotel with Jack and the Frasers."

All. She had not even thought about Christmas and Neil. Firmly she pushed him to the back of her mind.

"Are you sure?" Emma's voice had brightened.

"Of course I'm sure." Clare was suddenly full of energy. "It will be lovely to have a child up here! We'll form a Royland breakaway group." She laughed. "I've got so much to tell you, Em."

By the time Christmas came she would be sure one way or the other, and if the news was good, perhaps by then Emma would be up to hearing that another squawking brat was on the way.

Singing, Clare ran downstairs to find Jack. He was sitting in the office, his feet on the desk, reading the *Scotsman*. He put it down as Clare came in. "My, and aren't you looking bonnie today! You're glowing, lass."

"Am I?" Clare blushed. "I should be sad. Neil's not coming up this weekend."

"I know. He called me before the phones went off." Jack frowned. It hadn't been Neil who called, it had been Kathleen. "So, what can I do for you?"

"I came to tell you I've asked my sister-in-law and her daughter here for Christmas with us. I hope that's all right?"

Jack grinned. "Does that mean a Christmas tree?"

"Of course! You don't mean you weren't going to have one?" She was appalled.

He laughed. "Oh, I have one when I have guests, but I've not taken any Christmas bookings this year. With all the uncertainty I was afraid we might be closed by the end of December."

Clare stared at him, horrified. "With all my plans for the future?"

"Och, this was before your plans, Clare lass. People book up for Christmas months ahead."

She sobered for a moment, then she smiled. "Well, as it happens I'm glad. We'll have a small family Christmas, just you and me and Em and Julia and the Frasers, and—" She hesitated. "And anyone else who wants to come."

"That's fine by me." He stood up slowly and stretched. He could see how much she was in love with Neil and he didn't want to see her hurt. And he didn't want her to realize yet how vain was their attempt to save Duncairn. It was strange, but she still didn't seem to know that Paul had sold it. He edged the paper out of sight under some magazines. The news today had been, "Government to investigate new on-shore oil strikes in eastern Scotland. U.S. oil internationals start buying up Scottish land." Duncairn was the first name on a list of five.

That afternoon Clare took Casta for a long walk along the cliffs. They followed the footpath away from the village, around the cleft in the headland that carried the small tumbling river and back onto the cliffs, following them for several miles until they reached the Bullers of Buchan. The snow had melted everywhere but in some of the north-facing crevices of the rocks, and the ground was wet and cold. She didn't need to put the dog on the leash now. Casta trotted obediently at heel whenever asked. Neil had been scandalized by the leash that Clare, still used to London traffic, carried everywhere with her, and now she had abandoned it. Calling Casta to heel now, she began to walk slowly out along the narrow path that skirted the huge cauldron formed by the cliffs.

Far below the sea roiled and foamed against the rocks and she felt the wind tugging and sucking at her legs, trying to knock her off balance and draw her down into the maelstrom. Kittiwakes and gulls wheeled in the cold wind, their cries echoing off the cliffs. It was a place she normally loved, exhilarated by its wild beauty, but today she felt very much alone. Her depression had returned. She did not stay long.

Turning away from the wind, she retraced her steps onto the path. Heavy clouds piled up in the sky beyond the broad field now. It was going to snow again. Clare shivered, wishing suddenly she hadn't walked so far. Pulling her coat around her more tightly, she set off at a brisk pace, retracing her steps. Already it was growing dark and snowflakes were beginning to drift once more out of the north behind her.

When she got back at last the castle was almost dark. A drift of white was catching at the embrasure of the tower window. Beyond it the sea was quieter now, shushing against the rocks. It was very cold. Overhead the clouds were taking on an opalescent sheen as the moon, only three days after the full, rose high above them, backlighting the heavy sky. Clare glimpsed it, distant and cold, through a gap in the cloud. It was barely four-thirty in the afternoon.

She looked down at the dog and smiled, glad to be home. "Time for tea, Casta," she said as she turned with aching legs toward the hotel.

A figure was waiting for her in the shadow of the chapel wall. "How are you, my darling? It seems a long time since I've seen you."

Clare gasped. He was standing leaning against the stones, the rifle tucked under his arm. "Paul! What are you doing here?"

"I've come to see you." His voice was curiously flat. "How are you? You haven't told me yet." There was a mocking edge to his voice.

"I'm fine. I'm better than I have ever been." Defiantly she stepped off the grass onto the overgrown cobbles near him. Beside her Casta gave a throaty growl. "I was sorry to hear about your troubles in the City though."

"Were you?" He shifted his stance slightly, crossing his arms. Beneath his right arm the rifle barrel rose slightly. "But not sorry enough to help. This place takes precedence in your affections, I now realize."

"You don't need my help, Paul," she answered slowly. "You never did."

"Just as well, really," he said harshly. "Your help didn't amount to much even when you did give it. You've always been useless, haven't you? You've heard, I suppose, that Gillian has given my brother another son. You couldn't even do that, could you?"

Clare took a step nearer to him. "Couldn't I, Paul? Are you sure of that?" Either the tests had been wrong, or Paul had lied about the results. Was that possible? Could he have done such a thing? Her tone was suddenly cold. "Are you sure you got the results right when Dr. Stanford gave them to you? Are you sure the reason you never let me talk to him wasn't that it was you, not me, who couldn't have children?" One look at his face told her everything. "Oh, Paul! You lied to me! You couldn't bear the truth, so you blamed me! You told the whole world I was barren!" She was blazingly angry suddenly as the full realization of the truth hit her. "You bastard, Paul! You couldn't even spare me that misery!"

There was a long silence. Casta was growling uncomfortably in her throat, her hackles raised.

Slowly Paul straightened. "And what has led to this sudden revelation? Did you go for a second opinion?" His voice was heavy with sarcasm.

"I didn't have to, Paul." She spoke quietly suddenly. "I'm pregnant."

He narrowed his eyes with shock. "You're what?" Her words had come like a blow to his solar plexus.

"You heard me. I'm pregnant."

"By that raffish revolutionary, I suppose. You cheap, lousy little whore! What do you think everyone is going to say—"

"Everyone is going to say 'Oh, dear, so it was Paul after all,'" Clare said softly. "Perhaps you shouldn't have told quite so many people about our personal problems." She wanted to hurt him suddenly, wanted to give back a little of the terrible pain he had inflicted on her.

Behind them the moon rose higher. It found another gap in the thickening cloud and shone through onto the cold stone, glittering in the snow crystals, turning the sky around it mother-of-pearl.

Paul's face was in shadow. "Does Forbes know?" he asked. His voice was hard.

"Not yet. No one knows." As soon as she had said it she

could have bitten off her tongue. Hurriedly she rushed on. "Except Emma, of course. I told her this afternoon on the phone, and Jack."

"You haven't told anyone! You're not even sure yourself, are you? It could be a false alarm, like all those other times. It's wishful thinking, Clare. You wait and see. Another day or two and all your hopes will be dashed, just like all those other times."

"Not this time, Paul." She was more certain than she had ever been of anything. "This time I know."

"And what will Forbes say, do you suppose? I'll tell you what he'll say. 'Good-bye.' " He sneered. "You don't really think he loves you, do you? Do you know where he is this weekend?"

"Where?" In spite of herself Clare felt a quick flicker of fear.

"He's with a beautiful lady called Kathleen. You know Kathleen, don't you?" He smiled maliciously. "His girlfriend, his live-in lover, mistress, whatever you care to call her."

Clare felt suddenly sick. "If he is with her, I'm sure he had a good reason." She stared at him defiantly. "I'm going in, Paul. I'm cold—"

"You're coming back to Airdlie with me."

"No." She shook her head slowly, taking a swift step back. "No, Paul. I'm not going anywhere with you. Not ever again."

"You are, my darling." Paul moved toward her. "You are going to do exactly as I say." He grabbed her wrist.

Clare cried out in pain. "Paul, you bastard, let me go!" She struggled violently, kicking out at him.

Hampered by the gun, Paul let her go with a curse as Casta, who had been growling at him viciously, suddenly launched herself at him, teeth bared, in defense of her beloved mistress.

"Casta!" Clare screamed. She fell back against the wall, winded, as she saw the dog's teeth sink into Paul's sleeve.

Paul did not hesitate. Dragging himself free, he raised the rifle.

"No, Paul, no! *Casta!*"

Clare threw herself at him as he fired at almost point-blank range into the dog's head. The report was deafening, echoing across the ruins, reverberating from the cliffs as Casta collapsed at Paul's feet.

There was a moment's silence as Paul and Clare both stared at the dead dog, then Clare flung herself down, cradling the heavy lifeless head in her arms. There was a neat, scarcely bleeding hole through the skull above the left eye.

"Casta. Casta! Casta!" Clare was shaking with sobs. She rested her face against the dog's, willing life back into the still-warm, heavy body. Snowflakes were catching in the golden fur and on the dog's long eyelashes. Behind them the outside lights had come on at the hotel. Jack was striding across the dark gardens.

"Clare—it was an accident!" Paul stared down at the dog's body in horror at what he had done. Blood glistened on his sleeve, oozing from the bite.

"It was not an accident!" She looked up at him, her white face stained with tears in the moonlight. She was shaking like a leaf and her teeth were chattering suddenly. "You shot her deliberately. I'll never forgive you for this, Paul! Never!"

"What happened? I heard a shot!" Jack was panting as he ran the last few yards. "What the hell is going on here? Clare, are you hurt?"

Wordlessly she shook her head, cradling the dog across her knees.

"Casta?" Jack said the name in a whisper. "In God's name, man, what happened?" He took the rifle from Paul's hand and pulled back the bolt, ejecting the cartridge.

"It was an accident, a stupid accident," Paul said at last. "The dog attacked me. I had the gun under my arm . . ."

"You shot her, Paul. You took aim and you fired deliberately." Clare looked up at him, her face blurred with tears. There was a smear of Casta's blood across her raincoat. "What did you bring a loaded gun out here for? Shooting? In the dark? Who were you expecting to kill?" She broke off suddenly. "It was me, wasn't it? You were going to kill me! That was why it was loaded—"

"Clare—Clare, come on, lass, you don't know what you're

saying." Gently Jack bent and put his arm around her shoulders, trying to raise her to her feet. "Let be now. Come away to the hotel—"

"I'm not going to leave her here, in the snow." Suddenly she was sobbing again, burying her face in the dog's ruff. "She can't stay out here alone." She wrapped her arms tightly around Casta's body, clinging to her.

"I'll carry her back. Come on now." Jack took her arm and coaxed her to her feet. "We won't leave her here." He stooped and heaved the dog's heavy body up into his arms. Without another look at Paul he began to walk back toward the hotel.

Jack dug the grave in the garden near the terrace where Casta had loved to lie in the sun. Paul did not offer to help and Jack didn't ask. "I'd best do it straightaway, lass," he had said to Clare as he poured her a large brandy. "With the snow now and the freeze forecast for later, the ground will be too hard by tomorrow."

Wordlessly Clare nodded. Jack had wrapped the body in a tartan rug and laid it gently on the floor by the door. In the kitchen Catriona was sobbing audibly as she peeled the potatoes for dinner beside her mother.

Still wearing her bloodstained raincoat, Clare stood beside the grave as Jack carried the dog outside. Already the body was growing stiff and cold. She kissed the soft fur on the top of Casta's head once, then she turned away and went inside. She couldn't bear to watch the cold earth slipping from the spade onto the pathetically still form lying in the bottom of the dark grave, beneath a first quick shroud of snow.

She walked slowly upstairs and into her bedroom. After pushing the door closed, she moved in a daze toward the bed and threw herself down. Still wearing her boots and raincoat, her hair wet with snow, she rolled over and buried her face in the pillow.

~ Chapter Thirty-one ~

The patch of blood on the grass within the confines of the ancient chapel diluted slowly in the snow. It paled and ran and was washed clean. Within the castle the echoes were silent. The stones had witnessed too much blood for one more small murder to awaken them. But indoors Clare's unhappy sleep grew restless. The dream returned. The bars, the broken bird, the eyes. She recognized it now for what it was—another woman's nightmare.

Sleep came and went fitfully without regard to day or night. Cramped, weakened, disoriented, Isobel longed for the moment when sleep took her, but she feared it too, for to sleep meant to reawaken; meant again the sickening realization that it had not been a dream. That the reality was the nightmare.

In her dreams sometimes there was hope. Robert would come to rescue her; he would free her somehow. She did not think about him when she was awake. Then her mind was numb.

She had no idea of time. The grisly head on the spike near her had been picked clean by the kites and crows. Now the skull was white and dry.

Two Berwick women, implacable in their hostility, took turns bringing her food and sometimes a change of linen. She had no privacy beyond the shelter of the privy corner and there was no room to change there. She had to wait for the dark. They seldom spoke.

The same guards seldom stayed on duty for more than a day or two at a time. Sometimes she recognized a face; more often than not she did not see them at all. She had tried at the beginning to win their sympathy; she had tried to wheedle, to plead, to threaten. Nothing worked. Now she held desperately to her last shreds of dignity and sat unmoving at the back of the cage. The nights and days came and went. Some days were cold; she shivered. Some were wet and dank when her clothes and blankets were saturated and moldy, black creeping fungus threading its way inexorably through everything around her. Then the sun would come. At first she welcomed it. Then she feared it, hanging mercilessly in the blazing sky, moving slowly into the south and then around toward the west. There was no shelter, no shade. The sweat poured off her body and her head ached, pounding behind her eyes and between her temples. She asked often for water. Only once they brought it, cold from the well, in a jug.

She had no word of Robert or his followers. She knew neither of his escape nor of his return to Scotland. But she heard when King Edward died. The news flew around Berwick. Edward II was king! The young man who was her brother's friend. Sick with excitement and hope, she waited for news that the sentence of the sadistic old king would be overthrown and she would be set free. But nothing came. She begged her guards to bring her someone who would tell her what was happening, but no one came. Time passed.

The sun spun in the sky, a white blazing disc and King Edward II, embroiled in the wars with Robert, quietly confirmed her sentence. The Countess of Buchan would stay in her cage until she died. One of the women unbent enough to tell her, her eyes full of malice, that Robert's daughter had been held only a few weeks in her cage in the Tower before the old king had uncharacteristically relented and allowed her transfer to a nunnery in Yorkshire. Mary Bruce was still being held at Roxburgh Castle, but she too, so the woman told Isobel with glee, had been released from her cage and was being held in one of the towers. Only Isobel remained caged like an animal, victim of an old man's savage hatred and a young man's fear of the rebellion that festered on his northern border.

It was when the weather was gentle that she learned at last to pray. The mists would rise from the broad Tweed and flights of duck and waders would angle past the castle walls to feed on the mud at low tide. She would stare at the distant hills and watch the pink haze of dawn settle over them. The field below her cage was empty then, the dew silver in the grass. The air was pure, the wind carrying the stench of the open drains of Berwick away from the castle; carrying away the smell of her own body and the pile of rags she had to beg from the attendant women to staunch the heavy monthly bleeding that drained her, leaving her with each moon more pale and drawn and exhausted until, inexplicably, nature took pity on her and the bleeding stopped. She did not ask why. She thanked Our Lady for her mercy—and found herself praying more and more. Prayer occupied her mind, ordered her thoughts, gave her something to do.

And then she started to dream.

At first she had been afraid to think of Robert. She would not let herself cry and to think of him brought tears, but slowly now she began to build her fantasies. Her mind would leave the cage and roam free. She found that when the sun beat down she could close her eyes and conjure the cold brown waters of a highland stream, and lie beside it in the lushness of the grass. When the cage was cold and the bars were rimed with ice she built in her mind a huge, crackling log fire and a room hung with tapestries and a bed, soft with down-filled pillows and furs. And there, sometimes, her king would come to her. She sat cross-legged—it was the most comfortable pose in the small, hated cage—her eyes closed, her body relaxed, while her mind sped away.

Once or twice when the guards or her women came they looked at her calm empty face, so thin now, but still beautiful, and called her name, and when she didn't answer they knew she had escaped their reach. They looked at each other in fear and remembered this woman was a sorceress.

She was clutching at her sanity now. The fantasies returned again and again, but she could no longer control them. Sometimes she was at Duncairn, walking along the walls above the cliff, peering down into the boiling sea. Once she plummeted over the edge and flew, skimming the waves for a moment before plunging into the green weight of the water. She awoke spluttering and choking, a stream of rain running from the turf roof of her privy, angled onto her face. Only then did she realize she had been asleep. It was the first dream where she flew. Often after that she was a bird; but then she found suddenly that her wings were clipped and powerless, the muscles wasted; when she tried to stretch them they were useless and in her dream her eyes would fill with tears.

Again and again she saw herself walking the battlements of a castle, sometimes at Berwick, sometimes at Duncairn, but the castle was in ruins, the stones crumbled, overgrown with lichen and weed. Sometimes she was wearing her most beautiful gowns, silks and velvets, court dress, stitched with silver and gold; other times she was dressed strangely in woolen garments dyed bright vermilion and acid green, with hose on her legs like a man, and her hair was short. No, it wasn't her, it was someone else—another woman, a woman from another world who looked like her. She stretched out her hand across the mists and the other woman smiled. Their hands almost touched, then the mist swept back and Isobel was alone again. In frustration and disappointment she wept, then she saw the faces, the mocking, curious faces of the crowd who still came to stare at her, and she hid her tears.

One other piece of news they told her. The governor of the castle came to her and stood staring down at her as she knelt in the cage staring out at the English hills.

"Good morning, my lady." As she looked up, startled by his sudden presence, she felt a wild surge of hope. He saw it, and for a moment she saw compassion in his face. "I have some news, my lady, though not that for which you hope, I fear." He was uncomfortable now. He wanted to be gone. "Your husband, my lady, is dead." He stood awkwardly, feeling he should be able to say more, give some details perhaps of where or how, but he had none to give. Just the stark news that the Earl of Buchan was dead in England.

Her face was white with shock. There was no sorrow, no regret, only stark shock and the strange illogical feeling that now she was free.

Free!

Her hands clutched the bars near him, her knuckles white

as she pulled herself closer to him, and suddenly, hysterically, she began to laugh.

"I'm sorry, Kath, but you can't stay here." Neil had slept on the sofa again. "You've had plenty of time to find somewhere else—surely there is something suitable."

Kathleen looked away. "I'm sorry, Neil, I am trying. It's not easy just before Christmas." She smiled and tossed back her mane of hair. "I've been distracted by the rehearsals. You know what it's like. I'll take a couple of days off and find somewhere straightaway."

Neil nodded. "Thanks, Kath. I'm sorry it didn't work out."

"So am I." She smiled. "And I'm sorry about Duncairn. It was a beautiful place. Who would have thought that Clare would sell after all her protestations?"

"She hasn't sold. It's her husband."

"But her agreement was needed, wasn't it?" She smiled sweetly. "Poor Neil. You never understood, did you? Her fantasies weren't so special. Everyone has fantasies, for God's sake! She was using you. Using you against her husband." She stood up and reached for her coat. "I'll go out now and get the papers. I'm sure I'll find somewhere to camp over Christmas."

"Aren't you going home?"

She shook her head. "I have shows lined up right over the holiday. It's all right, Neil. I don't mind being alone. I'll get used to it."

He nodded. "Good. And, Kath"—he smiled apologetically —"please, can I have my key back this time, when you leave?"

Emma had phoned Rex at his apartment. It had taken her a long time to decide to call him. He was sitting on an easy chair near the window, staring out across the square. There had been a snow shower, and the trees in the gardens were outlined in white, clean and beautiful.

"Please, will you come with us to Duncairn, Rex? Julia and I would both like it."

He hadn't spoken once while she told him what had happened between her and Peter, his mind in a turmoil. Did this mean she liked him, after all? That she had made a decision?

The word *Duncairn* distracted him. Duncairn. The bastards had bought it after all. Sigma had double-crossed him. They had only gone ahead and signed because of him; their decision had vindicated everything he had said and done. He was hurt and very, very angry.

He frowned. "I doubt if your sister-in-law would want me there, honey." Why had she sold it to them and not to him? He cared for it; he would have restored it; he would have protected the environment when the drilling started. Was it because he was a Comyn? Was the old hatred still there?

"She knows the sale has nothing to do with you, Rex. It's not your fault. She knows you backed off because I asked you too. She'd like to thank you." Emma's voice was pleading.

Rex's eyes dropped to the newspaper on the coffee table. It was several days old, but still he kept looking at it. He had been to the Sigma offices and confronted Warner. "It wasn't my decision," Doug had said. "I'm sorry, Rex. It was the boys in Houston. One moment they said no, then they turned right around and said yes, go ahead, buy the place! You know the state of the oil industry over the last few months. It's been up and down, but after the latest developments they had to go for it. They couldn't afford not to when Royland suddenly offered it to me again."

"So, he finally talked his wife around, eh?"

"He sure did. I have all the documents right here." Warner had grinned, jerking his thumb in the direction of the safe.

Rex's knuckles tightened on the telephone at the memory. "Emma—"

"Please, Rex. You don't want to be alone for Christmas. If you can't go back to the States for some reason"—she hadn't probed why he had suddenly changed his mind about going home—"then come with me."

He could hear the tears hovering in her voice. Uncomfortably he stood up, the receiver to his ear. He stared out of the window. There was an icicle hanging from the guttering just above the French doors. A droplet of water appeared at the end of it. As he watched it filled suddenly and fell into a snow-covered flower pot.

"Okay." He sighed and turned his back on the scene. It was Mary's fault he wasn't going back. He had wanted to go home to the States, finish with Duncairn and with the unhappiness that was Emma, but Mary had told him she had arranged Christmas without him, and he had not argued. He had hung up on her and waited for her to call him back. She hadn't.

"I'll be through here and packed up by Tuesday," he said, suddenly brisk. "We'll fly up then. But check with Clare, my dear. If she doesn't want me there, then I'll understand."

"I'll ask her now." He could hear the relief in Emma's voice. "Take care, my love."

He frowned as he put down the phone and sternly squashed the sudden flutter of hope. *My love.* They were such easy words to say.

The phone at the Duncairn Hotel was busy. Emma tried time and again that evening to reach Clare, and at last she gave up. She would have to try again in the morning.

Paul was sitting by the fire in Jack Grant's small office, the phone on his knee. Outside, the snowflakes clung white to the window, slid a little, and compacted on the glass. He had stripped off his jacket and shirt and examined the bite on his arm. It was a bad one. He wondered briefly if his tetanus shots were up to date, then he gritted his teeth and poured some peroxide on the wound, binding it with the bandage Molly Fraser had grudgingly given him.

"Antonia?" At last she had answered. "Good news. I've found Clare and she is well." He had thought it all out so carefully. He smiled. "My dear, I want you and Archie to celebrate with us. Tomorrow. Will you meet us in Edinburgh? Guess what! Clare is going to have a baby!" He leaned back slightly in the chair and put first one foot then the other on Jack's desk, crossing them meticulously at the ankle. He was barely listening to Antonia's delighted clamor.

"I know, I know. We all thought she couldn't." He paused. "The doctors must have been wrong. And it's changed everything. She is so much better, completely calm. Antonia, we'll meet tomorrow—in Edinburgh, for lunch. Then I am going to take her back to London." His gaze focused on the corner of the office. Jack had propped the rifle there, behind the filing cabinet. "I'm worried about all this snow, so I'd like to get her home. Nothing but the best for my child!"

He picked the phone off his knee and, standing up, threw it down on the desk. The receiver dislodged, half off its cradle. He did not bother to replace it. After switching off the light in the office, he turned and made his way toward the stairs and the room he had been given on the second floor.

Clare was asleep when he went to her early next morning. It was still dark outside. Huddled in her bloodstained raincoat, she was lying across the bed, hugging the pillow, her hair tangled from the wind and rain. In the light of the single bedside lamp her face was pale and strained. He could see the stains of tears beneath her eyes.

"Clare, get up!" He shook her, hard. "Come on. We're going back to Airdlie."

She sat up slowly, pushing the hair back from her face, staring up at him blankly.

"Come on, Clare. Wake up." He was losing patience. "I've phoned your mother and told her what happened last night. She is expecting us."

"I'm not going anywhere with you, Paul." Wearily Clare swung her feet to the floor and paused a moment, swaying with fatigue and nausea. The events of the previous night flooded back, blotting out the bars, the loneliness, the despair. This new despair was quite different. This was reality. She looked up at him. "Why did you take that gun out to the castle last night? Was it me you meant to kill?"

Cold disdain showed for a moment on his face. "Don't be so melodramatic, Clare. Come on. Take off that raincoat, it's filthy. Where is your mink? You'd better wear that. It's bitterly cold out there."

"It's stained with blood too." Neil had told her about the mink cages, so small they couldn't turn around; told her how they killed them. She would never wear a fur again. She looked down at the Burberry and touched the brown stain with gentle fingers and her eyes filled with tears again.

Paul frowned. "It was an accident, Clare—"

"Of course." She stood up unsteadily. "Now please, leave me alone."

"No. Not this time. Your place is with me." Paul folded his arms. "Antonia and Archie are waiting at home for you. I've told them about the baby. *Our* baby."

"Oh no, Paul. Not ours. Mine. This child has nothing to do with you."

"I am your husband, my dear. And there is going to be no divorce. The child is mine. He is mine." When he awoke that morning he had been so sure. There could be no question about it. Clare might have been unfaithful to him in the last few weeks, but the baby had been conceived before she left him. Long before she left him. It must have been. He put his arm around her shoulders. "The unpleasantness last night has upset you, but you'll see it all more clearly when you've gotten over it." He was guiding her toward the door. Clare protested, but she was too dispirited and ill to fight him. Her head was swimming now that she was standing up, and she found herself leaning against him for support.

At the foot of the stairs Jack Grant, still wearing his dressing gown, was lighting the fire in the front hall. He looked up in surprise as he saw them. "It's very early to be going out," he said disapprovingly, glancing from one to the other. "The weather is closing in."

"That's why we have to leave now." Paul's fingers tightened on Clare's shoulder. "We don't want to get snowed in. It's better for all of us, I think you'll agree, if I take her home for a while, away from the scene of the accident." Already he was half guiding, half carrying her across the hall toward the door.

The car was still standing outside the front door where Paul had left it. The air was cold and sharp and very clear. Their breath hung in wisps in the darkness. Beneath their feet the snow was white and soft, a filmy blanket over the garden. Clare was only half conscious as he opened the car door. Too dazed to protest, she let him push her up onto the front seat of the Range-Rover, and she sat back, her eyes closed, feeling waves of nausea sweep over her. All she could think about was the dark hole in the garden and the warm golden fur sprinkled with snow crystals as Jack lowered the dog into the grave.

Paul started the engine. He glanced across at her. "Do up your seat belt. The roads will be slippery."

Automatically she obeyed, although her mind had not registered that he had spoken to her. She was far away. She hadn't looked at him once.

The windshield wipers were pushing the snow in white arcs across the glass, crunching slightly as their powerful strokes swept back and forth. Beyond them, the headlights swept across the drive and across the road as Paul swung the car onto it. The verges were white now, and the country beyond, but the tarmac was still wet and black as he pushed on the accelerator and headed south. On their left, beyond the trees, there was a slight lightening in the sky.

It was full daylight by the time Paul and Clare had driven through Aberdeen. The snow was falling steadily now, and a scattered whiteness was forming on the road. Clare's eyes were closed. Paul was driving fast, his gloved hands clutching at the steering wheel. The road was empty.

"Why, Paul?"

"Why, what?" He changed gear, throwing the Range-Rover around a steep double bend.

"The hatred. The anger. The trouble in the City. We didn't need more money."

"One always needs money."

"Will you go to prison?" She still hadn't looked at him. The snow was beginning to close across the road now that they had turned inland.

"I doubt it. I've got good lawyers."

"It's just as well Duncairn is still in my name. They might have taken it otherwise." She hunched her shoulders defensively.

"Duncairn is already sold." He smiled grimly. "Don't you read the papers?"

"What do you mean?" For the first time she turned and looked at him. He was startled by the whiteness of her face.

"I mean what I say. It is sold."

"But I signed nothing."

"No." He gave a perfunctory laugh. "I did. Your signature was remarkably easy to copy. No one questioned it."

Clare stared at him. "I don't believe you!"

"It's true."

"But I'll deny it—" She broke off suddenly, her eyes widening. "That was why you wanted to kill me—"

"Clare, I did not want to kill you. The gun was to persuade you to come with me, if you needed persuading."

He glanced at his watch. It was nearly eleven. Archie and Antonia would be halfway to Edinburgh by now.

The snow had settled heavily around Dunkeld and he was forced to slow up as he followed the gritted strip down the center of the slushy road and turned at last into the drive. For a moment he was afraid she might try to jump out, but she hadn't moved.

"I will tell my stepfather. He won't let you get away with it, Paul."

Paul swung the car around the front of the house. It looked empty, the curtains half drawn, and he smiled to himself with relief as he drove into the deserted stable yard and switched off the engine. He had been afraid for a moment that the snow would have stopped them from leaving.

He had made his plan so carefully. He had spied out the land, out of curiosity, weeks ago, before he knew what he was going to do, and now suddenly everything had fallen into place. It was all so obvious. All he had needed was the padlock.

"It looks as if they are out, I'm afraid," he said. "You may have to delay telling him for a while."

For a moment neither of them moved, then Clare reached for the fastening on her seat belt. She unlatched the door and pushed it open, wishing she felt better, wishing her mind were clearer. Her legs were weak and she still felt very sick. All she wanted was to get indoors and to a fire.

Paul tensed as he watched her taking deep breaths of the

cold air as she tried to will herself the strength to stand. He could feel his heart banging suddenly beneath his ribs. As he climbed out of the Range-Rover he felt suddenly very alert. Every sense was screaming. He walked quickly around to Clare and took her arm. "In fact, I know they are out. They are in Edinburgh for the day." He smiled. "This way, my dear."

"What? Where are we going? *Paul*—" Her words were cut off in a shriek as Paul stooped and lifted her off her feet. He turned away from the house toward the coach house and stables that formed the northern and eastern sides of the courtyard. "There is something here I'd like you to see, my darling," he said as she tried to struggle free. He could carry her easily, but in front of the coach house he put her down and, holding her arm tightly, he pushed open the old heavy doors. They both swung inward, creaking. Inside it was almost dark, lighted only by high dirty windows, almost lost beneath festoons of cobwebs. It was almost empty. An old rusting car parked in one corner and not disturbed for twenty years, two bicycles, a pile of torn apple boxes haphazardly stacked on the high cobbles on one side of the drain, that was all. The whole place smelled musty and damp.

Paul let go of the doors and they swung back creaking behind them. Abruptly he let go of her arm. Transferring his grip to her wrist, he twisted her arm sharply behind her. "Go on, over there. Through the side door."

Taken by surprise, she stumbled forward as he pushed her to the door and dragged it open. Beyond it was a small side yard formed by another range of old stone-built stables. Paul pushed her outside, and suddenly she understood.

In the far corner of the yard was a dog's cage, the iron bars rusty, the floor scattered with old rubbish. The door stood open.

"No! Paul, no! *No!*" Her voice rose in a scream as he pushed her toward it, and she began to struggle in earnest, kicking and lunging at his face with her free hand. With an oath he jerked her arm more tightly behind her, propelling her forward over the uneven cobbles.

After thrusting her inside so hard that she sprawled among

the rubbish headlong, he slammed the door shut and groped in his pocket for the new padlock. He clicked it into place, then stood back, panting. Then he began to laugh exultantly.

Clare struggled to her knees. She was sobbing desperately. "Paul, please, let me out! *Paul!* Someone will come. My mother will come. She'll see the car. Or Sarah! *Paul, please—*"

He stood, arms folded, watching her. He felt very calm now. There was no pity or affection for her, only a coldness as he saw her crawl to the bars and clutch at them. She shook them desperately, but they didn't move.

"Your brother told me about the cage," he said after a moment, over the sound of her sobbing. "Do you know, he still feels guilty about it, after all these years." He took a step nearer again. "I couldn't believe my luck when I found the cage was still here. You know how to get out, of course." He reached under his coat into the breast pocket of his jacket and pulled out a paper. "I have written it all out here. How you authorized me to act in your name. How you agreed to sell the castle and how any future negotiations are up to me." He pushed it at her through the bars.

Clare did not even see it. "Paul! Please, you can't do this! Please. Someone will come." She was crying hysterically.

"No one will come, Clare. Your parents have gone away for Christmas and Sarah has returned to London." He smiled at the easy lies. "We have all the time in the world. Either you agree to back me up all the way over the sale of that damn castle, or I shall leave you here." He paused for a moment to let his words take effect. "When everyone returns after Christmas they will find your body and assume that you were acting out your macabre fantasies while the balance of your mind was disturbed. God knows there will be enough witnesses to the state you were in. I shall be in London when they find you." He folded his arms. "I should sign, my darling. Think of the baby. Think of yourself. I have nothing to lose, you have everything." There was a strange, cold light in his eye.

She stared up at his face, numb with fear. "Don't leave me here, Paul—please—"

He did not reply. He merely shook the paper in her face.

"No." Her fingers were white on the iron of the bars. Small raw flakes of rust caught on her sleeve. Slowly Paul was putting the key of the lock into his pocket. After dropping the piece of paper through the bars, he watched it float to the ground beside her, then he pushed a pen after it.

"What shall we say? A couple of hours to think about it?" He pushed his hands into his pockets and hunched his shoulders against the cold. "If you haven't signed it by then, I'll have to leave you until tomorrow or the next day. There are things I have to do in Edinburgh before I go back to London." He turned away.

"Paul!" Her scream echoed around the small yard.

"Oh, don't worry, I'll leave you enough food to last a couple of days or so."

"Paul, for God's sake! Think of the baby—"

"Ah, yes. The baby." His jaw hardened. "My baby. You'd better keep calm, or you might lose it, mightn't you?" He turned on his heel. "Two hours, Clare, then I shall come back for your signature."

For a long time Clare didn't move. Her sobs had frozen in her throat; her hands were locked on the bars. It was bitterly cold in the yard, shadowy beneath the heavy sky, and completely silent. The snow was falling more thickly now, drifting past the high stone walls of the coach house as Clare closed her eyes, breathing deeply, trying to force herself to stay calm.

When Isobel came she welcomed her with a sob of recognition.

Paul had stopped beside the car. He stooped and picked up her shoulder bag, which had fallen to the ground in their struggle, and fumbled through it until he found her keys to the house. Slowly he walked around to the front and let himself in. He stood still and listened. The place was cold and dark, the curtains in each room half closed against the dull day, the fire in the living room out, a mound of pale ash behind the ornate fire guard.

He glanced around, then slowly he walked through to the

kitchen. The stove was still hot. After filling the kettle, he put it on to boil and sat down in the chair beside it, glancing at his watch. It was one hour and fifty minutes before he could go back to the cage. He had begun to shake like a leaf.

The dog's bowl still lay in the corner of the cage, as it had all those years before when James had locked her in. Chipped enamel, dirt encrusted, lying in the corner where it had lain since the last occupant of the cage had died.

She had tried to swallow her fear, to contain it, but she could feel it creeping up, cold, shivery, the panic closing in on her, turning her throat dry and her mouth papery with terror. Her hands were still clamped on the bars. She rested her head against them for a moment, then with an effort forced herself to let go, crawling to the back of the cage where she sat, her arms tightly around her knees, her face pressed against them to blot out the bars. She closed her eyes tightly. What had Isobel done? She had prayed. She had prayed to the Holy Virgin and to St. Bride, and to St. Fillan and St. Margaret. They had not helped her, but somehow she had kept her sanity.

Slowly Clare moved until she was on her knees again. She was still wearing the bloodstained Burberry.

Holy Mary, mother of God, pray for us sinners now and at the hour of our death . . .

My memories, your memories, merging in and out of the nightmare. Fear. Horror. Loneliness. Despair . . .

We are not alone. We have each other. . . .

Sancta Maria, Mater Dei, Ora pro nobis, pecatoribus, Nunc et in ora mortis nostrae . . .

A bird in a cage, an animal, a prisoner without hope. . . .

She buried her face in her arms.

Dear God in heaven, let her keep her sanity. Only let her keep her sanity. . . .

Libera me, Domine, de morte aeterna . . .

Behind her the folded paper lay in the rubbish, the pen beside it. She had not even seen it.

The snow was falling more thickly now.

* * *

Antonia, sitting at the bar in the George Hotel, looked for the tenth time at her watch before turning to look anxiously toward the door. She was ordering another gin and tonic when Archie appeared, pocketing some spare coins. "I finally got through to Grant. Apparently the phone has been off the hook. He says they left soon after seven this morning."

"Seven!" Antonia looked horrified. "Oh, Archie, do you think anything has happened to them?"

Archie picked up his own glass and drained it. He shook his head. "It's pretty bad up there, apparently, and drifting. But they've got the Range-Rover; they'll be all right. And Paul will stop if he gets worried. We'll give them half an hour, then if they're not here, we'll start without them. The hotel can keep the bubbly on ice until they arrive." He helped himself to a fistful of dry-roasted peanuts and smiled at her heavily.

Jack Grant had told him about the dog, but he wasn't going to tell the old girl, not yet. He eased himself onto a stool. He had seen the gun was missing at once, and he guessed Paul had taken it. But why the dog? Beautiful, affectionate creature that she was. He frowned as he pushed the glass across the bar to be refilled. There was something in all this he didn't like at all.

Halfway between Duncairn and Cruden Bay an old Scotch pine, groaning beneath the sudden fall of snow, suddenly shed one of its lower boughs. The edge of the branch caught the phone line near the telegraph pole and lodged there, hanging from the wires as the thick white blizzard whirled around it. For a radius of two miles, the phones went dead.

Paul, sitting in Archie's study, had tried to phone Grant and been told the lines were down. Smiling, he phoned a message through to the George: "Returned to Duncairn because the road south closed. Don't try to drive home tonight. Stay in Edinburgh. Will call again in the morning."

Conscientiously the young man at the reception desk copied down the message, twice offering to fetch the lady or gentleman to the phone, then he put down the receiver and, note in hand, went through to the bar.

Reassured, the Macleods went into lunch and broached the champagne alone.

The snow was drifting against the window frames high in the walls. The old buildings, lapped in snow, muffled sound and deadened it. It was very cold. Burying her face in her arms again, Clare slipped to the floor on her knees, her forehead in the litter with its thin mantle of wisped snow. The world was spinning, the bars closing in. She had screamed again and again, sobbing, until her throat had closed over the sounds. She was no longer rational, no longer conscious of the acres of empty garden with the snow-covered trees beyond the roofs of the stables, no longer thinking of the huge empty house where her husband was sitting in the kitchen, his wristwatch in front of him beside the whisky bottle, watching the minutes tick away. She was thinking now only of the cold angled sweep of the river Tweed and the harsh, echoing cry of the gulls as they swooped over the water and of the winter nights when skeins of geese flew high beneath the moonlit clouds, their wild bugling cries echoing across the cold countryside.

The soft whiteness of fog wrapped the cage, hiding it, lapping it in the cold wet of autumn, and Isobel felt her joints thicken and ache; her temperature soared and she lay in her rugs in a delirium of fever, her food and water untouched, alone inside her head with a myriad of demons who tormented and tortured her. The guards forbade the women to open the cage door and tend her, so she lay alone.

The touch of the sun healed her as the weather relented and the autumn sunshine entered the cage, drying the rugs, soothing her inflamed body, whispering in the fragrant wind that stroked her face, and she awoke, weak but sane again, and sipped the tisanes that a silent woman, on the order of the governor's wife, pushed through the bars in the old earthenware water jug.

The death of the king, the death of her husband. Neither

had brought her relief. Her captors kept her in complete ignorance of what was going on in Scotland. She did not know that Robert had swept to victory across northern Scotland. She did not know that he had beaten Lord Buchan so completely before the latter's retreat to England that Buchan had fled to die of shame. She did not know that Robert had gone on to lay the vast Buchan district waste—revenge against the man who had made her life a living hell; revenge for the woman he could not save.

Her body grew thinner and more wasted, but her courage was unbowed. Her prayers and daydreams kept her alive.

The next winter they brought her in sooner at the command of the governor's lady and she was given better food. Her frame was shaken with a cough that stayed for five months before the fresh air of spring soothed it as her cage was hung outside again and a new generation of Berwick's children came to torment her with their taunts and missiles. One boy, stronger and with a better aim than most, came back again and again with a catapult and a store of carefully selected smooth round pebbles collected from the shallow elbow of the Tweed near the ruins of the ancient bridge. She learned to recognize him and cower back in the cage when he came, protecting her head with her arms, but not before a flying stone had caught her full in the face, tearing her cheek and bruising the bone, causing her eye to swell until she could not see out of it.

Her pain had an unexpected side effect. For the first time one of the women who attended her, a new servant in the castle, showed open, defiant pity. She brought an ointment of crushed marigolds and pushed it through the bars with a sympathetic word, and this first kindness reduced Isobel at last to tears.

The first she knew of Robert's successes in the battlefield was an increase of hostility from the crowds below, then slowly the rumors began to reach her as her dulled ears picked up gossip from the guards behind her on the tower. The King of Scots—King Hob they called him—was gaining support on every side, and now at last he had held a parliament. Soon they were singing about him below the castle walls too, and the ridicule and scorn in the songs contained fear.

A parliament? She did not dare let herself hope. The bars were still there—too real, too absolute. Her whole world. But still, a tiny corner of her brain reasoned, surely, to hold a parliament implied a position of strength?

But if he was in Scotland, where was he? Why did he not come? Why had there been no message, no sign that he had not forgotten her?

In anguish as the sun set, her hands clutching the bars as they had when she was first imprisoned, she felt her eyes fill with tears again as she stared westward toward the golden hills and the Scotland she could not see.

Clare drifted back to consciousness, not knowing where she was, nor which the dream and which the reality. She flailed out in front of her with her hands as she had done on waking so often before, and this time they met the bars she dreaded, grazing her knuckles, jarring her fingertips.

Let me wake up. Please God, let me wake up.

She was cold, deathly cold, shaking. All around her there was silence.

Struggling to fight off the fog of fear and sleep and cold, she flung out her arms again.

"It's no use. They are still there. You can't get out." The cool voice cut through the fog. "And they'll stay there until you sign."

Crouching, Paul reached into the cage and picked up the paper, dangling it in front of her.

The dream closed over her again—Isobel's dream. The mist from the river, the rusty bars, the rain drifting in from the Northumberland hills. Desolate with disappointment, she began to cry.

"Sign the paper, then I'll let you out. Sign!" It danced in front of her eyes. She did not know what it said or where it came from; she did not recognize the man who held it. His face was shadowy, blurred in the twilight of the mist, unreal. It was not Robert.

Shakily she took the paper and then the pen that he pressed into her hand.

"Sign."

Her fingers were so cold she could barely hold it. "Where? What do I sign?"

"There." He was stabbing at the paper through the bars. "There. There."

Her hands were shaking so much she could not hold the paper as, trembling, she scrawled her name. Almost before she had finished he had snatched it from her and slipped it into his pocket. He was smiling with relief. At last the transaction was legal! They could not catch him out now. Duncairn was his to sell to whom he pleased! He was beyond thinking about witnesses. They could be added later.

He rose to his full height and searched for the key in his pocket, then he stooped again, this time to undo the lock. "Now you are free. You see, it was easy all the time." He swung open the door. "You've nothing to be afraid of now, as long as you keep quiet about all this." He hesitated, then he smiled again. Who would believe her? Who would believe anything she said at all? "Come on. I'm getting cold." He was impatient now, eager to get away.

She did not move. They had tried to trick her like this once before: opened the door and beckoned, only to push her back and slam it in her face, their mouths contorted with cruel laughter. She shook her wings; she moved back into the shadows and she closed her eyes. The cage was home. In there she would be safe.

Paul frowned. "Clare!" He stared at her, a sudden feeling of unease in the pit of his stomach. "Clare! Come on. You're free." He turned away from the cage, leaving the door hanging open, but she didn't move. He stopped and glanced back. "Clare, come on. You can't stay out here. It's freezing." Her face was a complete blank. Suddenly frightened, he turned back and, ducking under the low door, he went into the cage beside her. After putting his hands under her arms, he dragged her out of the cage and picked her up. Her face was white, her body limp. Not once as he carried her toward the house did her eyelids move.

He carried her upstairs and took her into her bedroom, laying her on the bed before looking down at her. She was still breathing. He fumbled for her pulse, holding her cold wrist for a moment, not attempting to count. It was there, weak but regular. "Clare. It is your own fault. You made me do it." He spoke out loud, wheedling. "If you'd done what any wife would have done and helped me, none of this would have happened—"

He dragged the cover from under her body and pulled it over her. "You'll be glad to be rid of the place in the end. You know you will. It was going to drain every penny we had. It wasn't realistic to keep it, Clare . . ." She did not respond. "Clare? Clare, are you all right?" Fear gripped him. Clare really was possessed. He stepped away from the bed and hurried toward the door. After closing it behind him, he turned the key, then he ran downstairs to the telephone. Suddenly he was in a blind panic. Geoffrey had to come now.

Henry was shocked at Emma's appearance. She was pale and exhausted, and her eyes were red-rimmed.

"You know what's happened between Peter and me, I suppose?" She smiled at him apologetically over the cups of coffee.

Henry nodded. "I'm sorry, Emma." He looked away, unsure what else he could say.

"It's for the best." She sounded as if she were trying to convince herself.

"And it will give you both time to think," he said guardedly.

She nodded. "I'm going up to Duncairn on Tuesday, to spend Christmas with Clare." She glanced up at him and saw the color rise in his cheeks.

"How is she?" He was trying to sound casual.

"She seemed well. Happy!" Emma shrugged. "Until I spoiled it for her by talking about myself. . . . I'm taking Rex Cummin with me."

"The man Sigma dropped?" For a moment Henry couldn't hide his astonishment. "Is it . . . I mean, are you . . . ?"

"No." She smiled. "We're not. Not yet. But it'll give us a

chance to get to know each other better, and besides, he was so depressed about losing Duncairn to Sigma I thought it might cheer him up just to spend a bit of time there before they complete the sale."

"What on earth made Clare change her mind and sell to them?"

She shook her head. "I can't think, unless it was guilt. She probably thinks it is because she didn't help Paul that he got found out, I suppose."

"How is he taking it all?" Henry had pushed away his cup almost untouched. "You know the board has asked for his resignation?"

She nodded. "Serves him right, if you ask me."

"What is he going to do?"

"You mean when they let him out?" Emma was totally unsympathetic. "I don't know and I don't care as long as he leaves poor Clare alone. She's happy without him. She's found this super man in Scotland. Her brother told me—" She broke off as she saw Henry's face. "Oh, Henry, I'm so sorry—"

"It's okay." Henry shook his head. "It's okay! I know I never stood a chance. Just so long as she's happy, that's all that matters. . . ."

Neil was walking down the Mound toward Princes Street, his shoulders hunched against the snow. Twice he had reported the line to Duncairn out of order; twice the exchange had told him the engineers would go out looking for the fault as soon as there was a letup in the weather. He crossed the road and cut behind the National Gallery, feeling the sting of the snowflakes hot against his eyes. Two more days to meet with antioil lobby people, then he would pack it in for the holiday. Usually he hated Christmas. For him the season was a lonely one without a family to go to. At New Year's Eve there were always friends, and that was the one time each year he would drink himself into oblivion, but Christmas was empty. He had no religious belief to console him, no mother or father to eat and drink with, no one. But this year there would be Clare.

He stood at the lights in Princes Street waiting to cross the road. She deserved a really nice present—something special —but what? He had puzzled over the choice for hours, then at last, the night before, he had thought of it. A silver bangle. It would cost, of course, but it was something he wanted very badly to give her. He headed across Princes Street at last and on up Hanover Street in the direction of Hamilton and Inches.

He was halfway up the street when Kathleen spotted him as she came out of a shop. She hesitated, then she threaded her way between the cars and ran after him. "Neil? I thought it was you! How are you?" Two days before she had moved out at last into her own apartment. She smiled at him, her red hair flecked with snow crystals beneath her green silk scarf. "I couldn't believe it when I heard the news. I'm so sorry, Neil, but you must have known she would go back to him."

He stared at her blankly. "What are you talking about, Kath?" He was impatient to move on.

"Why, Clare, of course." Her eyes were wide, carefully sympathetic.

"What about Clare?"

Kathleen looked at him incredulously. "You mean you don't know?"

"Know what?" His voice was edged with irritation.

"Paul Royland went up to Duncairn yesterday—" Suddenly she was blurting it out. "Apparently she's gone back with him. Back to London. I'm sorry, Neil."

Neil stared at her. "How do you know this?" He was startled by the shaft of fear that shot through him.

"I called Jack Grant last night. I've lost some of my music, and I thought perhaps I had left it up there." Kathleen looked down, unable to meet his eye. "He told me. Apparently she decided to go back with him because of the court case and everything. Jack said she had been going to speak to you—I suppose she didn't have time. . . ."

"I don't believe you." His face was ashen.

"It's true, Neil." She looked him in the eye again and was appalled by the pain she saw there. Suddenly she was less certain.

She had called Duncairn, it was true. Both times the line was busy, then the third time the line was dead. She breathed a silent prayer that by the time it had been repaired Paul would have gotten there and taken Clare away.

"Clare is beyond your reach, Neil. She never was yours. I did tell you. She was just amusing herself with you. She's out of your class. Out of *our* class. The moment Paul beckoned she ran back to him. She belongs to him. She belongs with him, Neil. Even in trouble he has money, influence, friends. He'll come out of this smelling of bloody roses—his sort always does! Don't betray yourself, Neil. Don't run after her!"

He had been standing completely still in the middle of the pavement, facing her, his face and hair wet with melted snow. Now, at last, he began to walk on slowly. For moment Kathleen stared at him, then she began quickly to walk after him.

"Neil—"

"Good-bye, Kath."

"Neil, if I come over to the office tomorrow, maybe we could have coffee together?" She was almost running now to keep up with him. When they reached the corner of George Street he stopped. "Maybe I could lend a hand with something at Earthwatch over Christmas," she called. "When the show is over? I'm alone over Christmas, Neil. Please don't leave me alone—" She despised herself for begging: A woman her age should be able to snap her fingers and summon a man, but she could not help herself.

"Maybe, Kath." He sounded very weary. "I just don't know."

When he crossed the road she didn't follow him. She stood and watched him, feeling the wind whipping her coat open, shivering as the snow slid down her neck. She saw him walk slowly down the street and stop outside the jewelers' for a long time, staring down at something in the window display, then at last he walked on without going in.

Biting her lip, Kath turned away, her hand in her pocket clenched around the keys to his apartment. He hadn't asked for them again.

* * *

Clare was lying in bed, her eyes fixed on the ceiling, when Paul returned to her bedroom. He had a cup of tea in his hand.

"Clare?" He felt light with relief at seeing her awake. He put the cup down on the table beside the bed. "Clare, Geoff is coming to look after you, darling."

She made no response.

"It'll be all right, Clare. They won't hurt the castle, you know. Once they've got the well drilled and the pipes laid and everything, you'll hardly be able to see anything at all—"

Her face was completely blank. Impassive. The fear had gone, and the cold pallor of sweat.

"We'll go back and visit it, darling, I promise, once all this stupid litigation is over. Nothing awful is going to happen to me, you know. I'll probably get a fine, that's all. And the case isn't spectacular. I doubt if the press will show any interest. They're getting bored with the City now. I don't suppose anyone will hear about it. And the child need never know." He paused and looked at Clare's stomach, hidden beneath the smeared raincoat. One of her shoes had fallen to the floor. He frowned. He approached her and stood looking down at her. Now that he had had his way he wanted everything to be the same as it used to be, before Clare and he had quarreled. They could be a perfect family now, with a baby of their own. A strange cold fear crept back into his stomach as he looked down at her still face. "Clare, can you hear me?" He reached out tentatively. The buckles of her belt lay on the counterpane below the knot that tied the coat around her. She did not move when he pulled at it. With cold, awkward hands he undid it and began to ease off the coat. She lay completely unresponsive, moving puppetlike as he pulled it from her arms, rolling to one side as he eased it from beneath her, then falling back onto the bed again. He bundled up the Burberry and pushed it into the back of the closet, then he removed her other shoe and pulled the counterpane over her again, tucking it in.

"Clare, you ought to drink something hot, darling. Please. You mustn't get chilled. Have your tea. It will make you feel better." He adjusted the counterpane again. "It will be all right. Geoffrey will be here soon, and he will help you."

The room was icy cold. He glanced around, feeling the hairs on the back of his neck stirring. The house was very silent.

"I'll go and make us some supper, shall I? And see the heating is on. It is very cold outside." He backed away from the bed. "You'll be all right, Clare?" He was begging her now.

Clare made no response. She had heard nothing.

The woman who had earlier brought Isobel the ointment brought her the news. "Your king has won a great victory!" she whispered, glancing over her shoulder toward the guards. Behind her the royal flag, flapping in the wind, proclaimed Berwick Castle still a stronghold of the English. "Scotland will soon be free!"

Isobel stared at her, almost too weak to hope. Her face, still bruised, was so thin and transparent now that her eyes were great black circles in her face. She stared at the woman without comprehension.

The woman smiled as she pushed the bowl of food through the bars. "Have courage, my lady. Have courage," she whispered.

Her tormentors were missing that day. A fine, wetting rain misted down across the river, soaking the stone of the castle walls, soaking her old faded robe and the cloak she wore around her day and night. Her bones ached, her joints were swollen and arthritic, and her throat was raw, but the open ground below was empty and that was a blessing to be counted. She sat staring southward across the Tweed, but the mist hid everything from her behind a damp gray wall and the world was silent.

Two days later the guard came at dawn. He unlocked the cage.

"Out."

She stared at him dully, not understanding.

"Out. We're changing your lodging, my lady." His tone was deliberately insulting as he held open the barred door. Behind him two other men were standing waiting, one armed, one dressed in a long, sober tunic.

Scarcely able to move for pain and weakness, she crawled toward the door of the cage and through it onto the battlements of the castle where the air was free. She still did not understand; she still did not allow herself to hope. Perhaps this at last was to be the death she had prayed for again and again of late as the pain ate into her limbs and despair closed over her in a black, heavy pall. She looked like an old woman; she was barely twenty-eight.

The second man stepped forward and took her arm as she straightened and stood upright painfully, swaying slightly. "It is the king's command, Lady Buchan, that you be taken from the castle and lodged at one of the convents within the city walls. King Edward has seen fit to show you mercy." He smiled for the first time, his austere face dissolving into a maze of wrinkles. "He feels you have had sufficient punishment for your treason. Your imprisonment will be henceforth in the hands of the Carmelite sisters."

Still she could not take it in. She thought it some new torment, a trick, a jape on the part of the governor, but they guided her slowly toward the door in the turret, and then she was carried by one of the men-at-arms down the long, long winding stair. At the bottom she was set on her feet again and for a moment she stood again upright, looking around in confusion, unable to believe it was all over. Then everything went black and she collapsed in a dead faint upon the herb-strewn flags.

They put her in a covered wagon in the end, and drove her in that, screened from the people of Berwick who had given her such torment for so long, to the convent that was to be her new prison.

There she was put in the infirmary and slowly at last she began to believe and to hope. The nuns bathed her wasted body and gave her nourishing food, pap at first as her teeth were loose and her gums sore. They gave her a feather mattress and soft sheets and new gowns, somber, undecorated, save for the beads and crucifix she wore at her waist as they did, but clean and new. They combed the lice out of her hair, still thick and without a trace of gray, and washed it, drying it in the lavender-scented sunshine of the herb garden before binding her head in a snowy wimple and veil. At first she could not walk more than a few steps, then slowly her body responded to its freedom. By the time the first snows came she was able to walk around the convent unaided and she had learned much of what had happened to Robert in the past four years.

She heard about his flight from Scotland, his winter in Rathlin, and his return. She learned of the death of two more of his brothers, Thomas and Alexander, both executed as Nigel had been. She learned of King Hob's victories. She learned some of the legend that was growing around him all the time as his exploits were discussed and related across the length and breadth of Scotland and northern England.

The nuns talked of his prowess in battle, of his chivalry— even his enemies acknowledged that—his love of Scotland— his brilliance as a king. She learned too that the other women who had been captured with her, the women about whom she had wondered so often, were all still prisoners of the English as she was, and that Mary had been removed from Roxburgh and taken south into England as Robert's victories had threatened to come nearer that border stronghold. Somehow they had all survived, though her own ordeal had been so very much the worst. And she learned from the garrulous old infirmarian, with her long nose and her deep, close-set eyes, of King Hob's love affair with his kinswoman Christian of Carrick and his two children by her, and of his much-talked-of dalliance with other ladies up and down the land. She was aware of the sharp eyes watching her, of the woman's curiosity and half-ashamed satisfaction at her pain, and she tried to muster some of her old pride, but nothing could hide her hurt that Robert had forgotten her and allowed her to hang so long in her cage at the mercy of his enemies.

There was no official explanation why King Edward had so suddenly ordered her release, but the gossip in the cloisters and by the fire in the warming house was that he was afraid, afraid of what King Hob would do if he took Berwick and found his beautiful mistress a living skeleton in a cage. The sisters were afraid too. Lest King Hob find Isobel and be displeased with their part in her captivity, they must take care of her and nurse her back to health, and so they gave her better food, another feather mattress, and they prayed for her with renewed ardor.

In her loneliness, however, Isobel could think only of Christian of Carrick, who had been Robert's mistress, and of their two children. Quietly in her small room in the infirmary she would at last allow herself to weep, and then she would sleep, and in her sleep she would find herself once more in the cage and see the eyes around her and feel her wings battering against the confines of the bars and in her dream too she would be crying.

Neil was sitting at his desk, gazing down at a pile of un-opened letters. In the corner Jim was supervising the elderly duplicator as it churned out copies of notices of a forthcoming meeting of Earthwatch. "Why don't you call the hotel again?" Jim straightened and shuffled a pile of posters onto the table near him.

"The line is still out of order."

"And her home in England?"

"There's no reply there either."

"Then she's still at Duncairn." Jim sighed. "There is no way I'd believe Kath's story, if I were you. She's lying through her teeth, Neil. She's a spunky lady, and she's fighting back the only way she knows how."

"I'll call the phone company again this afternoon. The weather has eased up, so they should have found the problem by now—"

They both looked up as the door of the office opened and a man and a woman walked in. Neil frowned, automatically categorizing them: woman, late fifties; man, mid-sixties; well off, middle class, ill at ease—not the kind who usually found their way into the office. He put down his mug and stood up.

The man glanced from him to Jim and then back at him, obviously making a similar train of deductions in his mind.

"Mr. Forbes?" He spoke with an barely perceptible Scots' burr, the accent almost refined out of existence.

Neil looked from the man to the woman and back and inclined his head. They both seemed uncomfortable in the office, but there was more to it than that. They were agitated about something.

"I'm Archie Macleod and this is my wife, Antonia." The man paused. "Clare's parents."

"We've been trying to reach them on the phone at Duncairn for a couple of days," Antonia blurted out.

"The line is down." Behind them Jim had switched off the duplicating machine.

"We're so worried, Mr. Forbes—" Antonia turned back to Neil. "We wondered if you knew anyone else near the hotel we could call. . . ." Her voice trailed away as she looked pleadingly up at his face.

Neil shook his head. "I'm sorry. The whole area is cut off. They say it should be back on by tomorrow—"

"Paul called us, you see, just before the lines went dead. They set out to meet us in Edinburgh, then they had to turn back because of the snow," Antonia rushed on.

"A bit of a blow for you, her going back to Paul, I daresay." Archie had noticed Neil's expression harden. "I'm sorry, old chap, but her place is with her husband, you know. Especially now."

"Is that how he persuaded her to go back with him? By blackmailing her with harrowing accounts of appearing in court wifeless?" Neil's voice was harsh. "I'm sure she hasn't gone back to him willingly."

His last hope that Kathleen had been making it all up had plummeted at Archie's words, and he found himself suddenly angry; angry with everyone, but especially with Clare.

Antonia said, "There was no question of blackmail, Mr. Forbes. Clare loves her husband." Her voice was soothing. "And of course she wants to be with him while all this silly misunderstanding is cleared up, but there is more to it than that. She is going to have a baby, so of course they want to be together."

For a moment Neil was stunned into silence. Three pairs of

eyes were fixed on his face. White to the lips, he took a deep breath. "I thought Clare couldn't have children."

"So the doctors told them, but apparently it was all a terrible mistake. The baby is due in August," Antonia added with just a trace of smugness. "So you see why we are especially concerned. We were going to meet them in Edinburgh to celebrate, but when we couldn't contact them we couldn't help but be worried."

Neil managed to keep his face impassive. "I can understand," he said with feeling. "But if I were you I should go home, then they will know where to contact you as soon as Duncairn's phone is working again."

"Poor Clare," Jim commented as the door closed behind them. "If I had parents like that, I'd join the Foreign Legion."

"She can't be pregnant!" Neil spoke through clenched teeth.

"Doctors make mistakes," Jim said softly.

"But she hadn't slept with him for months." Neil's voice was torn with anguish.

"Women have been known to lie, Neil."

"Not Clare. Not about that." He began to walk in agitation up and down the space between the desk and the window. "There is something very wrong. She wouldn't have lied to me. She wouldn't—" He turned suddenly. "I'm going up there, Jim."

Jim shrugged. "Are you sure that's wise? Quite apart from anything else, they're telling people to keep off the roads—"

"I've got to know! One way or another, I've got to know what's going on." Neil frowned angrily. If Clare was a liar, if she had gone back to Paul willingly, then it would confirm everything he had first thought about her. But if she wasn't . . . If Paul was forcing her in some way to go back to him as he had forced her before, then she needed help. Not only that: If she had been telling the truth and she had not slept with her husband for months, then the baby, if there was a baby, was his.

At Airdlie Paul put down the phone. He had tried a dozen times to reach Rex, but there was no answer in his apartment.

He wanted to give the man the chance to change his mind—just in case Sigma backed off. Supposing they had become suspicious about the signatures, after all? There had been too long a silence from their legal people and he was getting twitchy. He had not been able to get in touch with Doug Warner for two days and the Sigma offices were still empty.

Upstairs in her bedroom Clare lay completely still. She had not eaten for twenty-four hours. Twice Paul had lifted her head and put a glass to her lips. Both times she had sipped a little, but she did not speak or acknowledge him. She seemed to have slipped away into a world of her own.

He had taken the piece of paper she had signed and put it, still folded, into an envelope, sealed it, and locked it in his briefcase. Now that he had finally got it he was almost ashamed.

A day without using it, a day to contemplate his actions, the Sabbath day, the day of rest. Everything would be all right if he didn't rush it. That would make it seem better, make the whole transaction appear completely legitimate. He slammed down the phone and looked at his watch. Geoffrey should arrive within an hour if the roads were still open. It was already growing dark.

It was after six and pitch dark when the taxi from the airport deposited Geoffrey and Chloe at the end of the snow-covered drive and turned at once into the blizzard, making for home. Suitcases in hand, they trudged up the long, winding drive, exhausted.

Paul had left the light on in the porch. "Thank God you're here!"

Geoffrey let his bags fall on the hall carpet and shook himself like a dog. He shed his heavy coat, then helped his wife off with hers.

"How is she, Paul?" Chloe was shaking with cold.

"Come and see." He led them past the empty drawing room where a huge fire was blazing temptingly up the chimney, up the stairs to her bedroom, and pushed open the door. He had left it unlocked only the last time he had gone up there. Clare lay as she had before without moving. Geoffrey walked over and put his hand on her forehead. She didn't seem to notice him.

"Clare? Clare my dear, can you hear me?" He bent over her. His hands were cold, his face glowing from the walk up the drive through the snow. Some drops of melted ice fell from his dark hair onto her face. She blinked, but she didn't look at him.

He took her hands and chafed them gently. "Clare? I want you to look at me." He glanced up at Paul. "Has she said anything at all?"

Paul shook his head. Behind him Chloe was standing by the door. "Speak to Isobel. See if she is there," she whispered.

Geoffrey shook his head. "Not now. Not like this, unprepared. I must have time to pray. We don't know what kind of a spirit this Isobel is, if she's evil or unhappy, just a lost soul or one bent on destruction." He frowned. "We must all pray, then I shall contact the minister here. We must get her to the church."

"You mean you can't do it here?" Paul was appalled. "She can't go out like this. For God's sake, you've got to do it now. I need her in London! An insane zombie is not going to help my case any." Now that he was no longer alone, his fear had evaporated and his anger had returned.

"Paul, for God's sake!"

He ignored Chloe's shocked remonstrance. "I thought you said your bishop had given you permission to sort her out, Geoff. Surely he's told you what to do."

"It is not as simple as that, Paul," Geoffrey said patiently. "Clare needs time and understanding and prayer. I shall pray with her tonight, but if we need to take her to church we will have to wait for tomorrow—we can hardly take her there at night."

"Tomorrow?" Paul was shocked. "You're going to leave her like this for another night?"

"I'm not going to leave her, Paul, I told you. I shall stay with her and pray. Where are her parents, and Mrs. Collins? Perhaps they can help us."

"They aren't here. They went to Edinburgh."

"What?" Geoffrey looked up startled. "You mean there is no one else here?"

Paul shook his head. "No one. It's up to you, Geoff."

His brother frowned, with a strange feeling of unease. He glanced at Chloe, wondering if she had felt it too. Something here was not quite right, something quite apart from Clare and her shuttered, unhappy face. Paul was too bland, too innocent. He shrugged unhappily. Whatever it was, there was nothing he could do about it now.

Wearily he sat down on the edge of the bed. He felt in his pocket and after a moment brought out a silver cross on a chain. "Clare? Clare, I want you to wear this, my dear. Can you see it?" He held it out before her eyes and for a brief moment he thought he saw her eyes focus on the silver, glinting softly in the lamplight as it swung. He undid the small clasp on the chain, his fingers still clumsy with cold, and slipped it gently around her neck, bracing himself for some reaction. If Satan and witchcraft were at work here, the chances were she would scream or struggle and throw off the cross before it touched her, but she ignored it. He redid the clasp carefully, settling it beneath her hair, then he placed her hands gently over the cross on her breast. She made no move to avoid it, though for a moment he thought he saw the flicker of a smile cross her face.

The minister had been called away to a remote farm just before the snow started, to the bedside of a dying man. His wife did not think he would be back that day—even if the roads were plowed—and the farm did not have a phone.

Geoffrey was angry. "I told you to speak to him before we got here, Paul!"

"It was none of his business." Paul looked away, embarrassed.

Geoffrey, heavy-eyed after his night's vigil, was still sitting beside Clare's bed. She had barely moved in the night. One hand had fallen from the cross and dangled over the edge of the bed. He had not replaced it.

"You'll have to do it by yourself. Do it here," Paul whispered angrily.

"I don't want to do it here." Geoffrey shook his head. He had prayed again and again and there had been no response. "There is too much here—too much of her past, too much atmosphere."

"Too many ghosts, you mean." Paul was sarcastic. "Aren't you a match for them, then?"

Geoffrey frowned. In the night he had felt a cold that was not a physical cold and sensed a presence in the room besides him and Clare. Afraid, he had knelt and prayed harder than he had ever prayed before. The prayers had comforted him, they had surrounded him and safeguarded him, but they had not touched Clare.

He got up wearily from his chair and walked across to the window. "Do you know what day it is, Paul?" The river was black between the snowy banks beneath the trees.

"Monday." Paul was short-tempered. He had called Rex again and still there was no reply. And the Sigma offices were still closed, at nearly eight-twenty.

"It is the ancient feast of Yule," Geoffrey said thoughtfully. "A day of power."

"Good. Well, use it." Paul turned back to the door.

"*Their* power," Geoffrey went on. "The men and women who worshipped the old gods. Women like Isobel."

Paul stopped. He felt a sudden prickle of fear run across his shoulders.

"I have to take Clare to hallowed ground, Paul, to defeat her." Geoffrey wasn't looking at him. He frowned, still staring through the window. He was watching a fox running across the snow-covered lawn in the distance. It vanished between the trees.

Paul had raised an eyebrow. "Where better than Dunkeld then? The cathedral is pretty old, isn't it?"

"There has been a church here for more than a thousand years." Geoffrey had been reading up about Dunkeld. "But I have to have permission from the minister; I don't know his views—"

"I'll call him again." Suddenly Paul wanted to be out of the room. It still felt unnaturally cold, in spite of the radiator and the electric fire.

Chloe was in the kitchen frying bacon. A pot of coffee was warming on the stove.

"We have to try to get her to eat, Paul."

"She won't. I've tried."

"Even so, let me have a go. And anyway the rest of us could do with a good breakfast. Poor Geoff sat up with her all night."

"As I did, the night before." Paul took her remark as a reproach. It wasn't true. Afraid of the strange, hostile chill in the room, he had turned the key in the lock and left her alone.

This time there was a reply from the cathedral manse. The minister would definitely be away until the following afternoon, and no, sorry, he could not be contacted; if it was an emergency, could they suggest a neighboring minister. . . .

Paul put down the phone angrily. What now? He glanced toward the door. The house was eerily silent.

He dialed Rex's number again. Still no reply, but he managed at last to reach Doug Warner's secretary. She was sorry but Mr. Warner had flown to the States and would not be back until the New Year. Paul cursed silently, then as an afterthought he asked her about Rex. She didn't know where he was, but she did know that he would be in Scotland for the whole of the Christmas holiday. Sigma Aberdeen was sending a helicopter to meet him at Dyce Airport.

Paul tensed. "Dyce? Are you sure? When?"

There was a pause. "If you'll hold the line, Mr. Royland, I'll check for you."

The American voice the other end of the line was distracted by another phone in the distance and Paul heard her asking someone else to hold, then at last she was back.

"The helicopter is to fly Mr. Cummin and his guests to the Duncairn Hotel, Mr. Royland. I have the number here—"

"Don't bother." He slammed down the receiver. So, the bastard was still interested enough to spend Christmas there! And what a Christmas present he could give himself if Sigma dropped out. Paul smiled. He sat for a moment staring at his briefcase as it lay on the table in front of him. Suddenly he was filled with confidence.

* * *

They had propped Clare up in a sitting position and Chloe had gently sponged her face. "Come on, Clare, you have to eat."

Her firm tone seemed to reach Clare. Suddenly she focused on Chloe's face. "The cage—"

"There is no cage." Chloe's voice was bracing. "You've been dreaming. Come on, have a sip of coffee." She closed Clare's hands around the mug.

Obediently Clare drank. The strong hot coffee flowed into her, then suddenly her hands began to shake violently. "Casta? Where is Casta?"

Chloe glanced at Geoffrey. Geoffrey grimaced. "She's dead, Clare," he said gently. "She can't have suffered, my dear. It was just the most dreadful accident. But life must go on. You have to eat. Look. Chloe's made you some breakfast."

They watched her as she lay back against the pillows, her eyes closed, struggling against the tears as the memories flooded back. It was a long time before she could compose herself enough to sit up again and drink some more coffee. She pushed the bacon away in distaste, but eventually she managed to nibble some toast. She hadn't looked at Paul.

Geoffrey had a plate of bacon and eggs on his knee, still seated beside the bed. He was watching her closely. The atmosphere had lightened, he was sure of it; Isobel had loosened her hold. He glanced at the cross around Clare's neck. It lay on the soft blue wool of her sweater, glinting in the lamplight. She seemed completely unconscious of it. He nodded, relieved. She had not at any time recoiled from it or torn it off. It was a start.

Geoffrey stood up. "Why don't Paul and I leave you two for a bit. A good hot bath would make you feel better, Clare, I'm sure."

Clare nodded in agreement. Chloe had to help her out of bed. Her legs refused to function as she tried to walk across the bedroom, and she felt her head spin. Slowly Chloe helped her down the passage to the bathroom and bent to turn on the taps.

"Don't shut the door!" Clare's voice rose in panic as Chloe turned away.

Chloe stopped. She frowned. The terror had been very real. "I won't. I'll leave it open and wait out here till you've finished if you like."

Clare stood for a moment, her hand on the edge of the door while behind her the steam rose from the bath. "Chloe, have I been ill?"

"Ill?" Chloe shook her head. "Of course not."

"Then why are you here? Why is Geoffrey here? What's happened?"

"Nothing has happened, love. You were upset about Casta and Paul was worried about you."

"Paul! Worried!" Chloe was unprepared for the venom in Clare's voice. "He doesn't care about me. He doesn't care about anything. He—" She broke off abruptly. Whatever accusation she had been about to make had been blanked from her mind as if a black impenetrable shutter had come down. She fiddled with the door handle uneasily. "You will stay, Chloe?"

"Of course I will. Have your bath and get dressed and we'll go downstairs."

After her bath Clare rummaged through her closets and produced underwear and a soft white woolen dress with a flared calf-length skirt and a tie belt and slowly began to dress.

Chloe tensed suddenly. Clare was not wearing the cross. "Clare—" She had spoken before she thought.

"The cross, Clare. What have you done with it?"

Clare was brushing her hair. "Geoffrey's talisman against my evil ways? It's in the bathroom."

Chloe got up and edged past her toward the bathroom door. "Please wear it, Clare. To please Geoffrey. It won't do any harm. . . ." She stepped into the bathroom. The cross was lying on the glass shelf over the basin. The chain was broken. Chloe picked it up and looked at it. Her heart had begun to hammer in her chest. She faced Clare in the doorway. "You've snapped the chain."

"I'm sorry. It got caught." Clare threw down her hairbrush. "Don't patronize me, Chloe. I'm grateful for your being here. I didn't want to be here alone with Paul—" She paused. Again the strange blank. "But I don't need Geoffrey's help!"

"Don't you?" Chloe was suddenly angry. "Then what about Isobel? Don't you think she needs his help?"

Clare stared at her. The color had drained from her already pale face. "Isobel is imaginary, Chloe."

"Is she? What about the cage you were talking about—"

There was a long silence, then slowly Clare sat down on the edge of the bed. "*I* was in the cage. Me." She clenched her fists tightly, fighting the wave of fear that swept over her as the confused memories swirled inside her head.

Chloe frowned. "Don't be silly, Clare." She took a step toward her. "Don't you see, you need help! You don't know what is real and what is imaginary now. You've trapped yourself in some strange, masochistic dream! Please, let Geoffrey help you."

"Geoffrey thinks I'm a witch." Clare leaned forward suddenly and snatched the cross that was dangling from Chloe's fingers. "Doesn't he?"

Chloe shook her head. "No. He knows you were making that up," she said cautiously. Her hand had gone to her own small gold cross, nestling on her chest beneath her blouse. "But he believes in Isobel and he thinks you may have been experimenting with some dangerous practices to make her come to you."

"Dangerous practices that make me imagine things." Clare sounded almost thoughtful for a moment. "Like Paul shooting Casta." Her eyes filled with tears again.

"Clare, that was real."

"And so was the cage!" Clare threw the cross onto the bed beside her. "It was real, Chloe. Real! *I* was in it, not Isobel. It's out there now, in the stable yard. Go and see for yourself if you don't believe me! Dear God, do you think I could imagine that?" Her voice had risen hysterically. She slumped suddenly backward on the bed. "But I have, haven't I? It's the dream. God in heaven, it's the dream!" She brought her fists down on the bed covers. "But it was so real. Just like when

James—" She broke off. "I am so frightened and confused! I dreamed Isobel was free, and they took her to a convent where the nuns were kind. It was the end of the nightmare. . . . But when I woke it was real—the bars were real—and Paul, Paul was there—" She had begun to sob violently as she spoke.

Chloe leaned forward and put her arms around her, holding her tightly. "Clare, don't cry," she pleaded. "Whatever it was, it's over. You're safe now. You're at home, at Airdlie, and Isobel is long dead. She's dead and gone, Clare!"

"But she's not, don't you see?" Clare shook her head, the tears streaming down her face. "She's not dead!"

"She is dead, Clare, but she is not at rest," Chloe said slowly. "And Geoffrey can help her, I'm sure he can."

Behind them Geoffrey had appeared in the doorway and was standing listening to her. He frowned, seeing the cross on the bed.

"Chloe," he called softly.

Both women looked up. Clare picked up the cross and threw it at him. "Take your damn cross and go away. I don't need you!"

Geoffrey crouched and picked it up. He slipped it into his pocket. "Clare, you have to let me help."

"No! No, I don't have to let you do anything." Pushing Chloe aside, she stood up. "Go away, Geoffrey. Isobel is not evil. She prayed to the same God you do. Not that it did her any good. She'd have done better to call down vengeance from the moon goddess she worshipped when she was young, but she didn't. She accepted that she had been punished for her sins with Robert and she walked meekly into the chapel with the nuns!"

"Do you worship the moon goddess?" Geoffrey's voice was very quiet. "Is that how you summon her spirit to you?"

Clare laughed bitterly. "You really do want to believe it of me, don't you, Geoffrey! All right, then, if that's what you want, why not? After all it's a free country; people don't get burned for heresy anymore, do they? Your lot haven't got a monopoly of belief. Yes, I believe in the moon goddess. After all, she represents the feminine principle, doesn't she? She is all the vogue again these days. How apt. For a woman to summon a woman. Do you want to see me do it?"

"No, Clare!" Geoffrey's voice sharpened.

"Why not? After all, Isobel is happy now. She didn't die in her cage. She didn't die! She's still alive!" She faced the window suddenly and raised her arms. "Isobel! I want to hear you; I want to see you. I want you to tell them what happened. Come!"

Behind her Chloe screamed.

"Leave it, Chloe, it's all right." Geoffrey swallowed hard. "Clare? Clare—"

Clare did not hear him. Already she could see the old monastic buildings, hear the chanting of the nuns in the chapel. "Come to me! Come to me, Isobel. Now!"

Crossing her arms gracefully on her breast, she sank to her knees, her eyes on the pale sun that was shrugging itself out of the mist, dazzling on the settled snow beyond the window.

❧ Chapter Thirty-two ❧

Wrapped in her warm cloak, her hood pulled low over her face, Isobel walked the cloisters and the gardens whatever the weather, feeling the cold air catching at her lungs. She hated to be inside, and the sisters did not insist.

In Berwick winter had come early. Snow drifted across the hills and into the town, covering the dirty streets with a sheen of glittering white. The walls, black against the sky, were outlined with renewed clarity and the roofs of the houses were suddenly neat and uniform, beautiful until the ugly, melting gray began to creep across them from the heat of the fires beneath and drip off the reeded thatch. In the convent the herb garden was shaggy beneath the snow. Clumps of dead fronds arched above the ground and twigs and branches clustered over tiny nests of new green leaves, curled and blighted by the cold.

They had not tried to make a nun of this once-wild beautiful woman. When Isobel attended divine service the sisters gave thanks and made room for her as the smoke of incense wreathed around them. When she attended meals she was given her share and more of the simple fare. She was made welcome by the single fire in the warming room, and ushered toward the light of the cressets as the dark afternoons drew in. Only the portress who had official custody of the keys was unkind, turning her away from the door in the wall that led out into the streets of the town and making it clear that she was still, and would remain, a prisoner.

She made no special friends, asked no favors, not even of God. Inside her heart there was a terrible numbness that she dared not even question. From time to time she tried to pick up some embroidery or weaving, but they were not skills she had ever enjoyed. Occasionally she would sit by the cresset in the library, trying to fix her attention on an exquisitely illumined book of hours, but her head would ache and her vision, once so clear, would blur and she would find herself rising restlessly. Pulling her cloak around her, she would open the heavy door to walk out into the coldness of the still night and continue her slow patrolling of the sleeping herb beds.

She was stronger now; she could walk three times around the cloister without growing tired, and slowly her flesh was filling out and the shine was coming back to her hair. After a year her courses had resumed, hesitant and scant as those of a twelve-year child.

But still she had the nightmares.

As month succeeded month and the seasons turned full circle a second time, she was once more tall and light in her gait, composed and calm. She thought about escape; but she no longer had the courage or the strength to put the thought into action. That would have been the response of the younger Isobel. Now she was resigned to her captivity. She tried not to think of Robert. News of his exploits reached her almost daily, and her heart twisted with pain when she heard his name, but she merely smiled silently and hid her deepest feelings.

And still the nightmares came.

"My lady. The Countess of Buchan is here to see you."

The words made her smile. Holding her heavy veil close around her pale face for warmth, she stared at the novice who had stopped beside her seat in the frozen garth. "I am the Countess of Buchan, child."

The girl looked at the ground, abashed. "I'm sorry, my lady. That's what I was told. She's waiting in the parlor."

Isobel sighed. It didn't matter. Any variety in the awful monotony of her days was welcome. She made her way quickly through the dark passages toward the parlor near the main door and found the mother superior standing in the center of the room in earnest conversation with a woman, fashionably dressed in a velvet surcoat and pellison lined with squirrel furs, her hair hidden beneath a pleated fillet and a gold circlet. As Isobel appeared, both women turned to face her.

"Alice!" Isobel's cry of astonishment turned into a sob of joy as she ran toward her husband's niece and hugged her. "Oh, Alice!" Suddenly she was shaking like a leaf. It was the first time she had seen a familiar face in many years.

"You are to be released into Lady Buchan's custody, my dear. I am so pleased for you." The mother superior was smiling broadly.

"Released?" Through her tears Isobel stared at Alice incredulously. "You mean I am to go free?" She did not even notice this second use of the Buchan title.

"Not quite free." Alice's face was sober. "Sit down, let me explain." She took Isobel's hand and drew her to the window seat, her bright silks and velvets a sharp contrast to the sober gown and cloak that Isobel wore. "After Uncle John died, Henry was given the title of Earl of Buchan, since you and uncle had no heirs." Alice looked down suddenly.

"Given?" Isobel looked at her, puzzled. "By Robert?"

"Not by Robert. By King Edward of England. Remember" —Alice smiled ruefully—"my husband is King Edward's man. You are to live in our custody." She shifted uncomfortably on the uncushioned stone seat then hurried on. "But that means nothing. You shall be my guest—my honored guest! You will live with us, and meet my children—I have two daughters now—and you will get really well and strong."

"She is well and strong," the old nun put in tartly. "We have cared for her and given her every consideration, Lady Buchan!"

"I'm sure you have, but it's not the same as family!" Alice rushed on, not giving Isobel time to speak. She caught Isobel's hands in hers. "I can't tell you how excited I was when Henry told me we were to look after you. It's so wonderful! And you'll be able to leave Berwick at last!"

"And where are you taking me?" Isobel's voice was quiet. "Are we going north into Scotland, or do the Buchan lands lie only in England now?"

There was an uncomfortable pause. "Henry holds lands in

the north," Alice said at last cautiously. "But Buchan itself was most terribly laid waste by the Bruce. He ravaged the country and its people, and destroyed most of the castles, Isobel."

Isobel was silent. She had heard again and again now the story of the *herschip* of Buchan—and the romantic rumor that it was for her sake that Robert had wreaked such terrible vengeance on her husband's lands.

After a long pause she looked up. "Has Duncairn gone then?"

Alice smiled. "Duncairn still stands."

Their eyes met. Isobel bit her lip. If he had harried Buchan for her sake, he had spared Duncairn for her sake too.

"Where are you taking me, then?" Her voice was husky.

"South, into England." Alice's face mirrored the anguish she saw in Isobel's. "But at least you'll be free."

"Free?" Isobel was bitter. "I'm to be released into your custody, my lady"—she emphasized the words—"and I'm to be taken to the heart of the country of my enemies. Is that to be free?"

"You can ride. You can feel the wind in your hair and sun on your face. You can walk and run and laugh with my children. You can stop being afraid." Alice was reproachful. "Is that not something to thank God for?"

Isobel gave a little grimace. "Forgive me, Alice. It is just that I have thought myself so near—" Her voice broke. "From my cage, I could never see the hills of Scotland, but I could feel them, and they are still there, so close beyond these walls. . . . When the wind comes from the north it carries the smell of the heather, the salt of the seas that lap the cliffs below Duncairn. It is hard to turn my back forever on the land of my birth."

"You'll go back, one day," Alice whispered. "I'm sure you will." She stood up abruptly. "Come. You must collect your belongings and make your farewells. Our escort is waiting, and we have a long ride ahead of us."

It was the fear that the King of Scots might soon be strong enough to turn his attention to the liberation of Berwick that had made King Edward, in a fit of spite that would have done credit to his father, give the order that his prisoner should be moved south, forever beyond her former lover's reach.

The warm days of summer in the south, far from the Scottish wars, not touched even by the near civil war that racked England, were good for Isobel. Her health improved a little and her strength with it. She rode out with Alice often and flew her nieces' hawks, reveling in the untamed beauty of the birds, touching the glossy silk of their feathers and feeling her spirit soaring with them toward the sky. These birds had never known a cage.

She even tried to ride with the huntsmen as the autumn colors turned the forests of England to copper and gold, but the autumn brought mists and cold too and suddenly, unexpectedly, her strength began to fail again and her robust energy disappeared. Time and again, as winter drew on, she was forced to take to her bed at Whitwick as fevers and coughs ravaged her body.

Alice watched by her in anguish, seeing each fever take a little more of Isobel's precarious newfound vitality away, listening at the bedside as, in her delirium, Isobel cried again and again the two names she had never mentioned from the day they left Berwick, the names of her country and her king. In secret, at last, torn by fear and pity and love, and, still, by the guilt that would always haunt her for her betrayal of Isobel all those years before, Alice wrote a letter.

It took two months for the reply to come, carried by a messenger almost too tired to stand.

Alice read it and, smiling, threw the letter on the fire in her solar, watching the parchment blacken and curl to nothing before she went to find her aunt.

"Henry has been granted the stewardship of Duncairn," she said, clutching Isobel's hand. "The last of the Buchan lands. We can go back."

"Go back?" Isobel glanced at her. She had recovered from her last fever, but her face was pale and thin again and she was very weak.

"Back! Back to Duncairn! Don't you want to go?" Alice was laughing.

"But I thought Robert held Buchan. . . ." It was the first time she had mentioned his name since her last illness. She said it simply and without emotion.

"Robert is occupied elsewhere," Alice said impatiently. "He is too busy to bother with who holds one clifftop castle on the far side of his kingdom. He will pay no attention to a small detachment of retainers. Besides"—she paused—"he would never harm you."

The letter had been stilted, hardly the passionate outpouring Alice had hoped for, but at least he had not refused.

It took three weeks for the small party of riders to reach Duncairn. Isobel's weakness, the wild stormy weather, and Alice's terror that they would be apprehended—by English or Scots—made them travel warily and slowly, avoiding the more exposed tracks, keeping at last to the hills, but Isobel's delight grew as they traveled north in spite of her exhaustion, and that was Alice's reward. The brightness in her eyes was from excitement now, not delirium, and the color in her cheeks was from the wind and the sun, not fever.

Even so, when at last they reached Duncairn and rode wearily beneath the gatehouse arch, Isobel was swaying on her horse. Gritting her teeth with determination, she forced herself to walk to the clifftop postern and she stood there, staring down at the sea far below through the whirling wings of the sea birds.

It was a long while before, at last, she let them carry her to the bed in the lord's chamber that she had shared a lifetime ago with the Earl of Buchan.

Alice left three days later.

"But why?" Isobel was almost in tears. "I want you to stay."

"I can't, my dear." Alice kissed her fondly on both cheeks. "I have to go back. You'll understand why, I'm sure, soon." She smiled. "Take care of yourself, and may God bless you always." She hugged her one last time, then turned away. As she rode out and began the long journey south, there were tears in her eyes. She had a feeling she would never see Isobel again.

Behind her, Isobel stood alone in the courtyard, waving until the high iron-banded gates had swung shut and the heavy bars fastening them had fallen into place. She had no premonition that her next visitor would be the King of Scots.

"You have to do it, Geoff. The woman will go insane!" Paul was standing watching his wife as she knelt on the floor. "Go on. Do it. Now. Get out your holy water or whatever you use and drive Isobel out—"

"Clare—"

Shaking with fear, Chloe made as if to approach her, but Geoffrey put out a hand to stop her. "Leave her. It might not be safe to waken her." He felt absurdly at a loss as he looked down at her. She was not cursing or swearing or mouthing obscenities as the men to whom the bishop had sent him had warned she might. There was no feeling of evil in the room— only the sudden, strange, unearthly cold that they could all feel pressing in around them. There was a presence in the room, of that he had no doubt, but there was nothing to see, only his sister-in-law on her knees staring up with rapt face at the window, which was rapidly growing darker as the short afternoon closed in. Far from diabolic intervention, he was reminded of nothing so much as the pictures he had seen of St. Teresa. He shook himself sharply and quietly began to pray again, his mind reaching out to hers, trying to weave the protection of Jesus Christ around her, trying to touch the mind of the other woman who looked out now from her eyes —the woman who would not be dislodged.

Cautiously he approached her. "Clare. I want you to come downstairs." He laid his hand carefully on her arm. "Can you hear me, Clare?" He couldn't perform the exorcism here. He wasn't strong enough to fight the atmosphere. He would pray for the house later. Now they must go to a church.

At first she resisted, then slowly he felt her taut muscles relaxing. After a moment or two she began to rise to her feet.

"Get her something to put around her shoulders," Geoffrey directed Chloe quickly. "Paul, put my small black case in your car. We'll take her to the cathedral, minister or no minister." He had his arm around her now, guiding her to the door.

In a daze Clare obeyed him. She knew he was there; the

vision had gone, and yet part of it was still with her: the happiness Isobel felt as she looked around the castle home she had thought she would never see again; the joy at hearing again the sound of the sea against the rocks below; the heady scent of heather and salt and whin; the certainty at last of freedom.

She allowed Chloe to put a coat around her shoulders, deliberately clutching the daydream around her now, holding back from reality. Wherever they wanted to take her, it didn't matter. She, the hidden essential part of herself that they could not reach, could stay at Duncairn, with Isobel, in the castle that was not a ruin, where Casta had never existed and her pain and fear of Paul were things of the distant future.

Chloe sat with her in the back of the Range-Rover, her arm around her shoulders as Paul drove carefully down the snow-filled drive. The wind had changed and it was warmer suddenly. The icicles were dripping now and the trees were showering the car with soft drops of melting snow.

Paul drove slowly and carefully into the town and turned down toward the cathedral, parking outside the gates. It was almost dark. He turned in his seat and peered at Clare. "Is she all right?"

Chloe nodded. "She doesn't seem to know what's going on." Her hands were firmly clasping Clare's, which were cold and strangely still.

"Just as well." Geoffrey took a firm grip on the handle of his case. "Come on."

He and Paul helped Clare down from her seat, then they turned toward the wrought-iron gates. The wind was bitterly cold, the huge fir trees on the edge of the broad Tay moaning slightly as the four figures slipped through the gates, closing them behind them, and began to walk slowly up the path. Nearby one of the trees had been hung with Christmas lights. It swayed and curtseyed in the wind, tossing the lights in bright arcs in the darkness.

The snow was soft, unmarked in the twilight as they made their way toward the cathedral door. The huge bulk of the building, the tower, the ruined nave with its soaring pillars and crumbling arches, and the roofed choir, which was now the parish kirk, rose black against the sky.

Paul seized the door handle and turned it. It didn't move. "It's locked. Oh, Geoff!" Chloe bit back a sob.

Behind them the cloud was breaking up. A pale cold half-moon shone down on the river, throwing the colorless shadows of the huge old trees across the snow toward the closed cathedral.

"The key. We have to get a key." Geoffrey turned around anxiously.

"There isn't time, man, and they'd never give it to you." Paul had caught hold of Clare's arm. "The ruin! Do it in the ruin! It must be just as sacred, surely. It's hallowed ground, isn't it?" Almost at a run, he dragged Clare after him as he led the way along the long wall of the roofless nave, his feet squeaking in the snow.

The massive double arches of the walls reared up in the moonlight as Paul tried the gate that led into the ruins. It too was locked. With a muttered oath he put his shoulder to it, and they all heard the sharp crack as it swung open.

"Paul!" Geoffrey was dismayed, but his brother dragged him inside.

"I'll pay for the damage. Don't be such a fool. This is an emergency." He stopped, looking around awed at the huge pillars, the two-storied arches, the gravestones, white beneath the snow in the brightening moonlight. The place was very quiet.

"Will it work here?"

"It will work." His reluctance gone, Geoffrey set his case down on the snow and opened it. Crucifix, holy water, candles, the bread and wine. He brought them out quickly, his hands shaking with cold. Then he unfolded his stole, kissed it, and hung it around his neck. "Clare, my dear." His voice was gentle. "Come and stand here. Chloe, I want you with her. The bishop said it was important there should be a woman with her. Paul, you hold a candle. Here." He struck a match with trembling fingers and lighted the candles, sheltering the streaming flames as best he could, then he pushed one into his brother's hand.

Paul stood back, feeling the soft warm wax spill almost at once across his wrist as his brother and his sister-in-law fussed around Clare. The whole cathedral seemed to be listening as Geoffrey's voice, losing its diffidence, rang out suddenly among the echoes.

The candles threw a pale flickering orange glow across the moonlit pillars of a church, part of which had been built by Bishop Sinclair, Robert the Bruce's friend, then the moonlight strengthened and strayed even into the shadows and the candlelight was dulled.

Clare looked around her, dazed, and gasped as if she had only just realized what was going on. Pulling away from Chloe, she made as if to run.

"Hold her." Geoffrey's voice was peremptory.

Paul put his candle down on a tombstone and caught Clare's arm. Chloe stood beyond her in the darkness, and she groped for Clare's hand again and squeezed it.

They were both very frightened.

Geoffrey raised the crucifix and held it in front of Clare's eyes. "God our Father in heaven, we bow in your presence . . . direct your angels to gather all our deceased that seem to be lost, especially your servant Isobel. . . ." His voice echoed among the pillars, fighting the howl of the wind in the trees. "Bind and banish Satan and his minions to their appropriate place . . . Let the Body and Blood of our Lord heal all the wounds and torments inflicted by Satan and his minions, living and dead." He paused, his eyes on Clare's face. "Isobel, Countess of Buchan, in the name of Jesus Christ I bid you leave this woman, Clare, and go from this place," he called.

Holy water touched Clare's face and hair as she struggled to be free.

"No!" She was sobbing now. "No. You don't understand. Don't send her away. Don't! She's part of me. Please!" The cross was glinting in front of her eyes, the candlelight glaring, dazzling her. "Please, please." She could feel her strength going, her legs threatening to give way.

Geoffrey loomed hugely in front of her, his hand raised, his stole blowing in the wind over his coat. She could see the

sweat standing out on his forehead as he called out his
prayers.

"O Lord, grant rest to the soul of your servant, Isobel, that
she may repose in a place where there is no pain, no grief, no
sighing, but everlasting life." Behind him one of his candles
blew out and a stream of blue smoke escaped and dispersed
across the snow. "O Lord, grant to this Your servant, Isobel,
to rest with the righteous ones and to dwell in Your courts, as
it is written. Since you are merciful, God, forgive her sins and
all her transgressions that she has committed by thought,
word, or deed, knowingly or unknowingly, for you are the
lover of mankind, now and always and for ever and ever.
Amen."

Behind them the wind was rising, making the ancient firs
roar. She felt his hand, his fingers tracing a cross on her
forehead, then she knew no more.

In his apartment in the Barbican James was shaving; he
stared at himself in the mirror, ran an exploratory hand
across his chin, and, satisfied, unplugged the razor. For a
moment he went on standing there, staring into the mirror.
There was a slight frown on his face. He was thinking suddenly about Clare. Slowly he turned away and, after stowing
the razor in a drawer, he fished out a clean shirt. He put it on
and walked across his bedroom with it still unbuttoned, fid-
dling his cuff links into place. Why suddenly should he feel so
uneasy? He frowned and glanced at his watch, then he
reached for the phone.

There was no answer from Airdlie. As he sat listening to
the sound of the tone ringing away in the silence, he felt his
unease increase.

At Airdlie Paul had stayed downstairs and helped himself
to several stiff whiskies while Geoffrey and Chloe carried
Clare up to her room and put her to bed. He was thinking
about her panic-stricken struggling, her scream of anguish as
Geoffrey had made the sign of the cross upon her forehead,
and her heartbroken sobbing as they extinguished the remaining candles, before she had collapsed on the snow-cov-

ered ground. He had picked her up and silently they had made their way back through the moonlit snow toward the Range-Rover parked beyond the wrought-iron gates in Cathedral Street.

When Geoffrey called him at last, it was several minutes before he replied and reluctantly, glass in hand, climbed the stairs to Clare's bedroom.

The three of them stood around her in silence, gazing down at her still form.

"What have we done?" Chloe whispered.

"She'll be all right." Geoffrey put his hand on Clare's forehead. "She'll be all right when she wakes up." He sounded as if he were trying to convince himself.

He looked up, startled, as a log slipped in the fireplace. He had set match to the fire himself while Chloe was removing Clare's snow-wet clothes and putting on the nightdress she had found. It had caught and crackled cheerfully up the chimney, but he found that he was shivering again now, even though he still had on his heavy coat.

Paul stooped to turn on the electric fire. "I can't think why this room is always so cold," he exclaimed testily. "The whole house needs a new heating system—" He broke off abruptly as above him the light on the end of its short cord began to move jerkily from side to side.

They all stared at it speechlessly.

"What is it?" Chloe whispered at last. She moved closer to her husband. "What's happening?"

"It must be a draft." Paul strode to the window and opened the curtains. For a moment he stood staring out, transfixed, then he closed them abruptly. His face had turned a pasty yellow.

"What's wrong?" Chloe said softly. She could feel herself beginning to shake.

"Nothing. It's stupid. I . . . I thought I saw someone—"

Above his head the light was moving even more violently from side to side. The bulb began to flicker in protest and the room filled with swirling shadows.

"She's here!" Suddenly Chloe's voice was shrill with fear. "Isobel is here!"

"Rubbish!" Geoffrey had paled. He took a deep breath.

Clare's eyes had opened. She was watching them from the bed, a sad smile on her lips. "You've made her angry." Her voice was very distinct. Unexpectedly she began to cry.

"There is nothing to be frightened of." Geoffrey felt surprisingly calm as he turned away from the bed. "I believe it is because she has left you, Clare. She's almost free. . . ."

This time his prayers for Isobel were gentle, persuasive, kind. He blessed Clare and the room, sprinkling holy water around the bed, then he sent Chloe and Paul downstairs while he sat down beside the sobbing, incoherent woman to keep an all-night vigil. It was Yule, St. Thomas's Eve. The Longest Night.

Paul was standing in the drawing room, staring down at the dying fire, when Geoffrey came down the next morning. "How is she?"

Geoffrey shook his head. "She is still asleep. Chloe's going to sit with her for a bit." He threw himself down into one of the chairs. "How are you?"

Paul closed his eyes. "Exhausted." He frowned. "Is everything quiet up there now?"

Geoffrey nodded. "She . . . it . . . whatever it was has gone. It's all over. When are her parents coming back?" He sipped the coffee Chloe had left for him before she went upstairs.

Paul shrugged. "I don't know." Now that daylight was returning he wanted to get away. Above all, he wanted to corner Cummin at Duncairn. "I'm going to have to leave you and Chloe for a few hours. I know you'll cope."

"Paul! We have to get back to the parish! It's Christmas, my busiest time—"

"I know. Antonia and Archie will be back any moment. They will look after Clare. She doesn't want me, you know that."

"Is anything really so important you have to leave your stricken wife alone?" Geoffrey asked tartly.

He was still badly shaken. Clare's reaction to the service had not been what he expected. She had acted as if she had been violated—raped. He had not been sure what he really had thought would happen: a demon leaving might curse or swear or scream—he had been warned to expect that, but he had also expected a feeling of relief; a sense of evil departing.

But there had been no sense of evil in the first place, just those few angry moments when the light had so inexplicably swung to and fro below the ceiling. He shuddered and closed his eyes wearily. Perhaps the bishop had been right. He should have left it to the experts.

Paul was fidgeting restlessly with the poker, throwing more logs onto the fire, kicking them to settle them into last night's embers. His expression was brooding. He looked up suddenly. "When will you know if it has worked? Really worked?"

Geoffrey didn't pretend not to know what he meant. "As God is my witness, I don't know."

"Shouldn't God let you know, then?" Paul's voice was heavy with sarcasm. "So, I gather we have to wait and see if my wife's sanity has returned?"

"That's right." Geoffrey could feel his anger mounting. "And in the meantime she needs care and love and understanding."

"All things I'm renowned for not possessing," Paul said. "So, I leave her to you and Chloe who are loaded with an abundance of all three." He strode toward the door. "The roads are clearer now that it's thawing. I can be back tonight. If Archie and Antonia aren't here by then you can leave Clare to me and your adoring parishioners will have you back in time for the first carol service tomorrow."

Standing by the window in Clare's room, Chloe saw the Range-Rover leave with relief. She had never liked Paul; now she hated him with cold, clear, un-Christian loathing. There was no way she would leave Clare here alone with him. Either Clare must come back with her to London or if she wasn't well enough to travel, then Geoff could go back on his own and she would stay in Scotland.

There was a slight sound behind her from the bed. Clare was sitting up against the pillow, clasping her knees. She looked very wan. Chloe went toward her hesitantly. "How are you?"

Clare shrugged. "I don't know. How should I be?" She gave a faint smile. "Should I feel different? Shriven? Repentant?" She rested her chin on her knees, pulling her long nightgown around her feet and tucking it in with a shiver. "To be honest, I feel tired and rather sick."

"Would you like a cup of tea?"

Clare nodded. She didn't move when Chloe had gone. Nor did she look around the room.

Her mind was clear this morning. She remembered everything that had happened the night before, and everything before that. Casta. Paul. The cage. The piece of paper. Her signature on the paper making over Duncairn to Paul—

She scrambled out of bed, down the wooden stairs that were cold beneath her bare feet.

"Paul—"

Geoffrey appeared at the door. "Clare, my dear, what's wrong?" He stared at her, his heart thumping.

"Paul—where is he?"

Behind her, Chloe appeared from the kitchen, a tray in her hands.

"He's gone, Clare. He's gone."

"A paper! Did he have a paper with him?" She glanced frantically from her brother-in-law to Chloe and back.

"He had a briefcase," Chloe said. "I saw him from the window."

"Oh, God!" Clare subsided on the bottom step of the staircase and put her head in her hands. "I've signed away Duncairn. I remember it all now. I've signed away Duncairn!"

Geoffrey and Chloe looked at each other. "Clare, my dear. It is already sold," he said gently.

"No, you don't understand. It isn't. Paul lied. He forged my signature. . . . He told me. It isn't sold. Not legally."

"Where did Paul go?" Chloe looked at her husband, willing him to know.

"He was in an awful hurry to get away. He didn't say where. He promised he would return this evening—"

"Then he's gone to Edinburgh. To Mitchison and Archer—"

"Clare dear, even if he has, I doubt if a document such as you describe would be valid if it wasn't witnessed. Besides, you have only to say it is not genuine." He was trying to hide his shock.

"Are you sure?" Chloe looked at him hopefully. She turned to Clare. "There. So, you needn't worry. Look, we'll talk some more when you're back upstairs in the warm . . ."

Half an hour later Geoffrey went up with the breakfast tray. Clare's room was full of sunlight now. Chloe had taken one of the bowls of hyacinths from the piano in the drawing room and brought it upstairs. The scent filled the room. She took the tray from him when he came in and put it down beside the bed, then she glanced at him and shook her head. "You go back down. I'll call you when she's better." From the bathroom they could both hear the sound of agonized retching, followed by the rush of water from the taps.

When Clare reappeared she was white-faced. "I'm sorry, Chloe—"

"Don't be silly. Get into bed and keep warm. I've poured you out some tea. It'll make you feel better." Chloe twitched the covers over her. "The trouble is you have nothing in your stomach. You haven't eaten for days." She watched maternally as Clare drank the tea. "Paul's a bastard," she said suddenly. "An out-and-out unspeakable bastard."

"Praise indeed from you." Clare managed a rueful smile. "Did he tell you I'm pregnant?"

"Pregnant!" Chloe stared at her in genuine amazement.

Clare nodded. "It's not Paul's. Don't be shocked. Please."

"Oh, Clare—"

"I was so happy." Clare huddled under the covers. She was aching all over. "It was a dream come true. I love Neil. I never knew what love was with Paul." She was gazing into the distance. "It was Paul who couldn't have children, not I. He let me take the blame and I believed him." She lay back on the pillows and there was a long silence. Then she closed her eyes. "Will I stop having nightmares now?"

"I hope so." Chloe smiled reassuringly.

"And my daydreams about Isobel?"

"They were more than dreams, Clare." With a quick glance behind her at the room, now so bright and ordinary, Chloe reached for the teacup, refilling it automatically, hoping the gesture would be reassuring.

"But they weren't dangerous. They did no one any harm. She was part of me. Part of my inheritance, like Duncairn." She closed her eyes suddenly, trying to blink back the tears.

"I'm sure Geoff did the right thing, Clare." Chloe tried to sound cheerful. She changed the subject. "You know, I am glad Paul's gone—"

"He was prepared to kill me to get his way, you know." Clare said softly. "To inherit Duncairn."

"Oh, Clare, no."

"Why else was he out looking for me with a loaded gun?" Clare sighed. "I know him better than you, Chloe. He's capable of it when he doesn't get his way and now that he thinks he's won, he wants to claim my baby as his as well. I won't let him."

"Does Neil know all this?"

Clare shook her head. "He doesn't know about the baby."

Chloe frowned. "Where is he then? Shouldn't he be with you if he loves you so much?"

"I said I love him. I'm not sure that he loves me. It doesn't matter."

"I'd have thought it mattered rather a lot." Chloe was affronted. "I am sorry, Clare. Here I am being pompous and moralistic and all you want is to rest. We'll talk some more later."

After Chloe had gone Clare walked unsteadily to the window and looked out, thankful that she was alone at last. There were shreds of blue among the clouds, and a sharp wind had arisen, shaking the last of the melting snow from the dark fronds of the Scotch pines beyond the drive. The snow on the lawns was melting too, the soft glaze turning the surface to mirror brightness. She could see a crow plodding slowly across it, leaving a trail of footmarks as it paused every now and then to peck at something below the surface of the snow.

Isobel must have endured another winter at Duncairn, if

she lived. What had happened to her? Did she ever see Robert again? Clare groped for the thread of memory that would answer her questions, but there was nothing. It was gone. She glanced around the room. It was a cheerful, sun-filled bedroom, full of the scent of hyacinths. There were no shadows now.

The silver cross with the broken chain still lay on her bedside table. Clare picked it up and stared at it, then purposefully she put it down.

Moving swiftly, she pulled open her chest of drawers. There, at the back, was a half-burned candle. She took it out and, lighting it, melted some wax into the saucer from beneath her teacup. She set the candle down on the carpet beside the bed, then she tiptoed to the door and glanced out. There was complete silence from downstairs. Unconsciously she was murmuring a little prayer as she took the key from the outside of the lock and brought it inside. She turned it. Then she knelt before the candle.

"Oh Lord, let her still be there. Please, let her still be there."

Emma, Julia, and Rex arrived by Sigma helicopter at Duncairn. There was no Clare to meet them. As it landed on the side lawn at the hotel, whipping the snow into a small blizzard around it, Emma and Julia craned out of the windows to see.

"It's like fairyland with all the snow and the Christmas trees and there's the castle!" Julia cried, seeing the turrets and the Victorian battlements of the hotel.

"No, honey, there's the real castle, over there, behind the trees." Rex pointed. He felt a sadness at seeing it again, but a feeling of relief as well that it would never now be his.

It was a perplexed Jack Grant who came out to meet them. "Mrs. Royland is not here. Surely she called to tell you?"

"Not here?" Emma's voice was flat with disappointment.

"Her husband took her away after the accident."

"Accident? What accident? Was she hurt?" Emma stared at him in shock.

"Not Clare—the dog. Mr. Royland shot the dog, by mistake." His emphasis on the last two words spoke volumes.

"Oh, God!" Emma looked helplessly at Rex, then at Julia whose eyes had filled with tears, some for Casta and some for herself as she sensed the imminent collapse of all their fairytale plans.

She shook her head, confused. "I don't know what to say. I'll have to speak to Clare. I should have called—I tried."

Jack nodded ruefully. "The lines are down."

Rex turned and ran back toward the helicopter. He climbed stiffly back inside and had a word with the pilot, and moments later the idling rotor blades stopped. The pilot completed his close-down procedures and followed Rex back into the snow.

"I've told him to wait while we decide what's best," Rex called. "We can always use his radio to get a message to Clare, and then if necessary later we can get him to drop us somewhere else." Panting, he rejoined Emma and put his arm around her. "He's on loan to us for the rest of the day, so we can do what we like. Even if we can't get a message to Clare it could be fun to stay anyway, Emma, if Mr. Grant doesn't mind." He threw a longing glance in the direction of the castle.

"Mind!" Jack grinned. "It won't be Christmas without you here!"

After lunch, Emma peeked in at the open door of the room next to hers and noticed Clare's belongings scattered around it. She went in. Clare had obviously left in one hell of a hurry. Some of her makeup was there on the dressing table and her negligee was hanging behind the door. She opened the wardrobe and peered in. Two dresses hung there and right at the back, pushed almost out of sight, Clare's mink coat.

Emma pulled it out of the closet and buried her face in the silky chocolate fur. It smelled faintly of Clare's perfume. She must have left fast to leave that behind in this weather! Still holding the coat in her arms, she looked around the room again. Books, tissues, underwear, notebooks, sketchbooks were everywhere. Clare was a tidy person, she would never leave the room like this. Emma was suddenly suspicious. Of course, it could just mean that she intended to be back soon, to join them for Christmas after all. Cheered at the thought, she turned to leave the room. The mirror on the inside of the wardrobe door caught her eye and she realized she was still holding Clare's coat. Suddenly daring, she slipped it on and pulled the door father open to admire herself, turning the collar up around her ears, twirling a little to make the full-length fur swirl out around her. It was luxurious and warm and made her feel like a million dollars.

Rex had been standing in the doorway for several minutes before she noticed him. She blushed. "I know I shouldn't. It's Clare's, but I couldn't resist it."

"I'll get you one just like it, if you want one, Emma." Rex moved over to her and took her in his arms.

She was surprised by the shock of pleasure his action gave her and she found herself returning his kiss, almost shyly, suddenly confused. "It's a tempting thought," she whispered.

"Then it will be the first thing on my shopping list when we get back to London."

"You don't mind too much about me asking for a separate bedroom, Rex?" When she had told Jack Grant she wanted her own room, she had seen the disappointment in Rex's face.

"Sure I mind. I mind like hell! But I'll put up with it." He softened the words with a smile. "Just so long as I'm with you."

"Oh, Rex." Suddenly she knew she was going to cry. She turned and fled out of the room.

"Emma—"

"Don't worry. I just need to be alone for a bit, that's all. I've got to think, Rex," she called back as she sped along the hall. "Where's Julia?"

"Grant took her tobogganing with Bill from the helicopter. They're out front somewhere."

"Then I'm going out for a walk. Don't follow me, please, Rex. I'll be all right when I've had a walk. . . . I have to think."

It was only when she was outside in the snow that she realized she was still wearing Clare's coat.

Paul reached Duncairn just after three. The place was deserted. Twice he rang the bell in the hall, then he put his head around the door of Grant's office. It was empty. His gun, he noticed, was where Grant had left it in the corner by the filing cabinet. He narrowed his eyes, putting his hand into the pocket of his jacket. The remaining cartridges were still there, and he fingered them gently for a moment.

"Royland!" Rex had appeared in the doorway behind him. "What are you doing here? Where is your wife?"

Paul looked him up and down slowly. "I've come to see you. I've something here that might interest you."

"Indeed?" Rex was in no mood to trifle with Paul Royland, the man who had done him out of Duncairn. If they had completed the deal a month ago as Paul had promised, Duncairn would have been his by now. He took a deep breath, trying to control himself. "I can't think what you could possibly have that would interest me."

"Duncairn."

Rex laughed. "You've sold Duncairn to Sigma!"

"Supposing I haven't?" Suddenly Paul had forgotten the need for discretion. He had forgotten everything except the importance of telling this man that he had finally won, that in the end he had forced Clare to give in. "Supposing the documents I gave Warner weren't legally binding? Supposing the signature was false?"

"You mean your wife still wouldn't play ball?"

Paul smiled. "Now she has," he said softly. "Duncairn is mine to sell to whom I wish."

Paul still had that bad feeling about Sigma; his heart had almost stopped beating when he saw the helicopter outside the hotel. "I have the deeds to the hotel in my briefcase, together with Clare's signature on the document, giving me absolute authority to sell. She gave in in the end."

"Too bad she took so long." Rex eyed him with dislike. "I seem to remember telling you I wasn't interested in buying anymore. I haven't changed my mind."

Paul could feel the sweat breaking out between his shoulder blades. "So, the deal was too rich for you?" His mocking tone hid his panic.

"No, but it sure as hell stank."

"I suppose you think you're going to beat me down." Paul turned away to Grant's desk and sat down. His hands were shaking.

"I could beat you into the ground, my friend." Rex was growing bored with the conversation. "I could tell your DTI a few things about you, remember?" His tone was menacing. "I don't want your damn hotel."

"Then why are you here?" Paul's voice was silky. "Don't tell me you've come up to Duncairn for pleasure."

Rex was silent. So, Paul didn't know he was here with Emma. He certainly didn't want him to know. He wanted him to go away. "Okay. Say I'm interested." All he wanted now was to find out where Clare was and get Paul out of there. "Show me this famous agreement of your wife's."

Paul reached down, swung his briefcase onto Jack's desk, and snapped open the locks. He took out a manila envelope and handed it, still sealed, to Rex.

Rex tore it open. He unfolded the sheet and read it through carefully. Slowly he began to laugh. "What kind of a fool do you take me for, Royland?"

"What do you mean?" Paul stepped forward. Suddenly his stomach was churning.

"What do you think I mean?" Rex threw the paper down on the desk. "You didn't seriously expect me to fall for that? I'm beginning to think you're the one that is mad, Royland. Quite, quite mad." He turned and stalked out of the office, still laughing.

Paul grabbed the paper with shaking hands. He stared at it. There at the bottom of the page, in the space he had marked with a cross, was the one word ISOBEL in spidery, Gothic script.

He stared at it in disbelief. The bitch! The scheming, clever bitch! Even in her fear she could fool him! Why had he been such an idiot? Why hadn't he checked? How could he have been so confident? He picked up the paper and tore it across twice, tears of frustration in his eyes.

She had beaten him! He was through. There was nothing he could do. Even if Sigma hadn't made the discovery themselves, he had told Cummin now that the papers he had sent them were forged. He was finished.

He closed his briefcase slowly and as he did so his eye fell again on the rifle propped up in the corner. Grant was criminally irresponsible for leaving it there. Someone might have stolen it. He moved across the room and picked it up, weighing it in his hands. It was a beautiful piece of workmanship— the polished stock smooth as silk beneath his hand.

Slowly he felt in his pocket for a cartridge and slipped it into the breach.

The afternoon was nearly over, the sun almost gone, the snow streaked red from the sunset. The castle ruins were shadowy and dark, mysterious in front of the soft night-blue of the sky. He could hear the sea sighing at the foot of the cliffs. Somewhere a sea gull called out, a ringing, laughing cry that echoed among the ancient stones.

Then he saw her. Clare. Standing in the ruins of the old chapel, staring out toward the cliffs, and behind her another woman, a woman in a long cloak who moved slowly away from her into the dusk. He frowned, staring into the shadows. Was that Isobel? Had she shown herself to him at last? He shook his head with a shiver. Whoever it was she had gone, and Clare was alone. He didn't ask himself how she had got there or what she was doing. He just watched her. She hadn't moved. She was just standing there, gloating. Gloating over a pile of stones that could have saved him.

All his rage and self-pity and resentment boiled to the surface. Clare, in the mink coat he had bought her with his money, was probably laughing at him at this very moment. He raised the rifle to his shoulder and took slow and careful aim. She was moving now, hands in pockets, walking with a light, swinging gait—happy—

He squeezed the trigger so lightly it was a surprise when

the deafening report rang out. The figure in his sights dropped to the ground.

He smiled. Then slowly and methodically he took another cartridge from his pocket. He loaded it, turned the gun, and slipped the cold satin-smooth steel of the muzzle into his mouth. For a split second he wondered if the kiss of a gun would be more pleasant than the kiss of a woman.

Then he pulled the trigger.

Chapter Thirty-three

Isobel received King Robert in the castle great hall. A slim, solitary figure, swathed in a blue cloak—upright, proud, a little afraid, she was determined he would never know how her heart was crying out to him. For a moment she didn't move. Standing near the huge driftwood fire, her eyes fastened on his face, then as he stepped forward she came to him hesitantly and, taking his outstretched hand, she sank to her knees.

"I am so pleased to see Your Grace."

Behind them his three companions tactfully turned their backs, making for the huge fire in the eastern wall of the hall. The castle servants were less meticulous, staring openly as the tall, handsome king, graying now, his face marked by suffering, stooped and raised her to her feet.

"My Isobel. I thought I would never seen you again." His eyes sought hers again as she raised her face to his. "Holy Virgin! When I heard what they had done to you I thought I would go mad!"

"They did the same to Mary and your little Marjorie." Isobel could feel her heart slamming beneath her ribs.

He gave a half smile. It was very grim. "They were released from their cages long since, thank the Lord—but they are still captive." He did not mention his wife, Elizabeth, who was also still in England, and neither did she.

"I had thought I was still captive too." Isobel gave a faint smile.

"You are, my love." The last two words slipped out so naturally neither noticed. "At least, your fair jailer, the titular Countess of Buchan, and I have reached an agreement. Duncairn stands in a part of the country I hold, but for a while I am content to allow the castle a nominal English overlord!" He smiled. "We are to share rights, your Alice and I."

"Rights over who holds me?" She spoke in a whisper.

"Tonight I shall hold you." He put his hands on her shoulders. "And I share that right with no one." He swung to face the hall.

"My friends—I leave you to amuse yourselves," he called to his companions. "Lady Isobel and I have much to talk about in private." He took her hand. "Will you show me your solar, my lady?"

They talked until the night closed in around the castle, the darkness lying softly over the sea and over the cliffs, lapping with the cold dew over the walls as in the hall below the flares were lighted and the fires piled high. It grew late. They nibbled the foods she ordered brought to them from the kitchens, and drank some wine, and remembered the time they first kissed, here, in the chapel at Duncairn. Then at last he led her gently toward her bedchamber.

She never asked him why he had not tried to rescue her; she did not mention Christian of Carrick or his children, nor ask about his exploits over the years. He talked of some things. Of friends lost, and friends found again, of Isobel's mother, happy as far as Robert knew, far away in England, of her great-grandmother who like so many others in those fearful years had disappeared, never to be heard of again after Kildrummy had fallen, of battles and defeat and then of victory; surely and slowly victory after victory as more and more of the country was clawed back from the English. He did not mention his brothers' fearful deaths, and neither did she. He spoke most of all of the future—of the time when he would throw the English finally and forever out of Scotland and give his country back her liberty. Of their future together he did not speak and she did not even think. As he gently unlaced her gown and drew it down over her still-thin body, and then removed her shift, all she cared about was the present, snatched from fate.

He touched her with gentle hands, then drew her down onto the bed, pulling the feather-filled covers over their heads before he touched his lips at last to hers.

He stayed two days and nights at Duncairn that cold November, then he rode away. She waved to him from beneath the gatehouse arch until he was out of sight, then she turned back into the castle. He had promised that he would come back.

Three weeks later the first snow of the winter fell, and three weeks after that she knew that she was carrying the king's child . . .

"I have to find him! He has to know about the baby. He must . . ."

Clare had scrambled to her feet. She turned to the door and, leaving the candle burning on its saucer, she opened it and listened. The house was silent.

"Chloe? Chloe? Where are you?" She ran down the stairs and across the hall, into the drawing room. There was no one there. Sobbing, she turned desperately toward the kitchen. There was no one there either. The house was empty. "Chloe? I have to find him. I have to tell Robert about the baby!" She looked into her stepfather's study and the dining room. "Chloe? Where are you? I have to find him, don't you see?"

There was no reply.

After grabbing a coat from the hook in the hall, she pulled open the front door. "Chloe?"

The snow was falling thickly again and she stared at it, confused. She had forgotten it was snowing. "Chloe?"

Without thought of where she was going she set off up the drive, not feeling the soft snow catching on the hem of her nightgown and seeping through her leather slippers, not bothering to button the coat. Behind her her footprints were obliterated almost at once by the swiftly falling snow.

Chloe and Geoffrey stared aghast at the open front door. While Geoffrey paid off the taxi that had brought them back from their abortive trip to the station in their vain attempt to get Geoffrey back to London, Chloe ran upstairs. When Geoffrey joined her she was staring down at the guttering candle in the empty bedroom.

"Where do you think she's gone?" Chloe spoke in a whisper.

"I don't know." Geoffrey stood glumly looking down, his hands in his pockets. "I was so sure it had worked. I thought Isobel was at peace." He sounded stunned.

"We can't be sure that she isn't." Chloe stooped and picked up the saucer. She looked doubtful. "She could be sleepwalking, anything. We've got to find her, Geoff. She's in no state to be outside."

He nodded, turning toward the door. "The candle was still burning so she can't have been gone for long." Geoffrey looked outside but there were no tracks in the snow.

"What are we going to do?"

"We'll search the grounds, do a sweep of the gardens, and search the—" Geoffrey paused and glanced at his wife. "We'll have to search the riverbank. Then, if there is still no sign of her, we'll have to get help."

"Geoffrey, I want to call her boyfriend, Neil. She might have tried to go to him."

Geoffrey frowned. "I suppose she might, but what about Paul?"

"What about Paul? He and Clare are finished, Geoff. You know that as well as I do."

"I suppose so." He nodded reluctantly. "But I can't condone adultery, Chloe, or divorce."

"Then just for once turn a blind eye."

"I'm sorry, my dear. I know I'm being pompous again. You're right, of course. But do you know where he is? How are you going to get hold of him."

Chloe shook her head. "I don't know," she said miserably. "I just don't know."

Neil was tired after the long drive from Edinburgh to Duncairn, and his eyes ached from the glare of the sun on the snow. It was just beginning to fall again as he pulled in beside Paul's Range-Rover and sat for a moment staring at it. Beyond it there were two other cars. He opened the door and climbed out.

There was a man in the hall, wearing a uniform with a

sigma on the breast pocket. He stepped forward as Neil walked in. "I'm sorry, sir, the hotel is closed. I must ask you to leave straightaway."

"Where is Jack Grant?"

"I'm sorry, sir, he can't see anyone just now." The man was agitated.

"Look, I'm a friend of his. He'll see me—" Neil broke off as a door opened and Jack looked out into the hall.

He stared at Neil, barely recognizing him. "I thought maybe the police had arrived—"

"What the hell is going on here?" Neil strode toward him. "Jack? What's happened?"

Jack slumped down on the wooden settle by the front door. He made a helpless gesture with his hands. "Paul Royland. He shot his sister and then he killed himself."

Neil stared at him. "Shot himself," he repeated, dazed. "Dear God! Are they . . . are they both dead?"

Jack shrugged. "She was still alive. Just. Bill here rushed her to Aberdeen in the helicopter with our doctor." He shook his head, barely able to speak. "She's critically wounded. I left the gun in my office . . . I never dreamed he'd come back for it. . . . It never occurred to me. Not for a second." His hands were shaking badly. "I don't know what possessed him. Dear God, I just don't know."

"When did it happen?" Neil didn't know why he asked, but suddenly it seemed important to know.

Jack shrugged. "An hour ago perhaps—I don't know. Perhaps more. We all heard the shots. We were around the side, sledding in the snow with Mrs. Cassidy's daughter—"

"Clare!" Neil looked around suddenly. "Where is Clare?"

Jack shrugged. "She's not here. He came back alone, Mr. Cummin said."

"Cummin? Rex Cummin? What is he doing here?" Neil's eyes narrowed.

"He was here with Mrs. Cassidy. Clare seems to have asked him for Christmas too—"

"Do the police know?"

Jack nodded. "Bill got them on his radio."

Neil found he was shaking suddenly. He sat down next to

Jack. "I can understand Paul Royland's killing himself, I suppose—but his sister? Why in God's name try to kill his sister?"

"God knows." Jack shook his head.

As they were walking toward Jack's little office, Neil saw Clare's mink coat lying on the chair. It was covered in blood. For a moment he stared at it in horror. "Where did that coat come from?"

"Mrs. Cassidy was wearing it," Bill volunteered. "The hospital told me to take it away." For a moment all three men stood looking down at it, then at last Neil spoke.

"Paul Royland thought he was killing his wife," he said softly.

"You mean it was a mistake?" The broken voice from the staircase made them all look around. Rex was standing there, his eyes red, his body tense with anxiety. When they took Emma to the hospital the doctor had quietly insisted that he stay with Julia. He didn't want the distraught man in the small cabin of the helicopter with them. "Emma knew—she knew he was capable of killing Clare. That was why she begged me . . . she begged me . . ." His voice broke and he shook his head, unable to go on.

"Well, we'll never know for sure," Jack said at last. "Come on down, man. We all need a drink."

He poured them all triple whiskies in the bar.

Behind them there was a faint *ping* as the phone was at last reconnected. None of the four men noticed.

"How is the little girl?" Jack asked, suddenly reminded of Julia.

Rex shrugged. "The doctor is with her now. He's giving her something for the shock. I don't know how to contact Emma's husband. He's out in Singapore or somewhere. Em was trying to reach him. . . . She still loved him. If he'd even nodded she wouldn't have come with me. She'd still be okay." He did not notice that he was talking in the past tense.

"It was the piece of paper that sent him over the edge," Rex looked at them blindly. "He came to see me. I don't know how he knew I was here. He seemed to think I would still buy this place. He told me the sale to Sigma was a fraud. He'd forged the papers. Then he gave me a document he said his wife had signed, some kind of power of attorney. But Clare hadn't signed it at all. It was some woman called Isobel. . . ."

Neil stared at him. "Are you sure?"

"Of course I'm sure. God knows who she is, but she sure as hell doesn't have the authority to sell this place to me."

Neil smiled grimly. "Not now perhaps," he said slowly. "But she owned it once, every last stone, and had she but known it, the oil as well."

Chloe, after cudgeling her brains for five minutes to remember the name of the organization, got through to Earthwatch and learned that Neil had gone to Duncairn.

Jack took the call in his office and then came back to the bar to get Neil. "It's a Mrs. Royland, Neil. Not Clare. I haven't said anything."

When Neil at last hung up he went back into the bar. "Clare is at Airdlie. I'm going straight there before this damn snow gets any thicker. Geoffrey Royland and his wife will come up here as soon as I get there, to take care of Julia. Can you all cope till then?" His face was grim. Chloe had been incoherent on the phone after Neil had told them the news, and Geoffrey, when he came on the line, was almost speechless with shock. The story they had gabbled to Neil about Clare when they finally remembered made little sense. He did not ask for them to clarify it. He wanted only to get to her as quickly as possible.

"Whatever has happened we can't leave till he gets here, Geoff." Chloe was in tears. "And we have to find Clare. We have to."

"Emma." Geoffrey had collapsed on the edge of the sofa. "Why Emma? Paul loved her." He glanced at his watch. The hospital had told them to call again in two hours. Emma was in the operating theater and in critical condition.

"Paul obviously had no idea what he was doing, Geoff. Did you reach David?"

"He's flying straight to Aberdeen. He says we've got to

keep this out of the papers, Chloe. Will this chap Neil cooperate?"

"All Neil Forbes cares about is Clare," she said gently. She
had liked what she heard of him on the phone. "He might not
care about us, but he won't do anything to upset her."

"But where is she?" Geoffrey had been about to set out to
look when Chloe's anguished cry had brought him back to
the phone from the porch. He was still wearing his rubber
boots and heavy overcoat. "We have to find her."

With both was the unspoken thought: There could not be
another death.

The cold had cleared Clare's head. She stared around her,
suddenly frightened. It was dark and all around the whiteness of the snow hid the features of the land beneath the
starlight. She was shaking like a leaf. The thin coat she had
snatched from the hall stand gave her little protection over
her nightdress, and her feet were numb in the thin slippers.

She had climbed well away from the road. Behind her the
hill rose, its whiteness broken only by the blackness of rocks
and the gaunt shapes of the Scotch pine. The snow flurries
quickened, and the air was full of the sound of the wind.

She turned around, trying to still her panic, trying to see
her own footprints in the snow, but they were gone already,
the marks filled and blurred almost as soon as she had made
them.

How had she gotten here? She wasn't aware of having left
the house. All she remembered was the need for human
company, for Chloe, even Geoffrey, to comfort her. And
someone else. Who was it she had been looking for so desperately? She had forgotten now, and distracted by her whirling
thoughts, she had strayed up onto the hillside behind Airdlie
and not even noticed she was climbing.

"Go down. The road must be down there." She spoke out
loud to herself into the roar of the blizzard. "And go slowly.
I'm bound to come to the road. It must be there. It must
be. . . ."

She walked on for half an hour, getting colder and more
tired every moment. Twice she fell, soaking her coat, and the

second time she had to force herself to rise. Suddenly she was crying. Casta. Where was Casta? She wouldn't have allowed her beloved mistress to get lost.

Neil peered between the stubby wipers of the Land-Rover and gritted his teeth. Only another ten miles to go, then he would be with Clare again. The concentration required for driving through the blizzard had driven all thought of everything save Clare out of his head.

He had never been to Airdlie before. Leaning forward, his eyes straining in the darkness, he tried to make out the turn, seeking the gateposts between the whirling flakes in the headlights, following Geoffrey's garbled instructions. Twice he stopped, then at last he found it and set the old Land-Rover up the long drive.

Every light in the house was blazing as he came to a halt at the foot of the steps. There was a police car parked beneath the trees. Chloe was at the door before he had turned off the engine.

"Clare is still missing; we can't find her! Thank God you're here."

"Still missing?" Neil ran up the steps to her. "What do you mean missing? Missing where?" He felt as if his heart had stopped beating.

"I told you on the phone!" Chloe sounded faintly hysterical. "She went out this afternoon—we came back from the station and found the door open. I just don't know where she could have gone! There was no car to take, nothing. She was on foot!"

Neil glanced behind him into the night. "The police are looking?"

Chloe nodded miserably. "And Geoff is out with them. I shouldn't have left her, but she was asleep, and I thought she would sleep till morning, and she had been so calm, so rational. I thought it must have worked. . . ."

"What must have worked?" Neil was already turning and running down the steps. He paused at the bottom and looked back at her.

"The exorcism. To get rid of Isobel."

"Oh, my God!" For a moment Neil stood motionless. "Poor Clare."

"Find her, Neil. Please find her." Chloe was anguished.

Neil scowled. "I'll find her," he said grimly.

He threw himself into the still-warm world of the Land-Rover and backed it up, heading once more for the drive. Only at the bottom did he stop. Left or right? He had no way of guessing. If Clare was on the road she would have been found by now. On foot she could be anywhere.

Clare woke suddenly. She hadn't realized she had been asleep. She was kneeling in the snow, feeling its soft white-ness drifting around her. She stumbled to her feet with a sob. Where? Which way? Her strength was almost gone. The snowflakes were clinging to her hair, stinging her eyes, slid-ing down her neck; her face felt stiff and frozen. Brushing the snow away from her eyes with a numb hand, she gazed around, trying to see through the white-out, frowning. Some-thing had moved, there at the edge of her vision. She turned toward it in desperate hope. Was that a figure, there in the darkness beyond the snow?

"Help! Please, help me." Her voice was not much more than a whisper. "Where are you?"

It was there again. A shadowy figure, a woman's figure, almost invisible in the snow. Clare staggered toward it, floun-dering through the drifts. "Chloe? Chloe? Wait! Please. . . ." Her voice was husky with exhaustion.

She staggered on a few steps, and the figure seemed to drift ahead of her, moving steadily down the hill. "Wait! Please, wait!" Clare was almost running now. Her breath was burn-ing in her throat, her heart pounding painfully behind her ribs. Her foot slipped and she almost fell, then she was on her feet again and suddenly the ground beneath the snow was hard and even, and she realized that the dark shape she had seen close at hand, rising out of darkness whipped to white, was a telegraph pole. She was back on the road.

"Chloe?" she whispered. "Chloe?" She looked around for her guide, but the figure had vanished. She was alone.

* * *

There was a sudden total silence in the nearly empty bar as Clare pushed open the door of the lonely roadside inn and staggered in. She was painfully aware of how she must look; her hair was soaked and wild, her coat saturated and stiff with snow, her shoes caked, the long nightdress she wore beneath the coat torn and dragging on the ground.

"Please, I must phone—"

Her voice came out as a husky gasp as she made her way unsteadily to the bar.

"Over there." The girl behind the bar looked at her with suspicion and obvious dislike.

"I haven't any money." Clare was near to tears.

"Well, then, you'd better write a letter, hadn't you." The girl smiled at her customers, expecting admiration for her wit.

"Come on, Kirsty, what about a bit of Christmas spirit, eh?" A man farther along the bar slid off his high stool. He came and stood beside Clare. "You look all in, lass. Are you all right?" He had a kind face, weathered to a thousand wrinkles. "Let me buy you a drink."

Clare collapsed onto a bar stool beside him. "I got lost in the snow. I was up on the hill, then someone—a woman—led me back to the road, but she wouldn't wait—" The words tumbled out incoherently.

"Get the lady a Scotch, Kirsty," the man commanded. He held out his hand to Clare. "I'm Duncan Macdonald. I farm up by West Mains."

Clare had hardly heard him. "Please. Can I phone?" She was shivering violently.

"The phone, Kirsty—the bar phone. I'll pay," Macdonald commanded, "and get the lady a blanket, she's soaked to the skin." Pouting, the girl obeyed, slamming the phone on the counter before disappearing into the back to bring a tartan rug.

It did not occur to Clare to phone Airdlie. There was only one person she wanted and that was Neil.

The receiver was lifted the other end at Neil's apartment. "Neil! Thank God! Oh, Neil, please, can you come? Please."

She could feel the tears threatening again. She did not know how he could get to her; she just knew she needed him.

There was a moment's silence, then a woman's voice spoke. "The beautiful Clare, I presume! How are you, Mrs. Royland?" She stressed the last two words.

"Please, where is he?" Clare's hand was shaking on the receiver. Behind her Kirsty and the customers at the bar were all listening with undisguised interest. ·

"Before I tell you, you answer me one question, Clare Royland. Are you really pregnant?" Kathleen had seen the answer in the cards; she didn't want to believe them, but they had spelled it out—birth and death in the same spread. And again, death and birth. The cards still lay on Neil's kitchen table. The death was so persistent she had called Neil at Duncairn that afternoon, and he had told her what had happened.

"Yes." Clare's answer was monosyllabic.

"And is it true that it's Neil's?"

She had screamed at him when he had told her.

"Yes."

"So, your husband's death could not be more convenient!"

"My husband's death. . . ." Clare repeated the words dully.

"Didn't you know?" Kathleen frowned. "He shot his sister and then he shot himself, this afternoon."

Clare was staring at the rows of bottles behind the bar, not seeing them, not seeing anything. "You're lying. Paul's not dead!"

"I'm afraid he is."

"No—?" It was a plea.

Abruptly the receiver was taken out of her hand. Macdonald put it to his ear.

"Who is this? What are you talking about? You've upset this lady very badly!" He heard a soft laugh, and then the *click* of a receiver.

"Come on, lass. Throw back that whisky. I'm driving you home." He put the glass into her hand.

Obediently Clare swallowed. The whisky was like a shot of

adrenaline through her veins. "She said my husband had shot himself."

"Aye, I heard." He looked grim. "She hung up on me. Come on, if you're ready."

It turned out he knew Airdlie and he knew Archie and Antonia. Clare had roamed a long way across the hill; it was nearly ten miles back, by road. When they arrived there were two police cars in the drive.

"It looks as though they've missed you," he commented as he swung his car in next to theirs and climbed out. "Mrs. Royland is in my car," he called out as a young constable approached him. "She's in a bad way."

The police, exhausted and despondent after two hours of fruitless searching, were having a council of war with Neil in the hall before setting out into the dark again. It was Neil who carried her indoors and up to her bedroom, Neil who peeled off her wet, frozen clothes and put her to bed, then he told her again gently about Paul and about Emma, who was still hanging on to the brittle thread of life in a hospital in Aberdeen. He did not tell her that they suspected Paul had thought he was shooting her.

She cried most for Emma, and for Julia and Peter. For Paul her sorrow was more complicated. There was guilt and anger and regret and last of all relief. The memories of the good times would return later and then maybe she would mourn, but not now. Not yet. It was too soon and too sudden.

When she was at last asleep he went downstairs to the empty drawing room. The doctor had gone; the police were driving the Roylands to Duncairn; he and Clare were alone in the house at last.

He took a mug of canned soup and a stiff drink into Archie's study, then picked up the phone and called Kathleen.

There was no answer from his apartment, though he let it ring and ring. On Waverley Station Kathleen was waiting for the London train. The cards had predicted a long journey and a promise of change.

* * *

In her sleep Clare stirred. She huddled sideways in the bed and frowned, her arm across her face. Her hands were bandaged and still icy cold, but in her dreams the snows had gone and spring had already arrived.

Isobel walked often on the cliffs that spring, delighting in the sharp salt-sweet air and the flowers, the sea pinks, the campion, the golden honey-rich flowers of the whin, the delicate, frail bluebells of Scotland dancing in the grass around her. She was tired all the time now and the least exertion exhausted her, but her happiness was undiminished. The baby had begun to move. She could feel the sharp flutter as it changed position, and each time it moved she felt an upsurge of joy.

Twice Robert sent her messages; twice he promised to visit her again as soon as possible, but he never came. She tried not to mind. He had a kingdom to win. When the English were gone they would have all the time in the world together. She closed her mind to what would happen when Queen Elizabeth, comfortable still in her quasi-captivity in England, was at last returned to Scotland, and to Christian of Carrick and the other ladies who had solaced him over the past years. After all, she was his first love, his longest love, and now she carried his child.

Somewhere in the darkest corner of her mind, the corner where she kept the memory of the nightmare of the cage, there was another fear: the old fear, the sound of her mother's screams, and with it inseparably tangled now the blood, the terror, the pain of labor when she lost Lord Buchan's child. But the door on those memories was firmly bolted. They could not be allowed to escape. Nothing must spoil the glorious sunshine of this spring and summer.

She had made one friend in her neighbor, Lady Gordon, wife of the young man who years before had tried to persuade his mother to hold Isobel a hostage. Often the two women would talk together, and Isobel was reassured by Lady Gordon's calm description of her own four easy births. Her youngest son was two, her eldest seven, and she could see no reason for fear, even now that she was embarking on her own fifth pregnancy with yet again scarcely a break between them.

Sir Henry Beaumont, titular Earl of Buchan, found out that Alice had taken Isobel back to Duncairn just after Easter. He was speechless with rage.

"The king was specific! He said she was never to go anywhere near Scotland again. His father had sworn it!"

Quelling her apprehension, Alice shrugged as nonchalantly as she could. "He'll never know, unless you tell him. He's got other things to think about. Leave her there, Henry. Poor Aunt Isobel. Hasn't she suffered enough? She can do no harm up there."

Her spies had told her that Isobel was with child, and she had said a myriad of prayers for her friend. Half of her was glad for her and hoped Isobel had found even a little happiness at last with the man she loved; the other half prayed fervently that Henry would never find out. That kind of indiscretion he would call treason, and she doubted if he or his king would spare her for arranging it.

To the south the war raged on. Perth had fallen to the Scots, and Dumfries, Roxburgh, and Edinburgh. Scotland from the eastern to the western sea was now Robert's. Only Stirling Castle still lay in English hands, the subject of a truce that was to last until Midsummer's Day. Then, if the English king had not relieved the garrison, they were pledged to surrender to Robert.

But the English were massing their armies now, determined to win this one last battle and save their pride. Word came to Duncairn of the size of the English army gathering in the south, determined at last to defeat Robert and his claims once and for all. Huge divisions of men and a fleet of ships to service them were being brought together, the English lords united for once behind Edward II, and vowed to support him in his aim. They had all been summoned to gather at the beginning of June on the banks of the river Tweed.

Isobel, far away in her clifftop castle, knew of the approaching army. This time there was no place for her on the battlefield. Her lord would win or lose without her there.

Time and again she walked restlessly toward the cliffs or on the wall walks of the castle, dragging herself up the steep winding stairs. The baby's bulk wasn't large, she was too thin, but her breath was labored and her heart would pound agonizingly as she climbed.

The women who attended her begged her to rest. They tried to make her eat and drink nourishing things, but her restlessness would not be stilled, nor her feeling of unease, and she became afraid to sleep, sensing the thinness of the curtain that divided her nightmares from reality.

When the messenger came at last on the afternoon of Midsummer's Eve, he was a stranger. He brought a letter and a small package from the king.

> In haste, my love. These three days before I must decide where, and indeed, if, I meet with Edward of England. Know that I remember you in my prayers daily, with the child you carry. If anything should happen to me on the field of battle, I have left orders that you and your child be cared for. I pray that we meet soon and in a kingdom free and independent and proud. From my camp in the Torwood, this 21st day of June, 1314.

In the package was a necklace for Isobel and a carved ivory rattle with ribbons and silver bells for the baby to come.

Isobel took them and the letter and kissed them. "Go back to him, and give him my love and serve him with your life." She smiled at the exhausted messenger. He needed no second bidding. Already he had commanded a fresh horse.

Isobel watched him ride away until his horse was lost from sight, and then she turned sadly back into the castle. She knew in her heart that Robert would come back one day. But she would not be there.

Emma opened her eyes slowly. It still hurt to move, to breathe, but it was easier now. Beside her bed in the small hospital room Peter leaned forward and touched her hand.

"How is it?"

"All right." She gritted her teeth. Nearby, in three separate vases stood the flowers, gaudy and red among all the others, that Rex had sent her before he left for Houston.

Seeing Peter's eyes straying toward them yet again, she reached painfully out to touch his hand.

"He said he would still buy me a mink of my own," she said with an attempt at a laugh. "I said no thanks."

They were silent for a minute, both thinking about Rex. By the time Peter had arrived Rex had already decided to leave. Emma would never love him, he had accepted that. And Mary always would.

"Neil told Jack Grant at the hotel to burn Clare's mink coat," Peter put in thoughtfully. He had been rather impressed by the gesture.

"Good." Emma shuddered. "How did the funeral go?" It was the first time she had mentioned her brother, even obliquely.

"It was a cremation, Em." Peter's fingers tightened on her hand. "David arranged everything with the minimum of publicity—you know him, and Geoffrey took the service, what there was of it. Henry came. That was nice of him."

They had scattered Paul's ashes in the sea.

"Henry's a nice man." Emma nodded. "Was Clare there?"

Peter shook his head. "They wouldn't let her go. She wasn't well enough. She was damn lucky not to lose the baby. In fact, she was lucky to survive at all."

Emma was silent for a long time. "Is she over the exorcism and everything?" she asked at last. She hadn't been able to believe it when Peter told her the whole story.

He nodded.

"And you like Neil?"

Again he nodded. "He's the right man for Clare. He'll take care of her."

"No, Neil. I don't want to marry again." Clare was lying on the sofa at Airdlie. In the kitchen her mother was preparing tea. Archie had gone off on a private mission of his own.

She tried to soften the words with a smile. "I've been

someone's property too long. I want to try standing on my own feet."

He looked away, trying to hide his bitter disappointment. "You would never be my property, Clare." But it was no use. Her newfound determination was rock-solid. He sighed. "Where will you live?"

"Some of the time in Edinburgh with you, if you'll have me, but most of the time at Duncairn. I'm going to have my own apartment there, in the hotel. I'm selling Bucksters and the London house and Sarah is going to come up to work for Mummy full-time."

"But what happens if the oil comes?"

She smiled. "We're going to fight the oil, Neil, remember? You and me and Earthwatch. But if it comes, then so be it. We will have to put up with it. Everyone keeps telling me that once the wells are dug, so much of it can be hidden." She looked at him and gave him a wistful smile. "I'm sorry, Neil. Try not to mind too much. We can still be together as much as you like."

She had had a long talk with Geoffrey before he had left. "Are you going to marry Neil?" he had asked.

She had shrugged. "One day perhaps. Not now."

"But the baby, Clare."

"The baby is mine. Did you know that David wants the world to think it's Paul's?"

He frowned. "Is that what you want?"

She shook her head. "She's mine. That's all that matters."

A little shiver crept up his spine. He left the sentiment unchallenged, however. "You're sure it's a girl?"

She nodded. "Would you marry Neil and me if I asked you?"

He hesitated. "Would you really want me to?"

"No."

"Then why ask?" His tone was gentle.

"Because I want your approval, I suppose. Your blessing. Your absolution."

"You will have that unreservedly, whatever you decide to do."

"If I die, I don't want the Roylands to turn their backs on her."

He was visibly shocked. "Clare, my dear, you're not going to die!"

"People do, Geoffrey, in childbirth." Just for a second she had let her mask slip and he had seen her fear—Isobel's fear.

"Not these days, Clare. Not when you have the best treatment money can buy, which you will have." He took her hands. "You mustn't be afraid."

But, like Isobel, she was afraid.

Her mother realized it and so did James. James had come up to see her at Duncairn. He had brought the inevitable news that Sigma had been awarded the section of land containing Duncairn, and given the license. It was what they had all expected, but she could not hide her disappointment, even when he told her the astonishing fact that Sir David Royland had agreed to support their appeal against the planners who had granted provisional permission to test drill.

"What's wrong, sis?" he asked.

"There's nothing wrong."

"Are you sure?" He had been eyeing her with concern. He had grown much closer to his sister in the last few months.

She shrugged. "I'm just apprehensive, I suppose."

"Aren't you well?"

"Of course I'm well."

"Well, then." He pulled her down beside him on the window seat. "Why aren't you in Edinburgh with Neil, fighting?"

She shrugged again. "I don't want him to get too fond of me, I suppose. I don't want him to be hurt. So many people have been hurt."

"Clare!" He was indignant. "You are carrying Neil's child. Your place is with him and his with you! Don't you love him?"

"Oh, yes. I love him. More than I ever would have thought it possible to love someone."

"And does he love you?"

She smiled. "He says so."

"Then don't you think he's more unhappy away from you, worrying about you?" He stood up. "Is this to do with Isobel?"

Clare looked down at her hands.

"She hasn't gone, has she? Geoffrey never exorcised her. You still dream about her, just as you always did."

Clare shook her head. "No. There have been no more nightmares."

"And the others? The visions?"

She shook her head. "No," she whispered. "She's still there, but I can't see her. It's as if she's waiting for something. Waiting for the baby. My baby." She bit her lip.

"Rubbish! Why should she want your baby?"

"Perhaps her own died."

"It can't have. After all, we are descended from it, aren't we?" Seeing her rising panic now that the subject had been faced at last, James was crisply practical. "Aunt Margaret was so proud of our descent from Robert the Bruce and that was the way it came, wasn't it, through Isobel's daughter, so the child can't have come to a gory end. Listen, why don't you let me drive you down to Edinburgh in the Porsche. To be with Neil."

In spite of herself Clare smiled. "A recipe for a very gory end, the way you drive."

"Okay. You drive."

"James, it's sweet of you—"

"But—"

"But Neil is coming here."

It was the beginning of June when Isobel returned. Clare had spent the morning sketching on the cliffs. Neil was coming to join her that evening and she was looking forward to seeing him. The lengthy legal delays involved with appeal and counterappeal meant there had been no sign of any activity at Duncairn from Sigma. Everything was as it always had been.

The grass around the castle was neatly mown, and the walls hung with rambling roses in full flower. It was a place of peace and happiness. She had never asked anyone where Paul had died and no one had told her. Once, alone, she had brought a rose for him and laid it in the window of the chapel. That was all. A tribute to the years they had been happy.

It was a warm day—beautiful, a slight mist hanging over
the sea. Walking back toward the hotel slowly at lunchtime,
she had paused within the circle of the castle walls and
looked around. And suddenly she knew she was not alone.
The atmosphere had changed. The peace and tranquility had
gone. In its place she could feel a charge in the air. In the
distance there was a low rumble of thunder.

Isobel heard the thunder and shivered. It was Midsummer's Eve. Outside, the air smelled of hay and meadowsweet, of scented thyme and wild roses. Inside the solar,
where she sat idly playing with a skein of embroidery silks,
the air was heavy and rancid. Her ladies were gossiping quietly by the windows, and already someone had lighted candles in the darkening room.

Abruptly Isobel stood up, throwing her silks to the floor.
Silence fell on the room. "My lady, you should rest—" a voice,
querulous in the heat, came from the window.

"Time enough to rest later." Isobel put her hand to her
belly as a twinge of pain from the restless baby shot through
her. "I want to be outside. I want to ride."

"You mustn't ride, my lady!" Cries were raised in horror all
around her. "You're not strong enough! Please, rest—"

But rest was something she could not do. All her thoughts
were with Robert. Her prayers, her remaining strength, all
had gone to him with the departing messenger. Restlessly
she left the room, walking slowly down the stairs, her hand
on the stone newel post to steady herself, feeling even the
drag of her gown on the steps behind her as an intolerable
burden. She walked out into the courtyard and wearily bade
the gateward open the postern gate. She was too tired for the
wall walk tonight.

Outside a huge yellow moon was swimming up out of an
aquamarine sea. The evening was luminous, scented, completely still. Not even a bird's cry broke the silence now. The
sea itself seemed to be holding its breath. It was as if, if she
strained her ears against the silence of the intervening mountains, she would hear the chink of harness and the rasp of
weapons eased in the sheath as the armies waited for the day

to dawn, after a night without true darkness, like the night so long ago at Methven.

It was as she stopped and bent to pick a delicate bluebell from the grass near her feet that the pain hit her. Unable to stop herself, she let out a cry. At once her attendants, who had been following at a respectful distance, ran to her, and within minutes she was being carried back toward the castle as the first bright blood began to stain her kirtle.

Her body, which had been through so much, had no strength left for this last ordeal. The pain lifted her, carried her, till she was floating somewhere beyond its reach. She never saw the attendants who clustered around her; never felt the hands of the midwives as they probed beneath the stained sheets; nor did she hear the indignant wail of her tiny daughter as the baby slipped at last, two months too soon, from her exhausted body.

As the sun rose in a crimson haze from the sea, far away on the banks of the Bannock Burn Robert prepared to face the greatest battle of his life. At Duncairn the first red rays of light pierced the narrow windows of the great bedchamber where Isobel was scarcely breathing. The chaplain stooped over the bed; he was admonishing her to confess her sins. Dimly she heard his voice, coming and going from a great distance; she barely felt the man's finger trace a cross on her forehead. She could no longer see.

Shadows surrounded her now, shadows from the past; faces of people long dead, and with them other faces from the future—the faces of her child and her child's children. The shadows were growing darker now and, at last, she understood.

Her last vestige of strength rose as a wave of anguish and frustration and despair at the cruelty that was depriving her of life and love now, after she had lived through so much. She wanted to curse, to pray, to call out to her child and her child's children to live for her.

On the huge curtained bed where she had lain with her husband and then with her king she lay locked in silence, alone and afraid and angry as the sunbeams crept across the floor toward her. Then at last she rose from her pillow, throwing off the hands of the priest and the women who crowded around her, and she let out one last cry, a cry that contained all her hope and love and fear and all that was left of her life.

Clare was still very shaken when Neil arrived. Secure within the circle of his arms, she managed to tell him at last what had happened. "It was so awful, Neil." At the thought her eyes filled with tears again. "Poor Isobel. She had lived through so much, and to die then, just as Robert was winning his greatest victory. It was so unfair!"

"It explains why she has never been at rest." Neil pulled her close. "Is it all over now?"

Clare nodded. "It is all over. She has gone."

"Do you want to go back to the castle to make sure?"

She nodded.

The castle was bathed in a pearly mist from the sea. Clare walked slowly to the cliff's edge and looked over. Neil watched as she stood for a while staring out into the distance, then she turned and smiled at him. They walked slowly hand in hand over the newly mown turf.

"Do you think she came back to try to save Duncairn?" he asked as the walked inside the ruins.

"I think perhaps that was part it. She loved this place." Clare smiled again. "But mostly she just wanted to tell her story."

Neil sat down on a low wall and pulled her down next to him. "Was it Isobel who guided you in the snow?"

Clare nodded sheepishly. "I'd like to think so."

"She couldn't save herself, Clare, at the end of her life, but I have a feeling she's on your side now. You've nothing to be afraid of, you know." He too had felt her fear.

They sat silently for a while watching as the sun fought to disperse the mist, and it was some time before Clare realized that they were not alone. She glanced at Neil and saw that he had seen her too: a child, a little girl, playing in the grass in a patch of warm sunlight near them, a pretty, dark-haired child, with large gray eyes and a happy tinkling laugh. As they watched a man appeared, walking out of the mist, a tall, grave figure who played with her and made her giggle and then took her on his shoulder and walked with her back into the shadows and out of sight.

Clare glanced at Neil. "Did you see them too?" she whispered.

Neil nodded.

"Were they real?"

He was staring at the spot where they had disappeared. "They were there—" he replied cryptically.

"The king and his daughter?"

"Perhaps."

"She married Patrick Gordon, in the end, you know, and Robert gave them Duncairn."

"It was the least he could do."

"Oh, Neil." Suddenly she threw her arms around his neck. They were silent for a long time.

"My ancestors fought at Bannockburn," he said at last. "Did I ever tell you?"

She smiled. "About a thousand times."

He stood up slowly and helped her off the wall. "He was a fine figure of a man, wasn't he?" he said at last as they walked slowly on. "For a king."

Chapter Thirty-four

It was Midsummer's Eve. Neil and Clare had finished dinner and were alone in Clare's private apartment in the hotel. "Are you sure you want to go out there tonight?" he said. "You look so tired, Clare. Why not leave it until morning?"

She shook her head. "I want to show her we remembered the date, show her we still care. It must be tonight."

They planted the little rowan tree in the shelter of the wall that had once formed a part of the great hall, then they opened a bottle of champagne and toasted the tree and poured a little of the wine around its roots, and then they toasted Isobel.

"Rest in peace," Clare whispered toward the moon. "Be happy now, wherever you are—" She broke off abruptly, staring at the ground, her face white in the moonlight.

"Clare, what is it?" Neil called sharply.

She had dropped her glass, clasping her hands to her back as a wave of pain swept over her. "Oh, Neil—" She was suddenly terrified. "Oh, Neil, the baby!"

"Christ!" Neil let the bottle fall. "It's all right, darling, don't worry. I'll get you back to the hotel—"

"No." She closed her eyes and groaned. "No, Neil. It's no good. There is no time." She was clutching the rough stones of the wall. "It has to be here, don't you see? Oh, Neil, it's me she wants . . . I'm going to die!"

Neil stared at her, his face white in the moonlight. "Don't be silly! Don't even think such a thing! Come on, Clare, darling, you've got to let me take you back inside!"

She shook her head, biting her lips as another wave of agony swept over her. "Go and get Mrs. Fraser, Neil." She was sobbing now. "Please! Quickly—"

He stood for a moment, torn, then he turned away from her. "You'll be all right if I run? I'll only be a minute—"

"Yes, yes. Okay. Just go!" She was breathing deeply, trying to hide her fear and pain from him.

Already Neil was sprinting cross the grass.

Clare fell to her knees where she was, beside the wall, gasping as her body convulsed once more. So this was to be the end, after all. History was going to repeat itself. She too would die at Duncairn on Midsummer's Day, and Isobel would no longer be alone.

Closing her eyes, she let the pain take her, Neil already forgotten, as her mind focused inwardly on the very center of her being. She felt herself floating upward, away from the castle ruins and into the vast eternity of the sky above her.

Neil came back at a run, and with him were Jack and Mrs. Fraser and Catriona, all panting hard.

"Clare, are you all right? *Clare?*" Neil knelt beside her on the grass. *"Clare—"*

"She's fainted." Jack was directing a flashlight at her face with a shaking hand. "Poor lass."

"Aye, the baby's coming." Mrs. Fraser had laid a practiced hand on Clare's stomach. "It's coming soon. Away now and phone the doctor, Catriona, lass. She was right, it's too late to move her. Jack and I will see to things fine here."

She glanced up as her daughter disappeared into the darkness.

"Did you put the whisky in your pocket, Jack Grant? I think Neil there needs a wee drop, and so will you."

Neil tried to smile. "It's too early. The baby is much too early," he said anxiously.

"It's the seventh month; she'll be all right." Mollie Fraser has delivered babies before now, down in Duncairn village. "We'll cope fine." She glanced up at the luminous sky. "It's St. John's Eve—a night of magic. She'll be all right, you'll see."

Neil stared at her, astonished. How on earth had she, a good Presbyterian, known that?

He looked up and closed his eyes, stroking Clare's hand as

he knelt in the dewy grass. Was Isobel there somewhere in the darkness, waiting? Surely she did not want Clare to die?

"Please, spare her. Leave her for me. I need her. Please . . ." He was whispering into the silence. "You don't need her. Let her live. Please, let her live—"

"There." Mollie's voice was calm. They had managed to wrap Clare in blankets to keep her warm. "There we go. Hold the flashlight, Jack, lad. You don't have to look if you don't want to, man!" She chuckled comfortably. "One more push, lass, and we'll be there—"

Clare was staring up at the hangings over her head as the pain took her, wave upon wave. Someone was near her, holding her hand. Robert . . . it was Robert. He had come after all. No, it was Neil . . . Neil, and beyond him she could see the sky, sewn with stars. There was no bedchamber. She was outside . . . drifting . . . almost asleep. Her body convulsed suddenly with agony worse than she had thought it possible to bear, wrenching her back to wakefulness and she heard herself scream. Then it was over and she was floating again, floating in a painless dream.

"There we are! It's a little girl." Mollie's soft voice was jubilant. "A bonnie, tiny lassie. And she's fine." She was crooning now as she swaddled the crying baby warmly in a soft towel.

"And Clare?" Neil was almost too awed and afraid to ask.

"Clare's fine too," Mollie said comfortably. "Everything's going to be all right. Just you see if it isn't."

"Thank you." Neil stared up at the sky. "Wherever you are. Thank you."

Mother and daughter were taken to Aberdeen by ambulance less than an hour later. They were both pronounced fit and well within two days.

Clare never saw Isobel again.

REQUIESCAT IN PACE

The low morning sun slanted into the nursery at Duncairn, warming the carpet, reflecting on the toys on their shelves. A pink furry rabbit lay on the floor, and little Margaret Isobel Forbes stared at it happily as she lay kicking on her blanket, waiting for her mother to come and feed her. Near her lay a golden retriever puppy, sleeping deeply in the sunlight, Archie's slightly embarrassed present to his stepdaughter and his adored grandchild.

Bored with the rabbit, Margaret began to look around the room, her eyes caught by the movement of the curtains in the slight breeze and by the shadows of the bars of her cot, thrown obliquely across the wall.

As she frowned, on the point of tears, the puppy sat up. It stared for a moment into the corner of the room, then with a yelp of fear it fled for the door. It scrabbled it open with its small paws and vanished into the hall. Margaret didn't notice. A lady was standing near her suddenly, smiling, bending toward her, and the child held out her little hands for the toy she was offered, an ivory rattle, with a silk ribbon and silver bells.

She heard her mother's voice, laughing, in the hall and she turned her head away. When she looked back the lady and the toy were gone.

Historical Note

The story of the Countess of
Buchan's revolt against her husband, her desperate ride to
Scone to crown her king, her subsequent capture, and her
terrible fate are well known and matters of recorded history.
That she was Robert's mistress was the conjecture or inven-
tion of the more malicious English chroniclers; Robert's rov-
ing eye was well documented, although in later years he and
his wife Elizabeth were reconciled and she went on to bear
him four children.

Isobel disappears from history in 1313. The last time she is
mentioned in the records was when she was transferred to
the custody of Sir Henry Beaumont, Earl of Buchan.

When Robert reclaimed his surviving scattered family and
friends after Bannockburn, Isobel was not among them.

Brief Chronology of Historical Events

1286   Death of Alexander III.

1289   Duncan of Fife murdered.

       Marriage of Robert Bruce to Isabella of Mar.

1296   War between Edward I and Scotland; Battle of Dunbar; Balliol abdicates; King Edward tours Scotland, accepting homage.
Birth of Marjorie Bruce. Death of Isabella of Mar.

1297   Battle of Stirling Bridge. Wallace liberates Scotland.

1298   Wallace appointed Guardian of Scotland. Edward I returns from Flanders.
22 July: Battle of Falkirk.
Wallace resigns as Guardian. Robert Bruce and Comyn chosen as joint Guardians.

1301   John de Soules elected Guardian.

1302   Robert marries Elizabeth de Burgh.
Autumn: Scottish ambassadors, including Lord Buchan, leave for Paris.

1304   Scots submit to Edward I.
Lord Annandale dies.

1305   Wallace captured and executed.
Westminster Parliament.

1306   10 February: Robert Bruce murders Comyn in kirk at Dumfries.
25 March: Robert Bruce crowned at Scone by bishops.
27 March: Robert Bruce crowned at Scone by Isobel of Fife.
19 June: Battle of Methven.
August: Battle of Dail Righ.
September: Fall of Kildrummy; royal ladies and Isobel captured at Tain.
Isobel imprisoned at Berwick. Nigel Bruce executed.

1310   June: Isobel released into custody of nunnery at Berwick.

1313   Isobel released into Sir Henry Beaumont's custody.

1314   Battle of Bannockburn.